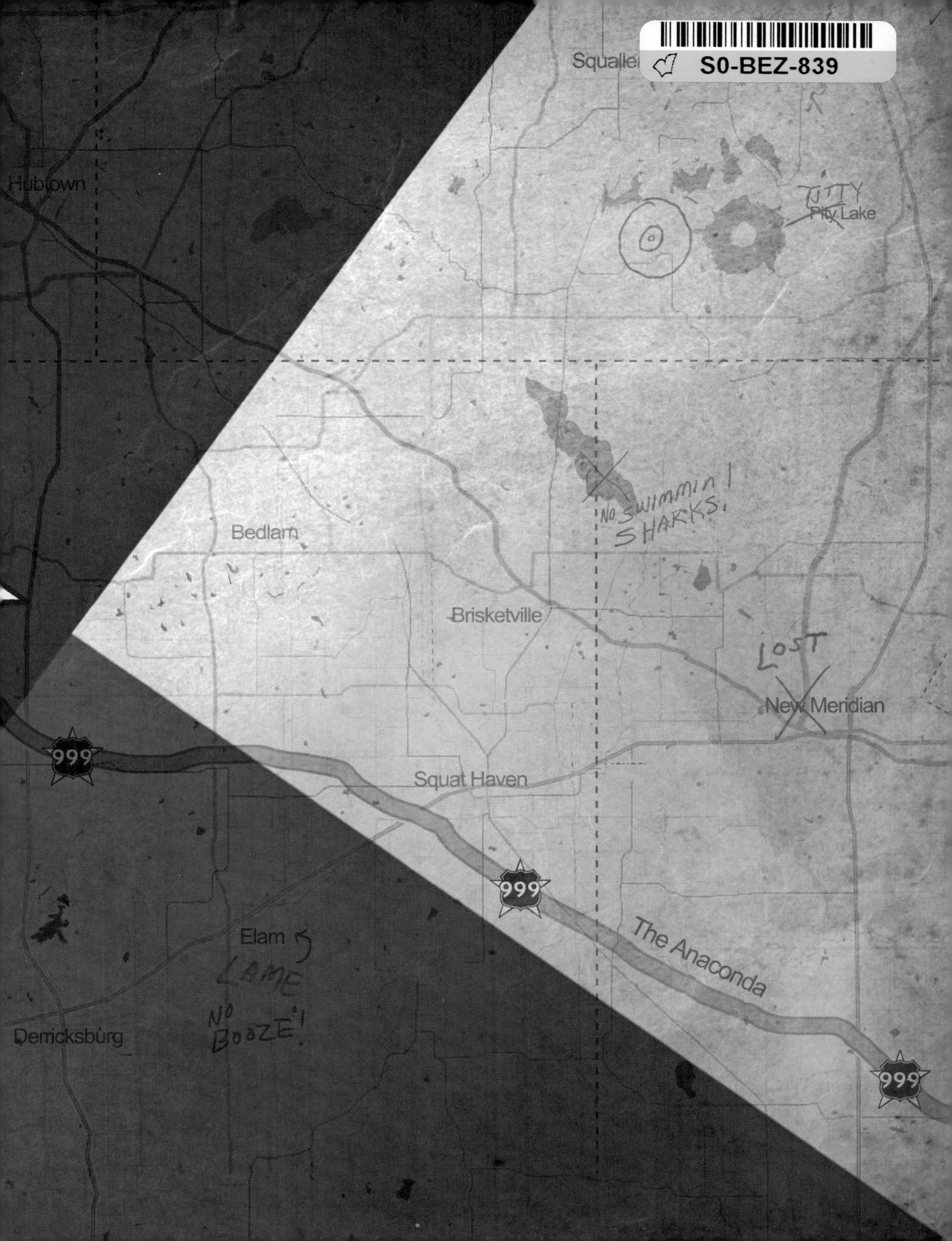
Hubtown
Pity Lake
NO SWIMMIN! SHARKS!
Bedlam
Brisketville
LOST
New Meridian
999
Squat Haven
999
The Anaconda
Elam
LAME
NO BOOZE!
Derricksburg
999

STRANGE HIGHWAYS

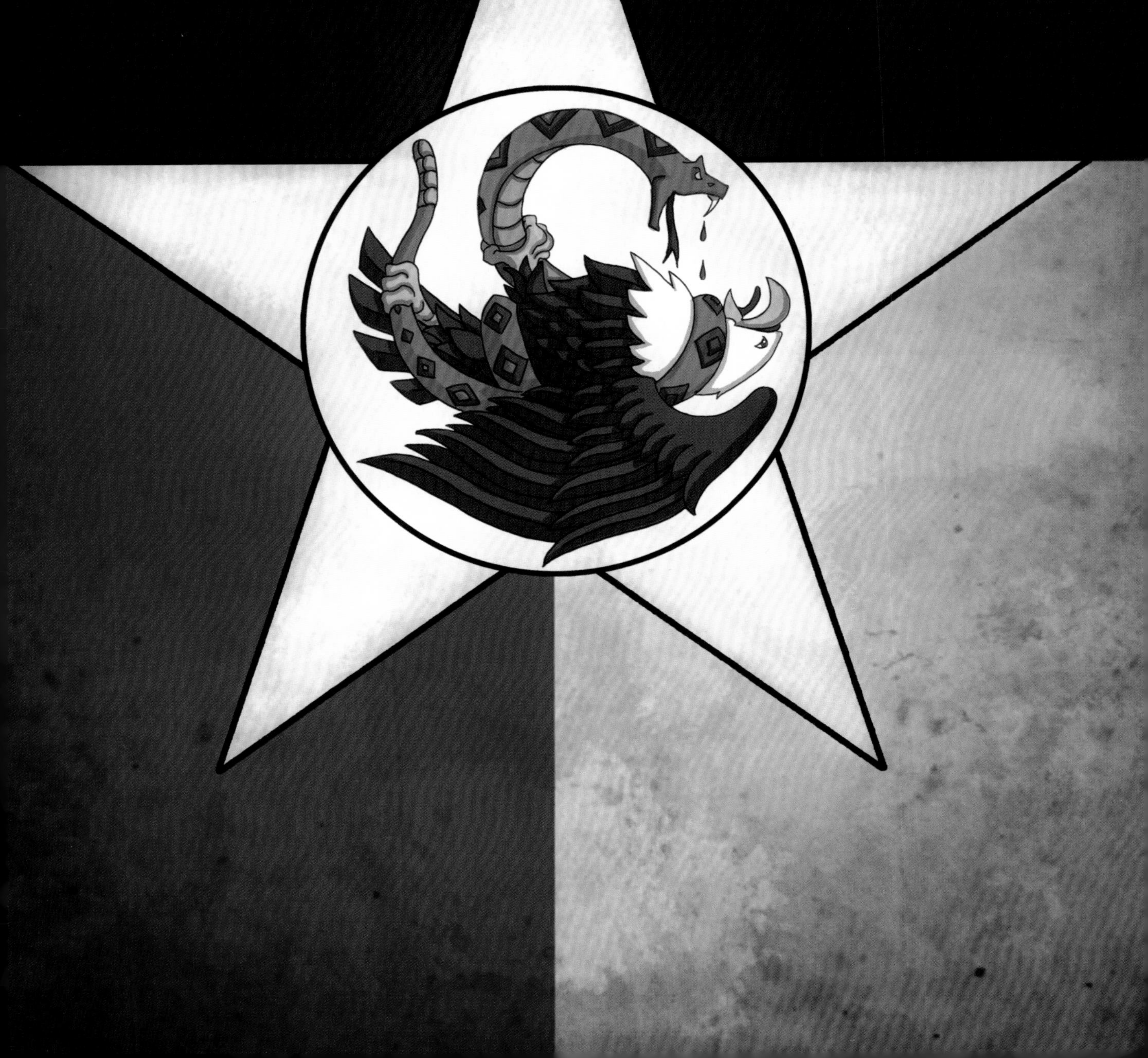

STRANGE HIGHWAYS

Written by
MICKY NEILSON and **SAMWISE DIDIER**

Illustrated by
SAMWISE DIDIER

INSIGHT
COMICS

San Rafael, California

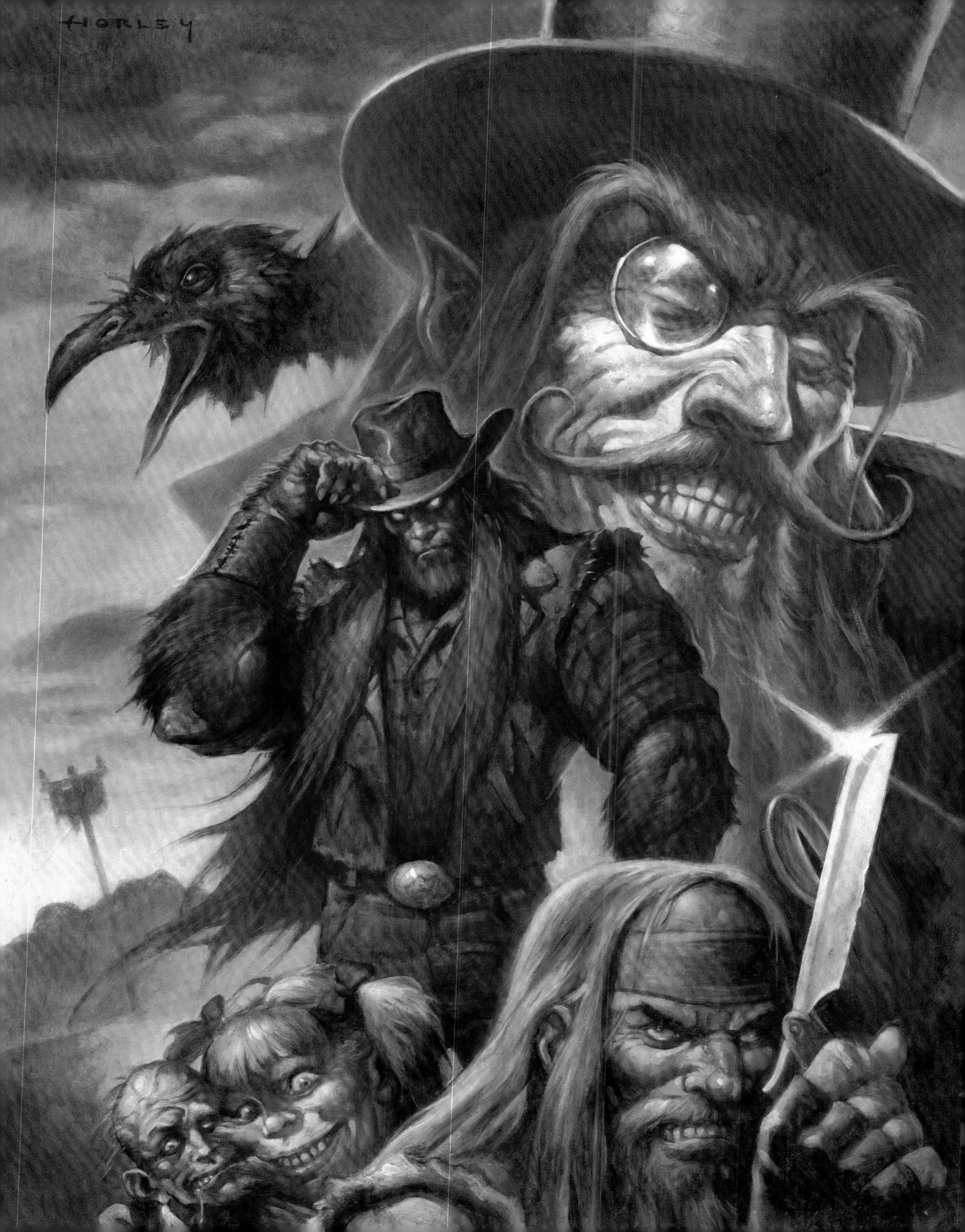
HORLEY

ACT I

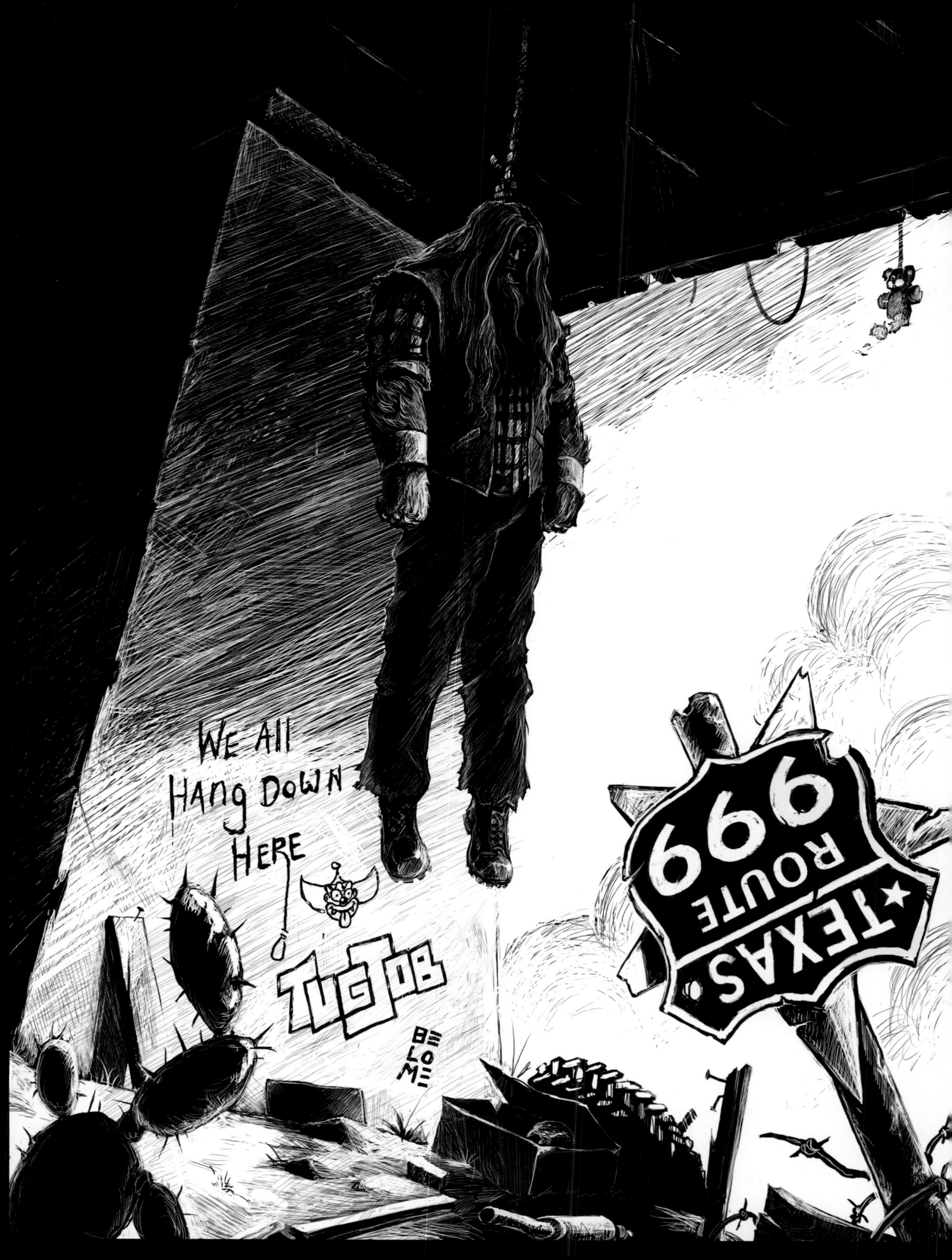
WE ALL
HANG DOWN
HERE
TUGJOB
BE
LO
ME
TEXAS
ROUTE
666

CHAPTER THE FIRST

It was in the mid-eighties that the world went to shit in a handcart.

Before that, things had been moving along okay, for the most part . . . then the Great Conflict happened. Things got real bad real quick; didn't matter if you lived in Montana or Mozambique. A whole lotta people died and a whole lotta maps got rearranged.

The folks who survived, well, many of 'em wound up wishin' they hadn't.

Let's take *this* sorry sonofabitch for example . . .

See him dangling there, full o' holes, bruises, broken bones . . . beat on, pissed on, shit on, stabbed, shot, hung by a rope off this here trellis bridge and left for dead?

"Nobody deserves that kind o' brutalizin'!" you might say. "No matter what he done. That there's overkill!"

Yeah, well, not in Texas.

After the Great Conflict, Texas finally got what it always aimed for: to be a real lone star.

The rest o' the world didn't want nothin' more to do with it. Hell, even the Mexicans got fed up. They all got together and built up the biggest, thickest wall you've ever seen.

Yessir, the Big T's a wasteland. Cut off from anything resemblin' civilization. And as far as the law goes . . . there's really only one law. The oldest one o' all: survival o' the fittest.

Thirty-five miles west of our lonesome hanged fella, just off the Anaconda—the main highway that cuts across the state—that endless, timeless struggle o' life and death is playing out under the bakin' sun.

What happened is, a desperate crow thought he'd make himself a meal o' a rattlesnake. Now crows ain't the smartest birds on their best day, but if you was to tell me this crow was especially feeble-minded to pick a fight with a rattler, I'd be inclined to agree.

What the crow mighta lacked in smarts though, he made up for in sheer cussedness. He ain't givin' up this fight, diggin' his talons into those scaly diamonds, a rippin' and a tearin' with that sharp beak . . . but I think you and I both know how this particular drama plays out: That's right, you don't pick a fight with a rattler. Once he sinks those teeth in—like he did just now—it ain't but a matter o' time 'til the fat lady sings.

That snake coils 'round those black feathers, emptyin' his venom. The crow lets out one strangled cry and then goes dead still. Right about now the fat lady is wailin' her ass off.

The snake, he don't pay no mind to the sound o' truck motors out on the Anaconda, don't pay much heed to the nails-on-chalkboard squeal o' brakes engaging. In the predatory world, rattlers don't pay no mind to anacondas anyhow, no sir.

But, as weather-worn boots crunch against the desert gravel, that rattlesnake senses somethin' awful comin' his way—somethin' meaner, smarter, and a whole lot deadlier than him. So he skedaddles, leaving a windin' trail in the dirt, well and gone by the time a tall, lean shadow falls over the stiffened blackbird.

After some heavier steps, that first shadow's joined by another—but this'd be about the strangest set o' shadows you've ever seen. That'd be on account o' 'em belonging to the Magi twins, Bo and Tweeny. They're what's called "conjoined," you see, so they make for quite a sight; Tweeny, she's the big one, holdin' her little brother—and I mean little in the literal sense o' the word, since they was born at the same time—like one o' them ventrily-quists holds a dummy. 'Cept a ventrily-quist and his dummy ain't o' course stuck together at the head.

The twins, they just had to come and see the handiwork of the Ringmaster. He'd be the one that the tall, lean shadow belongs to . . . dressed just as smartly as ever in his tux and top hat, monocle over one eye, carryin' a silver-tipped, dragon-headed cane. The Ringmaster goes by different names at different times, like the Ramblin' Man and Ledger DeMesne. Whatever name he goes by, though, you can bet it gets spoke on tremblin' lips, 'cause the Ringmaster ain't one to be trifled with.

While the Magi twins watch, fascinated, ol' Ledger DeMesne sets his cane to one side, where it keeps on standin' all by itself, and he bends down and picks up that crow, all gentle-like. He brings it close and whispers words that most folks forgot by the time that big pyramid was built in Giza. Then he puts his lips real close to the bird's beak and he blows . . .

And, see that? Those shiny black eyes just popped right open! The Ringmaster tilts his head up, throws his arms out, and lets that mangled bird fly, and damned if those wings don't flap. It don't fly right, not at first, jiggin' and jaggin' like a drunk leavin' a saloon after last call, but pretty soon it evens out, lets off a ragged squawk, and gets goin' with a purpose.

"Where's it headed?" Tweeny asks.

"East, dummy," says Bo.

"How far?" asks Tweeny.

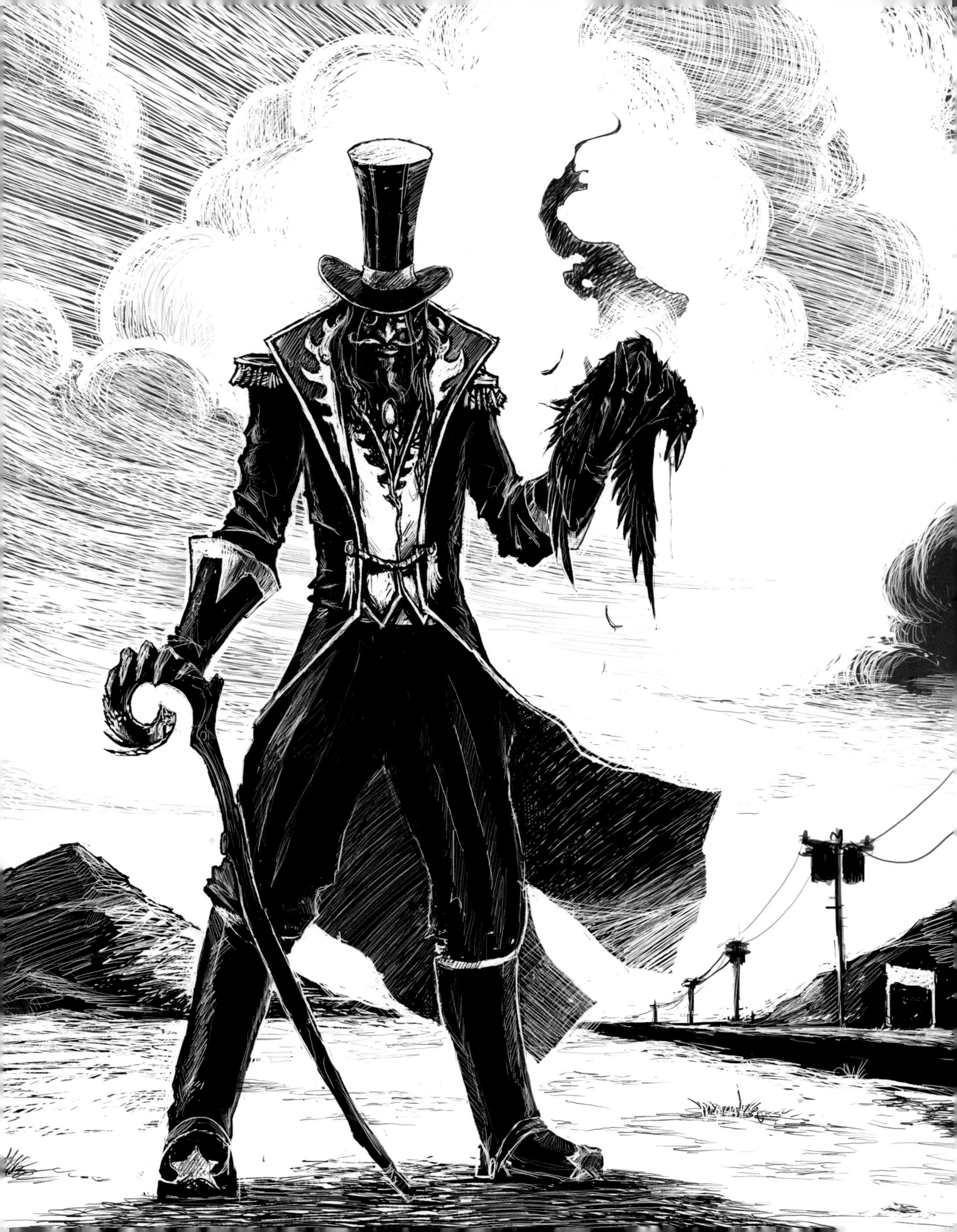

Bo grins. "'Bout thirty-five miles . . . as the dead crow flies."

Bo falls into one helluva fit o' gigglin' and guffawin' as the Ramblin' Man rambles his way back to the trucks.

★★★★�֍★★★★

A while later back at the trestle bridge, the damnedest thing happens: That hangin' corpse, well his hand gets to twitchin', followed pretty soon by his legs. Next thing you know he goes and opens up his eyes! You might think you seen some mind-bogglin' spectacles in your life, but until you've witnessed a hanged man climb hand-over-hand up his own rope, you ain't seen shit.

Our friend here, he ain't exactly no ordinary man, as you mighta surmised by now. His name's Jo Jo and he's what you'd call "different"—it's why he ain't dead, for one thing. It's also why he joined the Ramblin' Man's Barnstormers all those years ago. But we'll get to that later. Right now, Jo Jo has made it onto the bridge—takin' his time undoin' that noose but presently his persistence pays off. He tosses the rope aside and goes stumblin' west across the rails until he steps offa them tracks, relieved to feel solid ground under his boots. Eyes closed against the sun, his mind drifts back momentarily to the shootin' and the beatin', and he knows it's gonna be quite a spell 'til he feels anywhere close to normal once again, but mostly what he thinks about . . . is Her.

I gotta get back to Her.

He rubs his chest, plucks a lead slug or two off his hide, and casts his gaze west, where the rails continue on as far as he can see. But curvin' 'round the edge of the chasm he just crawled out of, sweepin' in and runnin' next to them train tracks, is the two-lane Anaconda. It's there that Jo Jo conducts himself next, eyeballin' a peculiar object just this side o' the blacktop.

Now, of all the shit-ass fortune Jo Jo's undergone in the last twenty-four hours, one tiny iota o' good luck has smiled on him: There ain't been but the slightest breeze overnight and Jo Jo's dusty, bullet-holed, beat-up cowboy hat is still sittin' right there next to the highway.

It's a small comfort, a man's hat, but at least it's one thing they didn't manage to take from him. That and the silver trinkets he wears.

In fact . . .

Jo Jo reaches into his jeans pocket and takes out his wallet, openin' it up to see . . . his money, his Johnnies, right where they're supposed to be. His picture o' Her, however, is missin'. They didn't wanna *rob* him, no sir, that ass whoopin' and killin' (or attempted killin', as it turns out) was some straight-up vindictive shit; but they did steal from him that image o' Her. And that alone's enough to make the bastards pay.

Jo Jo stands there, lookin' at the tracks in the dirt where the trucks pulled over. He bends down, scoops up some o' the earth in his hand, and sniffs. He knows where they're goin'. The Barnstormers run the same route, year after year. Ain't no way he can get to Hubtown before they've been and gone, but after that . . . Dead End, well he reckons he can catch up to 'em at Dead End. And it's there that he'll get Her back . . . and settle up with Ledger DeMesne once and for all.

Jo Jo tosses the dirt aside, pulls that cowboy hat down to block out the sun, and bends his steps to the west, along the Anaconda, so preoccupied with his own ruminations that he don't notice the scraggly crow that swoops in for a clumsy landin' on the road behind him, its feathers pointin' this way and that, lookin' for all the world like somethin' that done got chewed up and shit out.

Jo Jo's boots carry him on while the Ramblin' Man watches through the blackbird's dead eyes.

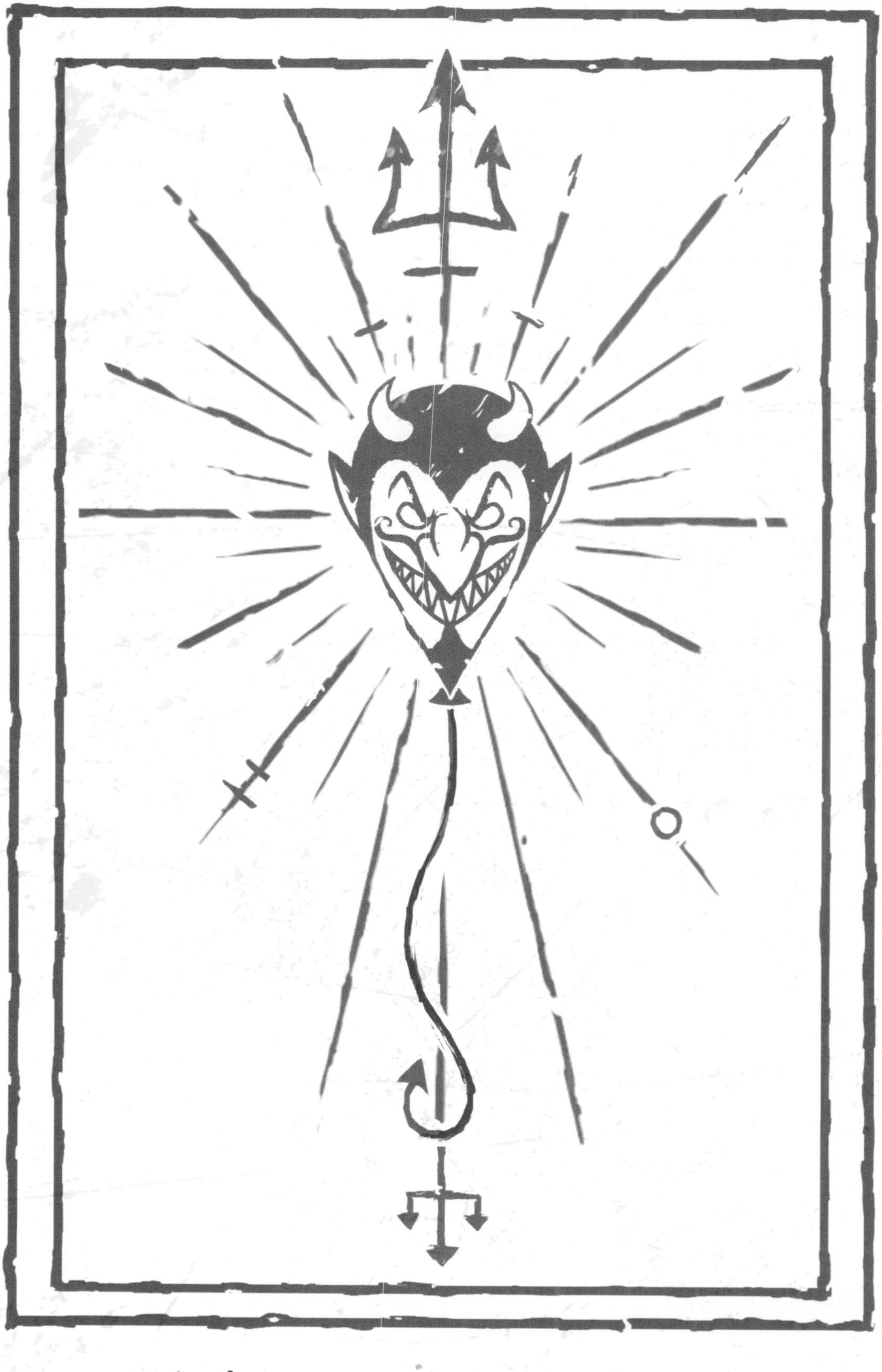

The Magician

CHAPTER THE SECOND

The Barnstormers' trucks are right smack-dab in the middle o' Devil's Tailbone when Ledger DeMesne, the Ramblin' Man, calls a stop.

Now the caravan'd been all fixed to roll right through the tiny town—you might even call it a hamlet—o' Devil's Tailbone. The people o' that little map stain had finally smartened up a handful o' years ago and decided that when the Barnstormers came through, why they'd just shutter the windows and lock the doors. Course, folks in Devil's Tailbone didn't get out much anyway, so no big loss there.

Now some o' you are askin' why the good people o' Devil's Tailbone would treat the caravan in such an unneighborly fashion. Well, it just so happens that the town's population was small enough to begin with, without their salt o' the earth and most especially their little tykes turnin' up missing every time the carnival set up shop. And when I say "missing," I don't mean missing entirely in the physical sense. The kids, they were there, but they weren't *there*, if you take my meanin'. It was like a mighty important piece o' em had been taken . . .

But for now, let's not meditate on such dark matters and return instead to the events at hand.

It's quiet enough on Main Street to hear a mosquito fart as the Ringmaster walks back a few wagons, to be met by the Magi twins.

Bo's all set to ask why the wheels ain't turnin', only to be silenced by the cold glare emanatin' from under the Ramblin' Man's top hat.

"Job's not finished," Ledger says. A shutter on one o' the houses facin' Main Streetcracks open, then quickly closes when the Ringmaster's head swivels over.

"Let me go fix it," says Bo. "It'll be fun!"

"Would I have to go, too?" asks Tweeny, soundin' unexcited by the prospect. Before the two o'em get to debatin' just how one half a pair o' conjoined twins might be capable o' undertaking any kind o' expedition without the other one, Ledger DeMesne cuts in.

"I'm sending the posse," says he.

The twins' eyes get real big and point in the general direction o' each other. "The posse?" Tweeny asks as if she didn't just hear them very words. "But they're insane."

"Insanity is a funny thing," the Ringmaster answers, looking back in the convoy to an ice cream truck, made by that same German company that makes them bubble cars. As the Ramblin' Man rambles toward the truck, the only sound bouncin' off the house-fronts that line Main Street is the titterin' o' Bo, as if he just got told the punch line to the world's most hilarious joke.

Now, see that sign? Not the NO DOGS OR GUNS ALLOWED sign but the other one—the big one on the metal pole that says PAPA BOEHNER'S DINER? Course I suppose it don't *say* that, it *reads* it, but let's don't get hung up on semantics. You see it? Well that's where we can find Jo Jo right about now, past all them big rigs in the parkin' lot and them motorcycles kicked out front.

Those semis, see, they're the lifeblood o' the Lone Star Nation. Yessir, without them eighteen-wheelers haulin' all manner o' necessities across the arid desert, everything from guns n' ammo to medical supplies to pork rinds—I did say necessities, mind—well, without them, the fine citizens o' this great land would either be dead or on the grim reaper's doorstep. Ask any military man about the importance o' supply lines and you're in for an earful.

Course, with such temptin' prizes as guns n' pork rinds in the offing, them trucker caravans attract all manner o' unsavory characters—vagabond types wantin' nothin' more than to take what ain't theirs by right. And that's where the biker gangs come in. Back in the old days, stagecoaches carryin' valuable cargo had what was called a "shotgun messenger" . . . a real grit-in-the-guts type whose sole charge was to protect the cargo with his life. (That'd also be the origin o' the term "riding shotgun," for all you trivia types.) Anyhow, you just think o' the biker gangs kinda like them shotgun messengers. They defend the trucker convoys against all types o' highwaymen.

Where the hell was I, anyway? Done gone off on a tangent. Jo Jo, that's right—he'd been left with his money—his Johnnies—if you remember, so he's staked himself a spot in that booth right there next to the window, with a good view o' the entrance. Course, behind him's where he should be castin' his attention. Sittin' a couple booths back, mad-doggin' Jo Jo's pelt-covered noggin, is Frankie. Frankie'd be the leader o' the Profits, one o' the very biker gangs I just spent that tangent on.

Somethin' you may already know about biker gangs: Not all them boys are 100 percent stand-up citizens. They still defend their trucker clients mind you, 'cause if they didn't they'd be out of a job; but some o' them steel-horse cowboys ain't above what you might call "supplementin' their income" via other means. And that holds especially true for the Profits. Just look at their name, for Christ's sake, and follow along—I can't spoon-feed you everything.

Now, Jo Jo's been sittin' for a while. Long enough to finish a plateful o' eggs and bloody steak and a heapin' helpin' o' coffee and water to boot. Long enough, too, for that coffee and water to be workin' its way south lookin' for an exit. Jo Jo gets up and heads back to answer the call, passin' by Frankie and three o' his faithful . . . and he can feel the impending violence as he walks by that booth, the way a lone wolf can sense a threat when it stumbles into some wild pack's territory—can smell the blood in the air that ain't even been spilt yet.

Jo Jo hears a voice like sand on a washboard: "The sign outside says 'No dogs allowed.'" This statement is accompanied by chuckles from the faithful.

Jo Jo stops in his tracks. True enough, he spent just about his entire life bein' called "animal," "feral child," "wild man," "dog face," and the like. ("Freak" was used most often.) But after bein' beat up and shot and pissed and shit on and hung and left for dead, but most especially after they took Her, well the words o' old Frankie don't cut no ice.

"Too bad they got nothin' against assholes," Jo Jo answers and keeps on walkin' . . . on into the bathroom and right up to a grimy mirror above the sink. He runs water to wash away some o' the Anaconda from his face, stoppin' briefly to look down at the dirt and hair and darker stains around the drain that look like blood.

Recall a while back when I told you Jo Jo was different? Well, somethin' I ain't shared about our man yet is his sense o' smell. Jo Jo can smell things in a way no one else can. You know how a bloodhound can track a man just by his smell? Well, Jo Jo puts any damn bloodhound to shame. Speakin' o' blood, Jo Jo dips his head and flares his nostrils, takin' in the particular odor o' that dark stain and sure enough, it's blood.

His blood.

The bastard stood here and washed my blood from his hands, Jo Jo considers. O' course, lookin' down at his own clothes, Jo Jo takes only the smallest comfort in notin' that he got a bit o' the Ramblin' Man's blood on *him*, too. At least the bloodlettin' wasn't no one-way street. Right about then that coffee and water get mighty insistent about evacuatin', and Jo Jo makes his way to the urinal.

The odors emanatin' from that cracked porcelain are a hundred times more pungent than anything he'd smelled in the diner, and he'd smelled plenty there. Somethin' else you don't know about Jo Jo's sniffin' ability: He can separate out a bunch o' scents, one from the other—what some fancy-pants types might call compartmentalizin'. And that's what he does now, honin' in on one particular emanation, one that reeks o' pain and death and despair and a black power that existed long before monkey men went walkin' upright, if'n you believe that sort o' thing.

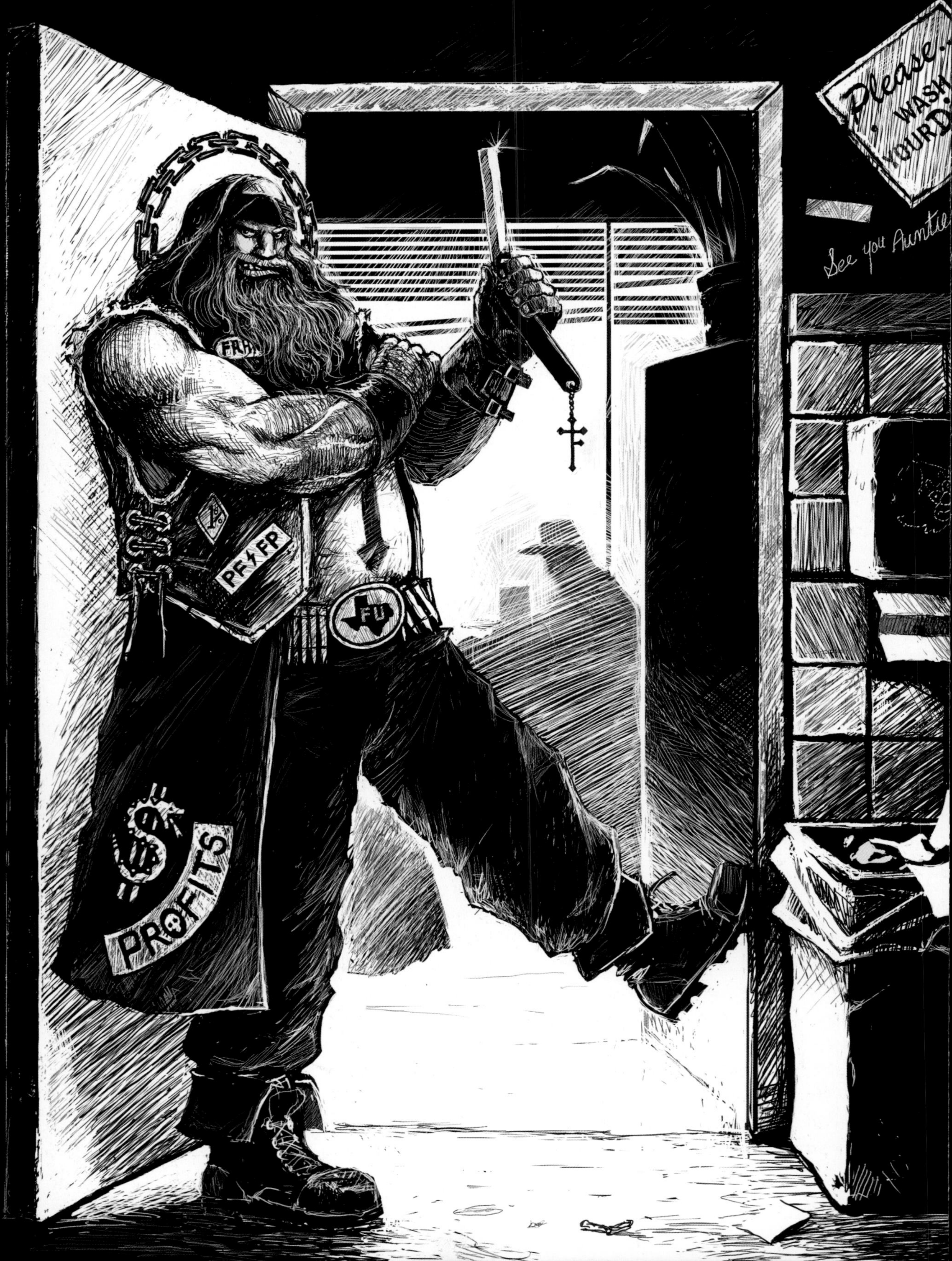
Please...
WASH
YOUR D
See you Auntie
PF/FP
PROFITS

The Ramblin' Man had pissed here, too.

As Jo Jo empties his bladder, feelin' a tiny bit o' satisfaction in covering up the Ringmaster's stench with his own, he hears bootsteps out in the hall. The door creaks open; someone comes in and leans against the groanin' wood and then he hears that gravel-pit voice.

"You know, what you said out there really hurt my feelings. By way of makin' amends, I'm gonna need you to make a donation."

Now Jo Jo, he don't even look up from the business at hand as he says, "Donation, huh?"

"That's right," the voice answers. "To the Church of Frankie, let's say. Nothing too extravagant, whatever you've got on you will do just fine."

Jo Jo's in the process o' shakin' off the last o' the libations when he says, "And what if I don't believe in Frankie?"

"That's downright offensive," Frankie says. It's then that Jo Jo hears him reach into his jeans pocket and draw somethin' out. Have I told you 'bout Jo Jo's exceptional hearing yet? No? Remind me. "Believing in me's just as good as believing any of the other crap people do. My dear old mama, may she rot in peace, said that the only *true* crime in life is not believing in anything at all."

Jo Jo puts all the important stuff back where it belongs, and as he buttons up his fly he hears metal spinnin' on a pivot. "People believe in some guy a bunch of crusty old scholars wrote about in a book of parables a few thousand years ago. Others believe in the nonsense sayings of some bald fat fella. Me, I believe in the almighty JC. Not Jesus Christ, of course. No, I'm talkin' about the one and only Johnny Cash."

Jo Jo makes his way to the mirror and squints at a gleam that cuts through its murky surface: the reflection o' the overhead lights on the straight razor in Frankie's hand. While washin' his mitts, Jo Jo pulls a couple rings off his fingers that look like they been there since before Texas went solo.

"What does it all mean, anyway?" Frankie carries on. "Does it mean people are stupid to believe in things they can't prove to be true? Just because they're desperate to hope that a part of them will continue after their time is up? I don't know . . ." Frankie rotates that blade round and round in his hand, mesmerized by the light glintin' off it. "Don't matter how you *cut* it, it always comes down to the same old shit: "You sin, you pay. You want through them pearly gates, you pay. One way or another, don't matter what you believe in, sooner or later we all pay."

Jo Jo turns to face Frankie. The gang leader finally breaks his eyes from the shiny metal and pushes his bulk offa the doorway, leather vest creakin'. He locks eyes with Jo Jo, and what he sees there looks an awful lot like two full moons, but that don't give him no pause as he moves in for the kill.

Not more'n thirty seconds or so later, the bathroom door opens, and Jo Jo comes walkin' out past the faithful, who stare wide-eyed, obviously not expectin' to see the stranger leavin' the crapper alive.

By the time Jo Jo reaches the door, he can hear the Profits gettin' outta their seats to go check on their fearless leader. The faithful hadn't noticed the flecks o' blood on Jo Jo's beard, or the dark patch coverin' the front o' his shirt, which is partially hid under his jean jacket. They most definitely didn't notice the key Jo Jo holds in his hand.

A motorcycle key.

It don't take much to find Frankie's chopper—marked as it is with Latin-cross *Fs* on the gas tank.

It's been a long time since I believed much of anything. But maybe Frankie's mom was right; maybe the only true crime in life is not believing in anything at all.

And so I choose to believe.

The bike's engine blasts across the desert like the roar o' some angry god.

Jo Jo hears the hollers o' the Profits, rushin' for the diner door as Jo Jo opens up the throttle and tears ass west on the Anaconda.

I believe I'll find Her.

I believe I'll make them pay.

Because, yes, sooner or later . . .

The engine roar o' Frankie's chopper fades away, as Frankie himself lies in the diner bathroom, his life leakin' out on the tile floor, pouring from a bite-sized hole where his throat used to be.

Sooner or later we all pay.

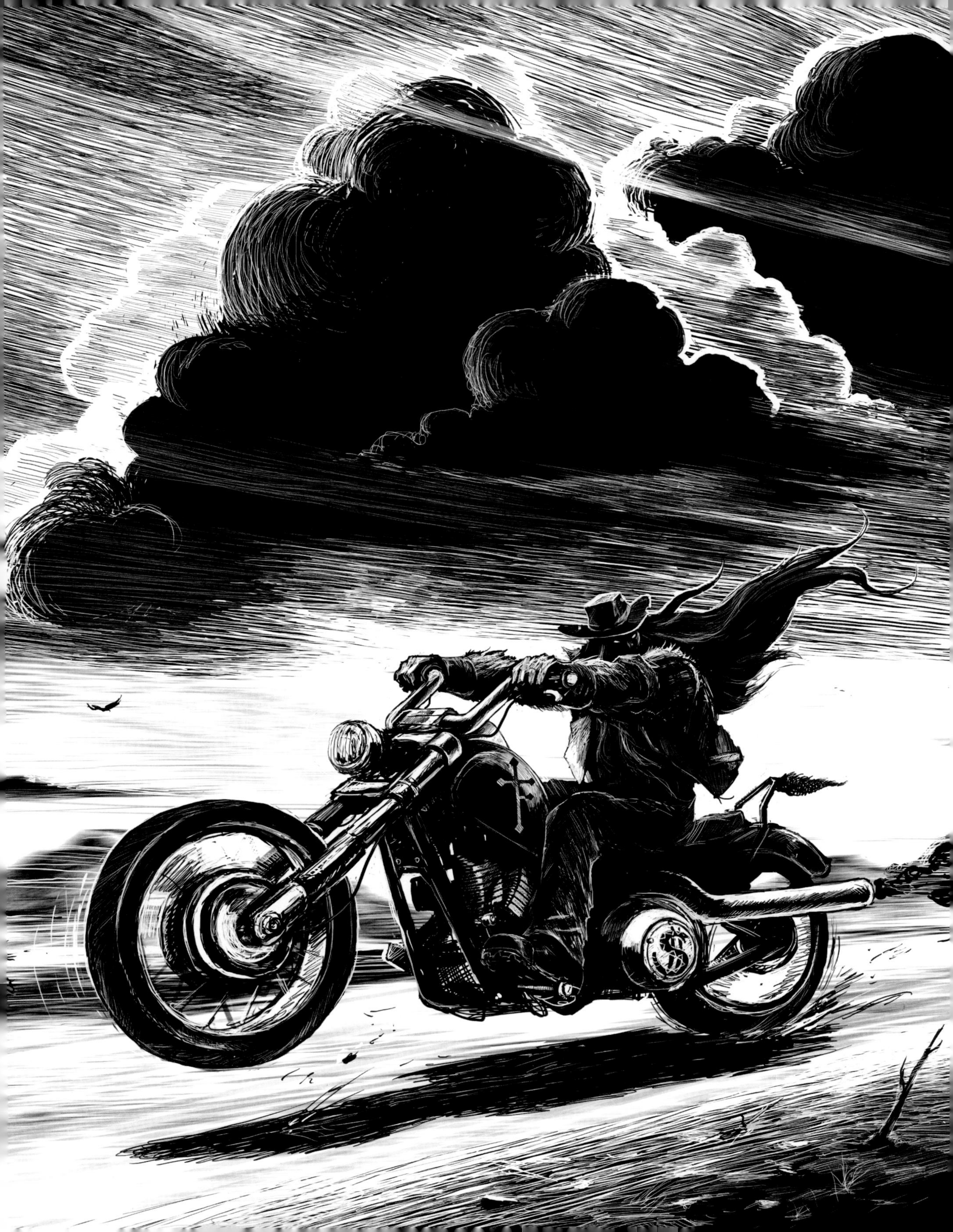

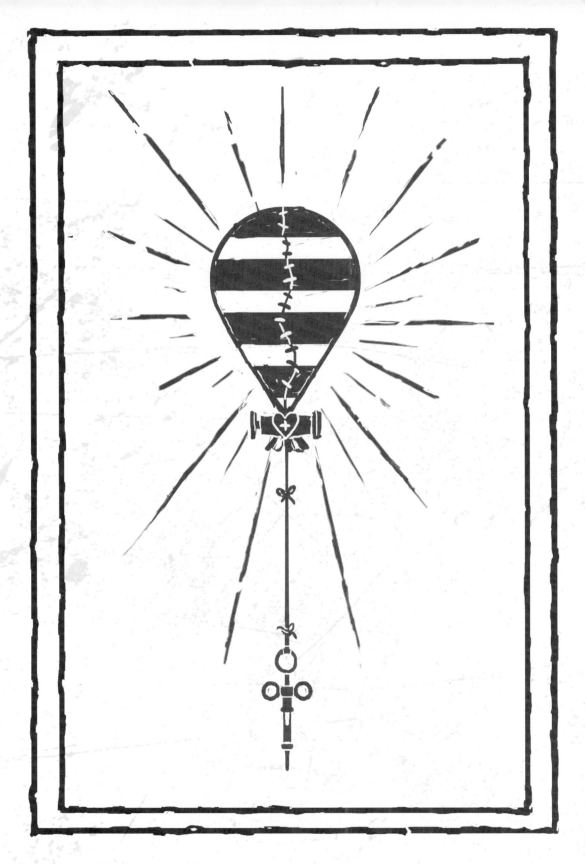

THE DANCER

CHAPTER THE THIRD

One hell o' a mighty wind blows down from the north as Jo Jo pushes the chopper for all its worth. He spots a gas station up ahead and thanks his lucky stars that Frankie's tank is full, 'cause he knows that the Profits are hot on his ass and stoppin' to top off the tank just ain't in the cards.

What Jo Jo don't know is, had he stopped he wouldn't o' found no attendant on duty anyhow. Reason bein', the attendant is in the garage, danglin' from a lift by his feet, dead as dead can be. There's an oil pan under him, put there to catch all his body fluids, but them fluids is gone. Course, Jo Jo mighta *smelled* the stench o' death with that special sniffer o' his, but that garage is locked up tight. So Jo Jo just blows on by. And as to why there's a corpse hangin' up in the Gas N Sip, well, you're just gonna have to sit on that for a spell while we get back to more urgent matters at hand . . .

Right about now, Jo Jo is cursin' them same stars he thanked a tick ago, on account o' the horizon due north has done been swallowed up by a two-mile long, barrelin' wall o' dirt—what some Texans call a "rollin' blackout."

Jo Jo's mighty familiar with the Anaconda, and knows all the stops along the way. He don't need no big-ass billboard with a mostly naked curvy gal and the words "Conway Titties" plastered on it to tell him that the roadhouse strip club is just a mile down that no-name dirt trail comin' up on his left. No sir, he don't need the billboard and the nipples with stars on 'em pointin' the way to the promised land for many a lonely traveler—but there it is anyway.

Cars, trucks, and bikes belongin' to just such lonesome folk occupy the parkin' lot o' Conway Titties as Jo Jo rolls on up. Now one o' them vehicles in particular catches ourman's eye, for the simple reason that it ain't like any he's seen—it's a hearse. Black as the Ramblin' Man's soul and reekin' with the stench o' death.

Just then Jo Jo's ears pick up on the sound o' a convoy, 'bout a mile out and closin' fast. Knowin' that Frankie's faithful are sure to find the bike if'n he don't stash it someplace outta the way, Jo Jo manages to get the chopper out back and behind one o' them giant-sized garbage bins as the winds kick up to beat the band. Now them bins, they got a wall around 'em, and sittin' just inside that wall, hunkering down for all its worth against the gale, is our dead crow, eyeballin' Jo Jo all creepy-like. Jo Jo stops and stares down, and he knows full and well just whose eyes it *really* is that are peepin' at him.

Ramblin' Man knows I'm alive. Damn.

He snatches that bird up by its scrawny neck, twists until he feels a pop, then tosses the carcass into the trash bin. And just before the rollin' blackout swallows everything in sight, Jo Jo lets himself into the back door o' Conway Titties.

A thumpin' bass assaults Jo Jo's ears as he hands the bouncer a few Johnnies and heads farther in. And inside—well let's just say there's a whole lotta female jiggly bits jigglin' the way god or nature or the devil intended . . . and a whole lotta Johnnies bein' spent to ogle 'em, while a bevy o' lonesome fellas hoot and holler and down Grim beers like they was goin' outta style.

Jo Jo ain't payin' much mind, though—even over the boomin' music he picks out the roar o' choppers and the rumble o' rigs outside and he decides to get himself hid.

But let's hold up right quick—you see that dark-skinned fella sittin' at the stage, suddenly not interested in the bouncin' betties two inches from his face but lockin' eyes on Jo Jo instead? The overly tall, unnaturally skinny one, with the tracksuit and the gold teeth? The one who looks like he's lickin' his lips? Well, that'd be Huxley, and he'd be the cause o' the blood-drained gas station attendant's state o' no longer bein' among the living. Huxley's taken a sudden, keen interest in Jo Jo, and for reasons that will become evident a bit later on, he's feelin' like maybe Lady Fortune is finally smilin' down on him.

Time now to catch back up with Jo Jo though, and not a tick too soon, 'cause our man's duckin' into a short hallway in that corner just as a whole gaggle o' bikers and truckers come bustin' in through the front and back o' the joint.

Now that hallway leads to a buncha booths, some o' which are empty, while others got curtains pulled across and noises comin' from behind 'em like . . . well, let's just say there's a fair amount o' moanin' and wet slappy sounds, like when you grab your cheeks and make smacky noises.

Jo Jo hurries on 'til he comes to a booth with a curtain pulled but no sounds comin' from behind it. When he pops in and pulls that curtain closed, he knows without even lookin' that despite the silence he ain't alone.

What confronts him in that booth is one helluva sight—two women', one o'em layin' on a couch starin' at the ceilin', which ain't all that strange by itself, 'cept for the fact that her naked body is facin' downward. Jo Jo then takes another peek at the woman's eyes, notin' how blank and doll-like they are and it don't take no rocket surgeon to surmise that gal number one is dead, probably by a broken neck,

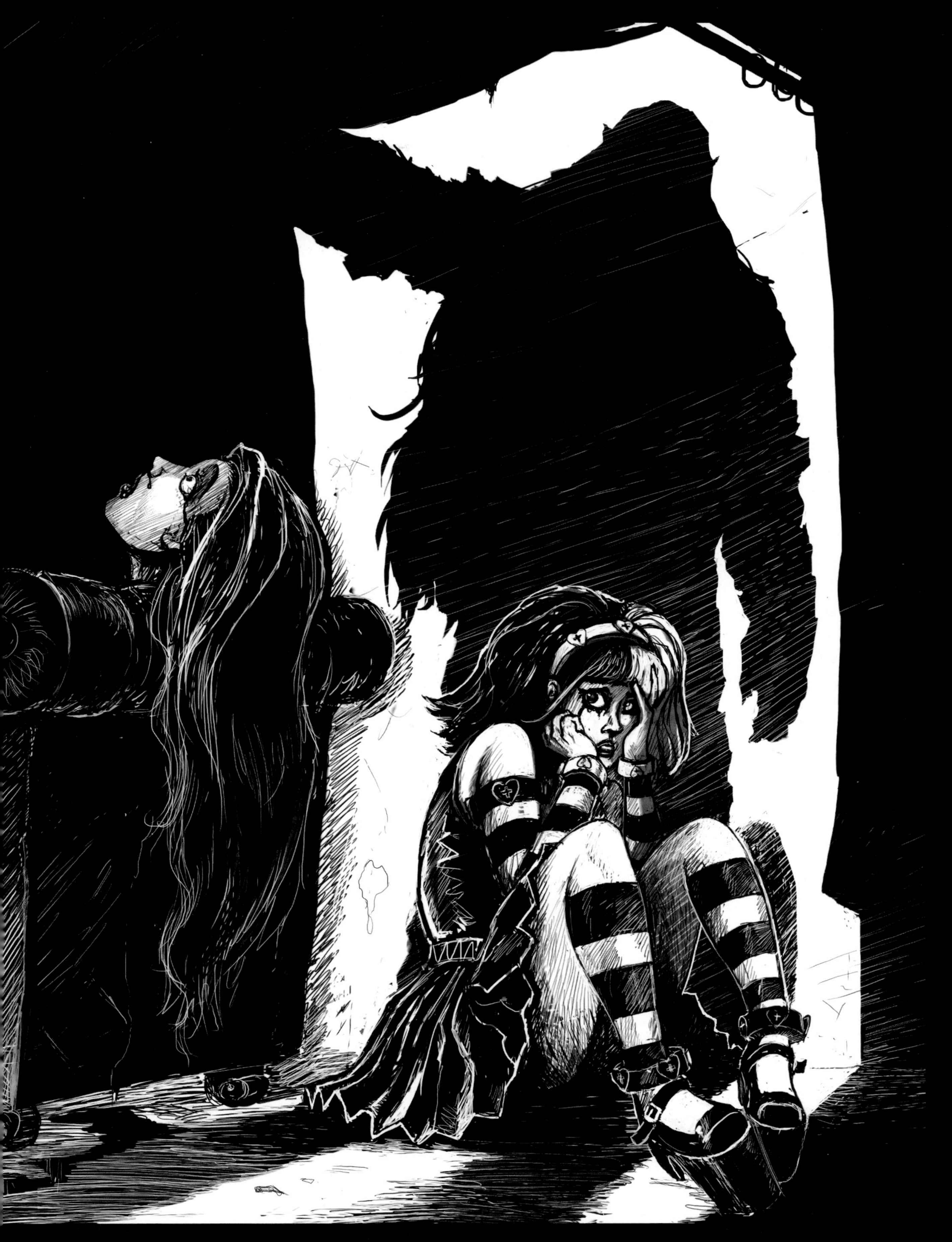

considerin' how it's all twisted. The other gal, well she's curled up on the floor, cryin' her eyes out, mascara runnin' down her pretty face.

"I didn't really have no choice," the not-dead dancin' girl says in a sobby voice. "Father sent her to spy, and she was gonna tell on me. I had to do it!"

Jo Jo, he don't quite know what he's stumbled into, and not surprisingly, he don't know precisely what to say neither. Consequently, nothin' more than an "umm" sound comes outta his mouth. Anyhow, while he's formulatin' a more intelligent response, let's get a better look at our teary-eyed assassin: Elsa'd be her name and as you can plainly tell, she ain't exactly your normal slice o' pie. That skimpy outfit don't hide much, and though our girl certainly is pretty, there's somethin' mighty peculiar about her as well—she kinda looks like a puzzle that got put together with a bunch o' different pieces. Her eyes is kinda mismatched for one thing. And then there's the body: one arm thicker than the other, one leg just a shade lighter than the other, and them funny clamps at the joints, like different arms and legs, and hell, even the head done been *attached* to the body and are all bein' held in place.

Unfortunately there ain't a whole lotta time to spend contemplatin' our patchwork executioner, seein' as how a couple o' Frankie's Profits are in the hall, rippin' booth curtains open one by one lookin' for Jo Jo.

Our man, he gives Elsa a stern look, leans in, and says, "You keep my secret and I'll keep yours." She just nods back and busies herself for a tick as Jo Jo squeezes himself to one side. When them bikers tear open that curtain, what they see is Elsa on top o' some naked gal, with her body facin' down and her head turned so's it faces away from 'em.

"Do you mind?" Elsa says to the Frankie Faithful, all angry-like. Them two give a look like they might wanna join in on the fun, but then one o' the truckers calls out: "Anything?"

"No," the one biker shouts back, and with one more glance inside the booth, they close that curtain and skedaddle.

CHAPTER THE FOURTH

It ain't too much later that Jo Jo finally makes his way out the front, havin' heard the bikes and trucks tearin' off the way they came. He checks to see if any o' Frankie's faithful done stayed behind, but far as he can tell, they all cleared out. The blackout's moved on, too, but it left behind a thick kinda haze, like the murky skies over Hubtown.

Jo Jo's grateful that the Profits and the truckers took off, but his relief don't last long. First, 'cause Elsa's been right at his side the entire time, askin' to go with him, carryin' an ol'-timey doctor bag that she grabbed on her way out.

"Ya gotta take me, Mister, I can't stay here."

"You need to get as far away from me as you can," Jo Jo answers. And the second reason he's gettin' anxious is 'cause he's hearin' a tinky-tonky melody, a jingle that makes the hairs all over his body stand up. He's heard that song before and he knows exactly what it means.

Ramblin' Man sent 'em back to finish me off.

Course it wasn't just anybody the Ringmaster sent.

Jo Jo knows it ain't no use runnin' as the ice cream truck pulls on into the parkin' lot. 'Cause these boys, they don't give up. They're the dirtiest, meanest, nastiest, and certainly most insane o' all carny types.

Clowns.

Elsa she takes a few steps back. Jo Jo cowboys up and takes a few steps forward, pullin' off a couple silver rings from his fingers and droppin' 'em on the ground as both the truck and the jingle come to a stop. Elsa asks why Jo Jo dropped them rings and he just replies that he's "gettin' ready." And then . . . well, then members o' the Posse start pourin' out, one after the other, a non-stop tide o' pom-poms and tutus and grease paint and polka dots and oversized shoes. They tumble and somersault and cartwheel and just when it seems like there ain't no way no more o'em could exit the vehicle, about twenty more come flippin' and frolickin' and gambolin' along until real quick-like they surround Jo Jo.

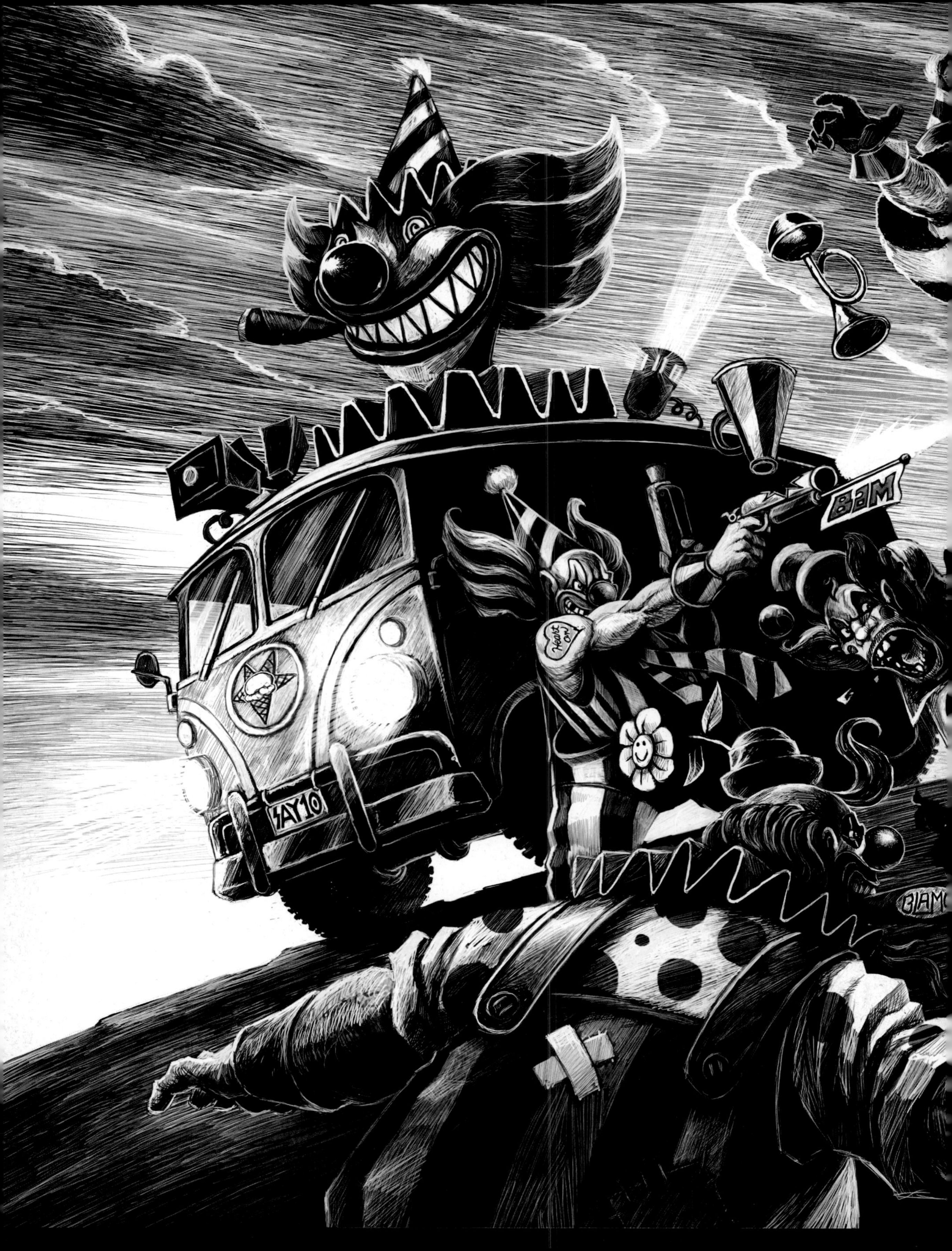
BAM
Heart on!
SAY10

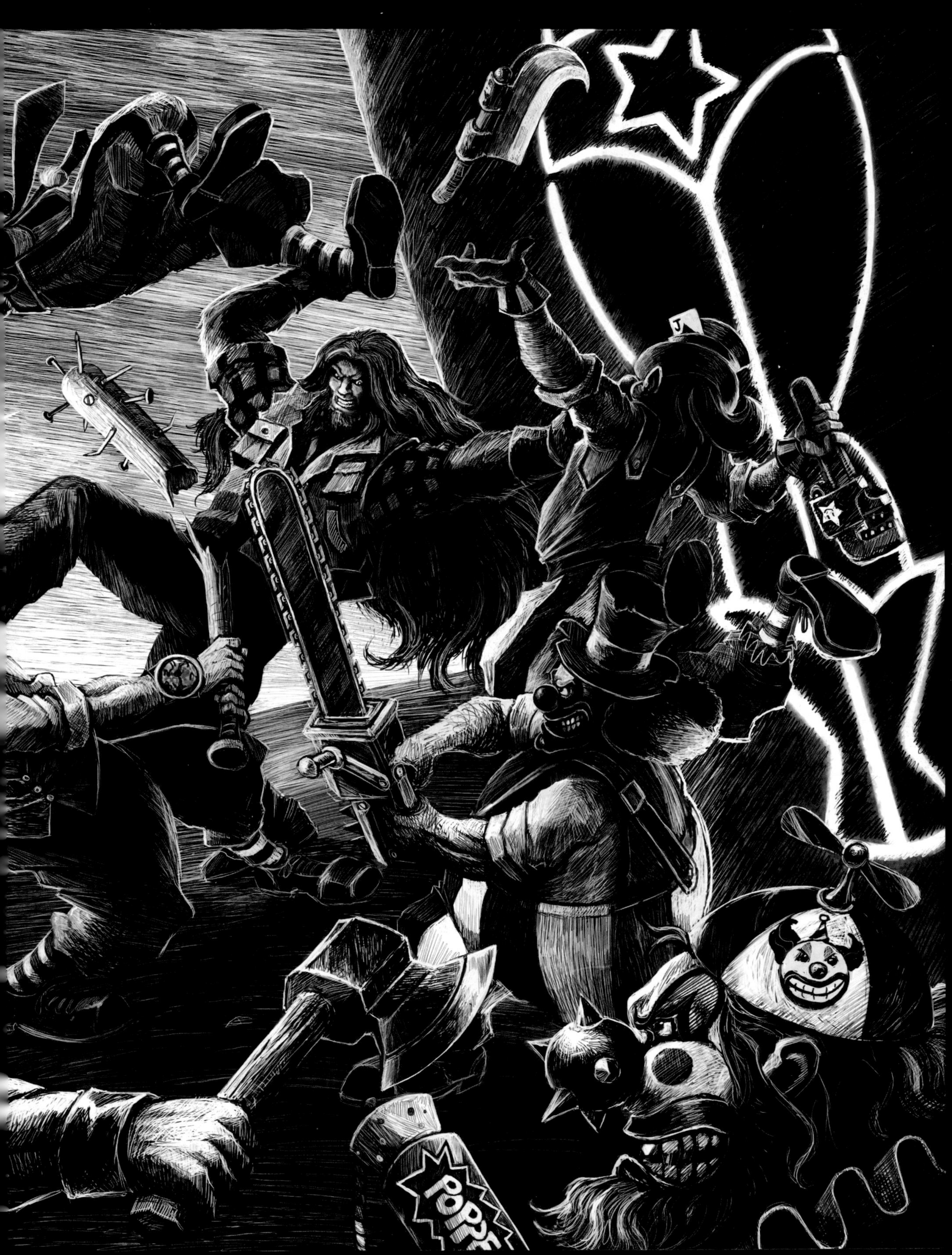

For a couple ticks there's silence, 'til General Custard squeezes the rubber ball on his bugle and the Posse moves in for the kill.

Jo Jo narrowly evades a bouquet of plastic flowers with a steel rod down the middle. He grabs Coco by the head and twists—just like he done with the dead crow not that long ago—until that neck snaps like a pretzel stick. Cuddles squirts acid outta a fake flower, but Jo Jo dodges to the side at the last second, and the caustic stream melts the face offa Professor Buttercup. Bubble Gum Dummy slips on his own banana peel and is out like a light. Bob the Gob Stomper is fixin' to stomp gobs when a poorly aimed explodin' pie blasts his own gob to giblets. Jo Jo proceeds to pound the daylights outta Big Bit o' Honey, while Captain Puff N Stuff mistakes his balloon sword for the real one and quickly gets his teeth kicked in. Boo Boo Goober tries to strangle Jo Jo from behind with a never-ending handkerchief but gets a poke in the eye before being flipped over Jo Jo's back and into the South African clown Ja Breaker, who—yeah you guessed it—he gets his jaw broke.

Bein' as occupied as he is, Jo Jo don't notice that two o' Frankie's gang done stayed behind and are now rounding the corner o' the buildin', pushin' Frankie's chopper ahead o'em.

Meanwhile, DJ Cheezy Squeeze has pulled the trigger on his gun, poppin' out one o' them flags that says (or reads) "Bang!" He's all set to pull the trigger again and shoot a real bullet, when Elsa shoves a scalpel from her bag into the middle o' his back. Jolly Dolly does get a shot off, and Elsa could swear it tags Jo Jo in the shoulder but it don't seem to slow him down none.

Elsa then makes a run for it, dodgin' hits and swings until she gets behind the wheel o' that ice cream truck. She fires it up, and while the Frankie faithful draw their guns, she plows that truck over the clowns she just ran through, right up next to Jo Jo, who's in the midst o' knockin' the wax lips offa Sassy Frass.

"Get in!" Elsa shouts. There's a gunshot, and Jo Jo hears somethin' like the world's fastest gnat go whizzin' by his left ear. He takes one look at Frankie's boys and decides to beat a hasty retreat. He hops into the truck, and that funky jingle starts up again as Elsa stomps the gas, leavin' behind Conway Titties and Frankie's lackeys and a pile o' beaten, battered, broken clowns.

But there's someone else, too . . . someone o' a dark complexion who's done been standin' in the doorway watchin' the whole confrontation unfold. Oddly 'nough, his tongue is flickin' in and out, and his eyes, they ain't watchin' the departin' clown car right now—no, his gaze is fixed on them rings Jo Jo discarded.

Meanwhile, Jo Jo and Elsa are back on the road when our man's keen vision picks up on a small black form teeterin' and totterin' back and forth on the blacktop. Its head's all swiveled 'round so its eyes are fixed on the truck, even though its body is pointin' the exact opposite way. As the truck bears down, Jo Jo yanks the wheel just enough to roll right over that damn crow.

And while the truck's unsettlin' jingle fades into the distance, our bedeviled blackbird lies still.

That is until one o' its wings gets to twitchin'.

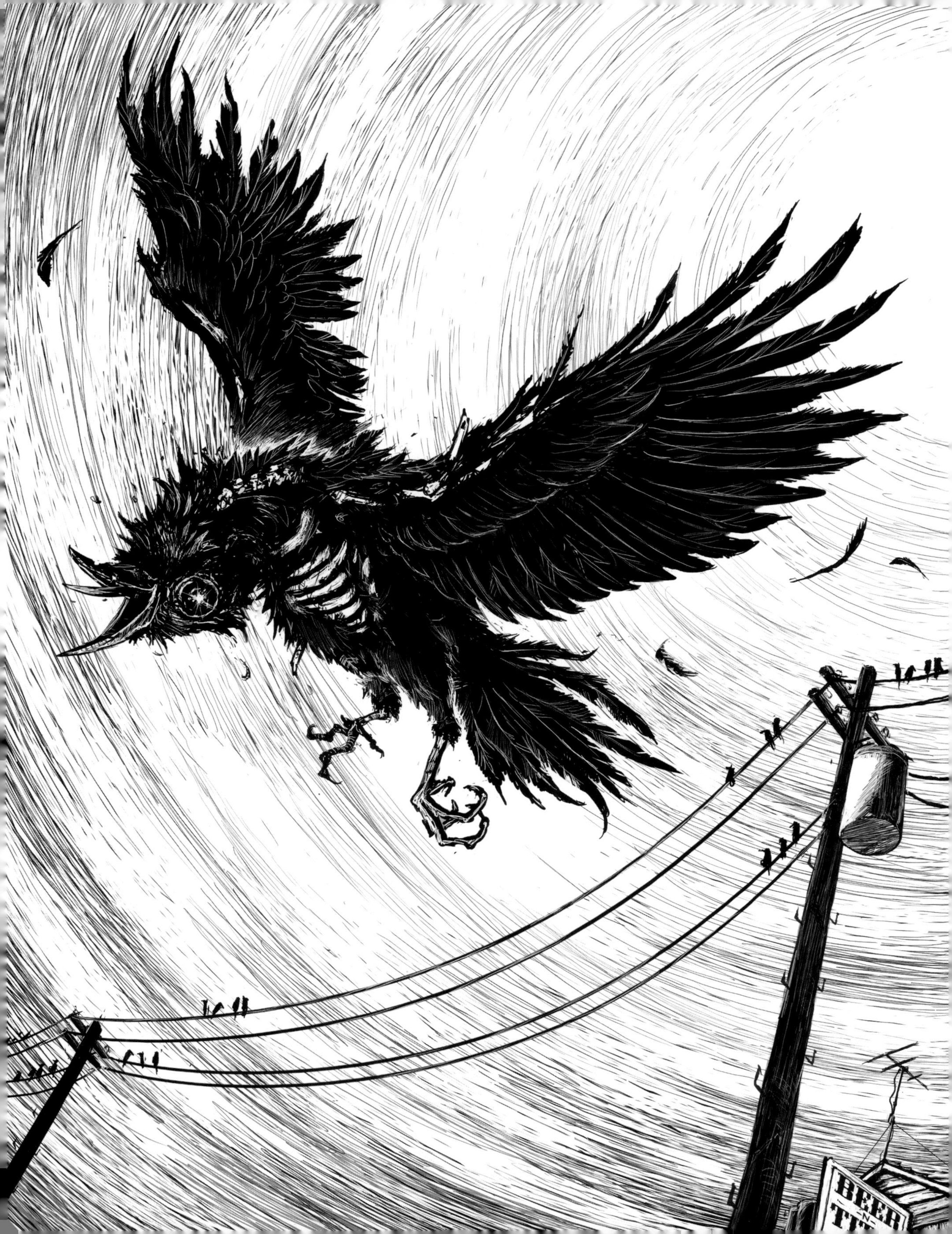
BEER
-N-

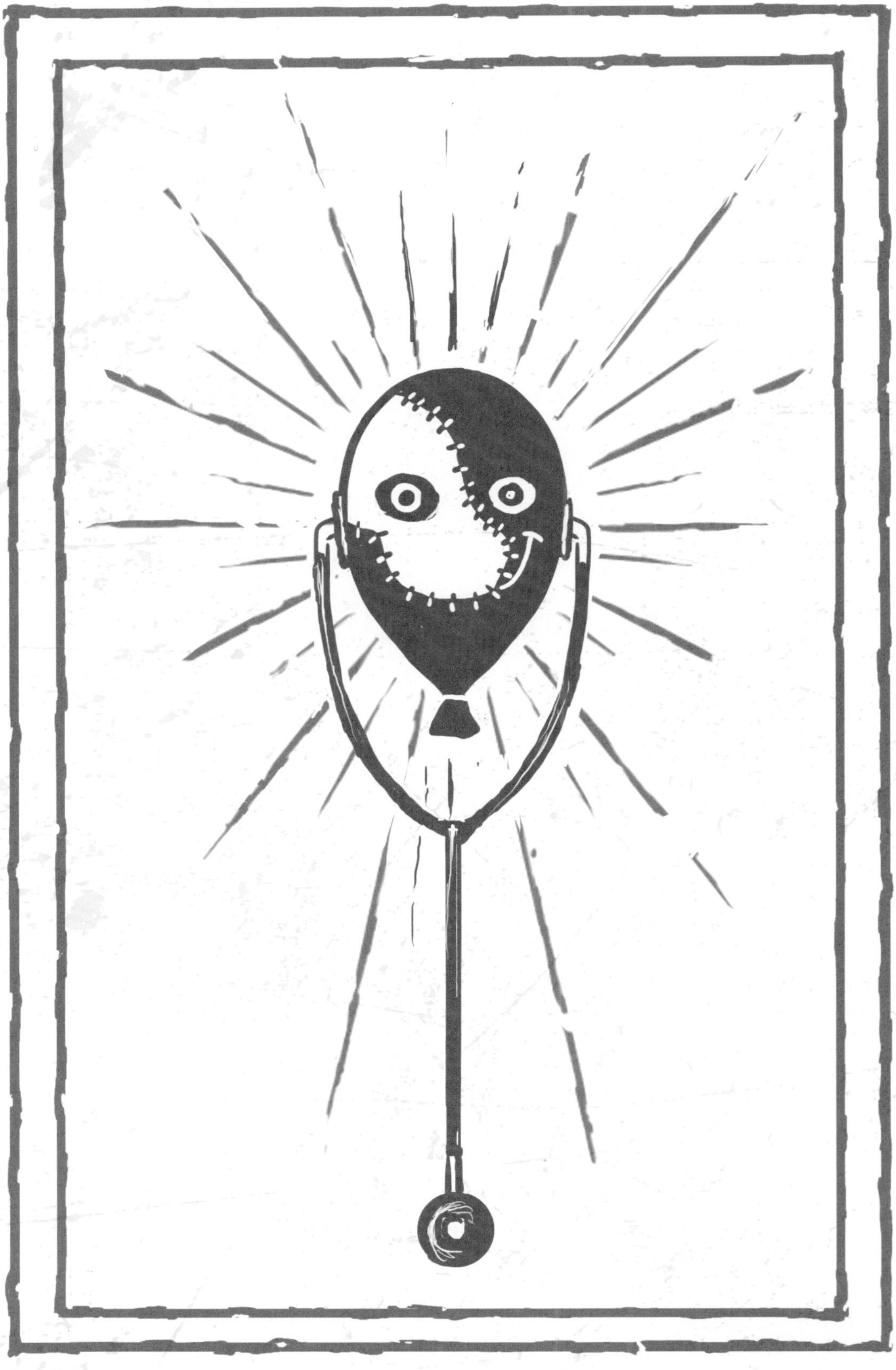

The Physician

CHAPTER THE FIFTH

Jo Jo takes a look out the back window o' the truck, checkin' whether or not Frankie's holdouts from Conway Titties are givin' chase, but it's all barren road as far as the eye can see. He takes a look at the inside o' the vehicle, tryin' to figure just how so many o' the damn clowns could fit, even squeezed in like sardines . . . but it still don't make no damn sense, so he faces front instead, ignorin' Elsa's eyeballs on him and tryin'—but failin'—to ignore the jingle-jangle tune playin' on a continuous loop.

"Mister are you okay?" Elsa asks.

"Fine."

"It's just . . . it sure looked like one o' them bullets hit you back there."

"Musta got lucky," Jo Jo answers. O' course, lookin' over, he can see that one o' them clowns sliced Elsa right across the arm. It's a good-sized wound, but she don't seem to pay it no mind. Not to mention there ain't nothin' comin' outta it. Jo Jo ain't no anatomical genius, but in his experience, most folks who get cut, bleed. That's when he gets to thinkin' that Elsa's different. Different like him in the sense that he's different too, but not different in the same *way* that he's different, if you get my meanin'.

Figurin' she wouldn't wanna talk about that, just like he don't really wanna get into it, he changes the subject to somethin' maybe she would be okay talkin' about. "What was it you said in the booth . . . 'bout your dad sendin' that girl to spy on you?"

"Oh . . ." Elsa gets real quiet while Jo Jo looks around the dash, tryin' to figure out how to shut off that damn annoying jingle. Jo Jo's thinkin' he picked the wrong subject anyway and figurin' maybe she don't wanna talk at all, when she answers.

"I been on the run from Father for quite a while and he don't like that, not one bit, so he sent spies out to find me."

"Why you runnin' from him?"

Elsa she looks down at a little box fixed to the underside o' the dash, with a red switch on it. She reaches into her doctor bag, pulls out a small metal hammer, and proceeds to pound the everlovin' shit outta that box, 'til the jingle don't jangle no more. Followin' that she turns to Jo Jo and taps the hammer against her noggin, sayin', "'Cause he ain't right in the head."

★★★★✷★★★

Not too long after, back at Conway Titties, a man in a real fine suit stands at the bar, waitin' on the establishment's manager, Demore Demerrier.

Demore, as you can imagine, done had his hands full explainin' to the Confederales just how a whole mob o' clowns ended up dead or dyin' on his doorstep. Once he's finished givin' his statement—which consisted mainly o' the phrases "I didn't see nothin', I don't know nothin'"—he finds his way to the bar where he addresses the dapper stranger.

The man hands over a fancy business card that reads "Doctor Victor Prometheus Hart: restorative, reconstructive, and cosmetic surgery."

The manager gets a good look at Doctor Hart, at first just kinda takin' him in, then scrunchin' up his face a bit like he's smellin' a particularly nasty fart. You ever get *Good from afar, far from good* syndrome? Suckered in by somethin' or someone that looks real pleasant at first and then when you take a closer look you realize you was sadly mistaken? Well Doctor Hart fits that bill to a tee, mainly 'cause half his face is fake. Kinda like a mask, but it fits on so good that at first you can't tell you're not lookin' at a normal, everything's-where-it-belongs face. But then when you lean in a bit and the doc starts talkin', well that's when the illusion crumbles 'cause them lips don't quite move right. In fact, half the face don't quite move right. And when the doc talks, the lack o' properly contributin' mouth muscles makes for a kinda mumblin' sound. Nevertheless, what Demore can decipher o' Doc Hart's speech comes out somethin' like this:

"I'm here for my daughter, Elsa. I have it on good authority that she entered your employ some weeks ago. She's an attractive young girl. Approximately five foot four."

"You'll need to be more specific," Demore says with his eyes still narrowed.

"She wears metal bracelets and a choker. Monolid on one side, the epicanthic fold—" The doc's pointin' toward his eyes but the manager's just standing there, all slack-jawed.

"Huh?"

"One eye is what you might call 'slanted.' Also, unless she dyed her hair it would be half-blonde, half-black. And she may have been using the name Shelly."

"Oh. That one. Yeah, well, she done took off. I suggest you do the same."

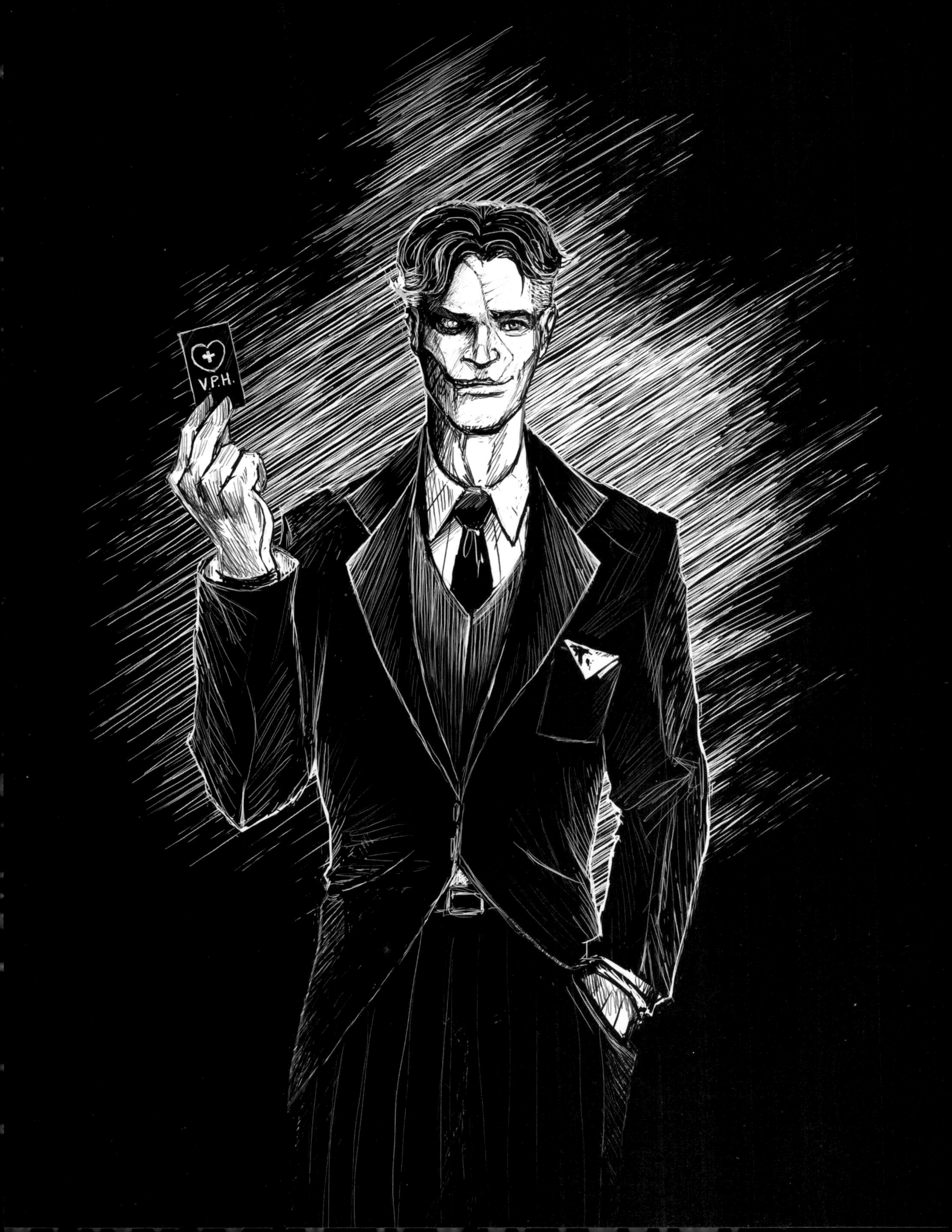
V.P.H.

"Details, good sir. I should like a fair bit more details. When did she leave? How? Was she accompanied by anyone?"

Now the manager, he's just about to tell Doc Hart to go piss up a rope when the doctor says, "I will of course compensate you generously for any information you provide."

Just imagine for a tick that this is one o' them ol'-timey cartoons where the character's eyes turn into dollar signs and their tongue rolls out. That'd be Demore. Once he collects himself, he pokes out a thumb and says, "Follow me to the back."

As you mighta guessed, the manager takes Doc Hart to the booth with that dead dancer. "Found her like this," Demore says and spins the gal's head around while the body stays in place. Our good manager, he wasn't keen on answerin' questions regardin' a dead body *inside* his fine establishment, so he didn't offer up that information to the Confederales.

Now the doc, see, there's a bit o' information he don't offer up neither. Like the fact that he knows this girl. Or that he hired her to find his daughter, just like Elsa said to our man Jo Jo not so long ago.

"Don't know if it was your girl that did this, or the stranger she left with," the manager offers.

"So she *was* accompanied. I require a full description."

A few ticks later Demore and Doc Hart are back on the main floor. The manager he's tuckin' a wad o' Johnnies into his pocket and the doctor's mullin' over the details he got regardin' this stranger that done ran off with his daughter. Hart says his goodbyes, but before he leaves, one o' the dancers—a gal with a chest that enters a room before she does—catches his eye. The two exchange a few words, another wad o' Johnnies changes hands, and the top-heavy gal accompanies the doc outside . . .

Doc Hart waves to his driver in the land-yacht tractor and then holds open the trailer door for his new companion. The two o'em get in and off they go.

They're damn near outta sight now, but if you listen real close you can barely make out a noise from inside that trailer, carried by the hot wind.

Sounds an awful lot like a scream.

CHAPTER THE SIXTH

It's just about nighttime outside Hubtown, though even when it's daytime you can't hardly tell, on account o' the thick smoke that hangs over the place like a death mask. Why all the smoke? Remind me and I'll come back to that.

First, let's focus on how the town got its name. If you was to look top-down on it—I know, I just told you about the smoke overhead. Use your imagination and pretend the smoke ain't there for a tick and work with me so we can move this along. Anyhow, lookin' down on it, you'd think you was lookin' at a wheel 'cause o' all the roads and rail lines and trails and paths that converge on it like spokes from every direction. People come to Hubtown from all over the Lone Star to buy, sell, trade, and make and lose fortunes. Lots o' people. And plenty o' the folks who come to Hubtown never leave, even when they got no place to stay. They become the Aimless, roamin' the dusky streets in their ratty, soot-covered clothes, talkin' to folks that ain't there, congregatin' down in the maze o' sewers, where if you listen real close, you'll hear a particular name gettin' whispered over and over: King Mo.

Now let's move on to the—oh, right. I did say I'd tell you 'bout the smoke. Well the town runs on coal and steam and pistons and hydraulics, see, and that'd be the explanation as to the perpetual blanket o' smog and smoke that hangs over the top o' it.

As I was sayin', let's move on to the outskirts o' town, out to where calliope music drowns out the chuggin' and clangin' o' the Hubtown machinery. Here you'll see that the Barnstormers have finally finished their setup and got the carnival ready for business. Hubtown, as I mighta mentioned, is their last stop before Dead End. So the Ramblin' Man's all set to make the most o' it.

And he seems to be off to a real fine start 'cause there's a whole lotta folks clustered 'round the boxin' ring there in the midway. Nothin' draws a crowd like a crowd, and as you can tell, more and more spectators are gatherin' to see what all the hullabaloo's about.

Now if you look real close, above the shiftin' tide o' men and women and kids, you'll see an assortment o' balloons movin' through the masses. Not too far below that you might take note o' a familiar top hat.

Yeah, the Ramblin' Man's makin' his way through the flock, stoppin' every now and again to hand off one o' them balloons to a boy or girl. See, there he is now with those three kids, leanin' down to that freckled one with the striped shirt. The freckled boy smiles as Ledger straightens and starts walkin' away.

"Uh, sir?" One o' the other two, the fat one, says. "Don't we get balloons?"

The Ringmaster comes, and he stands real close to that kid, his shadow from the lights on the Ferris wheel fallin' over the boy, who looks up like he mighta said somethin' bad, and the Ramblin' Man he says, "Why, no. No in fact, you don't get a balloon. Would you like to know why?"

Real reluctant-like, the kid nods his head.

"Because when you turn fourteen years of age you're going to sniff too much glue and fall into a coma. Two weeks later your parents give up on you and pull the plug."

Now that fat kid he don't say nothin' but his bottom lip scrunches up and tears start spillin' over his plump cheeks. Ledger turns to the other kid that didn't get no balloon, a taller skinny girl. "And would you like to know why you don't get a balloon?" he asks, the mornin' sun reflectin' off the monocle over his right eye. "No, sir," she answers in a quiet voice.

"A shame, since I'm going to tell you anyway. Your family falls on hard times. Early into your teens you sell your body for money. You're beaten repeatedly by johns until you stick the barrel of a .45 in your mouth and pull the trigger. You die penniless and alone, your life unmemorable and therefore unremembered."

The girl's mouth hangs open as the Ramblin' Man says, "Now if you'll excuse me," and departs.

The Ringmaster, see, he's in a foul mood for the simple reason that before the show opened, he peeped through the bobble-headed crow's eyes to see that his murderin' Posse done failed to dispatch Jo Jo. That was when he finally commanded Bo and Tweeny to finish the job. But we'll come back to that.

At this point, the midway's plumb full o' folks clustered 'bout the boxin' ring waitin' for the catch-rasslin' show. Ledger, he's made his way through the various spectators, castin' his gaze about, apparently not impressed enough with any o' the other kids to hand out no more balloons. So he just lets 'em go, and off they float, but instead o' goin' straight up they head along the midway toward the trucks and trailers and boxcars, and anyone observant enough to notice might take a gander at the billowin' banners and tent flaps nearby and note that them balloons is makin' their way *against* the breeze.

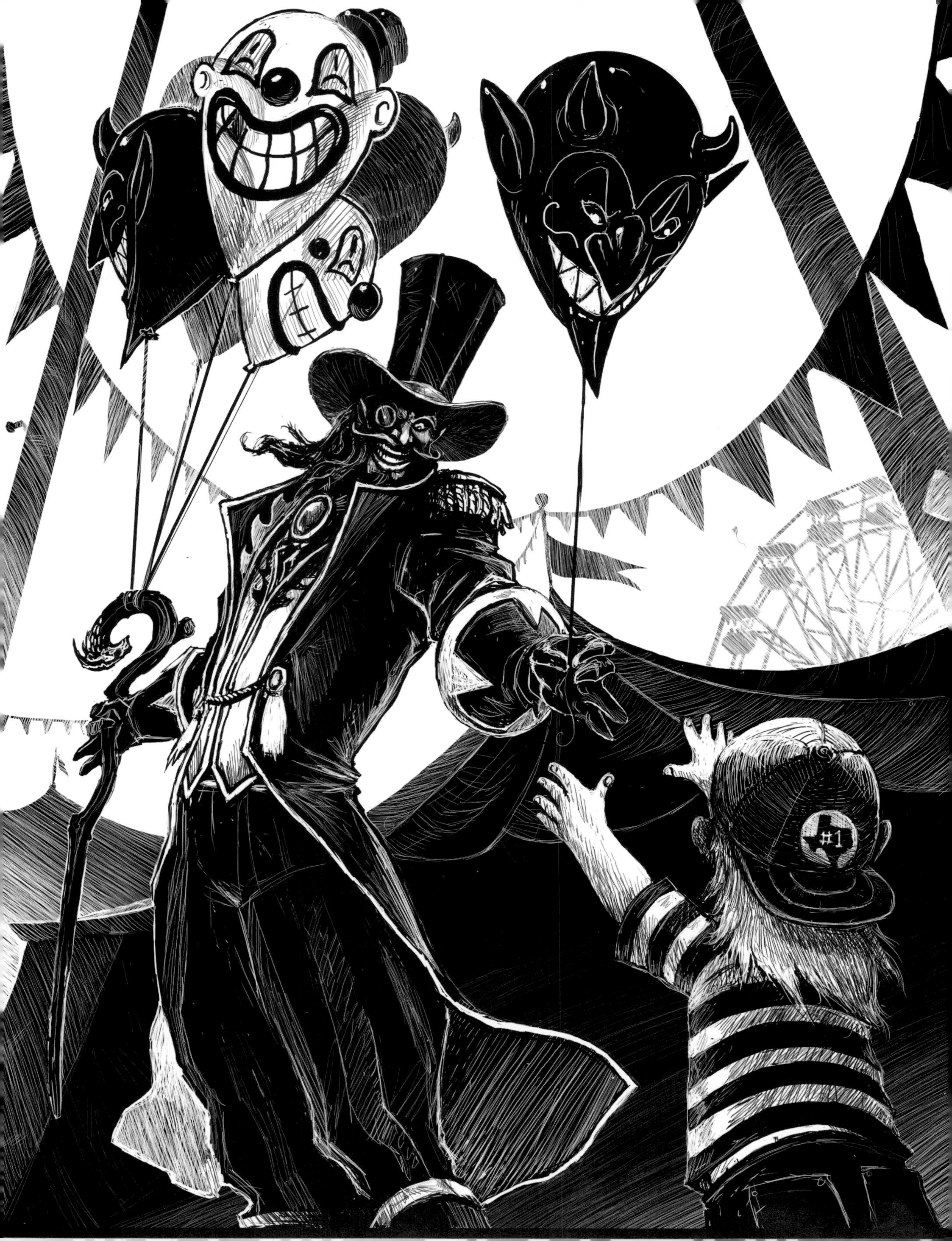
#1

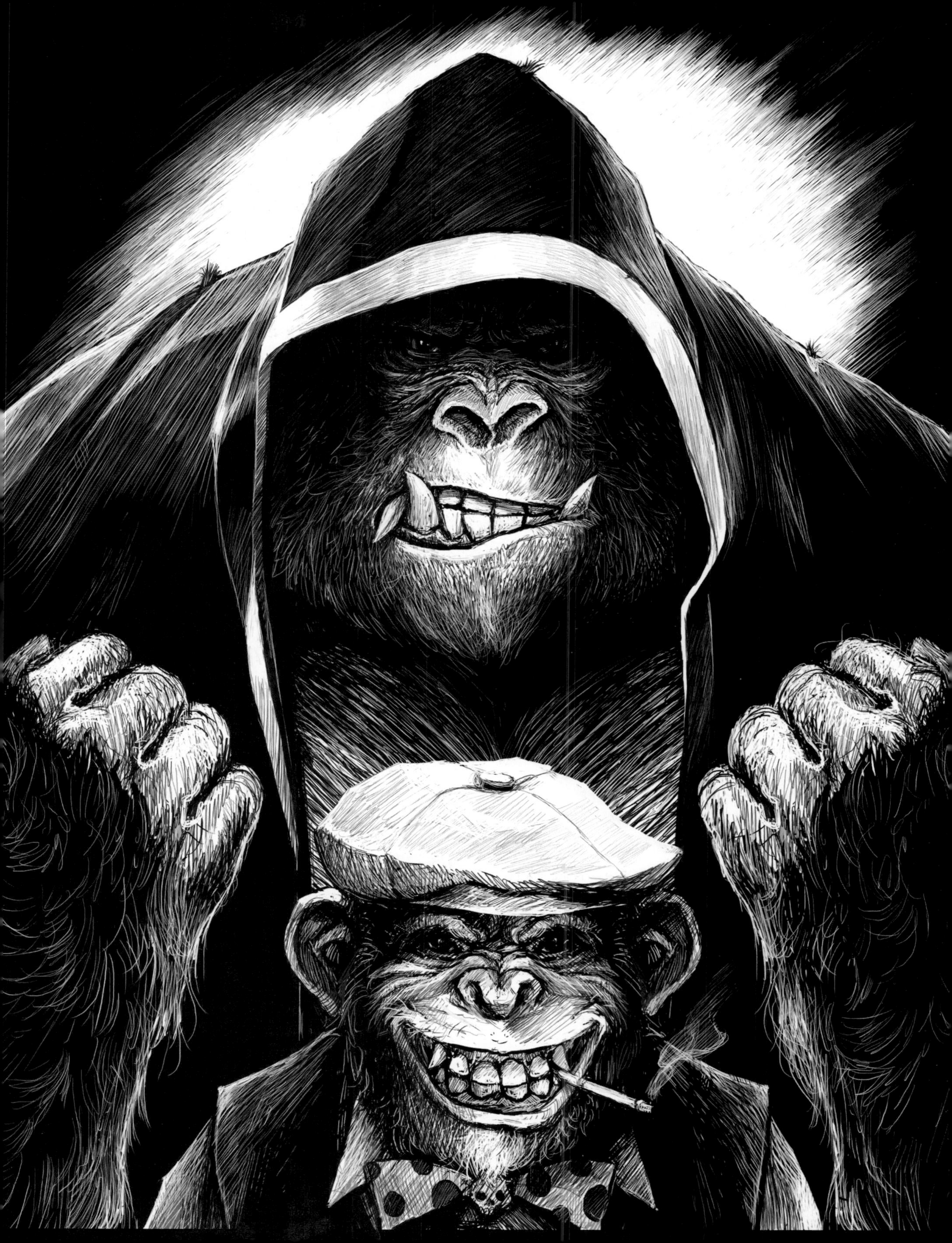

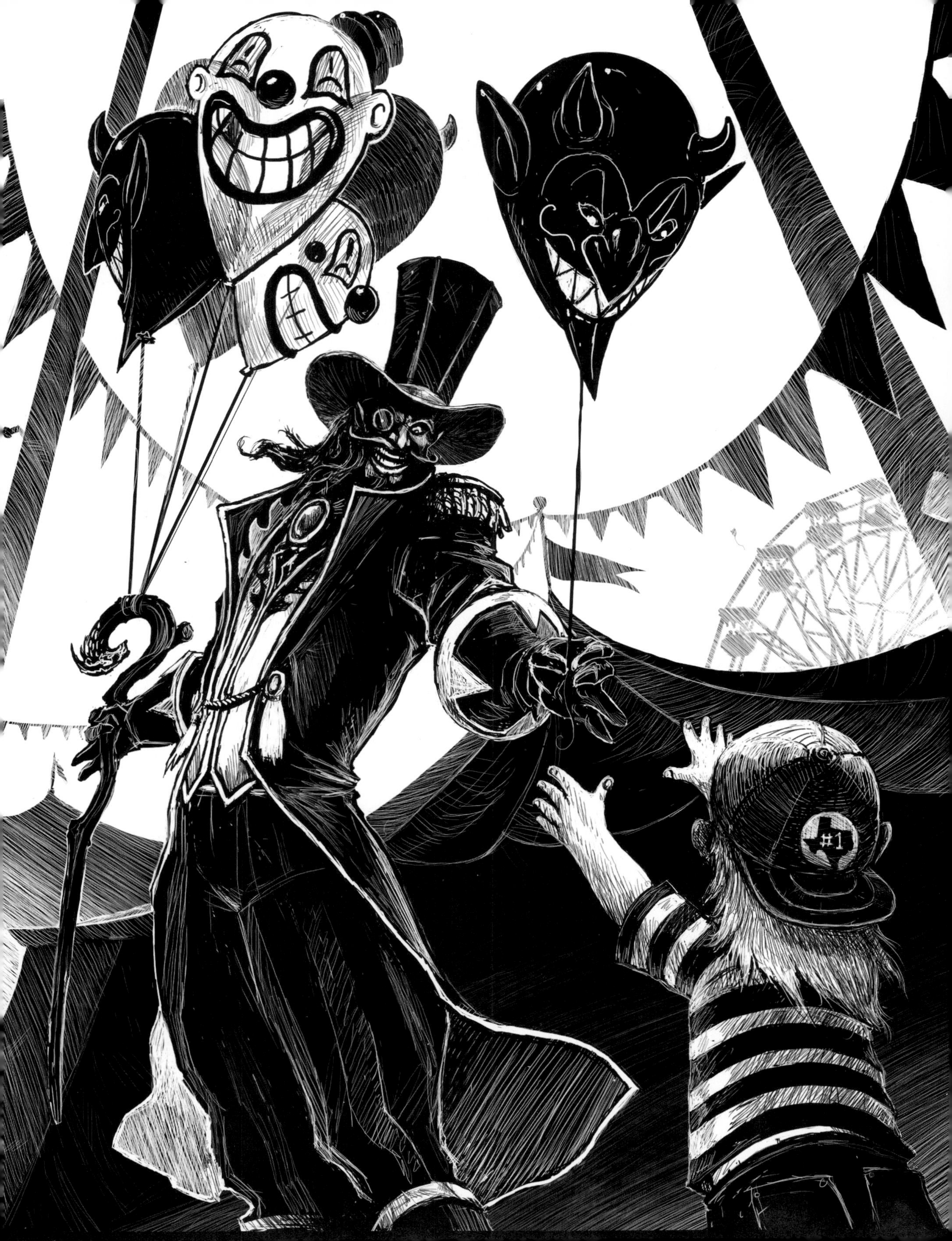
#1

If anyone does notice, they keep it to themselves as the Ringmaster hops up on top o' a crate and taps his cane against the wood for silence. Once he has the crowd's attention, he twirls the cane in front o' him and lets go, and damned if that cane don't keep on spinnin' in the air all by itself! This elicits plenty o' "oohs" and "ahhs" from the mystified spectators until Ledger takes the walkin' stick back and starts in on his spiel, in a voice that reaches far and wide, over the calliope and beyond the lights and the tents and the trucks.

"Ladies and gentlemen, boys and girls, gather 'round. The show is about to begin . . . with a test of strength! A match of wills!"

Now the crowd gets even quieter as a massive, hunched-over, cloaked figure appears. Fur-covered knuckles extend from under the cape and make like a set o' front legs as it stalks forward, followed by its corner man, a chimpanzee wearin' a newsboy hat.

The thing under the hood climbs into the ring. A black, knobby hand reaches up and unties the neck cord as the chimp hops up onto the corner ropes. The beast lumbers out while the chimp holds on so the cape comes slidin' off to reveal the biggest damn gorilla you ever laid eyes on.

The Ringmaster points his cane. "Who among you possesses the courage to climb into our ring and face the savage might of . . . *Terra Mungus*?!"

Terra Mungus stomps to the center o' the canvas. There he stands to his full height, tilts his head back, pounds his chest, and lets out a roar that makes little boys all across the midway piss their pants. After a fair bit o' chest poundin' he reaches down and smacks the heavyweight champion belt strapped 'round his waist, while the Ramblin' Man continues his ballyhoo:

"The challenge has been issued; the gauntlet has been thrown! Time now to see what you're made of! Time now to face your fear! *Men* are called for here. *Boys* need not apply. Who has the stones? One hundred Johnnies to the warrior who bests the beast!"

For a while there, it seems like the mere sight o' Terra Mungus has scared off even the meanest, drunkest bruisers in the bunch. Just when the Ringmaster's set to start in again, though, a gruff voice shouts, "One hundred each!"

The crowd parts to reveal three real rough-and-tumble types—the first one's bald and shirtless under a pair o' bib overalls. Whatever hair he ain't got on his head he makes up for on his back and shoulders. He's got a skinny fella to his left, and to his right, a shorter, immensely fat old boy in suspenders and a ball cap.

"Three against one!" The Ramblin' Man shouts. "Unfavorable odds to say the least! And yet . . ." Ledger swings his head over and points that cane again. "Our champion seems unconcerned." Sure enough the gorilla stamps his knuckles down on the canvas and huffs, puffin' his chest out even farther. The Ringmaster raises his arms like one o' them revival preachers sermonizin' to his flock. "So be it! The challenge is accepted!"

The crowd gets real excited and real loud at the prospect o' seein' a good ol' fashioned beatdown, whichever way it goes. The three men goad all them townies on as they approach and climb through the ropes. The challengers shout taunts from the other side o' the ring but Terra Mungus only answers with a steely, black-eyed gaze. "Gladiators to your corners," The Ringmaster shouts. "And when you come out, come out *fighting*!" The spectators erupt as everyone heads to opposite corners. Terra Mungus hands the championship belt to his corner man, who slings it over his shoulder and stands on the ropes massagin' his fighter until Ledger's voice breaks out over the deafenin' cheers: "*Fight!*"

Surprisingly Fat Boy's the first one to knuckle up. He squares off and aims a looping, meaty fist at the ape's noggin. Terra Mungus ducks the blow and spins the rotund fella around, chokin' the sad sack with his own arm. Skinny's the next one to step up to the plate, but he strikes out pretty quick as the gorilla grabs him by the top o' the head and tosses him back into the ropes. Baldy winds up a swing but gets backhanded and goes ass over teakettle, while Skinny rebounds and gets clotheslined. All the while, Terra Mungus has been chokin' poor ol' Fat Boy 'til his face has turned all different shades o' purple, and he finally just up and goes limp like a beached whale. Apparently not one to waste a good opportunity, Terra Mungus grabs the old hoss by the shirt and jeans and hoists him up over his head, holdin' him for just a tick like he's posin' for a photo, before tossin' the pile o' blubber onto Skinny, who emits one surprised grunt before all the air is done blasted outta his lungs.

Right about then, Baldy sneaks up and plants a punt kick right between the big ape's legs. There's a big "oooh" from the crowd as the gorilla takes one knee and blows out a gust o' breath. Thinkin' he's done won himself a hundred Johnnies, Baldy runs over to the chimp, snatches up the championship belt, then commences to whoopin' and hollerin' to the crowd as he puts the belt 'round his waist . . .

At this here juncture our overzealous volunteer spots one helluva big shadow fall over him. He turns and recognizes somethin' particularly murderous in the ape's eyes, and you can bet he sets to rethinkin' a whole lotta choices, right up to and includin' gettin' outta bed that mornin'.

Terra Mungus raises both arms, hands interlaced to make one giant maul o' a fist, and crashes the entire bundle down directly on top o' that shiny head. There's a loud crack as the big man's melon drops down a couple inches into his shoulders. He's got a mighty perplexed look on his face as he spits out a small gout o' blood. Terra Mungus snatches the belt from Baldy's waist and takes one step to the side as the vanquished challenger pitches face-first to the canvas.

A couple roustabouts run up into the ring and haul the man off while Terra Mungus beats his chest, hops up onto each corner post, and holds up the belt, lettin' loose a mighty roar. Meanwhile it takes about three more roustabouts to get Fat Boy offa Skinny.

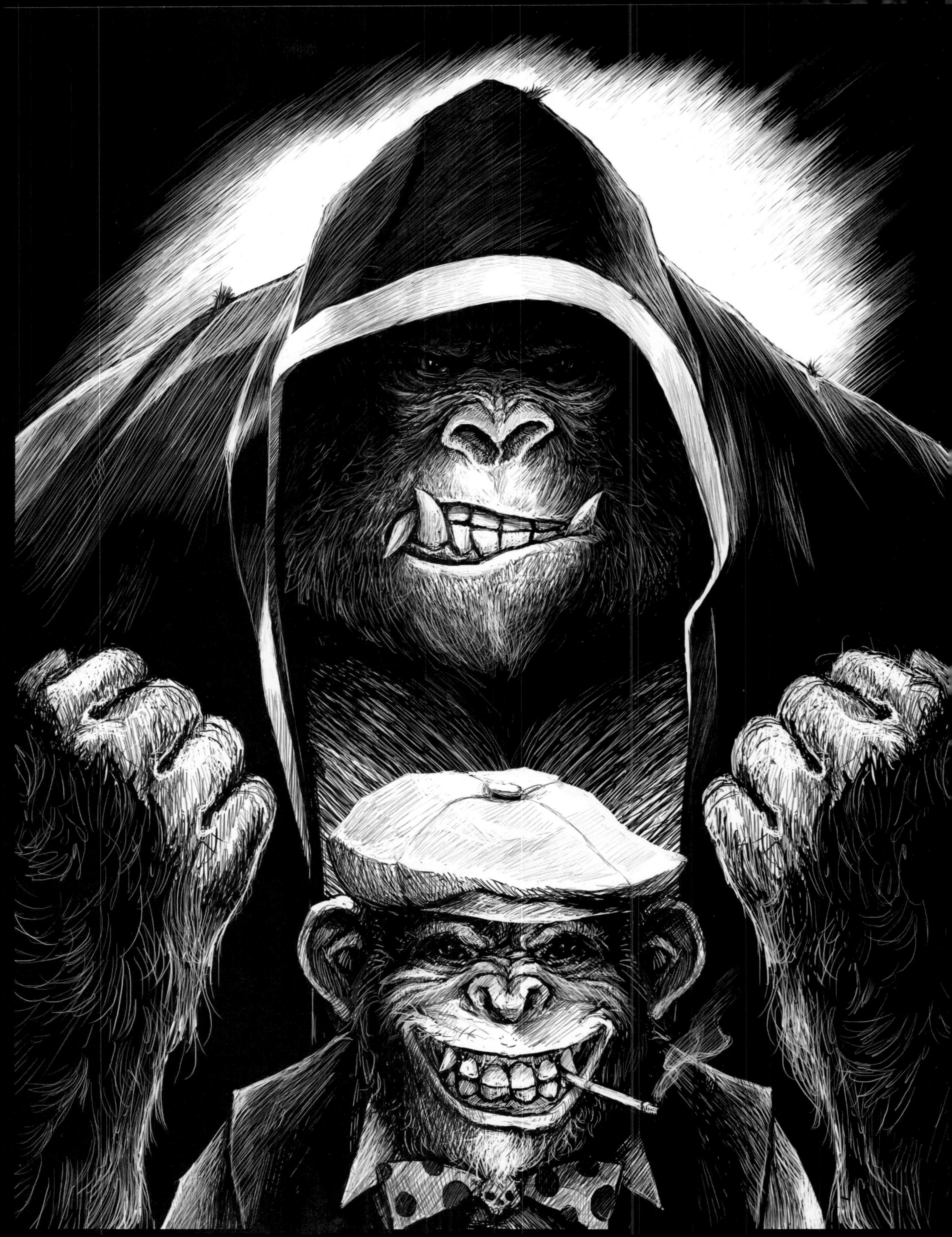

Now, in a typical catch-rasslin' show, what Terra Mungus is supposed to do is defeat his challenger—get the spectators all riled up and out for revenge—but not kill nobody. Unfortunately, Terra Mungus seems to harbor a pet peeve 'bout takin' a boot to Big Jimmy and the Twins and then havin' his championship belt paraded around his own ring. So Terra Mungus had done decided that Baldy had forfeited his right to continue breathin', and once that ape made up his mind, well that was that.

While the Ringmaster attempts to smooth things over a bit by assurin' the crowd that Baldy will wake up in due course, and movin' on to, "Hey, how about these upcoming acts? We've got an amazing show tonight!"—halfway 'cross the midway we're gonna set our sights on one trailer in particular. That black one with boards over the windows.

Here's where we'll find the Magi twins, in the candlelit space with the strange markings—what folks in the know call sigils—on the walls. After the Posse failed, see, Ledger DeMesne gave Bo and Tweeny their marchin' orders. And when the Ramblin' Man does that, the twins go to their special place to carry out his commands.

So here Tweeny stands, holdin' Bo, both o'em all quiet-like, eyes closed. That might seem odd but see, even though they're physically here in this trailer outside o' Hubtown, their minds in fact are somewhere else . . .

Yessir, their minds have just entered the head o' a dreamin' girl in Devil's Tailbone . . .

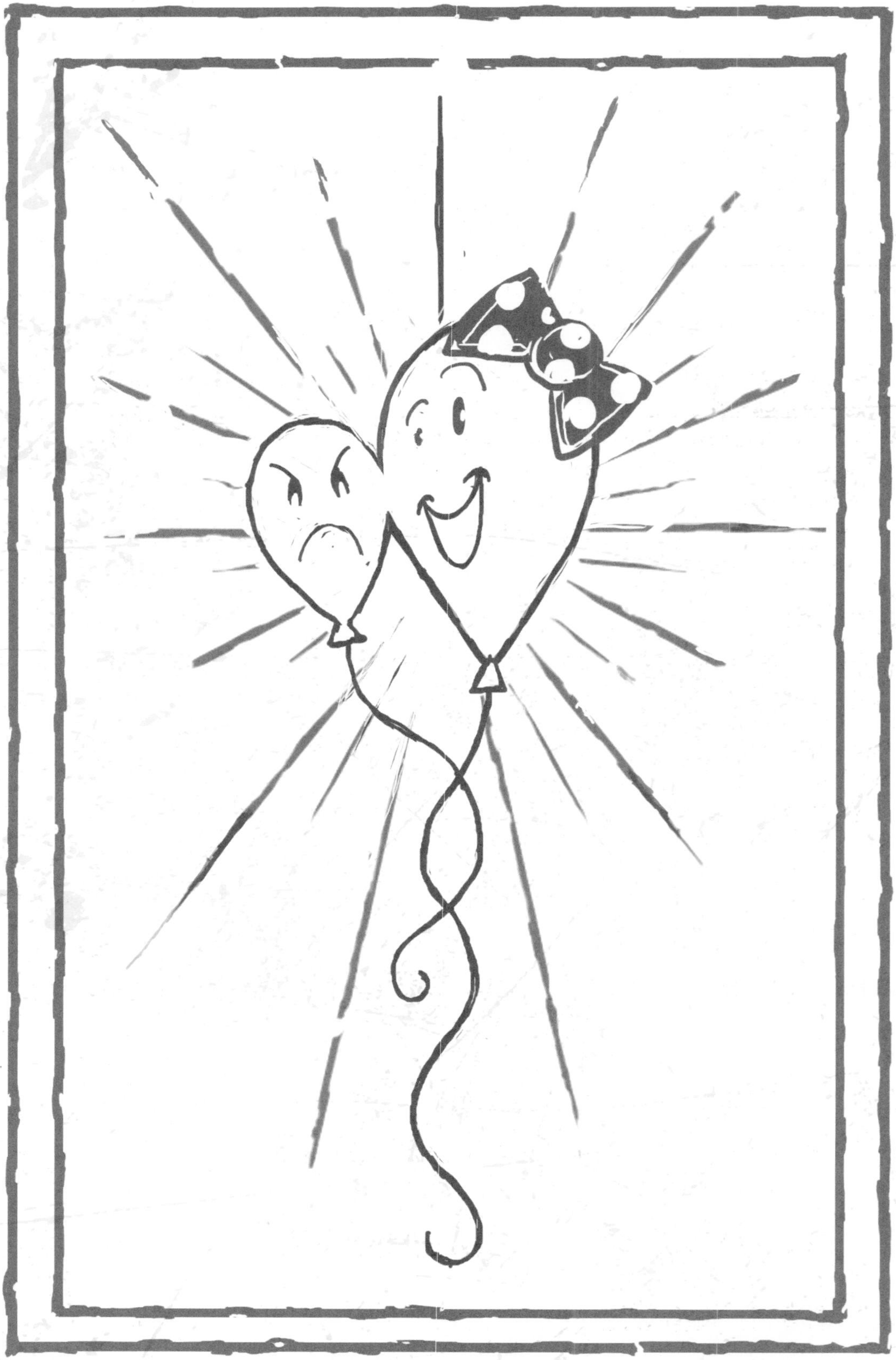

The Twins

CHAPTER THE SEVENTH

Jo Jo and Elsa are in the midst o' a disagreement as the ice cream truck pulls up to the only hotel in Devil's Tailbone.

All Jo Jo wants is to hightail it to Hubtown, so's he can catch up with the Barnstormers, get to Her . . . but him and Elsa done been on the road so long can't neither one o'em hardly keep their eyes open. So Elsa parks the truck there on Main Street and tells Jo Jo to wait while she sees about gettin' the two o'em a room.

Gotta keep moving, Jo Jo tells himself. *Gotta find Her. Save Her.* So what if he's noddin' off? If they can just find a diner, get him some coffee . . . he rubs his eyes and steps outta the truck to go tell Elsa that very thing when he happens to glance down the narrow road to see a kid-sized silhouette right in the middle.

Squintin' don't help him see no better, so Jo Jo heel-toes down to get a closer look. He stops a few feet away and sure 'nough, there's a kid standin' there in the moonlight in her nightgown, all blank-eyed and slack-faced.

"You okay, girl?"

The kid don't answer, and Jo Jo notices now the way she's holdin' her teddy bear; got it supported with her right arm, tiltin' her head to one side so's her head touches the bear's head. Now that's an anatomical configuration Jo Jo recognizes straight away.

The Magi twins.

He also recognizes somethin' the kid's holdin' down at her side, in the other hand . . .

A gun.

But before Jo Jo can do anything else, the twins reach out through that sleepwalkin', sleep-*standin*' girl, and work their yackle-dackle mind whammy. Jo Jo

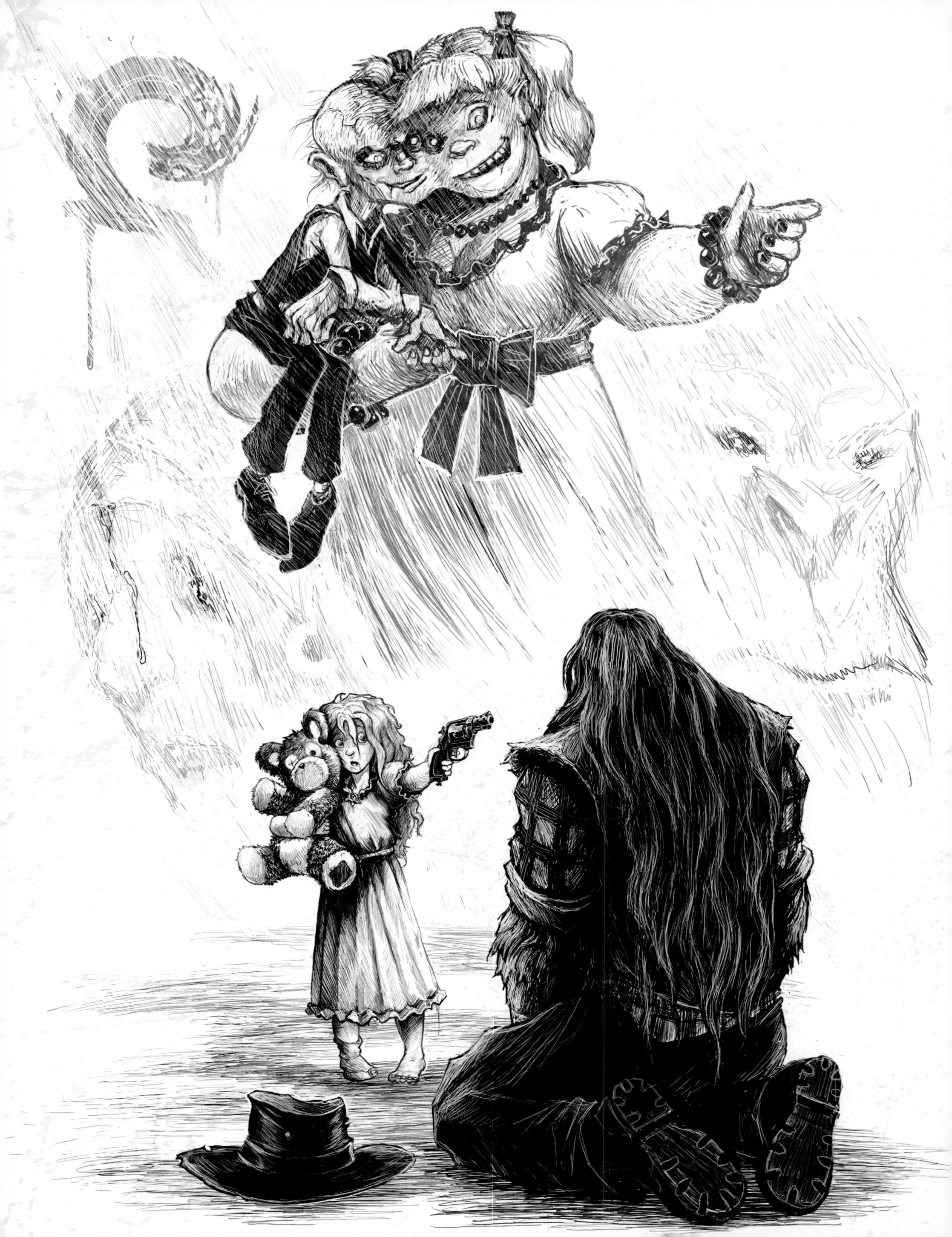

drops to his knees, his facial expression just as blank as the one on the kid. He stays in that position, like a windup toy that done ran outta go power. And if you look in his eyes, them lights ain't on, and there ain't nobody home, but we got us the special seats in the theater so I'm thinkin' we can sneak a peek inside our hero's noggin to see what's transpirin' . . .

And here we have it: memories . . . a whole parade o' painful, restless memories that done reared up and got to marchin' through Jo Jo's skull.

Now, there's rules to this mind whammy hocus-pocus. The Magi twins, they can't "see" what Jo Jo's seein'. No, they just reach in and grope around and start yankin', unravelin' threads one by one, pickin' at all the doubts and fears and regrets and haulin' 'em to the surface. They don't see none o' it, but Jo Jo does. More'n that, though, he relives it, every excruciating detail, in full Technicolor, with all the intensity cranked up as high as it'll go.

You might ask yourself just what kinda memories could be so devastatin'. Well I'm bettin' if we look a bit closer, we can find ourselves an answer.

It all starts when Jo Jo was just a tyke; not more'n a little ankle biter; homeless, Mom- and Dad-less—what you might call a street urchin, wild and mean, makin' his way by pickin' pockets and stealin' bread . . . when he gets snatched up by one o' the roustabouts and taken back to the carnival.

Now this part here, this part's key. Just trust me on this. The first carny to greet Jo Jo is the old gypsy Greta. And that's a fortunate thing, 'cause Greta tells Jo Jo that there's a bright light inside o' him, but he's gotta put a shade over it, 'cause if the Ringmaster sees that light, he'll extinguish it for all and for good.

Inside her boxcar trailer, Greta's got all sorts o' trinkets and baubles and curios. And the first thing she does after she offers Jo Jo that advice is, she modifies a silver bracer so's it'll fit the little ragamuffin, sayin', "Now pay attention so you can do this kinda thing yourself someday," and when it's done she takes it and puts it on him. He yells at her at first that it burns, but she tells him he'll shut up and bear the pain if'n he wants to live.

Despite the pain, it works, near as Jo Jo can tell. 'Cause Ledger don't do no light-extinguishin'. Yeah, but even though Jo Jo gets to live, his life ain't what you'd call enviable.

He gets billed as "Jo Jo the Feral Child." He "lives" in a two-by-three cage, doin' his business in the straw that covers the bottom, wearin' the same rags day in and day out, eatin' slop, snarlin' at the townsfolk who pass by, all o'em laughin' and pointin' and callin' him freak and throwin' horse shit or elephant shit at him.

These rememberin's are movin' on now, skippin' forward to a night when Jo Jo don't have the bracer no more but he wears special silver rings that Greta fashioned for him. We come to one night in particular, when one o' the roustabouts didn't latch up Jo Jo's cage right, and the starvin' kid done got out and set to wanderin' the back lot, trackin' the smell o' meat. A whole lot o' it.

Before long, he comes to a big-ass tent. Just inside, hangin' from a hook on one o' them poles, is a set o' keys.

Keys to what? Well, the animal cages is what. Jo Jo takes 'em and goes deeper in, where a lion, tiger, and hyena all eyeball him like they're ready for dinner and he's next on the menu. He walks past a cage with a chimpanzee readin' a newspaper upside down, and next to that he finds what he's lookin' for: the big pen. This one's got a tire swing and some weights and an enclosure in the back. But right out in the middle . . . sits a whole mound o' raw meat.

Our feral child can hear snorin', can smell the beast slumberin' inside the enclosure, but he bets if he's quiet enough he can sneak in, get him a helpin' o' that grub, and get the hell out.

Takes him a while to find the right key, but once he does, the cage door's open, and Jo Jo's in. And all too quick he's knee-deep in that mound, stuffin' all that bloody meat in his maw, oblivious to everythin' around him. Yeah, he's downright in dog heaven.

'Til a low, rumblin' growl gets his attention. Jo Jo looks over to the shadows o' the enclosure and sees two gleamin' pinpricks o' light starin' back at him.

The knuckles come out first, workin' like front legs, followed by a gorilla three times Jo Jo's size even though it's still a youth.

If you're guessin' right about now that this is Terra Mungus, well you'd win the prize. Only I ain't givin' no prizes so sit back down and shut the hell up.

Where was I? Oh, right. Big-ass gorilla. Well young Terra Mungus don't take too kindly to dog-boys comin' into his territory eatin' his food. He slams them fists o' his down on the ground and then leaps, landin' with all his weight on top o' Jo Jo, and the meat, and he commences to poundin' those fists on the feral child's chest. Jo Jo manages to slash his claws across the gorilla's face and wiggle out from under him, but Terra Mungus grabs him up by the ankles like he's nothin' and tosses him toward the back.

Jo Jo hits the tire swing and drops to the ground, but he recovers quickly, grabbin' up one o' them fifty-pound weights and swingin' it into the oncomin' gorilla's chest, takin' him by surprise and knockin' him back a couple steps. Jo Jo makes for the cage door, but gets caught up in a clench, Terra Mungus's arms wrapped tight around him like a python, squeezin' the air from his lungs. Real quick-like, spots start dancin' 'round the edges o' young Jo Jo's vision.

Now the gorilla's got Jo Jo from the side, so our dog-boy screws his head round and bites into the closest target, munchin' a quarter-sized chunk o' rubbery cartilage from Terra Mungus's left ear.

Terra Mungus cuts loose with a deafenin' roar, momentarily lettin' go and grabbin' at the wound. Jo Jo scrambles backward. Terra Mungus charges, and Jo Jo knows for sure that this is the end when one o' them oversized mallets, the kind used to ring the tower bell in the strongman game, lashes out, sendin' the dazed gorilla sprawlin'.

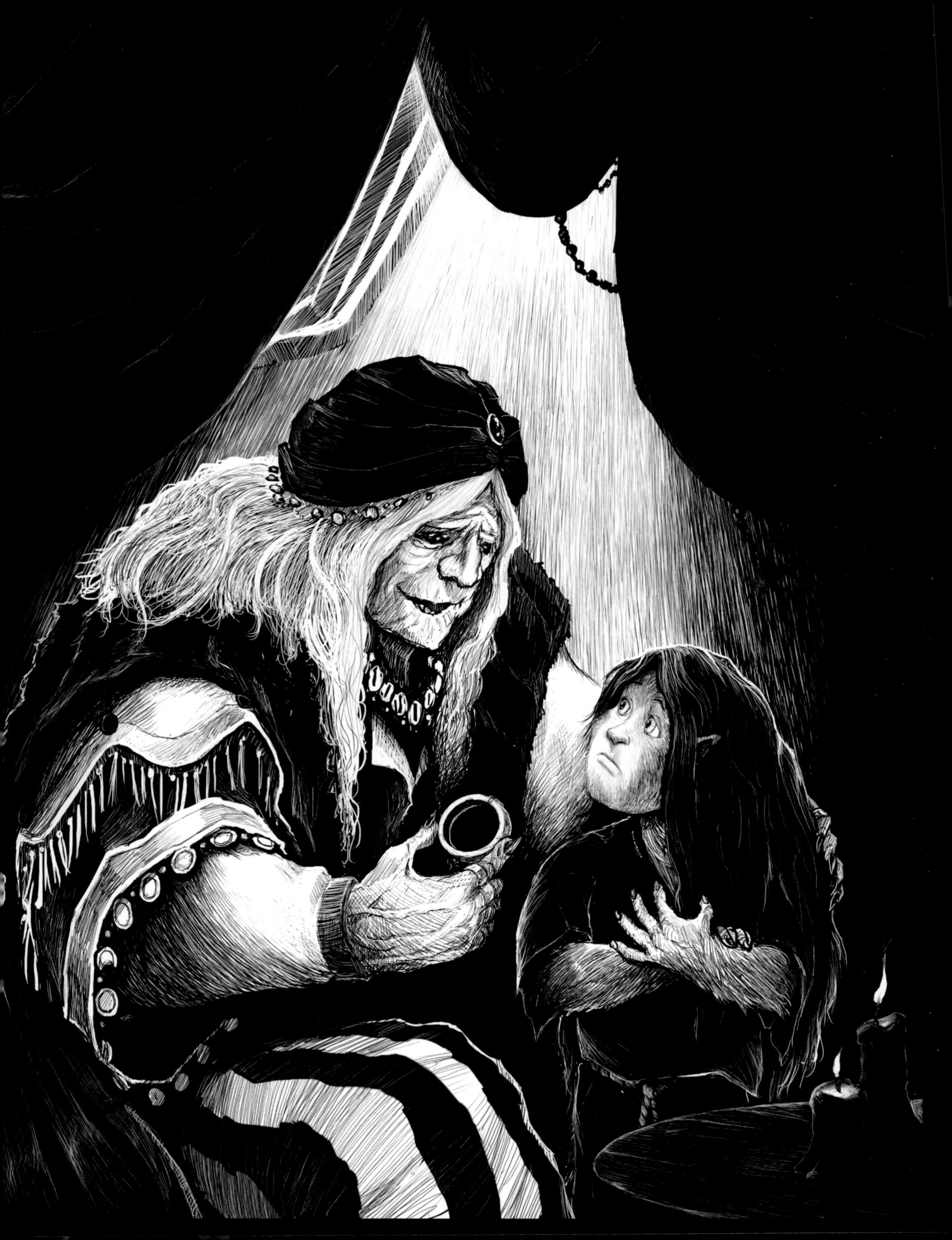

The Ramblin' Man drops the hammer, grabs hold o' the nape o' Jo Jo's neck, and hauls him out to the tent floor. He closes that cage door and locks it. Our feral child thinks he's got lucky and that maybe for once fortune's done smiled on him . . .

Until the Ringmaster turns, and Jo Jo sees the look in his eyes.

Ledger then snatches up his silver-tipped cane from where he had left it standin' up all by itself and commences to beatin' the dog-boy within an inch o' his life.

Before the next memory, let's pop out for a tick and see what the Magi twins are up to. See, that little girl done stepped up to where Jo Jo's kneelin' in the road, empty eyes not seein' anythin' in particular as she puts the gun barrel to Jo Jo's forehead.

That's bad news, folks. But the kid don't pull the trigger. Not just yet.

Meanwhile, back in the memory-parade, we've skipped forward 'bout a year, to a night near the end o' the carnival's annual run, when Jo Jo used a rusty nail to escape his cage once again.

He's sneakin' his way toward the exit and gets within sight o' it, when he stops. See, the thing is, he could run . . . but he's got nowhere to go. The carnival's done become the only life he knows. So the dog-boy just kinda stands there like a dummy, watchin' the roller coaster go rocketin' by, listenin' to the kids' screams that might be fun-type screams but might be some other kind too, and he finally turns and gets to wanderin' the grounds, headin' for the back lot . . .

Before long, he ends up near a trailer he's seen before. It's where the Ramblin' Man keeps his balloons. Struck with a sudden curiosity, Jo Jo uses that same nail to pick the lock on the trailer door, but before he can get in, a hand grabs him.

Now, first he thinks it's the Ringmaster, and he scrunches up, waitin' to take another ass-whoopin'. But it's Greta who done found him, and it's Greta who hauls him back to his cage and tosses him in. She points to the rings she made, and she says they're the only reason he's still alive, and he can't be doin' stupid shit like sneakin' outta his cage and breakin' into the Ringmaster's trailer. She scolds him good, but before she's done, who should show up, loomin' behind her like the specter o' death itself, but the Ringmaster.

"Someone's been to my trailer," Ledger DeMesne says. "You know which one I mean. The boy escaped again? Was anything taken?" And there's somethin' about him, somethin' about the way he can't stand completely still and the way that he keeps squeezin' his cane, that strikes young Jo Jo as . . . off.

Greta, she looks at the Ramblin' Man and she reads some kinda intent there, and she looks back at the boy and she seems to come to a conclusion. "No," she says. "No, he . . . he wanted a balloon. Wanted one real bad, and he begged me and I felt sorry for him but I didn't take anything . . ."

Now the Ramblin' Man, he laughs, the kind o' laugh that makes your balls—or your ovaries, dependin' on your anatomical orientation—shrivel up like raisins. "This cur isn't worthy of one of my balloons," he says. "Especially—" but he don't finish this next part. Instead, his hand briefly moves to his chest and Jo Jo thinks again that Ledger don't seem 100 percent like himself. He's been actin' anxious. Like he's got someplace to be and somethin' important to do. He tells Greta to follow him and hurries off.

Our next memory here, this one's the toughest, see, 'cause this memory is o' Greta's cries comin' from a nearby tent, The Ramblin' Man repeatin' over and over that she knows how important this night is, while young Jo Jo listens, knowin' that Greta's takin' this beatin' 'cause o' him . . . and when those cries stop but the sounds o' Ledger's cane strikin' flesh and bone continue . . . Jo Jo knows that Greta done gave up her life so that his miserable, worthless life could go on.

Yessir, Jo Jo's got scars, the physical kind from that cane-beatin' he took, deep scars that didn't never fully heal, but he's got emotional scars to boot; doubts and fears and regrets . . . our man's got 'em all in spades.

Back out in the street, the gun barrel against Jo Jo's forehead is shakin'. And over at Hubtown, Bo, who needs his sister's contribution to make the kid pull the trigger, is wonderin' as to the 'cause o' Tweeny's hesitation.

"What's the holdup?" he snaps. "Let off, I'm workin' on it!" Tweeny fires back, though she don't sound altogether convincin'.

And that's when Elsa comes outta the inn manager's office, havin' had no luck gettin' the two o'em a room. She shouts, "Hey!" runs over and snatches that gun from the kid's hand. It's enough to break the connection, and the girl becomes aware again, downright flabbergasted as to why in the holy hell she's standin' in the middle o' the road in her nighties while some kinda pretty but still kinda scary lady's yellin' at her. The girl plops down on her ass, and some piece o' the nightmare must come to her 'cause she tosses that teddy bear as far as she can throw. Meanwhile, Elsa makes ready to knock the daylights outta the kid when a voice shouts, "No!"

Elsa turns to see Jo Jo, standin' now, lookin' down at the girl with an expression that Elsa don't really understand.

"Leave her be," Jo Jo says. "Just leave her be." Elsa lowers her hand, but she keeps hold o' the gun.

"I'm awake now," Jo Jo continues. "I'm leaving. Going to get Her. With or without you." And he turns and walks back toward the truck.

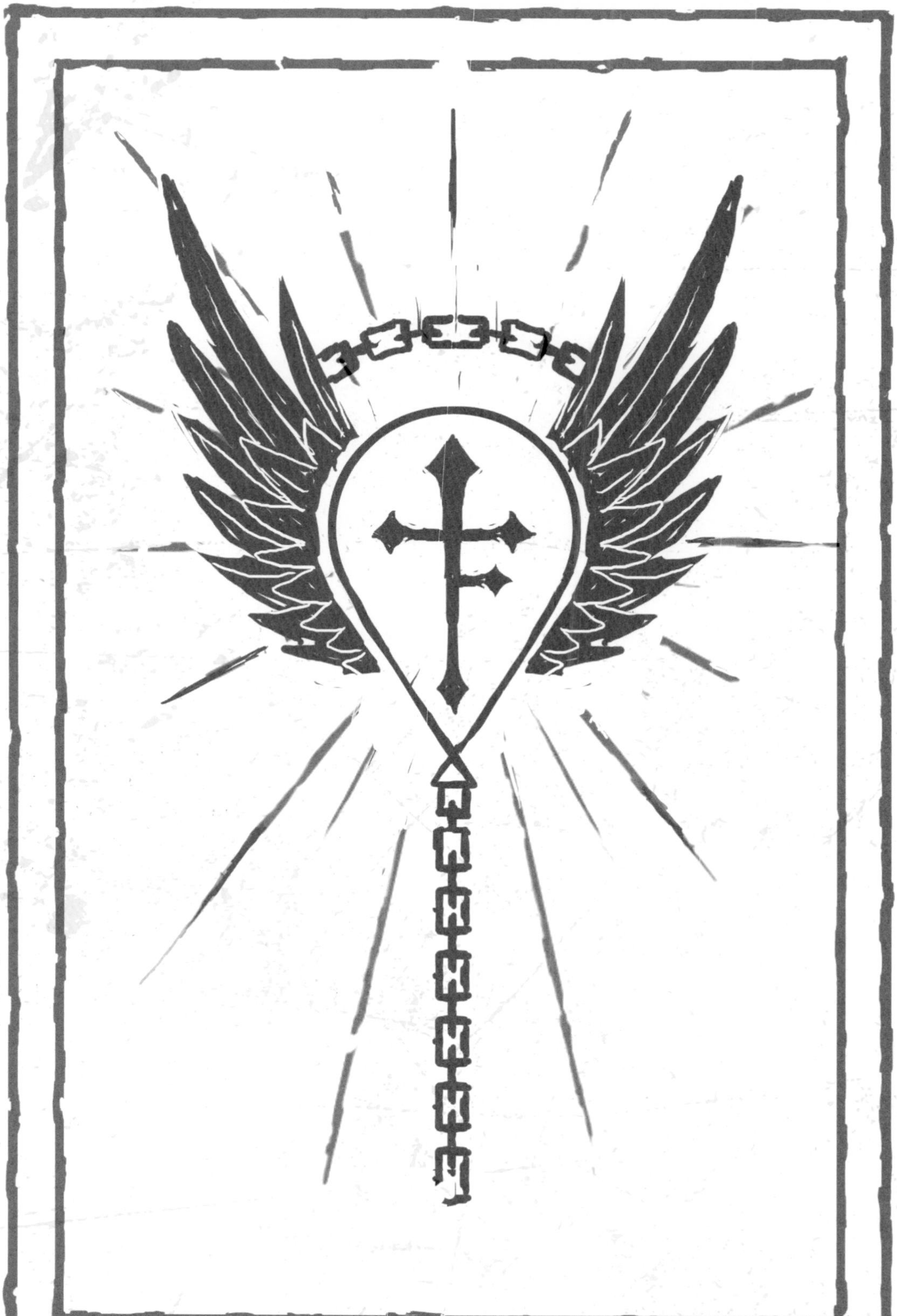

The Prophet

CHAPTER THE EIGHTH

Outside Hubtown, the carnival's comin' to a close.

Among the folks exitin' the gate—in fact, among all the townspeople that's been comin' and goin' the whole day long—there's been kids o' all ages. Course ain't nothin' peculiar 'bout that, no sir. But I'll share with you somethin' that *is* a might bit peculiar. The kids that Ledger DeMesne gave balloons to, well them kids, every single one o'em, done ended up balloon-less before they got home.

Sometimes it happened right as they left the gate, sometimes it happened just before they stepped into their house. But all throughout the day them balloon strings been slippin' right outta them kids' hands. And remember what I done told you back at the catch-rasslin' show? What I said 'bout the balloons that floated against the wind? Well it's the same with these. They go up and then head right on back to the carnival no matter which way the wind's blowin'.

But where exactly do they go? Let's find out. Fix your gaze on this freckled boy here, the one with the twinkle in his eyes and the spring in his step and the ear-to-ear smile. He's left the carnival with his pops, and he's got one o' Ledger's balloons, and there he goes out to the far end o' the parkin' lot, skippin' right along, hummin' a merry tune as he heads toward that truck and . . . yep, look there: That balloon just yanked itself right outta his little hand and off it goes. He runs after it, but that balloon moves quick, and pretty soon all the tired kid can do is watch it sail back toward the lights o' the carnival. The boy's face ain't nearly the same now—it done got all twisted up in despair; despair o' the gut-wrenchin' kind.

"Not fair! It's not fair!" Freckles yells. He cries at first but then, the farther away that balloon gets, the more he quiets down, 'til there ain't nothin' left but sobs. An outta-breath Pops catches up and pats him on the back sayin' it'll be okay as the boy turns, shoulders slumped, no more spring in his step, no more twinkle in his eyes.

If we leave Freckles behind and follow that balloon, it takes us over the carnival's main gate, down the midway to the back lot and on to a very specific trailer. Yeah, you knew already that this was where Ledger kept the balloons, but did you know this is where they come back to? I didn't think so. The Ramblin' Man's closin' up them back doors. And when that last balloon comes divin' in, he grabs it right up.

Ledger, he's collectin' these balloons, see. Collectin' for the Boss. The Boss . . . well that's a someone or maybe even a some*thing* that even I can't tell you much 'bout, 'cause to be honest, I don't know, and I'm not prone to makin' shit up. No, sir, I don't know a name; don't know too much other than it ain't from 'round here, and it ain't to be trifled with on account o' that Boss strikes fear even into the stone-cold black heart o' the Ramblin' Man.

Speakin' o' Ledger, he holds the balloon's string with one hand and locks them doors with the other, then he takes a few steps back and lets go o' that last balloon. It don't fly away, though. No it just floats for a tick and then slowly sinks until it's right at his face level.

Now, as I think I've communicated, the Ringmaster, he's got some special abilities, like seein' kids' futures and bringin' a kind o' life back to things that ain't got no more life o' their own. Well in order to maintain his particular gifts, in order to do what the Ramblin' Man does for as long as he's been doin' it, he needs to . . . *partake* every once in a while from the Boss's collection.

Most o' the carnival lights have done gone out now; the music's died and all we can see o' the Ringmaster is a silhouette. He grabs that balloon, unties the end, and sucks out some o' the contents. Then he stands there swayin' a bit. . . . Now you know when someone sucks in helium, and they talk in that squeaky voice? Well, the Ramblin' Man starts to talkin', and the voice is high-pitched, but it ain't that helium voice . . .

"Not fair! Not fair!" Ledger says, and it don't just sound *like* the voice o' Freckles. It *is* the voice o' Freckles. He hangs his head then lifts it and says, "I don't feel good. Somethin' ain't right," and just a few miles away in Hubtown, Freckles is at home sayin' that very same thing. "I'm not okay. Something's really, really wrong, and I want Mommy; I want Mommy to make it okay!"

Then Ledger takes that balloon and squeezes and bites into it. It don't explode, like you might think. No it just kinda shrivels up while Ledger sucks in more o' its contents. He discards what's left, and when he's done, he steps out and takes his cane from where it's standin' up by itself on the side o' the truck . . . and the more observant among you might note a particular spring in his step and a twinkle in his eyes.

Presently some heavy footsteps tell o' someone else's arrival as Tweeny carries Bo up for an audience. Now the Magi twins, they been with the Ramblin' Man for quite a while. Almost since the very beginnin'. And they ain't lasted that long by bein' dumb. No sir, they know that the best time to deliver bad news is right after the Ringmaster has done partook o' one o' his balloons.

"Her fault," Bo starts off. "We had the gun to his head and she, she hesitated!"

Those bright, inquisitive eyes o' Ledger's stare at Bo and Tweeny for long enough that the twins wonder if maybe they should just leave, when the Ringmaster says in that Freckles voice, "That true?"

"Well I, uh—I just wanted to make sure he was real dead this time. I wanted to be real sure, but then our connection got broke. Next time I won't mess up I swear. Next time I'll make real sure."

Ledger tightens his grip on the cane, and Tweeny looks at it with fearful eyes, but the Ringmaster just says, "Leave." And the twins, both o'em lookin' mighty relieved, do just that.

The Ringmaster he walks a bit, over to another trailer, the trailer where he's keepin' Her. He puts his hand up to its side and he thinks about what Tweeny said, about makin' sure. Ledger done thought he'd killed Jo Jo back at the bridge. He thinks about how Jo Jo don't seem to wanna die, and he thinks about Her, and he wonders if the "feral child" managed to hide somethin' . . . somethin' real special and real important, for all these years.

The next mornin', before the sun's peeked up over the eastern mountains, the carnival's done struck tents and loaded up and started a convoy outta town toward Dead End.

✸✸✸✸✲✸✸✸✸

At that same time, if we direct our attention elsewhere, back a ways and a mile or so down a dirt road off the Anaconda, we'll see a kinda ritual takin' place.

There's a bunch o' semitrucks and motorbikes gathered 'round, and Frankie's Profits are just finishin' buildin' somethin' there in the middle.

Now see, truckers and bikers got themselves all sorts o' rituals for when one o' their own goes to that almighty rest stop in the sky, but this particular ceremony is a damn sight more involved and meanin'ful than them others, 'cause these good ol' boys, they revered their leader Frankie. Thought o' him almost like he was superhuman, godlike, you might say.

So what've they built? Looks like a . . . yep, that's a throne. Made outta pieces o' Frankie's bike and various other chopper and big-rig parts, like them big smokestacks that make up the back. And what is it these four big ol' boys are carryin' out from that trailer there? Why that'd be the body o' good ol' Frankie himself.

See how all the faithful are kneelin' down now as Frankie's corpse is bein' sat in that throne? Yeah, all them loyal subjects are bowin' their heads to the one and only

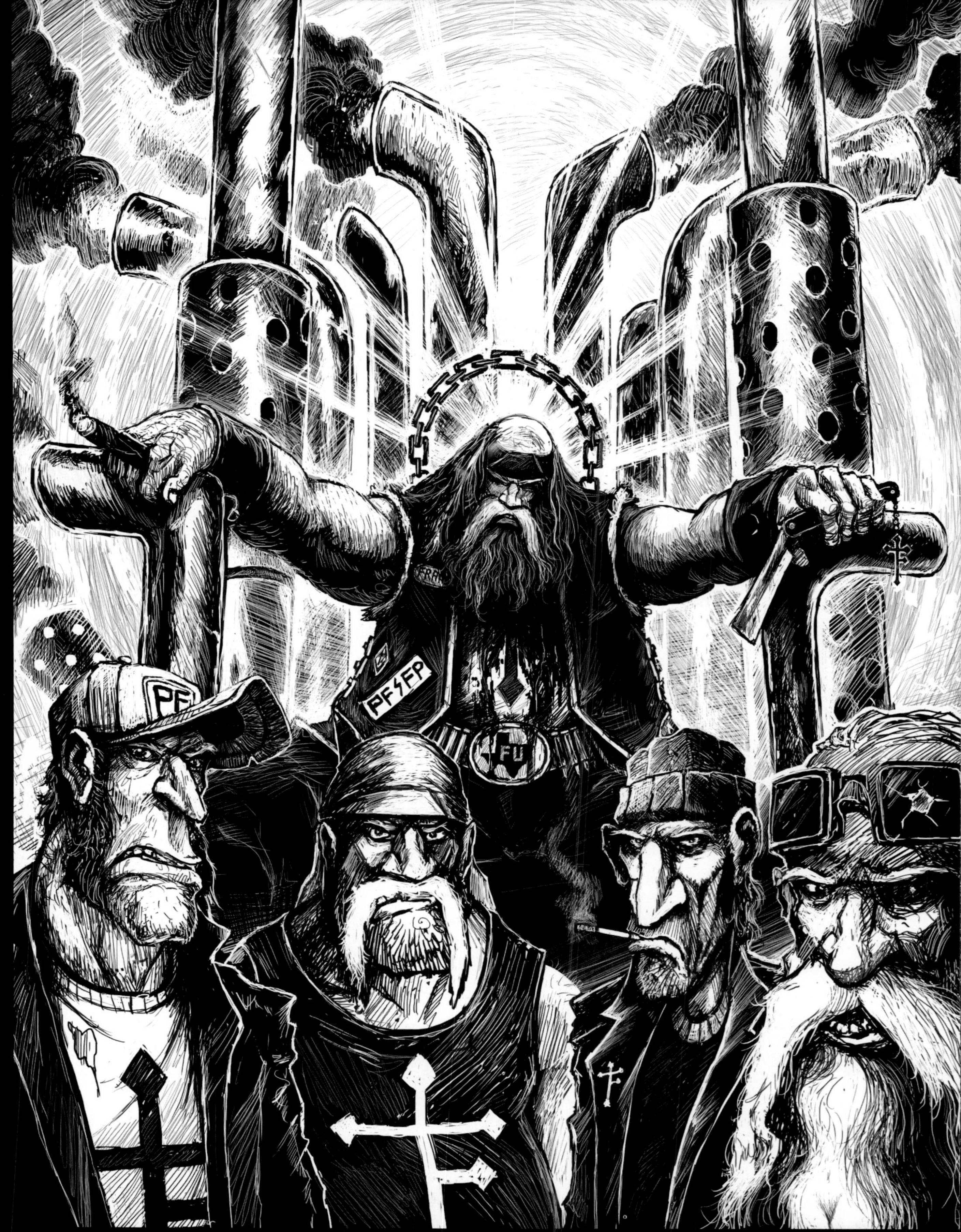
PF
PF FP
FU

Frankie, and a good bit o'em are convinced that their main man ain't completely gone and that he might come back, just like some folks say that ol' JC fella did. Not Johnny Cash, the other one.

We'll leave them boys to it for now and mosey ourselves to a familiar place, right here in Devil's Tailbone. That tractor and trailer are parked out front o' the inn, the same establishment Elsa was tryin' to get a room in. Now, if we head inside . . . see that skinny gal behind the counter? She's the one Elsa was talkin' to. Right now she's gabbin' with our ol' friend Doctor Victor Prometheus Hart, tellin' him what she can remember o' the conversation with Elsa. She's got a perplexed look on her face all the while, as if there's somethin' 'bout the doctor that ain't really sittin' right.

"And you're quite certain she didn't mention a destination?" Hart asks.

"Naw, she didn't. Just took off. You said she came from that titty bar, though, yeah? So there's prob'ly only one place she can be goin' to, and that's Hubtown, straight up the Anaconda. You should go there."

"I see. Your assistance is greatly appreciated." The doctor leans over the counter then, gettin' a closer look at the innkeeper and makin' her shy back. "May I say, you have the most magnificent facial structure?" the good doc says.

The innkeeper, most likely not bein' used to gettin' paid compliments, just kinda stares back. Finally the skinny woman decides she don't like the way our doc is eyeballin' her, and she says, "Uh-huh. You should go on."

"Of course. My sincerest thanks." The doctor heads out the exit and the innkeeper goes into the back room. And you'd think that'd be that. Before you get impatient to move on, though, let's hold up here just a tick and . . . see? The doc's back, and he's got a bag with him, a doctor bag like the one Elsa carries, 'cept this one looks newer. The little bell tinkles when he walks in, and he stops, turns 'round and flips the OPEN sign to say—all right, fine, "read"—CLOSED.

Before the innkeeper comes out, Doc Hart slips behind the counter and into the back room, removing somethin' from his bag as he goes. There's a little yelp and a *thump* and . . . well, maybe we should go ahead and move on now before we get to hearin' the sounds o' Doc Hart's bone saw goin' to work on that innkeeper's neck.

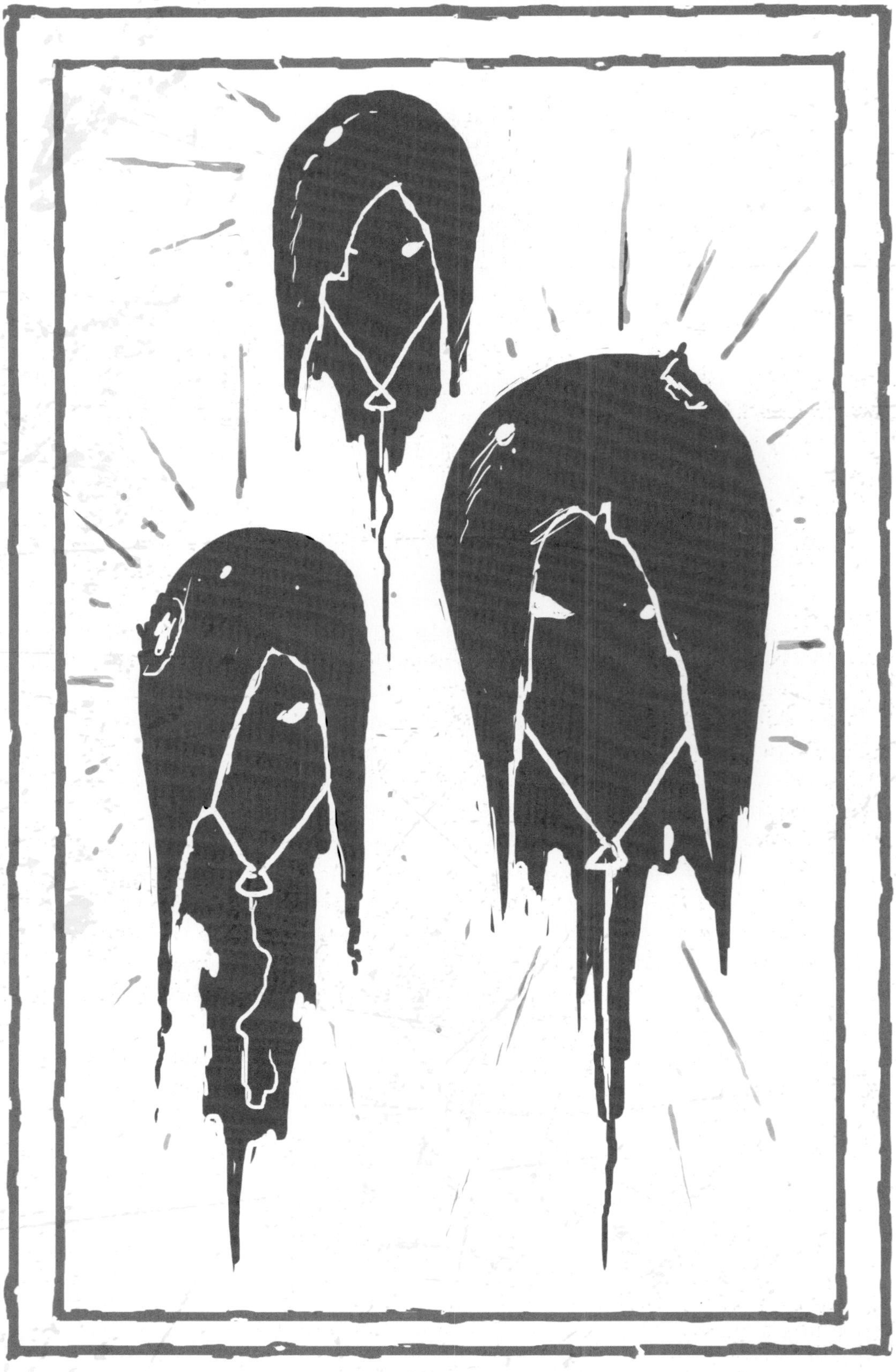

The Vagabonds

CHAPTER THE NINTH

Jo Jo had fought sleep as hard as he could for as long as he could, but after the mental tug o' war with them Magi twins, it hadn't been long before he done nodded off at the wheel, and Elsa took over.

Our hero's still out like a light as she pulls the ice cream truck into the outskirts o' Hubtown, drivin' through the empty lot where the carnival used to be, seein' all the flyers and leftover candy wrappers and animal shit and truck and trailer tracks . . . and she figures out right quick that the Barnstormers done moved on.

Now, prior to arrivin' at Devil's Tailbone, Jo Jo had told Elsa about Her. Elsa gets to thinkin' that before they head out toward Dead End, it might be worthwhile to ask 'round a bit for folks who went to the carnival, see if any o'em saw Her. Who knows, she coulda even escaped. If Elsa found Her, well then, the stranger would be more inclined to help out, should her father come callin'. Even better, though, she'd be some kinda . . . hero. That thought brings a smile to her crooked face and makes her sit up a little straighter.

So she drives into the clankin' and clangin' and hustle and bustle o' Hubtown, a place that's a bit overwhelmin' at first to someone who ain't been to no big cities. She finds herself a little outta-the-way spot just outside an alley market, not far from the massive locomotive turntable that makes up the hub o' Hubtown. She parks and takes her doctor bag and gets out, walkin' a bit and climbin' a short set o' metal stairs, 'til she comes to rows o' ramshackle huts and stands. A freight train rattles the trestle and rails overhead as Elsa asks some o' the shop workers 'bout the carnival. The first few folks just tell her to keep movin' if she ain't buyin'. So she moves on . . . and crossin' the grungy alley, shepasses near a dirty beggar woman wrapped in a blanket. The vagrant's talkin' to herself and Elsa manages to catch only snippets o' what the woman's sayin'.

"How many we been through already . . . ?"

"Give him what he wants or else it's the *gators* for us."

The woman sees Elsa and her jaundiced eyes get wide. "Say, you're kinda pretty . . ."

Elsa frowns at the bag lady and keeps her distance as she heads to the next shop. Here, a bald man in a leather apron tells her 'bout the carnival, and a big, mean gorilla layin' a beatdown on some good ol' boys. Unfortunately, the shopkeep don't have no info 'bout Her.

Elsa steps back out into the street when somethin' downright incredible happens.

It starts to snow.

Now, she ain't never seen real-life snow. She read 'bout it, heard Father tellin' tales 'bout it, and seen pictures o' it, but . . .

She puts out the hand that ain't holdin' the bag, catches a flake, and pulls her hand back to see. Her smile fades a bit when she realizes it ain't snow. It's ash. Hubtown's very own version o' snow.

But so what?

Thinkin' 'bout the books Father used to bring to her in the big ol' manor house that was more like a fancy jail . . . them kinda thoughts sure could dredge up all manner o' terrible memories, o' what Father's associates—what Father *himself*—did to her behind locked doors. But now that she's out, now that she's free, she's decided for all and for good that she ain't gonna focus on the bad stuff that was done, but focus instead on the fact that she's alive, and that's a pretty amazin' thing.

So she tilts her head up and that smile comes back now, bigger and better than ever, as she twirls 'round right there in the middle o' the street market, eyes closed, lettin' the ash tickle her skin like feathers, and in her imagination that snow's as real as can be. She opens her mouth and catches one o' them flakes on her tongue and you might think that'd ruin the illusion, but Elsa, she can't really taste nothin' anyhow (in fact she don't even eat or drink, but let's not get caught up in all that right now) and so she keeps on makin' believe that she's far away from anyone who can hurt her, on some mountaintop someplace where she don't have a single care in the world.

Elsa twirls for quite a long time but eventually she gets to thinkin' 'bout Jo Jo and Her, and she's more determined than ever to help. But to do that, they gotta keep movin'. Maybe find a few more people to talk to before they set out for Dead End. So she stops twirlin' and makes her way between stands tryin' to get back to where she parked . . . only she musta made a wrong turn somewhere, 'cause where she's at don't look familiar.

Thinkin' it must be up ahead, she walks on, through the steam risin' from grates and manhole covers, duckin' under pipes and then over by one o' them oil-pumpin' rigs, the kind that looks like them toy birds that bob up and down like they're drinkin' water, that ash-snow fallin' all the time. She keeps on, through and around piles o'

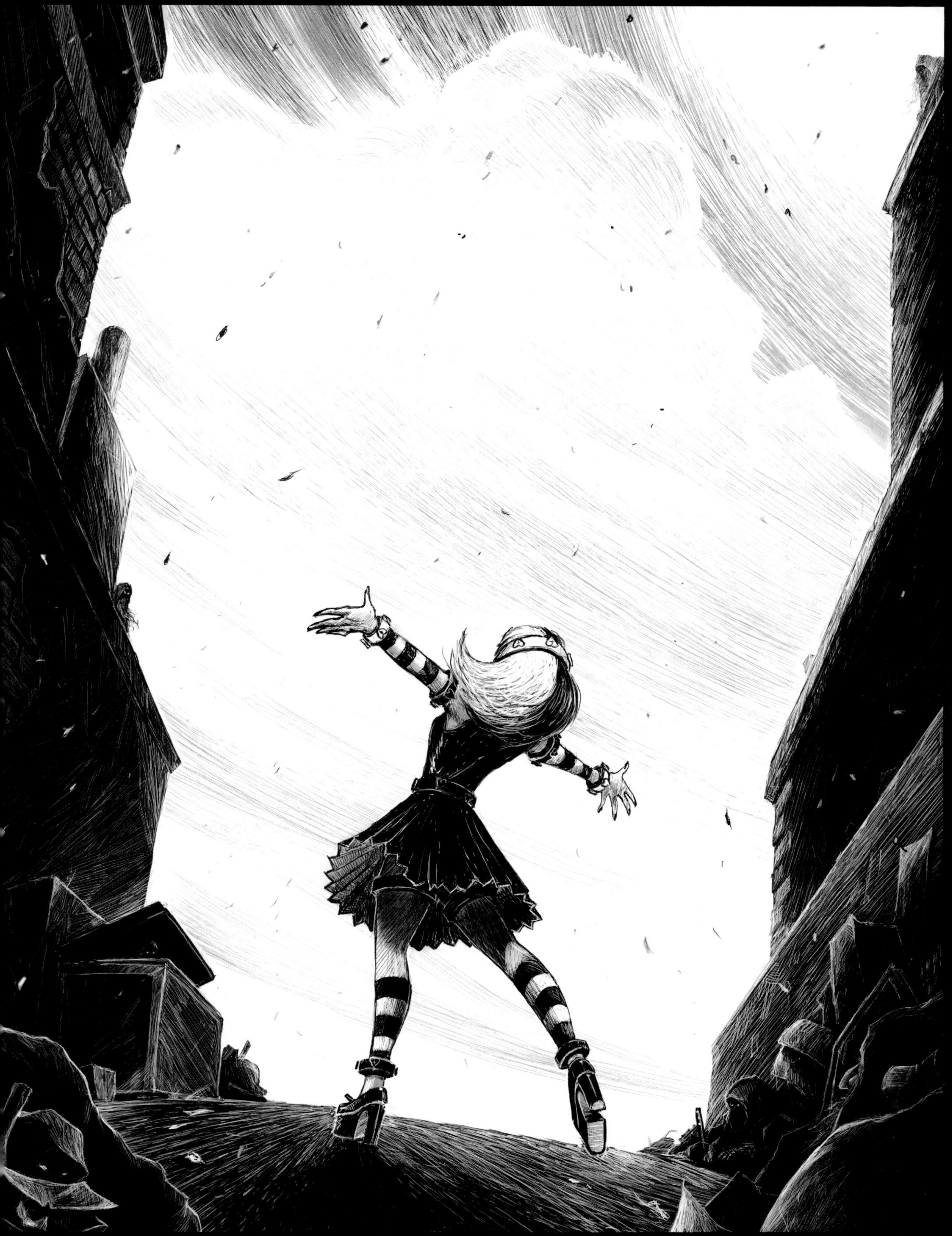

trash and junk, and just ahead she spots a soot-covered hobo in a long ratty coat, wild eyes fixed on her, barkin' out words to himself that don't seem to make no sense.

"I dunno . . . maybe. Little too close to the bone. He likes 'em cheeky! Worth a shot? Worth a shot? My opinion's shit. Yeah, fine, come an' get her."

The bum smiles open-mouthed, revealing a whole lot o' missin' teeth and Elsa gets a feelin' that maybe this ain't the best place for her to be. Off to her left side, a manhole cover lifts up and scoots aside silently. Fingerless-gloved hands reach out, and a grime-coated hobo hoists himself onto the cement, glarin' at Elsa while a metal door clangs open somewhere to the right, and that woman from the market steps out from under some steam pipes. "Told you, we gotta give him what he wants. Maybe her. Maybe the one."

"Maybe her."

Elsa hears the words repeated behind her and she turns 'round and she hears it over and over: "Maybe her, maybe her, maybe her," like it's comin' from everywhere at once. Just then, them piles o' trash and metal start to move and rise up, one after another, pieces fallin' away 'til she sees that a bunch more o' these scummy underworlders was hidin' in the junk, usin' it like camouflage. "Maybe her, maybe her," they keep repeatin'.

Elsa heard and read a few stories 'bout the Aimless, the underworld denizens o' Hubtown, some o' them stories sayin' that the sewer rats had some kinda powers. When she first came across these here hobos, she was thinkin' they were just crazy, talkin' gibberish or mumblin' to themselves or yellin' at folks that ain't there. But she realizes, watchin' and listenin' to these dwellers o' the deep and the dark . . . she realizes that these gutter-bums have been talkin' to each other.

Pretty soon, Elsa's done got herself surrounded like that Custer fella at Little Bighorn. A hand belongin' to the bum in the ratty coat snatches the doctor bag, and before she knows what's happenin', them dirty mongrels rush her. She swings and kicks and bites and she breaks more'n a few bones with the beatin' she dishes out, but then she sees a big ol' metal pipe come crashin' down and real quick-like she's on her back with dark faces lookin' down, and she's starin' up at that snow, the snow that now, now that she thinks about it . . . really is just ash after all.

The last thing she sees is a grimy, rapidly descendin' boot heel.

'Bout an hour later, Jo Jo wakes up wonderin' why the hell he's in the middle o' Hubtown and thinkin' that Elsa musta done upped and left him. He figures that's just fine, 'cause at least she ain't in danger no more, and she seemed nice enough, not withstandin' the murder and all, but who would he be to judge?

What he feels the need to do with a quickness is get to lookin' for the carnival and Her. He's fixin' to go when he notices another vehicle parked not too far away. Damned if it ain't that black hearse, the same one he saw parked outside o' Conway Titties. There's a figure behind the wheel, but he can't see who it is so good 'cause o' the ash-snow for one, but also 'cause whoever it is has got a hood pulled up and they ain't much more than a shadow in the seat.

Jo Jo wonders if this hooded stranger might be followin' him, and he figures that once he leaves Hubtown he'll know if he sees that hearse in his rearview mirror. Either way he needs to skedaddle.

He drives through the lot toward the exit, comin' round a big ol' bus, and that's when he sees that the way out is blocked by a rattletrap, flatbed truck with a steel-reinforced cage in back, a cage so heavy that the truck's ass end droops like a loaded diaper. A whole string o' curses escapes Jo Jo's lips as he sees that the driver is a chimpanzee wearin' a newsboy hat. And the cage . . . that cage is empty.

After what the Magi twins put him through, well, that little street urchin boy, the feral child, he ain't hidin' too far inside o' Jo Jo. And that boy remembers all too well what Terra Mungus did, and right 'bout now that little boy's balls are crawlin' up into his throat.

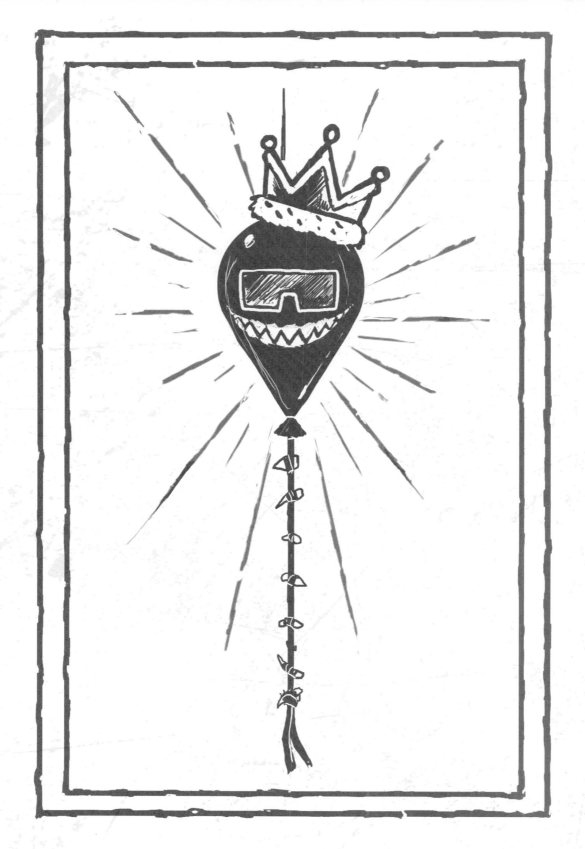

THE KING

CHAPTER THE TENTH

Hubtown is a city o' levels, see, and the bums, the Aimless, they live in the lowest o' the low. Elsa's gettin' her first look at the sewers, now that she's woke up, as the underworlders haul her down through the sublevels, each one dirtier and stinkier and nastier than the last, shit-and-piss water runnin' and gushin' all 'round.

Eventually it gets so dark there ain't nothin' but black. Them hobos though, apparently they don't need light to see. Down, down they take her until finally there's a little glow and then a bit more and a bit more 'til she gets brought to the mouth o' a huge tunnel.

They been carryin' her the whole way, but now they stand her on her feet and she realizes her wrists are chained and cuffed, like what they do to prisoners in some o' the books she's read. For the time bein', the bums just hold her there, the floor vibratin' underneath, a sound o' nearby machinery comin' through the walls.

Where they're at is a few steps up from a big flat concrete landing lit by some dirty kerosene lamps. There's a bunch o' pipes and spouts and then a kinda pool filled with brown shit water. The bums hold her there, tellin' her to keep still and keep her mouth shut.

Standin' on the cement space is a handful more o' the Aimless, and they got their grimy mitts on three women, city women by the looks o' em. More prisoners, Elsa's guessin', though they ain't chained like her; they're just bein' held real tight.

They're all facin' a raised area and another big tunnel. The openin' o' this one's got one o' them iron gates like the kind Elsa saw in books with pictures o' castles—a portcullis, she remembers. The same vibration that's shakin' the floor rattles that gate just enough for Elsa to hear.

Meanwhile, them bums down there, they're all mumblin' some name over and over . . .

"King Mo, King Mo, King Mo . . ."

There's an ear-stabbin' grindin' o' gears and metal teeth, and that portcullis raises up and disappears into the tunnel roof. A tick later, Elsa hears footstep noises, but there's more than one set, and some o'em don't sound *human*. Then she sees 'em come out—two critters, long snouts emergin' first, followed by long, knobby bodies carried forward by fat little legs. They got iron collars trailin' chains on 'em and they're covered in scaly hide from their heads to the tips o' their reptile tails.

Gators. Thirteen feet long if they're an inch. Elsa ain't never seen real gators before, kinda like with the snow. She just saw pictures and read 'bout 'em in them National Geography books. Now, seein' real-life ones not so far away, she's decidin' right quick that this is yet another new experience she could do without.

Then, comin' out behind them monstrous reptiles and holdin' onto them chain leashes, is a huge dusky-skinned fella in sunglasses, wearin' a knit cap and a thick fur coat with gator hide across the shoulders.

The gators come to the edge o' that stage, and they stop. The dark man, the one Elsa supposes must be "King Mo," keeps walkin', windin' the chains 'round his hands to choke up on them leashes, a coiled-up bullwhip swingin' on his hip as he comes to the edge and looks down on the bums and the captives.

"What this is?" Mo asks in a rumbly voice that bounces off the concrete; a deep voice, like what them soul singers have.

A few o' the bums just look at each other. One o'em offers up: "The . . . the hopefuls, liege."

"Hopefuls," the others agree.

"Hm," Elsa hears Mo say. The prisoners whimper, and the gator on Mo's right side lunges like it's gonna jump right off that ledge, but King Mo yanks the collar back. "Easy, Lizzy," he says to the scaly old girl. The one on the left lets out a kinda growlin' sound. "Quiet down, Lilah," Mo scolds. Then he gets back to lookin' out at them blubberin' women, and he lets out a big long sigh. Elsa's watchin', worried 'bout what's comin', straining against them chains and wonderin' just how much strength it might take to snap 'em.

"What hope?" Mo calls back. "How am I to ensure my legacy? How am I to continue my line with such meager offerings?" King Mo, he gets to shakin' his head. "This shit won't fly!" he yells, then cants his head toward the shit swamp. "Get 'em wet."

The hobos comply without hesitation, takin' the screamin' women to the edge o' that pool o' putrid human waste and tossin' 'em in. And while they do, King Mo's squatted down and he's reachin' to either side, unfastenin' them chains from the gators' collars.

Elsa makes to run out from the tunnel mouth, to try and do something, anything, but mongrel hands hold her back while a rusty blade tip touches her just under her right eye. A scratchy voice real close to her ears says, "Don't you make no moves, you wanna keep that eye."

Them eyes just watch while the gator Lizzy makes straight for the pool; Lilah takes off in the general direction o' the hobos that have backed up nearly to the landing wall but stops short at the crack o' a whip.

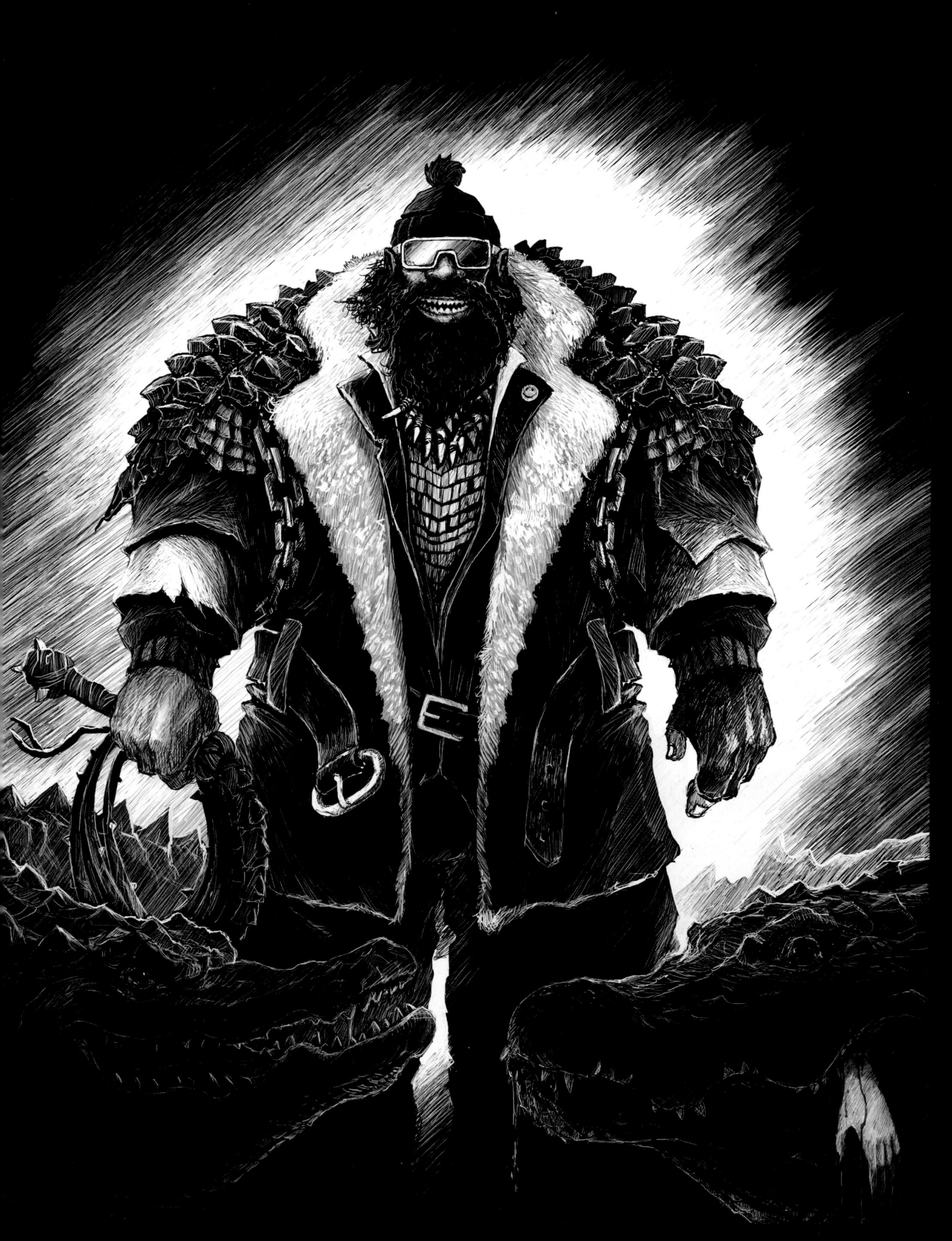

King Mo, he's standin' there, bullwhip in hand. "The pool, Lilah," he orders. Lilah just glares at him sideways for a tick, then like some faithful puppy dog, she obeys, runnin' off and plungin' in to join Lizzy, who's already in the turd pool, happy as a three-peckered rooster in a henhouse. Lizzy grabs one o' them flailin', caterwaulin' women by the arm and starts rollin' in that brown water, splashin' every which way and with a poppin' and a rippin' sound that arm comes clean off.

Lilah joins in on the fun, lungin' sideways and lockin' one of the wailin' gal's heads between them massive jaws, and if the women weren't screamin' so loud, Elsa would hear the crunch o' her skull crackin' open. Elsa's 'bout to close her eyes or turn away when she sees the third woman makin' for a metal ladder against the pool wall. Maybe . . . just maybe that last poor woman can make it, she thinks.

The woman succeeds in climbin' a couple o' them metal rungs. King Mo jumps off the stage, and a few long strides take him close enough to lash out with his whip, slicin' the back o' that woman's left hand so she's barely hangin' on with the right. Mo draws back for another thrashin' when Elsa decides she's had enough; they can take her eye if they want but she's done standin' and watchin'. She yells out, "No!" throwin' her chained hands up to knock away the knife tip, breakin' from the filthy hands holdin' her, stumblin' out into the light.

Mo looks over to Elsa, obviously surprised at bein' yelled at, while the woman manages her way up the ladder and through a hole in the ceilin'.

King Mo looks back to see the woman's gone, then turns and sends that whip flyin', and whether he means to or not Elsa ain't rightly sure, but he gets the tip to coil itself on the chain between her wrists. The king yanks, and Elsa comes pedalin' forward, nearly trippin' on her way down the stairs.

She stands there on the vibratin' floor tryin' not to look behind Mo, where the gators are gobblin' up bits o' what's left o' the two women in water that's turned a red brown that you might call "chestnut." Or hell maybe you'd just call it red brown, I don't know I ain't no artist.

Anyway, King Mo approaches real slow-like and with the hand that ain't holdin' the whip, he takes them glasses off, revealin' eyes as gray as a winter storm. And those eyes are roamin' all over Elsa, not in a lustful way, or at least not *just* in a lustful way, more like he's maybe seein' a member o' the opposite gender for the first time.

"Hold on now," he says when he's got close enough, still lookin' her over in an amazed kinda fashion. "Hold everything . . ."

He finally brings that wanderin' gaze to a stop, lockin' eyes with Elsa, drinkin' her in now, like she's some kinda fine wine. Not knowin' precisely what to do, Elsa just stares back. The hobos nearby wait so silent and still you'd think they was statues. "I didn't know," Mo says, kinda quiet-like. "I guess I didn't know what I was searching for . . ."

He smiles, a big smile showin' off a big mouthful o' pointed teeth.

"Until now."

CHAPTER THE ELEVENTH

Jo Jo's puttin' the pedal to the metal, lookin' for another way outta the parkin' lot. He done backed up and now he's pushin' the ice cream truck to its limits, drivin' through the snow-ash next to the parked bus, castin' his eyes this way and that. Outta the corner o' his vision Jo Jo thinks he sees somethin' come offa the top o' the bus. Right after, there's a deafenin' metal warpin' sound as the ice cream truck bounces, and the back half o' the roof bows in like a taco.

Bein' understandably preoccupied, Jo Jo don't see the old Ford pickup comin' round a row o' cars on the other side 'til it's too late, and he plows head-on into the jalopy, knockin' his noggin against the steerin' wheel and honkin' the horn, which plays a Dixie melody. A crusty old white-haired geezer gets outta the pickup, screamin' bloody tarnation 'bout his beautiful baby and who's gonna pay to fix her?

Jo Jo hears a groan o' metal, feels the suspension spring back up, and then he sees a big furry mass pass by the side windows. He throws the gear into reverse and backs up, while a massive, hunched form passes in front o' the ice cream truck, picks up the old goat like he's set to take out the trash, and tosses that Q-tip right outta the parkin' lot, out where Jo Jo can't even see him land; he just hears the hoarse screamin' come to a sudden end.

The terrifyin' beast levels them beady black eyes on Jo Jo's, lets out a mighty roar, and pounds his chest.

Jo Jo's sittin' still as can be; his heart's set to beat right outta his rib cage, and that little boy inside is tellin' him to run. But runnin' ain't gonna save Her. So Jo Jo tells the little boy to sack up or pack up, and when Terra Mungus takes a step in front o' the Ford, that's when Jo Jo guns it, blastin' forward, smashin' full-force into the ape and pinnin' him to the pickup.

Well, this has the effect o' seriously pissin' Terra Mungus off. The gorilla lets out a roar that damn near curls Jo Jo's hair as he pushes forward and lifts, heftin' the entire front end o' that truck 'til our hero can't see nothin' but the smoky dome o' Hubtown and fallin' ash. And that's when he remembers the gun.

The gun Elsa had took from the kid. The both o'em had agreed to just keep it in the back o' the truck for the time bein'. Jo Jo swings 'round and falls into the back, searchin' high and low for that gun among all the clown paraphernalia as the ice cream truck scoots backward and comes crashin' back down.

Finally Jo Jo finds the weapon under a rubber chicken just as the truck's rear door goes flyin' off. He aims and shoots, but Terra Mungus has turned as he reaches in, and the bullet just hits his shoulder. And what this does is—yeah you guessed it, this bullet just has the effect o' pissin' him off even more.

The ape clamps one meaty fist 'round Jo Jo's hand and the gun, squeezin' both 'til Jo Jo hears and feels bones snap while pieces o' the gun crack and grind together. Terra Mungus yanks, whippin' Jo Jo clean outta the truck and flingin' him across the parkin' lot.

Jo Jo goes tumblin', hat flyin' off, 'til he comes to a stop near the back end o' the bus. He forces his way up, tryin' to transfer the gun to his non-gimpy hand but havin' no luck, so when the gorilla leaps over and lands a few feet away, our hero just kicks as hard as he can, pushin' Terra Mungus back a step, and then he follows up with a solid left to the jaw that turns the ape's head. The irate primate snatches Jo Jo up by the neck like it ain't nothin' and throws him to one side, right through the bus's foldin' back doors, the useless gun clankin' down onto the pavement.

Terra Mungus charges into the bus, grabs Jo Jo by his feet, and proceeds to swing him like a bat over the seat tops, into one window, and then across into the other, bustin' the glass out and bustin' and slicin' Jo Jo up with every hit. When he gets to the end, the ape smashes Jo Jo up against the front foldin' door 'til it finally gives way and our man tumbles out.

Maneuverin' so he can try to push himself up, Jo Jo's got bits of bone stickin' out and he's bleedin' like a stuck pig, but he manages to get his feet under him just as Terra Mungus grabs him by the collar with one hand and the gonads with the other. The ape raises him up, flips him upside down, and smashes Jo Jo headfirst into the blacktop, producing a sound like a railroad tie gettin' snapped in two.

The limp body falls over. But Terra Mungus ain't done. He leaps up, fists together, and drops all that weight and them combined fists right down onto Jo Jo's spine. Them fists come down again and again like big ol' meaty sledgehammers, breakin' more and more bones underneath 'til it seems like there can't be nothin' else to break.

The ape stands up, breathin' heavy, eyeballin' Jo Jo, waitin' for him to move, ash-flakes gettin' caught up in his fur. He pokes at the body with his toe but there ain't no response. His big ol' nostrils flare as the wind shifts, carryin' an unmistakable smell his way.

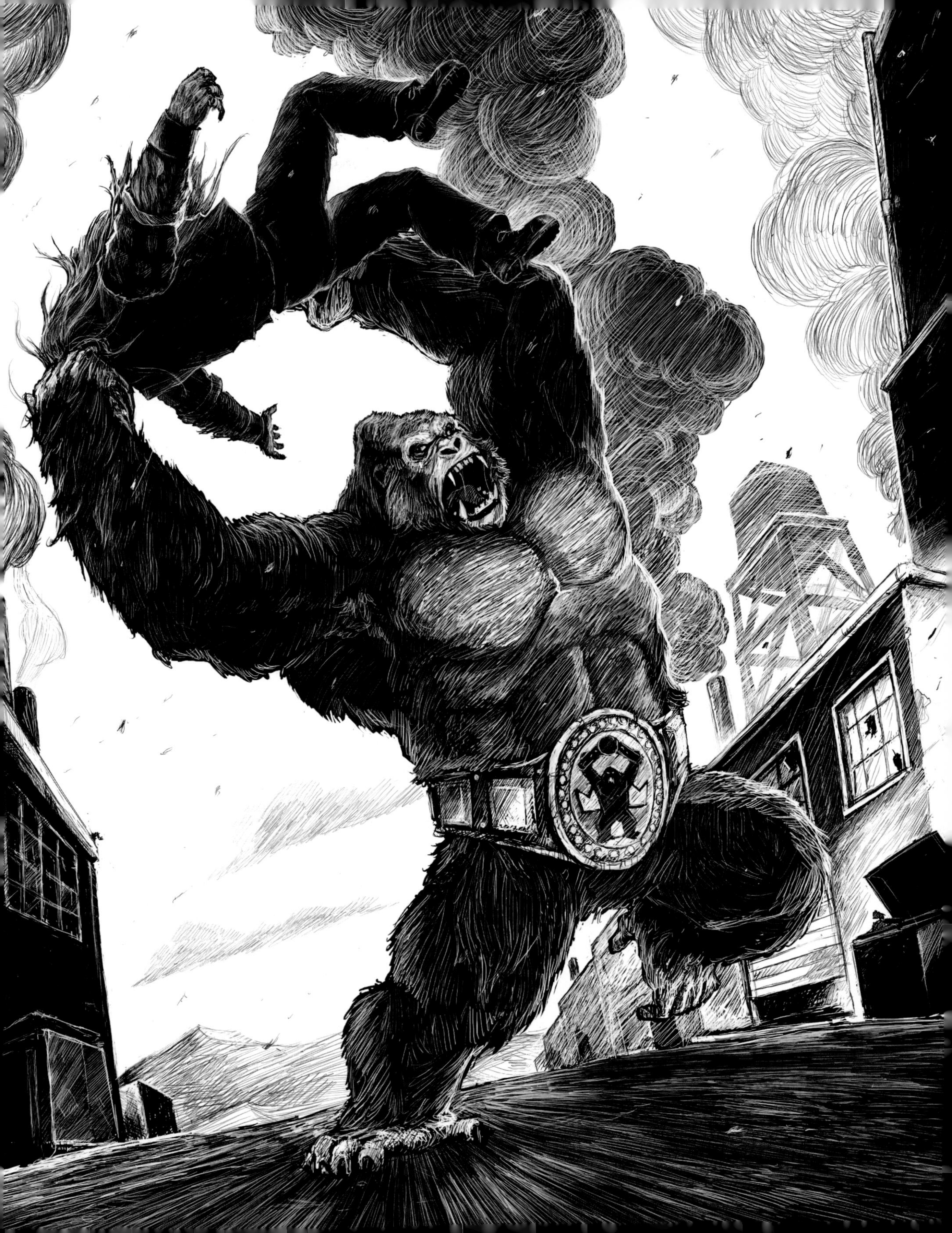

Shit.

Terra Mungus hears flowin' water not far off. Lookin' over his shoulder, he sees a low cement wall, like one o' them median strips, and he hears the water comin' from just past it. Gettin' himself an idea, the gorilla lifts the body by the back o' the shirt and drags. He passes the end o' the bus, lookin' over at his corner man behind the wheel o' the parked cage truck. The chimp offers a big grin and a thumbs-up as Terra Mungus drags Jo Jo over the wall.

There's a ledge and, in a cement channel below, a flowin' river o' shit. Terra Mungus lifts Jo Jo high up over his head, lets out one last nut-shrivelin' roar, and then tosses that body into the swiftly movin' muck, watchin' as it gets swept away into a tunnel and disappears.

CHAPTER THE TWELFTH

Elsa waits while the bag lady and a fat bum finish dressin' her up. She ain't got her chains on no more on account o' there bein' only one way outta the concrete room with its rusty pipes and mucky gauges. And with them gators waitin' at the end o' the tunnel outside . . . well, let's just say escape don't seem all that likely. Elsa don't know if gators are capable o' eatin' right away after they done got their fill, but she ain't exactly itchin' to find out, neither.

The bag lady and bum talk every once in a while to each other, but mostly they talk to folks that ain't there. Whoever it is they're chattin' with, everyone seems relieved that their liege mighta finally found what he was lookin' for. The bag lady takes a step back, givin' Elsa's outfit a critical eye in the dim lantern light. "Gotta be just right," she says.

It's a weddin' dress, or at least what gets by as one in King Mo's domain: a patchwork o' discarded rags and lace that mighta once upon a time been white but are now gray and brown and black, all joined together by electrician's tape.

Just as the fat bum puts on the cap and veil, Elsa hears familiar multiple footsteps comin' down the passage. Pretty soon them gators plod in, followed by the dark man in the coat, the king himself. He's got his glasses hangin' from the gold chains 'round his neck and he's grinnin' like a cat in a fish cannery.

He wraps the chain leashes 'round a wheel on a nearby pipe, and as he steps away, one o' them gators lunges, testin' the leash's hold. Mo stops, pivots his head, and barks, "Stay there, Elizabeth!" The gator lets out a low rumblin' growl and opens that tooth-lined maw nice and wide, the growl turnin' into a hiss. Mo turns to give the unruly reptile a good look at his bullwhip, and by way o' response the gator closes her mouth, turns, and heads back toward the pipes.

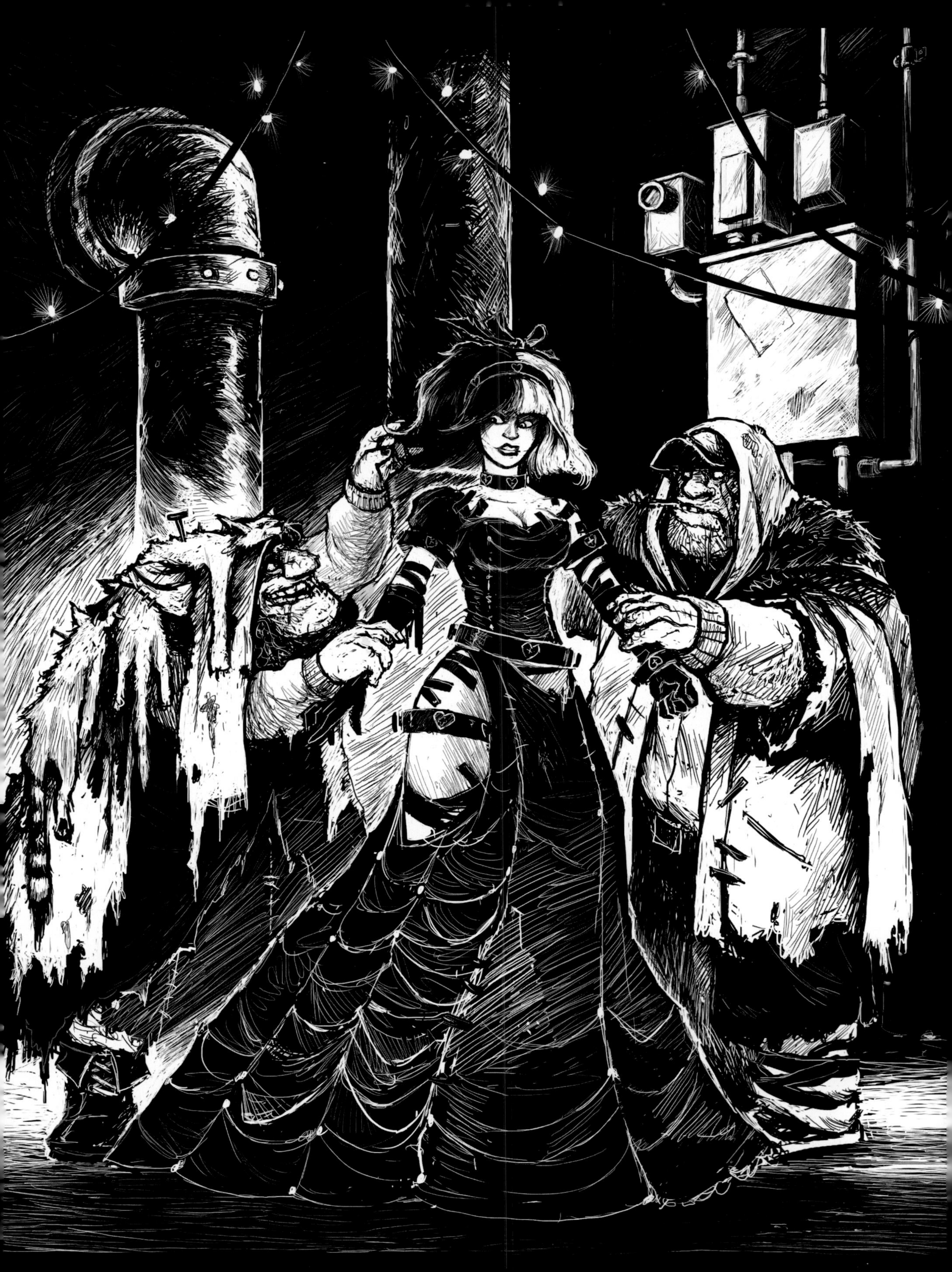

"Apologies," Mo says, returnin' his attention to Elsa. "She gets testy when I call her 'Elizabeth.'" Elsa hears one more growl, really faint-like from the other side o' the room.

The two bums step away as the king walks up, liftin' the veil so he can stare at Elsa. He reaches out and puts his grimy, calloused hand to her cheek. "You are a truly magnificent creature," he says in that baritone voice. "My expectations had been impossible, I see that now; I couldn't settle on one woman because I desired many women . . . but how? How to have all of those gifts in one package? And then, then you come along . . . and you are impossible. My beautiful miracle. My first, my last, my everything. Just imagine the children we'll have . . ." Mo takes his hand away and puts it behind his ear as if he's listenin' to something, and the next time Elsa hears his voice, she hears it inside her head even though Mo's lips stay closed. "I can hear it now," that deep voice flows through her mind. "The pitter-patter of little feet . . ." He spreads his hands wide, that grin growin' even wider, but the voice is still inside her. "Scampering through the scented gardens of my majestic kingdom!"

Elsa don't think that talkin' inside someone's head is normal, but she ain't seen enough o' the really real world yet to know exactly what's normal and what ain't. Besides, if the bums can talk to each other from far away, and that means they have special powers, it don't seem like much of a stretch for Mo to be doin' what he's doin' and have special powers too.

The king takes her cheeks in both hands now and he talks regular. "The ceremony will begin momentarily. And then . . . then, my baby girl, we will consummate." Another faint growl carries over from the other side o' the room.

Elsa don't answer. The ground under her starts to vibrate, and the pipes rattle, and what Elsa does next is the same thing she did while Father and the other men at the mansion had their fun with her—the very same thing she did while she thought about what she'd do to *them* when the time was right . . .

She looks into King Mo's steel-gray eyes, and she offers up her prettiest, most innocent smile.

★★★★✥★★★★

Now I hope you was payin' attention a ways back when I told you that Jo Jo was "different." In fact, I've done said it a few times now, but at any rate, this whole bit's gonna make a lot more sense if you cast your mind back on that simple fact.

Right 'bout now, Jo Jo's feelin' like he's just startin' to wake up from a dream, or more like a nightmare, I suppose, where he was swallowed up . . . kinda like fallin' into a well. It's real similar to how he felt after the beatin' that led to him bein' hung from that bridge way back when I first launched into this here yarn.

And now, just like then, Jo Jo's got the feelin' like he's floatin' back up outta that well, little by little, bit by bit, makin' his way back to the really real world. A voice drifts down, like it's comin' from a long ways away, sayin', "Yeah! Just floated in. No, he's mine! I saw him, he's mine! Screw you, anyway!"

As Jo Jo floats up farther, he realizes that he's got his eyes closed, and he ain't been breathin'. Right then he feels a little kick, a little spike o' energy, and he opens his eyes . . .

. . . scarin' the bejesus outta the bum who hauled him outta the shit, figurin' him for dead. The hobo was in the middle o' pullin' off Jo Jo's silver rings, them special ones that Greta made, that our man stretched and reshaped as he got older, just like she showed him; in fact the bum's holdin' onto one o'em right now when Jo Jo's eyes pop open and with a desperate gasp he sucks in a chest full o' air. The bum stumbles back, droppin' the ring and diggin' frantically in his own coat pocket for somethin'. What he pulls out is a blade, shinin' in the dim lantern light. At first Jo Jo can't get his limbs to respond, to mount any kind o' defense, and even when they do get to movin' they react all slow and sluggish-like.

The hobo lunges and drives that knife down as hard as he can on Jo Jo's chest but it don't go in—it just kinda skips off to one side. The bum gets a mighty confused look on his face while he holds the knife up, starin', and damned if the blade ain't just a smidge bent.

While the bum overcomes his confusion and gets set to stab again, Jo Jo's limbs finally kick into high gear; he grabs that incomin' wrist and twists, producin' a loud crack. The bum screams out, "He's got me! Sonofabitch!" while Jo Jo pries that crooked blade outta the vagrant's grubby grasp. "Wedding? Hang the wedding! Help! Spare some goddamned—" the bum don't get no more words out though as Jo Jo buries the unstraight knife as far as it'll go into the center o' the beggar's chest.

The sewer rat's eyes roll up into his head, as his body goes stiff and then falls limp. Jo Jo looks 'round to see who the bum was talkin' to, ready to take on another threat, but there ain't nothin' there. He's in a mostly empty little room; short-tunneled, bricked at one end, with some old blankets and dirty magazines (in the literal and figurative sense) and a kerosene lantern. Outside the little hidey-hole, Jo Jo can smell the overwhelmin' stench o' a whole lotta shit, and he can hear the crap rivers flowin'.

He ain't exactly sure how he got here; the last thing he remembers is gettin' the shit stomped outta him by Terra Mungus. What he does know is that the carnival's on its way to Dead End, and he needs to get movin'. Figurin' he'll need every weapon he can get, he pulls the knife outta the bum, but when he does he freezes, starin' at that blood-coated, bent steel blade. He recognizes it, see.

It's a knife from Elsa's doctor bag.

Elsa . . . he'd thought she left him but what if this hobo had taken her? Jo Jo retrieves his rings and crawls outta the little space onto a concrete ledge. Down below him is that swiftly flowin' river o' shit. The overpowerin' smell sets his head to poundin' and makes it tough to think. Forcin' his brain to cooperate, he figures that if the bum got to Elsa and took her stuff, she must be dead. What he's gotta worry 'bout now is gettin' back on the road.

So he heads along the ledge, goin' against the crap current until he comes to a side passage and little alcoves with metal ladder rungs bolted to the walls. One set o' rungs leads up, the other goes down. He's all set to climb up when he hears organ music driftin' outta the down-hole—music that he recognizes. It's old-timey music the gypsy woman Greta used to play in her trailer at night—this particular part— though the melody is distorted or kinda warped for lack o' a better word—is the bridal chorus from *Lohengrin*.

Jo Jo looks down at the blade, thinks 'bout Elsa, 'bout the bum talkin' 'bout a wedding, and hearin' that music. *Nah*, he thinks to himself. *Couldn't be.*

He can't be sure, though, can he? 'Less he goes and has a look for himself. He knows that he's gotta get on the road, get back to Her . . . but he also knows that if She ever found out he had a chance to save someone like Elsa and he didn't do it . . . well, he doesn't think he could live with the disappointment in Her eyes.

Jo Jo tucks the crooked knife into the back o' his jeans and starts climbin' down.

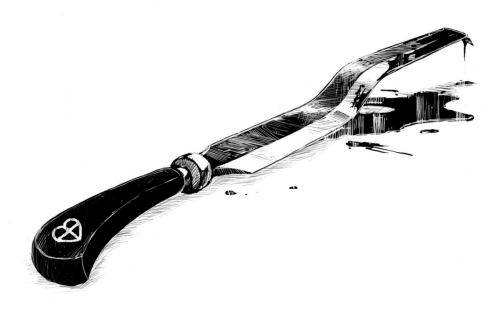

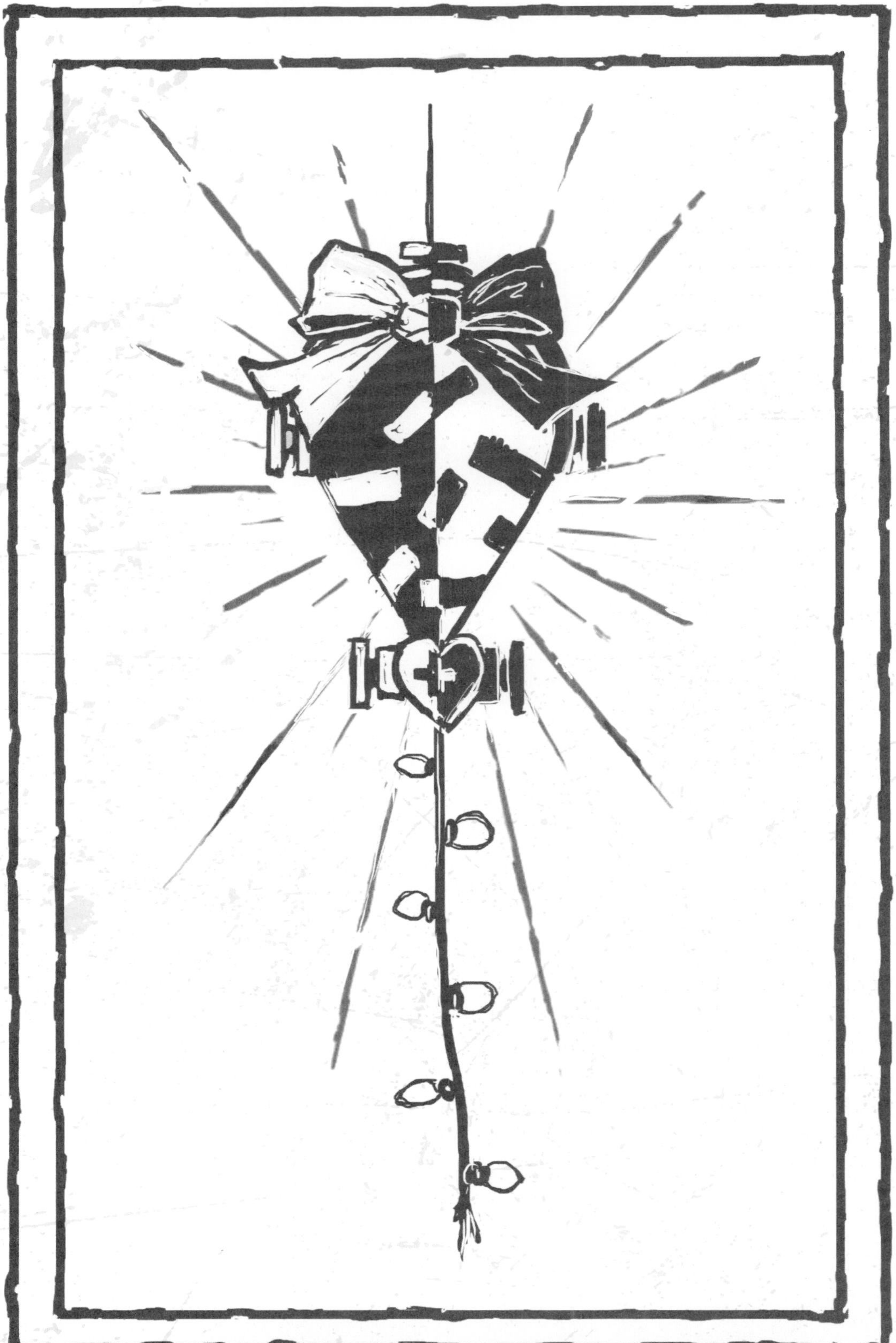

The Bride

CHAPTER THE THIRTEENTH

The weddin' music don't quite sound right 'cause it's comin' from a organ made o' rusty old pipes and various pieces o' junk and machinery the bums acquired and put together. Elsa ain't payin' much attention to the unharmony as she's led outta the tunnel though; no she's too busy gettin' a look at everything 'round her and workin' on a plan to kill whoever she needs to kill in order to get the hell out.

Under her feet is a metal grate, and below that's a whole lotta shit water. Directly on her right and then farther up on the same side are two big-ass pipe configurations—three times as big 'round as she is—that go down through the grate and disappear into the pool o' crap. On the other side o' the first big pipe is the organ and the bum playin' it, the scrap pipes linin' the concrete wall and reachin' up as high as the steel landin' that looks out over the big open space. King Mo is standin' up on that landin' with his shades back on, waitin' on Elsa to get brought up the metal steps. There's a hobo with a beard down to his nuts standin' next to Mo, wearin' a black robe, also waitin'. As Elsa comes to the top o' the stairs she sees Lizzy and Lilah on the other side o' the landin', their chains wound 'round the side rail. The robe-wearin' bearded fella's got a lazy eye and two nails welded to make a cross hangin' round his neck. He offers up a smile absent a whole lotta teeth, while Lizzy opens her mouth up as wide as it'll go, showin' off ten times as many teeth and pullin' against her chain.

"Lizzy, behave," Mo says. Elsa looks down 'bout twenty feet to where a whole mess o' dirty, stinkin' Aimless are gathered, all gawkin' up at where she's standin', the hobo priest on her right, and the tall, skinny, funky blade-wieldin' bum who escorted her up the stairs on her left. The weapon he carries is basically a pipe with machetes fixed to either end. Mo, he's facin' Elsa now, and she gets to wonderin': If this king can talk inside her head, what else can he do? Can he dig 'round in there and pick out secret thoughts, like her wantin' to escape?

While she ponders, the organ music stops, and King Mo turns and starts speechifyin' to the crowd 'bout how lonely he's been, not havin' no woman to bear his kids and carry on his line and so on and so on. While he keeps on gabbin' Elsa notices that the shit pool under the grate is *risin'*. In fact, it's risin' up closer and closer to where all them bums are standin'. And while Mo rambles, some o' them sewer rats sneak peeks at the risin' crap tide and then at each other with a bit o' what looks like concern, 'til finally Mo stops and looks at the fat bum that helped dress Elsa.

Lookin' mighty relieved, the hefty hobo tromps over to a big ol' lever attached to some gears and machinery next to the organ. Another vagrant on the other side walks over to another lever and both o' them bums pull them levers at the same time. Chains rattle and move up and down on pulleys, big-toothed gears grind, and an engine noise that sounds like a barrelin' locomotive carries over all and everything, while the whole shebang from floor to the ceilin' vibrates to hell and back and that crap water drains down, down, down, revealin' a big ol' square concrete well. Elsa can only guess that the shit is gettin' sucked into the fat parts at the bottom o' them two big pipes—gettin' sucked in and back up and out somewhere above where she can't see—cause that well ain't got no drains in the bottom.

No sooner is all that crap cleared out than a whole bunch more comes floodin' in, gushin' through openin's in the well wall. It comes in fast, too, the shit water line crawling its way back up toward the grate at a steady pace.

✶✶✶✶✤✶✶✶✶

Now, off to the side, in a corner and down a little tunnel that's small enough to make Jo Jo crouch, our hero's come to an old iron gate. He swings it open on squeaky hinges and makes his way out to where he can stand up again, out to where all the gathered bums are starin' up at some metal ledge, where there's a guy he ain't never seen before, standin' sideways. There's some kinda priest up there too, talkin' 'bout love or some nonsense, and there's a hobo with a mean-lookin' weapon, and he's pokin' it into the back o' . . . Elsa.

Jo Jo's mighty relieved when he sees her, and he's glad he made the choice to come down. While he's congratulatin' himself, though, that priest has done asked if the dark-skinned fella in the sunglasses will take "this woman" to be his wife, and he done answered, "Yes!" And then that holy asshole turns to Elsa and asks if she'll take the guy he calls "King Mo" as her husband. When she don't answer, the skinny vagrant with the blade gives her a little jab in the back and that's when our man decides he's seen enough.

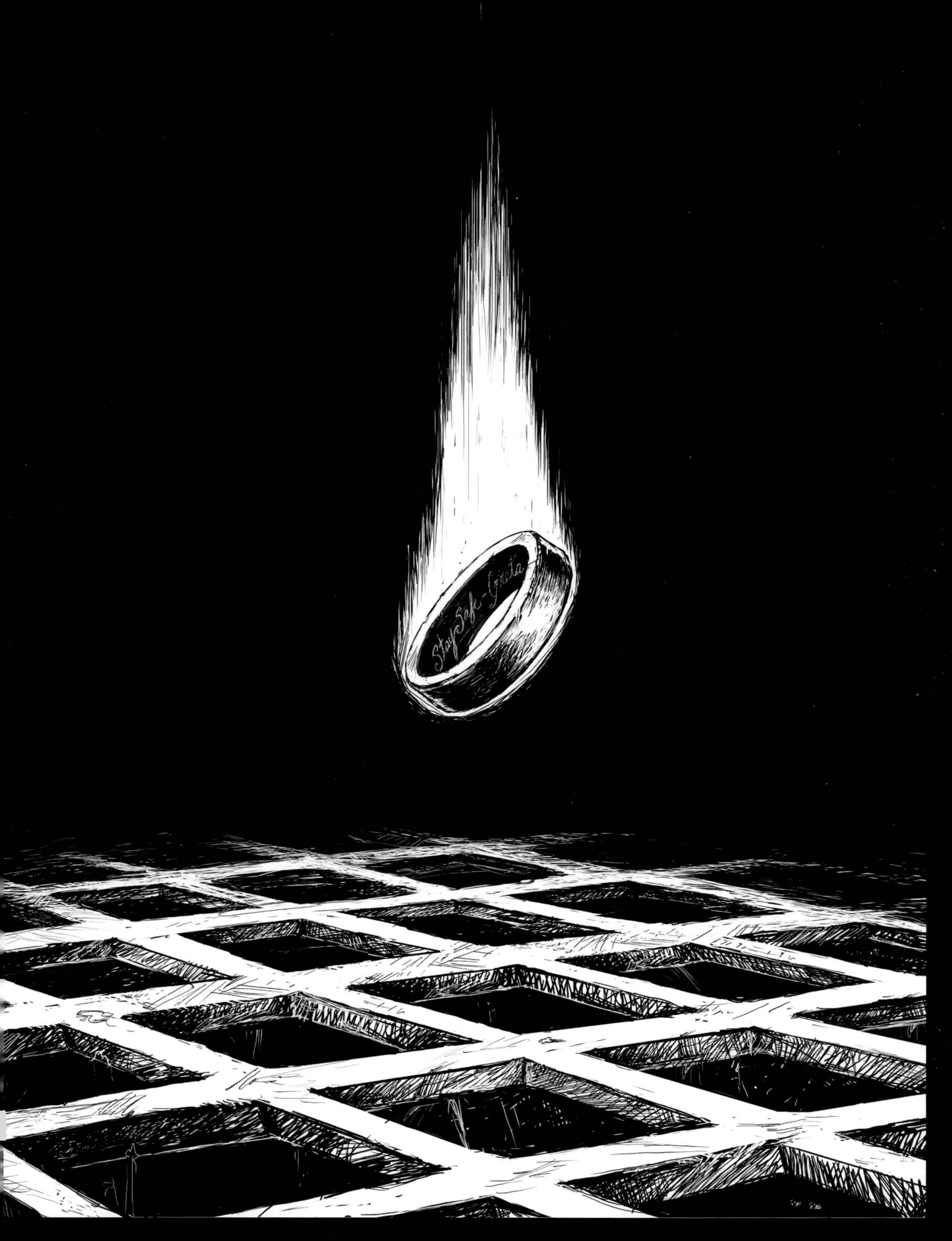
Stay Safe - Greta

He looks down at his fingers then, at the few rings he's got left, and he does somethin' that he realizes he shoulda done before he threw down with Terra Mungus: He slips one off and drops it. It goes through the grate under his feet and plunks into a whole mess o' raw sewage . . . raw sewage that's just a few feet away and inchin' closer but Jo Jo don't pay that no mind as he takes Elsa's bent blade and crams it into the neck o' the nearest bum.

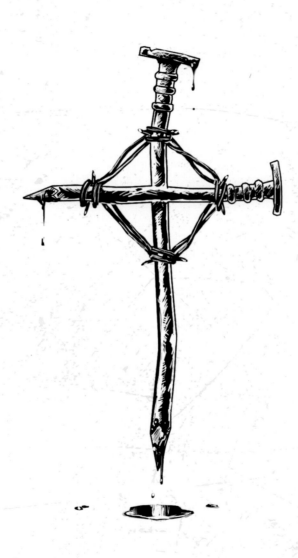

CHAPTER THE FOURTEENTH

"What this is?" the king asks, lookin' over the railin' as all hell cuts loose down below. Mo watches, flabbergasted, as a long-haired man in boots commences to kickin' the everlovin' shit outta his loyal subjects.

Elsa, she can hardly contain her excitement, lookin' down to see Jo Jo whoopin' a hundred different kinds o' ass on the scumbag masses. And she's thinking that right 'bout now might be a good time to make her move, when King Mo says, "Not to worry my love, I'll get this sorted *tout suite*." Mo reaches down and unclips the gator leashes at the collars. He takes out his bullwhip, and Lilah tears off first, boltin' down them metal stairs ahead o' Mo, followed by Lizzy, but damned if Elsa don't get the notion that Lizzy's beady green eye fixed her a look o' death before disappearin'.

Down below, Jo Jo's done stabbed and kicked his way through half o' the throng, when that crooked knife o' his finally breaks. He shoves what's left o' it into some fat bum's eye (the very same fat bum who assisted Elsa in gettin' her outfit on, though, 'course, he don't know that), and he heads off to the base o' the nearest metal stairs. Well up at the first landin' o' these particular stairs is the biggest goddamn alligator our man has ever seen, and it comes chargin' hellbent for leather straight at him! And just behind the determined reptile is that fella the priest called King Mo.

Mo's bullwhip lashes out and winds itself 'round Jo Jo's neck. Mo pulls, yankin' our man right toward the wide-open maw o' Lilah. Jo Jo slaps out, knockin' the jaws to one side where they shut with a loud snap. He pushes himself back up, wraps both hands 'round the leather a few inches from his neck, and jerks and twists with all his might. Mo comes flyin' off them steps, crashin' into Jo Jo, and the two o'em go tumblin' into the shit water that has by now worked its way up and over the metal grate.

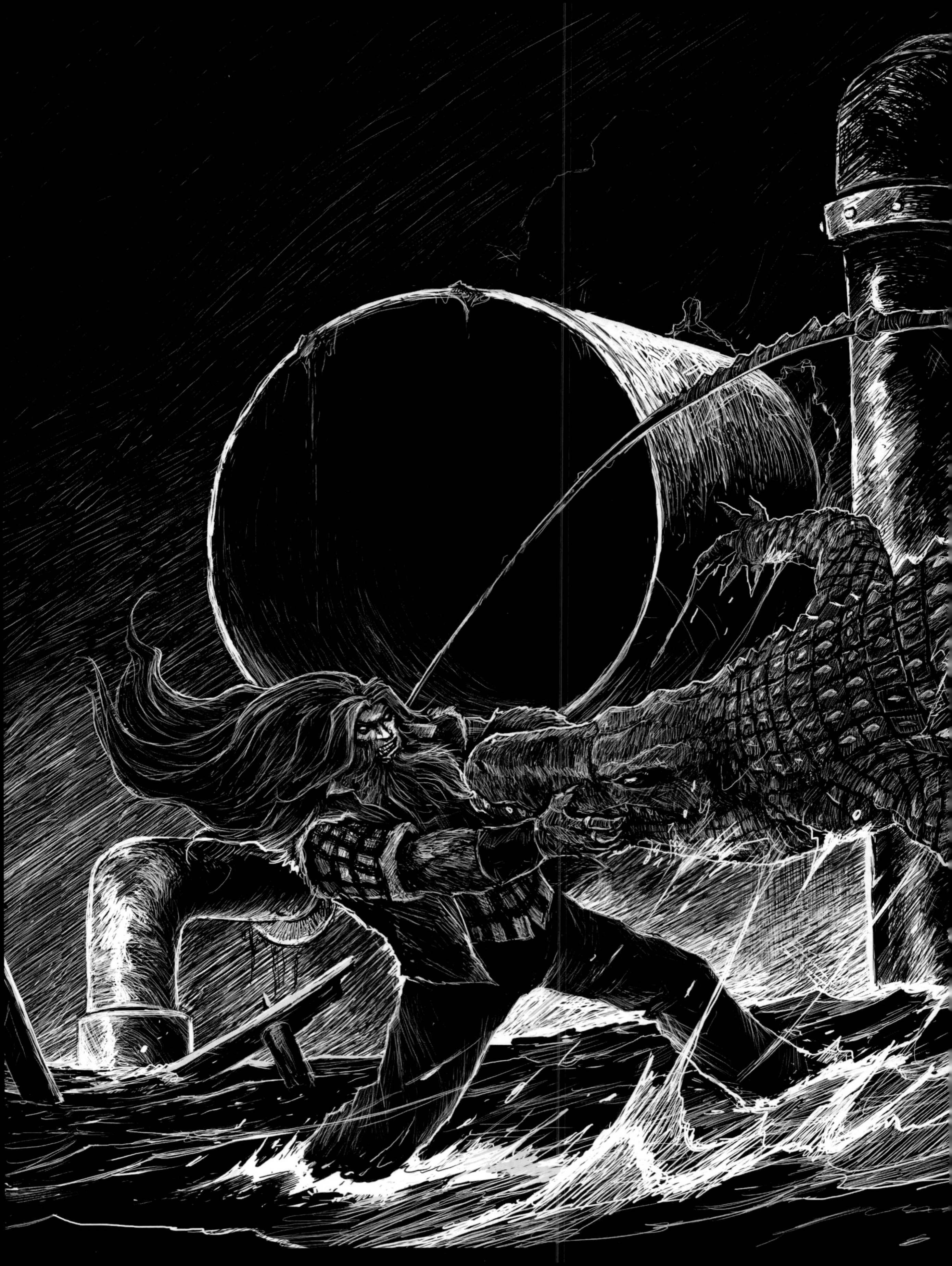

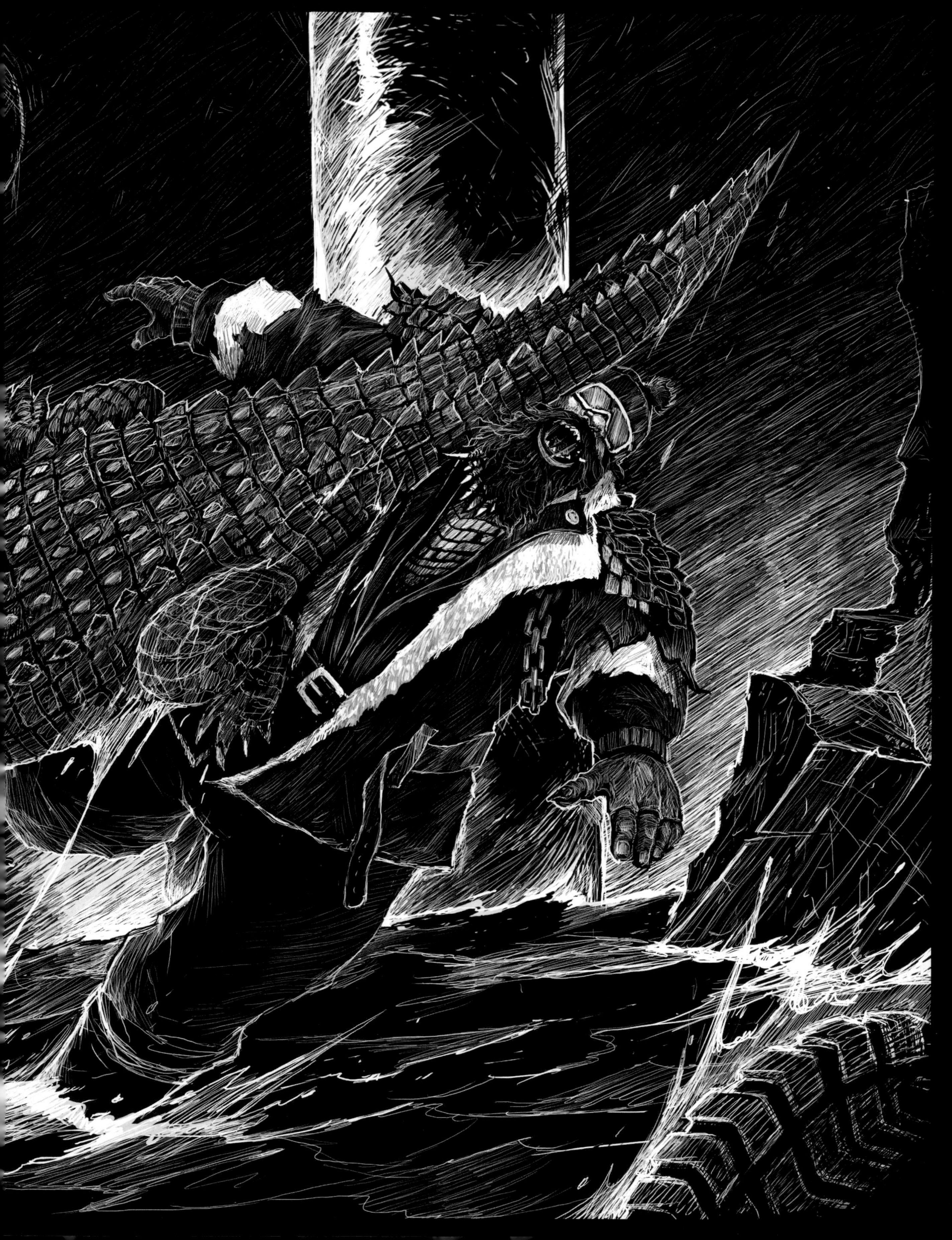

Elsa's ready to start her own fight up top when sure 'nough, Lizzy bolts back up the stairs and comes chargin' at her on them fat little legs.

Now you mighta worked this out on your own, but if you haven't, I'll fill you in on the fact that Lizzy is jealous. So jealous that she ain't ready to share her master with no other woman. And yeah, maybe you're thinkin' to yourself that she's just a dumb gator, but if you saw that behemoth chargin' at *you*, I doubt you'd waste time debatin' the finer points o' reptilian intelligence.

Seein' her chance, Elsa grabs the skinny fella who was guardin' her and tosses him in front o' Lizzy. The priest, he's so damn scared he's retreated all the way to the railin' and started screamin' like a teenage girl at one o' them boy-band concerts.

The skinny bum strikes down, but Lizzy, fast as can be, flips her snout sideways and bites down on the descendin' blade, twistin' and wrenchin' it right outta Skinny Boy's hands. She snaps her head to the side, and the blade goes out over the ledge, flippin' end over end 'til it buries itself in the skull o' the bag lady, who was splashin' her way over to pull one o' the pump levers.

Elsa kicks Skinny Boy in the back, into the waitin' maw o' Lizzy, whose bone-crushin' jaws split the skinny bum's skull in half.

The priest has opted to go over the railin' at this point and is barely hangin' on, too scared to let go and too scared to stay on the landin'. Elsa's decided she'd better make a run for it—thinkin' if she can make it down below, maybe she can get her hands on a weapon that'll dispatch the ragin' reptile. She sprints down the stairs as fast as her legs will carry her, riskin' a glance over her shoulder to see Lizzy hurdle over the body o' Skinny Boy and come gallopin' after her.

Down below and on the other side, Lilah swims through the shit to Jo Jo, jaws slammin' shut on thin air where Jo Jo's arm was a split second ago, while King Mo collects himself just a few feet away. Jo Jo gets himself an idea, grabs onto the closed snout o' that gator, and spins, liftin' the entire reptile up, swingin' it like a scaly baseball bat right into King Mo's noggin.

Now you might think you've been in some scraps, but until you've been bitch slapped by a six-hundred-pound gator tail, you've been through exactly jack shit.

Mo's glasses break apart and go flyin', bloody spit spews outta his mouth, and his head bobble-spins like when a fighter takes a heavyweight punch in one o' them boxin' movies. But Mo's made o' some seriously tough stuff, and he manages to keep his legs (now calf-deep in shit) under him.

Just then, Jo Jo remembers the whip. Thinkin' that he mighta just stepped on it, he bends down, reachin' into the god-awful muck and closin' a fist round the skinny leather.

Apparently Lilah didn't much appreciate bein' used as a blunt weapon, 'cause she comes tearin' after Jo Jo, jaws in search o' an arm or leg, but slammin' down on nothin' each time as Jo Jo dodges and pulls his limbs away. Our man's got more to worry 'bout than just Lilah though, as he knocks the daylights outta a couple more

Aimless who thought it might be a good idea to attack while Jo Jo was distracted. Our man dispenses with the lackeys, relieved to see that the remainin' few have decided they got someplace more important to be, leavin' our hero with just Mo and the gator to contend with.

Mo throws some blows and Jo Jo kicks out, knockin' the king off his feet and into the risin' shit swamp. Our man barely gets his arm outta the way o' a Lilah bite and manages to slap the whip 'round the gator's snout, wrappin' it up and leavin' Lilah temporarily unable to open her maw.

The crap-tide's up to their asses now as Mo and Jo Jo knuckle up and trade blow after thunderous blow, both men bloodied and battered . . . but it looks like Mo might be gettin' the better o' it, as he's forcin' Jo Jo toward the back wall while Lilah thrashes like mad to dislodge the whip wrapped 'round her snout.

Meantime, Elsa and Lizzy have both hit the water. Elsa, she's used to her father's big-ass pool, so she does know how to swim, but she ain't no match for a born-to-swim gator. She's lookin' 'round for a weapon, when that gator's jaws lock on her right arm; Lizzy goes into a death roll, and Elsa screams as the gator rips that arm right out from its clamp.

Remember not so long ago, when Jo Jo woke up from bein' dead, when I said it'd help quite a bit if you remembered that he was different? Well this is kinda the same thing . . . way back in the ice cream truck Jo Jo wondered why Elsa wasn't bleedin'. That'd be on account o' her bein' different. And it's why when her arm pops off, there ain't no fountain o' blood, and even though Elsa screams from the sudden shock o' it, she don't pass out or go into a fit o' cryin' and flailin' like most folks would.

The gator, though, she ain't happy with just a limb; no, she wants to pop Elsa's head off her shoulders. And that, folks, that *would* present a problem.

Mo and Jo Jo, now chest-deep in sewage, are still rearrangin' each other's facial features on the one side o' the stairs, but on the other side, up on the railin', that priest who was too weak to haul himself up finally lets go. Well as luck would have it, he falls right into the lever next to the organ and knocks it into the down position.

Elsa gets herself an idea. "Pull the other lever!" she shouts over to Jo Jo. Now see that space between the grate floor and the big pipe near Elsa? Course you don't, 'cause the floor's covered in sewage, but trust me, there's a ring o' space round that pipe and that's what Elsa's slippin' through right now, not waitin' to see if Jo Jo heard her, and hopin' the damn gator's determined enough to follow her through.

Elsa opens her eyes, grateful that she don't have to breathe like normal folks do—yeah that'd be that whole "different" thing again but let's not get hung up on the minutia right now. The muck she's in is thick, like shit soup, but there is enough actual water in it for her to see a reptilian shadow divin' her way. Elsa smiles and kicks herself downward.

Up topside, Jo Jo ducks down into the now slowly descendin' shit, under Mo's swing, and pushes the king into the chains hangin' on the wall. He heard Elsa's yell, and he's tryin' to comply, but first there's the business at hand. He wraps one o' them chains twice 'round Mo's neck, forcin' all manner o' garbled hackin' noises from the king.

Our man sees movement in the corner o' his eye and turns, but too late—Lilah's done shucked off that whip, and she locks jaws onto Jo Jo's left arm. It hurts like a sonofabitch and even after our hero pounds his fist into that knobby noggin time and again, the reptile still refuses to let go. Meanwhile, Mo's still gurglin', tryin' to get them chains unwrapped. Jo Jo eyeballs the gears and the lever and he gets one o' them "two birds with one stone" ideas. He swings Lilah up so half o' her's layin' over one o' them big gears, and then he reaches for the lever. He can't quite get it so he kicks out, bringin' his boot down and droppin' that metal arm.

Now all kinds o' things happen at basically the same time: Everything 'round Jo Jo gets to rattlin', joined by a deafenin' engine roar as the shit water plunges down at an accelerated rate; Lilah gets a taste o' what it's like to be caught in the jaws o' death as she gets chewed in half by them grindin' gears; and Mo gets yanked upward by them ascendin' chains, kickin' his feet and strugglin' mightily, but to no avail. Jo Jo tracks his ascent 'til somewhere up in the darkness o' rusty beams his body disappears.

Meanwhile, deep down in the shit, Elsa's gettin' whisked toward the fat section o' the pipe like she's caught in a rip tide . . . just like she intended. Down at the very bottom, the pipe don't go all the way to the well floor. It stops a few feet up, where all that raw sewage is gettin' sucked in, which was exactly what Elsa thought would happen. She grabs onto somethin' at the edge—she can't tell what at first. Then she sees that the bottom o' the pipe's covered with a steel grate that's done been worn away so that there's a big hole in the middle. She hangs on to the lip o' the pipe with her one good hand, and when she sees Lizzy comin' she tucks up her legs just as them jaws close, barely missin' her feet. The gator keeps goin', gettin' drawn over the grate and nearly bent in half before bein' sucked up into the pipe.

Darin' to peek over the edge and through the grate, Elsa sees a fast-spinnin' blade. Lizzy gets pulled right into it, and pretty soon all that's left o' the jealous leviathan is a whole lotta blood and a whole lotta bite-sized chunks that get swept on up and outta sight.

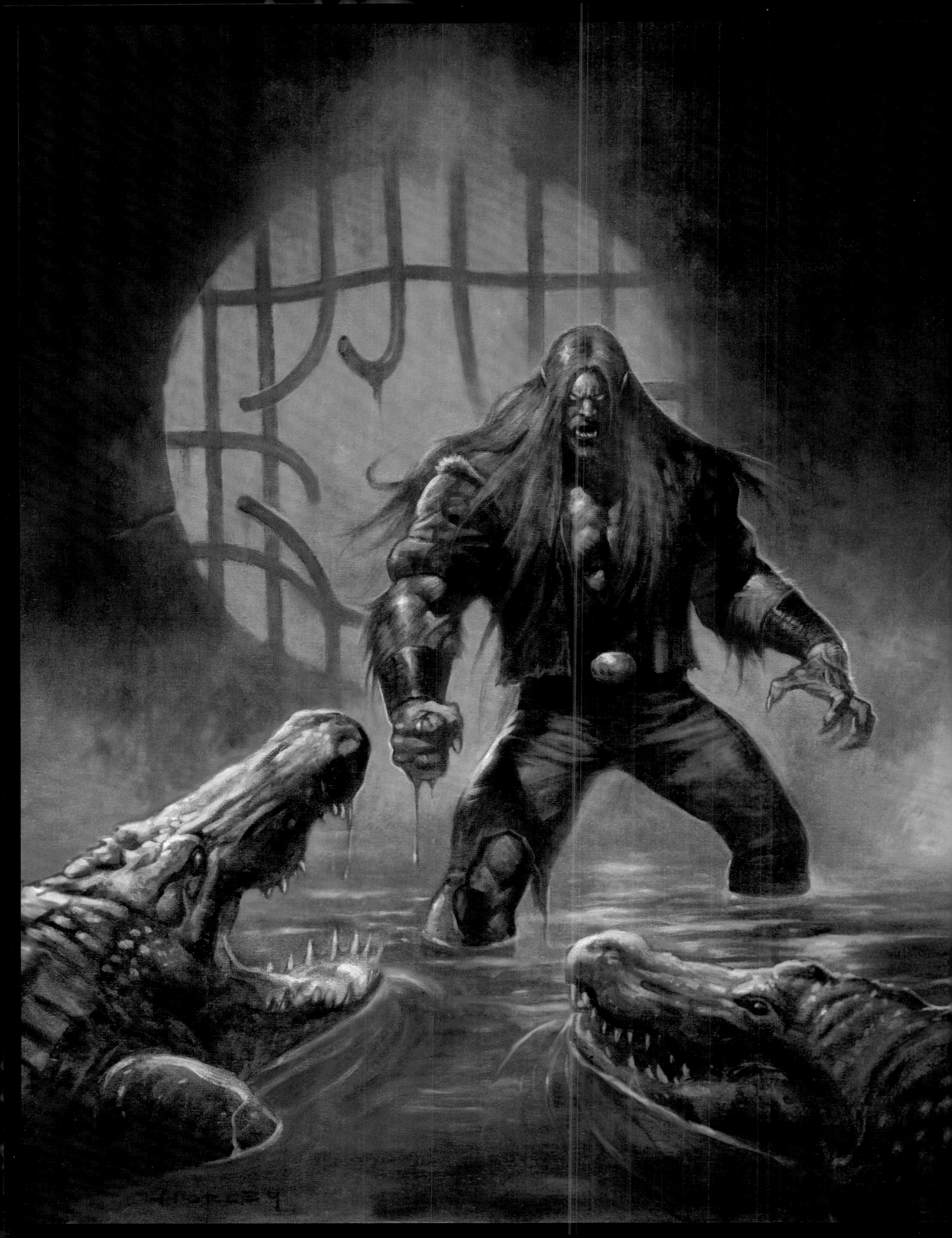

ACT II

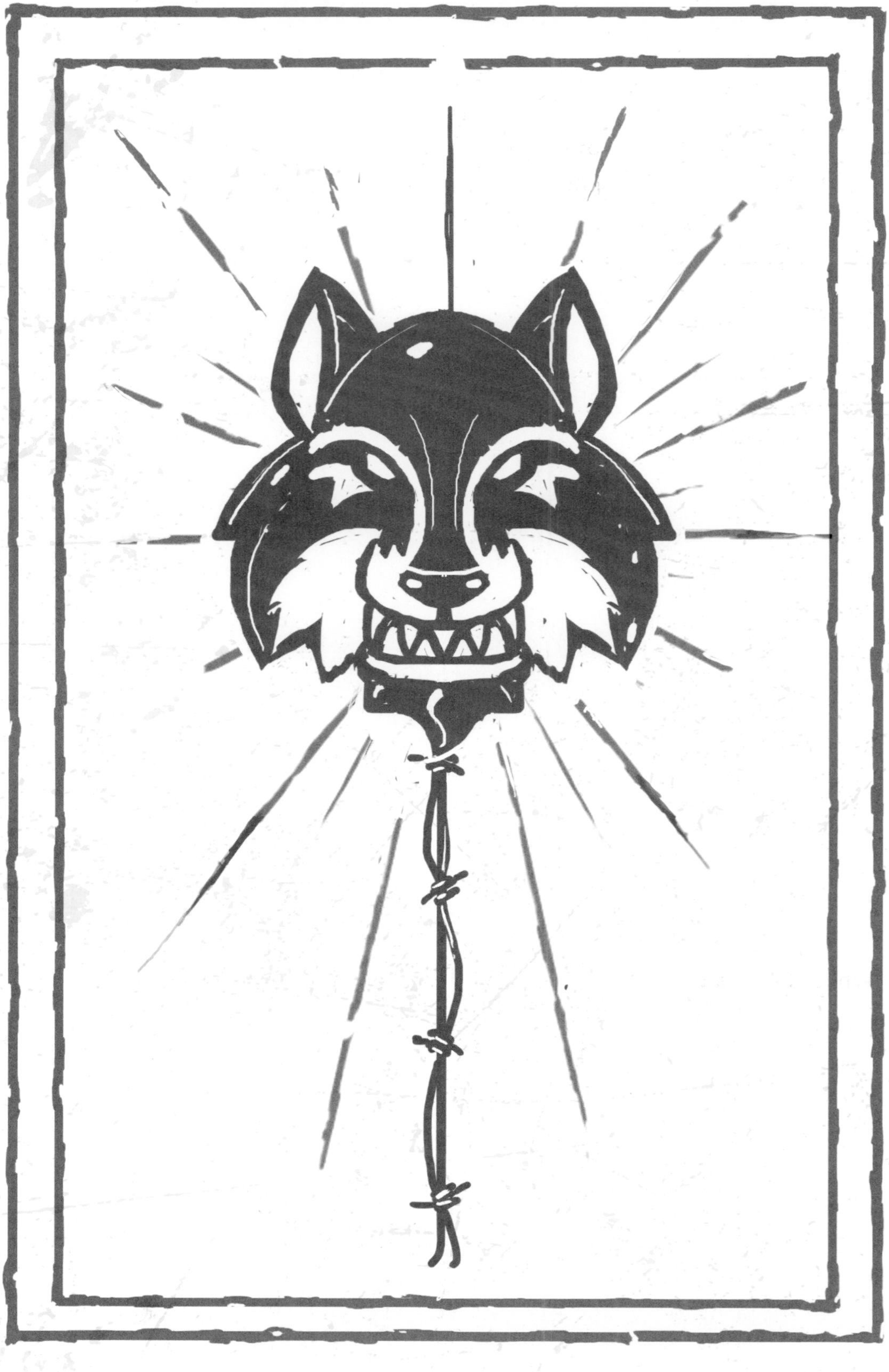

The Hellhound

CHAPTER THE FIFTEENTH

"I'm mighty glad you came to save me," Elsa says as they go through that portcullis Mo had stepped out from the first time our girl laid eyes on him.

Jo Jo just kinda mumbles in response, but Elsa can tell that he's glad he did what he did as they explore the handful o' passages, alcoves, and recesses o' Mo's "royal chambers." In one o' the pigeonholes, sure 'nough, they find Elsa's doctor bag. She grabs it up, looks inside, then cracks a big ol' grin and says, "Let's see 'bout gettin' me a new arm!"

They head on back to the pump room, where the two o'em pull the levers to drain the risin' shit, and they gather up all o' Elsa's missin' knives and surgical implements from the dead hands o' the Aimless. Then . . . then Elsa finds the bag lady that dressed her, puts the doctor satchel down, and gets to work on one o' the old gal's arms.

While she sets to amputatin' the old lady's limb up at the shoulder, Elsa looks over to Jo Jo and says, "I know you got bit by one of them gators. Just like I know you took a bullet when them clowns attacked," she eyeballs him with scrutiny in between scalpel strokes. "You ain't like other folks," she observes.

Jo Jo stays quiet, wonderin' if he oughta confide in Elsa or not as to the nature o' his differentness.

"Nothin' wrong with it," Elsa says, havin' removed the arm now. She attaches it via the metal clamp at her own shoulder stump. Now that arm don't actually move or do nothin' at first, 'til Elsa pulls a syringe with a tiny bit o' green liquid in it outta the bag. "This here's the serum," Elsa says. "It's what Father uses with all his creations." Elsa goes ahead and injects the arm, and then the two o'em wait, all quiet-like, and sure 'nough, within a few ticks those bag lady fingers start wigglin' and the arm starts to movin' like it was attached to Elsa since birth. She peers close at

Jo Jo, waitin' to see what his reaction'll be, like maybe she's wonderin' if he'll be disgusted or not. But Jo Jo can't hold back a smile as he says, "I imagine that comes in real handy."

Elsa grins back, and Jo Jo decides right then and there that he'll give this whole confidin' thing a try. He rolls up his sleeve and shows her his arm where he'd been bit, showin' that the wound is all healed, like it had never been. "Stuff that hurts or kills normal people, well, it just doesn't work that way on me," he says. And then he waits, the little boy inside him thinkin' back to all the times he had been called "freak." And just when he starts to get anxious, Elsa puts on an even bigger smile and says "Bet that comes in handy too!"

★★★★�֍★★★★

After what seems like a dog's age (no offense to our main man), Elsa and Jo Jo get on outta the sewers and back to the street level o' Hubtown . . . right up near where Terra Mungus done tossed Jo Jo into the crap channel in the first place.

Now after all the literal shit luck our man's had, a tiny speck o' good fortune does shine through the smog blanket o' Hubtown down onto Jo Jo, 'cause he finds his trusty cowboy hat, right where it'd gotten knocked off durin' the fight.

Jo Jo puts that hat right back where it belongs and the two o'em set about findin' some wash-up facilities and some clothes to change into. A bit o' wanderin' 'round the Hub leads 'em to an all-night, one-stop trucker facility, the Gas Grill n Gospel, where your average long-haul trucker or traveler can fill up on petrol, take advantage o' a hot shower, shove some barbecued brisket down the ol' gullet, and get hitched in the multidenominational chapel if the mood strikes.

Unfortunately the only shirts that'll fit Jo Jo are the XL souvenir T-shirts, like the one that says—or reads—"Everything's Bigger in Texas," with an arrow pointin' south, or the one that reads "I Got Your Longhorn Right Here." Jo Jo drops a few Johnnies on a couple o'em and a pair o' jeans and some engineer boots, takin' a moment to consider some alligator-skin cowboy kicks before thinkin' he's had enough o' gators and crocs and anythin' else in the big lizard family to last him a lifetime. While Elsa's cuddlin' up to a stuffed puppy Jo Jo picks up some o' the skimpy clothes she likes. Then, takin' the entire haul up to a clerk with a lazy eye named Lupita (she's named Lupita, not her eye; try to stick with me), Jo Jo inquires as to the fastest mode o' transport to Dead End.

Lupita informs him that there's a train headin' that way first thing in the mornin'. Elsa, she comes over and gushes on and on about how he didn't need to buy her them new clothes even as she swipes 'em up and heads over to a grimy stand-up mirror and holds the outfits in front o' her, posin' like she's on the cover o' some glamorous magazine.

While she does, Jo Jo pays for showers for the two o'em, then says, "One more thing to add," and spends an extra Johnnie on that stuffed dog.

After a shower and a change o' clothes and a whole lotta Elsa squealin' over her new "pet," the two are on their way to the train station when they realize that Hubtown bein' what it is, smoky roof and all, and them bein' down in the sewers for so long, neither one o'em knows just when "mornin'" is. Once they get to the ticket line, though, they find out pretty quick that mornin's set to break and they got no time to waste.

Now as they get into that line, let's take us a quick look at the rooftops. Yep, see there? Sure 'nough it's that damn bedraggled blackbird, spyin' down on 'em, head all lolled off to one side. It makes for one helluva sight, but unfortunately our travelers are too set on gettin' their tickets to pay it any mind.

Which makes the followin' bit even more unfortunate—Jo Jo, see, he just asked 'bout them tickets, but the ol' hag behind the counter, she just shakes her head and says, "Passenger train's full! Sold out! No room!"

"Make room," Jo Jo growls, leaning in. And though the crone shies back a bit, she must have a set o' balls that could fill a bathtub 'cause she sneers and says, "Full's full! No exceptions!"

"When's the next?" Elsa asks, hopin' maybe the trains run every half hour.

"Afternoon," the hag replies.

Now Jo Jo, he's fit to be tied. All he wants to do o' course is get to Her. Above all and everything his mind is fixed on Her and gettin' Her back . . . yeah and maybe settlin' a score with the carnies that done took Her in the first place and done beat his ass from hell to breakfast and left him hangin' off a trellis bridge. But ain't none o' that gonna happen if he can't find some kinda transport. And time is most definitely o' the essence 'cause when the Barnstormers get to Dead End, well let's just say that's the last stop and Jo Jo knows it.

It's right 'bout this time, as Elsa pulls Jo Jo away from the counter, that a raggedy bum in a peacoat and fingerless gloves comes hobblin' over and . . . well you'll forgive our two heroes for bein' set to plant their boots right in that ol' hobo's block and tackle on account o' him resemblin' one o'em Aimless vagrants. But before either o'em can deliver a punt kick to the tramp's coin purse, that fella up and says, "Couldn't help overhearin' as to your per-dicament." Now the bum leans in as if he's sharin' some state secret and says all low-like: "Ain't cause to drop Johnnies on no passenger train nohow! Freight's the way to go. Ride the rails, that's what! I'll show ya. Next freighter for Dead End leaves in thirty minutes."

The ol' hobo straightens back up and looks over to make sure the ticket hag ain't listenin' in while Jo Jo and Elsa share a look and both kinda shrug at the same time. The bum holds out a grubby paw and says, "Pleased to make your 'quaintence. Name's Bob," and he follows that first name with what sounds like a few vowels tossed in a blender and set to puree.

"What was that last part?" Elsa asks, shakin' the offered hand.

"I said, name's Bob Onminob!"

At this juncture, up on the rooftops, that broke-neck blackbird's apparently seen enough. It backs up to where it won't be observed and flaps them broken wings, losin' a few feathers in the process o' flyin' off toward the smoke canopy and then out to parts unknown. For now, anyway.

Before we take our own leave, though, you might be interested to know that there's another set o' eyes keepin' tabs on Jo Jo and Elsa—that fella standin' under the ripped awning over by that donkey boiler; yeah, the tall emaciated one with the dark skin and the hoodie and sunglasses. You'd recognize him as Huxley, the fella who's been shadowin' our man ever since Conway Titties, for reasons that ain't quite clear yet.

Whatever them reasons are, it most certainly has somethin' to do with Jo Jo, and maybe with his special rings too, 'cause the hooded stranger produces one o'em silver rings right now—one he musta "found" after the clown fight at the strip club—and he takes that ring, holds it real close to his mouth, sticks his tongue out . . . and licks the inside o' it. Whatever he tastes, it sets him to tremblin' all over, doin' a kinda herky-jerky little dance while he smiles big enough to reveal every one o'em golden teeth.

CHAPTER THE SIXTEENTH

For the time bein' let's cast our attention nowhere—I mean elsewhere. I mean nowhere *and* elsewhere, to this little patch o' dirt just off the Anaconda. Here we got ourselves a whole shitload o' eighteen-wheelers, all clustered up makin' a big, rough kinda circle. And if you look closer, you'll see the mornin' sun glintin' offa smaller motorized vehicles—the steel horses, hogs, choppers . . . motorcycles to all you common folk.

What's that, you say? The shoutin'? Yeah I was just gettin' to that. The more perceptive among you will take note that half the group is hollerin' at the other half, both sides wavin' clubs and knives and guns in a decidedly unfriendly manner.

These here shitstompers is the Profits. Frankie's gang. You remember how these faithful, they loved their fearless leader so much they set him up in a throne made o' truck and bike parts? Kinda like a big shrine? Well Frankie's corpse is still sittin' there, as dead and as stiff as can be. The body ain't quite reached that ripe stage just yet, where it starts stinkin' to high hell, but it ain't too far offa that neither.

So you're prob'ly wonderin' what the ruckus is all about. Well see that fella screamin' the loudest, the one with the mutton chops and the funky-shaped face that resembles one o' them Easter Island statues? That there's Cleeter, and he's convinced some o' these here Profits—mostly truckers but even a few o' the bikers—that there ain't no call to go on worshippin' Frankie. And that ain't all he's proposin' . . .

"Frankie's dead! Time we got us a *new* leader," Cleeter shouts, standin' at the head o' the *un*faithful with about twenty pounds o' air in his chest.

"Damnit, Cleeter! You shut yer brisket hole!" one o' the faithful retorts, the one with the tank top and the handlebar mustache. "That there's sacrilege!"

"Yeah?" Cleeter pipes back, "I say we need a new a president, and I got a good notion who!" He clomps over to Frankie's corpse, reaches out, and pries the straight razor outta Frankie's dead hand. Now there's a collective "oooohhhh" from the faithful, as if Cleeter had just gone and pissed on Johnny Cash's tombstone.

"Me! That's who!" Cleeter says, holdin' the razor up so the sun sparks right off it.

But before this here fracas can turn into an all-out brawl, a small shadow passes over Cleeter. The rabble-rouser looks up, nose all scrunched, and lowers the blade. "The hell's that?" he says.

It's enough to get both the faithful and the unfaithful to look skyward too, and what they see there is a dark mass, flippin' and flappin' and bobbin' and careenin' like it can't make up its mind whether it wants to zig or zag, bob or weave. Yeah, you guessed it; it's everyone's favorite death-defyin' blackbird.

So o' course these good ol' boys do what any rational-minded folks would do when presented with such a ponderous sight: They shoot at it.

Pistols, rifles, shotguns, just 'bout every one o'em takes aim. Gun smoke fills the air among deafenin' blasts as feathers go flyin' off the blackbird 'til finally it heads into a spiral like one o' them war planes goin' down over enemy territory.

Now it just so happens the blasted-up crow makes landfall smack-dab in the middle o' Frankie's lap. And Cleeter, he leans over, frownin'. "It ain't dead!" he hollers. Before he can take Frankie's blade to it, though, that crow pops to its feet, and Cleeter shies back a smidge, spyin' the danglin' head hangin' upside down off the broken neck. The mangled bird swivels that head 'round toward Frankie's gut so's it can see where the hell it's goin'.

The faithful and the unfaithful have gathered 'round now, watchin' all silent-like and dumbfounded while the crow, with a flurry o' wing-beatin', manages to fly itself up and latch onto Frankie's scraggly beard.

Then a few o' them boys' mouths drop open as the blackbird climbs up, swings that head into position, and pokes its beak inside dead Frankie's mouth. With a little help from one o' its talons, the crafty critter manages to pry that mouth all the way open, squeezin' its head and chest and then its ass end all the way in 'til there ain't nothin' stickin' out but tail feathers like Frankie's tryin' to deep-throat one o' them French maid dusters. Then, damned if the tail feathers don't disappear too.

Now, if we could peek under Frankie's beard, we'd spot a few feathers stickin' outta that hole in the big man's throat as the bird works its way down his gullet. Course you can't see that with the flavor saver in the way, so you'll just have to take my word for it.

There's a fair amount o' head scratchin' among the Profits, some o'em exchangin' confounded looks, not quite comprehendin' what the hell they just seen. 'Course what these boys witnessed so far ain't nothin' compared to what transpires next.

Frankie's fingers start to twitch. And when that happens, them good ol' boys all take a step back, eyes fit to pop right outta their skulls.

That twitchin' builds to a jump, like when a dog's dreamin' 'bout runnin' and its legs get to kickin'. And sure 'nough, Frankie's legs start movin' too. At this juncture a whole slew o' the faithful reach up with shaky hands and remove their hats.

And then, yep—we got our first fainter. That big fella just plumb falls over as Frankie's body stands right up and the fearless leader's eyes pop open. Everybody 'cept Cleeter takes more'n a few steps back now, as Frankie stomps all stiff-legged toward the upstart himself.

Cleeter lets out a kinda yelp and slashes with the razor blade, comin' down diagonal, openin' one helluva gash on Frankie's face, but that wound don't bleed, and it sure as shit don't slow Frankie down none. Cleeter tries for a backslash but Frankie's hands shoot out and clamp onto poor ol' Cleeter's wrist. Frankie rotates around then, with Cleeter's arm on his shoulder, and yanks down, causin' Cleeter to howl like a banshee as his elbow snaps.

Frankie faces forward again, lettin' Cleeter's useless arm dangle. Without a word or change o' expression, Frankie puts his left hand behind Cleeter's head and punches with his right, buryin' his fist in Cleeter's face with a sound that's a mixture o' someone stompin' in mud and crackin' their knuckles all at once.

When Frankie pulls his fist away, their ain't much left o' Cleeter's face 'cept a bloody, unrecognizable indentation. Frankie lets the limp body collapse to the sand, then casually picks up the dropped razor blade. He belches, spittin' out a single black feather, and raises that blade toward the sky all victorious-like.

Well, the faithful, they've just witnessed a bona fide miracle! A resurrection! All 'round Frankie, the Profits fall to their knees, chests to the dirt, arms in front, praisin' their newly risen messiah. And the unfaithful, well, they've been turned back to faithful real quick, joinin' the rest o' the gang face down in what religious types call supplication.

Now as Frankie holds that razor blade high, I wanna call your attention to a particular detail. Let's get real up-close and personal, right up in front o' that used-to-be-dead face, and take special note o' them eyes. They ain't the color o' old livin'-and-breathin' Frankie's eyes, no sir, these eyes is black, just like the crow's eyes, and as we get even closer—

Well, it's probably best we look away, 'cause what's starin' back at us ain't somethin' to be trifled with; no sir, them's the stone-cold, black-as-death eyes o' the Ramblin' Man. And the voice, the voice that comes outta Frankie next, well it sounds like taloned feet scrabblin' in dirt as Frankie gets to speechifyin'.

"I died for you. All of you," says he, and then he lets out a long, loud vocalization that you might describe as a mix between a caw and a yawp. And maybe a squawk thrown in to boot. Like a cawp-yuawk. Or a cawk-squawp. Anyway, it's a cross between a bird and human kinda noise, and after Frankie emits it, well, he kinda twitches his head like he's tryin' to work out a crick in the neck and then he continues.

"Your job was to avenge me but you couldn't get it done. So I came back . . . to help you sorry shits do it right! You . . . are weak," and Frankie raises his right hand,

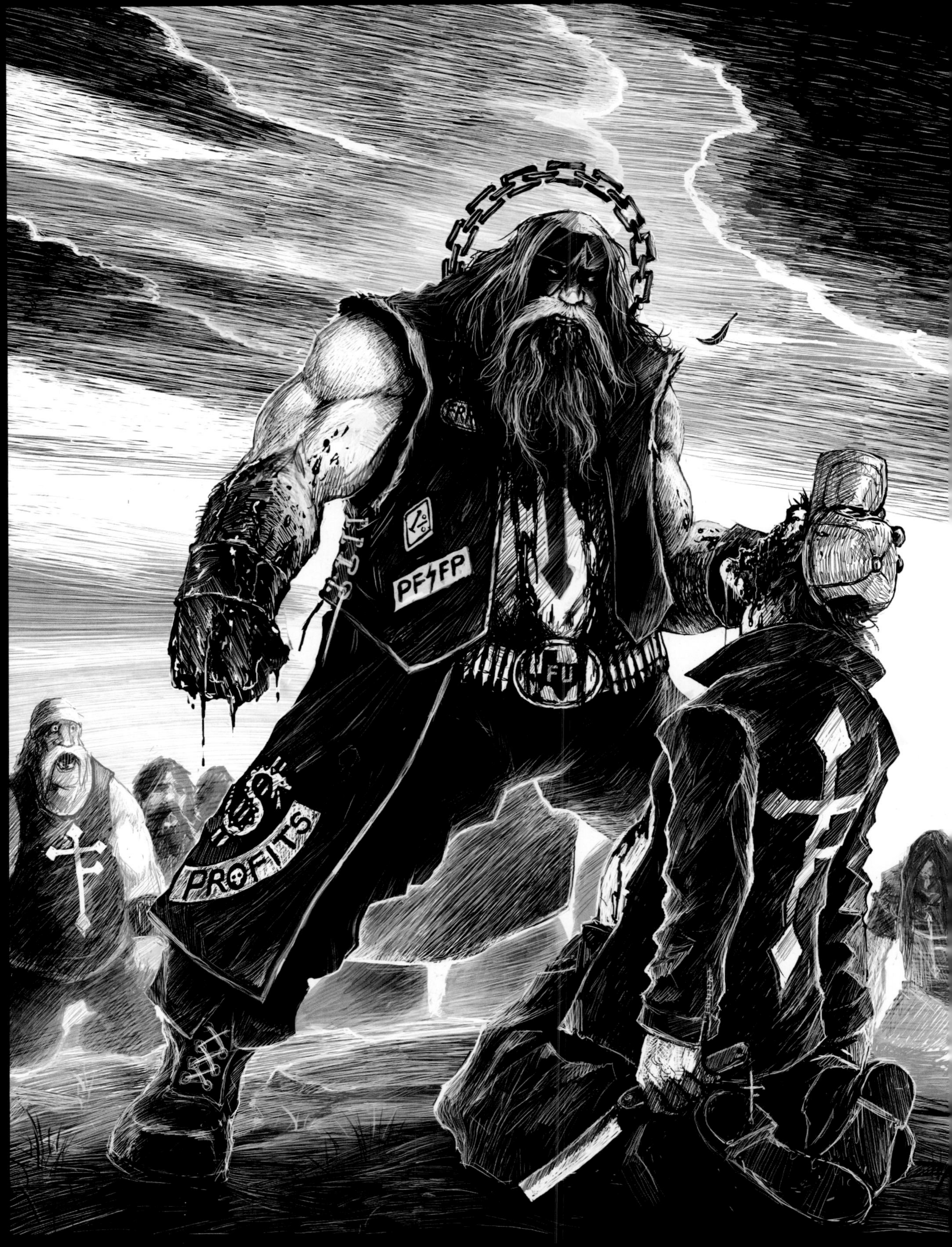

PF FP
FU
PROFITS

pokes out his pudgy pointer finger, and fans it across the faithful, all o'em still on their knees. "Thus I have come to give you strength." Now Frankie lifts up the razor blade in his left hand, puts it to the other arm, and slices out a chunk. "You . . . are empty." The big man motions for the nearest biker, a skinny fella in a mesh tank top, to step up. "But I will make you whole." Frankie holds out that little gob o' meat right in front o' that biker's face.

Ol' Skinny looks hesitant at first, but it don't seem like Frankie's takin' no for an answer, so the beanpole with the questionable fashion sense opens up his mouth and lets the boss man shove that meaty morsel right in. The biker swallows. At first nothin' happens, but then he starts to twitchin' a bit, then shakin' like he's caught himself a chill; his eyes bulge, he turns a few different shades o' eggplant, then he plops to the ground and gets to flippin' and floppin' like a flock member at one o' them revivals who's gettin' "saved."

Then all at once he just falls still; the other faithful they get up and come closer, waitin', starin' . . . and in just a few ticks, Skinny Boy starts movin' again. The gathered take a collective step back as he slowly gets to his feet. He just stands there, kinda slack-faced, and though he looks mostly the same, he looks kinda different too; his skin's got a ashy pallor to it, for one thing, and his eyes . . . well they've gone the opposite o' ol' Frankie's eyes; Skinny Boy's eyes have done gone bone-white.

The faithful wait and watch while the biker turns to look at Frankie, who takes his razor and slashes it right down the center o' Skinny Boy's chest. Now you'd think that a slice like that would be a killin' stroke, but Skinny stays standin', just kinda starin' dumbly down at the wound that ain't even bleedin'.

"Partake of my flesh!" Frankie yells, "and fear not the fangs and claws of our enemy! Together we shall seek out this dog . . . this lowly cur . . . and when we are done, my brothers, that dog shall never hunt again!"

The faithful let out a whole chorus o' whoops and hollers while Frankie takes his razor and commences to carvin' off another slice o' himself.

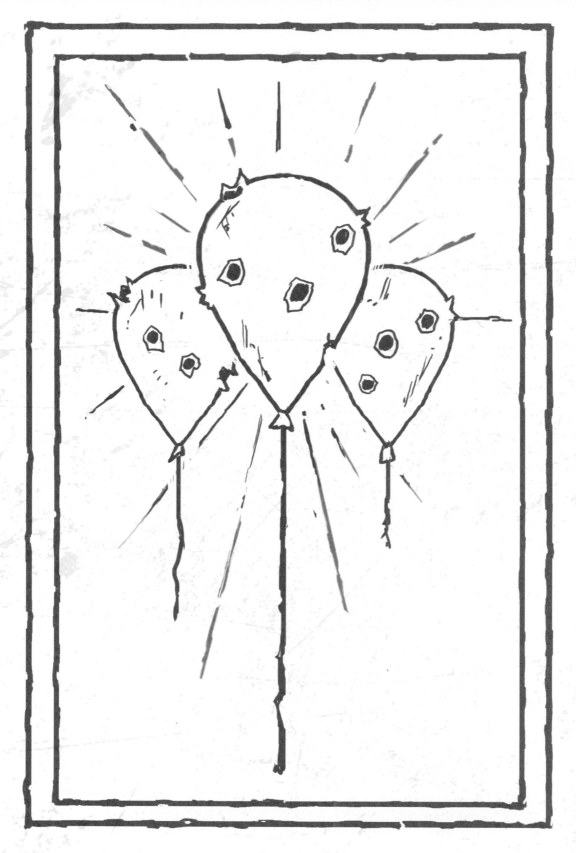

THE FAITHFUL

CHAPTER THE SEVENTEENTH

'Round 'bout the time the 8:20 a.m. freighter to Dead End is headin' outta Hubtown, while our mystery man Huxley's drivin' his hearse offa the lot where he'd parked it, Doctor Victor Prometheus Hart's tractor and trailer is pullin' in.

Now here Doc Hart's thinkin' he's gonna have to question damn near every citizen in the smoke city as to the whereabouts o' Elsa, when he wanders through an open spot in the maze o' alleys and happens to hear a fat vagrant woman mutterin' to herself 'bout "them damn outsiders." She's sittin' near a rusty flywheel, rockin' back and forth. The tramp's holdin' one arm, tryin' to stem the blood that's leakin' from her shoulder and poolin' on the oil-stained concrete.

"Ain't nobody left? That it?" the underworlder cries through missin' teeth. "Anybody upright you talk and come help, I got injured!"

"Madam," Doc Hart says, all smooth-like, leanin' over at first and then bendin' down. Now when he gets close, the old lady's eyes go big and her face scrunches 'til it resembles one o' them shar-pay puppies. "I'm capable of providing medical assistance," Hart continues, "should you be amenable to offering a faithful response to my inquiries."

"The hell nonsense you talkin'?" the woman barks.

"A few simple questions," the doctor continues. "You mentioned outsiders. A description could prove most helpful."

"Big hairy fella an' a skinny tart. She's just a hopeful at first but then she's the one! First last and ever-thing! Her and hairy slashed and cut and cut and slashed! Rent ma arm!" She lifts a shoulder, indicatin' her bleedin' limb. "All dead 'ceptin' me. I talk and talk, don't nobody answer no more!"

"And following the cutting and the slashing, these outsiders . . . departed?"

"De-what? Ya mean took off? Yeah they cut out! The tart she took a damn arm with her! Not her arm—took an arm fer the one she lost!"

"I see," Doc Hart says. He don't fully understand, but he does reckon that Elsa mighta used her skills and the purloined medical equipment to perform the kinda procedure this transient was describin'. And he gets to thinkin', knowin' damn well Elsa and her travel companion didn't pass him on the way in. He resolves to make sure they ain't still in Hubtown, but if not, there's only one direction for 'em to go.

"Tell me," Hart says. "What destination might one encounter next whilst traveling farther west on the Anaconda?"

"What's next? Ain't next, it's the end," the woman blurts. "Dead End! Dead End's the end!"

"Dead End . . ." the doctor repeats. "Very well, you have been quite helpful. And the . . . procedure you described, well it just so happens I'm capable of working similar miracles. That arm, for instance, I can make it as if the laceration never occurred." To this the woman just offers a quizzical kinda look. "My trailer is just this way . . ."

Now you might think that some o' the Aimless, like this hefty gal here, would be beneath our good doctor. But Hart, see, he's what you'd call "equal opportunity" when it comes to the women he . . . well we'll just say "collects." Race and age don't matter, and though he takes a special likin' to the pretty ones, looks don't matter that much neither. And as far as size . . . well he takes 'em all, big and small.

The sewer rat just kinda looks at the doc, not fully comprehendin', as he pulls her to her feet and sets off back the way he came.

★★★★✲★★★★

While Doc Hart marches the hobo lady off to some unknown but most likely gruesome fate, Jo Jo's sniffer is pickin' up on a whole host o' odors: rat, 'coon, cat, dog, taters, grass, and a buncha plants he can't immediately put a name to.

The source o' this scent medley is a pot suspended over a washin' machine drum. There's a fire in the drum, boiling everything in the pot, and right 'bout now ol' Bob Onminob is standing over the pot, takin' a big whiff.

Jo Jo backs up to the wall of the freight car and plops his ass down. He looks over to where Elsa's sittin', just inside the open doorway, cross-legged, watchin' the scenery fly by, clutchin' the stuffed dog to her chest. At first she had dangled her legs outside but ol' Bob informed her that the slidin' doors tend to slam shut on occasion and if this one did, why that'd be the end o' her walkin' sticks. Neither Jo Jo nor Elsa told Bob that she could get herself some new ones if push came to shove, but she decided to tuck 'em in just the same.

Bob spoons up a bowl o' soup and makes his way over to Jo Jo and says, "Jungle stew's what! Normally, see, ya can't have none if ya don't contri-boot. Everybody, see, contri-boots, like a rat or a tater or whatever ya can manage. But seein' as how you're a first timer, the gang gave the okay!"

With a big toothless smile, Bob hands the steamin' bowl down to Jo Jo. Our main man has certainly eaten a lot worse in his time, and it's been quite a while since he filled his gut, so he takes the bowl without protest. Lookin' across to where the four other rail riders are playin' craps, Jo Jo offers thanks, but them bums don't seem to take no notice, absorbed as they are in rollin' them bones. Only one hobo turns, a thin black lady with unkempt hair and an overbite. She flicks Jo Jo a thumbs-up then returns her attention to the dice.

"Girl can partake too!" Bob says, lookin' to Elsa, but she pops her head over her shoulder and says, "No thanks!" then goes back to oglin' the scenery. There ain't much other than sagebrush out past the door now 'cause the train has done cleared Hubtown and is headin' into the great wide open o' the Texas desert. Elsa stays put just the same, her mind occupied with the hope that this train will be enough to get her away from Father, for all and for good, but worried just the same that it might not be—that he's determined 'nough to chase her to the ends o' the earth. That fear gets to twistin' in her gut like it always does, and she pushes them thoughts away, switchin' her mental tracks.

She gets to imaginin' that she's a wealthy, exotic debutante on one o' them fancy passenger trains and that she's gazin' out at endless fields o' green, through the window o' her own private car, the kind with a real nice bed, just like she read 'bout in books. And the stuffed animal, it's one o' them dogs that rich foreign people have, like a chow chow or a bitchin' frise. Or maybe its "bee-shon frise," I don't know, I ain't rich. But the point is, in this little fantasy o' hers, she's free as a bird.

Meantime, ol' Bob has taken a seat next to Jo Jo and is carryin' on: "Lucky business we got an open car! Can't get an open one you gotta ride on top or ride the blinds. Ridin' the blinds, see, that's where—"

"Hey! Come look!" Elsa shouts just then.

Jo Jo muscles the soup down in a gulp, then heads over and steadies himself with one hand as he casts his eyes on the sunbaked sands.

Less than a mile out and just a bit ahead o' the train is somethin' that at first looks like another one o' them rollin' blackouts . . . although closer scrutiny reveals sunlight reflectin' offa metal and glass at the base o' the dust clouds. Now with that extra-special hearin' o' his, our man picks up on the unmistakable roar o' engines—some o'em belongin' to motorcycles, others to semitrucks.

Frankie's faithful.

But that ain't all: His ears are registerin' the same kinda' noises on the *other* side o' the train.

Jo Jo rushes 'round the jungle stew and shoves open the slidin' door opposite the one he just come from, lookin' out and seein' a similar sight: trucks and choppers inbound, kickin' big ol' plumes o' sand into the pale-blue sky.

He shoves the door closed, ignorin' Bob's questions as he goes again and peeps out over Elsa's head. The trucks and bikes are close enough now that he can clearly see the faces o' the faithful and can hear the whoopin' and hootin' o'

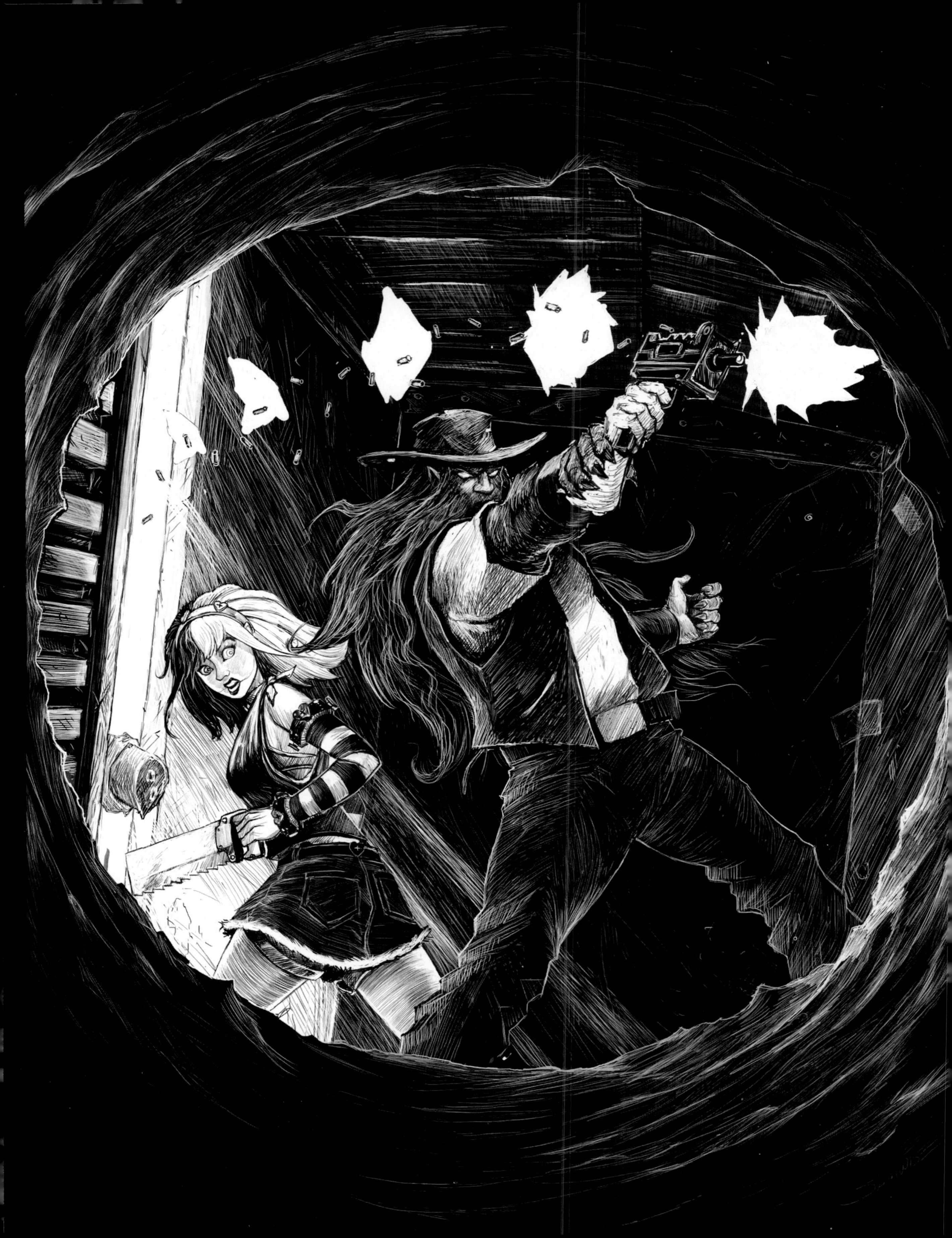

the good ol' boys climbin' up onto the truck roofs, wieldin' rifles and pistols and shotguns.

"We're gonna have trouble," Jo Jo says, and he hauls Elsa up under the armpits, sets her to one side, and shoves that door closed too. Bob gets a worried look on his face and says, "I, uh, I ain't never been good with confrontation," while Elsa sets her dog doll down, sayin', "Don't you worry, everything's gonna be just fine!" and she gets to thinkin' she's gotta give her new pet a name as she grabs a bone saw from outta her doctor bag.

Pretty quick-like the blast o' the motors is all 'round 'em, bombardin' Jo Jo's ears, but he's still able to pinpoint other noises . . . like bootsteps on top o' the car behind theirs, clompin' closer and closer. Just a tick later, a few sets o' them boots land on top and near the back. Shotguns boom, and two big-ass holes punch through the roof and stream thick beams o' sunlight right down to the dusty floor.

Bob and his gang are all bunched up in the far corner, mewlin' like a litter o' kittens.

There's a thump on the wall over by Elsa and the slidin' door goes crashin' open. One o' Frankie's gang sticks in a hand that's grippin' one o' them fancy new Uzi machine pistols. Elsa snags the wrist and shouts, "Make yourself useful!" to Bob, who lets out a little yelp, grabs the door, and shoves it back so's it pins the would-be intruder's arm.

While Elsa's wonderin' why the gunslinger ain't howlin' from the pain, the ivory-eyed attacker pulls the trigger, spittin' out a barrage o' bullets that narrowly miss Jo Jo, who dives away from that *and* the shotgun blasts.

At about the same time that Elsa realizes she's holdin' a bone saw and puts it to work on the biker's arm, Jo Jo decides that this particular uninvited guest ain't yet been introduced to the jungle stew. Not wantin' to be an ungracious host, he scoops up the entire pot, gets up behind Elsa and her furiously blazin' saw, and splashes the contents through the narrow openin' and into the outlaw biker's face.

But the machine pistol keeps rippin' off rounds as two more shotguns boom and two more holes open up in the roof. Elsa, meantime, she's still thoroughly perplexed as to why her "patient" is so calm regardin' the ongoin' amputation, but to her credit she sticks with it 'til that extremity, still clutchin' the fancy gun, plops right onto the floor. You might think that the trigger finger on that severed hand would relax and that the continuous gunfire would stop. Well, you'd be wrong. That baby keeps burpin', aerating the door on the other side, where a voice calls out, "Damnit Henry, stop shootin'!"

Elsa recloses the slidin' door on her side in the midst o' Henry respondin', "I cain't. It's doin' its own thing!"

Meanwhile them boys up top—well I won't bore you with a lecture on shot groupin', but let's just say they've put enough holes in close enough proximity that they've made room for one o'em to drop through.

And here comes this swarthy shit-kicker now. Right when he lands, though, Jo Jo snatches up the severed hand and points it *and* the bullet-spewin' gun it's holdin' at the filmy-eyed freak's face, creatin' a hole there big enough to shove your arm through. Jo Jo then raises the barrel, blastin' a full volley o' bullets at the remainin' Profits up top.

At this juncture I think you'd agree that with all that's transpired, our heroes have done a fine job o' fendin' off Frankie's faithful. But if we move our attention outta the freight car for just a tick and throw a look up ahead, past a buncha train cars and the locomotive and just a little ways down the tracks, we'll catch a mighty distressin' sight: See that eighteen-wheeler pullin' up to the rails, the one haulin' that tanker trailer? Well it just crossed over onto the tracks. And if you're guessin' that this particular tanker is plumb full o' highly combustible petrol, well you'd get the gold star.

Our dutiful engineer o' course he hits the brakes, but there ain't nothin' for it. The last thing he sees is that tanker rushin' up at him and then there's a boom big enough to rattle dentures for a hundred miles off, as a billowin' ball o' fire gushes up and out and then dissipates into black smoke. But the damage has already been done, 'cause all them cars ain't got no prayer o' stayin' on the tracks. While the bikes and semis peel off, the locomotive flips up, and everythin' behind it stacks up like poker chips that fly off and go tumblin' six ways to Sunday.

Now before all that shit went down, our heroes were thinkin' they just might stand a chance. Jo Jo had done emptied the fancy machine pistol's magazine at the boys up top when his balls got rattled by a thunderin' kaboom, followed by the ear-splittin' screech o' locked-up train wheels and then . . . well then everything went up and down and round and round and end over end and by the time all that tossin' and turnin' was complete, Jo Jo wasn't hearin' *or* seein' a damned thing.

CHAPTER THE EIGHTEENTH

At this particular moment, the Ramblin' Man ain't altogether privy to the goin's-on with his Frankie puppet and them Profits. He'd been holed up, see, meditatin' inside the ebony-draped confines o' his private trailer when the caravan came to an unscheduled stop.

Our villain's cane-walkin' his way right now to the front o' the convoy, peerin' through that monocle o' his, lookin' to surmise exactly why it is his driver hit the brakes.

He gets his answer right quick, as just over the crest o' where the lead truck is sittin', the Confederales have done set up a roadblock. Or to be more accurate, three Confederales have set up a roadblock, backed up by a whole host o' what appear to be well-armed, deputized, pissed-off locals.

The lawmen have their Bronco trucks sittin' nose to nose on the blacktop, and the rest o' these good ol' boys got their pickups parked helter-skelter on the highway behind 'em.

The Confederale sheriff—who goes by the name o' Lincoln Foxx—is standin' at the forefront. He's got a gut on him that looks like he done swallowed a small child. A greasy black handlebar mustache hangs from his upper lip damn near to his teets, and he's restin' the butt o' an elephant gun on one hip.

There's the sound o' a few truck doors openin' and closin' along the carny caravan, and just a tick later, Bo and Tweeny show up on the Ringmaster's left, and on his right . . .

Well you ain't made the acquaintance o' Diamond yet. She's a quiet gal, purty, with curves in all the right places, as evidenced by way o' her skimpy outfit, but if you look real close you can see that her skin has a flaky, almost scaly kinda texture to it. And the pupils o' her eyes are narrower than most folks'. And—what's that? You wanna know what she's holdin'? Well I was just gettin' to that. That there's a rattler tail she's rubbin' 'tween herfingers, up close to her mouth, and if you pay real close attention you'll notice that her lips are movin', makin' some kinda' whispery, hissin' sounds.

"Why do you barricade our path?" the Ringmaster calls out, and as he does, Bo and Tweeny eyeball the Confederales. When they do, them lawmen, every single one, feel a sudden, sharp pain in his head like a needle stabbin' into his brain.

"Well?" Bo blurts to his twin. "That one," Tweeny says, eyes fixed on one o' the Confederales, a tall, skinny, kinda scarecrow-lookin' fella name o' Jimmy.

"That one, that one!" Tweeny goes on all excited-like, shakin' her fist and hoppin' up and down a bit with anticipation. Course this jostles Bo, who quickly tells her to knock it the hell off. The twins turn 'round and head on back to their trailer and when they do, the pain in the heads o' them lawmen goes away.

Meanwhile Sheriff Foxx calls to the Ramblin' Man: "Heard some disturbin' rumors 'bout your little gang o' goons here. Word is, when you leave a town, kids ain't the same as when you showed up." This statement is met by various affirmations from the salt o' the earth at the sheriff's rear. "I don't know what the Sam Elliot's goin' on here but I aim to find out," the sheriff proclaims.

"Does their claim not strike you as ridiculous?" the Ringmaster replies to Foxx.

"Well it just so happens that investigatin' ridiculous claims is part o' my job," Foxx retorts. "Y'all just go ahead and exit your vehicles, nice and slow. Drop any weapons ya got right there in the dirt, and don't gimme no reason to let Nellie here join in on the conversation." At the mention o' Nellie, Foxx reaches over and pats the barrel o' his elephant gun.

Right 'bout now the Magi twins have done gotten into their trailer and started up their yackle-dackle, and that Confederale they was eyeballin' earlier, the scarecrow one named Jimmy, well he's hearin' a voice callin' out from the desert, a voice from the past that makes him start to question his sanity 'cause he knows that what he's hearin' can't possibly be real.

"An interesting ultimatum, Sheriff," the Ramblin' Man replies, while next to him, Diamond's still rubbin' them rattles and whisperin' whatever it is she's whisperin'. The only other sound is an elephant trumpetin' near the back o' the caravan.

"We have taken care not to cross paths with the law up until now . . ." Ledger says and unhands the cane, lettin' it stand up on its own. He raises that hand up, palm facin' him, fingers stuck together. "Still, I suppose this day was inevitable . . ." While them Confederales and the rest o' the mob watch, a cigarette rises up from behind the Ringmaster's fingers. "As is your demise." Ledger sticks that smoke in his mouth and flicks his thumb, causin' a tiny flame to ignite at the end o' it. He lights the cig and the flame disappears.

"Well, we done tried it the peaceful way," Foxx says, lowerin' the elephant gun barrel. The Ramblin' Man removes the cigarette and blows out a puff o' smoke that gets real big real quick, 'til it's big 'nough to cover up the Ringmaster completely. Diamond takes this opportunity to take a few steps back while the mob starts shootin'.

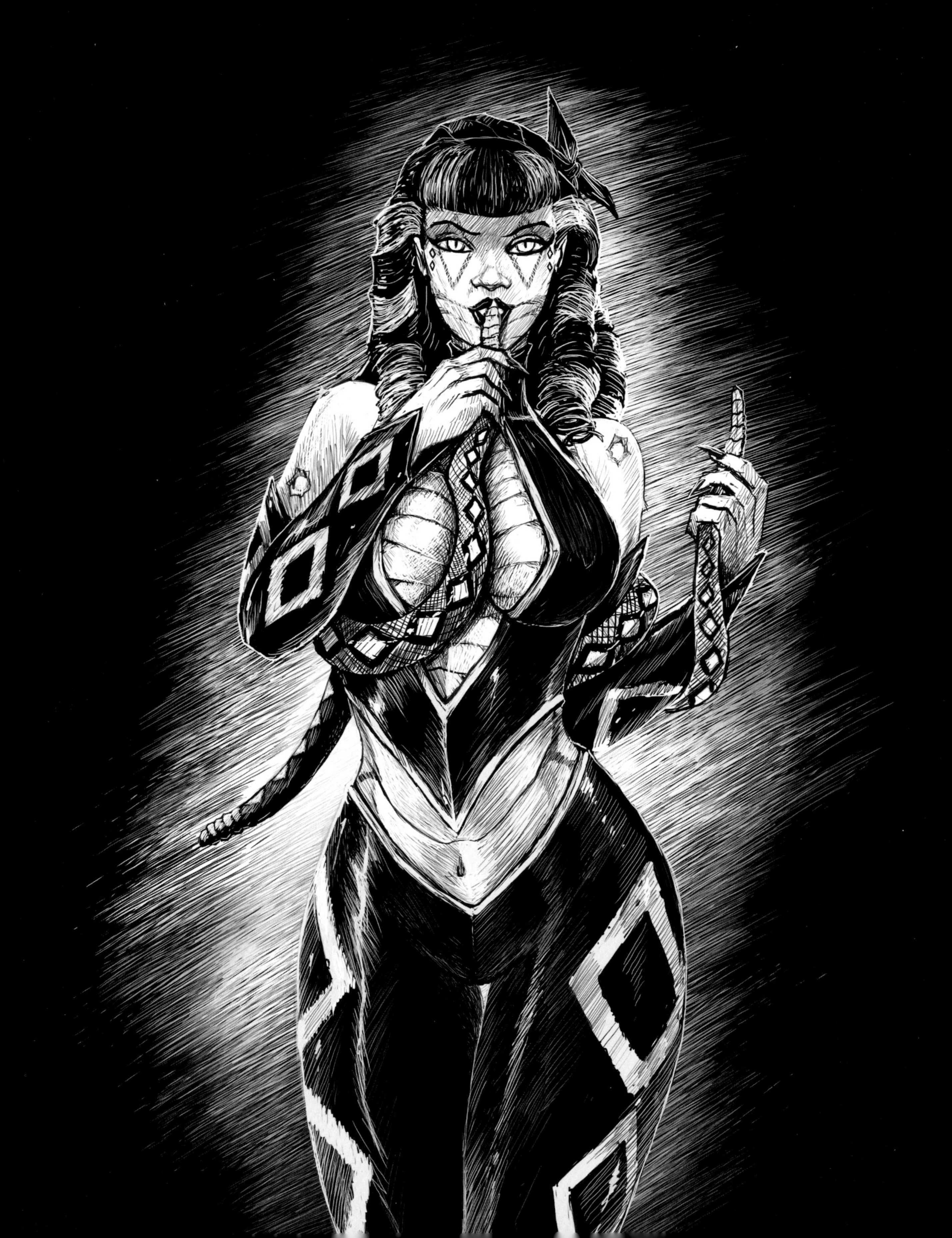

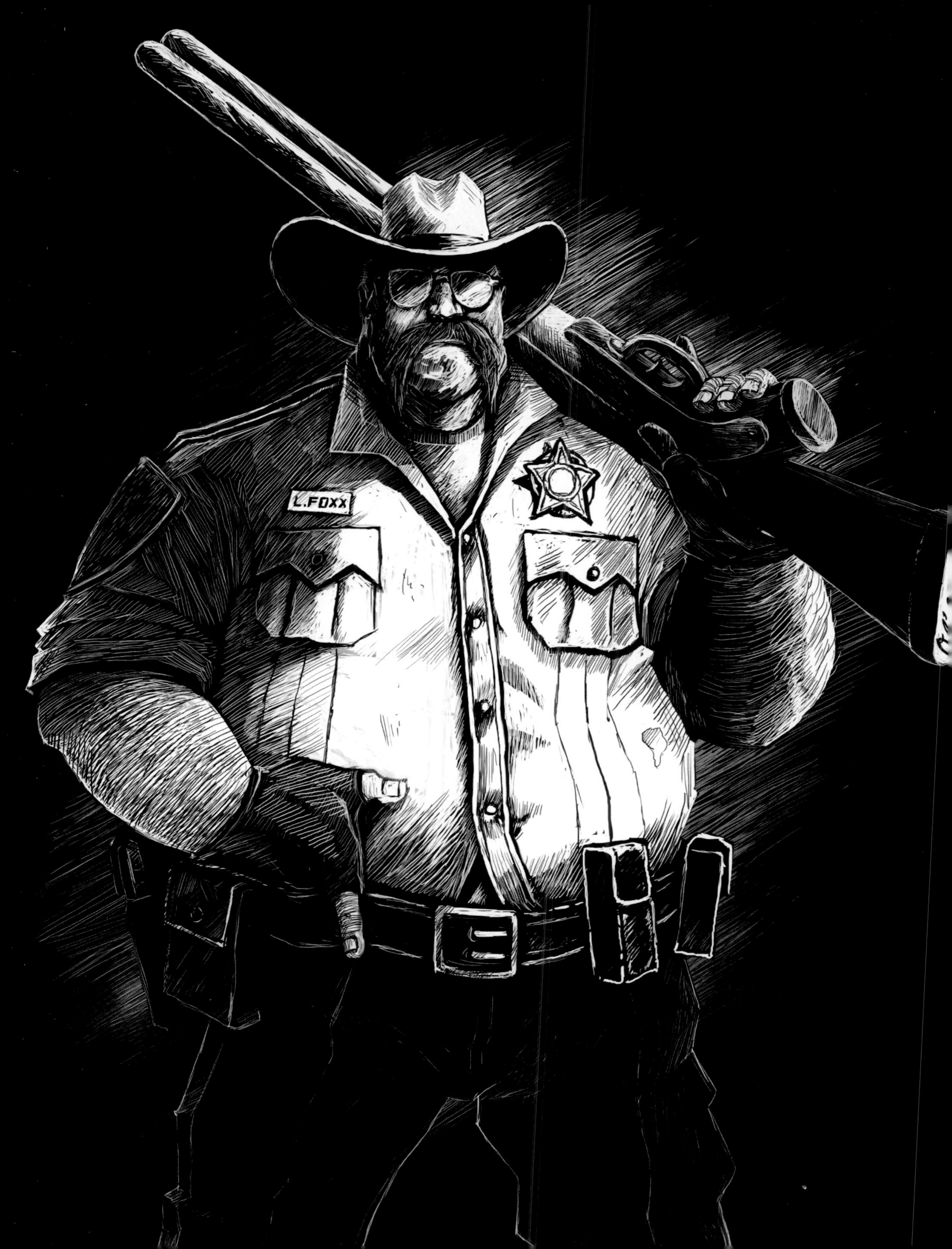
L.FOXX

A few bullets graze Diamond before she gets behind the truck. The smoke, meanwhile, dissipates enough to reveal that the Ramblin' Man *and* his cane ain't nowhere to be seen.

Deputy Scarecrow Jimmy, at this juncture, he's damn near shittin' his britches 'cause that voice he heard is drawin' closer. Jimmy, see, he spent a whole lot o' years cooped up in a shack with his ailin' mom. The cost o' medicine ate away at what few Johnnies he made as a deputy, and the older his mom got, the crazier she got, as dementia set in and she yammered nonsense at him nonstop until Jimmy decided he'd had enough. He drove her out to the remotest spot o' desert he could find, kicked her crazy ass outta the truck, and drove away.

Well as you mighta guessed by now, the noise he's hearin' is the haggard but unmistakable babblin' o' his not-so-dearly departed mama.

At that same time, one o' them local boys catches a glimpse o' somethin' movin' down by his boot. He lets out a yelp and aims his six-shooter at the fat, coiled-up rattler, but he don't get his shot off 'fore that diamondback sinks its fangs into his leg just under the knee, injectin' a heapin' helpin' dose o' deadly venom.

Right 'bout now, the rest o' the hoi polloi get to noticin' movement at the edges o' the road. The desert has done come alive, and a whole chorus o' shouts rises up at the sight o' twenty or so rattlesnakes o' various sizes slitherin' up onto the blacktop.

Meanwhile, the third Confederale, a handsome fella in the prime o' his youth, well he's turned 'round in response to a poppin' sound he heard a few feet off toward the highway shoulder. He spots the Ringmaster there, cane standin' next to him, three tarot cards juttin' out 'tween the fingers o' his right hand. A gun cocks to Ledger's left. The Ramblin' Man flicks out his left hand and the cane flies out like a bullet, bottom first, impalin' a leather-faced Texan who was fixin' to unload with a lever-action rifle.

The young lawman raises his own weapon, but not before Ledger DeMesne flicks his wrist and lets them cards fly, lodgin' all three o'em right in that pretty boy's face.

Foxx takes aim at the Ringmaster with his elephant gun as the cane comes flyin' back to the Ramblin' Man's left hand and a whole deck o' tarot cards suddenly appears in his right. Ledger squeezes, bendin' the pack and spewin' all them cards out in front o' him, so many cards so quick that the Ramblin' Man can't be seen no more. Foxx blasts that gun right into the card cloud, but as the pieces fall and flutter to the ground, our sheriff's mighty perturbed to find that once again Ledger DeMesne has done given him the slip.

Scarecrow Jimmy's firin' off his gun too, 'cept what he's shootin' at is a dried-up old husk o' a human that's still wearin' bits o' his mama's sundress. "Shouldn'ta left me, Jimmy!" the mummy woman rasps, even though her jaw's missin'. The mama thing gets closer with every step no matter how many bullets Jimmy sends her way. Course, the bullets he's firin' ain't actually hittin' her, even though he don't know it. He's already done shot two o' the locals and sent a handful more o'em scatterin' for cover.

Sheriff Foxx is set to go and rip that rifle right outta Jimmy's hand when he hears a thumpin' sound accompanied by a creakin', like one o' the caravan trucks is settlin' under a heavy weight. He hears that sound again and again, growin' louder, 'til he looks to the head truck and sees the biggest damn gorilla he's ever laid eyes on land on the cab roof.

Terra Mungus leaps; Foxx raises the elephant gun and shoots, but the ape twists in midair, takin' a .458 slug to the shoulder instead o' the chest. Foxx leaps to one side, barely evadin' the swingin' arm o' Terra Mungus as the behemoth beast lands. The ape moves quicker'n the sheriff, though, and before the lawman can get off another shot, the gorilla's done swiped out, snatchin' that gun by the barrel and breakin' it in half over one knee. Foxx pulls a revolver but that gets batted away next, and then, then Terra Mungus grabs the sheriff by his coat lapels and lifts up, tossin' the Confederale one-handed into the windshield o' his own Bronco.

The locals that ain't been shot by Jimmy or bit by snakes or impaled by the Ramblin' Man or scared shitless by the sight o' the giant ape have decided that there ain't no shame in livin' to fight another day—that squealin' sound you hear is their tires grindin' pavement as those good ol' boys hightail it for the hills. Course there ain't many hills in these parts so they'll be drivin' for a while.

Terra Mungus, in the meantime, has hopped up on the hood o' the Bronco and extricated Foxx. The ape flips the sheriff over, wraps his arms 'round him like he's givin' him a big ol' hug, then jumps offa the truck, landin' on his ass on the blacktop . . . 'cept the sheriff's head o' course hits first, and that loud crack you hear is the sound o' the lawman's neck gettin' snapped in half.

Right 'bout this same time, Scarecrow Jimmy can be seen kneelin' on the pavement, his rifle flipped upside down, barrel pointin' under his chin. "I'm sorry, Mama! I'm sorry!" he shouts and pulls the trigger.

After all that, things kinda quiet down a bit. The Ramblin' Man appears from behind a truck and calls out to a few caravan drivers and roustabouts who've exited the vehicles. "Find the keys to the trucks and remove these obstructions—we're burning daylight!"

And there you have it folks, the last stand o' Lincoln Foxx and his overambitious posse. You can bet your last Johnnie that tales o' this showdown will soon be proliferatin' all across the land. The Confederales o' course will be itchin' for revenge, but the Barnstormers ain't stickin' around for round two—as soon as that blockade's cleared, they'll be in the wind. Before we leave, though, let's check in on Diamond. You might remember she got nicked by a couple rounds. Well there she is, near the Ramblin' Man's trailer, lookin' fresh and fit as a fiddle. Hell, her skin's damn near glowin'. You might wonder why that is, and if so I'll give you a hint. There's somethin' layin' on the road not far away—a pile o' some see-through material. . . . If we get a real close look, well you might be surprised to find that it resembles a human—in fact, a Diamond-sized snakeskin.

CHAPTER THE NINETEENTH

"What 'bout this'n here," a voice asks.

"She dead too," another answers.

A shotgun boom rolls 'cross the desert.

"Yep, dead as all get-out."

"Well grab ol' dog-boy and let's move."

A bunch o' minutes later, after the sound o' truck motors have faded into the distance, Elsa opens her eyes and looks at her left leg, where the skin and muscle on the thigh's been blasted away clear to the broken bone from the Profit who was testin' to see if she was alive or not.

She moans a bit in frustration, lookin' 'round. She got tossed outta the freight car when it went off the tracks, and she woulda ended up without so much as a scratch if not for the overly inquisitive, trigger-happy biker. She quickly surmises that sittin' here ain't gonna help Jo Jo, who's been hauled off to who knows where and for who knows what (though she assumes it's somethin' most likely bad for his health). And Jo Jo, why he came down to the sewers and he fought for her, so she's determined that come hell or high water she's sure as shit gonna fight for him.

But first things first: She's gotta find the doctor bag. And what about her stuffed animal? When she sits up and looks 'round, she spots the puppy dog doll's head, layin' just a few feet off. She crawls a little closer and notes that not only is the head separated from the body, but one o' the critter's eyes is missin' to boot. The body's not far away, sittin' with its little feet spread out, bits o' stuffin' protrudin' from where the head used to be.

Rather than bein' distressed by the sight o' her decapitated pup, Elsa don't seem too put off as she says to the head, "Don't you worry, Mama's gonna fix us both up." She maneuvers to a standin' position then and gets a look at the wreckage.

Train cars done got tossed all over creation. There's a lotta smoke driftin' up into the sky, and there's a bunch o' metal pieces, some o'em all twisted, and smaller parts and wheels and such, along with some o' what the cars was carryin', like coal and grain from the open-top jobs and bags o' beans and rice and canned food and fruits and hell yes even bags o' pork rinds from some o' the boxcars. The big ol' boxcar she had most recently occupied is just a few feet beyond the stuffed dog's body, layin' on its side, bottom facin' her way.

Elsa gets to a standin' position and hop-drags her way 'round to the other side o' that car, and that's where she finds the rail riders. Or what's left o'em.

Ol' Bob Onminob and the black lady and all the rest are scattered about, all broken and limp and dead. Now this *does* cause Elsa distress. She scrunches up her face, shakin' her head at the unfairness o' it all. Ol' Bob and the gang was just tryin' to get along as best they could and now look at 'em. Their bodies look . . . abandoned. Elsa don't know much about souls and all that, but she wishes that whatever they had inside 'em that gave 'em life and personality, she wishes that it's just moved on.

"I hope you've gone to someplace real good," she says and then crawls into the boxcar to set 'bout findin' her doctor bag.

She spots it pretty quick, along with all the implements lyin' 'round, includin' the syringe with the serum. Once all o' that's gathered up, she goes back out into the sunlight . . . 'cept the sunlight ain't as bright as it should be, so she looks to see what's causin' the interruption . . .

It ain't a rollin' blackout and it ain't another Profit attack. No, this here's an actual storm. Something the likes o' which this dried-up ol' desert prob'ly ain't seen in quite a long spell.

Elsa decides it's time to get movin'. But there is the matter of her leg. She hates to do it, 'cause it seems . . . disrespectful, but there are parts layin' all 'round. If whatever was inside the rail riders has moved on, then really, that's what's left. Parts. She's about to head over to the black lady when her attention shifts to Bob Onminob, and she hesitates, gazin' down to the syringe in her hand.

She really liked Bob, and she wonders if she were to head over and stab that needle into his heart and inject the serum if it wouldn't bring him back. And if it did bring him back, would his soul, if that was what it was, come back too? Hell, what if he didn't *want* to come back?

All these deep thoughts is makin' Elsa's head hurt. Besides all that, there's only enough serum left for one more injection.

She looks up at the rapidly darkenin' sky, then hops over to the black lady, removes the woman's pants, and sets to work with the bone saw.

By the time the first drops o' rain hit the wreck site, Elsa's done swapped out her own busted drumstick for the black lady's leg, and she's used the last bit o' serum to get that leg back in walkin' shape.

Now it just so happens that along with all the surgical equipment in the doctor's bag is a needle and thread. Handy for sewing sutures, but also useful for puttin' back together busted-up, decapitated stuffed puppy dogs.

First off, Elsa sews the head back on. Then, focusin' on the missin' eye, she takes a button from the peacoat o' the nearest rail rider and sews it in the empty spot. The rain gets to fallin' a bit heavier as Elsa holds up the mismatched, stitched-up pup, and a big ol' grin spreads itself 'cross her face.

"Not a bad patch job if I do say so. Hey! We gotta name for you now," she says, all happy-like. "Patch!"

She hugs the dog tight and gets to treadin' 'cross the wet sand, followin' all the sets o' tire tracks that head off toward the horizon and outta sight.

"C'mon, Patch," she says. "Let's go get our friend!"

She follows them tracks as fast as her new and old leg will take her, gettin' more and more drenched as she goes, thinkin' that she shoulda taken a coat offa one o' the rail riders. She's also worryin' that the rain's gonna wash away the tracks before she can get to Jo Jo.

"We'll make it," she tells Patch. "You'll see. Stop your worryin'!"

Lightnin' cracks overhead as she comes up to a thick dividin' line in the desert. . . . Damned if it ain't the Anaconda. The truck and bike tracks, though, what's left o'em, don't curve up and onto the blacktop. No, they cross over and keep goin' off toward the horizon on the opposite side. Elsa's fixin' to follow, but before she does, her eyes catch somethin' just up the road. A black mass huddled in the misty rain . . .

A closer look shows it to be an automobile. Parked just offa the highway.

Elsa marvels at just how familiar the car is—familiar 'cause it's just the kinda vehicle some o' Father's friends, the ones in the funeral profession, would make "deliveries" in.

A hearse.

Abandoned. Just like them bodies back at the crash site.

Elsa goes and tries the doors. They're all locked, but a sizable rock through the driver's side window takes care o' that little problem right quick.

She sits Patch in the passenger seat and then lets out a squeal when she finds a key in the ignition. Her smile fades as she thinks that maybe the car's broken down and that's why it was on the side o' the road, but the engine turns over on the first try. "We're in business, Patch!" Elsa affirms and hits the gas, tearin' off into the desert, so preoccupied with savin' our main man that she don't bother to glance into the back o' the vehicle.

If she did, she damn sure woulda noticed that there's a coffin sittin' there.

★★★★✯★★★★

The rain wakes our Jo Jo up—big, fat droplets smackin' him right in the kisser.

He opens his eyes to find himself starin' at the sky, blinkin' against the fallin' water. There's some faces lookin' down on him, an assortment o' pug-ugly mothers that he instantly recognizes as Frankie's crew.

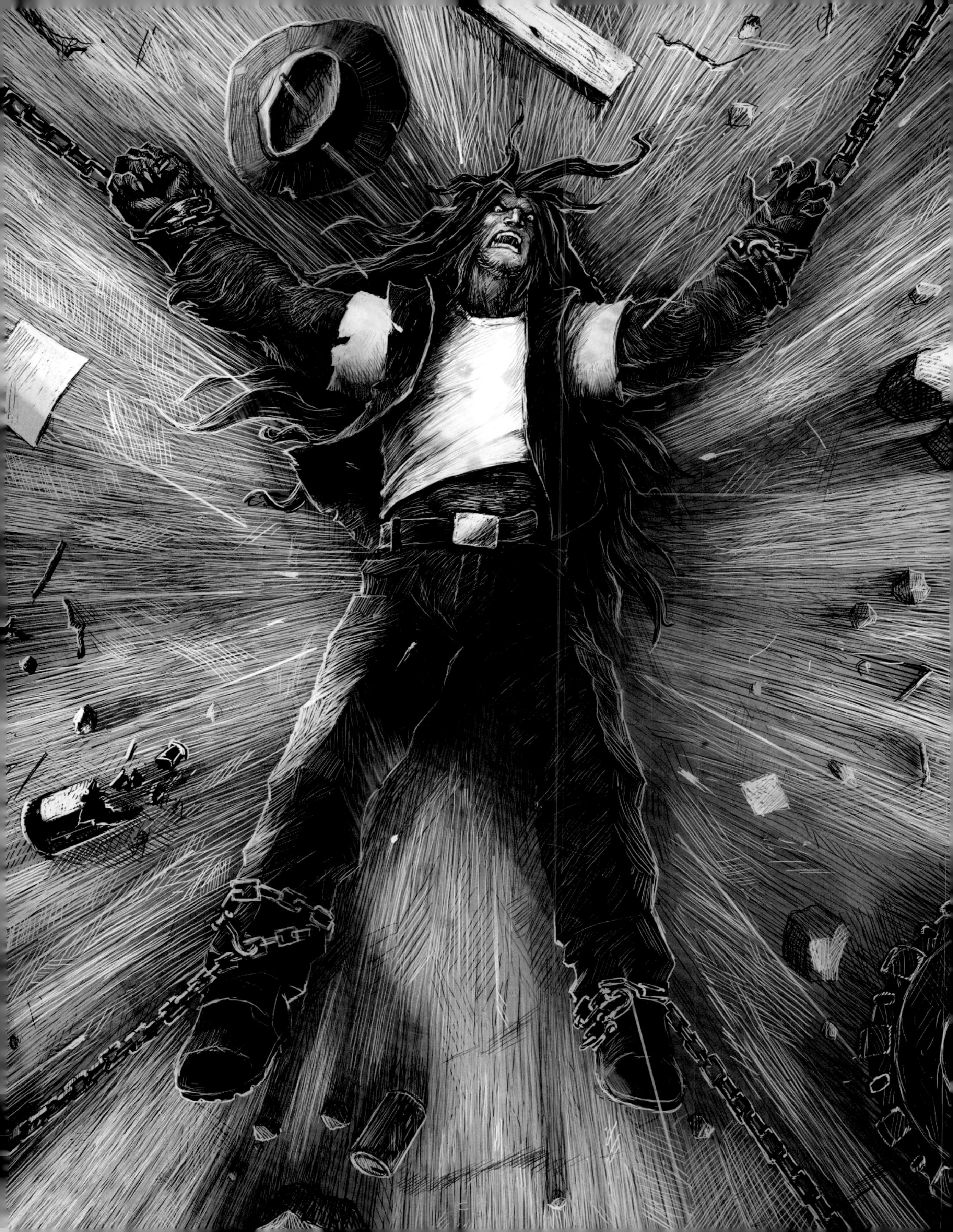

The smell o' exhaust is thick in the air, joined by the rumble o' truck motors.

"He done come 'round," one o'em says—the mesh-tank-top fella I told you 'bout earlier, the first one to partake o' Frankie's flesh. 'Cept now he's missin' one arm—presumably, Jo Jo surmises, from the train derailment. In fact, a few o' the milky-eyed faithful have ugly gashes and gouges and various gruesome-lookin' injuries, but it don't seem to bother 'em none, and Jo Jo notes that there ain't no blood. And though our man acknowledges that these hardy boys can survive a bona fide train wreck, that don't discourage him from dishin' up a good ol'-fashioned knuckle sandwich . . .

Or at least tryin' to.

When he goes to clobber Mesh-Top, he's surprised to find that his hand won't budge. Lookin' to either side, he sees that his wrists are done chained up. And when he tries kickin', he finds that his legs is bound too.

What the hell?

Liftin' his head, he spies more chains wound 'round his ankles. In fact his arms and legs are done spread out like he's 'bout to make a snow angel. Or a dirt angel I s'pose, seein' as how he's layin' on the desert sand.

The rain falls heavier as the Frankie faithful on one side disappear, makin' way for the ugliest mug o' all. It's Frankie that's lookin' down on Jo Jo now, 'ceptin' o' course that it ain't. Jo Jo recognizes the black-death stare o' the Ramblin' Man, and though he's got no earthly clue how, our man knows sure as shit that the Ringmaster *moved in* to Frankie, and that whatever mighta been left o' the ol' gang leader has done moved out.

The somehow-not-dead biker messiah gets real close, breath smellin' like recycled puke and somethin' akin to spoiled chicken, and then with a voice like bricks in a cement mixer, he says:

"I see for you a dark and dismal demise. A *final* termination, at last. I see you ending in pieces. Five graves with not a single mourner, except . . . Her." (Just a little side note here, folks—if we was to pop over to the Barnstormers' convoy right now, back on its way to Dead End, if we was to eavesdrop on the shadowy recesses o' the Ramblin' Man's personal trailer, well, we'd hear ol' Ledger DeMesne speakin' these exact same words.)

Anyway, Jo Jo hears the gunnin' o' engines and the furious spinnin' o' tires and the clinkin' o' chains and he smells the rush o' exhaust; Frankie's face rises up outta the way as Jo Jo's entire body pops a few inches offa the dirt, arms and legs yanked out in different directions, damn near bustin' outta the sockets. He thinks 'bout what Frankie-Ledger said 'bout "five graves" and he realizes what the Ringmaster's up to.

The wily bastard plans to rip Jo Jo apart and bury the pieces.

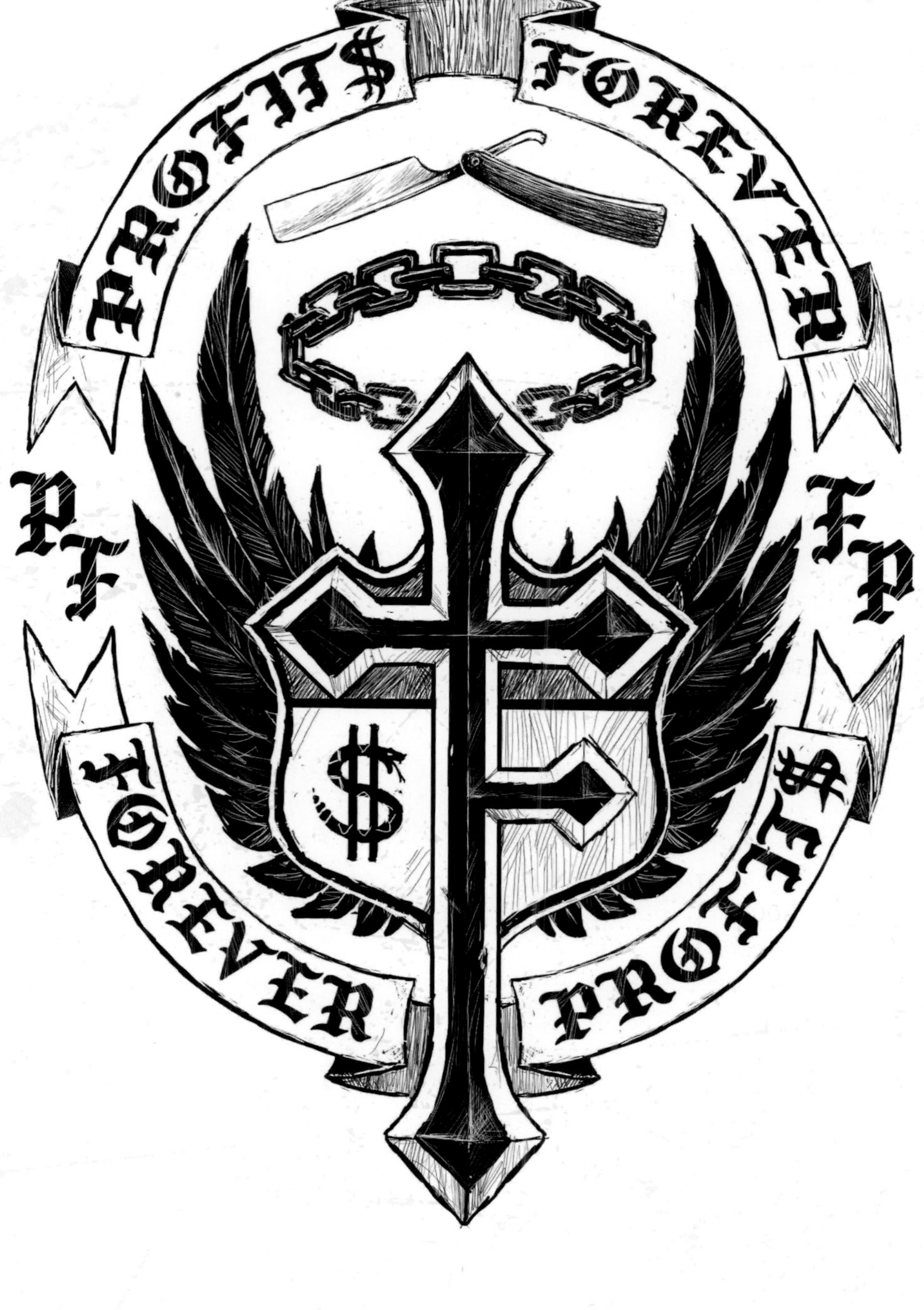
PROFIT$ FOREVER
PF
FP
FOREVER PROFIT$

CHAPTER THE TWENTIETH

Well it's safe to say that Jo Jo's more'n a bit concerned.

Most o' the time he can walk away from the kind o' damage that'd kill just 'bout anybody else, but he's pretty sure that havin' his arms and legs separated from his torso and buried in separate locations would qualify as the kinda injury you'd call unrecoverable. So yeah that's got him worried, but that ain't all; what with the thunder crackin' and pealin' the way it is, he's even scared that lightnin' might strike the chains and electrocute his hairy ass.

Somehow, though, for now at least, he's literally holdin' it together, veins standin' out on his neck like ropes, his teeth clenched damn near tight 'nough to break, his limbs barely holdin' strong against the force o' thousands o' horses that are threatenin' to rip 'em loose. And Frankie—by way o' the Ringmaster—is thinkin' that this show shoulda been over already and he's plumb tired o' waitin'.

"Time for the backup," he says.

A few ticks later, Jo Jo's still barely in one piece when one o' the faithful shows up with an ax, and another with a chainsaw.

Before them ol' boys can set to work on Jo Jo's joints, however, Frankie's black eyes dart away and he holds up his hand for the men to wait. Jo Jo cranes his neck and gazes down between his legs so's he can see what Frankie's lookin' at, and damned if he don't spot two o' the gang walkin' up in the open space ahead o' where the semitrucks are tryin' to yank our man's legs off. The men are holdin' Elsa by the arms, and one o'em—a peanut-shaped biker with a big-ass pipe wrench in one hand—is yellin' somethin' that gets swallowed up in the engine roar.

Mesh-Top yells, "What?" and Peanut yells again, with nobody hearin' a damn thing.

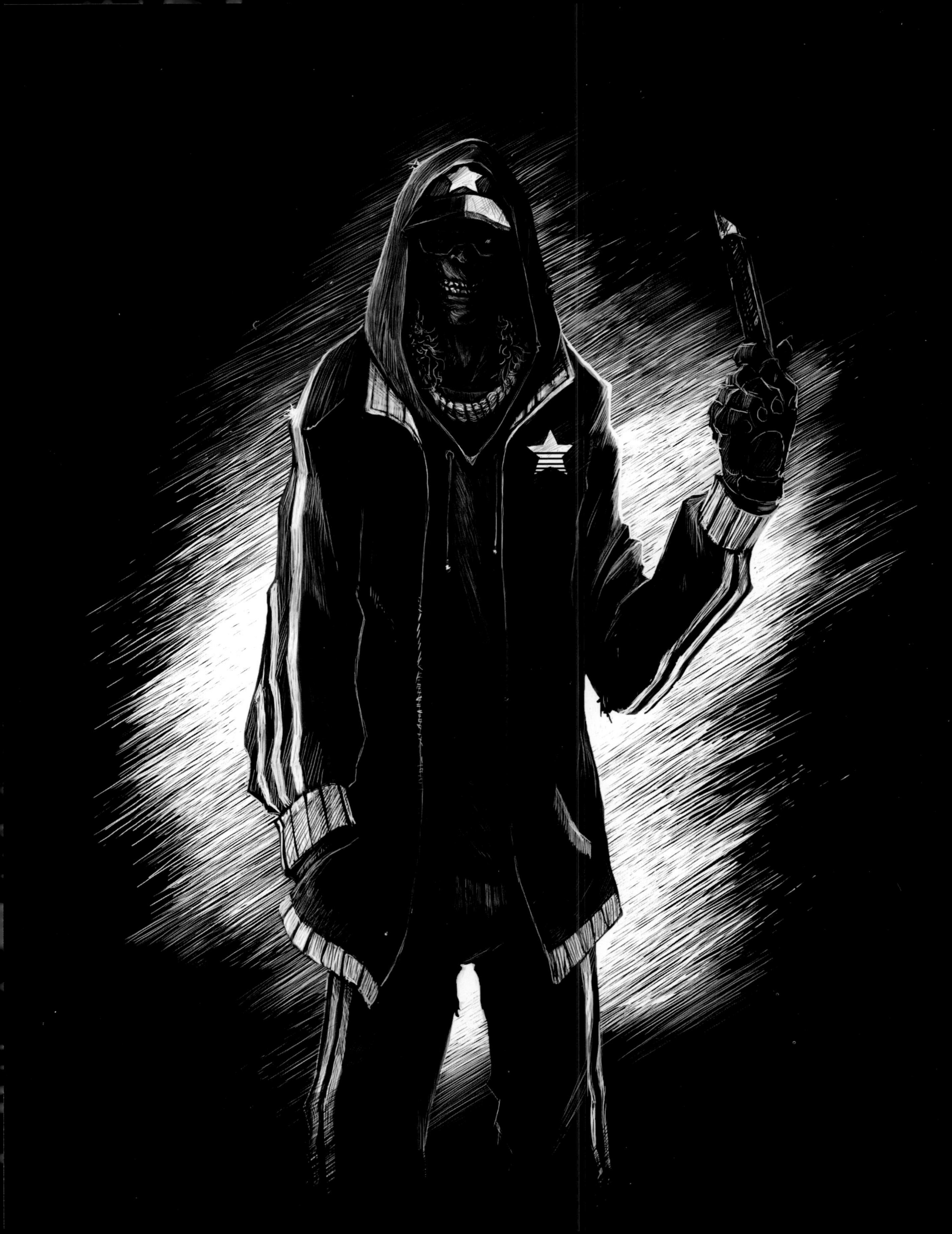

Frankie swats Mesh-Top upside the back o' the head, and when the lackey turns with a "what'd I do" look on his face, Frankie motions toward the semis. Mesh-Top nods and points with his one hand to a few other faithful, and they all run in different directions. A couple ticks later the four motors cut off and the tension on Jo Jo's arms and legs eases up a bit, though he's still suspended a few inches off the ground, feelin' like one o' them moths that's been pinned inside a display case.

"We found this'n here, but that ain't all," Peanut yells, and Jo Jo's surprised to see a black hearse—the same one he spotted at Conway Titties and then again at Hubtown—pull up behind 'em. A fat trucker with a gray beard gets outta the driver's seat, sayin', "Wait'll y'all see this!"

Frankie's still hangin' back with Jo Jo, who can't lay eyes on much o' what happens next, though you and I can plainly see Gray Beard as he heads to the rear o' the vehicle and opens up the door there to reveal the coffin . . . which is now open.

"Hey," Gray Beard says, "It wasn't open a second—"

Just then, a blur comes outta nowhere, shootin' through the heavy rain, disappearin' into the open driver's side door. A tick later the sounds o' Axel F blare out from the car's speakers, and some hydraulics kick in, makin' the front end o' the hearse hop up like a dog beggin' for treats.

"What the shit?" Gray Beard says, backin' up . . . and the two bikers holdin' Elsa actually let go, movin' away from the possessed automobile as that black streak returns, stoppin' in a clear spot where Jo Jo can finally see, takin' the form o' the tall, dark-skinned fella in the hoodie and sunglasses—now wearin' gloves too—that our man spotted behind the wheel at Hubtown. Huxley by name, as I've said, but o' course Jo Jo don't know that.

Huxley, holdin' a rusty box cutter in one hand, gets to movin' . . . doin' some kinda funky dance, gyratin' and toprockin' before he disappears once again. The blur zips to Peanut—who grabs at his throat—then whooshes back to become Huxley again. This time he lays down the wave and the robot before streakin' off to the other fella who was holdin' onto Elsa; this guy looks down at both his wrists all curious-like as the blur returns, and then Huxley busts out the runnin' man and the "Thriller" dance before blazin' off to Gray Beard—who starts rubbin' his neck—and then whizzin' right on back . . .

At this point, our hooded newcomer's appearin' mighty confused. Rather than doin' anything fancy, he just kinda looks to Peanut and Gray Beard and the other fella and says, "How y'all still standin'? Normally I kill with these moves."

Jo Jo's also downright perplexed as to what the hell's goin' on, but he's noticed somethin' . . . in all the chaos, Elsa's done vanished. The faithful are so caught up in the spectacle o' the newcomer that they haven't seemed to notice, includin' Frankie, who's just starin' and growlin', no doubt irritated that all his fun got interrupted.

Lightnin' flashes overhead while the stranger pulls a flask from his jacket pocket and takes a sip. Peanut decides to nut up and charges, swingin' that big ol' pipe wrench overhead. Well the mystery man blurs again, and all sudden-like, Peanut ain't holdin' his wrench no more. He's lookin' kinda dumbly at his empty hand when the hooded man appears behind him and buries that pipe wrench in Peanut's head.

Peanut plops facedown like a sack o' taters, while Huxley smiles, says, "That's more like it," and blurs again. Frankie takes a few steps away from Jo Jo to get a handle on the situation, while Jo Jo, he's surprised to feel the tension on one o' the chains give way. He looks over his left shoulder to see Elsa, kneelin' down, a chain and S-hook in one hand, with the pointer finger o' the other on her lips warnin' our man to stay quiet.

As Elsa goes 'bout unhookin' the rest o' the chains, the blur goes on bashin' in noggins with that pipe wrench. Frankie, not appearin' too concerned, strolls up next to the trucker holdin' the ax and he stops, waitin' and watchin'. He's got his razor blade out and unfolded and sure as shittin', when the blur comes for Ax Man, Frankie's free hand shoots out almost faster than the eye can catch, his meaty paw snaggin' the descendin' pipe wrench before it can cave another skull. Huxley's standin' there, holdin' the wrench, but his grin's done disappeared. Before Frankie can hack and slash, though, there's a rattlin' sound as a chain lashes out and catches Frankie's razor blade, sendin' it smackin' down to the wet sand. Frankie looks over his shoulder at Jo Jo, who's stood up with one of the chains still wound 'round his left wrist.

Frankie don't take his eyes offa Jo Jo as he casually jabs that wrench into Huxley's forehead and drops the newcomer flat on his back.

The rumblin' sky lights up as Frankie ditches the wrench and snags the ax from the poor sap next to him. The messiah belts out a war cry and charges. Jo Jo answers the call. A colossal bowlin' ball o' thunder rolls overhead as the two titans engage. Frankie swings the ax once, twice—but Jo Jo dodges both times. Frankie follows with a kick that damn near knocks our man off his feet.

Meantime, outta one o' the open trailers that was set to yank Jo Jo's legs off, the erstwhile Ax Man is withdrawin' a double-barrel shotgun. Unfortunately for him, when he turns 'round, Elsa's there waitin'. She yanks that double-barrel outta his hand, reverses it, shoves the barrels under his chin, and pulls both triggers. The doomed desperado's head and a whole buncha skull bits fly out into the downpour.

Elsa turns to Frankie and Jo Jo, but them two are a ways off now and Elsa, she's got her own problems: The remainin' Profits, includin' Mesh-Top and Gray Beard, are closin' in on her. She pulls them triggers again, but nothin' happens, and she realizes right quick that in the midst o' all the excitement she done forgot to reload.

Returnin' our attention to Jo Jo, though . . . you might remember the fella from earlier who got sent to retrieve the chainsaw. Well he's done fired that puppy up and he closes in on our hero's left side, arcin' the saw and them deadly teeth right at Jo Jo's head.

CHAPTER THE TWENTY-FIRST

Jo Jo thrusts his chain-wrapped arm up at the last second, causin' a shower o' sparks to shoot offa the coiled links.

Frankie takes advantage o' this distraction to drop the ax down at a diagonal on the right side o' Jo Jo's neck. Our man grimaces and growls as the combined power o' Frankie and the Ramblin' Man behind that woodcutter manages to break Jo Jo's skin. This particular oak don't topple, though. No sir, instead he rotates to the left, grabs hold, and wrenches the chainsaw outta the surprised biker's grip. Frankie yanks his ax back while Jo Jo jabs out, crackin' the former saw-wielder in the forehead with the chain brake.

Jo Jo squares off once again with Frankie as the rain pounds down, and time and time and time again, rippin' whirlin' saw teeth meet woodcutter blade and woodcutter blade meets chain links and sparks fly.

The back and forth goes on, both men slippin' in the wet sand, blinkin' the water outta their eyes, ax versus saw and grit against grit.

Poor Elsa's thinkin' that she's just 'bout done for, when that blur returns and all o' a sudden Gray Beard's got the chisel edge o' a crowbar stickin' outta his forehead. Takin' full advantage, Elsa sets to swingin' that shotgun by the barrels, wallopin' Mesh-Top upside the head so hard his mama gets a concussion . . .

Not far away, Frankie hacks into Jo Jo's hide repeatedly, thinkin' he might even have the upper hand, 'til he swings low and Jo Jo gets the notion that instead o' pittin' the saw blade against the ax-head, he should adjust his aim. Sure 'nough, as Frankie swings, Jo Jo shifts the saw, and them teeth shear right through the ax handle, causin' the useless ax-head to drop like a stone and leavin' Frankie holdin' nothin' more'n a flat-ended stick.

The gang leader pauses and looks down, contemplatin' how his weapon went from blade-edged to blunt, just as Jo Jo dives in with the saw, slicin' Frankie's stick-holdin' hand off at the wrist.

Continuin' that same motion, our hero brings the blade up in an arc, takin' just a tick to appreciate the look o' surprise on Frankie's face before he swipes the chainsaw across and through the doomed messiah's neck.

The black-eyed head tumbles offa them thick shoulders. The body sways and wobbles and then falls back, slappin' down into the wet earth.

The rain lets up a bit while Jo Jo shuts off the chainsaw motor. He drops the machine and the chain to the ground, then gazes 'round, notin' that as far as he can tell, every single one o' the Profits is layin' prone, heads all busted open. And Elsa, she's kneelin' next to one o' the men, loadin' two shotgun shells that she done liberated from the corpse.

Lookin' to his right, Jo Jo realizes the mystery man's standin' there, starin' down at Frankie's corpse, whistlin' before he says:

"Damn, man, you ain't got no ruth."

Jo Jo throws him a quizzical look. "What?"

"You ruthless," Huxley answers and busts into a golden-grilled grin.

"Who the hell are you?" Jo Jo asks, but the stranger ain't payin' him no mind. No, he's still gazin' down at the leader as he says, "What kinda shit is this?"

Jo Jo glances down to see that Frankie's body has done sat up! The one hand gropes 'round and plants itself in the dirt, and pretty soon the headless carcass maneuvers to a standin' position.

Elsa has joined the two now. All three watch and wait, no doubt wonderin' just how the one-handed, decapitated death dealer plans on dealin' any more death.

But then they hear a few squishy sounds, followed by a pop, as somethin' wet and black juts up from Frankie's neck stump. Jo Jo squints, disbelievin' his own eyes as the upside-down crow's head swivels 'round and a raggedy caw escapes its beak.

Frankie's hand lunges forward as Jo Jo snatches the shotgun away from Elsa.

The bird wriggles its way outta Frankie's neck and manages to take flight. Jo Jo blasts Frankie's body point-blank in the chest with one shot, sendin' it back to the ground, then he lifts them double barrels, gettin' off a second shot that sends a few feathers flyin' from the battered blackbird. It keeps on, though, gainin' altitude, and before long it becomes nothin' more'n a speck against the dissipatin' clouds.

Huxley, he's tiltin' his head back, holdin' that flask o' his upside down over his open mouth, tongue out. Unfortunately for him, his reserve is dry as a bone and don't nothin' come out.

"Well," Elsa says, "at least that's over."

Yeah you might think so, but it's lookin' like Elsa spoke to soon. 'Cause one tick, Jo Jo's watchin' Huxley put the flask away, next, the stranger's done disappeared again and our man feels his hair and beard pulled away, teeth against his throat as Huxley bites and slurps up some o' the blood from the ax wound in Jo Jo's neck.

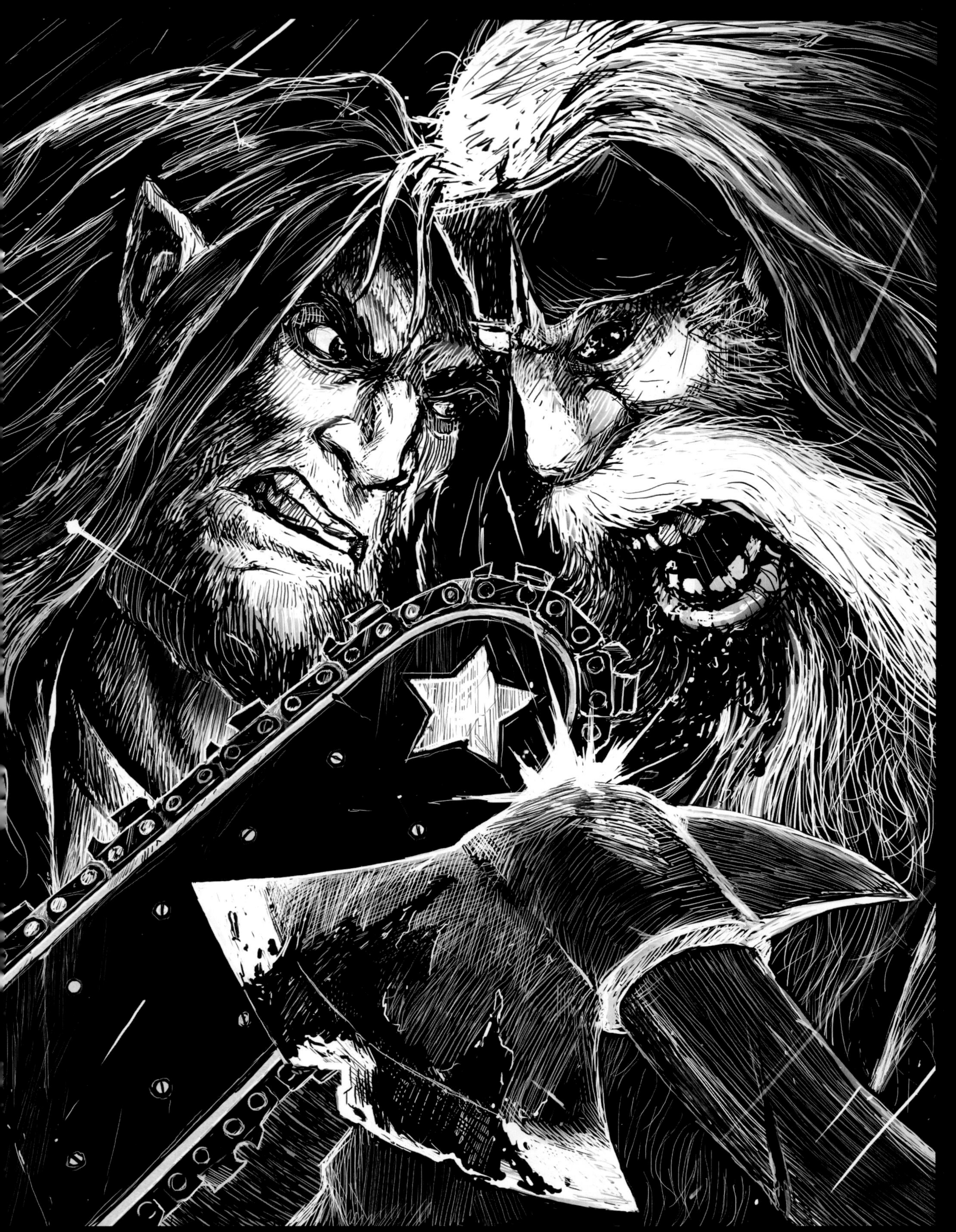

Jo Jo reaches up and over his shoulders, grabs Huxley, and flips him onto the ground next to the shotgun-blasted body o' Frankie. Our man's got Huxley by the throat but the mystery man still manages to vocalize, "Gawd-damnit, I don't feel no different!"

"Why have you been following us?" Jo Jo asks through clenched teeth, leanin' into the stranger's grill. "Why'd you try and kill me?"

Jo Jo lets up his grip just enough to let Huxley speak. "Name's Huxley. I got me a kinda gift, see, when it come to blood. Can't smell it, 'cause I don't smell. I mean I don't breathe. But I can taste it. Tasted it on yo rings back at that titty bar."

Huxley grabs hold o' the hand on his neck, pulls it away and then draws it to his mouth, probin' with his tongue at one o' Jo Jo's rings. Our man yanks his hand back like he touched a pipin' hot stove.

"What do you want with the blood?"

"I need it!" Huxley pleads. "Need it 'cause I got a, a . . . condition. But I just drank some and like I said, I don't think it did nothin'."

Jo Jo stands up, lookin' at his hand, specifically at the ring that Huxley tried to get his tongue on. He pulls that ring off and looks at the inside and sure 'nough there's dried blood in there.

Now Jo Jo gets to thinkin'. He recalls Papa Boehner's Diner, in the bathroom where he washed blood down the sink, and he remembers that some o' the blood on his hands was his own, but some . . . some belonged to the Ringmaster. And he wonders if *that's* what the skinny fella's goin' on 'bout.

Then Jo Jo gets to thinkin' that this mystery man might just come in handy as he says, "You want the blood that's on these rings? I know how to get it."

CHAPTER THE TWENTY-SECOND

Once Jo Jo convinced Huxley that the blood he got all worked up 'bout was the Ramblin' Man's and not his, and after invitin' the stranger to join their little party, our man was mighty anxious to get back on the road.

As far as transport goes, seein' as how neither Elsa nor our hero had a clue as to how to drive a semi, Huxley agreed to take 'em all to Dead End.

So here they are now, motorin' down the Anaconda like a bat outta hell. You might recognize Frankie's razor blade hangin' from Huxley's rearview mirror. Well that's on account o' Huxley askin' if he could use it to replace his rusty box cutter before they all upped and left.

Jo Jo, anyway, he's ridin' shotgun, while Elsa's in back with the coffin and some guns they took offa the Profits and a whole heap o' pork rind bags they done liberated from one o' the Profits' trailers. She leans up on the bench seat, makin' barkin' noises and havin' Patch make-believe lick Jo Jo's face.

Our hero, he's just kinda sittin' with his thoughts, mullin' over somethin' that's been buggin' him ever since the stranger arrived at the trucker camp. He didn't pay it much mind then, what with all the ax and chainsaw shenanigans and such, but when the wind shifted just right, Jo Jo could smell Huxley, and what he sniffed— under the maskin' scent o' Wackarr Noarr cologne—was the faint odor o' a corpse. In fact, both the cologne *and* the corpse scents are particularly pungent right now, in the confines o' the cab.

Jo Jo considers that in all fairness, he himself had been left for dead not so long ago . . . but he had never died *for real*. Huxley, though, he smells like he went tits-up a long ways back—not somewhat freshly dead like Frankie had been, but way past the expiration date.

All o' this gets our man to wonderin' just how it is their new companion can be alive and not alive at the same time. Jo Jo, though, he ain't much o' one for conversation so for now he just keeps his mouth shut, content that Huxley, like Elsa and himself, is simply different.

"How long you been wit yo breezy?" Huxley asks.

Not understandin' what the hell Huxley's on about, Jo Jo simply raises an eyebrow and glances sideways in response.

"Yo girl," Huxley explains.

"We're not—"

"We've been pals for a while now," Elsa interjects helpfully.

"Oh, okay."

"Hey what's in the coffin, anyway?" Elsa asks, turnin' to look at the fancy casket she's sittin' just in front of.

"Me, mosta the time," Huxley answers. "That's where I count sheep."

"You sleep in it?" Elsa asks, incredulous.

"Yeah, that's right."

"Is that 'cause of your condition?"

Huxley quiets down when he says this next bit—"Yeah you could say that"— then he pipes up again: "I's born with my, uh . . . affliction. Made me all skinny and weak and shit . . . been battlin' it my whole life."

"You poor thing!"

"I get by, you know . . . gotta drink blood to live. Keeps me goin' but it ain't no ideal kinda life. If I was to get ahold o' the right *kinda* blood though—special blood, see—it'd be a cure."

"So you wouldn't have to drink it no more?" Elsa asks.

"'Xactly right," Huxley confirms.

"We'll get you what you need," Elsa says, pokin' Jo Jo in the shoulder with Patch. "Ain't that so?"

"Mm," Jo Jo replies. 'Cept he ain't convinced. He can't rightly explain why, but he suspects that Huxley's story ain't true. Or that maybe he ain't tellin' them the *whole* truth.

Outside, meantime, the hearse is drawin' within a couple miles o' the ghost town o' Ojo Rojo. This little berg ain't like Devil's Tailbone, where the occupants just shut up their windows and wait for the Barnstormers to pass on through. No sir, this is a bona fide, deserted ghost town; time was, it'd been one o' them touristy spots, made up to look like an Old West boomtown, but after the Great Conflict, luxuries like vacations became a thing o' the past and so did vacation destinations. When the residents' incomes dried up, they moved on, leavin' behind wooden facades and hitchin' posts and boardwalks . . . all fallin' apart now, collectin' dust, and crumblin' away to nothin'.

Yessir, there ain't a single livin' soul inside o' Ojo Rojo . . .

'Cept one.

Up on the balcony above the general store stands a fella you might recognize. That there's none other'n Doc Prometheus Hart, peepin' through a spyglass so's he can see who's in the front seat o' the approachin' vehicle. The Barnstormers, o' course, he done just let them pass right on through a few hours ago. But this car, this might be just what he's been waitin' for, he reckons. He don't know nothin' 'bout the driver, but the hirsute gentleman on the passenger side, well he certainly fits the description o' his daughter's travelin' companion. And what's that behind him, in the backseat? Someone holdin' a stuffed animal . . .

Elsa.

Doc Hart lowers the spyglass, his slightly off-kilter features distortin' into a smile. Now like I said, our doctor's the only livin' soul in town. But he did at one time have himself a driver, a not-so-bad-lookin' lady . . . one o' them bodybuilder types. In order to finish his special project, however, well, it was necessary to make use o' her, like he done with all the others.

Anyway, on account o' not havin' no driver, Doc Hart's forced to head on down to the street, then to the side alley where he parked his tractor and trailer. He gets in, fires up the engine, and pulls out so's the back end's blockin' off the road halfway up Main Street.

Havin' already stashed the surprise he's got waitin' for Elsa inside the saloon and brothel, the doc takes up a spot downstairs in the general store, and when that hearse comes to a stop, the good doctor steps on out into the street.

Inside the hearse, Elsa looks at the trailer and the man standin' before it, and her gut gets to twistin' in that familiar way.

"Oh. Oh, no," she says.

"Is it him?" Jo Jo asks.

"Him who?" says Huxley.

"Yeah. It's Father."

"Somebody you don't wanna talk to?" Huxley inquires. "I can zip down one o' these alleys—"

Now a whole lotta thoughts are goin' through Elsa's mind, like all the possible ways they can escape, but there's other considerations too, like, even if they do get away, how long 'til Father tracks her down again?

And that fear, that wrenchin' in her stomach, well she knows that as long as Father's chasin' her, that nest o' snakes in her gut won't never go away. And though it may seem a simple thing, the sudden realization hits her full-force—the undeniable truth that she's sick o' livin' with that fear, sick o' the knowledge that she can't never truly be free.

And so she makes a choice, right then and there.

"I want out," she says.

"You sure?" Jo Jo asks.

"Yeah I'm sure."

"Not by yourself," Jo Jo replies.

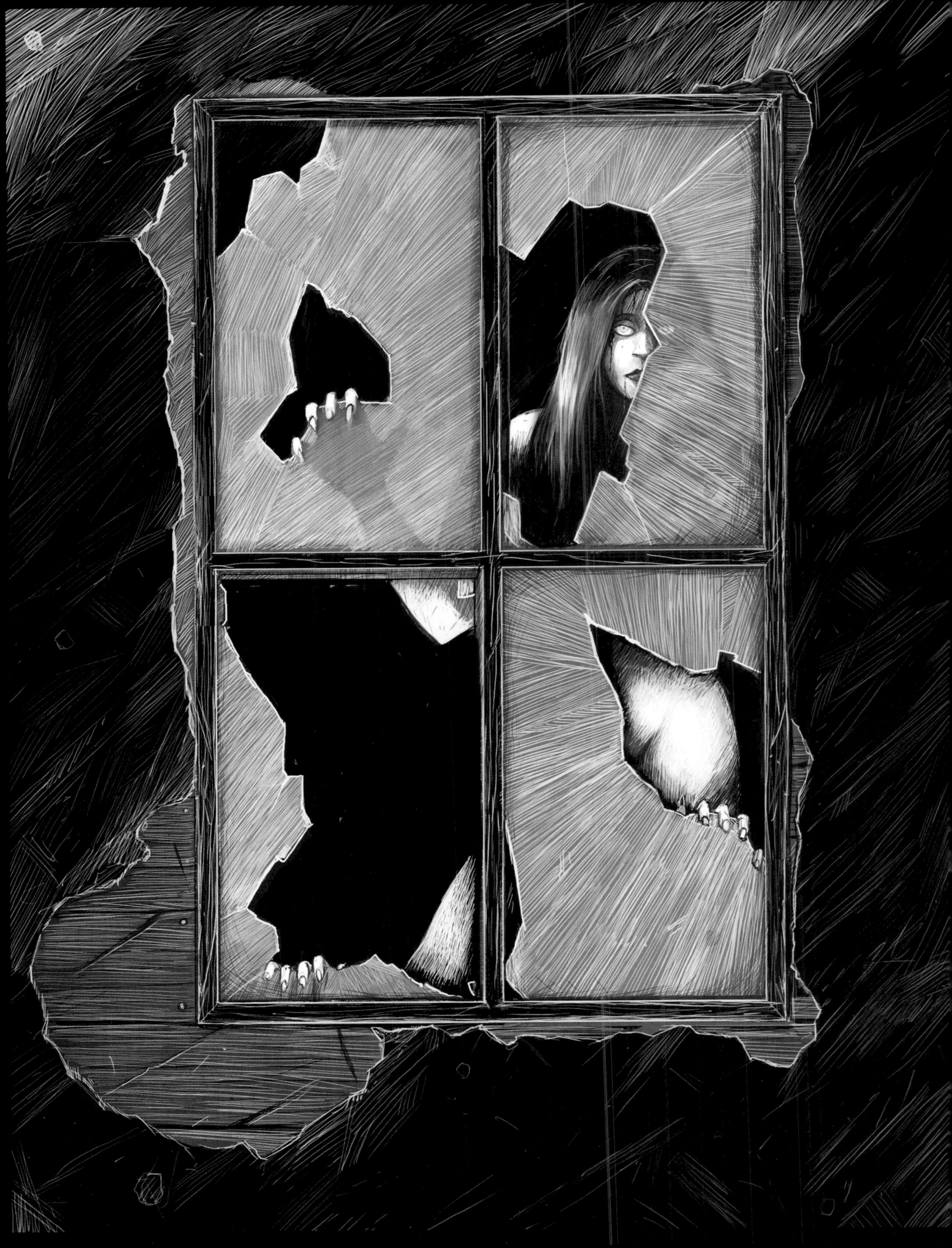

"Damn straight," Huxley adds, grabbin' Frankie's razor offa the rearview mirror and pullin' up his hood.

Huxley and Jo Jo and Elsa all pile outta the hearse then and stand in front, facin' the doctor who's 'bout twenty paces away. Elsa, she's got Patch clutched to her chest as she steps forward, and if we look real close, we can see a steel handle stickin' up from Patch's back, just behind his stuffed head.

Anyway, at first everyone just kinda' stands there starin' at each other and Elsa's reminded o' them old Westerns where two gunslingers face off at high noon and draw their six-shooters.

"Playtime is over!" Doc Hart calls out. "The hour has long passed for you to return home."

Elsa works up her gumption and she says, "I ain't never comin' back! Why would I?"

"Because we're family," Hart says. "Because I am your father and because I say so."

"Well I got me a new family!" Elsa yells back. "And they know how to treat people. Not like you! You . . . you're sick. Always were. You don't deserve no family."

Hart lowers his head just a bit, then says, "It grieves me to hear you say these things. You never truly learned discipline. Respect, appreciation. I tried to raise you correctly but I failed. I have asked myself why, but when you left, that's when the realization dawned on me . . . you never had a mother."

Now the doc turns his head as he says this, lookin' to one o' the open windows above the saloon. There's a real pretty woman standin' there, kinda half in shadow, only her head and naked shoulders visible, and she's smilin' down at Elsa and starin' at her kinda glassy-eyed.

"You never had a mother because I never provided you one. That is an oversight I have seen fit to remedy. Mother will teach you what I could not. And your first lesson, beloved daughter, will be . . . obedience."

On that cue, the lady in the window *sinks* down, as if she's lowerin' herself right through the floor. This is a fair bit confusin' to our gang, but what they don't realize is that the inside o' the saloon and brothel has done deteriorated to the point where there ain't no floor. So that head disappears, and all's quiet for a tick . . . until somethin' comes blastin' through the saloon facade, scatterin' timber from hell to breakfast, somethin' big and strong and downright unnatural.

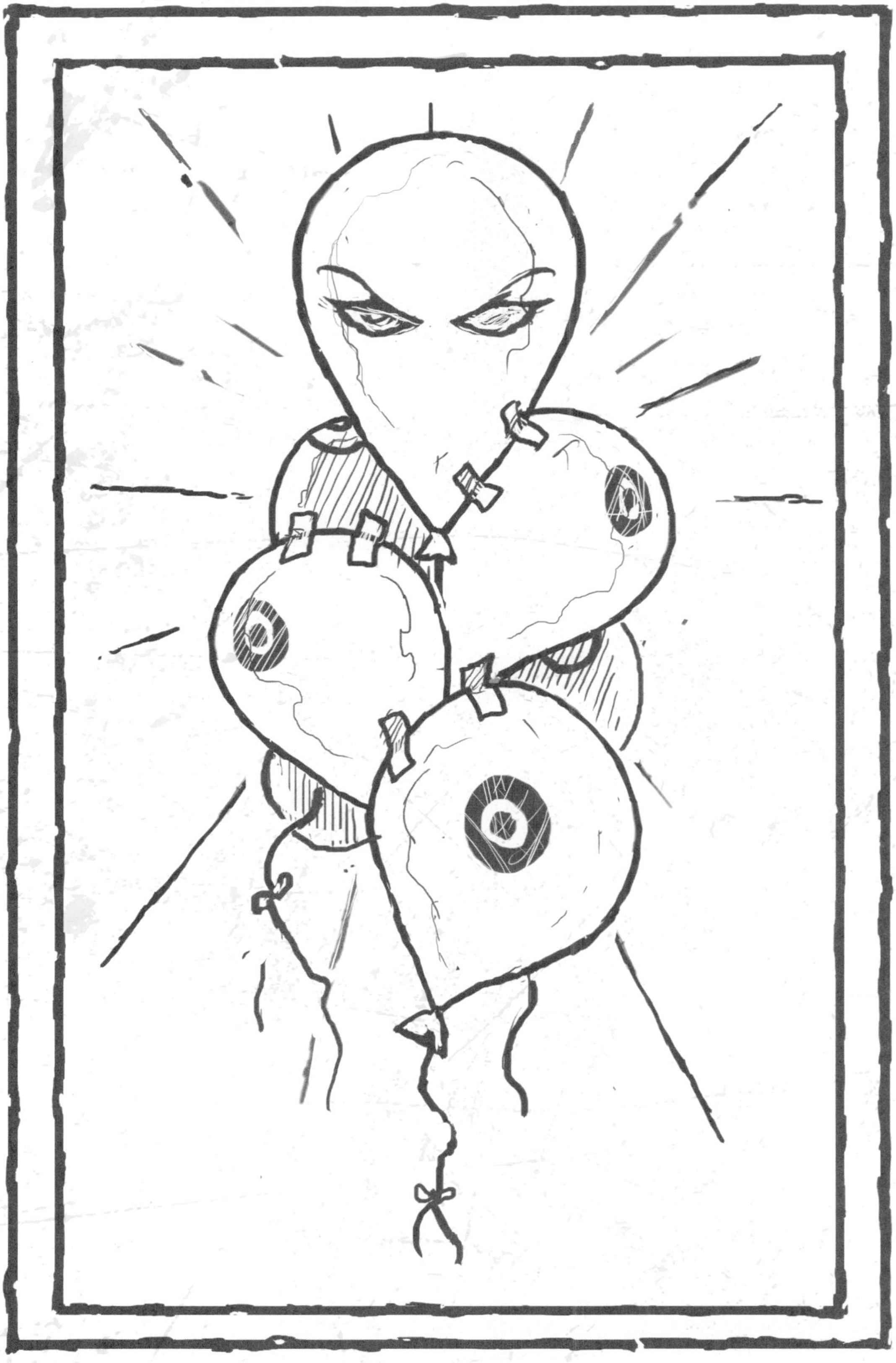

The Matriarch

CHAPTER THE TWENTY-THIRD

"Gawwwd-damn, that ain't right!" Huxley hollers as Doc Hart's creation lumbers out into the street.

The monstrosity is a damn near unrecognizable mish-mash o' female body parts. Its main trunk is composed o' a whole mess o' torsos all stitched together to make one giant, misshapen, tubelike body. Haphazardly attached to that whole shitshow is a buncha' arms and legs—half on top and half on bottom. If that ain't weird enough, well them limbs, see, some o'em is legs with hands on the end, some is arms with feet on the end, and some o'em, hell some o'em have heads on the end. Take for instance that appendage in the back, topped off with the slack-faced melon o' the wounded hobo lady from Hubtown. At the front o' the freak-show configuration is a smaller female upper torso, naked. The head on top, well that's the same as what was starin' at our heroes from the window. And now that Elsa gets a closer look—as the thing's lower limbs propel it forward like a big-ass centipede—she sees that it's the head o' the innkeeper from Devil's Tailbone.

"Kill her companions first," Doc Hart orders.

Mother barrels down on the gang, a few o' the front appendages grabbin' hold o' Jo Jo. The thing rears up so the front half o' it is two stories high, and as it descends, it throws our main man into a horse trough, bustin' that container to kindlin'.

Huxley, he sees an opportunity to guzzle some blood, so he blurs on over to one o' them limbs, draws Frankie's razor across, and sinks his grill right in. What he sucks outta that appendage causes an instant reaction, as the skinny fella doubles over, retchin' up a greenish liquid. "Gotta be kiddin' me!" he blurts before vomitin' another stream o' green goo. Now the more astute among you mighta caught on that what Huxley consumed wasthat special serum the doc used on Elsa, and what she uses on herself when she reattaches body parts. But for some damn reason, that concoction don't sit well with our bloodthirsty break dancer. Anyway he gets himself so caught up in spittin' and spewin' that he don't move outta the way quick enough to prevent gettin' swept up and tossed into the livery.

Mother beelines for Elsa then, but our girl runs underneath, clutchin' Patch to her with one hand, crawlin' fast as she can through the appendages, squealin' when a skinny white leg with a brown hand on the end grabs hold o' her arm. Now you might remember that steel handle I mentioned stickin' up behind Patch's head. Elsa reaches over and she pulls out the scalpel she hid in her faithful pet's back, and she cuts through the fingers o' that hand 'til it can't hold her no more.

Jo Jo, meantime, he's taken up two pieces o' the wooden remains o' the trough and he runs over and jumps onto the monstrosity's body at right 'bout the halfway mark. He's ridin' Mother like a bull, takin' the pointy ends o' them sticks and stabbin' for all he's worth, but it don't seem to be havin' much effect.

Elsa crawls her way to the ass end o' Mother, but before she scurries out, she looks up to see Doc Hart, standin' there, waitin'. She ducks back in, scootin' on her butt, knife in one hand, Patch in the other. The fleshy roof over her head spins 'round and disappears as the monstrosity rotates and then reverses, allowin' Mother's two front arms to scoop our girl up.

"Remove her legs," Doc Hart yells. "So she can run no longer."

The freaky creature holds Elsa up at eye level o' the primary head, and our girl can see a little shaved spot in the hair with a stitched-up incision scar. She don't know precisely what Doc Hart did to the poor woman's brain, but she imagines he removed part o' it so's she couldn't disobey his orders—somethin' he threatened to do to Elsa a time or two.

Anyhow the upper arms hold Elsa by her shoulders while a couple o' the monstrosity's other appendages get to twistin' on her legs, in the midst o' which, the thing rears up again, liftin' Elsa so's her back's against the wooden rail o' the balcony Doc Hart was lookin' out from not so long ago.

Elsa's swipin' like mad with the scalpel but she can't quite reach anything vital. Jo Jo in the meantime has stopped stabbin' at the lower torso and moved up, usin' both sticks on Mother's back the way an ice climber uses them pointy tools to scale a glacier.

Jo Jo fights off the limbs that try to snatch at him and gets all the way to the innkeeper's torso. Just as Elsa gets her right hand free and plunges her scalpel into Mother's eye, Jo Jo thrusts one o' them stakes through the back o' the creature's throat, shovin' it clear through to the other side less than an inch from Elsa's wide-eyed face.

The thing twists and wails in agony, allowin' Elsa to wrench free, fallin' off to the side where she lands on the roof o' Doc Hart's trailer. Jo Jo corkscrews that head 'til it finally comes loose, and him and what's left o' the freakish monstrosity come crashin' down.

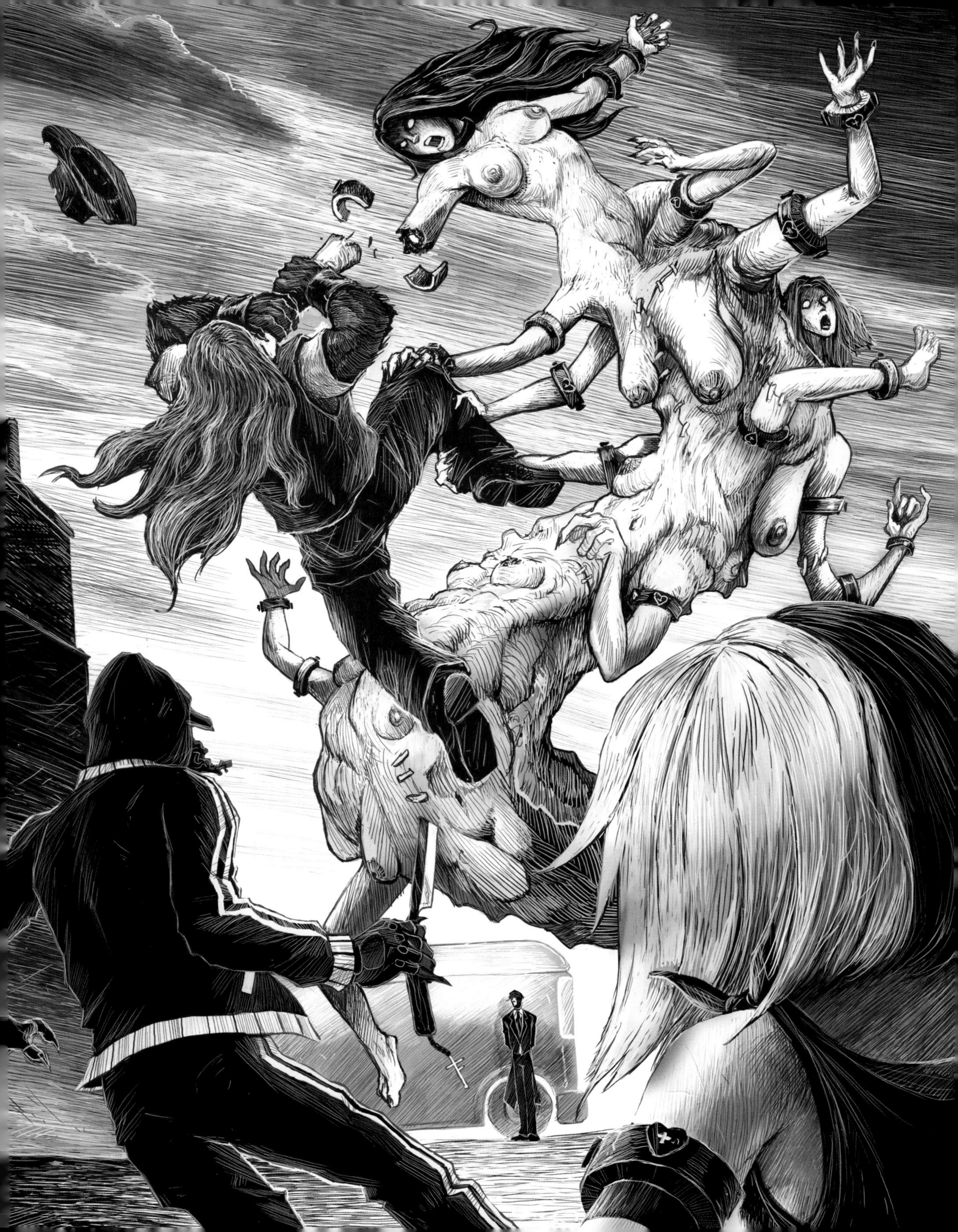

Doc Hart takes heed o' the fact that his current efforts have ended in failure and starts sneakin' off toward the boardwalk, only to be confronted by Huxley, covered in hay and lookin' none too happy, a little glint o' gold shinin' from his grill as he smiles and says, "Where you think you're goin'?"

The doctor turns to go the other way, and stops cold when he spots Jo Jo, feet planted, mouth grimacin'. "You got a lot to answer for. 'Doc.'"

Hart starts backin' up, nice and easy, palms out, toward the shadowy hole left by Mother's exit from the saloon, when Elsa slinks outta them shadows and slices the scalpel across the tendons at the back o' the doctor's knees.

"Daaamnn," Huxley says. "Way to go, girl. Now let's bleed him! Bleed him real slow . . ." and his tongue gets to flickin' in and out 'tween his grill.

Jo Jo takes a step back as Elsa comes round to face Hart, who's collapsed to all fours.

The doctor lifts his vaguely unsettling face to her and says: "Stop this . . . foolishness and return home with me at once. You were not meant for this world. You need my shelter. My protection."

"You ain't got nothin' I need," Elsa says, and she reaches once again to Patch, replacing the scalpel in the pocket she created in her pet and withdrawing something she had found in the trailer: a syringe with a familiar-lookin' green liquid inside. Huxley puts his hands out, sayin', "No, don't, I need his—" but Elsa jabs that needle into the doctor's carotid artery and sinks the plunger as far as it'll go.

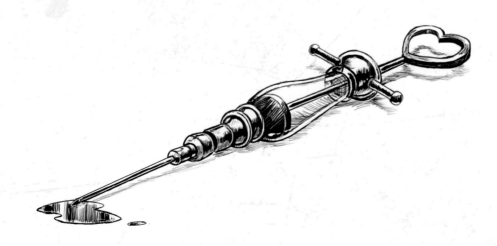

CHAPTER THE TWENTY-FOURTH

Dead End's known all across the land for two things: bein' the last stop on the Anaconda before the gigantic-ass wall that separates the big T from everything else, and for bein' the brisket capital o' Texas. Course, only one o' them things is altogether pertinent to our story. And it ain't brisket.

In a big patch o' desert 'tween the Wall and the domiciles on the outer fringe o' the city, the Barnstormers are sweatin' balls now in the wanin' sunlight that finally broke through the departin' clouds. You might also notice that a large section o' the Wall here is missin'. Nobody knows just how the Wall got compromised in this particular spot, but seein' as how there ain't nothin' just beyond 'cept the Ohelno Arroyo, apparently no one saw fit to patch it up.

Anyways, the Ramblin' Man's pressurin' the roustabouts to get shit done and get it done quick, 'cause they've got a schedule to keep. 'Course it don't help that these boys is workin' double duty—not just erectin' the usual tents and such, but settin' up all the rides as well. Most important o'em is the rollercoaster. Now that's not somethin' the Barnstormers normally bother with, but tonight . . . tonight at the end o' the run, they pull out all the stops. 'Cause tonight marks the comin' o' the Boss, and for Ledger DeMesne it could mean the settlin' o' a centuries-old debt.

The Boss's forthcomin' visit ain't the only thing that's got the Ringmaster's nose outta joint. No, there's a particular fly in the ointment that's got him madder'n a three-legged dog trying to bury a turd on a frozen pond:

Jo Jo. Somehow, some way, despite all o' Ledger's efforts to the contrary, Jo Jo remains among the livin'. And on such an important night as tonight, a rogue element like the dog-boy simply ain't to be suffered.

Bo and Tweeny are sittin' outside their trailer, playin' checkers and arguin' on account o' Bo accusin' Tweeny o' cheatin', when the Ringmaster slams his cane on the board and sends checkers flyin'.

Tweeny lets out a little yip and both o' the twins cast fearful eyes on the loomin' presence o' the Ringmaster.

"I tasked you with breaking the mongrel," he says. "And you failed." He's holdin' the cane's dragon head right up close to Tweeny's eyeballs, and she believes that deep in the grooves and creases o' that likeness she sees old, dried-up blood. "I suggest you dig deeper. Unravel—"

And right at this instant, just for the slightest tick, Ledger's left hand flies to his heart. His features twist slightly and he lowers the cane a smidge, but the whole o' it only lasts for a breath and then his left hand's balled into a fist and the cane is back up and that face is grimacin' once more, and both Bo and Tweeny are too damn scared to ask him if everything's alright as the Ramblin' Man concludes—

"Unravel him. Nothing, *nothing* may be allowed to interfere with tonight's show."

"Okay," Bo says. "Sure thing. We'll get started right now." The Ringmaster, though, he don't stick around; he's already gone, long strides carryin' him straight back to his private trailer, where he ducks in through the black drapes, doffin' his coat and vest as he heads deeper in to stand in front o' a gilded mirror. He tears open his shirt to stare at the reflection o' his chest, and see there? Just over his heart is a black spot as big as one o' Terra Mungus's fists. And if we look real close, we'll see that it's slowly *spreading*.

Like I told you, Ledger's got a debt to pay, and this here, this happens once a year. It's a visual reminder, a warnin' to the Ramblin' Man that the final countdown has begun and that the hands o' the doomsday clock are once again approachin' midnight.

★★★★✤★★★★

Back at Ojo Rojo, 'bout a quarter mile south o' the outskirts o' town, Elsa's standin' at the edge o' a well that she spotted on their way in. Huxley's there next to her, leanin' on the low wall, lookin' at the object Elsa's holdin' in her hands. It's an old mason jar that our girl found in the general store, and inside that jar, lookin' back at her, is the head o' Doctor Victor Prometheus Hart. His mouth's movin', but there ain't no sound comin' out 'cause there ain't much o' the neck attached, and even if there had been, Elsa wouldn'ta wasted serum on her father's vocal chords. She *did*, however, inject two syringes worth into the doc's diseased brain.

"I been doin' some thinkin'," Elsa says quietly, lookin' down at her father. "About souls. I wonder if maybe when you do bad things and you die, your soul, if you have one, goes to a bad place. I don't know, but you can think about that. I want you to think about all of the bad things you done for a really long time. I want you to think about somethin' else too: that everything a father should be . . . you were none of that." She brings the jar just a bit closer and says, "But you coulda been."

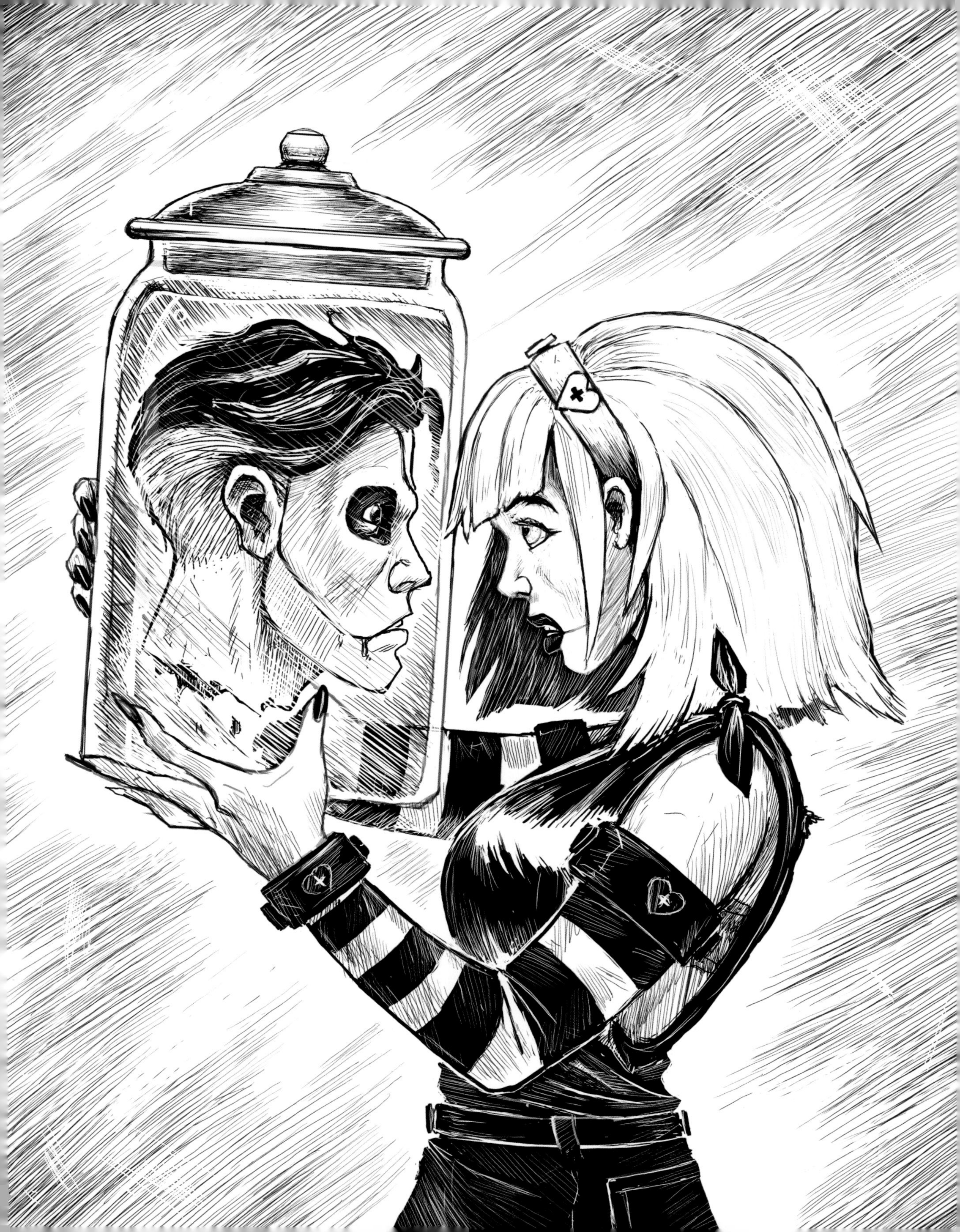

Now the recent rain deposited a hefty amount o' water into the well's bottom, which is a lucky thing, 'cause Elsa knows it'll break the fall. She reaches down to the wall, picks up the jar's lid, and screws it on real tight. Then she takes one last look into the eyes of her father, and she don't know if it's a hint o' regret she sees reflected in that pained gaze or if it's just her imagination. Either way, I'd be lyin' if I said she isn't sheddin' a tear as she drops that jar into the depths.

Everything else is quiet as it splashes down. The silence carries on a bit until Elsa says, "Maybe I'm finally quit of him," and wipes at her eyes. "Sorry for the detour, but now we can go get Her." She looks over to where she thinks Jo Jo should be standin', but Huxley's the only one there.

"Where's Jo Jo?" Elsa asks.

Huxley shrugs his shoulders, lookin' 'round. "I coulda swore he was right behind me when we walked out here."

"I'm sure he's back in town," Elsa says with confidence, but there's already a sinkin' feelin' in her gut.

The sun's nowhere to be seen and the light is quickly fadin' as Elsa and Huxley head on back to Main Street. Huxley, he's movin' a fair sight slower'n normal . . . or, at least what Elsa figures as normal, considerin' she ain't known him that long. He's also shakin' like a meth head at a rehab clinic and she's fairly sure *that* ain't normal. At any rate, she asks if he's okay and he just answers in a low voice.

"Yeah just gotta get me some blood and I'll be straight."

"Oh well there's plenty of blood in Father's trailer," Elsa says. "From his work. He has it sealed up in big plastic barrels."

Huxley looks over, and though Elsa can't see it, his eyes get real wide behind them sunglasses. "Damn, girl, why didn't you say so? Now I can—"

Right 'bout then Elsa and Huxley get through the alley and onto Main Street. Mother's collapsed remains are there. Huxley's hearse is there. But the truck and trailer are gone . . .

And so's Jo Jo.

Right 'bout now it might be a good idea to back up for just a tick: See, right as the three o'em had started walkin' out toward the well, Jo Jo, he had done got a sharp pain in his noggin. He had stopped just a few steps offa Main Street, all woozy-headed. Memories came back 'round on him, like they had at Devil's Tailbone, 'cept this time the recollections was later on, snippets o' when he was older, and not confined to his cage so much, after he had started gettin' to know some o' his fellow freaks and performers; hell he'd even been conversatin' on a fairly regular basis with

140

the Magi twins, and although Bo couldn't give two shits what he had to say, Tweeny seemed to warm up to him just fine. All this socializin' had made him less self-conscious, to the point where he even struck up the nerve to start chattin' with a gal he thought was the most beautiful creature on Earth . . .

Henna was her name. The Painted Lady. She had ink runnin' over her entire body from head to toe—fire and bones and razors and barbed wire. And that was just what she had *before* she joined the Barnstormers. After, well, after she joined, Ledger DeMesne made it a personal project o' his to add more "illuminations" o' his own. Arcane, esoteric symbols and glyphs and runes, and rumor was, the Ramblin' Man started talkin' to Henna 'bout bein' a "vessel" . . .

So anyway as them memories got to flowin', causin' Jo Jo to stop followin' Huxley and Elsa, somethin' else was happenin' at that very same time; an underlyin' imperative was drivin' Jo Jo's actions:

Her. Gotta get to Her.

He wasn't altogether himself 'cause o' the yackle-dackle takin' place inside his head, perpetrated by none other'n them Magi twins, but his desire to get to Her was so overwhelmin' that he done turned 'round, ambled his way back to Main Street, got into the driver's seat o' Doc Hart's truck, and maneuvered it so's it was headin' west.

And that's where we catch up to him now, eyes open as you can plainly tell, but drivin' on a kinda autopilot, 'cause what his *mind's eye* is seein' is somethin' else: His brain's runnin' through the events that led up to him gettin' beat and shot and stabbed and hung under that bridge.

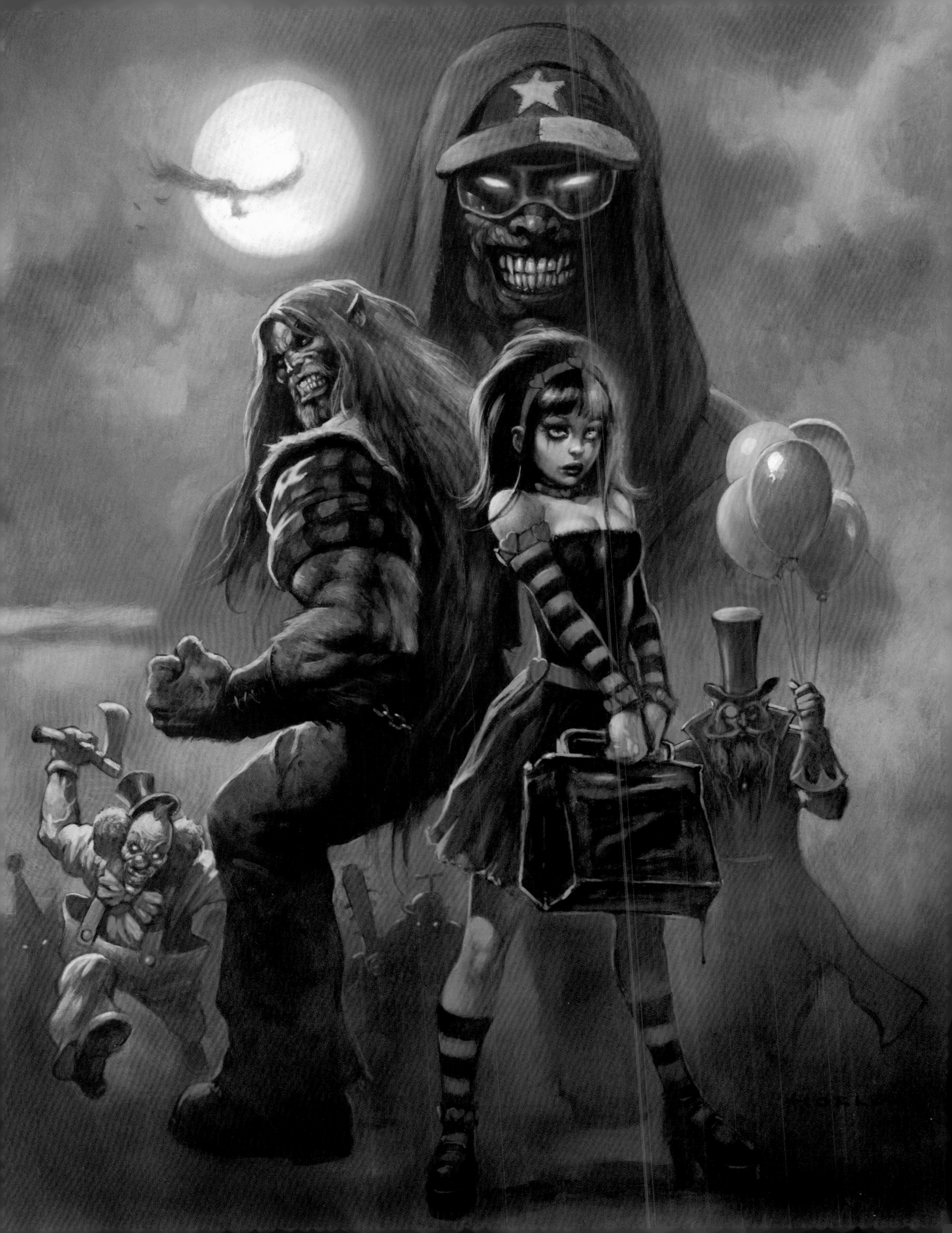

ACT III

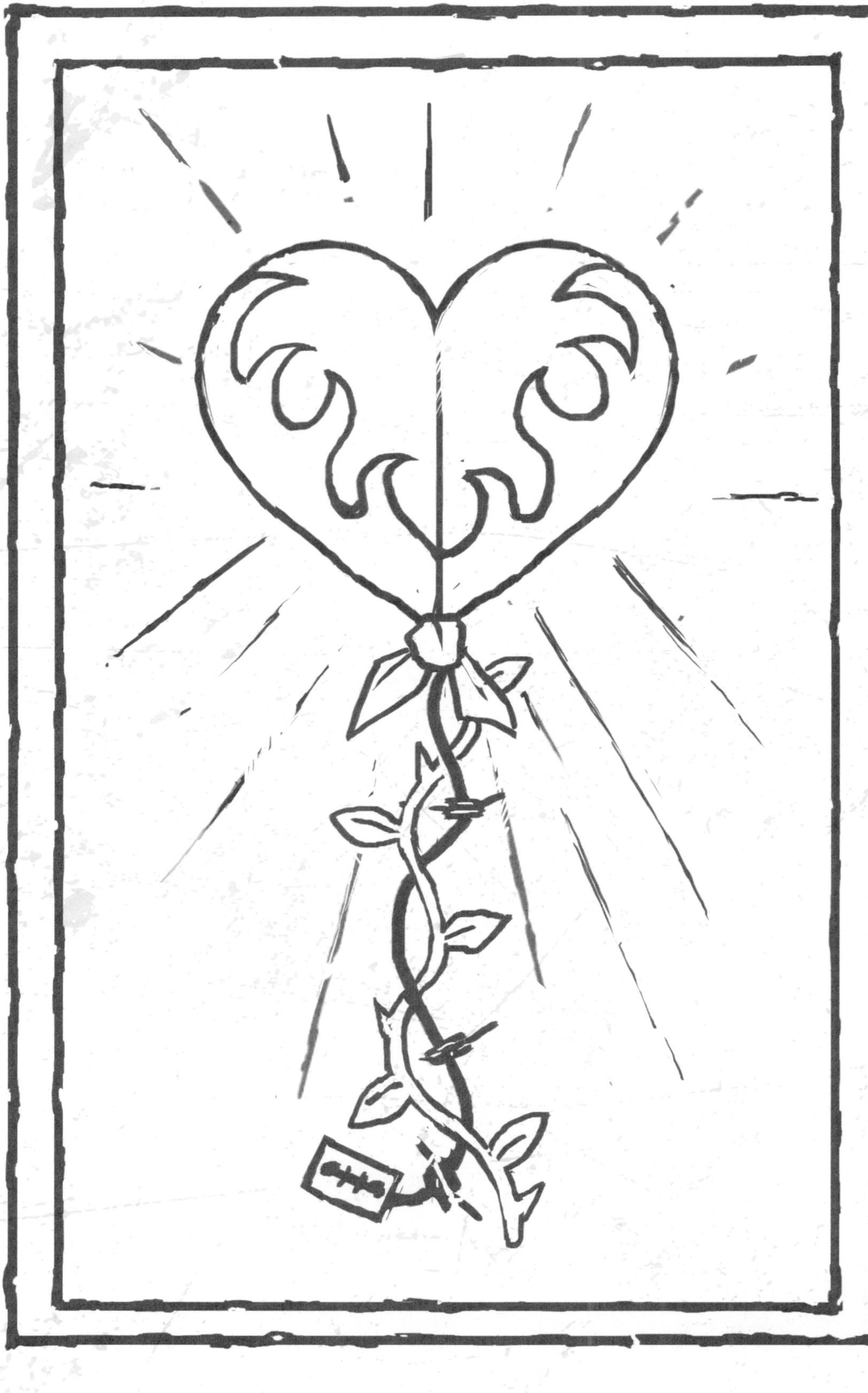

The Harlot

CHAPTER THE TWENTY-FIFTH

The ride construction's finally complete, and the calliope's singin' its merry song as a host o' townies gather near the sideshow banners that mark the carnival entrance. Two Barnstormer trucks are parked just outside, noses facin' each other. A roustabout sits on the hood o' one, waitin' on . . .

Well here he is now. Ledger DeMesne emerges from between the rollercoaster supports, lookin' all dapper and put together once again as he sashays into the truck headlights.

A few o' the carnies and freaks—includin' Diamond and a sword swallower and a fire breather and a juggler and a kid with lobster hands—come out to stand behind Ledger in the glare o' the lights as he strikes a pose between the trucks, thrustin' out his cane while he starts his ballyhoo.

"Ladies and gentlemen, gather 'round!" The crowd draws in a bit, and lookin' out at the kids, Ledger sees the sparks out there that mark them little ones as special, and he thinks that they'll do nicely to fill his balloons, and he's feelin better now that the coaster's complete but he's still anxious—about Jo Jo and most especially about his plans to settle his debt with the Boss once and for all. All o' his careful preparations, decoratin' Henna all them years ago with just the right symbols and sigils and marks o' power—

He wonders if everything he's done will be enough; he ignores the blood in his veins slowly turnin' to an icy black sludge and he ignores the fist squeezin' his heart and he smiles, always the showman, and he gets to pacin' back and forth, tossin' his cane from hand to hand.

"Listen, and listen well! I declare that fate has brought you to my doorstep this very evening!" And the Ringmaster stops, facin' the crowd, and he tosses the cane

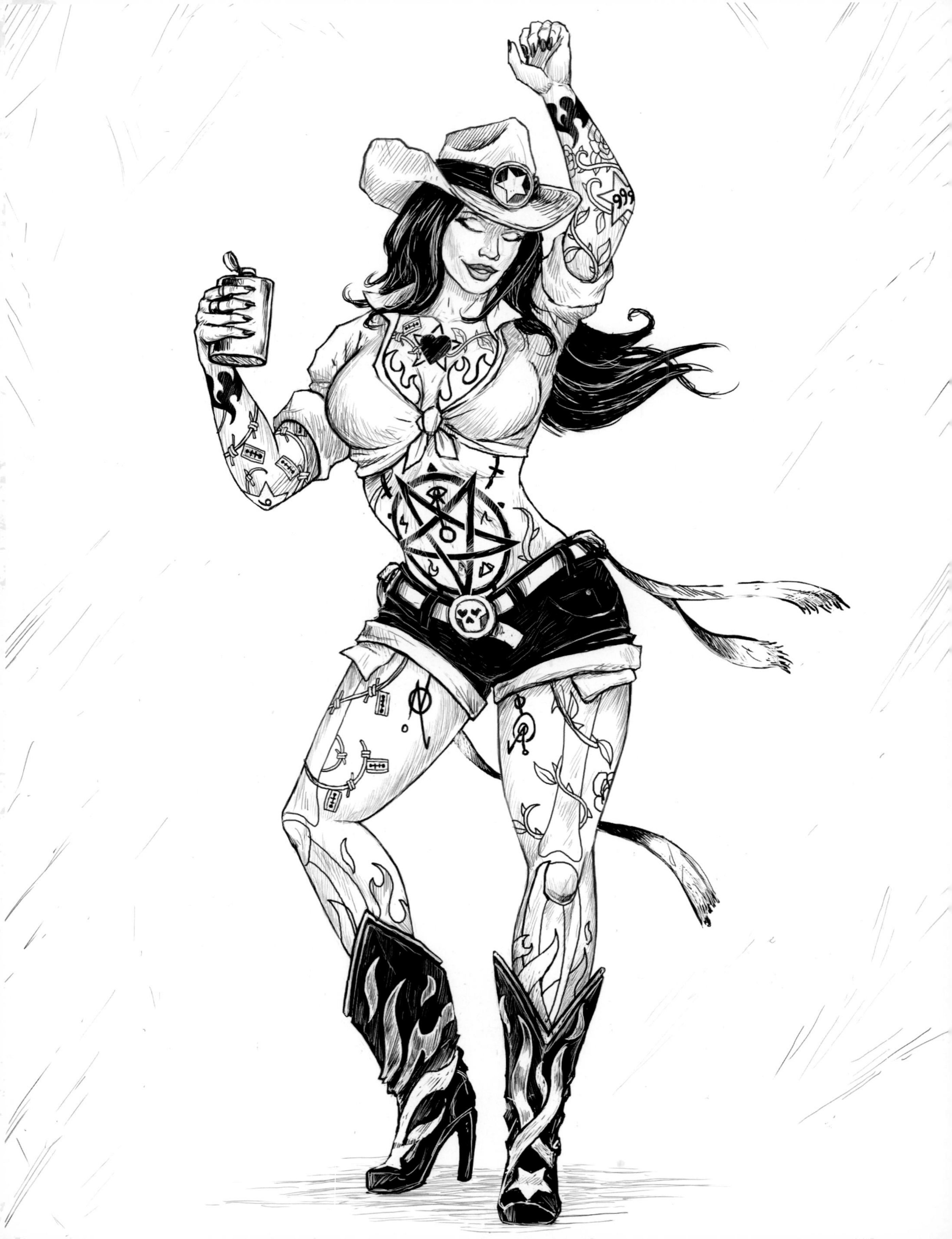

but it freezes in midair, makin' the little kids' eyes go wide and their hands fly to their mouths.

Ledger grabs the cane and hops over to the truck on his right, up onto the bumper and then the hood and then the cab and the trailer roof and he spins the walkin' stick . . .

"Yes, you will witness freaks of every description! You will behold wonders beyond your imagining!"

Then he tosses that spinnin' cane up into the air, and right on cue, the roustabout sittin' on the hood o' the opposite truck flicks on a big-ass flashlight that he uses to light it up while the crowd voices their wonderment that it ain't come back down yet.

As they're watchin', mesmerized, the Ramblin' Man says: "Most important of all, you will arrive at a crossroads this very evening, a momentous, unimaginable point of no return, before which your lives will have been as nothing and beyond which, as nothing they will be."

Some o' them carnies and freaks look to each other questioningly, not rightly sure what it is the Ringmaster's talkin' 'bout 'cause this ain't his typical ballyhoo. The crowd, they ain't payin' a lick o' attention to the words comin' outta the Ringmaster's mouth, so captivated are they by the still spinnin' cane.

"And now, ladies and gentlemen, boys and girls . . ." Ledger holds up his hand and lets the cane fall right into it, and his voice booms so loud it breaks the spectators outta their trance and causes the little ones to clap their hands over their ears as he bellows, "On with the show!"

✷✷✷✷✲✷✷✷✷

The tractor and trailer rattles west, bypassin' the scene o' the Confederale roadblock. Jo Jo don't notice all the dead bodies and good ol' boy trucks and the Confederale Broncos off the side o' the blacktop, no he don't see that 'cause he's too deep into the imaginin's o' days past—or one specific night, to be more accurate, a night when the Ringmaster was in one o' his deep meditations inside his trailer . . .

In his recollection, Jo Jo's sittin' 'round a bonfire with the other freaks, and Henna, she's been hittin' the hooch and she's dancin' in her skimpy outfit to the music o' drums bein' played by that kid with the lobster hands. Our man's mesmerized by the gyrations o' the beautiful Painted Lady, and every once in a while, her eyes flicker over to him and a smile tugs at her lips.

When the music's done, Henna grabs a flask from the pint-sized sword swallower and leaves the circle, but as she passes Jo Jo, she brushes a finger against his cheek. He turns to watch her go, and she looks over her shoulder, smilin' in a way that our hero understands is an invitation to follow.

And follow he does. Pretty soon him and Henna are seated in the back o' one o' the roustabout's trucks, watchin' the stars. Henna confides in Jo Jo the Ramblin' Man's talk 'bout makin' her a "vessel."

"He says a vessel's gotta be pure," she says, takin' a swig from the flask and then holdin' it up. "So this'll be our little secret." She turns her painted face to Jo Jo, kinda drinkin' him in the way she's drinkin' that hooch. "Right now I just want to forget all this shit. You wanna help with that? We can have some fun, you and me, and that can be our secret too," she says, and her eyes get to twinklin' just like them stars. Jo Jo, well he gets kinda lost in there, and before you know it, the two o'em are lockin' lips and gettin' real comfy in the back o' that truck.

Now you might think, "Hey that memory don't sound half bad!" Especially considerin' Jo Jo hadn't never been with a woman before. In the biblical sense, if you take my meanin'. Well that might be, and yeah that particular memory is one humdinger, but Jo Jo ain't smilin' as he recalls 'cause he knows, see . . . he knows what comes *after*.

✱✱✱✱✿✱✱✱✱

"Stupid!" Huxley blurts, his hands shakin' against the wheel o' the hearse. "I'm so stupid. Screwed it up, just like everythin' else. All I had to do was keep him in my sights, follow him to the blood, but no. . . . How many times I gotta fail 'fore I get one thing right? One goddamn thing!"

"Hey, jeez, stop beatin' yourself up," Elsa says, Patch sittin' in her lap. The vehicle's approachin' the site o' Sheriff Foxx's demise, and in fact as they get closer and Elsa peeks out the window, there's just enough light left that she can see the good sheriff layin' by the side o' the road, his head all bent in an unnatural fashion. A little ways down from him is Deputy Scarecrow Jimmy, the top o' his head missin', rifle still clutched in his hands. Course there's a whole lot more bodies and all the trucks parked just offa the blacktop, and Elsa, she's wonderin' just what on God's green Earth happened out here, but Huxley don't seem to notice as he keeps on jaw jackin'.

"You don't understand. I need this. Can't screw it up. My whole life, I's a failure. Back in the day, 'fore the Wall went up, this weird dude with messed up teeth bit me and I died. I thought things'd be different . . ."

"Did you say you died?" Elsa asks, slightly delayed in realizin' what Huxley just said.

"Yeah and then I came back, good as new, and the man said I could be like him, I could live forever, all I had to do was drink blood sometimes. I didn't wanna at first but my body *needed* it, like it ain't never needed nothin' before. Right around that time the Wall went up. Shit went crazy everywhere. Martial law. Everything shuttin' down, people like me losin' my damn job and gettin' railroaded outta the city . . . drugs all over the place. I had to drink but it wasn't like I had a lotta options. Had to drink offa damn bums! Caught some kinda blood-deficiency disease. Got so sick my damn teeth fell out!"

148

Huxley turns on the headlights as they leave the abandoned vehicles and the carnage behind, and Elsa's givin' her full attention as Huxley keeps on goin'. "I got all skinny, started wastin' away. Been like that near as long as I can remember. Can't die. I drink blood it gives me a little boost, but when it's gone I'm back to bein' weak and slow."

Elsa at first don't like that Huxley lied to her and Jo Jo, but she also understands what it's like to be so ashamed o' somethin' that you'd do just 'bout anything to keep it hid.

"You asked about the coffin," Huxley says, pokin' a shaky thumb toward the back. "Reason I sleep in it is 'cause I just want it to be over, you know? I sleep in a coffin 'cause I wish I'd stayed dead."

✶✶✶✶✻✶✶✶✶

Doc Hart's tractor don't even have its lights on as it barrels down the now moonlit Anaconda. In the cab, the imperative to find Her continues to propel our man onward, even as the sorcerous memory parade carries on in bits and pieces . . .

Takin' him back to the day after him and Henna played hide the popsicle. Jo Jo's tryin' to find her 'cause he's got somethin' important to say. He looks and looks but he can't find her nowhere, 'til that night, as the roustabouts are strikin' tents, he sees her on the back lot. All excited-like he runs over and he says, "Hey I've been looking everywhere for you. I've been thinking, we should run away. Just go as far as we can. I tried a long time ago but then I kind of gave up on the whole idea, but then I met you and . . . well you make me feel like I can do anything." Henna eyeballs our man and she lights up a cigarette and blows the smoke out and says, "Look, don't make a big deal outta what happened, okay? You and me . . . that was the booze, okay honey? I got a pretty good thing goin' here so don't mess it up for me." Without waitin' for an answer she heads off toward the Ramblin' Man's trailer, and Jo Jo realizes that the reason he couldn't find her all day was 'cause she didn't *wanna* be found. Least not by him.

After that, Henna don't show up at the freak fires to dance no more. Jo Jo takes a bit o' comfort in the fact that he plowed the same field as the Ringmaster, and in fact one day he sees Ledger spit and he thinks to himself, *Must be some hair of the dog.* The next time he does see Henna, she's got new runes on her body, and a few months after that, her belly starts gettin' big, and the Ramblin' Man, well even he seems to be in a good mood. As more time moves on, Henna gets to where she's so big she don't even come outta Ledger's trailer no more . . .

Meanwhile the tractor's at the outskirts o' Dead End now, passin' by cow pastures and corrals and over the train tracks and closin' within view o' the town's low, squat huts and monstrous meat smokers and ol' brick slaughterhouses. In fact, if Jo Jo was altogether *present,* he'd be hearin' the sounds o' the bolt pistols against the cows' skulls; but the only sound fillin' our man's ears right now is the memory-wailin' o' Henna comin' from the Ramblin' Man's trailer as the Painted Lady gives birth . . .

Jo Jo stands outside, anxious, waitin' along with all the other carnies for the Ringmaster to emerge. Time goes by 'til eventually a cryin' noise issues from inside, and when the Ramblin' Man finally does make an appearance, his eyes are burnin' hellfire. He sights our hero and stalks right up, flingin' out his cane, which flies, upright, to a spot just a few inches to the right o' Jo Jo's face. Our man looks over and because he does, he don't see the fist that crashes into the side o' his head and knocks him flat.

The shadow o' Ledger DeMesne falls over Jo Jo, and that silver-tipped cane comes outta nowhere, strikin' him upside the head, knockin' him senseless. "Pray as you might," Ledger says, and that cane wallops him again, this time from the other side. "Your death will not be quick. Your suffering . . ." *Bam!* That cane hits him again. ". . . will seem interminable."

There's a brief respite then as the Ramblin' Man shouts, "Bring them out!"

Jo Jo tilts his head and blinks blood outta his eyes. A couple roustabouts go into the trailer. One o'em comes out with the Painted Lady, who's hunched over, coverin' herself with a ratty robe, and the other carries a little sheet-wrapped bundle, hollerin' for all its worth.

The one fella hauls Henna down from the trailer steps. The other brings the baby, still covered up. The rest o' the carnies get closer, formin' a circle 'round the spectacle that's surely 'bout to unfold.

"It was him!" Henna yells, pointin' at our man, who's still got his ass parked in the dirt. The woman Jo Jo had thought was the most beautiful creature on Earth, well let's just say that there's an insane rage that's got them pretty features all twisted up and our poor hero he's seein' her now for the ugly piece o' work she really is as she goes on: "He forced me! Raped me! I was too afraid to say!"

The circle cinches in. Ledger steps up 'til he's standin' uncomfortably close to the Painted Lady, and he says, "Is that so? It wasn't your intention, then, to defy my wishes?"

Henna, she's started tremblin' at this point, her mouth quiverin' as she responds, "No! Of course not, I would never—"

The Ringmaster reaches out and grabs her lower lip 'tween his left thumb and finger. "These lips . . . are quite accomplished at hiding the truth."

He lets go and gets even nearer, stickin' his cold-as-death unflinchin' eyes right up to hers as he says, "But your soul is not."

She don't see the cane come crashin' down, she just crumples under the weight o' it. Next thing she knows, it's in his hand and he lashes out, again and again, and this time the Ramblin' Man don't stop; he gets down on his knees and he grits his teeth and anything about him that mighta ever seemed sane simply disappears as he rains down blow after vicious blow 'til the Painted Lady is fully painted in her own blood.

Ledger stops to catch his breath and compose himself just a bit, then turns his attention to Jo Jo . . .

'Cept Jo Jo ain't there.

Ledger stands. The carnies widen the circle and the Ramblin' Man spots the roustabout who'd been holdin' the baby, layin' flat on his back, out cold.

And that hellfire flares once again in the Ramblin' Man's eyes when he sees that the baby's gone too.

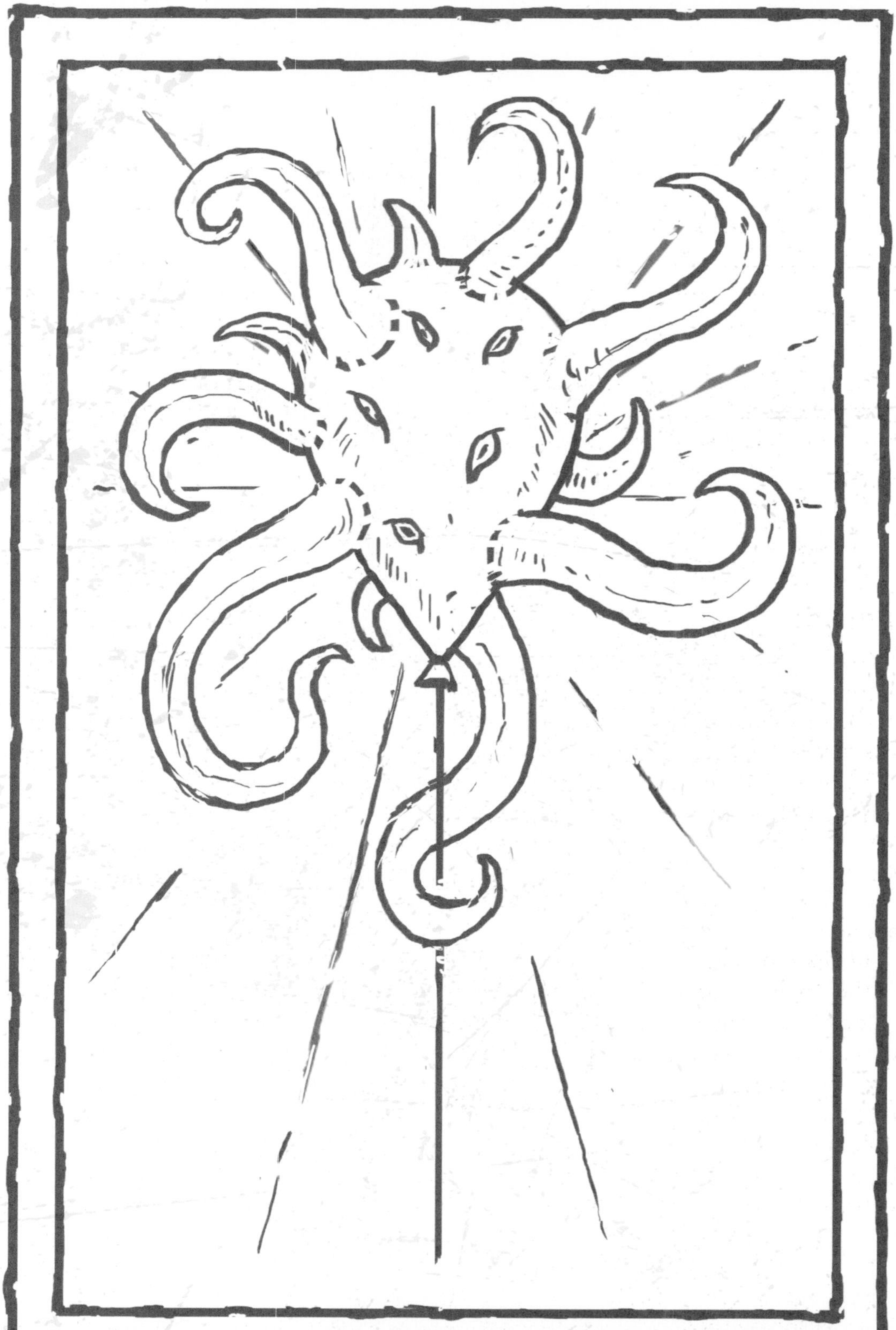

THE BOSS

CHAPTER THE TWENTY-SIXTH

Back in real time, broken feathers are beatin' against the night air. Spastic wings barely keep the blackbird airborne, and sometimes it damn near rolls to an upside-down position, even though the head remains in the same orientation, starin' down at the tractor and trailer that's steadily passin' through town, just a few miles east o' the carnival, which is in full swing.

The Ramblin' Man, takin' a quick peek through the blackbird's eyes, he's surprised that even in the midst o' the assault bein' levied against him by the Magi twins, Jo Jo's still givin' chase. And for that very reason, the Ringmaster is once again entertainin' the idea that Jo Jo might have that spark inside o' him that Ledger should o' recognized the first time he laid eyes on the ragamuffin all those years ago.

But them thoughts are too little too late, and right now all that matters is makin' sure the stage is set for the arrival o' the Boss.

Not wantin' any chance o' delays, the Ringmaster informs Terra Mungus—standin' in the center o' the boxin' ring, thumpin' on his championship belt as a barely breathin' local gets hauled out—to make sure Jo Jo don't make it past the entrance.

He hurries on then, bendin' his steps down the midway as the full moon slips behind some thin clouds. He casts his gaze to either side, movin' with purpose, bathed in the neon lights o' the fun house, eyeballin' the carousel and Ferris wheel and the rides on either side and the rollercoaster that circumnavigates the whole shebang, listenin' to the kids' cheerful screams. He hears the barkers announce that the rides are free for the next ten minutes only and he hurries on . . .

He passes by the main tent, heads beyond the animal cages in the back lot, and comes finally to the trailer full o' them special balloons, the final batch o' which he collected this very night. Sittin' in the drivin' seat o' the truck attached to that trailer is Terra Mungus's corner man, the chimp in the newsboy hat. The worthless animal is currently dozin' and it takes a hard rap on the hood o' the truck to wake the simian up. The ape shakes his head and, in response to Ledger's angry glare, offers a yellow-toothed smile and an overly enthusiastic thumbs-up.

The Ramblin' Man bustles to a spot just in front o' that gapin' hole in the giant wall overlookin' Ohelno Arroyo, and he motions for a nearby roustabout to come over. "Bring Her," he says. The fat man nods and waddles off and the Ringmaster takes a long, deep breath o' the night air, pushin' his mind past the numbness that's begun spreadin' from his chest down through his limbs. He unhands his cane, lettin' it float off to one side as he starts speakin' in that tongue that was ancient before ancient was even a word. Pretty quick-like he rises up, levitatin' just a bit offa the ground, hands extended, while behind him, the screams o' joy on them rides and on the rollercoaster . . .

. . . turn to screams o' terror.

The coaster's movin' faster and faster. Jagged streaks o' lightnin' arc over the cars as the kids and adults cry their lungs out. There's a hum o' electricity in the air and the ground's vibratin' like it's 'bout to tear loose. If we could slow down that coaster, we could take a peek at them riders and see that they've started gettin' a bit *thinner* and kinda grayish, as their mojo or life force or whatever the hell you wanna call it is slowly gettin' sucked right out o'em. The same thing, in fact, is happenin' all over—the Ferris wheel's spinnin' like a pinwheel in a strong wind, the horses on the carousel are gallopin' at a heart-attack pace, and the Tiltin' Whirl and the Jawdropper and the Racin' Rockets are all movin' at breakneck speed, enveloped in that lightnin' current, 'cause them rides, see, they're all pieces that make up a kinda machine, powered by the life they drain, and created with just one purpose: to open a gateway to the Boss's world.

★★★★✹★★★★

The tractor barrels through the carnival entrance while, behind the wheel, Jo Jo's still caught up in the past, relivin' the aftermath o' him takin' that baby—five years o' layin' low, sleepin' in fleabag motels, doin' odd jobs to pay for skimpy meals, and then, then . . .

The memories fade just a bit, and Jo Jo kinda comes to his senses, realizin' where he is—*I made it, made it to Dead End*—but not before his vehicle plows into the ring toss stand.

At that same exact moment, inside the Magi twins' trailer, Bo breaks concentration long enough to hiss at Tweeny: "You're hesitatin' again! Holdin' back!"

"But he was always so nice to us," Tweeny replies.

"I knew it," Bo blurts. "You're soft on him! That's why you couldn't finish the job last time. Oversensitive oaf, you'll get us both killed."

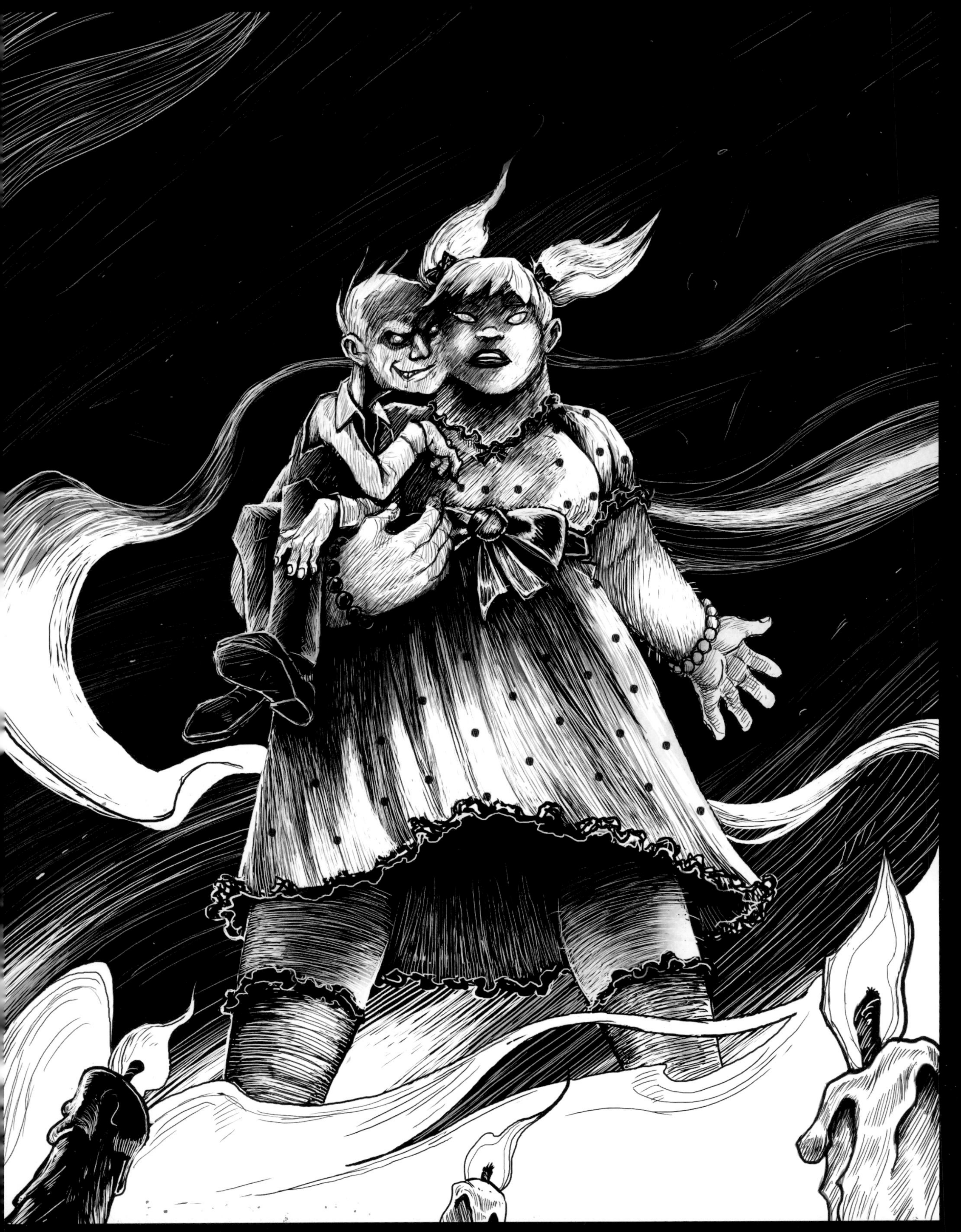

And ol' Bo, well he's hit on the truth here, folks. Fact is, Tweeny's had herself a kind o' crush on Jo Jo for quite a long spell, and it did in fact dissuade her from usin' her sorcerous ways to make that kid in Devil's Tailbone pull the trigger.

But let's not get too caught up in that just now. The pertinent information is that their hold on Jo Jo's done slipped enough that our man regains his wits. Inside the tractor, he hears a hummin' noise and the cracklin' o' electricity. Up to his left beyond the ruined stand, he sees the support structure for the rollercoaster. Terrified wailin' fills the air as the coaster shoots by, nothin' more'n a blur. Jo Jo catches movement in his peripheral and looks to see some rough-and-tumble roustabouts closin' in on him, but before they reach the rig, the big fellas stop and take a few steps back.

It's right 'bout then that two big-ass gorilla feet crash down and pulverize the tractor's hood.

✶✶✶✶❋✶✶✶✶

If we was to look real close at the Ramblin' Man's eyes—which o' course I don't advise—we'd see little arcs o' electricity there, seein' as how the powers bein' drawn by the coaster and the rides are bein' channeled through him.

There's a hole openin' up several feet in front o' the levitatin' Ringmaster, not far above the gap in the Wall. It's small at first, like somebody's pokin' an invisible finger into our reality, but then it gets bigger and bigger, like that same invisible someone's rippin' away the wrappin' on a Christmas present, 'til pretty soon the whole thing's 'bout the size o' a movie theater screen, and that gateway offers up a glimpse into a whole other world: a land you might call Ultima Thule, meanin' outside o' the world as we know it. This other world is made up o' varyin' shades o' gray and lookin' into it is like watchin' a movie on an old black-and-white TV. In that other world, it ain't really daytime or nighttime, it's kinda like what's called the gloamin', in between when the sun's gone down and the sky goes full black. There's what looks like a road laid out in front o' us, stretchin' off into the distance. It's made up o' white objects, maybe bones, it's hard to tell. And far off on the horizon, if we squint, we can spot a figure, movin' real slow, but definitely gettin' closer, and gettin' bigger. A dark figure, but one we can't keep our eyes on for very long without goin' absolutely stark-ravin' nuts. 'Cause that figure . . .

That there's the Boss.

CHAPTER THE TWENTY-SEVENTH

Terra Mungus stands on the demolished tractor hood, thumps his chest, and lets out a thunderous roar. He punches through the windshield like it's paper and rips the roof o' the cab clean off, then reaches down to yank Jo Jo outta the seat. But he stops, gettin' a quizzical look on his primate face, realizin' the seat's empty.

Jo Jo, see, he opened up the passenger door and rolled out while Terra Mungus was busy destroyin' the windshield. And once he was out, he did somethin' else, too: He slipped off the remainin' silver rings from his fingers and dropped 'em to the ground.

Gotta get to Her. Can't fail. Gotta save Her!

Though it ain't what you would call strikin', there is a sudden difference in our man's appearance. He looks a tad bigger—and not just 'cause the electricity in the air's got his hairs standin' up. He looks meaner too. His teeth are just a smidge pointier, he's more hunched, and there's a particularly feral, predatory gleam in his eye. Yessir, Jo Jo's gone into what you might call "beast mode," and the beast Jo Jo, well, the beast Jo Jo ain't afraid o' Terra Mungus the same way the other Jo Jo is. So with a roar o' his own, our new man lashes out and grabs hold o' the ape's meaty ankle and yanks the baffled brute's feet out from under him, sweepin' him all the way down to the dirt.

Terra Mungus recovers right quick, gettin' his bearin's and unloadin' a vicious uppercut that sends Jo Jo flyin' 'cross the midway into a cotton candy booth.

Jo Jo wastes no time rushin' back into the fight as the ape charges. The two juggernauts crash together like planets collidin', and though Jo Jo's lighter than his foe, he don't give an inch o' ground. They tussle and pummel as the roustabouts draw close and watch, ready to pounce on our man should he get the upper hand.

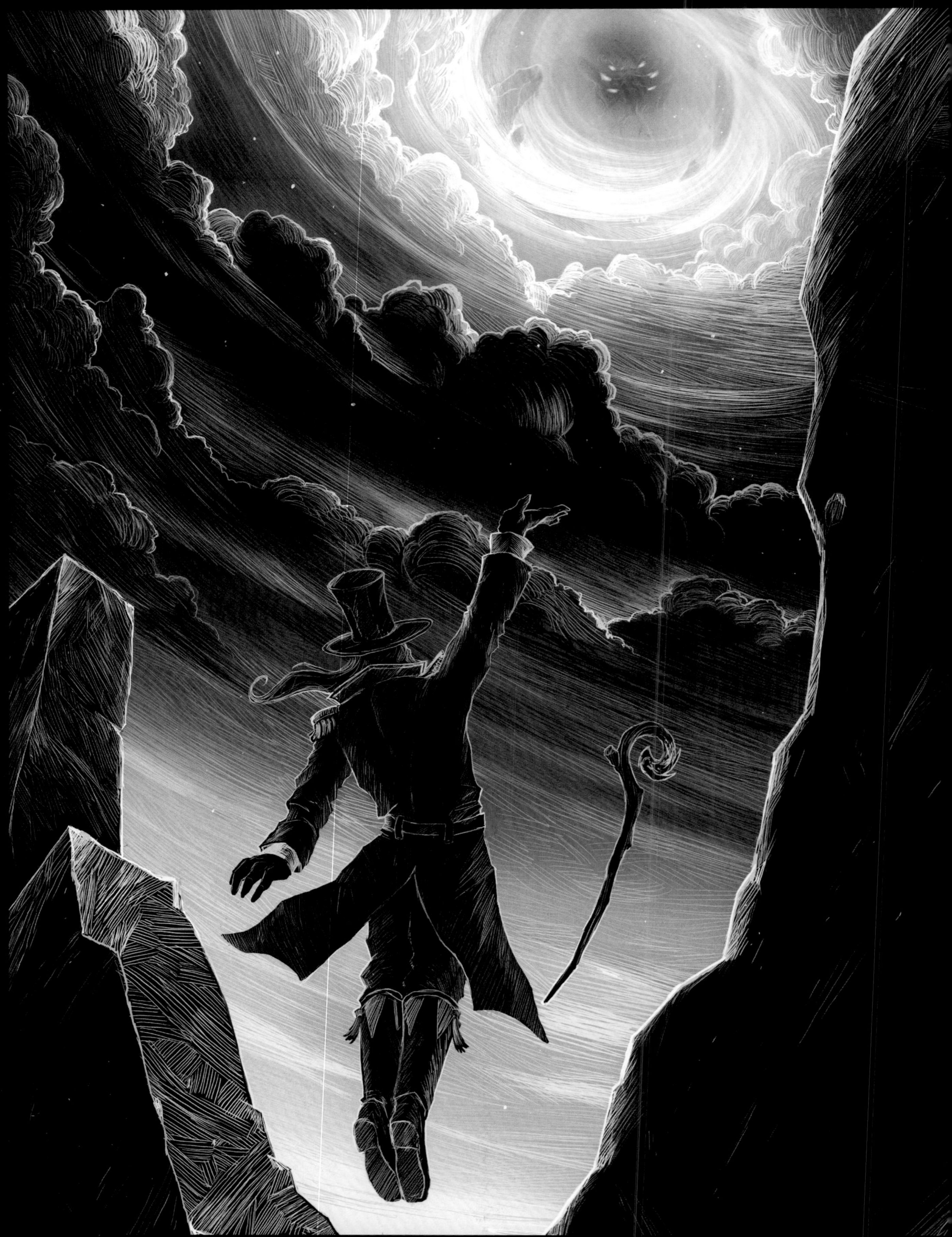

The sudden appearance o' headlights causes the roustabouts to turn 'round, as a black vehicle plows into the few who were still gathered closest to the entrance. The car hops and jumps with a whole lotta boom-chicka-boom music comin' from inside, generally causin' a shitload o' confusion amongst the carnies. Jo Jo and Terra Mungus, however, ain't payin' no mind.

Jo Jo works his way 'round to Terra Mungus's back and executes a suplex that dumps the ape onto his head. This has the not-at-all-surprisin' effect o' sendin' Terra Mungus into a blind rage. The rabid animal drops a hammer fist onto our man's skull, grips him by the neck, and flings him down the midway, then chases after, snatchin' up the mallet from the strongman game and barrelin' down, smashin' Jo Jo's left knee. Our man crumples as Terra Mungus hefts the hammer in a two-handed grip, ready to cave in Jo Jo's melon.

At this same instant, Elsa and Huxley exit the hearse. Elsa's got Patch strapped on kinda like a backpack and she's blastin' away with a shotgun in one hand and a revolver in the other, mowin' down the nearest Barnstormers. In between shots, she takes special note o' the coaster as it goes rocketin' past, her ears pickin' up the hoarse, raspy screams o' the terrified townies. She's realizin' that somethin' seems awful wrong but *not* knowin' that with every clock tick more and more o' the riders' life force is gettin' sucked away.

Huxley, movin' a fair bit slower, gets up next to Elsa and holds up Frankie's blade. The roustabouts have spread out now, but to their credit, they ain't turned tail. In fact, a couple o'em are lookin' at each other as if they know somethin's comin'. "Aight, remember," Huxley says as Elsa tosses the now-empty shotgun to the ground, "We cold as ice. Ice, baby. Too legit to quit." And he's eyeballin' the trailer as he says this, thinkin' back to what Elsa said 'bout it havin' them barrels o' blood. He grins, rotatin' the razor in his hand. "Let's work. Time to get me some bl—" Huxley's takin' a step as he says this but he gets cut off midsentence as a roarin' tiger leaps outta nowhere, latchin' onto the back o' his neck, rollin' in the dirt and then draggin' him off behind the demolished ring toss stand.

Elsa hears a chuckle and looks over to see Ledger's animal wrangler, a pudgy Texican fella with a thick black mustache, lookin' mighty pleased with himself. Him and the other carnies move in for the kill but immediately regret that decision, as Elsa empties the last bullets in her revolver then reaches back and pulls one o' Father's surgical knives from its hidin' place in Patch. She sets 'bout slicin' throats, includin' that o' the mirthful Texican animal wrangler, who finds nothin' more to laugh about as he dies chokin' on his own blood.

Just as our girl turns to go lend Huxley a hand, she hears a chorus o' noises, like a buncha folks playin' maracas. She sees a gal standin' in front o' her, patchy skin lit up by the surroundin' neon. The weird-lookin' woman's holdin' somethin' to her lips and whisperin'. As Elsa wonders what fresh new shit sandwich this is, she hears slitherin' sounds all 'round, accompanied by more o' that chatterin' noise. A quick look reveals the source o' the ruckus: a whole mess o' fat rattlesnakes, mouths open, fangs bared, coiled and ready to strike.

✱✱✱✱✤✱✱✱✱

We can make out enough o' the Boss now to take note o' things that look like tentacles or tendrils or the like, wavin' and rollin' offa the thing's blob-like body. And though it's still too far away to make out any real details, the unidentifiable mass is most definitely gettin' closer.

Havin' succeeded in creatin' the gateway, the Ramblin' Man settles back to the ground, placin' a palm to his heart, bendin' over slightly at the waist, feelin' drained but rallyin' nonetheless, knowin' his moment is soon at hand.

Presently, he acknowledges the approach o' the fat roustabout he sent to get Her. 'Cept She ain't alongside him like She's supposed to be.

The roustabout's chubby jowls are quiverin' a bit, and despite the lack o' any real heat, he's sweatin' like a whore in church.

"What happened?" Ledger hisses, keepin' one wary eye on the doorway and the inexorably approachin' Boss. "Have you not found Her?"

"She—she kicked me in the dangly bits and ran off!" the fat man confesses.

The Ramblin' Man feels his heart clench. 'Cause She is, after all, the key. The key to his liberation, to settlin' the debt once and for all.

A whole lot o' work and research and expertise went into decoratin' Henna with symbols that would imbue her with the necessary arcane energies to pass into the baby, energies that would in turn infuse the child's life force with enough potency to make a suitable offerin' to the Boss . . . a spark powerful enough to put paid to Ledger's account, for all and for good. Yessir a lot o' careful plannin' done went into this tribute, but Ledger's dreams o' bein' well and truly free are sure as shit doomed to failure if he can't produce Her.

The fat roustabout, well he must see somethin' murderous in Ledger's eyes, 'cause he *does* turn tail and run. And the Ringmaster, well he's got enough gas left in the tank to flick his wrist, sendin' his cane like an arrow straight through the base o' tubby's neck and out his mouth, ejectin' a handful o' teeth in the process.

Ledger then casts his fiery gaze at the few other carnies gathered 'round and roars, "Find Her!"

Them roustabouts scatter like cockroaches under a flashlight, leavin' the Ringmaster starin' at the Boss's steady approach, graspin' his chest while the surroundin' silence is broken only by the carnival sounds in the background: the calliope, all but drowned out by the barrelin' o' the coaster on its tracks and the whooshin' o' the Ferris wheel and the whirrin' o' the carousel and other rides . . . and the desperate but fadin' wails o' the doomed passengers.

CHAPTER THE TWENTY-EIGHTH

The fact that Bo and Tweeny are still arguin' in their trailer allows our hero to stay focused on the only objective that matters: Stay alive so he can rescue Her.

Just as that big-ass mallet comes crashin' down, Jo Jo rolls outta the way. Now the force o' the hammer's impact done broke the head of the mallet off, so Jo Jo, kneelin' on his good leg, reaches out to the busted end o' the shaft, then strikes out with his other hand—right where the ape has ahold o' it—bustin' that piece o' wood away and givin' our man a jagged stick, which he shoves up into the meat o' the ragin' gorilla's right bicep.

Terra Mungus roars. Jo Jo yanks the stake out, pops up, hobbles 'round, and buries it as far as it'll go into the ape's ribs. While the primate tosses the stump o' wood that was left in his hand, Jo Jo gets his arms up under his foe's pits, lockin' in a full nelson and preventin' the gorilla from removin' the stake.

With a ball-shrivelin' bellow, Terra Mungus turns and bolts, smashin' through the entrance o' the fun house with Jo Jo still attached. They bounce off a wall or two and end up in the now aptly named Barrel o' Monkeys, a large, horizontal rotatin' cylinder that tosses 'em 'round and round like they're in a washin' machine. This also has the effect o' dislodgin' some o' the carnival-goers who was inside the ride. When them folks get forced out from the . . . we'll say "influence" o' the ride, there's a kinda zappin' sound and a crisscross o' electrical energy, and if we was to take a quick peek at the gateway out by the Wall, why we'd see just the slightest *flicker* in it. And Ledger, standin' there with little currents o' electricity in his own eyes, well he feels it too.

Anyway, back to the business at hand: Jo Jo and Terra Mungus tumble out the other side o' the Barrel o' Monkeys and onto the Tip Tripper, a floor trick that moves up and down and side to side. All the jostlin' and jarrin' is enough to loosen Jo Jo's grip, so when the dizzy ape at last stumbles outta the fun house, he manages to reach back and toss our man into the boxin' ring.

Spins or no spins, Terra Mungus is determined to finish Jo Jo once and for all. He yanks out the mallet handle and tosses it, then climbs into the ring and scoops Jo Jo up in a bear hug—or I suppose it'd be an ape hug, but let's not get too technical. Point is, he aims to break our hero's back. And he's damn close to doin' just that when Jo Jo smashes the beast's ears, thumbs his eyes, and follows up with a head butt that makes the gorilla let go and shuffle back. Jo Jo grabs at the championship belt, rips it free, and cracks his enemy over the head with it. The ape grabs hold o' the belt and the two play tug o' war with it for a tick 'til finally it tears right down the middle. Both o'em discard the pieces, and Terra Mungus cuts loose a bellow that'd straighten your short and curlies, as he goes for a one-handed choke . . . but before he can lock onto Jo Jo's neck, our man grabs two o' them beefy fingers in one hand, and two in the other, holdin' all four o'em like a couple o' joysticks. He then pries them fingers away from each other, snappin' the ape's hand like a wishbone.

For the first time, we hear Terra Mungus wail out in true pain as Jo Jo gets to the beast's back once more, this time securin' a rear naked choke and droppin' both o'em to the crimson-coated canvas.

The ape thrashes and kicks and bats at our man, but his retaliations get slower and slower, 'til, knowin' he's 'bout to pass out, Terra Mungus does the one thing he ain't never done in his entire life.

He taps out.

Jo Jo lets go o' the hold and rolls out under the ropes and onto the ground, exhausted. Despite his victory, despite barely bein' able to move, our man still has only one thing on his mind.

Gotta get to Her.

He gets to his feet and limp-runs as fast as he can toward the back lot, leavin' Terra Mungus behind, sittin' and sulkin' in center ring, a bloodied, defeated, and altogether demoralized former catch-rasslin' champ.

✯✯✯✯✤✯✯✯✯

What about Huxley, you ask? Well right 'bout now the frisky feline's havin' a field day swattin' the skinny fella, pickin' him up in its teeth, tossin' him a few feet away, then leapin' onto him and startin' the whole routine all over again. Somewhere in the process o' cat and mouse, Huxley done got Frankie's blade knocked outta his hand, and though he's tried a few times to bite the cat, he just ends up with a mouthful o' fur.

Back over by the tractor and trailer, Elsa's fairin' a smidge better, for now at least: Them rattlers, see, they're pumpin' all kinds o' venom into our girl but it don't have no effect. In fact, the serum in Elsa's body acts like a kind o' venom on the snakes! That's right, half them reptiles have detached themselves and gotten the

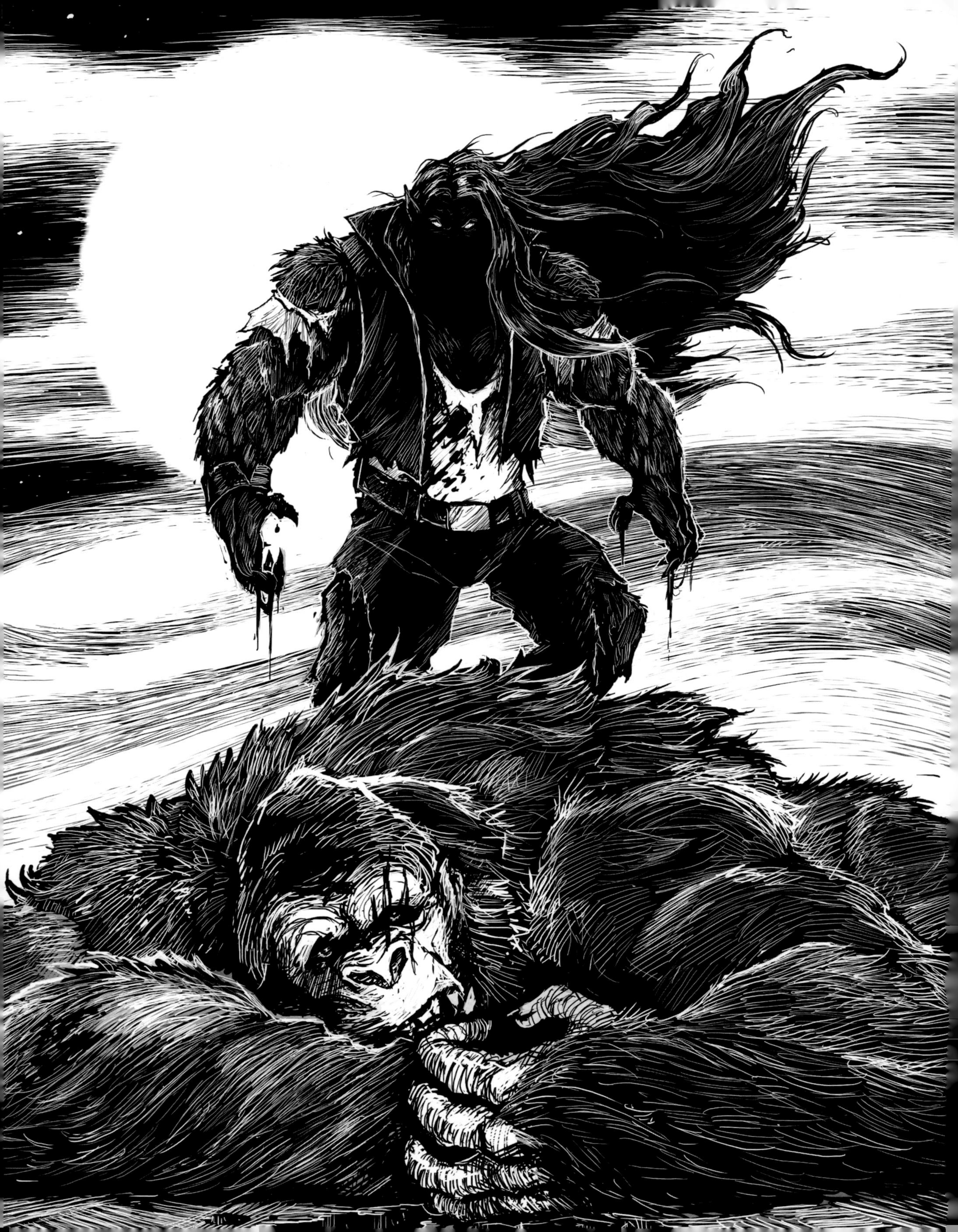

hell outta Dodge, and most o' the others have died while still bitin', so some o'em's still latched onto her body as she faces Diamond.

The coaster shoots by as Elsa goes on the attack, swipin' with that blade o' hers and openin' up a couple cuts on Diamond's arm. But the snake lady manages to lash out and grab hold o' Elsa's wrist, twistin' and wrenchin' our girl's arm off with a pop! Somewhat surprised to be holdin' a limb, the snake lady nevertheless has the presence o' mind to begin slashin' and clobberin' at Elsa with our girl's own arm.

★★★★✤★★★★

Bo and Tweeny are still bickerin' in their trailer when the whole contraption gets to movin'. The twins look around, kinda dumbfounded, 'til realization hits Bo. "Oh sh—" he starts but don't get to finish before the back door o' the trailer gets ripped off its hinges.

The twins catch a quick flash o' the Ramblin' Man's blazin' eyes before he yanks the two o'em out into the dirt, draggin' 'em up to the gateway. "Look," he says.

Tweeny and Bo obey, seein' that the unthinkable monstrosity is now close enough to make out what might be mouths, lined with needle-sharp teeth. There ain't much road left between that thing and our world. In fact, those tentacles look like they could reach through at just about any instant if they stretched just a smidge more.

"Years ago I spared your light, when I could just as easily have extinguished it. Continue to fail, and I'll not be the only one you answer to," Ledger warns. And Bo and Tweeny, they stare just a smidge too long at the Boss and somethin' inside their brains starts to stretch like a rubber band that's damn near ready to snap. They both shut their eyes tight and Tweeny yells, "Okay! Okay! Okay!"

And just now, back toward the carnival, our man Jo Jo stumbles into sight.

"Ledger DeMesne!" Jo Jo thunders. And although his leg has started to heal itself already, he still has a noticeable limp as he stalks forward, clothes covered in Terra Mungus's blood.

"I've come for Her!" Jo Jo declares.

The Ringmaster smiles. Jo Jo sees the massive thing drawing closer in the portal behind him. Now Jo Jo, though he heard whispers 'bout it in years past, he ain't never laid eyes on the Boss 'til now. Be that as it may, our man knows better than to let his gaze linger on it for more than a tick.

The Ramblin' Man responds, "What does it matter?" just as Jo Jo feels a pain in his head, sharp enough to drive him to his knees.

"You couldn't save Her before," Ledger continues, as our man clutches at his skull.

"And you won't save Her now."

Now you might be wonderin' 'bout Bo and Tweeny's trailer, and them sigils, and thinkin' that the symbols are necessary in order for the Magi twins to wield their arcane magic. Well that holds true when the magic's bein' cast over long distances.

But with Jo Jo in close proximity, them sigils ain't needed. Anyway if you're done nitpickin', we can get back to the action, 'cause at this particular moment Jo Jo's heart feels like it's 'bout to split in two.

Tweeny sheds a tear and then closes her eyes, and the Magi twins force our man to relive the single most painful recollection o' all . . .

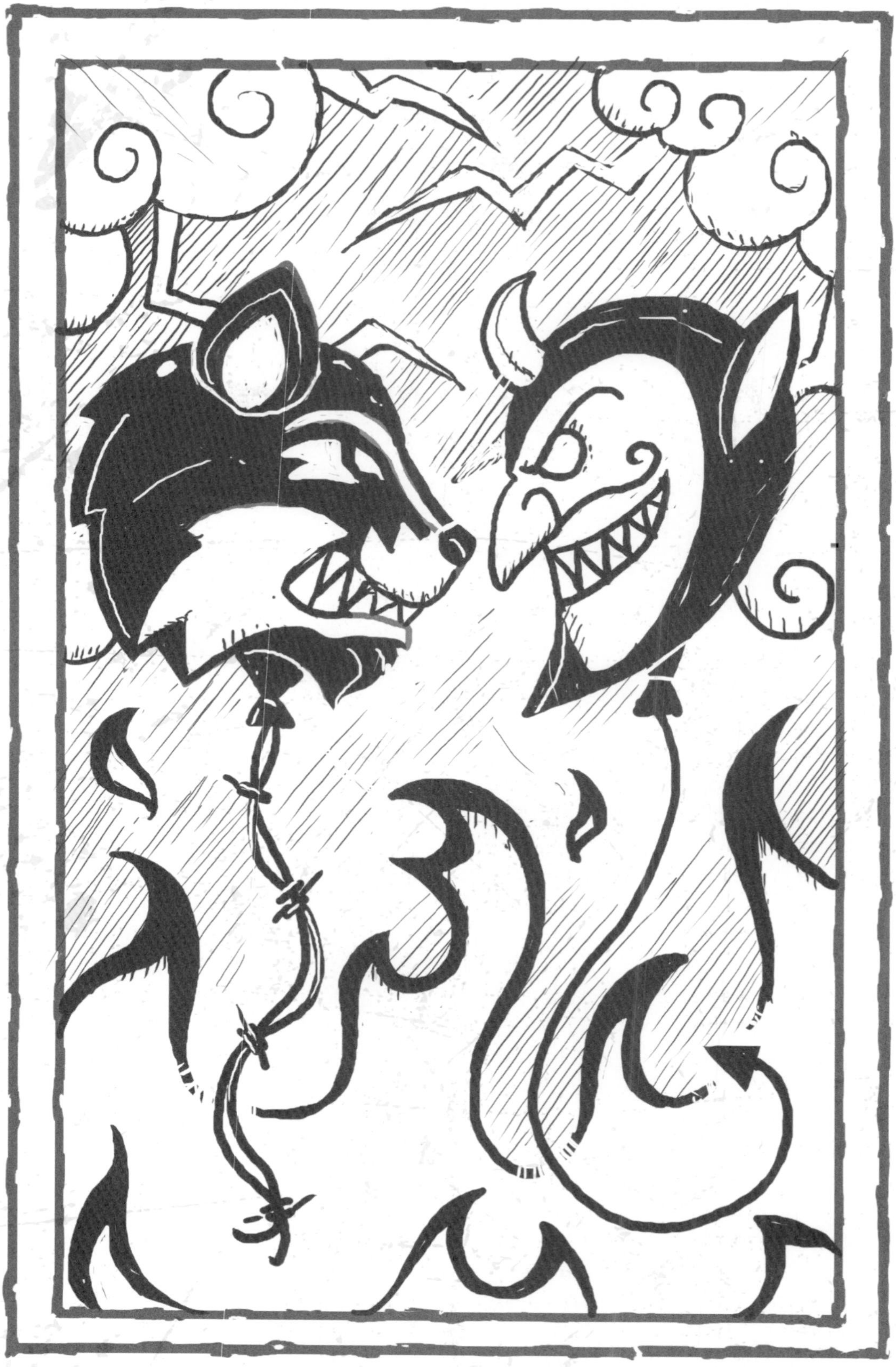

THE CONFRONTATION

CHAPTER THE TWENTY-NINTH

Bo and Tweeny's yackle-dackle takes Jo Jo back to where they had left off.

Five years o' layin' low, sleepin' in fleabag motels, doin' odd jobs to pay for skimpy meals, and then, then . . .

He had finally given in and taken her to an arcade. They couldn't afford to play no games, but he hoped maybe they'd find some quarters left inside the machines or maybe some that rolled underneath. He had just wanted her to have the chance to play one game, maybe two.

It's more crowded inside than Jo Jo thought it'd be. She's so excited she goes runnin' off and he loses sight o' Her for just a tick and when he looks up and realizes that it's a balloon she's chasin' after, well that's when his heart shrivels up inside his chest.

He runs this way and that, feelin' like the arcade all of a sudden got a hundred times bigger, that there's no way he'll ever find Her. Then he spots a tiny figure darting through the crowd and he shoves folks aside to get to Her, but when he finally reaches the tyke . . . it ain't his little girl. He's double-scared now, knowin' he's looked everywhere, breathin' heavy, weak in the knees, and that's when he notices the front door o' the place swingin' closed.

His deepest fears are confirmed as he runs outside and sees the Ramblin' Man in the parkin' lot, standin' there with the Magi twins and a couple o' them creepy-ass clowns, their shadows long in the settin' sun.

Ledger DeMesne has one hand on the back o' Her neck, the cane held high in the other. She's screamin' and cryin' but Ledger tells her that everything's gonna be okay.

"Don't resist," he says. And then with a nod to the other clowns and roustabouts emergin' from behind parked trucks: "Take him."

And now the memory train skips to another track: Jo Jo's on the bridge. He's been gettin' beat on and spit on and pissed on and shit on by the carnies, until he can't hardly see or breathe no more, but now it's the Ramblin' Man's turn to whoop on him. Jo Jo fights back at first and he even manages to draw blood, but it ain't no use. Ledger DeMesne soon gains the upper hand and rains down blow after blow with his cane, its silver tip gleamin' in the truck headlights . . .

"You want to know where She is?" Ledger's voice says, but it sounds like it's comin' from far away—reason bein', that voice is travelin' across the Magi twins' mind whammy. Yessir, the very same thing—this new thing—he's sayin' in Jo Jo's memory, is bein' said by the Ringmaster right there in front o' the gray gateway.

"She's dead and gone!"

Now it ain't the pain or the beatin' that sends Jo Jo to the edge o' the abyss: It's the very thought that they've taken Her, that he failed Her . . . and the feelin' that if anything happened to Her, well, there just ain't no use in goin' on.

The Ringmaster continues bludgeonin' Jo Jo in his memory, while in the really real world, out there in front o' the gray gateway, he does the exact same thing. "Dead and gone!" he shouts. And that double-whammy assault is havin' the desired effect o' breakin' our man down, mind, body, and spirit, bit by bit, chippin' away 'til Jo Jo's very soul is in danger o' bein' swallowed in the void.

✴✴✴✴✢✴✴✴✴

That big ol' cat's still havin' a field day with its new toy, when it finally tosses Huxley close enough to where he dropped Frankie's blade that he can snatch hold o' it. Once he does, he opens up a slice on one foreleg and manages to lap up a couple drops o' blood. "That's some good shit!" he says. "Got me a different constitution now!"

He fights his way to a stand, the tiger on its hind legs, and he tries to fling it off but the two o'em end up spinnin' into the back side o' the distribution panel that's gettin' power from the nearest generator and in turn feedin' it to the closest rides. Huxley and the cat hit these terminal blocks, normally used for—okay fine, I'll spare you all the technical mambo jahambo and say it like this: They get juiced! Cooked! Fried like cakes on a griddle! Huxley's doin' a whole new kinda dance move, muscles all spasmin', while the big cat's gone stiff like one o' them animals that's been stuffed by a taxidermist.

✴✴✴✴✢✴✴✴✴

While them two are ridin' the lightnin', Elsa and Diamond are still engaged in hand-to-hand combat ('cept Diamond's got an extra hand 'cause she stole Elsa's) over by Doc Hart's tractor and trailer. Now Diamond's quick as can be, but nevertheless, Elsa's able to grab the incomin' wrist that was recently hers, and she disarms (yeah, I saw the shot and I took it) Diamond by pullin' her own limb back!

Now the land-yacht tractor, as you can plainly see, is nose-deep in the remains o' the ring toss stand. Diamond's got Elsa backin' up, even though Elsa's got her arm back, 'cause the snake lady's bigger, stronger, and faster, and them cuts our girl opened up on Diamond's arms didn't seem to slow her down none.

Well the way the tractor and trailer are bent just slightly, with Elsa backed up to where they're connected, don't leave her no place to go 'cept . . . see that curved space where the back o' the land-yacht and the trailer is hitched? Well Elsa's got her an idea. One-handed, she removes Patch from her back and shoves him through, then she takes her arm and she crawls through that openin', 'round the fifth wheel, and out to the other side. Diamond comes slinkin' after her, but like I said, Diamond's a bigger gal than Elsa is and she gets slightly stuck.

This o' course was Elsa's plan, but somethin' bizarre happens next when Elsa hears rippin' and tearin' sounds in that dark place where the moonlight don't reach. There's a couple o' softly glowin' eyes approachin', the pupils o' which are just vertical slits. Diamond's head emerges, but the skin o' her face splits down the middle and parts to either side as the snake lady keeps comin', forcin' her way out, not really altogether human no more. Her mouth opens wide . . . and then wider, and then wider still, her jaw unhingin' as the cuspid teeth extend, curvin' downward, and them crazy eyes o' hers, they fix on Elsa with cold, murderous intent.

Elsa she sticks her detached arm 'tween her legs and holds it there while she removes the blade from that hand. She lets the arm fall, and then she steps up and rams her good hand and blade down Diamond's throat all the way to her shoulder, swirlin' and lashin' and battin' and flailin' like she's whippin' up an omelet.

Now even though the snake lady can withstand a fair amount o' damage on the *outside,* the same don't rightly hold true for the *inside.* As Elsa draws her gore-coated arm back, Diamond's eyes roll up into her noggin and the snake lady slumps down, dead as dead can be.

Elsa takes a tick to reattach her limb, but before she sets out to find Huxley she hears an explosion off to one side—that'd be the distribution panel Huxley and the tiger crashed into, though o' course she don't know it—followed by a cracklin', sizzlin' sound just down the midway. She grabs up Patch and replaces him on her back as she hurries 'round the tractor and the booth debris. When she comes to the Tiltin' Whirl, she notices the calliope music's stopped just before she hears a loud, short-circuitin' kinda sound. The jagged arcs o' electricity at the Tiltin' Whirl fade out; the hummin' and vibratin' decrease, and the ride gradually starts slowin' down.

★★★★✲★★★★

The Ramblin' Man pauses, feelin' a disruption in the channelin' o' power while the gateway behind him jitters and flickers for just a tick. At his feet is the limp, bloodied form o' Jo Jo. The Ringmaster knows that the former feral child's spark o' life ain't no more'n a glimmer now, but lookin' back, he also sees that the Boss is drawin' ever

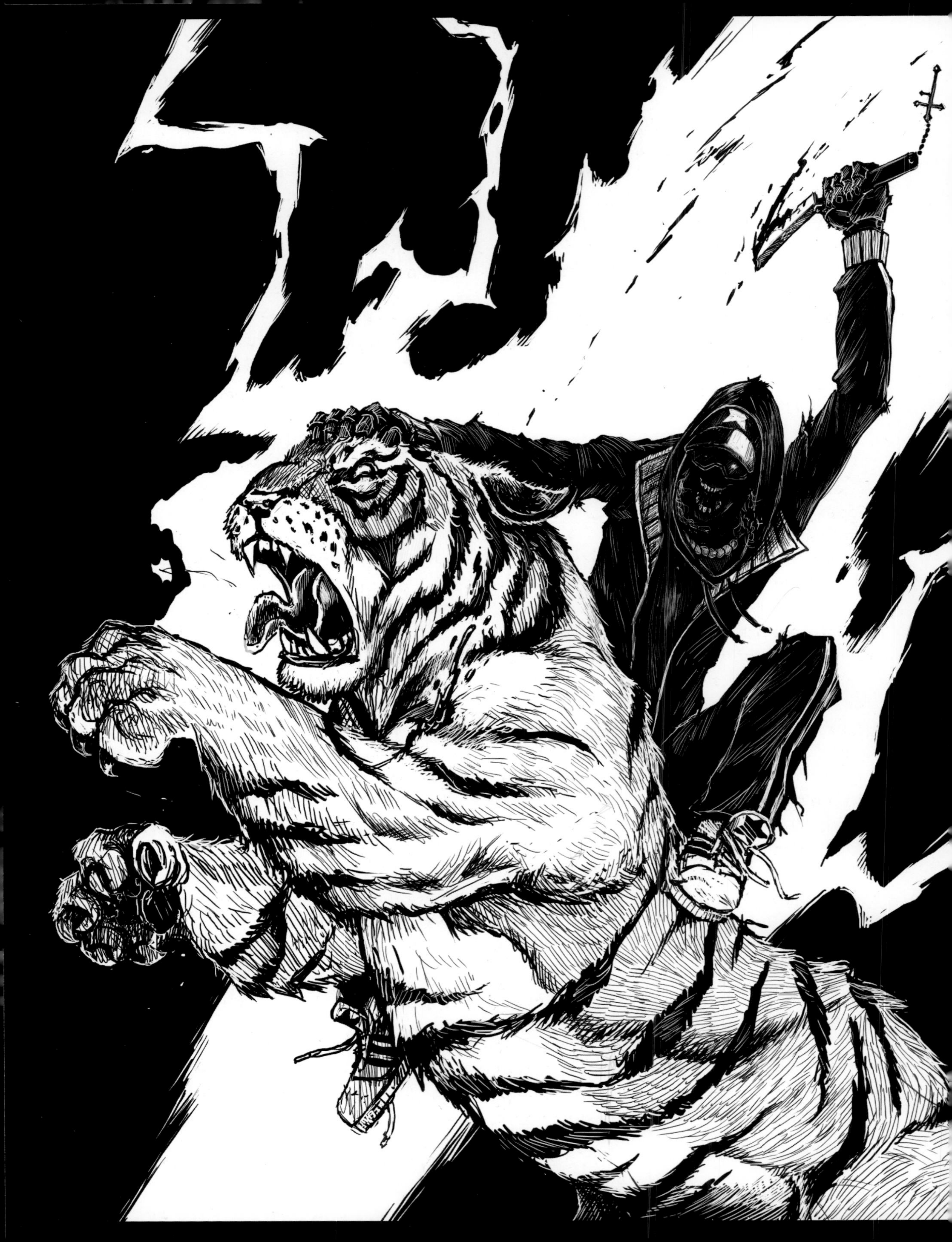

closer to the gate, its mouth-orifices openin' and closin', hungry for the first part o' its tribute. Not to mention the black stain has worked its way down Ledger's wrists now, into the veins on the back o' his hands.

So the Ramblin' Man whistles for the chimpanzee driver to pull the truck up. The ape complies, coastin' in, turnin' 'round, and backin' the trailer toward the rift. The tips o' some o' the Boss's tentacles reach out from the portal, chillin' the air and movin' kinda herky-jerky as if they're havin' trouble maintainin' a presence on our side o' the gate.

Ledger leaves Jo Jo, with the bloody cane floatin' nearby, hurryin' to open the trailer—but he can already see that somethin' is very, very wrong.

The lock ain't on the trailer door.

His black heart shrivels just a bit in dread, and sure enough as he opens it up, he sees . . .

The balloons are all gone.

Now he suspects that the brat did it, but 'tween the drain from openin' the gate, the disruptions in the channelin', and the blight consumin' him from the inside out, ol' Ledger just don't have enough go-juice left to detect where them balloons are, much less summon 'em back.

One o' the Boss's gropin' tentacles flickers, jitters, and reaches toward Ledger, who quickly moves away. The tendril's swiftly joined by another, and the two lash out faster than the eye can follow, wrappin' 'round the truck and trailer and yankin' 'em into the other side where all them tentacles set to squeezin' and twistin' the truck and trailer 'til they rip it apart.

The chimp gets ejected, grabbed by one o' them appendages, and we can hear a distorted scream just before the ape pukes its guts out. And I don't mean in the figurative sense. No it hacks up its insides and those get scooped up by a smaller tendril, and then teeth appear along the big tentacle that's holdin' the chimp, and pretty soon that maw-like appendage closes 'round the corner man and just like that, he's gone.

The truck and trailer pieces then get tossed back through the gateway, crashin' and bouncin' and narrowly missin' Ledger and the twins and Jo Jo.

The Ramblin' Man puts a hand to his throat, where the black stain has begun spreadin' up into his face, and he knows full well that his continued existence now depends 100 percent on Her.

He rushes to the barely clingin'-to-life Jo Jo, grabs him by the scruff o' the neck, and lifts, shoutin' to the surroundings, "Come out! I meant to give you over, but I believe . . . I believe there's just enough of a spark left in him to feed what's on the other side!"

Poor Jo Jo, he's just 'bout completely lost in the abyss. Silver, see, silver can hurt him, and under the right circumstances maybe worse, but the one thing that can outright terminate Jo Jo is Jo Jo himself. By givin' up. She gives him a life worth livin', so without Her, what's the damn point? Yessir, Jo Jo, he's at that threshold, on

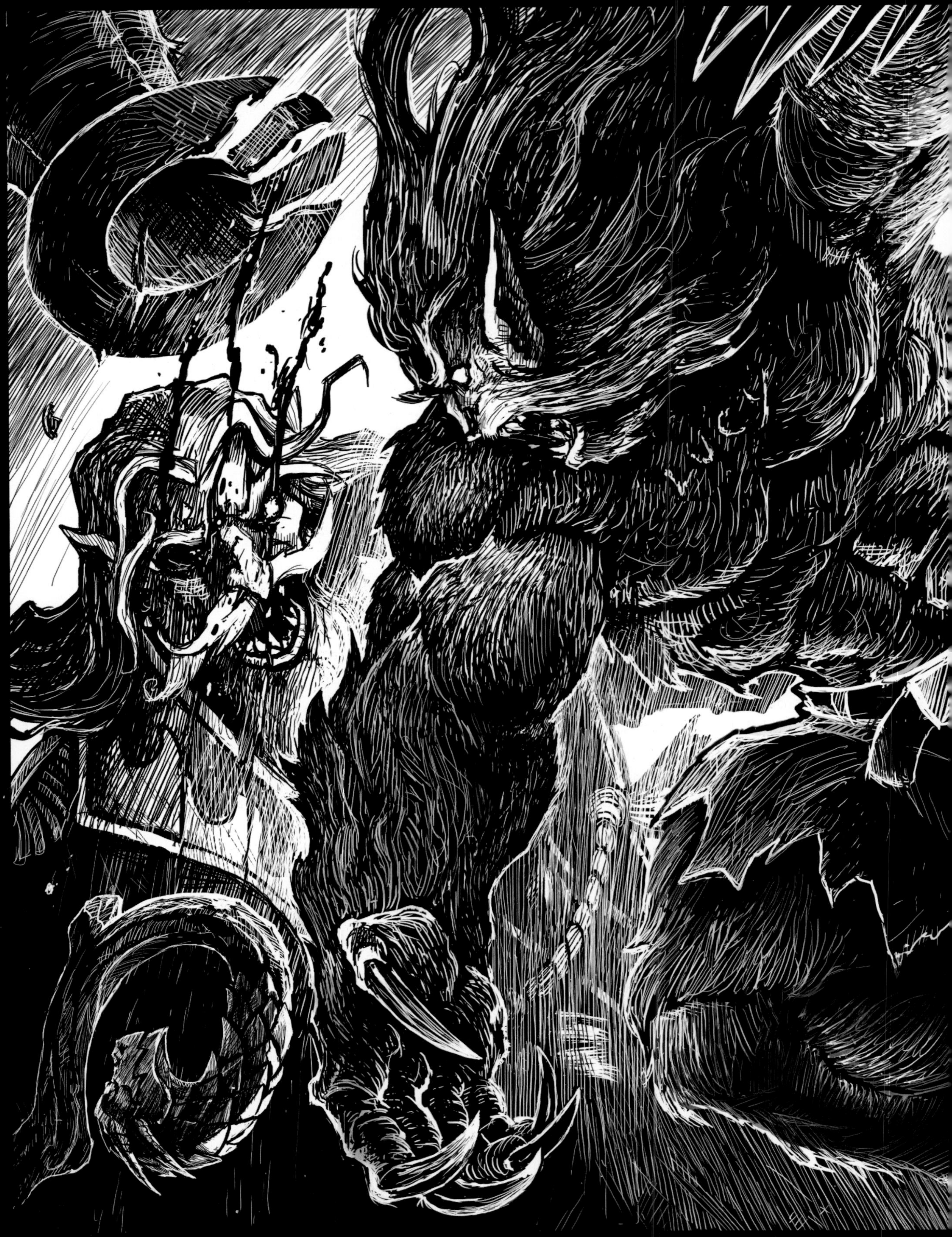

the very brink o' passin' that point o' no return, when suddenly a voice, not unlike that o' an angel, rings out through the void.

"Daddy!"

Now that voice pulls our man back up and outta the gulf. That voice *always* brought him back—brought light to Jo Jo's darkest days—and I'll tell you what, durin' them five years Jo Jo was runnin' from the Barnstormers, there were plenty o' dark days. But those were also the years he spent with Her, and 'cause o' that, them five years were the best damn years o' his life.

Ledger, havin' trouble breathin' now, he looks over by some o' the trucks, where a tiny little girl has made an appearance. She's wearin' a ragged little dress, and she's covered in a thin pelt o' fur. She's as cute as cute can be, even though right now her eyes are wet and her face is all scrunched up in worry over her daddy.

Ledger wheezes like he's got emphysema and beckons. "Come, girl! Come and take his place. Come to me . . . and I'll let him live." Course the Ringmaster don't plan to do no such thing, but that darling little girl knows that she's got to save her daddy, no matter what, so she takes a hesitant step. "That's it!" Ledger coaxes. But then she stops as she hears her daddy's voice.

"Her . . . name . . ." and Jo Jo's gotten to all fours, diggin' 'round under his shirt for somethin' . . .

"Is Lucy!" Jo Jo declares as he stands up and rips off a silver necklace, bearin' a rough kinda pendant that our man fashioned himself after his girl was born, a crude piece o' craftsmanship that forms the letters *L, U, C,* and *Y.* And as Jo Jo rips the necklace and his shirt away, we can see that them letters are burned into his chest. This piece, this is the last one, the only one that was still containin' any part o' the beast inside o' Jo Jo.

The Ramblin' Man's black eyes go wide. He makes a feeble motion with his right hand and the cane hovers over to one side o' Jo Jo—just like it had when the Ringmaster discovered that the baby wasn't his. This time, however, Jo Jo don't wait; he punches first, offloadin' every iota o' pain, torment, and heartache into one solid punch that demolishes Ledger's nose and smashes his monocle into his own eye.

Then our man grabs hold o' that cane at either end; he smashes it over his knee and he hurls them pieces into the gateway, where they get snatched up.

As the full moon slips out from behind the clouds, our man lowers a glare on the Ringmaster that spells unequivocal doom. He don't see nothin' but the enemy as he unleashes the beast, pummelin' and bashin' with his bare fists . . . unaware o' the two tentacles that have taken a keen interest in Lucy. They skip and jitter and unfurl in her direction, stretchin' and gropin', but before the tips can make contact with Her, Elsa comes rushin' outta nowhere, scoopin' the little ragamuffin up in her arms and backpedalin' 'til her heels go out from under her.

The little girl, she don't seem concerned for her own safety. She's eyeballin' the coaster that's still speedin' along the periphery o' the carnival grounds. The nearest tentacle flickers and jerks and disappears for a tick, but when it reappears, it's latched onto Elsa's right ankle. Where it touches, Elsa's skin turns black, and the serum becomes a frigid blight that spreads up her leg . . .

Elsa reaches to the clamp up near her hip and detaches the lower limb before the black taint can infect the rest o' her body. While she does, Lucy helps drag her farther away. In the midst o' all this, out by the carnival's rear gate, Huxley appears. He's lookin' over to where Jo Jo's still beatin' the piss outta the Ramblin' Man, that tongue o' his flickin' at his lips.

Lucy, she leans down and whispers in Elsa's ear. Elsa looks over her shoulder and shouts to Huxley, "The rides! You gotta shut down the rides!"

Huxley dares a glimpse at the thing just beyond the gray gateway, but he don't like what he sees so he looks away quickly, back at the coaster and the Ferris wheel and them other rides, where the cries are so faint now you can't hardly even hear 'em no more.

Finally he nods, and, still hopped up on tiger's blood, he blurs out . . .

Lucy recommences to pullin' Elsa away as the tentacle skips and whips and disappears and reappears.

Jo Jo, meantime, he's standin' over the battered Ringmaster, who's kinda crumpled at the base o' the Wall. The Ramblin' Man's face, underneath the bruises and blood, is almost completely black, swallowed up by the taint. He don't give up though, raisin' his left hand, which holds three tarot cards. Jo Jo slaps the cards away as Ledger scoots back. He's eyeballin' the carnival, where the lights o' the rides have somehow gone out. The cracklin' o' electricity in his one remainin' good eye has gone out too. Above him, the gateway's flickerin' like a neon sign with a faulty tube.

The Ramblin' Man turns away, facin' the ground. Jo Jo reaches down to the Ring-master's shoulder and pulls; when he faces our man, Ledger's got a lit cigarette in one hand. He blows smoke that forces Jo Jo to close his eyes for just a tick, and when Jo Jo opens 'em again . . .

The Ringmaster's gone.

Well it took everything Ledger DeMesne had left in him to pull off that last trick. Still, he wasn't able to go far. No sir he's reappeared just a ways away, over by the animal cages. He's on his knees, strugglin' to stand, hopin' if he can just find out where She hid them balloons, if he can get to even just one, maybe it'll be enough to buy him some time, just a little bit more time, and maybe then he can—

"What's up playa?"

Ledger struggles to his feet, turnin' to face Huxley.

There's a big-ass, golden grin on the skinny fella's face just before he swipes Frankie's razor blade across Ledger's throat. The Ramblin' Man just goes kinda limp, hangin' there like a rag doll as Huxley bites in with his grill, guzzlin' like a drunk at last call.

The moon's done disappeared over the horizon as a confused Jo Jo looks 'round, but he don't see the Ringmaster nowhere. Bo and Tweeny, they've disappeared too. Hell, in his beast mode, Jo Jo realizes he was kinda out of it, but he's back to bein' aware now. Somethin' else he don't see no more is the Boss's tentacles. Up and behind him, the gateway has faded to the point where it—and the Boss—can't hardly be seen no more. Just then, there's a kinda sizzlin' sound and one final flicker before the gateway's gone altogether.

Our man looks to Lucy, who comes runnin' with the world's biggest, lovin'-est smile on her face.

"Come here, baby!" Jo Jo says, droppin' to his knees. And he don't look quite so big and beastly no more as he embraces Her in his arms. "I thought you were gone."

"I'm here, Daddy. I'm okay."

"You always were and always will be the greatest part of my life. My big girl. My best girl. My supergirl."

A little ways away, Elsa sits up on her one good leg, watchin' with a dreamy kinda expression on her face as Jo Jo and Lucy hold each other real close.

This is the happiest Jo Jo's been in a mighty long time. He knows damn well though that there's one particular black-hearted sonofabitch who's still capable o' stealin' that happiness away. He knows the Ringmaster's hurt, and probably couldn'ta gone far, so he listens real close with that special hearin' o' his . . . and then he picks it up, just barely—a kinda' groanin' noise, and some slurpin' sounds.

"Go to that young lady right there," Jo Jo tells his girl, pointin' at Elsa. "I'll be right back."

Lucy does as she's told and by the time our man finds the source o' them noises he detected, Huxley's done drained every last bit o' blood outta the Ramblin' Man. What he drops to the ground is a shriveled corpse that kinda resembles one o' them old Egyptian mummies.

Now I'd be lyin' if I said Jo Jo didn't feel a bit robbed for not bein' the one to snuff out Ledger's flame. He puts that behind him, though, takin' comfort in the fact that the Ringmaster is gone, for all and for good. Huxley, meanwhile, he just stands there, all quiet-like, and he pulls up his hood. "Did it work?" Jo Jo asks him. "You feel okay?"

Huxley's eyes shine behind them sunglasses as he says, "Oh, I'm better than okay! I feel like I can do anything. Go anywhere! I ain't felt this good in my whole damn . . ." he pauses for a tick, then says, "life." He looks down at his hands, flexin' his fingers as if he's feelin' 'em for the first time, and then he voices, kinda to himself: "Dyin' . . . dyin's for fools."

And just like that, Huxley blurs away, leavin' Jo Jo starin' at the Ramblin' Man's cadaver, which degrades to a fine, dark dust.

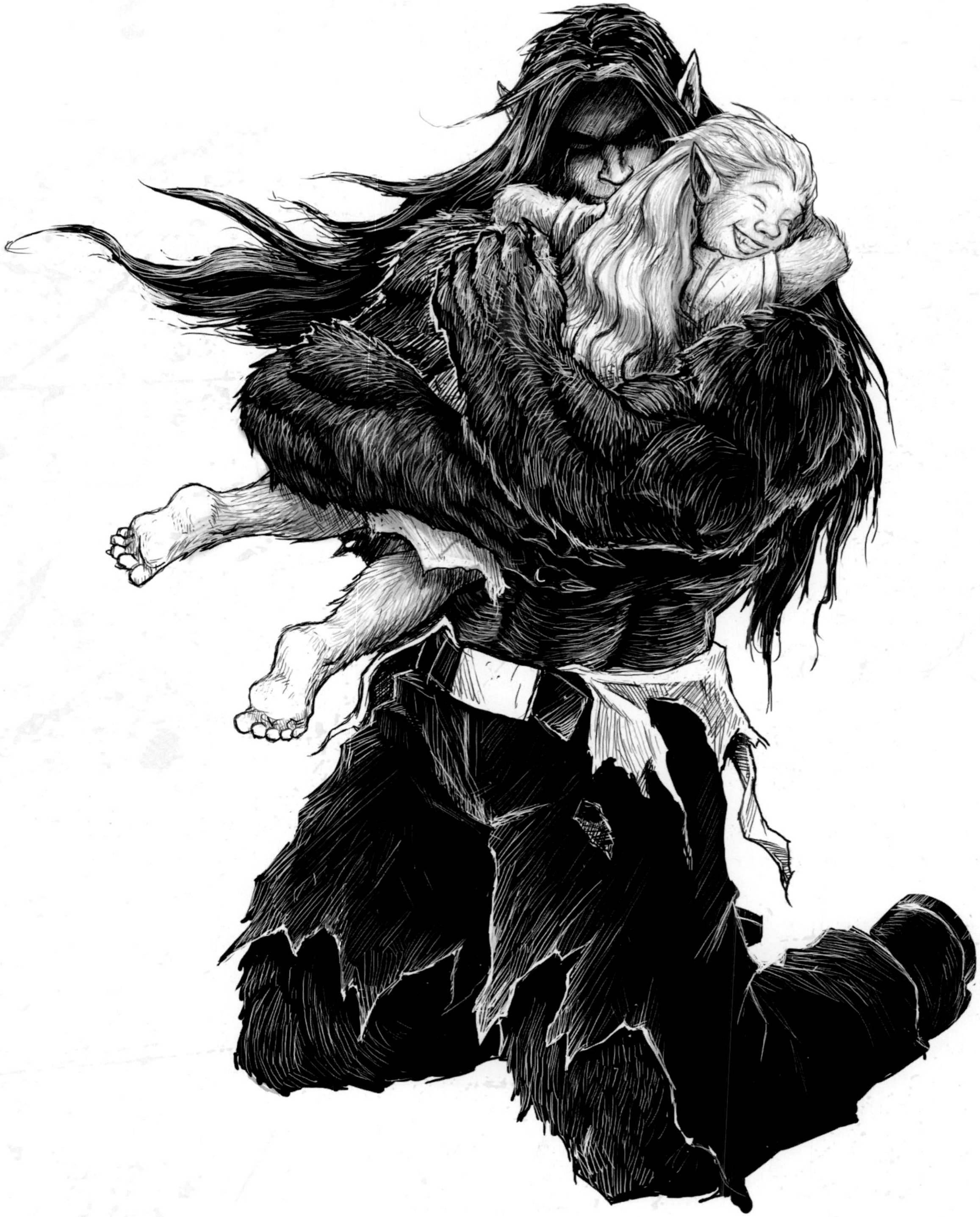

THE PART AFTER THE BIG ENDIN' ACTION PART

Or, I s'pose you could call it an *epy-log* if you're into them fancy words.

While Jo Jo's off starin' at the disintegratin' remains o' Ledger DeMesne, Lucy's standin' with the still-seated Elsa and she's cryin'. When Elsa asks why, the little girl points and says, "Your leg."

"Oh, sweetie, it's okay," Elsa says. She thinks for a minute and then she takes Patch off her back. "See Patch? How he lost parts but they got reattached?"

Lucy nods, wipin' at her tears.

"Well I'm kinda like that. I can get me a new leg." Elsa smiles. "And I know just where to get it."

Not far away, a handful o' the Barnstormers' trucks, includin' the ones with the animal cages, fire up their engines and drive off, back toward town. Jo Jo meanwhile, he comes back and when Lucy asks him if everything's alright, our man answers that everything's just fine. He then tells Elsa that Huxley's gone.

"Just like that?" Elsa asks. "'Fraid so," Jo Jo answers. "He got the blood he needed, though." Elsa nods and gets all quiet, saddened by the fact that Huxley left without tellin' her goodbye.

Lucy breaks the silence, sayin', "You gotta see somethin'! If it's okay," she says, lookin' down to Elsa. "Yeah, okay," Elsa answers. "It's not far," Lucy promises.

Jo Jo carries Elsa like it ain't no trouble at all as Lucy leads the two o'em to a particular truck trailer—probably Diamond's, judgin' by the snakes painted on the side. Once there, Lucy opens up the back to reveal a whole bunch o' balloons.

"So that's where they went," Jo Jo says, puttin' Elsa down so she can see.

"I knew he needed 'em so I hid 'em," Lucy replies. "I used a nail to pick the lock."

Jo Jo thinks back to when he did the very same thing, when he wasn't much more'n an ankle biter himself. He smiles proudly. "Smart, baby girl, real smart."

Lucy smiles, looks at the trailer, and says, "It's okay, you can come out now, you're safe."

Well right quick them balloons get to stirrin' and wigglin' like a soft breeze has got ahold o'em. Jo Jo helps Elsa step back as one by one them balloons break away, exit the trailer and float up, and even though there ain't no wind to speak of, they slowly start headin' east, 'cept for a few that break off and scud toward the carnival.

Jo Jo's not sure if his baby really talked to the balloons and they kinda answered her, or if they just floated away on their own. Then he thinks about the fact that she was able to get 'em from one trailer to another, thinks some more about Lucy's mom and them special sigils, and just kinda smiles, thinkin' that he's proud o' his girl either way.

Lucy smiles at Elsa and says, "We should get your leg."

The three o'em head back along the midway 'til they come to the empty boxin' ring, and Jo Jo takes note o' the fact Terra Mungus ain't nowhere to be found, and he wonders if he's seen the last of the catch-rasslin' gorilla.

They move on, stoppin' for a tick at the Jawdropper—basically a bunch o' seats that go up real high and then fall real fast. There's a bunch o' kids sittin' in the seats at ground level, lookin' like they're sleepin'. Well three o' them balloons that broke off from the rest, they've come floatin' up to three o' them little faces, and then the balloons pop, makin' Lucy jump.

The three kids breathe in, and then they moan and start movin' just a little, openin' their eyes and blinkin' at the sun. Next to them three, the other kids get to doin' the same thing.

Elsa smiles, relieved to know the ride-goers are alive. Up above, some o' the kids and the adults on the stopped rollercoaster get to moanin' and wakin' up as well.

"We better keep movin'," Jo Jo says, not particularly wantin' to get stuck with all the questions when them ride-goers get all their wits back.

Elsa has Jo Jo take her to Father's trailer and the ruined ring toss stand, and the body o' Diamond.

Now, the upper half o' the snake lady looks like seven kinds o' hell, and Elsa knows that her insides are done ground up to mincemeat, but Diamond's lower half, just as our girl was hopin', is still normal.

Elsa has Jo Jo retrieve all the surgical implements and serum she'll need from Father's trailer. Before settin' to work, she hands Patch to Lucy, tellin' her, "This might be too gruesome for my friend Patch to watch. Can you make sure he doesn't see?" Lucy nods solemnly and hugs Patch close, turnin' her back on the operation.

Not more'n a few minutes later, Elsa tests out her new leg, wonderin' if the skin on it will act the same for her as Diamond's "special" skin did. Lucy's fixin' to hand Patch back when Elsa says, "Why don't you hang onto him for me?" Well that puts another big ol' smile on the little one's face as she says, "Really? Thanks!"

A cursory inspection o' the tractor and trailer confirms it to be drivable, despite the smashed hood, windshield, and missin' roof. Jo Jo asks Elsa if she's okay with them usin' the rig for transport, knowin' that anything her father owned has got some not-so-happy memories attached to it.

But Elsa don't seem put off in the least. "You bet!" she says. "It'll be good to have the supplies."

It takes just a minute o' maneuverin' to get the tractor and trailer out from the wrecked stand and to the entrance, nose pointed east. Jo Jo's drivin', Elsa's in the passenger seat, and Lucy's sittin' between 'em with Patch in her lap, lookin' at the balloons, which ain't much more'n specks now in the distance.

"You think Huxley's gonna be okay?" Elsa asks.

"He'll find his way," Jo Jo says. "And so will we."

"Think we'll see him again?"

"Never can tell," Jo Jo answers as he puts the tractor in gear and sets off in the direction o' the brightenin' sky.

★★★★✾★★★★

And that, folks, is what we call a wrap. We've done come to the end o' our tale, the fat lady's warmin' up them vocal chords, and that's where we're gonna leave our heroes for—oh, hold up, there is just *one more* thing . . .

See the top o' them sideshow banners there at the entrance? Yeah well a pair o' eyeballs up there is watchin our heroes depart. Them eyes are black and beady, gazin' from an upside-down head, and them eyes, yeah you guessed it . . .

. . . are attached to the body of a not-so-dead crow.

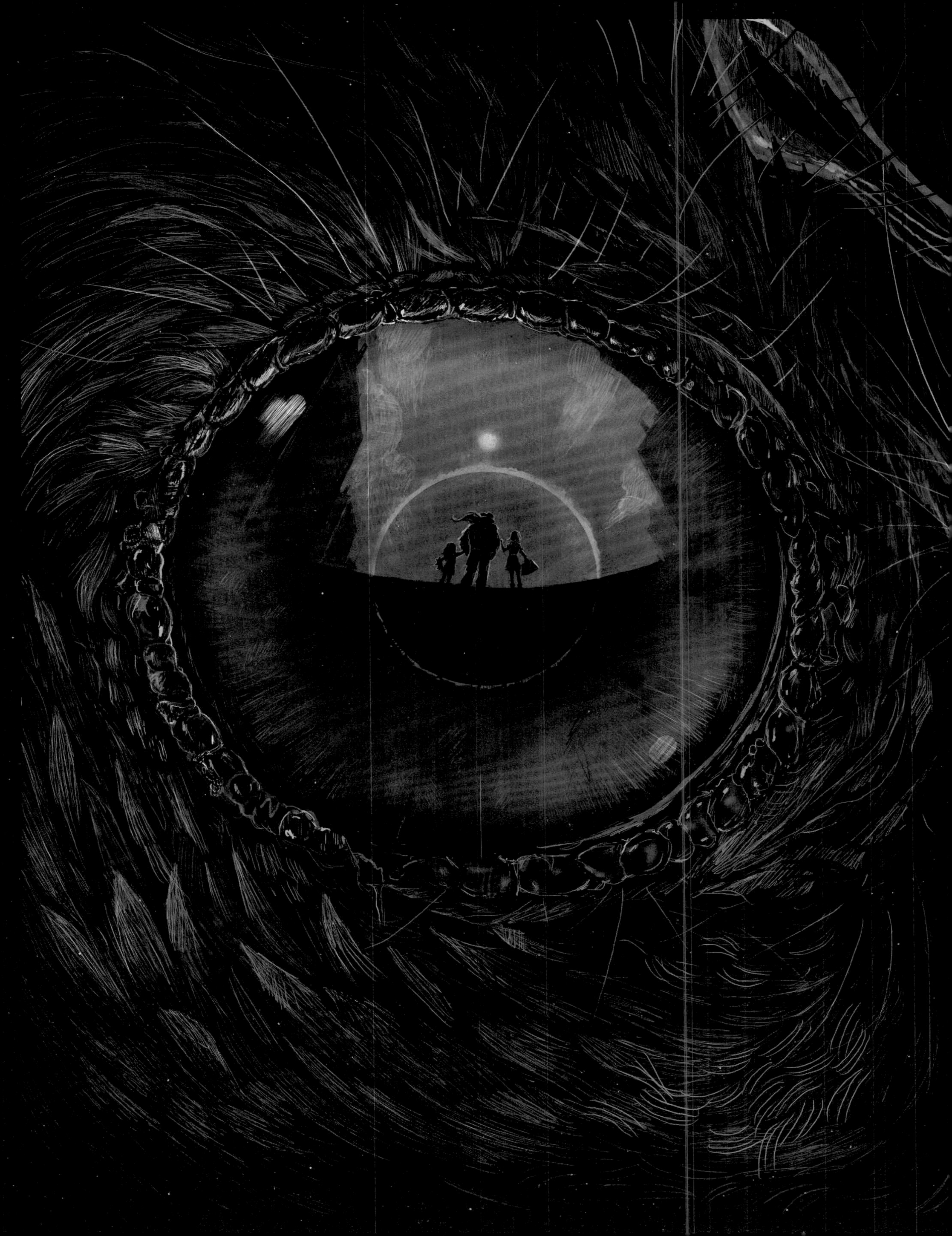

(for the time bein', anyhow)

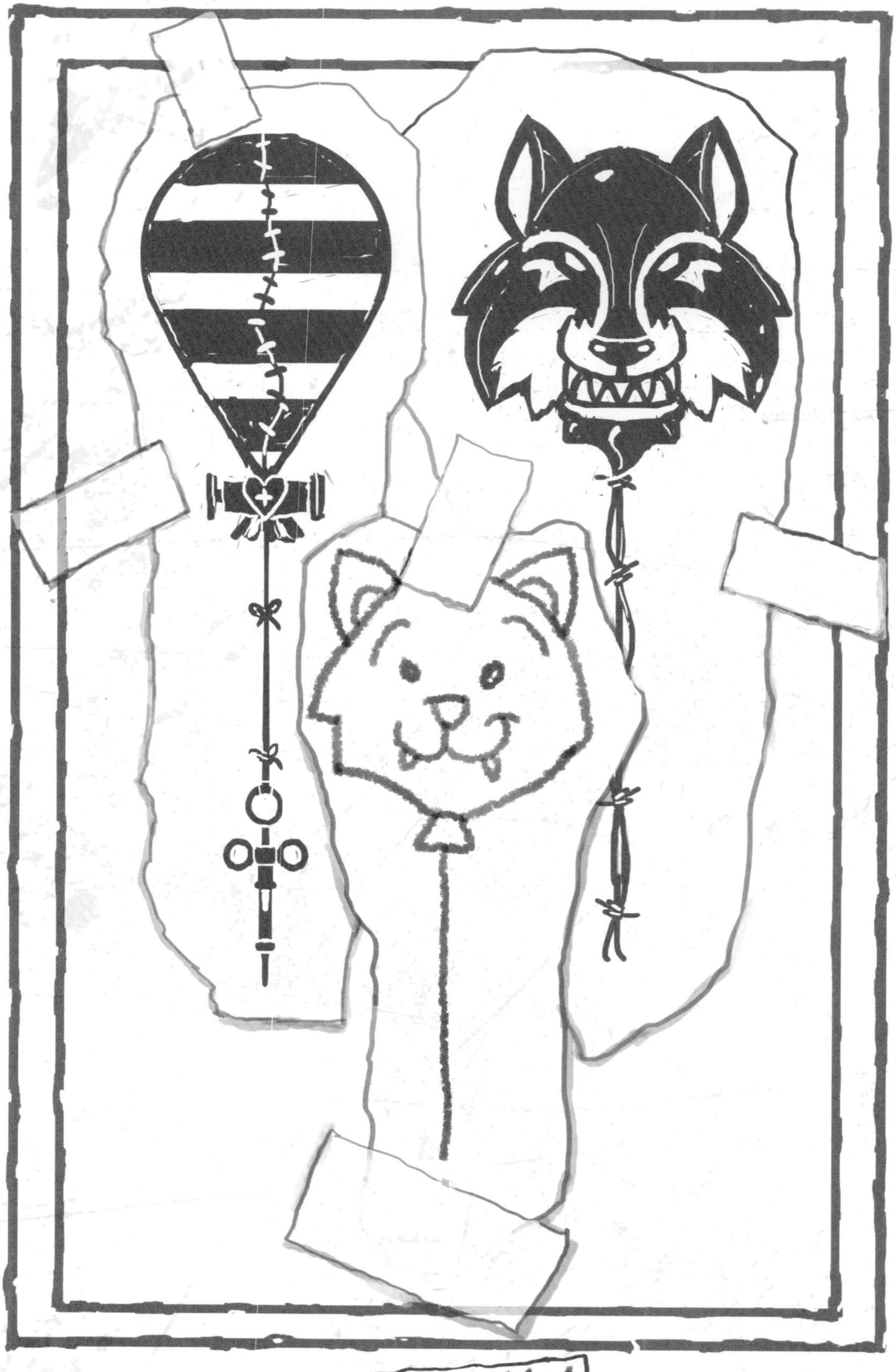

THE FAMILY

ACKNOWLEDGMENTS

All my thanks to Sammy D (aka Samwise), who started this whole shebang with some kickass art of a circle of cactuses (okay, fine, cacti) that he called the Crown of Thorns. Our man Jo Jo woke up inside that circle, with various birds—buzzards, crows, an owl—all staring down at him. We knew that Jo Jo had been beaten and left for dead, and that a mysterious traveling carnival had taken Her, but we didn't have many details beyond that. Nevertheless, those concepts were the seed of what would grow into *Strange Highways*. What an amazing journey it's been, from those early thoughts and images, through the evolution of the narrative to the final product that you now hold in your hands. Huge thanks to all the folks at Insight Editions for their dedication and hard work in putting this book together, and a massive thanks to you, the reader, for dropping your hard-earned Johnnies on our crazy tale. I hope you all enjoyed your journey along the Anaconda, and I look forward to whatever destination the Strange Highways lead to next.

—Micky Neilson

Thanks to the following human oddities who helped bring this carnival sideshow from dead-end towns in Texas to the rest of this wasteland of a world.

To Bernie Wrightson for a lifetime of horrific inspiration and for showing me that the world is most beautiful (and terrifying) in black and white.

To Tom Waits for the decades of musical madness, melodious maladies, and devil's lullabies. Those tunes kept me company while riding the dawn patrol down the Anaconda.

To the keeper of *Magica*, Ronnie James Dio, the traveler who shared with me how to get to the Strange Highways.

And to Brother Mick, my loquacious carnival barker, for writing wondrous words for this fabulous freak show and riding double barrel shotgun and the graveyard shift with me down Route 999.

—Samwise Didier

An Imprint of Insight Editions
PO Box 3088
San Rafael, CA 94912
www.insightcomics.com

Find us on Facebook:
www.facebook.com/InsightEditionsComics

Follow us on Twitter:
@InsightComics

Follow us on Instagram:
@Insight_Comics

ISBN: 978-1-68383-125-9

PUBLISHER: Raoul Goff
ASSOCIATE PUBLISHER: Vanessa Lopez
CREATIVE DIRECTOR: Chrissy Kwasnik
DESIGNER: Amy DeGrote
PROJECT EDITOR: Greg Solano
EDITORIAL ASSISTANT: Jeric Llanes
SENIOR PRODUCTION EDITOR: Elaine Ou
PRODUCTION MANAGER: Sadie Crofts

Insight Editions, in association with Roots of Peace, will plant two trees for each tree used in the manufacturing of this book. Roots of Peace
is an internationally renowned humanitarian organization dedicated to eradicating land mines worldwide and converting war-torn lands into
productive farms and wildlife habitats. Roots of Peace will plant two million fruit and nut trees in Afghanistan and provide farmers there with
the skills and support necessary for sustainable land use.

Manufactured in China by Insight Editions

10 9 8 7 6 5 4 3 2 1

CONTENTS

BONILLA, Tony
Lawyer, Activist

Tony Bonilla is a prominent Hispanic congressman and civic leader in Texas. One of eight children of Maria and Ruben Bonilla, Sr., he was born and raised in Calvert, where he attended public high school. On graduating he enrolled at Del Mar Community College in Corpus Christi. Within a year he was elected president of the student body by his classmates. He went on to take his first degree at Baylor University, Waco, and then graduated in law from the University of Houston. He later became an attorney.

Throughout his life Bonilla has been involved in national politics. He has campaigned on behalf of every Democratic presidential candidate since 1960, when he became active in the Viva Kennedy Club. After John F. Kennedy won election to the White House, Bonilla was a cofounder of the Mexican American Political Association (MAPA), and its successor, the Political Association of Spanish Speaking Organizations (PASSO). In 1965 he became the first state representative of Mexican ancestry to be elected in Nueces County.

National leader

Bonilla was also a leading member of the League of United Latin American Citizens (LULAC), a national civil rights organization with a focus on education. So, too, were his brothers William and Ruben. William was elected national president of LULAC in 1964; Ruben entered the same office in 1979, and Tony succeeded him for two annual terms from 1981 to 1982, after having been state president in 1970. In 1983 Tony and Ruben founded the National Hispanic Leadership Conference (NHLC). Together with the Reverend Jesse Jackson, Bonilla lobbied for more business for Latinos from major corporations.

▲ *Tony Bonilla (right) is pictured with President Lyndon B. Johnson.*

Bonilla has dealt with several U.S. presidents and other heads of state. He attended President Lyndon B. Johnson's signing of the Voting Rights Act in 1965, played a leading role in President Jimmy Carter's White House Conference on Latino Issues, and participated in President Bill Clinton's White House Conference on Hate Crimes. In 1988 Bonilla became one of the first Mexican Americans to speak at a National Democratic Convention. President Jose Lopez Portillo of Mexico awarded Bonilla the Aztec Eagle, the nation's highest honor for non-Mexican citizens.

While still campaigning vigorously on behalf of the Hispanic population of Corpus Christi, Texas, Bonilla has undertaken numerous missions to promote Latino interests abroad. He has twice visited Israel to encourage closer ties between Jews and Latinos. He has also visited Colombia, Bolivia, and Ecuador several times, and made three trips to Germany. Bonilla attended the 1988 Peace Conference in Vienna, Austria, and has visited Madrid, Spain. In 2005 he went on a trade mission to Shanghai, China.

KEY DATES	
1936	Born in Calvert, Texas, on March 2.
1967	Elected State Representative from Nueces County.
1970	Elected state president of LULAC.
1981	Elected national president of LULAC.
1988	Speaks at National Democratic Convention.
2005	Visits Shanghai, China, on a trade mission.

Further reading: http://rattler.tamucc.edu/dept/special/bonillat. html (biographical Web site).

BORDER, MEXICO–UNITED STATES

The border between the United States and Mexico has been a matter of controversy in varying degrees for two centuries. It assumed its current form—a line extending 1,951 miles (3,140km) between Brownsville/Matamoros on the Gulf of Mexico and San Diego/Tijuana on the Pacific Ocean—in 1854, and since then its actual course has not been substantively challenged. Yet the division between the two nations remains contentious for a variety of reasons, even in the 21st century, when the physical frontier is more clearly demarcated than ever before. Meanwhile, the area surrounding it, to the north and south, has assumed a unique character distinct from that of the U.S. or Mexican heartlands. The border lands and border culture have become the subjects of academic study.

Early difficulties

When Mexico won independence from Spain in 1821, its northern provinces were too remote from Mexico City, the capital of the republic, to be governed effectively. Independence movements began to flourish, principally in the areas that would become the U.S. states of California, New Mexico, and most importantly, Texas. As the United States expanded westward in the early 19th century, many non-Hispanic Europeans crossed the Red River from Oklahoma and settled in Texas. Among them were the brothers Haden and Benjamin Edwards, who received

This sign on the bridge over the Rio Grande between Laredo, Texas, and Columbia, Nuevo Leon, marks the boundary between the United States and Mexico.

permission from the Mexican government to colonize Nacogdoches; in the face of local opposition to their presence, they later declared the short-lived Republic of Fredonia.

Although the Mexican government at first encouraged such immigration, it later became alarmed by developments. The population of Texas soared from 7,000 in 1821 to 35,000 in 1836; most of the newcomers were U.S. citizens. The Mexicans, fearing that they would be overwhelmed, imposed restrictive laws that provoked the 1836 Texas revolution and led ultimately in 1845 to the incorporation of Texas as the 28th state of the Union.

The Mexican War (1846–1848)

Mexico objected to the annexation of Texas, a substantial part of its territory, and broke diplomatic relations with the United States. Despite some bellicose political rhetoric, it wanted to avoid open

conflict, but the situation deteriorated when the U.S. government tried to extend the new frontier to the southern bank of the Rio Grande. Mexico insisted that the boundary was the Nueces River, which flows roughly parallel to the Rio Grande an average distance of 100 miles (160km) to the north.

The United States now also wanted to annex two other outlying Mexican republics, California and New Mexico. The claim was fueled by the idea of Manifest Destiny. "Manifest Destiny" was a phrase first used in 1845. It encapsulated a vague but powerful set of beliefs. First was the idea that it was natural for the United States to expand west across the continent. This was underpinned by a feeling that the United States had a moral right to do so because of the superiority of its society and government. In December 1845, President James K. Polk sent an emissary to Mexico City to offer up to $40 million in return for California and New Mexico and recognition of the Rio Grande boundary. The Mexican government refused to deal, however, and Polk ordered U.S. forces to advance to the north bank of the Rio Grande. On April 25, 1846, Mexican troops crossed the river and attacked U.S. soldiers in the disputed area. On May 13, 1846, the U.S. Congress declared that "by the act of … Mexico" a state of war existed.

The ensuing conflict led to the temporary occupation of Mexico City and an overwhelming victory for the United States. The Mexican War was formally ended on

This photograph, taken in 1913, shows trams on Oregon Street, El Paso, Texas. In the later years of the 20th century, the city developed a strong link with its Mexican neighbor, Ciudad Juárez.

February 2, 1848, by the Treaty of Guadalupe Hidalgo, which established the Rio Grande as the boundary of the United States. Mexico ceded to the United States one-third of its territory: all of present-day California, Utah, and Nevada, and most of what is now Arizona and New Mexico. In return, the United States paid Mexico $15 million, and canceled all outstanding Mexican debts.

The Gadsden Purchase
One lasting consequence of the boundary changes that followed the Mexican War was that millions of Mexicans became U.S. subjects. Many of them subsequently had their land expropriated, and ended up working in menial capacities on property they had previously owned.

The border region remained militarized—both countries stationed armed forces on their side of the line in case of further trouble—but in many ways the new frontier was no more effective than the old one had been before the conflict. Under the terms of the Treaty of

Guadalupe Hidalgo, the United States had pledged to discourage crossborder incursions into Mexico, but in the event it made little or no effort to do so. The situation was complicated by the fact that, although the treaty had agreed to the general course of the U.S.–Mexico border, subsequent boundary surveys failed to achieve consensus on the detail. A substantial disputed area remained. In 1853, when the governor of New Mexico Territory threatened to occupy the disputed regions, his Mexican counterpart in neighboring Chihuahua sent in state troopers.

The ensuing confrontation was ended by the Gadsden Purchase (December 30, 1853), the acquisition of about 30,000 square miles (77,700 sq km) by the United States from Mexico for $10 million. The land later became part of southern New Mexico and Arizona.

Since the Gadsden Purchase, the U.S.–Mexico frontier has remained substantially unaltered. Yet although the modern borderline has not moved on the map, it has remained a source of

conflict. For long periods it has been more or less porous. One of the problems was the ease with which the armed forces of one of the nations could still enter the other's territory. In the 1880s, the U.S. Army pursued the Apache chief Geronimo into Mexico; from time to time, Mexican forces also chased Apaches into the Southwest United States. As a result, there was continuing friction between the two governments.

Water supply

A more bitter and lasting source of contention, however, was the way in which the scarce resources of the border region were apportioned. From the 1850s, and particularly after the Civil War (1861–1865), the cultivation of land on the U.S. bank of the Rio Grande increased enormously. In the 1870s, there were disputes between Texans and Mexicans over ownership of salt deposits in the El Paso–Juárez valley, and in the following decade, U.S. farmers claimed that Mexicans were building dams to divert the course of the Rio Grande. Since the Treaty of Guadalupe Hidalgo made no provision for the cross-border effects of irrigation, there was no obvious remedy. Irrigation schemes on one side of the border had a corresponding detrimental effect on the availability of water on the other bank. Droughts became regular and increasingly severe. In 1889 an International Boundary Commission (IBC) was set up to resolve outstanding territorial disputes, but its task was complicated by the fact that the course of the Rio Grande was constantly altering, and slowly transporting large quantities of sediment from one of its banks to

the other. On the recommendation of the IBC, in an attempt to distribute the river water fairly, the Elephant Butte Dam in Sierra County, New Mexico, was completed in 1916. The waters of the reservoir thus created were used by the citizens of both the United States and Mexico.

The Elephant Butte Dam eased the problems of the upper Rio Grande, but the lower stretches of the river, as well as the Colorado and the Tijuana rivers, remained contentious. In 1905, the U.S. government announced plans to build a dam on the Colorado River and divide its water between the seven U.S. states that bordered the waterway (Arizona, California, Colorado, Nevada, New Mexico, Utah, and Wyoming). By the time Boulder Dam was completed in 1936 (it has been known since 1947 as Hoover Dam), treaties had been signed that guaranteed a proportion of the water to Mexico. However, disputes later arose about the level of salt that the supplies contained. In 1961, for example, Mexico claimed that the United States was extracting so much water that the remainder was too salty for agricultural or domestic use.

The problem of the changing course of the Rio Grande has reemerged from time to time. In 1963, the Chamizal Convention resolved a dispute over El Chamizal, a parcel of land near El Paso, by running the Rio Grande through a 4.4 mile (7km) concrete channel, and assigning 437 acres (177ha) to Mexico. More recently, the discharge of domestic sewage and industrial waste into rivers along the border became a source of tension. In 1996, the two countries reached agreement

under the U.S.-Mexico Border XXI Program to foster ecological resource management.

Migrant labor

The prosperity of the United States attracts poor people from all over the world. One of the main sources of migrant labor has always been Mexico. Mexican workers found it easy to cross the vast and incompletely guarded border. That remained true even after 1924, when the Border Patrol was established under the Bureau of Immigration in the Department of Labor to monitor movements. The welcome the Mexicans received varied according to the state of the U.S. economy. In boom times, they were used to perform mainly menial jobs; during recessions, many were deported, and those who remained were often the victims of xenophobia (fear of foreigners).

One of the low points for Mexicans in the United States came in the Great Depression, during which unemployment rose from 1.6 million in 1929 to 12.8 million in 1933, from 3 percent to 25 percent of the workforce. Farmers faced disaster as agricultural commodity prices fell by half, and thousands of farms had to be sold to pay debts. Many former landowners were forced to work for very little, and the availability of cheap labor forced Mexicans out of the market. Thousands of Mexicans were deported, including many who had U.S. citizenship.

Mexican immigration was most welcome after 1941, when the United States entered World War II (1939–1945), and many railroad workers and farmhands went off to fight in the U.S. armed forces

TWIN CITIES

Since the 1960s, the Mexican side of the border has become one of nation's most urbanized regions, with 80 percent of the people living in cities with more than 800,000 inhabitants. Three of the biggest new population centers have developed close to a metropolis on the U.S. side. Each set of urban twins has become economically and socially interdependent with its counterpart, as millions of residents cross the border daily to work, shop, and visit friends. Civic amenities, such as firefighting forces, are also shared.

In Texas, El Paso is twinned with Ciudad Juárez, and Brownsville with Matamoros; both Mexican cities are now larger than their U.S. neighbors.

San Diego, California, has a similar relationship with Tijuana, but the seventh most populous city in the United States overshadows its Mexican twin.

Commuters make the short trip over the border from El Paso, Texas, to Ciudad Juárez, Mexico. Millions of similar crossings are made both ways daily.

against Japan and Germany. In order to fill the jobs thus vacated, in 1942 the United States reached an agreement with Mexico known as the Bracero Program, which offered temporary work to millions of Mexican migrants. The idea was that the guest workers should return home at the end of their contracts; in practice, however, many settled permanently in the United States.

Forced deportations

Although the Bracero Program was maintained until 1964, it was widely abused after the war: Employers often exploited workers, and many workers quit their jobs to find better-paid jobs elsewhere. In response to a growing outcry against Mexicans taking work from U.S. citizens, in

1951 the Border Patrol seized 280,000 illegal immigrants; by 1953 the number had increased to 865,000. By 1954, the number of illegal aliens coming from Mexico had increased by 6,000 percent over the previous 10 years. The U.S. Immigration and Naturalization Service (INS) introduced "Operation Wetback," which aimed to remove from Texas illegal Mexican immigrants (known disparagingly as "wetbacks," because they were reputed to have swum the Rio Grande). In practice, however, the operation became a long series of raids on Mexican *barrios* that resulted in the deportation of one million people in its first year. As in the Great Depression, many of those deported were U.S. citizens and legal immigrants. The pattern of

illegal immigration from Mexico to the United States was thus established: Impoverished families on the border sought work in the United States; U.S. industries were willing to pay cheap illegal workers; meanwhile, the U.S. government condemned illegal immigration and demanded that all Hispanics prove that they were U.S. citizens on pain of deportation. The pattern persists in the early 21st century. The promise of work in the United States continues to draw Mexicans across the border.

The third major repatriation episode occurred in 1982, when another economic downturn inspired "Operation Jobs," an attempt to ensure that U.S. citizens were employed in preference to Mexicans. During

KEY DATES

1845	Having seceded from Mexico, Texas becomes a U.S. state.
1848	By the Treaty of Guadalupe Hidalgo, Mexico loses California, Utah, Nevada, and much of Arizona and New Mexico.
1853	The United States buys further territory in New Mexico and Arizona.
1924	Border Patrol established to police the Mexico–U.S. frontier.
1941	Bracero Program encourages Mexicans to take U.S. jobs; ends 1964.
1954	Operation Wetback: more than a million Mexicans deported.
1966	First maquiladora opened in Mexico on U.S. border.
1994	North American Free Trade Agreement (NAFTA) implemented.

the 1990s, another wave of anti-immigrant sentiment caused more than one million undocumented workers to be deported.

Cross-border trade

The mobility of labor across the border has been one of the main problems that has blighted U.S.–Mexican relations since the mid-19th century. Yet throughout the period, trade has remained one of the most stable and important links between the two countries. The 1980s saw the growth of the maquiladora industry (*see box on page 10*), in which factories were set up on the Mexican border by U.S. and multinational companies to assemble goods that were then exported to the United States. Although criticized by some observers as sweatshops that operated outside U.S. regulations, maquiladoras have been successful for their owners, and have allowed many Mexicans the opportunity to work in nonagricultural industry.

As Mexico developed its natural resources and increased its political stability in the 20th century, it gradually realized its economic potential. The

implementation in 1994 of the North American Free Trade Agreement (NAFTA) abolished tariffs and trade barriers between Mexico, the United States, and Canada. Mexican imports to the United States increased dramatically, and the U.S. trade surplus with Mexico turned into a large deficit. Although opponents of NAFTA claimed that many more U.S. jobs had been lost to lower-paid Mexican workers than had been gained by the increase in exports to Mexico, supporters of the agreement maintained that the benefits to the United States would take longer to emerge, but were inevitable.

Border culture

The unique conditions that prevail along the frontier between the United States and Mexico have created an ambience that is unlike that of either country. In Mexico, the land known as La Frontera became regarded as an alien place populated by people who were neither Mexican nor American, but a breed apart. Residents played up to their image, being always quick to rebel against any perceived injustice. They commemorate their resistance in *corridos*, a variant form of an established Mexican ballad style. The best-known *corrido* is the "Ballad of Gregorio Cortez." Admirers maintain that the work does not celebrate the lawlessness of a border bandit, but the right to defend oneself and live independently.

Border culture is distinguished above all by an independence of spirit that perhaps compensates for the inhabitants' historical lack of political power. Its art and cuisine, for example, are

A man from Michoacan, Mexico, talks with an agent of the Border Patrol (now part of Homeland Security) through the U.S.–Mexico border fence near Tijuana, Mexico.

MAQUILADORAS

First set up in 1966, the earliest maquiladoras (assembly plants) in Mexico were confined by law to within 15 miles (24km) of the border. In the 1980s, however, the Mexican government relaxed its rules, and by the end of the 20th century there were 3,655 maquiladoras as far south as Guadalajara, 400 miles (650km) from the border.

Maquiladoras created a boom in the Mexican economy. They attracted unprecedented levels of foreign investment, notably from Japan and South Korea, which the Mexican government welcomed as a way to diversify its interests and reduce its reliance on the United States. By 2000, maquiladoras generated 40 percent of the nation's exports and employed 1.3 million Mexican workers.

Their major limitation was that their fortunes were still inextricably linked to the performance of the U.S. dollar. When the currency took a downturn between 2000 and 2003, 850 maquiladoras closed, and employment declined by more than 20 percent.

Although maquiladora workers are generally paid more than four times the Mexican average, they earn much less than wages in the United States. Critics of the program regard it as exploitative, and the term maquiladora is sometimes used as a synonym for sweatshop.

A Mexican worker on an assembly line at the Samsung maquiladora plant located near Tijuana, Mexico.

discernibly different from those of Mexico and the United States, even though they are often misidentified by those unfamiliar with the nuances. The language is different, too: The Spanish spoken in New Mexico retains words and idioms of the colonial period; Tex-Mex in Texas and Calo in California are more than minority dialects. They are established regional variants.

Border studies

The development in the late 20th century of border studies as an academic discipline is partly a reflection of growing interest in a region that is unlike any other. It is also a response to altered perspectives. Historically, the United States was regarded as a melting pot, in which immigrants of various nationalities gradually became Americans; more recently, however, the nation has been seen as more of a salad bowl, in which the ingredients are mixed but retain their own distinctive qualities. There may no longer be any need for Mexican traditions to be Americanized: Immigrants can retain their ethnicity while becoming part of an increasingly cosmopolitan U.S. culture. Border studies is also in part a response to postcolonialism. In the 1960s and 1970s, it was generally thought that a culture was either indigenous or imposed by an imperial power. By the end of the 20th century, however, it became apparent that native and colonial cultures could be synthesized into a new entity. Border studies are part of the effort to chart such processes and to find out what causes them.

See also: Cortez, Gregorio

Further reading: Davidson, Miriam. *Lives on the Line: Dispatches from the U.S.–Mexico Border*. Tucson, AZ: University of Arizona Press, 2000.
Fatemi, Khosrow (ed.). *The Maquiladora Industry: Economic Solution or Problem?* New York, NY: Praeger, 1990.
Gutierrez-Jones, Carl Scott. *Rethinking the Borderlands: Between Chicano Culture and Legal Discourse.* Berkeley, CA: University of California Press, 1995.
http://smithsonianeducation.org/migrations/bord/intro.html (migrations in history).
http://www.tsha.utexas.edu/handbook/online/articles/OO/pqo1.html (Handbook of Texas Online article about Operation Wetback).
http://www.tsha.utexas.edu/handbook/online/articles/EE/fed4.html (article on Haden Edwards).

BORI, Lucrezia
Singer

Lucrezia Bori was a leading soprano at the New York Metropolitan Opera. Spanish by birth, she lived most of her life in the United States.

Lucrecia Borja y González de Riancho was born in Valencia, Spain, in 1887. Her family was descended from the powerful Borgia family of Renaissance Italy, and her father was a wealthy army officer. A talented singer from an early age, Bori made her first public appearance at age six.

Educated at Valencia Conservatory, when she was 16 Bori decided to pursue a singing career. She moved to Milan, Italy, where she studied with Melchiorre Vidal. She made her professional debut in 1908, and joined the city's La Scala Opera House the following year. In 1911 she

created the role of Octavian in the Milan premiere of *Der Rosenkavalier* at the request of the opera's composer, Richard Strauss (1864–1949).

Career with Met

Bori's career changed after she stood in for an indisposed colleague at a performance by New York's Metropolitan Opera in Paris, France, in 1910. Her portrayal of the heroine of Puccini's *Manon Lescaut* was so well received that the performances sold out. She was offered a job with the Met and moved to New York.

Bori made her New York debut in the same role on November 11, 1912, singing opposite Enrico Caruso. The combination of her delicate voice and charismatic stage presence made her a popular favorite at the Met. In 1915, at the peak of her career, she was forced to quit singing when nodules on her throat required surgery. A long period of convalescence followed.

She was unable to sing for the next six years, and had to endure two months of complete silence. She finally made a triumphant comeback at the Met in 1921, and over the next 16 years appeared in nearly all the leading soprano roles.

Bori retired from singing on March 29, 1936, after a gala performance. She later worked as a fund-raiser for the opera house. In 1935 she became the first woman and the first performer to be elected director of the Metropolitan Opera Association. She held the post until her death.

▲ *Spanish-born soprano Lucrezia Bori spent most of her career with the Metropolitan Opera in New York.*

Further reading: Hamilton, D. Metropolitan Opera Encyclopedia. *New York: Simon & Schuster, 1987.* http://www.bookrags.com *(comprehensive biography).*

BOTERO, Fernando
Artist

Fernando Botero has achieved international recognition as an artist. His achievement has been to unite sophisticated European and American art movements with the naive thematic and aesthetic concerns associated with Latin American folk cultures.

A precocious talent, Botero was expelled at the age of 16 from his Jesuit school in Medellín, Colombia, for his "immodest" illustrations for *El Colombiano* newspaper. He lived a bohemian life among the brothels and bullfights of Medellín while studying at the Liceo de la Universidad de Antioquia. Botero worked briefly as a set designer for the touring Spanish theater group Compania Lope de Vega before moving to Bogotá in 1951; his work showed the influence of Pablo Picasso (1881–1973) and Paul Gauguin (1848–1903). In 1952 Botero went to Barcelona and Madrid, Spain, where he studied at the Academia de San Fernando and discovered the work of the Spanish artists Francisco de Goya (1746–1828) and Diego Velázquez (1599–1660). He then went on to Paris, France, and Florence, Italy, where he encountered the work of Italian artists Giotto (about 1266–1337), Paolo Uccello (1397–1475), and Piero della Francesca (about 1420–1492). In 1957 Botero moved to New York City; there his career was launched when the Museum of Modern Art purchased *Mona Lisa, Age Twelve* (1961), a work that exemplified the fashionable movements of abstract expressionism and pop art.

▲ *Sculptor Fernando Botero stands in front of one of his works, the* **Sphinx,** *during an exhibition in Florence, Italy, in 1999.*

Mature work

By 1964 Botero had reached his mature style. His figures were painted in a rotund and primitive manner that deliberately evoked the folk culture of his native Colombia, but which used compositions derived from his European historical studies. In *La familia presidencial* (1967) he satirized the social pretensions and the naive depiction of figures of Latin American painting within a composition reminiscent of Goya's court portraits. His still lifes such as *Still Life with a Cabbage* (1967) are reminiscent of the work of Francisco de Zurbarán (1598–1664). Other themes included brothels (*The House of María Duque*; 1970); nudes (*Venus*; 1989); and a further take on Leonardo da Vinci's most famous work (*Mona Lisa*; 1971). In 1973 Botero returned to Paris, where he devoted more time to sculpture, which gradually replaced painting as his main medium of expression. He also returned to bullfighting subjects in works such as *Bull* (1987) and *Broadgate Venus* (1990). In 2005 Botero unveiled a series of paintings inspired by the torture of Iraqi prisoners by U.S. soldiers in Abu Ghraib prison, Iraq.

KEY DATES	
1932	Born in Medellín, Colombia, on April 19.
1961	First major work, *Mona Lisa, Age Twelve*.
2005	Unveils paintings inspired by Abu Ghraib scandal.

Further reading: Fernando Botero: *Monograph & Catalogue raisonné: Paintings 1975–1990.* Edward J. Sullivan and Jean-Marie Tasset. Lausanne: Acatos, 2000. http://karaart.com/botero/index.html (comprehensive Web site detailing the artist's life and work).

BRISEÑO, Rolando
Artist

Rolando Briseño is one of the best-known Chicano artists in the United States. His work encompasses a wide variety of media, from small-scale paintings and ceramics to monumental public sculptures and installations. Much of his work deals with his Chicano heritage, examining the often uneasy relationship between Mexican and mainstream U.S. cultures.

Early life

The son of Mexican immigrants, Briseño was born in 1952 in San Antonio, Texas. He studied art at the Universidad Nacional Autónoma de México (UNAM) in Mexico City, and went on to take two BA degrees at the University of Texas at Austin. In 1977 he completed a master's degree in fine art at Columbia University, New York. During the following decades he lived mainly in Brooklyn before returning to his hometown in the late 1990s.

In his work Briseño often depicts food, which he sees as a commodity that connects people with their traditions and culture as well as with each other. The table is a central image, which he uses to express complex, often divided identities and the problems of communication among members of families and communities, especially in hybrid border cultures such as those of Texas and New Mexico.

Bicultural Tablesetting (1998) sums up many of Briseño's preoccupations. The work depicts a table from above, half of which is covered by a brightly colored, flowery Mexican mantel, or oilcloth, and half by a blue-and-white checkerboard American picnic cloth. Two hands—one pale, one dark—are poised to take tomatoes—a traditional staple of Mexican cuisine—from a plate.

Public art

In the 1990s Briseño became well known for his public art, which was commissioned for display in multicultural cities such as New York and San Antonio. In 1991 he designed the platform for the North White Plains, New York, Railroad Station, turning the columns into trees with Mexican-blue leaves; in 1995 he created for the Cypress Hills Library, Brooklyn, a pair of aluminum and steel gates depicting a family gathered round a book spread open on a table. More recently Briseño has created sculptures for San Antonio's Trinity University (2004) as well as for the city's International Airport.

▲ **Galaxy Way *(2005), an artwork by Rolando Briseño, is located at the train station attached to Houston's Bush Intercontinental Airport.***

KEY DATES	
1952	Born in San Antonio, Texas.
1977	Graduates from Columbia University, New York, with an MFA degree.
1991	Designs North White Plains Railroad Station, New York.

Further reading: Keller, Gary D. *Contemporary Chicana and Chicano Art: Artists, Work, Culture, and Education.* Tempe, AZ: Bilingual Review Press, 2002.
http://www.artco.org/sa/briseno/briseno2.html (artist's official Web site).

BUJONES, Fernando
Ballet Dancer

Second-generation Cuban American Fernando Bujones is widely considered to be among the greatest male ballet dancers of modern times. As principal dancer with New York City's American Ballet Theatre, his athleticism, grace, and sheer masculine presence won him comparisons with all-time greats such as Rudolf Nureyev. Although Bujones gave up dancing professionally in 1995, he has continued to be a vital presence in contemporary U.S. ballet. In later years he has worked as artistic director of the Orlando Ballet, one of the foremost of the smaller dance companies in the United States.

Principal dancer
The son of Cuban immigrants, Bujones spent his early childhood in his native Florida and in Cuba, where, at the age of eight, he took his first ballet lessons at the school of the Ballet Nacional de Cuba (BNC). The BNC's founder, Alicia Alonso, had done much to popularize ballet among ordinary Cubans, and her high profile had attracted many youngsters into the profession.

In 1967 Bujones won a Ford Foundation scholarship to study at the School of American Ballet, the educational wing of the New York City Ballet. Just a year before Bujones's arrival the Ford Foundation had granted the

▼ *Fernando Bujones performs with Janette Mulligan in a production of Adolphe Adam's* **Le Corsair.**

KEY DATES	
1955	Born in Miami, Florida, on March 9.
1972	Joins American Ballet Theatre (ABT).
1974	Appointed principal dancer at ABT.
1995	Retires from the ABT and makes only rare subsequent appearances.
2000	Becomes artistic director of Orlando Ballet, Florida.

organization almost $8 million to promote professional ballet in the United States, and both school and company now stood at the forefront of the country's vibrant dance scene. While undertaking the vigorous training needed to become a ballet dancer, Bujones also followed the regular education program at the Professional Children's School on New York City's West 60th Street.

After graduation Bojones's talent took him rapidly to the top of his profession. In 1972 he joined the corps de ballet (ensemble) of the American Ballet Theatre—the troupe in which Alonso had made her name in the 1940s—and the following year he was promoted to the rank of soloist. In 1974 he became one of the company's principal dancers alongside the émigré Russian Mikhail Baryshnikov. At the age of 19, Bujones was the youngest principal dancer in the company's history.

"Latin Lightning"
By this time Bujones had already acquired an international reputation. Shortly before his promotion to principal dancer, he had astounded both jury and public with his performance at the Seventh International Ballet Competition in Varna, Bulgaria, where he won a gold medal for the United States. Invitations to perform as a guest dancer followed from companies all over the world. In 1974 he made his European debut at the London Palladium, England, and two years later won his first encore at the Maracanā Stadium in Rio de Janeiro, Brazil.

Everywhere Bujones performed, his exhilarating, technically accomplished performances garnered him critical superlatives, along with the affectionate nickname "Latin Lightning." In 1980 he was one of the recipients of the Outstanding Young Men of America Awards, and in 1982 he became the youngest winner of the coveted *Dance*

INFLUENCES AND INSPIRATION

Fernando Bujones has often paid tribute to the many great male ballet dancers who have inspired him throughout his career, including the Dane Erik Bruhn (1928–1986) and the American Edward Villella (born 1936). His greatest influence, however, is acknowledged to be Rudolf Nureyev (1938–1993), whose athleticism, technical mastery, and good looks made the male ballet dancer the focus of attention as never before.

In 1961 Nureyev defected from his native Soviet Union and began to make guest appearances with dance companies across Europe and the Americas. As a boy, Bujones saw Nureyev perform in the ballet *La Bayadère*, and was immediately and deeply impressed by the Russian's formidable energy and presence. Later Bujones would work with Nureyev, notably at the Paris Opéra Ballet and the National Ballet of Canada.

The influence of Nureyev on Bujones has often been noted by critics. For example, in 1985 one British critic, writing of Bujones's debut with the Royal Ballet in London, wrote that "Not since Nureyev in his prime have we seen such a combination of voluptuous movement with an absolutely firm classical style." Another reviewer declared: "We have not looked upon the like since the young Nureyev astounded the West."

Magazine Award. In 1987 the illustrious French choreographer Maurice Béjart created a work specially for Bujones. By this time the dancer was producing his own choreography, including his debut work, "Grand Pas Romantique" (1984).

Bujones continued to dance through his late thirties. In 1991 the Boston Ballet celebrated his two decades as a dancer with a gala performance entitled "Bravo Bujones." Finally in 1995, just a month after his 40th birthday, he gave his farewell performance with the American Ballet Theatre at the Metropolitan Opera House, New York. His outstanding performance career with the company ended with a 20-minute standing ovation.

Dance administrator

Many retired dancers continue their involvement with the art by directing a ballet company; few, however, have shown themselves as able and astute in the role as Bujones. Even before his official retirement in 1995, he had served as the artistic director of the Ballet Mississippi in Jackson. His choreographic flair, management skills, and commercial sense really came to the fore, however, with his appointment as artistic director of the Southern Ballet Theater (later renamed the Orlando Ballet) in Orlando, Florida.

Under Bujones's direction, the Orlando Ballet rapidly became one of the finest troupes in the United States, attracting some of the best young dancers from around the world and establishing a varied repertoire that contrasted established classics, such as *La Fille Mal Gardée*, *Giselle*, and *Coppélia*, with contemporary pieces of choreography, some of which, such as "Jazz Swing" and "Splendid Gershwin," were the work of Bujones himself.

At the Orlando Ballet, Bujones has tried to reach out to Florida's large Hispanic community. A third of the company's dancers are themselves Hispanic, and the repertoire often has a strong Latin flavor as, for example, in "Let's Dance Salsa," and the jazz ballet *To the Rhythm*, which incorporates the work of the group Santana. Bujones works closely with Orlando's flourishing Hispanic businesses, some of which are sponsors, and uses bilingual English and Spanish publicity material and advertising. The ballet company's attendances and revenue have doubled during his time in charge.

Fame and posterity

Bujones's influence has also been felt across the United States in the increasing numbers of Hispanic dancers—especially males—now working for ballet companies. The American Ballet Theatre itself has taken up many Hispanic dancers in Bujones's wake—among them the Argentine Julio Bocca (born 1967) and the Cuban José Manuel Carreño (born 1968).

Bujones's more recent honors have included an Artistic Achievement Award from the Chicago National Association of Dance Masters (1998), a Lifetime Achievement Award from the Southern Ballet Theater Company (1999), and the ¡Qué Pasa! Hispanic Award (2001).

See also: Alonso, Alicia; Santana, Carlos

Further reading: Elizabeth Godley: "Fernando Bujones: Cuban Fire Meets Anglo-Saxon Practicality." *Dance International*, Summer 2005.
http://www.fernandobujones.com (official Web site).

BURCIAGA, José Antonio
Painter, Poet, Essayist

From the 1970s until his death in 1996 José Antonio ("Tony") Burciaga was a leading figure of the Chicano movement, which asserts Mexican American identity, culture, and rights. Although primarily an illustrator and artist, Burciaga became best known as a poet and essayist, and for his outspoken opposition to perceived injustices such as California's Proposition 187, passed by voters in 1994, under which undocumented immigrants were denied state benefits.

A second-generation Mexican American, Burciaga was brought up in his native El Paso, Texas, where his father worked as a caretaker in one of the city's churches. In 1960 Burciaga joined the Air Force, serving two years at a radar station in Iceland. He later took a bachelor's degree from the University of Texas at El Paso, and studied illustration at the Corcoran School of Art in Washington, D.C. For a time he worked as an illustrator for the Central Intelligence Agency (CIA).

Early work

During the 1960s and 1970s Burciaga began to write poetry. In his work he explored the difficulties of being Chicano—an identity which he once humorously defined as "Mexican by nature, American by nurture, a true 'mexture.'" One of his most famous poems is "Stammered Dreams/Sueños tartamudos", in which he describes the awkwardness some Chicanos feel when communicating in either Spanish or English.

While in Washington, D.C., Burciaga met and married the Latina educator Cecilia Preciado, and in the early 1980s the couple settled in California, where Preciado worked as a senior administrator at Stanford University. In 1984 Burciaga helped found the Chicano comedy theater group Comedy Fiesta, which would later evolve into the popular Culture Clash.

▲ *José Antonio Burciaga works on his controversial mural at the Casa Zapata.*

In 1985 Burciaga became a resident fellow at Stanford. In 1989 he attracted controversy when he painted a mural of the Last Supper in the university's Chicano residence, the Casa Zapata, in which he replaced Christ and the Disciples with Chicano and Chicana heroes, including Ché Guevara and Frida Kahlo. Burciaga gained a national reputation with the publication of *Drink Cultura: Chicanismo* (1993), a collection of essays and anecdotes about the Chicano movement.

In 1994 both Burciaga and his wife lost their jobs at Stanford amid some acrimony, and soon after he was diagnosed with cancer, from which he died two years later.

Further reading: Burciaga, José Antonio. *Drink Cultura: Chicanismo*. Santa Barbara, CA: Joshua Odell Editions, 1993. online.sfsu.edu/~josecuel/chicanismo.htm (discussion of Burciaga's ideas in relation to Chicanismo).

KEY DATES	
1940	Born in El Paso, Texas, on August 23.
1989	Paints *The Last Supper of Chicano Heroes*, Casa Zapata, Stanford.
1993	Publishes the essay collection *Drink Cultura: Chicanismo*.
1996	Dies on October 7.

BUSTAMANTE, Cruz
Politician

Cruz Bustamante is a leading Latino politician. He was the first Latino speaker of the California State Assembly, and when he was elected as the Democratic lieutenant governor of California he became the first Latino to take a California statewide office since 1878. As lieutenant governor Bustamante also served as a regent for the University of California, a trustee for the California State University, and a member of the State Lands Commission.

Early life
Bustamante was born in 1953 in Dinuba, California. The son of first-generation Mexican Americans Cruz and Dominga Bustamante, a barber and homemaker, Bustamante grew up in San Jaoquin with five siblings, one of whom, his sister Nao, later became a well-known performance artist. Bustamante's parents were both community activists and Cruz, Sr., ran for political office: He was elected a city councilman and also ran unsuccessfully for a county supervisor position.

Cruz Bustamante attended public high school and California State University, Fresno. To help his family's finances he had to work in the fields in his free time,

▼ *Cruz Bustamante takes part in a march held to commemorate the birthday of Martin Luther King, Jr.*

KEY DATES	
1953	Born in Dinuba, California, on January 4.
1993	Elected to 31st Assembly District.
1996	First Latino speaker of the California Assembly.
1998	Elected lieutenant governor of California.

an experience that influenced his later policies on immigration, education, agriculture, health care, and business practices.

Political career
Through his father, Bustamante found an internship in Washington, D.C., working for congressman B. F. Sisk. The experience changed his life and redirected his career path from that of a butcher to a politician. He went on to work for assemblyman Rick Lehman, the Fresno Summer Youth Employment Program, and assemblyman Bruce Bronzan. Bustamante ran successfully for Bronzan's seat in the 31st Assembly District in a special election in 1993.

As a member of the Democratic Party of California, Bustamante has been characterized as a moderate. He has repeatedly tried to shed the notion that his policy interests are part of an "ethnic" agenda. The issue was the center of vitriolic debate in his 2003 run for the governorship of California, particularly surrounding his membership of MEChA (Movimiento Estudiantil Chicano de Aztlán) while a student at Fresno. Bustamante has also strived to make the lieutenant governor a position of more authority by supporting educational initiatives, suing energy generators and tobacco companies for harming California consumers, and founding the Commission for One California to foster racial diversity and tolerance in schools, the media, and law enforcement.

Cruz Bustamante has received several awards for his work, including in 2003 the National Legislative Award from the League of United Latin American Citizens (LULAC).

Further reading: Bustamante, Cruz. *Fresno: Heartbeat of the Valley.* Memphis, TN: Towery Publishers, 2000.
http://www.lta.ca.gov (Web page of California Lieutenant Governor Cruz Bustamante).

CABANA, Robert
Astronaut, NASA Administrator

Ever since his days as a pilot for the U.S. Navy, flying everything from bombers to experimental aircraft, Robert Cabana believed he was destined for space. A graduate of the U.S. Naval Academy in 1971, Cabana showed outstanding aptitude from the start of his career, winning numerous medals and awards. His ability to fly a multitude of aircraft and his distinguished service record made him an ideal candidate to become an astronaut.

Robert Cabana was born on January 23, 1949, in Minneapolis, Minnesota, where he graduated from Washburn High School. He received a bachelor of science degree from the U.S. Naval Academy in 1971, before he went on to become a Navy pilot in 1976. Cabana was chosen for astronaut training in June 1985. Once qualified, he served in a number of important positions at the National Aeronautics and Space Administration (NASA), including deputy chief of Aircraft Operations at the Lyndon B. Johnson Space Center in Houston, Texas, and spacecraft communicator in Mission Control.

Shuttle mission

Cabana went into space on October 6, 1990, when he piloted the Space Shuttle *Discovery* on a five-day mission. The five-man crew deployed the spacecraft *Ulysses* at the start of its four-year journey to explore the Sun. The crew also conducted several experiments, including studying the effects of microgravity on plants. Cabana piloted *Discovery* again on December 2, 1992. He was later mission commander on the shuttle *Columbia* when it launched on July 8, 1994, for a 15-day mission, a new record for time spent in space. Cabana's crew conducted experiments that involved the cooperation of six space agencies around the world. Cabana's last flight was aboard the Space Shuttle *Endeavour* on December 4, 1998. The mission was a cooperative venture by the United States and Russia.

▲ *Robert Cabana receives assistance from a suit technician as he prepares for a space mission.*

By the end of his flying career Cabana had logged over 1,000 hours in space. More recently he has supervised space operations for NASA. After serving in a range of technical and administrative capacities, he was appointed deputy director at the Johnson Space Center in 2004.

Further reading: Cassutt, Michael. *Who's Who in Space.* New York: Macmillan, 1993.
http://www.jsc/nasa.gov/Bios/htmlbios/cabana.html (Official biographical website for NASA)

KEY DATES	
1949	Born in Minneapolis, Minnesota, on January 23.
1986	Completes initial NASA astronaut training.
1990	Pilots Space Shuttle *Discovery* on his first space flight, commencing on October 6.
1998	Serves as mission commander on the space shuttle *Endeavour*.

CABEZA DE BACA, Ezekiel
Politician

Ezekiel Cabeza de Baca was a leading Democratic politician in New Mexico in the early 20th century. When New Mexico became a U.S. state in 1912, he was elected its first lieutenant governor, and in 1917 he was sworn in as its second governor. Cabeza de Baca's abiding concern throughout his civil and political career was with the educational, economic, and political rights of Mexican Americans.

Early life

Cabeza de Baca was born in 1864 on a ranch near Las Vegas, New Mexico. He was the son of Estefana Delgado and Tomás Cabeza de Baca, a rancher, politician, and judge. They belonged to one of the most illustrious Spanish families in New Mexico; among their ancestors was the celebrated 16th-century Spanish explorer Alvar Nuñez Cabeza de Vaca.

Having completed his education in Las Vegas schools, Cabeza de Baca worked as a teacher and later as a clerk on the railroad. In 1889 he married his cousin, Margarita Cabeza de Baca. He then took a job as a journalist for the popular Spanish-language weekly newspaper *La Voz del Pueblo* (The Voice of the People), whose proprietor was Felix Martínez.

Into politics

Cabeza de Baca quickly established himself as a leading member of the Las Vegas community. In 1895 he helped form the Sociedad por la Protección de Educación (Society for the Protection of Education), an organization that provided schooling for the children of low-income Hispanic Americans. He also became involved in politics, joining the Partido del Pueblo Unido (United Peoples Party), which was led by his friend Martínez. The fusion of the party with the U.S. Democratic Party in 1892 led Cabeza de Baca to the forefront of New Mexico politics.

KEY DATES	
1864	Born near Las Vegas, New Mexico, on November 11.
1911	Is elected lieutenant governor of New Mexico.
1916	Is elected governor of New Mexico.
1917	Dies in Santa Fe, New Mexico, on February 18.

▲ *Ezekiel Cabeza de Baca was an important figure in the early political history of New Mexico.*

For much of his political career, Cabeza de Baca acted mainly as a spokesman and party organizer and did not himself take public office. In 1911, however, as New Mexico prepared for entry into the Union, he won election as the state's first lieutenant governor. While in office he carried through several progressive reforms, including a bilingual education bill. In 1916 he beat the Republican candidate, Holm Bursum, in the gubernatorial elections. By then, however, Cabeza de Baca was gravely ill. When he was sworn in in January 1917, he was receiving treatment at the St. Vincent Sanitarium in Santa Fe. At the inauguration ceremony, he told officials: "I want the people to be informed that I will be 'Governor of the People'—I mean, 'The People's Servant.'" Ezekiel Cabeza de Baca died only 49 days after being elected into office.

See also: Martínez, Felix

Further reading: Gómez-Quiñones, Juan. *Roots of Chicano Politics, 1600–1940*. Albuquerque, NM: University of New Mexico Press. 1994.

CABEZA DE BACA, Fabiola
Writer, Nutritionist

An important early figure in "Nuevomexicano" literature, Fabiola Cabeza de Baca belonged to a generation of women Hispanic writers who, from the 1930s, sought to record the culture and traditions of New Mexico, which they feared were facing eradication by rapidly advancing U.S. colonialism. Her best-known work is *We Fed Them Cactus* (1954), a richly detailed and nostalgic account of her childhood spent on the family ranch near Las Vegas, New Mexico.

The Nuevomexicana

Cabeza de Baca was born into a wealthy family of landowners and ranchers whose ancestors included the famous Spanish explorer Alvar Nuñez Cabeza de Vaca (about 1490–1560). Her father was Graciano Cabeza de Baca y Delgado (1867–1935). Her mother, Indalecia Delgado, died when she was four, and she was brought up by her formidable grandmother. Cabeza de Baca was educated in Las Vegas, Mexico, and graduated from high school in 1912.

By this time her family had lost much of its wealth, and to support herself Cabeza de Baca became a schoolteacher. The work gave her the independence to pursue her own education, and in 1921 she graduated with a bachelor's degree in pedagogy from the New Mexico Normal University in Las Vegas. In 1929 she gained another degree, in domestic sciences, from New Mexico State University, Las Cruces.

In the same year Cabeza de Baca became the first Hispanic woman to be employed by the New Mexico Agricultural Extension Services (NMAES), a state government department that taught modern farming practices to native peoples. For the next 30 years Cabeza de Baca traveled through New Mexico teaching Hispanic and native Pueblo women about food preservation and hygiene. As part of her work, she compiled some of the first books of traditional New Mexican cuisine, including *Historic Cookery* (1939). The publication was of great significance because some of the recipes it contained had been used by native peoples since the earliest times but had never previously been written down.

Vanishing way of life

The unexpected success of *Historic Cookery* and other, similar works led Cabeza de Baca to write further books in which she sought to give a detailed account of the way of life of the Hispanic population of New Mexico, which was rapidly changing under the impact of U.S. rule. In *We Fed Them Cactus* she created a warm and celebratory picture of ranch life and of the resilience of Hispanics in the face of hardship and social change. The book—written in English for a largely non-Hispanic audience—takes its title from the severe drought of 1918, during which ranchers were forced to feed their cattle the watery branches of cactus in order to keep them alive.

In the 1940s Cabeza de Baca was severely injured when the car in which she was traveling was hit by a train on a crossing in Las Vegas. She suffered facial disfigurement and had to have a leg amputated. Undeterred by her disability, she remained as active as she had been before the accident, and thereafter appeared in public with an old-fashioned artificial wooden limb. She found the prosthesis uncomfortable, however, and in private she took it off, and moved around on crutches.

Fabiola Cabeza de Baca retired from NMAES in 1959, but continued to lecture widely into advanced old age, and was a founder member of La Sociedad Folklorica (The Folklore Society). She died at the age of 97, and was buried at the family ranch in Newkirk, New Mexico. An important archive of her unpublished papers is housed in the Center for Southwest Research at the University of New Mexico in Albuquerque.

KEY DATES	
1894	Born near Las Vegas, New Mexico, on May 16.
1929	Begins work as an agent of Agricultural Extensions Services.
1939	Publishes *Historic Cookery*.
1954	Publishes *We Fed Them Cactus*.
1991	Dies in Albuquerque, New Mexico, on October 14.

Further reading: Cabeza de Baca, Fabiola. *We Fed Them Cactus*. Albuquerque, NM: University of New Mexico Press, 1954. http://elibrary.unm.edu/oanm/NmU/nmu1%23mss603bc (collection of Cabeza de Baca's papers at University of New Mexico).

CABRERA, Lydia
Ethnographer, Writer

During her long career Cuban ethnographer Lydia Cabrera wrote numerous short stories, essays, and studies about the culture, folklore, and languages of the Afro-Cubans (the African peoples of her native land). Although in later life Cabrera lived largely in the United States, she wrote primarily in Spanish. As yet only a small part of her influential and pioneering work has been translated into English.

Telling tales
Cabrera was the daughter of wealthy white Cuban writer and lawyer Raimundo Cabrera (1852–1923). She grew up in a household of black servants, and became fascinated by the magic-filled folk stories they told each other. At this time her brother-in law, the distinguished Cuban anthropologist Fernando Ortíz Fernandez (1881–1869), was also conducting research into the island's Afro-Cuban heritage.

▼ **Lydia Cabrera's stories were influenced by the folk tales of her native Cuba.**

In 1927 Cabrera went to study painting at the Ecole du Louvre in Paris, France, where she lived with her lover, the Venezuelan writer Teresa de la Parra (1895–1936). When de la Parra became fatally ill with tuberculosis, Cabrera wrote a series of tales based on black Cuban folklore to entertain her. The tales were eventually published in Spanish under the title *Cuentos Negros de Cuba* (*Black Tales of Cuba*) in 1940, a year after Cabrera had returned home.

In 1948 Cabrera published another collection of tales, *¿Por Qué?* (*Why?*), in which she drew on interviews with black Cubans carried out during her ethnographic fieldwork. The stories are full of magic and marvels, and sometimes have a sharp, satirical edge—in one story, a turtle defeats a pompous official, while in another the pope sends out an encyclical (papal document) about pumpkins.

A lifetime's labors
From the 1950s Cabrera increasingly turned her attention to Afro-Cuban religion. Her book *El Monte* (*The Wilderness*) (1954) was one of the first in-depth studies of the black Cuban religion Santéria (properly known as Lokumí), which derives from traditional African Yoruba beliefs and encompasses secret rites, hymns, and animal sacrifice. Cabrera also made important contributions to the study of Afro-Cuban languages and made several valuable recordings of the island's black music.

In 1959 Cabrera—a political conservative—fled Cuba after Fidel Castro established a Communist regime in the country. She settled first in Spain, but later moved to Miami, Florida, where she remained for the rest of her life.

KEY DATES	
1900	Born in Havana, Cuba, on May 20.
1927	Settles in Paris, France.
1954	Publishes *El Monte* (*The Wilderness*).
1991	Dies in Miami, Florida, on September 19.

Further reading: Rodriguez-Mangual, Edna M. *Lydia Cabrera and the Construction of an Afro-Cuban Cultural Identity.* Chapel Hill, NC: University of North Carolina Press, 2004. www.library.miami.edu/umcuban/cabrera/cabrera2.html (biography and bibliography).

CALDERÓN, Alberto
Mathematician

A cofounder of the so-called Chicago School of Analysis, Alberto Calderón was a mathematician who made significant contributions to calculus, infinite series, and the analysis of functions.

Born in Argentina, Calderón was the son of a medical doctor. He took his first degree, in civil engineering, at the University of Buenos Aires, and then traveled to the United States, where he completed a PhD in mathematics at the University of Chicago. On graduating he became, successively, a visiting associate professor at Ohio State University, a visiting member of the Institute for Advanced Study, and an associate professor at Massachusetts Institute of Technology (MIT). In 1959 he returned to Chicago as professor in mathematics. Apart from brief and occasional returns to MIT and the country of his birth, he remained at Chicago for the rest of his life.

Historic meeting

In 1948 Calderón was visited by the distinguished Polish American mathematician Antoni Zygmund (1900–1992), who had been impressed by Calderón's simple proof of a complex mathematical problem that he himself had devised. Zygmund supervised Calderón's subsequent research, and they worked together to create what became known as the Calderón–Zygmund Theory of singular integral operators. A singular integral is a mathematical object that may seem to be infinite, but that is finite when properly interpreted. Calderón later showed how singular integrals could be used to obtain estimates of solutions to equations in geometry, and to analyze functions of complex variables. He also demonstrated how they could provide new ways of studying partial differential equations. His work had wide-ranging theoretical and practical applications, being used to solve problems in pure

▲ *Mathematician Alberto Calderón spent much of his life teaching at the University of Chicago.*

mathematics and in engineering and physics. The two men's work offered mathematicians a better understanding, and spawned an informal school devoted to its study.

Calderón was widely honored for his achievements. In 1989 the American Mathematical Society awarded him the Steele Prize. In 1991 he received the National Medal of Science for his contributions to the field. Argentina honored him as well, awarding him the Consagracion Prize in 1989 for his work. Calderón was the author of more than 80 papers on mathematical theory and research. He died in Chicago after a short illness at the age of 77.

Further reading: Christ, Michael, Carlos E. Kenig, and Cora Sadosky (eds*.*). *Harmonic Analysis and Partial Differential Equations: Essays in Honor of Alberto P. Calderón.* Chicago, IL: University of Chicago Press, 1999.
http://www.mathunion.org/Organization/ICMI/bulletin/47/ Calderón_El-Pais_article.html (International Commission on Mathematical Instruction Bulletin translation of *El Pais* article "The Genius that Only Read the Titles").

KEY DATES	
1920	Born in Mendoza, Argentina, on September 14.
1950	Receives PhD in mathematics from the University of Chicago.
1958	Publishes paper on the solution of the Cauchy problem for partial differential equations.
1998	Dies in Chicago, Illinois, on April 16.

CALDERÓN, Sila María
Politician

Sila María Calderón was the first female governor of Puerto Rico, winning election in November 2001 and holding office from January 2002 to January 2005.

Early life

Sila María Calderón Serra was born in 1942 in San Juan, Puerto Rico, and attended high school at the Sacred Heart Academy in Santurce. She continued her education in the United States, taking an undergraduate degree in political science at Manhattanville College in Purchase, New York, in 1964. She then returned to her homeland to study at the University of Puerto Rico, where she completed a master's degree in public administration in 1972.

Calderón was then drawn into politics, and followed her father into the Popular Democratic Party (PPD), which then held power in Puerto Rico. In 1973 her former professor Luis Silva Recio became Puerto Rico's secretary of labor, and hired her as his assistant. She also worked as special assistant to Governor Rafael Hernández Colón. Under his administration she gained broad practical experience in public administration, especially in the areas of labor and economic development.

In November 1976 the PPD lost the general elections, and in January 1977 Hernández Colón quit the party. Suddenly out of a job Calderón went to work for Citibank Corporation and became president of Commonwealth Investment, Inc. She remained away from public administration until 1984, although she was in the meantime a prominent member of the Estado Libre Asociado (ELA), a political lobby group that works to preserve Puerto Rico's status as a commonwealth of the United States and opposes statehood for the island.

KEY DATES	
1942	Born in San Juan, Puerto Rico, on September 23.
1985	Appointed chief of staff by Puerto Rico governor.
1988	Becomes secretary of state and lieutenant governor.
1996	Elected mayor of San Juan.
2001	Elected first female governor of Puerto Rico.
2005	Leaves office on completion of first term.

The PPD won the general elections in 1984. In January 1985 Hernández Colón again became governor of Puerto Rico, and one of his first appointments on returning to office was to make Calderón chief of staff. She was the first woman to hold the post in Puerto Rico. In 1988, still under Colón's administration, she also served as secretary of state and lieutenant governor.

Return to corporate work

In 1990 Calderón resigned her jobs in the administration and returned to work in the private sector. From 1990 to 1992 she served on the board of directors for many profit and nonprofit organizations, including BanPonce (BPOP), Banco Popular de Puerto Rico (BPPR), Pueblo Internacional Inc., and The Sister Isolina Ferré Foundation. Until 1995 Calderón also worked for a consortium investing in the reconstruction of impoverished areas of San Juan.

By the mid-1990s Calderón was looking for a return to politics. The opportunity came in 1995 when she was nominated as the PPD candidate for mayor of San Juan.

INFLUENCES AND INSPIRATION

The life and career of Sila María Calderón are dominated by family influences. She inherited her interest in politics from her father, and passed it on to her children, two of whom—Sila Mari González and María Elena González—served in ceremonial capacities as "first ladies" while their mother was governor of Puerto Rico. Sila Mari was later elected to the Senate of Puerto Rico, and took her seat in January 2005.

Calderón's achievement in becoming the first female mayor of San Juan and later the first female governor of Puerto Rico have demonstrated to her compatriot women that the traditional social order is not unalterable, even in a strongly patriarchal society. As she herself has recalled: "When I was a little girl everybody who had power was male. Now girls know that it is very normal for power to be shared between men and women."

▲ *Sila María Calderón has campaigned vigorously to preserve Puerto Rico's commonwealth status.*

She won the election in November 1996, and took office the following January.

As mayor, Calderón focused on urban development and community outreach. She sponsored the revitalization of Río Piedras, Santurce, and Condado. She also proposed and initiated "Special Communities," a program intended to assist impoverished communities and promote community volunteerism. In 1998 Calderón led opposition to Governor Pedro Roselló of the New Progressive Party (PNP). Roselló wanted annexation of Puerto Rico by the United States, but a referendum did not support him: 50.3 percent of Puerto Ricans voted in favor of retaining commonwealth status.

Election victory

In 2000 Calderón ran for the governorship of Puerto Rico. Her campaign was based on three main platforms. She pledged to preserve the commonwealth relationship with the United States, undertook to end corruption in the public administration, and promised to address the problem of Vieques, an island near the Puerto Rican mainland used by the U.S. Navy for bombing exercises. In the election on November 7, 2000, she narrowly defeated the New Progressive Party candidate Carlos Pesquera to become the first woman elected governor of Puerto Rico.

Gubernatorial record

Calderón took office in January 2001, and three months later Puerto Rico filed a lawsuit against the U.S. government under the Noise Control Act of 1972. Her attempt to force U.S. withdrawal from Vieques was made despite a previous accord between Roselló and President Bill Clinton. They had agreed that a referendum would be held in February 2002 in which Puerto Ricans would be asked to choose between U.S. troops leaving the island by May 1, 2003, and allowing them to remain on the island indefinitely. If the people chose the latter option, Puerto Rico would receive a $50-million package of U.S. aid. Calderón's assertive initiative was at first resisted by President George W. Bush, who succeeded Clinton in 2001, but on May 1, 2003, the United States vacated Vieques without the proposed plebiscite.

Calderón also had some success in the fight against government corruption, but the overall effectiveness of her administration was hampered by frequent changes of personnel, and she was widely criticized for doing too little to combat increasing crime. In 2003 she announced that she would not stand for reelection, and at the end of her term of office in 2005 she withdrew completely from public life.

Personal life

Sila María Calderón has three children by her first husband, Francisco Xavier Gonzales Goenaga, to whom she was married from 1964 to 1975. Three years after they divorced she married Adolfo Krans, and the couple had five children. Divorced again in 2001, Calderón married Ramón Cantero Frau in 2003, but separated from him a few months after she completed her term as governor of Puerto Rico.

See also: Hernández Colón, Rafael; Roselló, Pedro

Further reading: Alexander, Robert J. (ed.). Presidents, Prime Ministers, and Governors of the English-speaking Caribbean and Puerto Rico: Conversations and Correspondence. Westport, CT: Praeger, 1997.

CALLEROS, Cleofas
Activist

Cleofas Calleros was a historian, writer, and community activist who is best remembered for his work to prepare Mexican immigrants for U.S. citizenship.

Early life

Born in 1896 in Mexico, Calleros was one of four children. In 1902 he immigrated with his family to the United States. They settled in El Paso, Texas, where his parents worked on farms. In 1904 diphtheria broke out in the city, and health officials deported many people of Mexican origin to Ciudad Juárez, regardless of whether they were U.S. citizens. Among the victims of the epidemic were Calleros's brother and two sisters, who all died in a single week.

Calleros attended the Sacred Heart School, from which he graduated as valedictorian in 1911, and then Draughton Business College. He had to work his way through school and college because his parents were so poor.

Wartime bravery

In 1917 Calleros lied about his citizenship in order to enlist in the Army when the United States entered World War I (1914–1918). He was wounded in action and was awarded a Purple Heart. He became a naturalized citizen in 1918. From 1920 to 1938 he was a member of the U.S. Army Officers Reserve Corps, and then worked for 20 years as a border representative for the Department of Immigration of the U.S. Catholic Conference. One of his main responsibilities was organizing free citizenship preparation classes for immigrants. His commitment to the activity was so great that he maintained his involvement for another 20 years after leaving government service.

▲ **Cleofas Calleros won a Purple Heart for his military service in World War I. In later civilian life he worked as a community activist and historian.**

Meanwhile Calleros wrote numerous works of regional history. In the late 1920s he contributed the first of an award-winning series of articles to the *El Paso Times*, and in the 1950s he coauthored two important books: *Queen of the Missions* (1952) and *Historia del Templo de Nuestra Señora de Guadalupe* (1953). The latter had an introduction by Carlos E. Castañeda.

Cleofas Calleros died in 1973, and was buried with full military honors. His only daughter later donated his papers to the University of Texas at El Paso.

See also: Castañeda, Carlos E.

Further reading: García, Mario T. *Desert Immigrants: The Mexicans of El Paso, 1880–1920.* New Haven, CT: Yale University Press, 1981.
http://www.tsha.utexas.edu/handbook/online/articles/CC/fcadb.html (Handbook of Texas Online).

KEY DATES	
1896	Born in Rio Florido, Chihuahua, Mexico, on April 9.
1918	Acquires U.S. citizenship; wins Purple Heart.
1920	Joins U.S. Army Officers Reserve Corps.
1938	Joins U.S. Department of Immigration.
1952	Publishes his first book, *Queen of the Missions*.
1958	Wins American Association for State and Local History merit award for articles in the *El Paso Times*.
1973	Dies on February 22.

CALVILLO, María del Carmen
Rancher

At the end of the 18th century, women owned one-fifth of the ranches in Spanish Texas. Few of them, however, took an active part in the daily business of cattle ranching, which was performed principally by men. One exception was María del Carmen Calvillo, who in 1814 undertook the management of her family's estate. Her determination and independence have today made her an icon of empowered Latina womanhood.

Early life

María del Carmen Calvillo-Arrocha was born in 1765 in San Fernando de Béxar (modern San Antonio, Texas). She belonged to an important family of Spanish settlers from the Canary Islands, who had first come to Texas—then part of the Spanish colony of New Spain—in the early 1730s. She grew up on a ranch that was part of the Mission San Juan Capistrano, one of a cluster of church-led communities that had sprung up on the land around San Fernando.

Ranch life was arduous, and European settlements were often vulnerable to raids from Comanches and Apaches. The Spanish colonists of Texas were not as wealthy as those in other parts of New Spain, but from the 1790s they were able to buy up the mission lands as the colonial rulers implemented a policy of secularization. In 1794 María's father, Ygnacio Calvillo, acquired the extensive Rancho de las Cabras (Ranch of the Goats) near present-day Floresville.

The early life of María Calvillo was typical of that of many colonial Hispanic women of the time, who were brought up to be primarily wives and mothers. In about 1781 Calvillo married another San Antonio colonist, Juan Gavino de la Trinidad Delgado (born 1760). The couple raised five children, two of whom— Juan Bautista and José Anacleto—were their biological sons, while the other three—Juan José, María Concepción Gortari, and Antonio Durán—were adopted.

KEY DATES

1765	Born in San Fernando de Béxar, Texas, New Spain, on July 9.
1814	Takes on management of the family ranch.
1856	Dies on Rancho de las Cabras, Texas, on January 15.

In the early 19th century Texas entered a troubled and uncertain period. In 1811 and 1813, in the wake of the Mexican uprising led by Miguel Hidalgo, revolts broke out in the province against Spanish rule. Spanish royalist forces quickly suppressed the insurrection, and many of the rebels were executed or imprisoned. Juan Gavino played an important part in both revolts, and María Calvillo seems to have used his downfall as an opportunity to separate from him.

Woman of property

In 1814 Ygnacio Calvillo was murdered during a raid on the Rancho de las Cabras. The assailants were at first thought to have been Native Americans, but subsequent inquiries implicated one of his own grandsons. María del Carmen Calvillo then took effective control of her late father's estate, and petitioned the Mexican government for formal rights of possession. The ensuing legal process was very slow, but she was eventually granted formal title to the ranch in September 1828. Further land grants made in 1833 gave her control of a vast area. Instead of hiring a ranch manager or calling in a male relative to help her, Calvillo took on the job of running the enormous ranch herself. She proved an able ranchera: an excellent equestrian as well as a skillful manager. She oversaw the installation of an extensive irrigation system and the construction of a granary and a sugar mill. While the owners of neighboring ranches had constant trouble with native peoples, Calvillo established a good relationship with them by sharing surplus cattle and grain in times of shortage.

Legacy

María Calvillo died in 1856 at age 90. Her land passed to two of her children, one of whom was her adopted daughter. The family later sold the ranch but it remained in private ownership until 1977, when it was purchased for about $86,000 by the Texas Parks and Wildlife Department, which now runs it as a Spanish Colonial Heritage site.

Further reading: Ríos McMillan, Nora E. "María Del Carmen Calvillo: How an Independent Spirit Emerged." *Journal of South Texas*, Vol. 13, No. 2 (Fall 2000). http://www.tsha.utexas.edu/handbook/online/articles/CC/fcabz.html (Handbook of Texas Online).

CAMACHO, Héctor
Boxer

Flamboyant and often controversial, Héctor "Macho" Camacho is considered one of the greatest fighters in the history of boxing. His record includes 79 victories and three major world titles between 130 and 140 pounds (59 and 64kg), and two lesser titles at between 147 and 160 pounds (67 and 73kg).

Early life
Héctor Luis "Macho" Camacho was born in Bayamon, Puerto Rico, on May 24, 1962. His family immigrated to New York when Camacho was a child. He grew up as a troubled youth, serving 3½ months in a New York prison for auto theft when he was 16. Boxing allowed him to channel his aggression in a positive manner.

Camacho rose from the streets of Spanish Harlem to become a top amateur fighter, winning the New York Golden Gloves tournament in his division three times before turning professional on September 12, 1980. He continued his success, moving from the featherweight class to the junior lightweight division. After just 12 fights he emerged as the National American Boxing Federation champion by beating Blaine Dixon in 12 rounds on December 11, 1981.

Ten fights later Camacho would capture his first major title by defeating Rafael Limon in dominating fashion to win the World Boxing Council title in August 1983. He put Limon down in the first and third rounds before the referee stopped the fight in the fifth. Camacho won his second major world title as a lightweight, defeating Mexico's Jose Luis Ramirez in a 10-round decision for the World Boxing Council title on August 10, 1985.

Shortly after Camacho scored another significant victory—a split decision against Edwin Rosario in Madison Square Garden in June 1986 to retain his title—his bad-boy reputation surfaced again. He was charged with possession of drugs after the fight, although the case against him was later dropped.

In March 1989 Camacho became a three-time world champion by defeating Ray "Boom Boom" Mancini for the vacant World Boxing Organization junior welterweight title with a unanimous 12-round decision.

Always a showman as well as a fighter, the flamboyant and controversial Camacho endeared himself to fans throughout the world. Leopardskin loincloth trunks, bikini briefs, Roman-soldier headpieces, and other outrageous

▲ *Héctor "Macho" Camacho (left) fights fellow veteran Roberto Duran in July 2001.*

outfits, a buzz cut accented by curly locks, and colorful banter were among the image-defining trappings of "The Macho Man." He was less popular with critics, however: Many of them disliked his extrovert nature, which they condemned as a poor imitation of Muhammad Ali.

Fights outside the ring
On the flip side of "Macho Madness" were the boxer's many out-of-ring spats, which were followed by carefully considered public declarations that he was a maturing and changed man. His subsequent actions did not often reflect any such changes, however. A scuffle with police officers in Dade County, Florida, led to charges of disorderly conduct and battery before a January 29, 1994, fight against Felix Trinidad. At stake was Trinidad's International Boxing Federation (IBF) welterweight title. Allowed to box under house arrest, Camacho went on to lose a lopsided 12-round decision.

INFLUENCES AND INSPIRATION

Héctor Camacho's showmanship and flair were undoubtedly influenced by Muhammad Ali, boxing's most famous extrovert. Camacho went far beyond the verbal flourishes that made Ali so famous. Camacho's wardrobe was elaborate, including loincloths, bikini underwear, and a Captain America outfit, which he wore for his fight against Julio César Chávez.

That legacy of flamboyance in and out of the ring has been passed on to other fighters, including Roy Jones Jr., Naseem Hamed, and Camacho's own son Héctor Camacho, Jr. Love him or hate him, Camacho has been a unique figure in boxing's circus. "I have this trademark," the fighter told *KO Magazine* in 1997, "Everyone wants to be like The Macho Man."

Camacho beefed up his record with 16 victories against mostly nondescript opponents before facing another Latino icon, Roberto Duran, in Atlantic City, New Jersey, on June 22, 1996. Camacho outscored his legendary opponent to gain a 12-round decision, setting up another high-profile fight.

With a guaranteed purse of $1.75 million dangled as an incentive, Camacho scored a fifth-round technical knockout (TKO) against Sugar Ray Leonard. By then Camacho was also well into the process of nurturing the career of his son, Hector Camacho, Jr., who turned professional in 1996 after failing in his bid to make the U.S. team for that year's summer Olympics in Atlanta, Georgia.

A family concern

The Camachos became only the third father and son in modern boxing history to fight on the same card when they each scored victories on October 1, 1996, in Fort Lauderdale, Florida. Camacho senior stepped into the ring wearing a silver cape, silver boots, and matching bikini underwear. Junior was dressed in his father's hand-me-downs, a teal loincloth with white tassels and matching boots.

The elder Camacho kept punching away, though he clearly could not sustain the charge of his younger days. He lost badly in Las Vegas, Nevada, on September 13, 1997, when Oscar De La Hoya ended his 21-fight winning streak with a unanimous decision.

Despite Camacho's periodic protestations that he had put his past behind him, his personal struggles continued to resurface; they were reflected in various arrests on charges ranging from domestic assault to cocaine possession. On January 6, 2005, Camacho was charged in Mississippi with trying to rob an electronic goods store and with possession of the drug ecstasy. Despite having entered his fifth decade, Camacho continued to fight occasionally, defeating Raul Jorge Munoz on July 9, 2005. He has been quoted as saying that, when he finally quits boxing, he would like to pursue a full-time career in acting, but to date he has had few opportunities in that area. After the Munoz fight Camacho had a career record of 79 wins, five losses, and two draws, with 38 wins by knockout.

"I'm going to leave my mark in boxing history as one of the greatest ever, after Muhammad Ali," Camacho told *The Orlando Sentinel* in September 1997. "I was in that category and never got the credit for it. People just don't want to talk that high about me because the flash and dash intimidates them. They really don't know me as a person. They know me as this bad-boy image, the center of attraction. It bothers them. It's too heavy. It's too real."

See also: De La Hoya, Oscar; Trinidad, Felix

Further reading: "Hector Camacho: 'I've Learned to Respect Myself.'" Interview in *KO Magazine*, August 1997. http://www.latinosportslegends.com/stats/boxing/Camacho_Hector_career_boxing_record.htm (career statistics).

KEY DATES

1962   Born in Bayamon, Puerto Rico, on May 24.

1980   Makes professional debut with a win against David Brown on September 12.

1983   Captures his first major title by defeating Rafael Limon to win the World Boxing Council super featherweight championship.

1989   Becomes a three-time world champion by defeating Ray "Boom Boom" Mancini for the vacant WBO junior welterweight title.

1996   Camacho and his son, Héctor Jr., become only the third father and son to fight on the same card in modern boxing history.

1997   Loses fight against Oscar De La Hoya for the WBC welterweight title.

CAMPECHE Y JORDÁN, José
Artist

The painter José Campeche was one of the earliest and greatest exponents of the style now known as Latin American colonial art. He was originally inspired by the artisan decorative traditions of his native Puerto Rico, and his greatest mature work deals with both religious and secular subject matter.

Early life

Born in 1751, José Campeche y Jordán was of mixed race, the son of a black former slave and a white mother. His father was an artisan who had prospered sufficiently to own his own house. He sent his son to the Covent Real de Santo Tomás de Aquino, the oldest and most important school in San Juan. There Campeche learned philosophy, Latin, anatomy, and music, while also receiving instruction from his father in the craft of decorating *retablos* (altarpieces). The young man excelled as a painter, learning from contemporary Spanish source books such as *Principios para estudiar el nobilisimo y real arte de la pintura* by José García Hidalgo. From 1775 to 1778 Campeche worked with Luis Paret y Alcázar, the exiled Spanish court painter, who introduced him to the rococo, a European style of painting characterized by delicate shapes and pastel colors.

Campeche benefited from the period of economic prosperity in Puerto Rico that followed the liberalization of the island's trade. His work became popular with the local political, military, economic, and religious elite, members of which were anxious to embellish the churches with, and to be depicted in, paintings. Although Campeche worked in the contemporary European style, his paintings allude to local conditions. For example, *Gobernador Ustariz* (1792), his portrait of the colony's governor, shows a view of San Juan through a window; *Exvoto de la Sagrada Familia* (1778–1780) depicts Puerto Rican slaves in adoration of the

▲ *This portrait of José Campeche by Ramón Atiles depicts Campeche with a painting of the Virgin Mary.*

Holy Family. Campeche was also in great demand by patrons in Venezuela following the death of that nation's most popular painter, Juan Pedro López (1724–1787).

Posthumous reputation

José Campeche died in 1809. His importance was established by a biography written in 1854 by local historian Alejandro Tapia y Rivera, and he has been honored continuously since. Manuel Gregorio Tavarez (1843–1883) composed "Rendención," a funeral march dedicated to Campeche's memory, and schools and streets in Puerto Rico have been named after the artist. Campeche has also been a source of inspiration to 20th-century artists, most notably Lorenzo Homar (1913–2004).

See also: Homar, Lorenzo

Further reading: http://www.yale.ws/ynhti/curriculum/units/ 1984/3/84.03.08.x.html (article on Puerto Rican art and artists).

KEY DATES	
1751	Born in San Juan, Puerto Rico, on December 23.
1775	Begins working with Spanish court painter Luis Paret y Alcázar.
1787	Enters the period of his artistic maturity.
1809	Dies in San Juan, Puerto Rico, on November 7.

CAMPOS, Juan Morel
Musician, Composer

One of the most acclaimed exponents of the Puerto Rican *danza*—a musical genre associated with European classical music that arose in Puerto Rico in the mid-19th century—Juan Morel Campos was a musician and composer. He is thought to have composed more than 500 works.

Early life

Born in the southern metropolitan town of Ponce, Puerto Rico, on May 16, 1857, Campos developed an interest in music at an early age. At age eight, he began taking lessons from Professor Antonio Egipciaco. Over the next few years, Campos developed his talents and became an accomplished musician, mastering the flute and the bombardino (baritone horn). He became the local church organist, and for a short time conducted the municipal band of Ponce.

Danzas

Campos was most influenced by "father of the *danza*" Manuel G. Tavárez. By the time Campos became his student in the 1870s, Tavárez was an established pianist and composer in Puerto Rico. Tavárez first popularized the *danza* in Puerto Rico with compositions such as "Margarita" (1870). Tavárez gave the *danza* a romantic classical slant that made it suitable to be played in concert salons as well as in less formal surroundings, such as clubs and dance halls. Under Tavárez's tutelage, Campos himself began to compose *danzas*. Tavárez died at age 39 in 1883, after which Campos became director of Bazar Otero's music department, where he sold musical instruments and accessories. Campos continued composing and developing new *danzas*, often incorporating a variety of modern rhythms and styles in his music.

Development

Campos originally composed *danzas* for his own dance orchestra, La Lira Ponceña. However, he was eager that his work should not be forgotten, and so with an eye on posterity he transcribed many of his compositions for the piano, thus enabling them to be played at domestic gatherings. Many of his musical works were inspired by romance, among them "Felices Días" (Happy Days), "Vano Empeño" (Persistence in Vain), "No Me Toques" (Do Not Touch Me), "Mis Penas" (My Sorrows),

"Tormento" (Torment), "Alma Sublime" (Sublime Soul), "Idilio" (Romance), "Maldito Amor" (Damned Love), and "Laura y Georgina" (Laura and Georgina). The subjects of these pieces were influenced by women and love. Campos was also inspired by African music rhythms; they can be heard in "No Me Toques," and in other pieces, such as "La Conga" (The Conga), "Si Te Toco" (If I Touch You), and "El Torbellino" (The Eddy). Of the hundreds of musical pieces that Campos composed, including waltzes, *zarzuelas*, symphonies, and overtures, more than 300 were *danzas*.

During a concert in Ponce on April 26, 1896, Campos suffered a stroke; he never recovered, and died 16 days later, at just 38 years of age.

Honors

Among the numerous honors and recognitions given to Campos were the creation of the Juan Morel Campos Free School of Music in San Juan, the Juan Morel Campos High School in Brooklyn, New York, and a junior high school in his hometown of Ponce. Morel Campos was also inducted posthumously into the International Latin Hall of Fame. To Puerto Ricans today, November 23 is known as the "Day of the Composer" in memory of Campos. Even now, Campos is considered one of the most renowned and influential composers of Puerto Rican *danzas*.

Further reading: Thomas, Donald (ed.) *Music in Puerto Rico: An Anthology*. Lanham, MD: Scarecrow Press, 2002. http://www.guitarpeople.com/classical/contrdanza.asp (article about *danzas*, featuring Morel Campos).

CANALES, José T.
Politician, Activist

Widely regarded as one of the outstanding Mexican American leaders of the 20th century, José T. Canales served in his native Texas as a lawyer and legislator. He was also a landowner and a founder of the League of United Latin American Citizens (LULAC), a pioneer civil rights organization.

Border-raised

José Tomás Canales was born in 1877 on a ranch in Nueces County. His parents were Andreas and Tomasa (Cavazos) Canales. On his mother's side Canales was descended from José Salvador de la Garza, one of the recipients of Spanish land grants made in the 18th century to pioneers willing to settle on the northeastern frontier of New Spain (modern Mexico).

The land held by the de la Garzas, the Espíritu Santo Merced, was an enormous tract that occupied most of what is now Cameron County in the Rio Grande Valley of south Texas. After the conclusion of the Mexican American War (April 1846– February 1848), the landholding was no longer in Mexico but was now part of the United States.

Canales attended schools on both sides of the border— in Nueces County, Texas, and Tampico, Matamoros, and Mier, Tamaulipas. In 1890, while still a teenager, Canales was sent by his family to study at the Texas Business College in Austin. While there he obtained employment with a cattle company as a driver, and traveled to Oklahoma, where he became friendly with a cattle dealer. His new acquaintance invited him to Kansas City, where he completed his studies in a Midwestern milieu through which he assimilated much more American culture than he would have experienced in his native surroundings. Along with improving his spoken English, Canales converted from Catholicism to Presbyterianism.

▼ *Lawyer José T. Canales helped found the League of United Latin American Citizens.*

After finishing school in Kansas, Canales was accepted at the University of Michigan, where he obtained a law degree in 1899. After returning to Texas in 1900, he practiced law in Corpus Christi and Laredo, and in 1903 received his first public position at the Cameron County Assessor's office in the border town of Brownsville. At this point Canales began to devote his energies to a political career by accepting the support of James B. Wells, Jr., who ran the Democratic Party in Cameron County. In 1905 the voters of the Ninety-fifth District (Cameron, Hidalgo, Starr, and Zapata counties) elected Canales to the Texas House of Representatives, in which he served until 1910. During his tenure Canales proved himself a progressive reformer when dealing with irrigation laws, education, and judicial and tax legislation. Before his term ended Wells withdrew his support when Canales did not follow the dictates of the south Texas party machine. Undeterred, Canales struck out on his own, and ran unsuccessfully for county judge as an independent.

Working for poor Hispanic Americans

Canales soon recognized that he could not succeed politically without the Democratic Party. Consequently in 1912 he returned to the fold, and was shortly afterward elected superintendent of public schools as a party candidate. During his time in office, which lasted until 1914, he stressed the need to educate the predominantly Spanish-speaking population of south Texas in the English language. He reasoned that if his poor rural Hispanic constituents impressed the United States with their loyalty,

INFLUENCES AND INSPIRATION

One consequence of José Canales's conversion as a young man to Presbyterianism was that it persuaded him to support the Eighteenth Amendment, which brought in Prohibition in 1920. His antialcohol stance did not endear him to local bosses of the Democratic Party.

The evenhandedness with which Canales represented the interests of Hispanic Americans became a model for subsequent generations of Tejano politicians. While he strenuously opposed white vigilantes who threatened his constituents, he believed that Mexican Americans should commit themselves unequivocally to the United States. He did everything in his power to ensure that migrant workers were prevented from fleeing back across the border to escape the draft that was introduced in 1917 when the nation entered World War I (1914–1918) against Germany.

sense of duty, and patriotism, they would obtain improved access to educational services.

Canales served as a county judge from 1914 to 1917, in which year he was again elected to the Texas state legislature, this time representing the Seventy-seventh District, Cameron and Willacy counties. Once back in office, Canales continued to support the rural agricultural and educational programs.

Ideology of assimilation

José Canales was a leading proponent of "Mexican Americanism," an ideology that stressed that ethnic Mexicans in the United States should assimilate American values and reduce their traditional dependency on Mexican culture. During Canales's lifetime a new generation of Mexican Americans grew up who were either born in the United States or who immigrated at a very early age from Mexico and became U.S. citizens. They were eager to make their presence felt as a political force, and Canales was prominent among a group of Mexican Americans who took up the civil rights struggle on their behalf. For example, on January 31, 1918, at special hearings held in response to unprovoked attacks on Mexican civilians, Canales called for curtailment of the authority of the Texas Rangers,

members of which were held responsible for the brutality. In the hearings, he filed 19 charges and demanded a legislative investigation and the reorganization of the force. As Canales put it in a letter to C. H. Pease, a legislator who opposed his efforts, "I want to clear out a gang of lawless men and thugs from being placed… in the character of peace officers to enforce our laws." Such mounting public criticism tarnished the Rangers' romantic image, but it also damaged Canales's political career. The Tejano (Mexican Texan) legislator received threats from Ranger officials, who were bent on silencing his outspoken criticisms, and he was even opposed by hearing committee chairman William H. Bledsoe of Lubbock. Demoralized by attacks from every quarter, and increasingly unpopular in the state assembly, Canales did not seek reelection in 1920.

New outlets

Although personal setbacks drove Canales out of politics, nothing could dampen his desire to help his people, and he turned his attention to civil rights activism. He drafted the League of United Latin American Citizens (LULAC) Constitution in Corpus Christi in 1929, then served a term as the fourth president of the organization. Elected in 1932, at the height of the Great Depression, Canales regarded education as the best hope for Hispanic Americans, and promoted the establishment of the LULAC Scholarship Fund, which provided young people with opportunities for higher education.

José T. Canales died in Brownsville, Texas, three weeks after his 99th birthday. He left one son and a widow, Anne Anderson Wheeler, to whom he had been married for 66 years.

Further reading: Anders, Evan. *Boss Rule in South Texas: The Progressive Era.* Austin, TX: University of Texas Press, 1982. http://www.tsha.utexas.edu/handbook/online/articles/CC/fcaag. html (Handbook of Texas Online).

KEY DATES	
1877	Born in Nueces County, Texas, on March 7.
1905	Elected to the Texas House of Representatives.
1914	Starts to serve as county judge.
1929	Drafts constitution of League of United Latin American Citizens (LULAC).
1932	Elected LULAC's fourth president.
1976	Dies in Brownsville, Texas, on March 30.

CANALES, Laura
Singer

Laura Canales was a leading Latin singer from the 1960s to the 1990s. For much of that period she was known as *La Reina de la Onda Tejana* (The Queen of Tejano Music). During her distinguished career she won more accolades and awards than either of the previous holders of the nickname, Chelo Silva and Lydia Mendoza.

Texas-born Canales began her singing career with encouragement from her high school choral director, Milicent Wiley. From an early age her main ambition was to be the lead singer with a Tejano band, but in her youth musical groups of all types were almost exclusively male. However, her talent was so outstanding that it could not be ignored for long: Canales joined Los Unicos shortly after graduating from high school and cut her first record in 1973. She was invited to sing with El Conjunto Bernal, but the trio of brothers could not make room for her at the front microphone. She joined Snowball (Ramiro de la Cruz) and Company in 1975, and recorded a version of Linda Ronstadt's "Blue Midnight," which became a hit single in 1977. From then on any song Canales recorded or any album produced with her material skyrocketed to the top of the charts.

Married life
In 1981 Canales married Balde Munoz, a drummer with Snowball, and together they formed the group Laura Canales and Encanto. Again she enjoyed hit after hit. She won both the Female Entertainer of the Year and Female Vocalist of the Year at every Tejano Music Awards event held between 1983 and 1987. That record run of accolades stood until the 1990s, when it was surpassed by Selena (Quintanilla Perez).

▲ **Known as the Queen of Tejano Music, Laura Canales was one of the genre's greatest exponents.**

In 1989 Canales separated from Balde, and Encanto broke up. She then went into semiretirement, although she recorded occasionally with Los Fabulosos Cuatro and took part in a special one-time Leyendas y Raises tour with fellow Tejano performers Carlos Guzman, Freddie Martinez, Mario Montes, Sunny Ozuna, Agustin Ramirez, and Grupo Sierra.

Early death
Canales retired completely in 1992 to return to college and her hometown. She earned a bachelor's degree in clinical psychology in 1997, and then began a master's degree. She did not live to complete it, dying from complications during bladder surgery at the age of 50.

See also: Mendoza, Lydia; Ronstadt, Linda; Selena

Further reading: Clark, Walter Aaron (ed.). *From Tejano to Tango: Latin American Popular Music.* New York, NY: Routledge, 2002.
http://www.washingtonpost.com/wp-dyn/articles/A10756-2005Apr22.html *(Washington Post obituary).*

KEY DATES	
1954	Born in Kingsville, Texas, on August 19.
1973	Releases first record.
1977	Releases first hit single, "Blue Midnight."
1981	Marries Balde Munoz; together they form Laura Canales and Encanto.
1989	Splits from husband and group.
2005	Dies in Corpus Christi, Texas, on April 16.

CANALES, Nemesio
Writer, Lawyer, Activist

Nemesio Canales was a man of many talents who achieved distinction as a lawyer, unionist, essayist, poet, journalist, and, posthumously, as a playwright.

Born in Jayuya, Puerto Rico, Canales was the son of Rosario Canales and Francisca Rivera. His younger sister, Blanca, became a nationalist leader. After completing high school, he moved to Spain to study medicine at the University of Zaragoza. Two years into his medical studies, and in the midst of the Spanish–American War of 1898, Canales decided to return to his native island without completing his degree. He changed careers by moving to the United States and graduating with a law degree in 1903 from the Baltimore College of Law in Maryland.

Canales then returned again to Puerto Rico, where he worked as a lawyer in Ponce, and later joined the law offices of Miguel Guerra Mondragón and Luis Llorens Torres in San Juan. Like many lawyers of the time, including both his colleagues, Canales was active in politics and had a strong urge to write. He joined the pro-worker Unionist Party and, after being elected to the Puerto Rican House of Representatives in 1909, advocated the political rights of women and introduced legislation that would allow them to vote.

Writing career

Meanwhile Canales developed a parallel career as a journalist. He had been associated with the newspaper *El Eco de Puerto Rico* since 1905, and later wrote a regular column, entitled "Paliques," for *El Día*, the leading newspaper in Ponce. His writing reflected the whole vast spectrum of his interests—social science, culture, economics, and politics—and was informed, witty, and generally light-hearted. Many of the critical essays that appeared in the "Paliques" column were anthologized in book form in 1913. Canales further collaborated on various other publications in Puerto Rico, and he cofounded the newspaper *Juan Bobo*, which later became the journal *Idearium*. In 1913 Llorens Torres founded *Revista de las Antillas*, and invited Canales to work for the new magazine. Canales wrote "Vendimia literaria," a column in which he aired his views about the world of letters, books, authors, and literary movements. His contributions were extremely popular and greatly enhanced his reputation. Formerly perceived as a lawyer and an occasional journalist, he became one of Puerto Rico's leading writers.

KEY DATES	
1878	Born in Jayuya, Puerto Rico, on December 18.
1909	Elected to Puerto Rican legislature.
1922	Becomes assistant attorney general, Puerto Rico Department of Justice.
1923	Dies in New York on September 14.

Canales was a forerunner of modernism in Puerto Rican literature, a movement that was characterized mainly by poetry. Among his best-known poems are "Mi caballo," "Por el camino," and "En tu oído," which were published in *Revista de las Antillas* and another journal, *La Semana*. Canales was now internationally acclaimed, being published, and making personal appearances in many countries of Latin America: Argentina, Costa Rica, Honduras, Panama, Paraguay, Peru, and Venezuela.

In 1922 Canales became assistant attorney general of Puerto Rico, but resigned from the position soon after his appointment. He died in New York City in 1923 en route to Washington, D.C., where he was to have served as legal counsel in a Puerto Rican legislative commission on U.S.–Puerto Rican labor relations. Shortly after he died his play *El Heroe Galopante* (The Traveling Hero) was staged in San Juan.

Achievement and legacy

Nemesio Canales made an important mark on the literature of Puerto Rico through his versatility and use of innovative writing techniques, and on its politics through his radical progressivism. His posthumous reputation has grown: A major avenue has been named for him in San Juan, and in his birthplace, Jayuya, there is a commemorative statue of him sculpted by Tomas Batista. The Nemesio Canales Award in Literature is presented annually to outstanding young Puerto Rican writers.

See also: Batista, Tomas; Torres, Luis Llorens

Further reading: Canales, Nemesio. *Obras Completas.* San Juan, Puerto Rico: Instituto de Cultura Puertorriqueña, 1972. http://www.preb.com/qs/qsoy90.htm (brief biography in Spanish).

CANSECO, Jose
Baseball Player

Jose Canseco is one of baseball's most controversial players. He played 16 seasons for seven teams, drawing fans with his thunderous home run power. Although he fell only 38 home runs short of the 500 benchmark, Canseco gained more celebrity, if not infamy, for his writing. In 2005 the self-proclaimed "Godfather of Steroids" wrote a best-selling book implicating a number of prominent superstars. The book helped spark congressional hearings into alleged abuse of performance-enhancing drugs.

Jose Canseco Capas, Jr., was born in Cuba in 1964 but was brought as an infant to the United States when his family fled Fidel Castro's regime. Although he played baseball for Coral Park High School in Miami, Florida, he did not emerge as a legitimate prospect until signing with the Oakland A's in 1982.

Success and controversy

After being named American League Rookie of the Year in 1986, Canseco became the first big-league player in the modern era to hit 40 homers and steal 40 bases in the same season (1988). He played in three consecutive World Series with the A's from 1988 to 1990, winning the title in 1989.

Despite his talents, Canseco is generally considered to have squandered his true potential with a carefree lifestyle.

▼ *Jose Canseco (right) is congratulated by New York Yankees teammates after a home run in 2000.*

KEY DATES	
1964	Born in Regla, a suburb of Havana, Cuba, on July 2.
1982	Drafted to the Oakland A's.
1985	Makes Major League debut on September 2.
1988	Becomes the first 40-40 player in major league history when he hits 42 homers and has 40 steals; is elected American League MVP.
1989	Wins World Series with Oakland A's.
1993	Injures right elbow and misses half a season.
2005	Canseco tells a Congressional committee that steroids were as acceptable in the 1980s and 1990s as "a cup of coffee," and urges Congress to take action to stop their use.

Persistent rumors of steroid use, a social life that included an aggravated assault charge for ramming his Jaguar XJS into a new car driven by his former wife, and a late-night outing with Madonna made Canseco a gift for paparazzi and the tabloids. Of the media attention, Canseco said: "I love playing baseball, but sometimes I feel like the gorilla in the zoo. People watch the gorilla, stare at it, point at it, trying to figure out why it's doing what it's doing."

His last truly successful season was 1998, when he had 46 homers, 107 runs batted in (RBI), and 29 steals for Toronto, coinciding with the first time since 1991 that he played as many as 120 games in a season.

After his release by the California Angels in spring training during 2001, Canseco played with Newark of the Independent Atlantic League and worked his way back to the majors, hitting 16 home runs at the end of the 2001 season for the Chicago White Sox.

In 2005 Canseco wrote *Juiced: Wild Times, Rampant 'Roids, Smash Hits, and How Baseball Got Big*. The book contained numerous accusations of steroid abuse in Major League Baseball and named several leading players. It increased scrutiny into possible steroid abuse in baseball, led to Congressional hearings, and went to the top of the *New York Times'* best-seller list.

Further reading: Canseco, Jose. *Juiced: Wild Times, Rampant 'Roids, Smash Hits, and How Baseball Got Big.* New York: Regan Books, 2005.
http://www.historicbaseball.com (baseball history Web site).

CANTOR, Andrés
Broadcaster

▲ *Andrés Cantor has been used in various advertising campaigns by companies such as Pepsi and Snickers.*

Immortalized by his trademark cry of "GOOOAL!" in the soccer World Cup, popular Spanish-language broadcaster Andrés Cantor is among the most recognizable sports commentators in the United States. Cantor broadcast the play-by-play for matches during the 1990, 1994, and 1998 World Cups on the Miami-based U.S. Spanish-language station Univision. Broadcaster Bob Costas once timed Cantor's goal call at 26 seconds (Cantor has, however, made even longer calls). At the end of each half, Cantor delivers another signature line: "El arbitro dice que no hay tiempo para mas"—"The referee says there is no more time."

Early life
Cantor was born in Buenos Aires, Argentina, on December 22, 1962. When Cantor was a teenager his father, who was a doctor, moved the family to the affluent Los Angeles suburb of San Marino, where Cantor attended San Marino High. He went on to attend the University of Southern California in Los Angeles, where he majored in journalism.

A lifelong love of sports
Cantor never forgot his Argentine soccer roots. He recalled watching soccer matches on TV and being enthralled by the announcers' spirited goal calls. He put this to use when he was hired by Univision as a soccer broadcaster in the late 1980s. Although Cantor had worked at an Argentine sports magazine for a few years, he did not have much broadcasting experience. The station loved his energy, enthusiasm, and knowledge of soccer, however. Cantor began incorporating his childhood memories of thrilling goal calls into his broadcasts. The lively style was Cantor's route to U.S. and worldwide fame. Cantor's calls

were eventually played on television networks across the globe. Cantor was teamed with Argentina-born sportscaster Norberto Longo, and the duo earned a reputation as the best Spanish-language sports team in the United States. Cantor quit Univision after 13 years in 2000 to join the Spanish-language network Telemundo. Longo joined Cantor at Telemundo; however, he died of a massive heart attack in April 2003.

Cantor, who won an Emmy for his work in 1994, has estimated that he broadcasts approximately 150 games a year. He served as a soccer analyst for NBC during the 2000 Olympic Games in Sydney, Australia. In 2004 Cantor was a studio analyst and broadcaster in Athens when Telemundo became the first U.S. Spanish-language station to broadcast the Olympics.

KEY DATES

1962 Born in Buenos Aires, Argentina, on December 22.

1990 Broadcasts his first soccer World Cup for Univision.

1994 Receives an Emmy for Individual Achievement.

2000 Olympic soccer announcer at the Sydney Games for NBC.

2004 Broadcasts Olympic soccer for the U.S. Spanish-language network Telemundo.

Further reading: Cantor, Andrés. *GOOOAL: A Celebration of Soccer.* New York: Simon & Schuster, 1996.
http://www.laradiodelmundial.com/andres.htm (Fútbol de Primera Web site).

CANTÚ, Norma Elia
Writer, Academic

Norma Elia Cantú is one of the best-known Chicana authors and educators today. She has been active in promoting Chicano/a culture for more than three decades.

Early life
Cantú was born on January 3, 1947, in Nuevo Laredo, Tamaulipas, on the Mexican side of the Texas–Mexico border. The following year she moved to the United States with her parents, Florentino and Virginia Ramon Cantú. She became a naturalized U.S. citizen in 1968.

Cantú received a BS in English and political science from Texas A&I–Laredo in 1973; she received an MS from Texas A&I–Kingsville in 1976. Cantú then graduated in 1982 from the University of Nebraska–Lincoln with a doctorate in English.

Academic career
Cantú began teaching while in college, first as a teaching assistant and then as an instructor. In 1980 she began teaching at Laredo State University. She received tenure in 1987, and became a full professor in 1993. In 2000 she took a position at the University of Texas, San Antonio. Cantú has taught as a visiting professor at a number of other schools, such as at Georgetown University. She has also worked in administrative posts, serving as interim dean of education and arts and sciences at Texas A&M (1991–1992) and as acting director of the Center for Chicano Studies at the University of California at Santa Barbara (1998–1999).

▲ **Norma Elia Cantú has won several awards for her work as both a writer and an academic.**

The emergence of a writer
Cantú began writing and publishing book reviews of Chicano texts in graduate school. In 1983 she published the poems "Untitled" and "Unemployed" in the journal *Huehuetitlan*. Following this she published several short stories. Her first major work, *Canícula: Snapshots of a Girlhood en la Frontera,* was published in 1995 to critical acclaim. The book was later reprinted in Spanish in 2000. Cantú published *Soldiers of the Cross: Los matachines de la Santa Cruz* (Texas A&M University Press) in 2005.

Cantú considers being bilingual in English and Spanish an asset for a writer. She says that it allows her to draw on the richness of two languages and cultures. Cantú has served on the editorial boards of many journals and publishers. She has delivered many papers at professional conferences and is a popular guest speaker. Cantú's work has won several awards.

Further reading: Cantú, Norma Elia. *Canícula: Snapshots of a Girlhood En La Frontera.* Albuquerque, NM: University of New Mexico Press, 1995.
http://colfa.utsa.edu/cantu/ (University of Texas at San Antonio's page on Norma Elia Cantú).

KEY DATES

1947 Born on January 3 in Nuevo Laredo, Tamaulipas, Mexico.

1973 Receives a BS from Texas A&I–Laredo.

1976 Receives an MS from Texas A&I–Kingsville.

1982 Awarded a PhD in English from the University of Nebraska–Lincoln.

1995 Publishes *Canícula: Snapshots of a Girlhood en la Frontera.*

2001 Receives the Outstanding Alumni Award from Laredo Community College.

CAPETILLO, Luisa
Labor Organizer

Luisa Capetillo was an intellectual, writer, and feminist. One of the most important Puerto Rican labor organizers of her generation, Capetillo is more popularly known as the first woman in Puerto Rico to wear pants.

Born in Arecibo, Puerto Rico, on October 28, 1879, Capetillo was the daughter of Luisa Margarita Perone, a French teacher, and Luis Capetillo Echevarria, a Spanish immigrant. Educated at home, Capetillo was encouraged to think and speak freely by her unorthodox parents, who lived together but never married. Capetillo was attracted to the idea of a society organized on a cooperative basis rather than by a government-run system. Aged 19, Capetillo fell in love with Manuel Ledesma. The couple had two children before they parted three years later.

Activist

Capetillo took a job as a reader in Arecibo's tobacco factories to support her children. She read newspaper articles, novels, and political essays aloud to factory workers. She met many unionists through her job. In 1905 Capetillo began working for the Free Federation of Workers. Her intelligence and commitment to labor rights soon made her stand out as a natural leader. She began traveling around Puerto Rico to encourage workers to unite for positive change. She also argued that unions were the best means by which women could achieve equality.

In 1909 Capetillo published her opinions on unions and other major issues in the essay collection *My Opinion about the Liberties, Rights, and Responsibilities of Women*. She called for an end to the exploitation of women and argued for a workers' revolution. She also demanded the legalization of divorce. These views were also expressed in

▼ *Luisa Capetillo's insistence on wearing pants offended many people and led to her arrest in 1905.*

La Mujer, a short-lived magazine that Capetillo founded.

The United States

In 1912, a year after she gave birth to her third child, Capetillo moved to New York City. She wrote for several newspapers. In 1913 she began reading in a tobacco factory in Tampa, Florida. Over the next few years she traveled to Cuba and the Dominican Republic to support striking workers.

In 1916 Capetillo helped organize a strike of more than 40,000 sugar-cane workers, resulting in an average wage increase of more than 13 percent. In 1919 she also helped secure legislation for a minimum wage in Puerto Rico. Capetillo also ran a guest-house and cafe in New York City before her death in 1922.

KEY DATES

1879 Born in Arecibo, Puerto Rico, on October 28.

1909 Publishes *My Opinion about the Liberties, Rights, and Responsibilities of Women.*

1916 Helps organize a large-scale strike by Puerto Rican sugar-cane workers.

1919 Helps secure a minimum wage in Puerto Rico.

1922 Dies on October 10.

See also: Political Movements

Further Reading: http://www.lucyparsonsproject.org/anarchism/ aldebol_luisa_capetillo.html (article on Capetillo).

CAPÓ, Bobby
Musician

Born Félix Manuel Rodríguez Capó in Puerto Rico in 1922, Bobby Capó was a popular singer and composer. His professional career began in his native country when he replaced vocalist Davilita in the Victoria Quartet directed by Rafael Hernández. In the early 1940s Capó immigrated to the United States, where he worked with numerous Latin bands and vocal groups in New York City.

Rise to stardom
Capó became famous after he was hired as a singer by Xavier Cugat, whose orchestra appealed to all kinds of audiences. Over his long career Capó recorded mambos, popular music, and boleros. He not only sang the top songs of the period—most famously a cover of "Besame mucho" (Kiss Me a Lot)—but also wrote much of his own material. Cugat's band toured the United States, the Caribbean, and Latin America, bringing Capó's vocal abilities to the attention of a vast international audience.

By the 1950s Capó was an established solo vocalist, and his compositions brought him even greater popularity. His own songs included "El Negro Bembon," "El Bardo," "Luna de Miel en Puerto Rico," "Sin Fe," "Triangulo," and "María Luisa." The work for which he was best known, however, was "Piel Canela," which became his signature song. It was a hit when first released in 1952, and has since been reprised by many other singers, including Plácido Domingo, Nat King Cole, Eydie Gorme, Linda Ronstadt, José Feliciano, Trío Los Panchos, and Vicki Carr.

Soon after the inauguration of President John F. Kennedy in 1961, Bobby Capó composed "Jacqueline," a song dedicated to Jacqueline Bouvier Kennedy, the first lady. After reaching age 40, Capó gradually reduced his performing schedule. He worked increasingly in television, hosting his own show on Channel 47 in New Jersey. He also served as musical director to various bands and continued to compose original work.

▲ *Singer Bobby Capó found fame when he began to perform with bandleader Xavier Cugat. He later enjoyed solo success.*

Bobby Capó retired from show business in the early 1970s. He subsequently worked in the Puerto Rican Department of Labor's Division of Migration in New York. He died in 1989 at age 77. His reputation grew posthumously, and in 1997 Governor George E. Pataki of New York established the Bobby Capó Lifetime Achievement Award honoring Hispanics who have distinguished themselves in the arts and public service within the state.

See also: Carr, Vicki; Cugat, Xavier; Feliciano, José; Ronstadt, Linda

Further reading: Roberts, John Storm. *The Latin Tinge.* New York, NY: Oxford University Press, 1999.
http://www.musicofpuertorico.com (eclectic Web site featuring numerous references to Capó's work).

KEY DATES	
1922	Born in Coamo, Puerto Rico, on January 1.
1941	Immigrates to the United States.
1952	Releases "Piel Canela," his theme song.
1989	Dies in New York City on December 18.

CAPOBIANCO, Tito
Opera Director

One of the world's foremost opera directors, Argentine Tito Capobianco is best known for his long association with the Pittsburgh Opera, which he helped transform into one of the foremost companies in the United States. While his innovative productions and support for young and lesser-known singers have frequently won him plaudits, his fiery, aggressive management style has often entangled him in controversy.

Innovation and provocation

Tito Capobianco was born in 1931 in La Plata, Argentina, and named after his father's favorite singer, the Italian tenor Tito Schipa (1889–1965). In 1954, at age 23, he directed his first opera production at La Plata's Teatro Argentino. Capobianco quickly gained a reputation for his striking and sometimes provocative interpretations of classic operas. One of his most famous productions in Argentina was his 1957 modern-dress *Tosca*, which he used to attack the oppressive regime of Juan Perón, who had only recently been overthrown. In 1959 Capobianco was appointed technical director of the Teatro Colón, the world-renowned opera house in Buenos Aires.

In 1962 Capobianco's burgeoning reputation brought him to the United States. From 1965 he directed a series of bold productions for the New York City Opera, including *Don Rodrigo* (1966) and *Manon* (1977), working with some of the greatest names in modern opera, such as Spanish tenor Plácido Domingo and American soprano Beverly Sills. Meanwhile, Capobianco had also become an important figure in musical education, especially after his appointment in 1968 as director of the Julliard School's American Opera Center.

In 1975 Capobianco became the general director of the San Diego Opera in California. There his outstanding

▲ *Tito Capobianco poses during rehearsals at the Pittsburgh Opera.*

achievement was the launch of an annual festival celebrating the operas of Giuseppe Verdi. However, other ambitious plans for the San Diego Opera soon faltered owing to lack of funding, and in 1983 Capobianco left to become director of the Pittsburgh Opera in Pennsylvania. Having learned from his mistakes in San Diego, he embarked on an aggressive fundraising campaign and concentrated the company's resources on the high-quality production of popular operas. Under his direction the Pittsburgh Opera flourished as never before. He introduced innovations such as "supertitles" (simultaneous translations projected above the stage) and matinée performances, which helped bring in a wider cross-section of the community. In 1985 he opened the Pittsburgh Opera Center, the company's educational wing.

Capobianco left the Pittsburgh Opera in 2000, and in the following years focused much of his work on education. In 2004 he returned to Argentina as director of the Teatro Colón, but resigned the following year amid much controversy. Capobianco has received many honors, including honorary doctorates from the University of Duquesne, Indiana, and Roche College, Pennsylvania.

Further reading: Stanley Sadie, ed. *The New Grove Dictionary of Opera*. New York, NY: Oxford University Press, 1998. www.post-gazette.com/magazine/20000402tito2.asp (article about Capobianco's directorship of the Pittsburgh Opera).

KEY DATES	
1931	Born in La Plata, Argentina, on August 28.
1962	Immigrates to the United States.
1965	Produces the first of a series of works for the New York City Opera.
1983	Appointed general director of the Pittsburgh Opera.
2004	Is briefly director of the Teatro Colón, Buenos Aires.

CARA, Irene
Singer, Actor

Irene Cara is best remembered for her role as Coco Hernández in Alan Parker's *Fame* (1980), a film about New York's High School of the Performing Arts (now the Fiorello H. LaGuardia High School of Music & Art and the Performing Arts). Cara sang the film's title song as well as its first hit single, "Out Here on My Own." She is also well known as the singer and cowriter of "What a Feeling," the song from the movie *Flashdance* (1983), for which she won an Academy Award, a Golden Globe, and two Grammies.

Early life
Born in 1959 in New York City, Irene Cara Escalera was raised in the South Bronx by her Puerto Rican father, Gaspar, and her Cuban American mother, Louise. Her musical talent was evident from an early age. By five she had learned to play piano by ear. At age seven she began singing and dancing on local Spanish-language television.

▼ *Irene Cara stars as Coco Hernández in* **Fame.** *Cara performed the movie's title song.*

A year later Cara made her Broadway debut in the musical *Maggie Flynn*. Her performance led to her first appearance on national TV, a part in *The Electric Company*, an educational series with Bill Cosby and Rita Moreno. At age eight she recorded her first song for the Spanish market; at 10 she appeared with Stevie Wonder and Roberta Flack in a concert tribute to Duke Ellington. As a teenager her first lead role was in *Aaron Loves Angela* (1975), which led to the title role in *Sparkle* (1976). She also participated in two TV miniseries: *Roots: The Next Generation* (1979) and *Guyana Tragedy: The Story of Jim Jones* (1980).

Hitting the heights
Cara became a major star in 1981, when she was the first performer to sing two Academy Award nominated songs—"Fame" and "Out Here on My Own"—at a single Oscars night. In 1982 she won the Image Award for Best Actress when she costarred in *Sister, Sister*, a TV movie, and the following year won an Oscar for the song "What a Feeling," which she cowrote. Next she portrayed Myrlie Evers in *For Us the Living*, a TV movie about civil rights leader Medgar Evers. Cara also starred opposite Clint Eastwood and Burt Reynolds in the gangster comedy *City Heat* (1985).

In 1985 Irene Cara sued her recording company over unpaid royalties. In 1993 the case finally went to court in California. She was awarded $1.5 million, but much of the money went to cover legal fees. Since 2002 Cara has written scripts and scores for musicals, and performed as lead singer in the all-female band Hot Caramel.

KEY DATES	
1959	Born in New York City, New York, on March 18.
1980	Stars in *Fame*.
1983	Wins Academy Award for lyrics to "What a Feeling."
2002	Forms Hot Caramel.

See also: Moreno, Rita

Further reading: Desmond, Jane C. (ed.). *Meaning in Motion: New Cultural Studies of Dance*. Durham, NC: Duke University Press, 1997.
http://www.irenecara.com (official Web site).

CARBAJAL, José María Jesús
Tejano Patriot, General

During the Texas Revolution of 1835–1836, a large number of Tejanos joined the American colonists in their revolt against Mexican rule. A leading Tejano revolutionary was José María Jesús Carbajal, who was one of the signatories of the Goliad Declaration of Independence of December 2, 1835. Carbajal's checkered, freewheeling career is suggestive of the divided loyalties and shifting sense of identity experienced by many Hispanics living in the U.S.–Mexican border region in the early 19th century.

Early life

José María Carbajal was born in or about 1810 in San Antonio de Béxar (modern San Antonio, Texas). His father died while he was still a child, and he was bought up by his mother. Carbajal's intelligence won him the patronage of local U.S. colonists. In 1823 one of them, Stephen Fuller Austin (1793–1836), the so-called father of Texas, sent

▼ *José María Carbajal took part in the Texas rebellion against the rule of Santa Anna.*

KEY DATES

1810 Born in San Antonio de Béxar, Mexico, at about this time.

1835 Takes part in the Texas Revolution.

1874 Dies in Soto la Marina, Tamaulipas, Mexico.

Carbajal to Kentucky to learn a trade. Carbajal later went to Virginia to study with Protestant reformer Alexander Campbell (1788–1866).

On his return to Texas in the late 1820s, Carbajal was so Americanized that his countrymen regarded him as a "un Norte Americano" (a North American). With Austin's support, Carbajal trained as a land surveyor, and from 1830 he helped the Mexican colonist Martín De León (1765–1833) lay out the settlement of Guadalupe Victoria in south Texas. Carbajal later married one of De Léon's daughters, Refugio De León.

In 1835, U.S. colonists led by Austin rebelled against Mexican rule, which under the presidency (1833–1836) of Antonio López de Santa Anna had become despotic. Carbajal and the De Leóns supported the rebellion, and helped the Texan forces by chartering a ship, the *Hannah Elizabeth*, to bring them arms. The Mexicans seized the vessel, but Carbajal managed to escape capture.

Changing sides

For the remainder of his career Carbajal served as a military leader in the frequent disputes that broke out along the Mexican–U.S. border. A liberal, Carbajal disliked interference by central governments of whatever nationality, and as a result he sometimes changed his allegiance. In the 1860s he became an important figure in the Mexican government. He was governor of the state of Tamaulipas and San Luis Potosí, and in 1865 he was sent as a special envoy to negotiate a loan from the United States.

See also: De León Family

Further reading: Reséndez, Andrés. *Changing National Identities at the Frontier: Texas and New Mexico, 1800–1850.* New York, NY: Cambridge University Press, 2005. http://www.tsha.utexas.edu/handbook/online/articles/CC/fca45.html (Handbook of Texas Online).

CARBAJAL, Michael
Boxer

Michael Carbajal was a junior flyweight boxer who won an Olympic silver medal in 1988 and was later four-time champion of the world.

Early life
The child of Mexican American parents, Michael Carbajal was born and raised in Phoenix, Arizona. He showed precocious talent as a fighter, and was picked at age 19 for the U.S. team at the 1988 Olympics in Seoul, South Korea. He was the strong favorite to win gold in his weight division, but had to settle for silver when he lost his final bout on the referees' decision.

Back home Carbajal turned professional, and launched his new career in February 1989 with a win over Will Grigsby, another future world champion. Carbajal's next fight ended spectacularly when he knocked out Silviano Pérez in the first round. In 1990 Carbajal stopped South Korean Maungshai Kittikasem, the International Boxing Federation (IBF) World Junior Flyweight champion, in the seventh round to become champion of the world.

Carbajal successfully defended his IBF title six times. In March 1993 he faced World Boxing Council (WBC) champion Humberto "Chiquito" González. Carbajal went down in the first and fifth rounds, but in the seventh a series of punches felled González. In winning the WBC crown he unified the two boards' titles and became the first junior flyweight to win $1 million for a fight.

In a rematch with González, Carbajal lost a split decision, but bounced back to earn a shot at World Boxing Organization (WBO) champion Josue Camacho. The fight went 12 rounds, with Carbajal winning a split decision to

▲ *Michael Carbajal celebrates after his victory over Domingo Sosa in October 1993.*

take the title. In November 1994 he tried to win back his IBF and WBC championships from González in yet another rematch, but lost for a second time on a split decision.

Glorious career
In January 1997 Carbajal beat two-time IBF Junior Flyweight champion Melchor Cob Castro by a unanimous decision. At the end of the year he fought WBO World Junior Flyweight Jorge Arce. Carbajal sent Arce to the canvas in the eighth round. In the 11th Carbajal struck with a right that ended the fight. For the fourth time in his professional career Michael Carbajal had won a world championship title. When he finally retired in 1999, his career record was 49 victories, 33 by knockout, and only four defeats.

Further reading: Mullen, Henry. *The Ultimate Encyclopedia of Boxing.* Edison, NJ: Chartwell Books, 1996.
http://www.hboarchives.com/boxing_fights_details/carbajal_michael.html (complete career record).

KEY DATES

1967	Born in Phoenix, Arizona, on September 17.
1988	Wins Olympic silver medal for boxing.
1990	Wins International Boxing Federation (IBF) World Junior Flyweight Championship.
1993	Wins World Boxing Council (WBC) title, but loses both that and the IBF crown in a rematch.
1997	Regains IBF title and wins World Boxing Organization (WBO) title.
1999	Retires as world champion.

CAREW, Rod
Baseball Player

▲ *This photograph of Rod Carew was taken in May 1983 during his time with the California Angels.*

Known for his crouching stances in the batter's box, Rod Carew was one of the best hitters in the history of Major League Baseball (MLB). Carew batted .300 or better for 15 consecutive seasons, a feat matched by only five other MLB players. A first and second baseman with the Minnesota Twins and the California Angels, Carew was named to the All-Star Game 18 consecutive years in a career that lasted from 1967 to 1985.

Early life

Born on a train in the Panama Canal Zone in 1945, Carew was named after the doctor, Rodney Kline, who delivered him. His full name is Rodney Cline Carew. His Panamanian mother had been traveling to a hospital in Colón when she gave birth. Growing up poor, the 16-year-old Carew immigrated to New York City, where he was spotted playing sandlot baseball by Minnesota Twins' scout Herb Klein. Carew was impressive in his tryout and signed with the team. He spent the next few years in the minor leagues. On reaching the majors in 1967 Carew made an immediate impact. He collected 150 hits in 137 games, and was named American League (AL) Rookie of the Year.

Over the next 10 years Carew carved his niche as an aggressive baserunner (he stole home 17 times in his career) and expert bunter. He also reached base on numerous chopped ground balls, and had many other ways of utilizing his speed. In 1977, after Carew had already won five of his seven batting titles, he had one of the finest hitting seasons ever recorded, ending with .388, the

highest average since Ted Williams in 1950, and the most hits (239) since Bill Terry in 1930. Carew also led the AL in runs (128), triples (16), and on-base percentage (.452), and was named AL Most Valuable Player (MVP).

In 1979 Carew was traded to the California Angels, where he mainly played first base. On August 4, 1985, he made his 3,000th career hit off his former teammate, Twins' lefthander Frank Viola. Carew retired at the end of that season, and was elected to the National Baseball Hall of Fame on the first ballot in 1991. He later served as a roving hitting coach, and landed with the Angels again in 1992. In late 1995, Carew's youngest daughter, Michelle, was diagnosed with acute non-lymphocytic leukemia, and the family was told she needed a bone marrow transplant. Michelle died in 1996, and Carew has since been an active campaigner on behalf of the National Marrow Donor Program for more diverse backgrounds among donors (Carew has West Indian and Panamanian roots, and his wife, Marilynn, is of Russian-Jewish heritage).

KEY DATES	
1945	Born in the Panama Canal Zone on October 1.
1961	Drafted to the Minnesota Twins.
1967	Gets his first major league hit on April 11.
1977	Bats .388, the highest batting average since Ted Williams in 1950.
1979	Traded by the Twins to the California Angels on February 3.
1985	Makes 3,000th hit off Twins' lefthander Frank Viola; retires at end of season.
1991	Inducted into the National Baseball Hall of Fame.

Further reading: Carew, Rod, and Ira Berkow. *Carew.* New York, NY: Simon & Schuster, 1979.
http://www.baseballhalloffame.org/hofers_and_honorees/hofer_bios/carew_rod.htm (Hall of Fame biography page).

CAREY, Mariah
Singer, Songwriter

With a remarkable five-octave vocal range and a string of awards, Mariah Carey has proved herself one of the most popular singers of all time. In sales terms she is the most successful female artist in music history. No artist since Elvis Presley and The Beatles has had so many No. 1 singles and albums. Carey's achievement has been recognized with many of the most prestigious accolades in the industry, among them two Grammy Awards, the World Music Award for "Best Selling Female Artist of the Millennium," eight American Music Awards, and *Billboard*'s "Artist of the Decade" Award. Since her meteoric rise to superstardom, however, Carey's career has been a rollercoaster of ups and downs.

Early life
Born in 1970, Mariah Carey was the youngest of three children of an Irish American mother and a half-African American, half-Venezuelan father. Her formative early years were troubled by the divorce of her parents when she was three and incidents of racism in the mostly white suburb in which she grew up. Carey found solace in music and from an early age showed extraordinary abilities, singing from the age of four. Her mother, a vocal coach and former opera singer, encouraged the young Carey to build on her innate talent. The child honed her songwriting skills while at middle school, and immediately after graduating from Greenlawn's Harborfields High School she set off into the heart of New York City to pursue her dream of a glittering musical career.

After a series of short-lived jobs, Carey's break came when she was hired as a backup singer for Brenda K. Starr,

▲ *Mariah Carey performs at Radio City Music Hall, New York City, in September 2003.*

who passed her demo tape to Tommy Mattola, the head of Sony Music Entertainment. Mattola was reportedly so impressed by Carey's voice that he tracked her down at a party and signed her to Columbia Records.

Record breaker
Released in 1990, Carey's self-titled debut album was a massive and immediate hit, spawning four No. 1 singles: "Vision of Love," "Love Takes Time," "Someday," and "I Don't Wanna Cry." It also led to two Grammy Awards for Best New Artist and Best Female Vocalist. *Mariah Carey* was followed by *Emotions* (1991) and *MTV Unplugged* (1992). These albums brought Carey two top-five singles

KEY DATES	
1970	Born on Long Island, New York, on March 27.
1990	Releases first album, *Mariah Carey*.
1993	Releases *Music Box*, her biggest selling album to date.
1999	The release of the single "Heartbreaker" makes Carey the first person to have a No. 1 single in every year of the 1990s.
2001	*Glitter* flops at the box office.
2005	Releases *The Emancipation of Mimi*.

INFLUENCES AND INSPIRATION

Although Mariah Carey cites Stevie Wonder, Whitney Houston, Janet Jackson, and Madonna as major influences, soul diva Aretha Franklin was probably her biggest inspiration. In 1998 she appeared with Franklin on the VH1 show *Divas*, duetting on "Chain of Fools." Carey, who herself has established a reputation as a sometimes difficult diva, observed of Franklin: "A diva has to have talent, you know."

Born in Memphis, Tennessee, on March 25, 1942, Aretha Franklin is regarded as one of the best vocalists ever, and is often known as "the Queen of Soul." She is also renowned for her R&B recordings, and has been successful with pop, hip-hop, gospel, jazz, rock, blues, and even operatic works.

Franklin has won 16 Grammys (including an unprecedented 12 for Best Vocal Performance). On January 3, 1987, she became the first woman to be inducted into the Rock and Roll Hall of Fame.

and two more number ones, making her the first performer in pop history to have chart toppers with their first five singles.

Marriage and divorce

In 1993 Carey married Tommy Mattola, 20 years her senior, before releasing her best selling album to date, *Music Box*. In the same year she recorded a version of Diana Ross's "Endless Love" with Luther Vandross. It became one of the year's most widely played singles. After *Merry Christmas* (1994) came *Daydream* (1995); "Fantasy," a track from the latter album, entered the charts at No. 1 on the day of its release—this was the first time a woman had achieved this feat, and only the second time that it had ever happened (the first record to do so was Elvis Presley's "Jailhouse Rock" in 1958). A further Carey single, "One Sweet Day," a duet with Boyz II Men, remained at No. 1 for a record 16 consecutive weeks.

A two-year hiatus saw Carey divorce from Mattola, but in the first of her comebacks she released *Butterfly* (1997) and followed it in 1998 with *#1's*, a collection of her greatest hits. Carey then released *Rainbow* (1999), which contained some hip-hop numbers as well as more traditional style pop. The success of "Heartbreaker," the single from the album, made Carey the first artist to have a number one single in every year of the 1990s. In the meantime she launched her own record label, Crave Records, but despite signing several bands, including the female quartet Allure and the male trio 7 Mile, the venture struggled from the start and was closed down in 1998 by the parent company, Sony.

All that glitters

In the 1990s Carey's career and personal life entered another turbulent period. After signing a deal with Virgin worth $80 million—at the time the biggest recording contract in history—she experienced a very public breakdown in 2001. She starred in the movie *Glitter*, which loosely mirrored her own rise to fame, but it flopped at the box office and earned her an unwanted award: a Razzie for worst actress. The accompanying soundtrack was also financially disappointing—it struggled to make gold sales, and prompted Virgin to cancel Carey's contract in early 2002, paying her $28 million to break the deal.

Later that year Carey signed a new record deal with the Island Def Jam Music Group. She released her ninth album, *Charmbracelet*, which also failed to replicate the success of her earlier recordings. However, in 2003 the single "Through the Rain" topped the charts, and at the Soul Train Music Awards Carey was honored with the Quincy Jones Award for Outstanding Career.

Comeback queen

Although Carey took nearly three years to produce a follow-up, she once again struck gold with *The Emancipation of Mimi* (2005). The album, which was entirely written and coproduced by Carey, was her most successful record in years, topping the *Billboard* 200 album chart and the Top R&B/Hip-Hop Albums chart, and selling more copies (404,000) in the United States in its first week of release than any of her previous works.

Later in 2005, Carey performed in London, England, as part of the worldwide Live 8 concerts to raise awareness of poverty in Africa. She has refused to let the failure of her film debut hold back her ambitions of becoming a movie star: In 2005 she took roles in both *The Sweet Science* and *State Property 2*. She was slated to start work on the movie *Tennessee* in early 2006.

Further reading: Wellman, Sam. *Mariah Carey* (Galaxy of Superstars). Northborough, MA: Chelsea House, 1999.
http://www.mariahcarey.com (official Web site)

CARMONA, Richard H.
U.S. Surgeon General

Richard Carmona was appointed in 2002 as U.S. Surgeon General. In that role he was responsible for providing all U.S. citizens with the best information available on medical matters, maximizing the nation's health, and minimizing illness and injury. A physician, educator, and decorated veteran, Carmona braved many difficulties in his early years.

The grandchild of Puerto Rican immigrants, Richard Henry Carmona was born in 1949 in New York City's Spanish Harlem. After dropping out of DeWitt Clinton High School in the Bronx, he held a number of odd jobs, including selling hot dogs at Yankee Stadium. His life soon changed after he enlisted in the U.S. Army in 1967.

Green Beret in Vietnam

The seeds of Carmona's subsequent career were planted when he was a teenager serving in Vietnam. He hoped to join the Special Forces as a combat medic, but lacked the basic requirement—a high school diploma. After gaining a General Educational Development (GED) equivalency diploma, he provided medical care to American soldiers on counterinsurgency and intelligence-gathering operations.

As a 19- and 20-year-old medic in the Green Berets, Carmona treated tropical diseases and trauma wounds, and even delivered babies. Later on his tour of duty he joined the Navy, in which he rose to the rank of vice admiral. He was twice wounded in Vietnam, and was awarded two Purple Hearts and a Bronze Star for his exemplary service.

Returning to New York, Carmona was encouraged by his family to train as an electrician. He was determined to become a doctor, and so he attended Bronx Community

▲ *Richard Carmona rose from humble origins to become U.S. Surgeon General.*

College through an open enrollment program for veterans. By the mid-1970s he was a young married man, juggling schoolwork and jobs to support his family. In 1977 he graduated with a Bachelor of Science degree from the University of California at San Francisco. Two years later he was honored as the top graduate of the university's medical school.

Outstanding trauma Surgeon

Many opportunities then arose for the newly qualified doctor. San Francisco Mission General Hospital chose Carmona as a resident to train in general vascular surgery, treating diseases of the arteries, veins, and lymph vessels.

During his residency training Carmona encountered many unusual symptoms and previously unknown forms of cancer, which medical science later identified as AIDS. At the start of 1985 he was honored as the Outstanding Chief Resident and Teacher at the hospital, and later that year he secured his next position—an ideal job that enabled him to combine his unique medical and military experience.

KEY DATES	
1949	Born in New York City on November 22.
1967	Serves as medic in U.S. Special Forces in Vietnam.
1979	Earns medical degree from University of California, San Francisco.
1997	Becomes CEO of Pima County (Arizona) Health Care and Hospital Medical Director.
2002	Appointed U.S. Surgeon General by President George W. Bush.

The new post, which Carmona took up at the start of 1986, was as a trauma surgeon and deputy director of Special Weapons and Tactics (SWAT) in the Pima County Sheriff's Department in Tucson, Arizona. There he became a licensed peace officer, completed with honors a masters degree in public health at the University of Arizona, and held a succession of positions covering trauma care and surgery, law enforcement, disaster care, and emergency medical support.

Pima County borders Mexico for 200 miles (320km) along its southern perimeter. Part of Carmona's responsibility was to oversee "border health," working to optimize the medical welfare of citizens along the frontier. Among his principal concerns were the treatment of victims of rattlesnake bites and scorpion stings, the organization of effective responses to environmental conditions affecting health, and restricting the transmission of communicable diseases such as HIV–AIDS and tuberculosis among migrant workers, travelers, and citizens. In pursuit of those objectives, Carmona established the first Basic Emergency Medical System along the U.S.–Mexico border, a program that served as a model for numerous subsequent initiatives elsewhere.

Memorable rescues

Carmona's work in southern Arizona often took him out into the field. In 1992, while suspended on a rope from a helicopter, he rescued a crash survivor clinging to the side of a cliff on a snow-covered mountain. The event attracted national publicity and inspired a made-for-TV movie. In 1999, while driving through Tucson, he stopped at a traffic accident and quickly realized that an armed man was holding a woman hostage at the scene. He shot and killed the suspect, who, it subsequently emerged, had just murdered his own father and was searching for another victim. For these and other remarkable acts of leadership and valor, Carmona earned numerous awards. In 2000 he was named the best U.S. police officer by the National Association of Police Organizations.

While serving with the Pima County Sheriff's Department, Carmona also taught clinical surgery and public heath at the University of Arizona. There he developed and implemented a community preparedness program to manage the effects of a possible attack by weapons of mass destruction (WMD).

In 2002 Carmona was nominated by President George W. Bush to champion the nation's health care concerns as U.S. Surgeon General. One of the most important responsibilities of the office of U.S. Surgeon General is to raise public awareness of important health and safety issues. Long before his appointment to this key executive role, Carmona was already an influential opinion-maker in these areas. He was an outspoken advocate of disaster-preparedness long before the terrorist attacks on the United States of September 11, 2001, and he has voiced warnings about the threat of bioterrorism since the mid-1990s.

While recognizing that his role was necessarily political, Carmona was adamant that all his decisions were reached through consideration of the scientific evidence, not as a response to party pressures. For example, he said that he was not opposed in principle to stem-cell research or the medical use of marijuana, but merely insisted on weighing all the facts before reaching an informed decision. During his time in office Carmona has made a substantial contribution to programs designed to prepare Americans to manage threats of terrorism and WMD.

Further reading: Whitlock, Charles R. *Police Heroes.* New York: Thomas Dunne Books, 2002.
http://www.surgeongeneral.gov/aboutoffice.html#biosg (U.S. Surgeon General's official site).

CARR, Vikki
Singer

Mexican American Vikki Carr was one of the most successful Latina singers of the second half of the 20th century. She worked with some of the leading names in the music business and had the rare distinction of performing live for five U.S. presidents.

Background
Born Florencia Bisenta de Casillas Martinez Cardona in 1941, Carr was the eldest of seven children. She grew up near Los Angeles, California. In her teens she began singing with Pepe Callahan's Mexican-Irish band, taking the stagename Carlita. She also sang with the Chuck Leonard Quartet in Reno, Nevada. Her performances led the Liberty label to sign up the 21-year-old. Shortly after, she changed her stage name again, this time to Vikki Carr, although she always made it clear that she was extremely proud of her Mexican American heritage.

Carr's first single, "He's a Rebel," was not a huge success in the United States but did well in Australia, where Carr toured. She began to appear on TV shows with singers such as Dean Martin and the comedian Bob Hope; she was also a regular on the *Ray Anthony Show*. Singing fluently in English and Spanish, Carr became increasingly

▼ *Vicki Carr appears on British television in 1973; the Mexican American singer enjoyed international success.*

popular during the 1960s. In 1966 she traveled to Vietnam with actor Danny Kaye to entertain U.S. troops. The following year she played for Queen Elizabeth II at The Royal Variety Performance in London, England. Also in 1967 Carr's first album, *It Must Be Him*, received three Grammy nominations, while the title track reached No. 3 in the singles chart. Carr was named Woman of the Year by the *Los Angeles Times* in 1970.

Spanish language success
In 1972 Carr recorded her first Spanish album, *Vikki Carr en español*. In 1980 *Vikki Carr y el amor* became a huge success throughout Latin America, and in 1985 *Simplemente Mujer* won a Grammy for Best Mexican American Recording. In 1991 her single "Cosas del Amor" spent more than two months at No. 1. on the U.S. Latin charts. Carr also won Grammys in 1992 and 1995 for Best Latin Pop Album (*Cosas del Amor*) and Best Mexican American Recording (*Recuerdo a Javier Solis*) respectively.

Throughout her career Vikki Carr has been dedicated to philanthropic work and has spent much time and money helping children's charities. She continues to fund-raise for the Cross High School in San Antonio, Texas, and has helped fund more than 280 Hispanic American students in college through the Vikki Carr Scholarship Foundation, established in 1971.

KEY DATES	
1941	Born in El Paso, Texas, on July 19.
1966	Tours Vietnam with actor Danny Kaye.
1967	Nominated for three Grammys for "It Must Be Him."
1971	Establishes the Vikki Carr scholarship fund.
1991	"Cosas del Amor" spends 2 months at No. 1 in U.S. Latin charts.

Further reading: Mendoza, Sylvia. *The Book of Latina Women: 150 Vidas of Passion, Strength, and Success.* Avon, MA: Adams Media, 2004.
http://www.vikkicarr.net/biography.htm (official Web site)

CARRASCO, Barbara
Artist

Barbara Carrasco is a leading Mexican American artist who rose to prominence in the 1980s as part of the Chicano mural movement. Her work ranges from small drawings to prints to monumental murals, and addresses themes of Chicano and Chicana identity and culture.

Early life
Carrasco was born in Texas but raised in Culver City, California, where she lived with her family in the Mar Vista Gardens housing project. She attended public schools, and then studied art at the University of California, Los Angeles (UCLA), taking a BA degree in 1978.

On graduation Carrasco became involved in mural painting. She assisted John Valadez and Carlos Almaraz

▼ *Chicano artist Barbara Carrasco is best known for her work as a muralist.*

KEY DATES

1955	Born in El Paso, Texas.
1981	Begins her controversial mural, *Los Angeles History: A Mexican Perspective*.
1989	Her computer animation *Pesticides* is shown in Times Square, New York City.

with *Zoot Suit* on the outside of the Aquarius Theater in Los Angeles. She also joined the Public Art Center, where she worked with Mexican American painters on the creation of public murals. In 1981, as part of a regeneration project funded by the city, Carrasco received a commission of her own. She produced designs for a mural entitled *Los Angeles History: A Mexican Perspective*, but the city agency responsible for the project objected to parts of her design—including a scene of Japanese Americans being interned during World War II. Carrasco refused to remove the contentious images, viewing them as a true reflection of the city's history, and the mural, which she painted on panels, was never installed.

Carrasco was influenced by César Chávez and Dolores Huerta, leaders of the United Farm Workers (UFW) union, and from 1979 she painted banners and murals for the organization's conventions and campaigns. In 1989 *Pesticides*, her computer animation showing the effects of agricultural chemicals on farmworkers, was shown on electronic billboards in Times Square, New York City.

After Carrasco completed an MFA degree at the California Institute of Arts in 1991, her work increasingly challenged traditional patterns of male domination in Chicano society. *Self Portrait* (1994) expresses the exclusion that she felt growing up with fair skin in a Hispanic neighborhood. Her paintings have been exhibited throughout the United States and worldwide.

See also: Almaraz, Carlos; Chávez, César; Huerta, Dolores

Further reading: Del Castillo, Richard Griswold, Teresa McKenna, and Yvonne Yarbro-Bejarano (eds.). *Chicano Art: Resistance and Affirmation, 1965–1985.* Tuscson, AZ: University of Arizona Press, 1991.
http://138.23.124.165/exhibitions/broadterritories/default.html (Broad Territories: Images of Identity Web site).

CARRERA, Barbara
Model, Actor, Painter

One of the few women to succeed in making the switch from fashion modeling to the cinema screen, Barbara Carrera is an internationally acclaimed actor, painter, and fashion icon. The Nicaraguan supermodel started posing when she was 17 and appeared on the covers of more than 300 magazines, including *Vogue*, *Cosmopolitan*, and *Harper's Bazaar*.

Born Barbara Kingsbury in Managua, Nicaragua, on the last day of 1951, she was the daughter of an American diplomat father and a Nicaraguan mother. She moved to the United States, where she finished conventional schooling at age 10 before taking lessons at a convent in Memphis, Tennessee, where she excelled at art.

Modeling career
At age 17 Carrera embarked on a modeling career, dropping her father's name, Kingsbury, in favor of her mother's maiden name. Her beauty and natural grace saw her rise quickly through the modeling ranks, and before long she came to the attention of Hollywood producers through a series of Chiquita Banana commercials. Carrera made her film debut in 1970 in *Puzzle of a Downfall Child*, but her first major role came when she was cast in *The Master Gunfighter* (1975). Her performance garnered her the first of two Golden Globe nominations, and she was voted Most Promising Newcomer in a Leading Role by the Hollywood Foreign Press Association. Carerra next appeared alongside Rock Hudson in the horror film *Embryo* (1976). International success followed with *The Island of Dr. Moreau* (1977). Big roles continued in Hollywood features such as *Condorman* (1981), *I, The Jury* (1982), and *Lone Wolf McQuade* (1983). However, Carerra's best-known role to date is undoubtedly that of Fatima Blush in the 1983 James Bond film, *Never Say Never Again*, for which she earned her second Golden Globe nomination. On television, Carrera has appeared in several popular miniseries.

Nicaraguan ambassador
In 1997 Carerra was appointed ambassador-at-large for her native Nicaragua. Alongside her ambassadorial duties, she developed a career as a successful artist. Her paintings have won much acclaim and have been exhibited internationally. She continued to act into the 21st century, appearing in the film *Paradise* in 2003.

▲ *Nicaraguan American Barbara Carrera made a smooth and successful transition from modeling to the world of movie acting.*

KEY DATES	
1951	Born in Managua, Nicaragua, on December 31.
1968	Embarks on modeling career.
1975	Appears in *The Master Gunfighter*, and earns first Golden Globe nomination.
1983	Appears as Fatima Blush in *Never Say Never Again*, and earns second Golden Globe nomination.
1997	Appointed ambassador-at-large for Nicaragua.

Further reading http://www.hollywoodcultmovies.com/html/barbara_carrera.html (biography on Hollywood Cult Movies). http://users.skynet.be/sky82359/UK_index.html (Career details).

CARRILLO, Elpidia
Actor

Elpidia Carrillo is a movie actor who began her career in her native Mexico. She made her Hollywood debut in *The Border* (1982), directed by Tony Richardson, in which she starred opposite Jack Nicholson. She is best known in the United States for her role as Anna in *Predator* (1987), with Arnold Schwarzenegger.

Early life

Carrillo was born in 1961 in Michoacán, Mexico. She made her first screen appearance at age 16 in *Deseos* (1977), a surrealistic movie by Mexican director Rafael Corkidi. While still in her teens she also worked for established directors such as Gabriel Retes and Sergio Arau. She began working in Hollywood in the early 1980s. After *The Border* she next appeared in *Beyond The Limit* (1983) with Richard Gere and Michael Caine. She then played a Sandinista (a left-wing Nicaraguan revolutionary) in Roger Spottiswoode's *Under Fire* (1983) with Nick Nolte, Ed Harris, and Gene Hackman. In 1986 she acted opposite James Woods in Oliver Stone's *Salvador*. Next came *Predator*, which, despite its blockbuster status, received mixed reviews. In the following years Carrillo acted in a string of smaller roles, sometimes returning to Mexico.

▼ *Elpidia Carrillo starred with fellow Hispanic American Jimmy Smits in* **My Family** *(1995).*

Carrillo's next major role was in *My Family* (1995), a saga of Hispanic American immigrants directed by Gregory Nava and starring Jimmy Smits, Edward James Olmos, and Esai Morales. Following that Carrillo returned again to Mexico, where she played opposite Gael García Bernal in Antonio Urrutia's *De tripas, corazón* (1996), and then in two celebrated movies: Carlos Carrera's *Un embrujo* (1998), and Salvador Carrasco's *La otra conquista* (1998). In the meantime she returned to the United States to star with Marlon Brando in Johnny Depp's *The Brave* (1997).

Coming of age

In 2000 Elpidia Carrillo appeared in Rodrigo García's *Things You Can Tell Just by Looking at Her* with Holly Hunter and Glenn Close, and in Ken Loach's *Bread and Roses* with Adrien Brody. The movies marked a watershed in her career: While previously she had been cast for her Latin looks, she had now acquired a reputation as a substantial character actor. In 2002 she appeared in Steven Soderbergh's remake of Andrei Tarkovsky's *Solaris*. Subsequently Carrillo has acted in the TV mini-series *Kingpin* (2003) and in García's *Nine Lives* (2005).

See also: Morales, Esai; Nava, Gregory; Olmos, Edward James; Smits, Jimmy

Further reading: Keller, Gary D. *A Biographical Handbook of Hispanics and United States Film*. Tempe, AZ: Bilingual Press/Editorial Bilingüe, 1997.
http://www.imdb.com/name/nm0001990 (International Movie Database [IMDb] Web site).

CARRILLO, Leo
Actor, Conservationist

Leo Carrillo first came to pubic attention as an actor, and was honored with his own star on the Hollywood Walk of Fame. In later life he became well known for his work to protect the environment of his beloved California.

Background
Born in Los Angeles in 1880, Leo Carrillo came from a distinguished Hispanic American family that claimed direct descent from the conquistadors. His great-grandfather was the first provisional governor of California, and his father was the first mayor of Santa Monica. Carrillo grew up proud of both his heritage and the state in which he lived.

A talented student with a particular gift for drawing, Carrillo went to study at Loyola University. Although his family wanted him to train to be a priest, Carrillo took a degree in engineering instead. After graduation he went to work as a political cartoonist at the *San Francisco Examiner*, but quit the newspaper after his friends encouraged him to try his hand at acting. Carrillo first appeared in comedy reviews and vaudeville shows, but before long moved into film. He would eventually act in more than 90 films, theater productions, and TV series. Carrillo was most frequently cast as stereotypical

▼ *Leo Carrillo enjoyed a long and illustrious career in acting, appearing in theater, television, and movies.*

Spaniards or Italians, but he was no carboard cutout and brought distinction to the roles he played. In 1950 he landed the part of Pancho, sidekick to Cisco (Duncan Renaldo), in the popular TV series *The Cisco Kid*. He lied about his age to get the part, pretending to be in his 50s rather than over 70 so that the studio could get insurance. The series ran for six years and made Carrillo's face instantly recognizable throughout the United States.

Conservationist
Away from acting, Carrillo spent much of his life working to conserve California and to promote its natural attractions to the public. He was a member of the California Beaches and Parks Commission, working for 18 years on key developments such as the Los Angeles Arboretum and the Anza-Borrego Desert State Park. He was also instrumental in the state's acquisition of the spectacular hilltop castle at San Simeon, which had formerly belonged to newspaper tycoon William Randolph Hearst (1863–1951). Governor Edmund G. Brown called Carrillo "Mr. California," and appointed him as a goodwill ambassador for the state.

In 1937 Carrillo bought the Rancho de Los Kiotes, about 28 miles (45 km) northwest of Santa Monica in what is now southeast Carlsbad, with the intention of turning its 840 acres (340 hectares) into a working ranch. By the time of his death in 1961 he had increased its land area to 2,538 acres (1,027 hectares). Sixteen years later the property was turned into an educational and recreational center and named the Leo Carrillo Ranch Historic Park.

KEY DATES	
1880	Born in Los Angeles, California, on August 6.
1937	Buys Rancho de Los Kiotes, California.
1950	Cast as Pancho in *The Cisco Kid*.
1961	Dies of cancer in Santa Monica, California, on September 10.

Further reading: Carrillo, Leo. *The California I Love*. Englewood Cliffs, N.J.: Prentice-Hall, 1961.
http://www.carrillo-ranch.org (Carrillo's ranch site, including biography).

CARRILLO, Leopoldo
Businessman

Leopoldo Carrillo was a successful businessman who made a major contribution to the development of Tucson, Arizona, in the 1870s and 1880s.

Mexican immigrant

Carrillo came to Arizona from his native Sonora, Mexico, in 1859 at the age of 23. He worked for the U.S. government as a freighter, organizing consignments of goods and chartering transportation. He was so successful that within 10 years he became one of the richest men in Tucson. He invested in property, eventually owning about 100 houses in the town, including its first two-story building, construction of which he personally supervised. He also bought extensive tracts of farming land around Tucson, including a large cattle ranch at Sabino Canyon. His most profitable enterprises, however, were a wide range of amenities, including an ice-cream parlor, a saloon, a bowling alley, and a feed stable.

▼ *The entrepreneurship of Leopoldo Carrillo left a lasting impression on the city of Tucson, Arizona.*

In 1875, on a return visit to Mexico, Carrillo was captured by bandits who demanded the then massive sum of $25,000 for his safe release. His wife raised part of the ransom by selling some property, and made up the balance with the family jewels.

Tucson history

The site of an ancient settlement, the modern city of Tucson started to grow up after 1775, when a presidio (military garrison) was established on the banks of the Santa Cruz River at the foot of the "A" Mountain. The project was supervised by Hugo O'Conor, commandant inspector of the King of Spain's presidios along Mexico's northern frontier. Tucson became a part of the United States with the Gadsden Purchase of 1854; from 1867 to 1877 it was the capital of the Arizona Territory.

Carrillo skillfully took advantage of the commercial opportunities created by Tucson's spurt of urban growth. At the height of his fame as a businessman he tried to diversify into politics, but although he ran for several civic offices he never won an election. Historians have debated the reasons for this strange failure in a life that in nearly all other aspects followed what the 20th-century scholar Thomas E. Sheridan has described as "a basic trajectory of success." Some have speculated that the commercial acumen that made Carrillo attractive to business partners was viewed with suspicion by voters.

Carrillo is commemorated in Tucson by two schools that are named for him, and by a museum located in one of the few traditional adobe houses that survived extensive reconstruction of the downtown area in the mid-1960s.

KEY DATES	
1836	Born in Moctezuma, Sonora, Mexico, on May 25.
1859	Immigrates to Arizona.
1890	Dies in Tucson, Arizona, on December 9.

Further reading: Sheridan, Thomas E. *Los Tucsonenses: The Mexican Community In Tucson 1854–1941.* Tucson, AZ: University of Arizona Press, 1986.
http://www.arizonahistoricalsociety.org:80/default.asp (Sosa–Carrillo–Fremont House Museum Web site).

CARTER, Lynda
Actor, Singer

One of the most recognized faces of the 1970s, and widely regarded as one of the most beautiful women in the world, Lynda Carter shot to fame first as a beauty queen, and then in the title role of *Wonder Woman*, the TV adaptation of the comic book series.

Born Linda Jean Cordova Carter in 1951 to an Irish father and Mexican mother, she was the youngest of three siblings. After showing an interest in music at around the age of 10, Carter joined local choirs and took part in school plays; she also composed her own songs.

Miss World–USA

Carter went to Arizona State University, but left after just one semester to launch a career as a full-time singer. She joined several bands, but had little commercial success. Carter then participated in her first beauty contest, the Miss Phoenix Pageant, before going on to be crowned Miss Arizona. In 1973 she became Miss World–USA. Carter then decided to try acting, and went to study in New York. In 1975, after playing a few minor roles on TV shows such as *Starsky & Hutch*, she beat out almost 2,000 hopefuls to the role of one of the 1970s' most fondly remembered icons.

Wonder Woman is arguably the most popular female superhero of all time. Carter first appeared in the role in the ABC-TV pilot, *The New Original Wonder Woman*, in 1975. When the show went into production, she was catapulted to stardom. *Wonder Woman* ran until 1979.

During this time Carter made her big-screen debut in *Bobbie Jo and the Outlaw* (1976). However, she continued to make more of an impression on the small screen. She appeared in several TV movies, her most notable performance being in *Rita Hayworth: The Love Goddess*

▲ *Lynda Carter appears as Wonder Woman. The role earned the former beauty queen international fame.*

(1983). Carter's success as an actress gave her the time and money to return to her first love, music, and she released *Portrait*, a solo album, in 1978. She also took part in various musical specials, such as CBS's *Lynda Carter Celebration* (1981). Her contribution to Hispanic culture was recognized with several awards.

Carter continued to act into the 21st century. She had a major role in the movie version of *The Dukes of Hazzard* (2005). She also acted on stage, achieving popular success in the musical *Chicago* in London in 2005.

See also: Hayworth, Rita

Further reading: http://www.wonderland-site.com (information and guide relating to Lynda Carter's career).
http://www.imdb.com/name/nm0004812 (biography and full career listing on the Internet Movie Database).

KEY DATES

1951	Born in Phoenix, Arizona, on July 24.
1973	Crowned Miss World–USA.
1975	First appears on TV as Wonder Woman, the role for which she became most famous.
1980	Wins the Ariel Award for International Entertainer of the Year (Mexican Academy of Motion Picture Arts and Sciences).
1983	Voted Hispanic Woman of the Year (Hispanic Women's Council of Los Angeles, Inc.).

CASAL, Lourdes
Political Activist, Poet

Cuban-born Lourdes Casal was a progressive intellectual—a professor of psychology, a poet, an activist, and a writer.

Early life

Born in Havana, Cuba, on April 5, 1938, to a middle-class Afro-Cuban family, Casal was of mixed African, European, and Chinese decent. She studied at the Catholic University of Santo Tomas de Villanueva in Havana for seven years, and concentrated in biometrics before turning to psychology. As a student, Casal supported Fidel Castro in his efforts to overthrow the corrupt Fulgencio Batista dictatorship, but she reluctantly chose exile in the United States after the 1959 revolution brought communism to Cuba.

Life in exile

Casal moved to the United States in 1961. She settled in New York, where she completed her studies, receiving an MA and PhD in psychology from the New School for Social Research in New York.

In the United States Casal encountered a vastly different society from the one to which she had been accustomed in her native land, and she never really felt that she belonged in her new environment. The feeling of deracination is expressed in Casal's poetry, which often portrays a deep sense of nostalgia and of loss. The poem "Definición," for example, describes exile as "living in a place where there is no house/ in which we were children." Despite this feeling, Casal grew to love New York and became very active in the city's literary, intellectual, and cultural life.

In 1971, Casal completed her first book, *El Caso Padilla: literatura y revolución en Cuba*. A compilation of essays, the book exposed the official hostility of the Cuban government toward certain writers, most notably the poet Heberto Padilla (1932–2000), who was forced to make a public confession of his "crimes" against the revolution.

After studying, Casal taught psychology at Dominican College, Brooklyn College, and Rutgers University, where she spent the majority of her professional career.

Activism

In the mid 1970s Casal helped create *Revista Areíto*, a progressive Cuban exile magazine that reassessed the Cuban Revolution in light of its socioeconomic and political achievements in the context of the Cold War and the radical student movements of the 1960s and 1970s. At about the same time, Casal cofounded the Antonio Maceo Brigade, a group of progressive Cuban American youths who were invited back to Cuba in the late 1970s in order to understand the revolution.

Casal returned to Cuba with the brigade on a number of occasions. She continued to work with the Antonio Maceo Brigade in the late 1970s. She wanted to help other young exiles share her experience of reencountering Cuba. Not everyone shared Casal's views, however, and Casal and her supporters became a target of hate for some of the more conservative members of the Cuban American community. In May 1976, *Areíto*'s office in Miami was the target of three bomb attacks, and in 1979 one of Casal's cofounders of the magazine and the brigade, Carlos Muñíz Varela, was assassinated.

Going home

In the late 1970s, Casal negotiated visitation rights for exiles with the Cuban government. In 1979s she returned to Cuba after suffering kidney failure. She died in Havana in 1981. In honor of her achievements, New York's Center for Cuban Studies named its collection the Lourdes Casal Library.

KEY DATES

1938   Born in Havana, Cuba, on April 5.

1961   Moves to New York, where she later becomes a professor of psychology.

1974   Founding editor of *Revista Areíto*.

1981   Dies in Havana, Cuba; poetry collection *Palabras juntan revolución* published posthumously.

1982   *Itinerario Ideológico*, an anthology of work, is published by the Instituto e Estudios Cubanos in Miami.

Further reading: Decosta-Willis, Miriam (ed.). *Daughters of the Diaspora: Afra-Hispanic Writers*. Miami, FL: Ian Randle Publishers, 2003.
http://www.palabravirtual.com (Web site featuring Latin American poets).

CASALS, Jordi
Medical Researcher

Jordi Casals was a Spanish American epidemiologist who created a system of classifying viruses that cause diseases of the central nervous system. He is most famous as the doctor who identified the virus that causes Lassa fever: The discovery almost cost him his life.

Jordi Casals-Ariet was born in 1911 in Viladrau, near Girona, Spain. He served in the Spanish army, and later took a degree in medicine at the University of Barcelona. In 1934 he moved to the United States, where he spent two years working in the department of pathology at Cornell University Medical College before joining the Rockefeller Institute of Medical Research in New York City. When the Rockefeller Foundation moved its program to Yale in 1964, Casals went with it to become the university's professor of epidemiology. He remained in Connecticut until his retirement in 1981.

Historic breakthrough

At Yale Casals studied thousands of viruses that were sent to him by researchers from all over the world. In 1969 he and his team identified a previously unknown virus in the blood of three U.S. missionary nurses. They named it Lassa fever after the village in northern Nigeria in which the victims had been working. Lassa is a rare and often fatal viral disease characterized by a high fever, headaches, mouth ulcers, aching muscles, small hemorrhages under the skin, pneumonia, and kidney and heart failure.

Two of the nurses died, but the third, Lily Pinneo, was flown to Columbia-Presbyterian Hospital in New York City. She recovered nine weeks later.

Shortly after he started working with the virus, Casals became ill and checked himself in to the same hospital. As his symptoms worsened, the doctors determined that Casals had also been infected with Lassa. The medical team brought Pinneo back in from her home in Rochester, New York, and gave Casals a transfusion of her blood. It was a desperate, kill-or-cure measure, but it worked: The professor recovered, and as soon as he was strong enough to travel he flew to Africa to study another outbreak of the disease in Sierra Leone.

The mystery of how Casals acquired the disease raised questions about laboratory safety, and procedures were tightened up as a consequence.

Further research

In the latter part of his career Casals worked with the World Health Organization (WHO) to establish a reference center for viral diseases. He also taught at Mount Sinai School of Medicine in New York. He collaborated with numerous scientists in his work to classify viruses and make that knowledge available to researchers. He helped provide new information on mosquito and tick-borne viruses. His research helped demonstrate that such viruses as poliomyelitis, rabies, Japanese encephalitis, and other diseases of the central nervous system are not linked, as had previously been suspected, while certain other strains were related to each other. Such classification techniques greatly increased the fund of knowledge of viral-borne diseases. Casals was responsible for the classification of viruses in general and for establishing the taxonomy of nearly 10,000 viruses that affect virtually every living thing on Earth. He won numerous honors, including the 1969 Richard M. Taylor Award, given once every three years by the American Committee on Arthropod-Borne Viruses.

Jordi Casals died in 2004 at the age of 92. One of the many tributes to him was paid by Dr. Gregory Tignor, a former colleague at Yale, who said: "Before Casals ... we had no way of telling the difference between rabies encephalitis, polio encephalitis, or other causes of encephalitis. But Jordi found ways, using antigens and antibodies, to figure it out. His work was so meticulous that to this day nobody has changed his classifications because they have all held up."

KEY DATES	
1911	Born in Viladrau, Spain, on May 15.
1964	Becomes professor of epidemiology at Yale University.
1969	Contracts Lassa fever while researching the disease.
1981	Retires.
2004	Dies in Manhattan, New York, on February 10.

Further reading: Casals, Jordi. *Resistance to Viral Challenge in the Days Immediately Following Vaccination.* New Haven, CT: Yale University Press, 1992.
http://www.med.yale.edu/external/pubs/ym_fw04/capsule.html (Yale quarterly bulletin).

CASALS, Pablo
Musician

Pablo Casals was one of the world's greatest cellists. He was also a distinguished composer, conductor, pianist, and humanitarian.

Early life
The second of 11 children, Pau Carlos Salvador Defilló de Casals was born in 1876 in the Catalan town of Vendrell, southwest of Barcelona, Spain. ("Pau" is the Catalan form of the Spanish "Pablo.") He first learned piano from his father, an organist in the local church. Casals's mother had been born in Puerto Rico of Catalan parents.

By age four Casals had learned to play violin and flute as well as piano, and by age five he was singing in the church choir. He did not start playing the cello until 1887. The following year his mother took him to Barcelona, where he enrolled in the Escuela Municipal de Música (Municipal School of Music). At age 13 Casals became fascinated by the scores of six unaccompanied cello suites by Johann Sebastian Bach (1685–1750). He practiced them for 12 years before he dared play them in public because they were so difficult. They became the pieces with which he was most strongly associated.

After graduating from Barcelona in 1893 Casals moved to Madrid, where he acquired the patronage of the Spanish royal family. He moved to Paris, France, in 1895, but returned to Spain the following year to teach at his former school. In 1899 he spent further time in the French capital working with conductor Charles Lamoureux.

Casals then embarked on a worldwide career, performing for, among others, the British royal family and U.S. President Theodore Roosevelt. He worked outside Spain until after World War I (1914–1918). In 1919 he founded the Orquestra Pau Casals in Catalonia and became its conductor. He also set up the Workingmen's Concert Association, which reduced admission charges to live classical music performances so that the poor could attend.

▲ **Spanish-born cellist Pablo Casals eventually immigrated to Puerto Rico, his mother's homeland.**

Politics and humanitarianism
At the outbreak of the Spanish Civil War (1936–1939), Casals made no secret of his support for the Republican cause. When the conflict was won by the Nationalists under General Francisco Franco, who became the dictator of Spain, Casals went into exile in France, where he remained throughout World War II (1939–1945). When France was occupied by Germany in 1940, Casals largely abandoned music in order to help victims of the Nazis.

Pablo Casals fully resumed his musical career in 1950, when he was one of the leading lights in celebrations to mark the bicentenary of the death of Bach.

In 1956 Casals left France for Puerto Rico, his mother's native country, where he established the annual Festival Casals and set up a musical conservatory. From Puerto Rico Casals traveled the world giving master classes. He performed for President John F. Kennedy at the White House in 1961, despite the United States's continuing support for the Franco regime in Spain.

In his later years Casals gained a reputation as a composer, particularly with his "Himno a las Naciones Unidas" (Hymn to the United Nations), which he first conducted in 1971. Pablo Casals died in 1973.

Further reading: Kirk, H. L. *Pablo Casals: A Biography*. New York, NY: Holt, Rinehart and Winston, 1974. www.bach-cantatas.com/Bio/Casals-Pablo.htm (detailed biography).

KEY DATES	
1876	Born in Vendrell, Catalonia, Spain, on December 29.
1939	Moves to France at end of Spanish Civil War.
1956	Immigrates to Puerto Rico.
1973	Dies in San Juan, Puerto Rico, on October 22.

CASALS, Rosemary
Tennis Player, Activist

Rosie Casals is popularly remembered as a spirited tennis champion of the late 1960s and 1970s who challenged the staid tennis world with her multicolored, sequined dresses and her acrobatic, aggressive style of play. Casals's greatest legacies, however, are her pioneering work to professionalize women's tennis and her activism for gender equality for all female athletes.

Early challenges

Rosemary Casals was born in 1948 in San Francisco, the daughter of indigent, immigrant parents from El Salvador. Given over to the care of her great-uncle and great-aunt Manuel and Maria Casals, Rosie grew up in an economically deprived African American neighborhood near Golden Gate Park. She had no access to the largely "country-club" environment where much tennis was played, so she played all her early tennis in public parks, where she displayed obvious skill and talent. Casals never fit in to the tennis establishment: That she overcame deep-seated ethnic, class, and gender-based prejudice to reach the top of the sport was a tribute to her physical skill and personal tenacity.

By the time she was 18, Casals was traveling the world playing and winning tennis tournaments, and in 1967 she won her first Wimbledon doubles title with partner Billie Jean King (born 1943). Consistently ranked in the top ten in singles over a two-decade career, Casals is also one of the sport's most accomplished doubles players, winning 12 Grand Slam titles, including seven Wimbledon titles. In 1996 Casals was inducted into the International Tennis Hall of Fame.

Legacy

Casals's off-court battles were as important as her tennis victories. They won great advances for generations of women tennis players and other female athletes. On September 23, 1970, during the early years of the women's rights movement, Casals and King formed the Virginia Slims Professional Women's Tennis Circuit. It was the first professional organization of its kind for any women's sport. Female tennis players had always been paid less than men, and Casals fought successfully to achieve equal prize money at the four Grand Slam tournaments (the U.S., Australian, and French opens, and Wimbledon). Casals was also a leading advocate of Title IX, legislation passed in

▲ *Rosie Casals is pictured here in singles action. Her greatest successes, however, came in doubles.*

1972 by the U.S. Congress that guaranteed gender equality for women in athletics at elementary through college levels. Today's greatly increased financial opportunities for girls and women in such sports as soccer, tennis, golf, and basketball—and the increased popularity of women's sports in general—are a direct result of Casals's pioneer activism for female professionalism and equality in sports.

KEY DATES	
1948	Born in San Francisco, California, on September 16.
1967	Wins her first Wimbledon doubles title.
1968	First woman tennis player to receive prize money.
1970	Launches the Virginia Slims Tour and wins the first singles title at the Virginia Slims of Houston.
1996	Inducted into the International Tennis Hall of Fame.

Further reading: Lichtenstein, Grace. *A Long Way Baby: Behind the Scenes in Women's Pro Tennis.* New York: Morrow, 1974.
http://www.edwardsly.com/casalsr.htm (Casals biography).

CASARES, Oscar
Writer

Descended from a long line of Mexican storytellers, Oscar Casares has earned a great deal of respect from both critics and readers for his debut collection *Brownsville: Stories*, which pays homage to his hometown in Texas. He said, "I prefer to write about things I've lived, that I have some sort of intimate emotional connection to."

Early life
Born in 1964 in Brownsville, Texas, a small city bordering the Rio Grande, Casares grew up in a predominantly Hispanic region. He initially struggled to define himself culturally, however. Tall and light-skinned, he felt great pressure to fully assimilate into mainstream Anglo society. Since Mexico was so close to where he lived with his family, Casares was also very aware of his ancestral roots and heritage. As he grew up, Casares developed a bicultural consciousness that led him to believe that it was possible to coexist properly in both worlds.

An advertising man
In 1984 Casares left Brownsville to study at the University of Texas at Austin; he received a bachelor's degree in advertising in 1987. Over the next 10 years, Casares traveled across the United States, writing and producing national advertising campaigns for GSD&M, an Austin-based firm.

Recalling the stories that some of his master-raconteur uncles used to tell him as a boy, Casares began entertaining friends with family legends and tales of everyday life in South Texas. Sharing the stories of his youth helped awaken Casares's own talent as a storyteller. He said that writing was about "going home. It was about trying to reclaim a part of myself."

The emergence of a writer
In 1996 Casares quit his advertising job to pursue writing full-time. Two years later he was selling stories to well-known literary journals, including the *Threepenny Review* and the *Northwest Review*.

By 2001 he had finished a Master of Fine Arts (MFA) degree from the respected University of Iowa Writers' Workshop. At Iowa he wrote several of the stories featured in the collection *Brownsville: Stories*. The stories predominantly focus on Mexican immigrants

or on the children of immigrants, and deal with the themes of love, death, birth, and the bicultural experience. Casares carried on writing after he left Iowa while he taught at the University of Texas at San Antonio.

Brownsville: Stories
After winning a Dobie Paisano fellowship, Casares finished writing the collection of stories at the Paisano Ranch, west of Austin. When he found out that his book was going to be published, he asked that it be distributed through HEB, a supermarket chain with stores in Texas and Mexico. This made the book particularly accessible to people in the border region, where bookstores were few. The unconventional choice to sell a work of high literary value in such a nontraditional outlet drew welcome publicity, but also reflected Casares's ability to use his experience in advertising to market the book properly.

The Brownsville stories are both quintessentially American and Mexican. With skill and economy, Casares depicts the common desire "to get ahead, to fall in love, to try and learn from mistakes, and [to] be a better person … these [are] things that go into being human." He claims that these are all universal experiences and that his characters just happen to be Mexican American.

Further reading: Casares, Oscar. *Brownsville: Stories.* New York, NY: Back Bay Books, 2003.
http://www.dailytexanonline.com/media/paper410/news/2005/04/18/Focus/Author.Brings.Border.Experience.To.His.Stories-928030.shtml?norewrite&sourcedomain=www.dailytexanonline.com (an article that discusses Oscar Casares's influences, background, and success).

KEY DATES

1964 Born in Brownsville, Texas.

1987 Graduates from the University of Texas at Austin.

1998 Publishes his first short story, "Yolanda," in *The Threepenny Review*.

2001 Graduates with an MFA from the University of Iowa Writers' Workshop.

2003 Publishes the highly acclaimed collection of short stories *Brownsville: Stories*.

CASAS, Juan Bautista de las
Tejano Revolutionary

In 1811 Juan Bautista de las Casas was briefly governor of an independent Texas after leading a revolt against the province's Spanish rulers. Lacking both the idealism and charisma of contemporary revolutionaries such as the Mexican priest Miguel Hidalgo y Costilla (1753–1811), Casas has never gained heroic or legendary status. Nonetheless some scholars regard the uprising that he led—the Casas Revolt—as an important precursor of the Tejano (Hispanic Texan) struggle for civil rights in the 20th century.

Little is known about the early life of Casas. He was a criollo (a North American of Spanish ancestry) of Nuevo Santander (a province of New Spain comprising the modern Mexican state of Tamaulipas and the southern tip of modern Texas), where he was a captain in the local Spanish militia.

Revolution in Texas

In the early 19th century many inhabitants of Mexico became increasingly dissatisfied with Spanish rule. The criollos, in particular, wanted greater political power, which had long been largely concentrated in the hands of the peninsulars, the European-born elite. On September 16, 1810, in the village of Dolores, Hidalgo y Costilla made a famous speech in which he called for independence from Spain and popularized the slogans "Viva Mexico" and "Viva la independencia!" His rallying call—later known as the Grito de Dolores (cry of Dolores)—sparked rebellions throughout the Mexican provinces.

In Texas the revolt was led by Casas, who had retired from the militia and was now living in San Antonio de Béxar (modern San Antonio), the provincial capital. He roused local criollo citizens and disgruntled troops in the city's garrison, and on January 22, 1811, they marched on the government headquarters and arrested the Spanish governor, Manuel María de Salcedo. The revolt soon spread to other areas of Texas, and Casas was declared the new governor. Following the example of Hidalgo he ordered the arrest of the peninsulars and the confiscation of their property.

Counterrevolution

Casas, however, soon proved himself an inept ruler. He failed both to reward those criollos who had helped in the revolt and to suppress those who continued to support Spanish rule. In San Antonio royalist counterrevolutionaries were rapidly able to exploit divisions among the rebels, and on March 2—little more than a month after the revolt had begun—Casas was arrested and Spanish rule reimposed.

Casas was sent to Monclova (now Coahuila state, Mexico), where he was imprisoned, tried, and executed by firing squad. His head was severed from his body and sent back to San Antonio, where it was displayed in the central plaza as a warning to other would-be revolutionaries. By that time Hidalgo, too, had been caught and shot as a rebel. While the priest's actions are commemorated annually on Mexican Independence Day (September 16), those of Casas are largely forgotten, yet his involvement was of crucial importance in Texas history.

▼ **This painting depicts the capture of Juan Bautista de las Casas in March, 1811.**

KEY DATES	
1811	Seizes power in San Antonio on January 22.
1811	Suppression of the Casas Revolt on March 2.
1811	Is executed by the Spanish authorities on August 3.

Further reading: Chipman, Donald E. *Spanish Texas, 1519–1821.* Austin, TX: University of Texas Press, 1992.
http://www.tsha.utexas.edu/handbook/online/articles/CC/jcc2.html (Handbook of Texas Online account of Casas revolt).

CASTANEDA, Carlos
Writer

Carlos Castaneda was a 20th-century author who wrote a series of best-selling books on mysticism. He was controversial during his life, and even after his death there remained a sharp division between readers who venerated him as a great guru and those who thought he was little more than a con man.

Early life

At the height of his fame, Castaneda actively misled the public about the details of his early life. He claimed that he was born in 1935 in São Paulo, Brazil, that his father was a literature professor, and that he studied sculpture in Milan, Italy. However, an investigation by *Time* magazine in 1973 revealed the truth: Carlos Cesar Arana Castaneda was born on Christmas Day, 1925, in Cajamarca, Peru. His father was a goldsmith who in 1948 moved the family to Lima, where he established a jewelry store. Castaneda graduated from the Peruvian Colegio Nacional de Nuestra Senora de Guadalupe, and studied briefly at the National Fine Arts School of Peru. In 1951, he immigrated to the United States, settled in California, and enrolled at Los Angeles City College, where he took classes in creative writing and journalism. He transferred to the University of California at Los Angeles (UCLA), where he received a BA, and then pursued graduate studies in anthropology.

Meeting Don Juan

In 1960, while conducting field research on medicinal plants used by Native Americans of the Southwest United States, Castaneda met Don Juan Matus, a Yaqui Indian from Mexico, at a bus depot in Nogales, Arizona. This chance encounter developed into an apprenticeship when Don Juan revealed himself to be a shaman. In many traditional religions, shamans are believed to be able to communicate with the spirit world, often while in an ecstatic state. Don Juan claimed to be the last in a line that could be traced back to the pre-Hispanic Toltec people who inhabited central and northern Mexico 1,000 years earlier. In 1961, Castaneda began his formal training under Don Juan. The education process involved the heavy use of psychoactive drugs, including peyote, jimson weed, and psilocybe mushrooms. Under the influence of the drugs, Castaneda experienced a series of bizarre hallucinations. Among the apparitions he claimed to have seen were a bilingual coyote, a 30-foot (9m) gnat, and columns of singing light.

KEY DATES

1925 Born in Cajamarca, Peru, on December 25.

1951 Immigrates to the United States.

1960 Meets Don Juan Matus in Nogales, Arizona.

1967 Submits *The Teachings of Don Juan: A Yaqui Way of Knowledge* as his master's thesis.

1969 *The Teachings of Don Juan: A Yaqui Way of Knowledge*, published the previous year, becomes a best seller.

1973 *Journey to Ixtlan: The Lessons of Don Juan*, Castaneda's third book, is accepted by UCLA as his PhD dissertation. Don Juan Matus supposedly dies the same year.

1998 Dies in Los Angeles, California, on April 27.

In 1965, fearing for his sanity, Castaneda cut short his training. The experience was not wasted, however. UCLA accepted *The Teachings of Don Juan: A Yaqui Way of Knowledge* as Castaneda's master's thesis in anthropology, and it was published in 1968 by the University of California Press. The work, which chronicled Castaneda's drug-induced visions and provided an analysis of Don Juan's belief system, became an underground classic. In 1969, at the height of the psychedelic era, it was reissued by a trade publisher and became an instant best seller.

Further investigations

Castaneda developed the mystical themes in his subsequent writings. His second book, *A Separate Reality: Further Conversations with Don Juan* (1971), was followed by *Journey to Ixtlan: The Lessons of Don Juan* (1972), which was accepted by UCLA as his PhD dissertation. He then wrote *Tales of Power* (1974), at the end of which he described throwing himself off a cliff, an act that symbolized his progression from disciple to shaman. That seemed to mark the end of the Don Juan series, but three years later Castaneda produced another book about the shaman, *The Second Ring of Power* (1977). He eventually wrote 12 books, including *The Eagle's Gift* (1981), *The Fire from Within* (1984), and *The Power of Silence: Further Lessons of Don Juan* (1987). Among his later publications were *The Art of Dreaming* (1993) and *Magical Passes: The Practical Wisdom of the Shamans of Ancient Mexico* (1998).

INFLUENCES AND INSPIRATION

Carlos Castaneda claimed to have learned from Don Juan about shamanism, a range of practices that are found in indigenous cultures based on the belief that the visible world contains invisible forces and spirits that affect the living. Shamans are medicine men and women who can access hidden spirit worlds that are otherwise known only through myths, dreams, and near-death experiences. While shamans have been credited with abilities that include divination, astral projection, shape-shifting (turning into animals), and the capacity to interpret dreams and other psychic phenomena, most are healers who help cure illness in their tribal communities through the use of song, dance, music, and herbal medicines.

Each successive book became less anthropological, and displayed an increasing range of influences, including philosophy, existentialism, and Eastern mysticism. Don Juan—who died in 1973 but remained the central figure in the series—changed in the books from a mysterious, barely literate, Mexican shaman into a sage familiar with the vocabulary of analytical philosophy and linguistics.

Castaneda explained that Don Juan instructed him in the use of psychoactive drugs to help him break through his rigid, rationalist Western mindset. The objective was to experience the alternate realities that shamans attain by a variety of means, including the use of drugs. The insights revealed in the first three books impressed academics and the general public alike. Timed perfectly to coincide with the peak of the drug-fueled 1960s, they made Castaneda a rich and famous author.

Truth or fiction?

The objective accuracy of Castaneda's works was widely questioned, but the author's skill in presenting what novelist Joyce Carol Oates has called "another way of reality" made him a successful, if controversial, writer in the 1970s and a guru of the New Age movement.

By the mid-1970s, doubts about the authenticity of Castaneda's accounts had been raised by numerous critics. Castaneda's refusal to reveal the whereabouts of Don Juan—a pseudonym he used to protect the privacy of his teacher—or to allow other anthropologists to examine his field notes added to the general suspicion. In 1976, psychology professor Richard de Mille published *Castaneda's Journey: The Power and the Allegory*, which detailed numerous inconsistencies in Castaneda's supposedly scientific writings and concluded that the Don Juan books were works of fiction. In 1993, Courtney Jay Fikes, an anthropologist who worked with Native American healers, published *Carlos Castaneda: Academic Opportunism and Psychedelic Sixties*. Fikes decided that many of Don Juan's insights were taken from various esoteric and occult traditions, and that Castaneda was "in the business of turning shamanic experience into a consumer product to be sold in the marketplace." In the 1990s, Castaneda suggested that the last assertion might be true. Having spent most of his adult life as a recluse, he suddenly emerged into the public spotlight to propagate "Tensegrity." This was a system of bodily movements that he claimed had been taught to initiates over 27 generations, in conditions of utmost secrecy, and passed on to him by Don Juan. Marketed by the Cleargreen Corporation, Tensegrity was taught in seminars and workshops in which participants paid large sums of money to hear Castaneda lecture.

Posthumous reputation

Carlos Castaneda died of liver cancer in 1998 at age 72. No one knows what happened to his body, although it may have been cremated and his ashes scattered in Mexico. His death was kept secret for several months until an adopted son publicly contested his will because he was not named as a beneficiary. A different picture of Castaneda then began to emerge, one that featured a cult of personality and a band of followers who were controlled and manipulated by the self-styled guru. Despite persistent rumors, and accusations that Castaneda was a fraud—which led to UCLA stripping him of his PhD—he was revered by millions and continues to be widely read. Carlos Castaneda may have been, in the words of one critic, "a sham-man bearing gifts," a trickster who "lied to bring us the truth." Yet to date his books have sold eight million copies worldwide and have been translated into 17 languages; he left an estate reportedly worth $20 million.

Further reading: Castaneda, Carlos. *The Teachings of Don Juan: A Yaqui Way of Knowledge.* New York, NY: Simon and Schuster, 1973.

http://users.pandora.be/gohiyuhi/nafps/articles/art03.htm (New Age Frauds and Plastic Shamans Web site).

CASTAÑEDA, Carlos E.
Historian

Carlos E. Castañeda was a 20th-century historian of Texas during the colonial period. He overcame poverty and discrimination to become professor of Latin American History at the University of Texas at Austin.

Early life

Born in 1896 into a poor family in Mexico, Carlos Eduardo Castañeda went to school in Matamoros until 1906, when his family crossed the Rio Grande and settled in Brownsville, Texas. There he quickly learned English and graduated as a valedictorian from Brownsville High School in 1916. He won a scholarship to the University of Texas at Austin but, owing to financial problems caused by the death in 1910 of both his parents, he instead taught for a year at a school in Las Palmas.

Castañeda finally enrolled in the university in 1917 as a student of civil engineering, and worked in his spare time translating Spanish colonial documents for a professor of history, Eugene Campbell Barker. In April 1917, however, the United States entered World War I (1914–1918). Castañeda dropped out of school and enlisted in the Army,

partly in the hope that by so doing the U.S. immigration authorities would grant his application for citizenship. At the end of the war, with continuing financial difficulties, Castañeda began working for an oil company in Tampico, and did not return to the university until 1920. He had decided in the meantime to change to history, a tough choice since that subject, unlike his original discipline, offered no clear career path. Nevertheless he was singleminded, and graduated with a BA in 1921. While studying for his degree Castañeda helped the University of Texas acquire the archive of the scholar Genaro García (1867–1920), which contained a wealth of important documents relating to the cultural and political history of Mexico from the 16th to the 20th century.

After graduation Castañeda taught Spanish in high schools in San Antonio, while studying part-time for a master's. His thesis, which he completed in 1923, was entitled "A Report on the Spanish Archives in San Antonio,

▼ *Carlos E. Castañeda (left) is pictured in discussion with an unidentified priest in October, 1941.*

INFLUENCES AND INSPIRATION

Carlos Castañeda depicted the importance of the Spanish and Catholic foundations of Texas. He deliberately expanded the field of Spanish borderlands' studies, originally defined by the historian Herbert Eugene Bolton at the University of California at Berkeley. Castañeda's first book, *The Mexican Side of the Texas Revolution* (1928), drew on the testimonies of the Mexican generals Antonio López de Santa Anna and José Maria Tornel, and argued that the Mexicans were defeated not by a superior military force but by internal conflicts between clerical and progressive movements. Castañeda expanded this theme in volume six of *Our Catholic Heritage in Texas: Fight for Freedom, 1810–1936* (1950), which portrayed how Mexicans in Texas had rebelled against corrupt governments in both Spain and Mexico. This countered both the stereotype of Mexicans as inherently undemocratic and the predominant view of American history as uniquely "Anglo." It was, moreover, a direct attack on the "frontier" school of American history associated with Frederick Jackson Turner. In other respects, however, Castañeda was less critical of the Spanish inheritance; he portrayed the missions of the Southwest as noble institutions, and the missionaries who ran them as heroes. His interpretation endeared him to many Catholic organizations, but did not find wider acceptance among contemporary historians.

Texas." He then became an associate professor of Spanish at the College of William and Mary, Virginia. Texas remained his true home, however, and he began looking for a way to return there. The chance came in 1927, when he was invited to become librarian of the Genaro García Collection in Austin. Although the job paid less and was a substantial reduction in academic status, Castañeda was persuaded to accept it by an offer of support from the Knights of Columbus of Texas, who commissioned him to carry out a study of the Catholic church in the state. The result was his principal work, *Our Catholic Heritage in Texas*, which was published in seven volumes from 1936 to 1958. Back in Austin, Castañeda also studied for a PhD; his dissertation, "Morfi's History of Texas," completed in 1932, was a translation of a manuscript by Fray Juan Agustín Morfi that Castañeda had discovered.

Castañeda remained librarian of the Genaro García Collection while serving as associate professor of history from 1939 until 1946, and developed what became the Benson Latin American Collection into one of the most important historical archives of its kind in the United States. In 1946 he became professor of Latin American history, a position he held until his death.

Honors

Castañeda was awarded honorary doctorates by St. Edward's University in Austin (1941) and the Catholic University of America in Washington, D.C. (1951), the presidency of the American Catholic Historical Association (1939), and knighthoods in the Equestrian Order of the Holy Sepulchre of Jerusalem (1941) and the Order of Isabel the Catholic (1950). He also received the Junípero Serra Award of the Americas from the Academy of American Franciscan History (1951). The Perry-Castañeda Library at the University of Texas at Austin, which opened in 1977, was dedicated to Castañeda and Ervin S. Perry, the university's first African American professor.

Castañeda's Mexican background and Texan upbringing gave him a unique insight into contemporary problems: He campaigned to improve school conditions in the barrios of San Antonio, and served as regional director of the Fair Employment Practice Committee, set up by President Franklin D. Roosevelt during World War II (1939–1945).

KEY DATES

1896   Born in Ciudad Camargo, Tamaulipas, Mexico, on November 11.

1927   Becomes librarian of the Latin American Collection at the University of Texas at Austin.

1936   Publishes first volume of *Our Catholic Heritage in Texas, 1519–1936*.

1946   Appointed professor of Latin American history at the University of Texas at Austin.

1958   Dies in Austin, Texas, on April 3.

Further reading: Almaráz, Jr., Félix D. *Knight without Armor: Carlos Eduardo Castañeda, 1896–1958.* Austin, TX: Texas A&M University Press, 1999.
http://www.tsha.utexas.edu/handbook/online/articles/CC/fca85.html (The Handbook of Texas Online).

CASTILLO, Ana
Writer

Ana Castillo emerged as one of the most prominent Latina writers of the second half of the 20th century. In often challenging and experimental poems, novels, and essays she explored themes of Chicana identity, feminism, sexuality, and power.

Castillo was born to working-class, Mexican American parents in Chicago, Illinois, on June 15, 1953. She attended Jones Commercial High School, Chicago City College, and Northeastern Illinois University, from which she graduated with a BA in art and education in 1975. While at university Castillo became involved in Hispanic American artistic and activist circles. She abandoned her early ambition of becoming a visual artist and turned increasingly to writing. After completing her first degree, Castillo taught ethnic studies at Santa Rosa Junior College in Sonoma, California, and from 1977 to 1979 was writer in residence for the Illinois Arts Council. Also in 1979 she received a master's in Latin American and Caribbean studies at the University of Chicago.

Published work

Castillo self-published her first collection of poetry, *Otro Canto,* in 1977, and followed it two years later with her second, *The Invitation.* Her later volumes of poetry include *Women Are Not Roses* (1984), *My Father Was a Toltec* (1988), and *I Ask the Impossible* (2001). Castillo's first novel, *The Mixquiahuala Letters,* was published in 1986 and won the Before Columbia Foundation's American Book Award in 1987; she followed it with *Sapagonia* (1990), *So Far from God* (1993), and *Peel My Love Like an Onion* (1999). Her other works include *Loverboys* (1996), a volume of short stories, and *Massacre of the Dreamers* (1994), a collection of nonfiction essays about women in Chicano society. She also edited *Goddess of the Americas* (1996), an anthology of writings about the Virgin of Guadalupe, Mexico's most sacred religious image.

▲ *A central theme of the works of writer Ana Castillo is the place of women in Chicano culture.*

In her work Castillo presents a forthright and often challenging look at Chicano cultural identity. She is preoccupied in particular with the changing place of women in Chicano culture—she terms her brand of Chicana feminism "Xicanisma." Drawing on the storytelling traditions of Mexico, as well as European and American literary forms, her style is direct, informal, and often experimental, making extensive use of dialogue and mixing English and Spanish with Chicano dialects. With their look at universal themes such as love and power, Castillo's works have found an increasingly wide audience. Her most recent novel, *Watercolor Women Opaque Men,* was published in 2005, the year in which she also brought out two short plays in a work entitled *Psst—I Have Something to Tell You, Mi Amor.*

Further reading: Spurgeon, Sara L. *Ana Castillo.* Boise, ID: Boise State University Press, 2004.
http://www.anacastillo.com/ac/index.htm (official Web site).

KEY DATES	
1953	Born in Chicago, Illinois, on June 15.
1977	Publishes first collection of poetry, *Otro Canto.*
1986	Publishes *The Mixquiahuala Letters.*
1992	Publishes *Massacre of the Dreamers.*

CASTILLO, Leonel
Public Servant

Leonel Castillo was the first person of Mexican ancestry to head the U.S. Immigration and Naturalization Service (INS). He was appointed to that position by President Jimmy Carter in 1976.

Early life
Leonel Castillo was born in 1939 in Victoria, Texas. His family came originally from Spain and lived in Linares, Nuevo León, Mexico, until the early 1900s, when his grandparents immigrated to the United States and settled in Brownsville, Texas. Leonel's father, Seferino Castillo, later moved to Victoria and then to Galveston, where he worked on the docks. The young Leonel helped him maintain the records he kept for the local union.

On graduating from public high school in Galveston in 1957, Leonel Castillo attended St. Mary's University in San Antonio. There he joined the Young Democrats and became an active opponent of segregation at the city's Majestic Theatre. He was also a member of the Viva Kennedy Club, which helped the 1960 presidential campaign of John F. Kennedy. The following year Castillo graduated with a degree in English and hitchhiked to New York City in search of a job. When he failed to find one, he joined the Peace Corps, which sent him to teach in the Philippines.

After four years abroad Castillo returned to the United States and took a master's degree in community organization at the University of Pittsburgh, Pennsylvania, which he completed in 1967. He then moved to Houston, where he was appointed director of the Catholic Council

▲ **Leonel Castillo served as head of the Immigration and Naturalization Service between 1977 and 1979.**

of Community Relations in 1970. Meanwhile he became involved with the Chicano movement in its confrontations with the educational authorities. He organized the Mexican American Education Council (MAEC), established Huelga (strike) schools to teach boycotting students, joined the Political Association of Spanish Speaking Organizations (PASSO) to support striking farmworkers in the Rio Grande Valley of Texas, and founded the Chicano Family Center, an organization that serves poor Hispanic people.

Public office
Through his activism Castillo acquired a reputation as a shrewd politician, and his popularity with Hispanic Americans helped him win election in 1971 as comptroller of Houston. The comptroller's main responsibility is to certify that funds are available for public expenditures by the city council. Castillo's success in the post inspired him to seek the leadership of the Democratic Party of Texas in 1974. Although his attempt failed, he was elected party treasurer in 1976. In the same year president elect Jimmy Carter invited Castillo to serve in Washington, D.C., as commissioner of immigration and naturalization. Leonel Castillo took office on May 13, 1977. He remained in the post until October 1, 1979, when he resigned and returned to Houston, where he has since served in an advisory capacity to several mayors of the city.

Further reading: San Miguel, Guadalupe. *Brown, Not White: School Integration and the Chicano Movement in Houston.* College Station, TX: Texas A&M University Press, 2001.

KEY DATES	
1939	Born in Victoria, Texas, on June 9.
1961	Graduates from St. Mary's University, San Antonio.
1963	Joins the Peace Corps and serves in the Philippines.
1966	Returns to the United States.
1967	Graduates from the University of Pittsburgh with master's degree.
1971	Elected comptroller for the City of Houston.
1976	President Jimmy Carter appoints him to head the INS.
1979	Leaves INS; returns to Houston.

CASTRO, George
Scientist

George Castro is an industrial scientist who made his name in the 1970s and 1980s while working for the International Business Machines Corporation (IBM), a multinational corporation that manufactures and sells computer hardware and software, and provides related consulting services. In the latter part of his career he became prominent as a highly efficient and inspirational university administrator.

Early life

Born in Los Angeles, California, and raised by Mexican American parents, George Castro had a fascination with science from an early age. He was particularly absorbed by mechanics. After graduating from public high school he attended the University of California, Los Angeles (UCLA), where he started out studying physics but changed in his first year to chemistry, the subject in which he completed his BS degree in 1960.

Although Castro had not, by his own account, been an outstanding student at UCLA, he was offered a chance to go to graduate school at the University of California at Riverside with his tuition paid in full. The only stipulation was that he maintain a B average grade in all his courses. Castro accepted the offer, and graduated in 1965 with the necessary overall mark.

Into industry

During his PhD studies, Castro became involved in various research projects, including one that used organic matter to simulate solid-state effects. That area of expertise was of special interest to computer pioneers IBM, and in 1972 the firm hired Castro to help develop a new form of film made from organic photoconductors and to find new techniques of photocopying. His work broke ground in both areas, and as a direct result of his findings IBM installed new charge carriers into its electrophotographic copying machines and laser printers in the early 1970s. By the end of the decade the same innovations had been adopted by Eastman Kodak and other competing firms.

Laboratory management

In 1975 Castro was promoted to manager of physical sciences at IBM's world-renowned research laboratory in San Jose. In the 11 years between Castro's appointment and 1986, scientists at the center produced more than 3,000 learned publications and won many major national and international awards. Their productivity was in large part a reflection of Castro's inspirational leadership and management techniques.

In 1986 IBM charged Castro with the construction of a new synchrotron X-ray facility (synchrotron radiation is electromagnetic radiation produced by the acceleration of high-energy charged particles in a magnetic field). After five years' planning and experimentation carried out in close cooperation with members of the faculty at Stanford University, Castro installed new X-ray machinery at IBM. It became fully operational in 1993.

Work in education

After 27 years with IBM, George Castro left the company in 1999 to take up an appointment as dean of the College of Science at San Jose State University. There his main responsibility was to help allocate grant money to high schools with students showing promise and ability. The job could have been merely administrative, but Castro was characteristically proactive, addressing young audiences and fostering in them a love of science. In both phases of his professional career Castro distinguished himself both as a creative genius in his own right and as the inspiration of originality in others. He has been widely honored with a host of industrial and civic awards. Since taking up his university post he has lived in San Jose with his wife, Barbara, and their four children.

Further reading: Kirk, Raymond E. *Encyclopedia of Chemical Technology.* New York, NY: Wiley, 1984.
http://www.jascc.org/hall/hfgcastro.htm (Santa Clara County, California, Hall of Fame).

KEY DATES

1960   Graduates from University of California, Los Angeles (UCLA), with a bachelor of science (BS) degree in chemistry.

1965   Completes PhD in physical chemistry at the University of California at Riverside.

1972   Joins IBM.

1975   Becomes manager of IBM San Jose Research Lab.

1999   Appointed dean at San Jose State University.

CASTRO, José
General, Political Leader

General José Antonio Castro was an important political and military leader in the Mexican province of Alta California in the turbulent times that led up to its annexation by the United States in 1846. Castro is chiefly known for his role in military engagements, such as the Battle of La Providencia of 1845, and for his friendship with Juan Bautista Alvarado (*see box on page 70*).

Living in turbulent times

The exact birth date of José Antonio Castro is unknown. Records show that he was baptized in the mission at Soledad, California, on August 7, 1808. His father, José Tiburcio Castro, came from a distinguished family of soldiers who had helped colonize the region around Monterey in the late 18th century, and himself became the leader of a presidio, or Spanish military post. Castro's mother was María Rufina Álvarez, who came from a prominent Spanish family in Los Angeles.

Castro was raised in Monterey, which since 1775 had been the provincial capital. There he became friends with Juan Bautista Alvarado, who later became his closest political ally. In 1821 Mexico achieved its independence from Spain, and Alta California entered a tumultuous period as local factions fought for power. Between 1822 and 1846, the Mexican province had no fewer than 12 governors.

Many Californios, as the Hispanic inhabitants of California began to call themselves, believed that the province should become an independent state. They resented any interference by the Mexican government in Mexico City. However, the situation was complicated: Very few Californios agreed on the form that independence should take. In particular, there was a deep-seated rivalry between the north—centered around Monterey—and the south—centered around Los Angeles. The division repeatedly brought the province to the brink of civil war.

By the 1830s, increasing numbers of foreigners, including American, French, and English traders and merchants, were settling in California, especially in the port city of Monterey. The United States made little attempt to disguise the fact that it wanted this attractive and lucrative province for itself; especially as Britain and France, its colonial rivals in North America, were also showing an interest in its affairs. However, it was not

KEY DATES
1808   Baptized in Soledad, Alta California, on August 7.
1835   Briefly serves as interim governor of California.
1845   Defeats Micheltorena's troops at the Battle of La Providencia and is appointed commandante general of California.
1846   Flees to Mexico after the U.S. annexation of California.
1860   Dies in California.

until the early 1840s that significant numbers of U.S. settlers began to stream down into the province from the neighboring territory of Oregon.

Political allegiance

Castro and Alvarado became involved in the province's complicated politics as young men. Both eventually served on the small but powerful provincial assembly known as the *diputacíon*. Both Castro and Alvarado were firmly allied to the northern faction and both supported some measure of independence for the province. The friends' political machinations often got them into trouble, however: In 1831, for instance, both Castro and Alvarado had to flee Monterey for San Francisco when Governor Manuel Victoria ordered their arrest after he discovered their involvement in a plot to unseat him.

A charismatic leader

Castro was an able and charismatic leader. In 1833 another governor, José Figuero, appointed Castro president of the *diputacíon*; after Figuero's death in September 1835, Castro became acting governor. He remained in the position until January the following year, when the Mexican government sent Nicolás Gutiérrez to replace him. In November 1836 Castro and Alvarado led yet another revolt. They surrounded the presidio in Monterey and forced Nicolás Gutiérrez to resign. Alvarado had himself appointed governor and Castro was made the province's commandante general, or military leader.

While northern Californios supported the new regime, their southern countrymen opposed it. In 1837 civil war broke out, and in the skirmishes that followed, Castro and Alvarado were easily victorious.

INFLUENCES AND INSPIRATION

Throughout his political career, José Castro was influenced and abetted by his friend and ally Juan Bautista Alvarado. The two men grew up in the cosmopolitan climate of Monterey, Alta California, where traders of many different nationalities lived and worked. Of the two, Alvarado was in many respects the dominant figure, although his habitual drinking often marred his career, particularly during his tenure as provincial governor.

Both Castro and Alvarado were strong and colorful characters. Some critics say that their actions, although courageous, were often driven by personal ambition rather than by any high-minded political ideals for their country.

Like Castro, Alvarado ceased to play a part in political or civic affairs after the province became part of the United States. In later life, Alvarado ran his wife's estates at Rancho San Pablo, and concentrated on business and agriculture.

The Mexican government formally recognized Alvarado as governor, and he continued to hold the position until 1841, when the central government appointed Manuel Micheltorena (d.1852) the new governor. This time the government also took the precaution of sending a force of 300 former convicts with Micheltorena to help him maintain power. Micheltorena proved even more unpopular than earlier appointees, however, and both northern and southern Californios were united in wanting to get rid of him.

On February 19–20, 1845, Castro and Alvarado defeated Micheltorena's troops at the Battle of La Providencia (also known as the Second Battle of Cahuenga Pass), and the governor finally agreed to withdraw from the province. This time the southern leader Pío de Jesús Pico was appointed governor and set up his headquarters in Los Angeles. Castro once again became commandante general; his headquarters were in Monterey. Pico and Castro were soon at loggerheads, each plotting the other one's downfall.

The Gavilan Peak Incident and after

Governor Pico and Comandante General Castro were soon embroiled in an even more threatening crisis. In the summer of 1844, Captain John Charles Frémont of the U.S. Army led a party of soldiers into California, ostensibly on a scientific and exploratory mission. In January 1845 Castro, Alvarado, Pico, and the U.S. consul, Thomas O. Larkin, met with Frémont, who requested permission to remain in the uninhabited valley of San Joaquin over the winter. Castro took this to mean that, as soon as winter was over, Frémont and his men would follow the Sacramento River back to Oregon and the United States. Castro did not reply in writing to the request and Fremont took this to mean that he had permission. In February 1845, Frémont and his men camped at the Rancho Laguna Seca. Contrary to what he had told Castro, Frémont led his party west to Santa Cruz, then south on to Salinas, where he made camp early in March 1845. For Californios his actions inevitably conjured up fears of an American invasion and Castro ordered Frémont to leave, copying his order to the U.S. consul, Larkin, so that there would be no misunderstanding. Frémont refused to comply. In March 1855, he set up camp on Gavilan Peak, outside Monterey. Castro responded by leading troops to the foot of the peak, and conflict was only avoided by some last-minute mediation by Larkin.

Tensions between the Californios and U.S. settlers now reached crisis point. On June 14, 1846, a group of settlers occupied the northern town of Sonoma and declared California independent, rechristening it the Bear Flag Republic. By then, Mexico and the United States had declared war on each other. Despite last-ditch attempts to present a united front by Castro and Pico, U.S. forces quickly seized control of first Monterey, then San Francisco, Los Angeles, and San Diego. Castro initially fled to Mexico; he later returned to Monterey to live with his wife and children.

Last years

Castro was never again active in politics. He gradually sold off most of his property and lands to U.S. settlers. Castro died in 1860; he was buried in the San Carlos Mission, Monterey.

See also: Alvarado, Juan Bautista; Pico, Pío

Further reading: Chapman, Charles E. *A History of California: The Spanish Period.* New York, NY: Macmillan, 1991. www.inn-california.com/Articles/history (various articles on Californian history).

CASTRO, Raúl
Politician, Diplomat

Raúl Castro was the first Mexican American to be elected governor of Arizona. He held office from 1975 to 1977.

Early life
One of 14 children, Raúl Héctor Castro was born in Mexico in 1916 and immigrated to the United States with his family at age 10. They settled in Arizona. Castro worked his way through Arizona State Teachers College at Flagstaff, graduating in 1939. Despite his qualification and the fact that he had become a naturalized U.S. citizen, he could not obtain a teaching job because of the state school board policy that prohibited the hiring of Mexican Americans. Instead he worked for the U.S. State Department as a foreign service clerk at Agua Prieta, Mexico, for five years before enrolling at the University of Arizona College of Law. He graduated with a JD degree in 1949, and was admitted to the Arizona Bar in the same year.

While practicing law in Tucson, Castro became increasingly involved in politics and served in various positions with support from the Democratic Party. He was elected Pima County Attorney in 1954, and held the post until 1958. In 1959 he was elected judge of the Pima County Superior Court. After Castro had spent six years on the bench President Lyndon B. Johnson appointed him U.S. ambassador to El Salvador in 1964. At the embassy in San Salvador Castro showed immense skill as a diplomat, and he was rewarded four years later with another posting as U.S. ambassador to Bolivia.

▲ *Raúl Castro is pictured on his appointment as U.S. ambassador to El Salvador in October 1964.*

From Arizona to Argentina and back
Castro spent a year in La Paz before returning to Tucson in 1969 to practice international law. He resumed his political activities, too, and in 1974 sought election as governor of Arizona. Few commentators expected him to carry the state—there was thought to be still too much prejudice against Mexican Americans—but a spirited campaign brought him victory. After Castro had completed two years as governor in 1977, President Jimmy Carter selected him to be U.S. ambassador to Argentina. His period of service in Buenos Aires coincided with some of the worst human rights abuses during Argentina's "dirty war," which began as an attempt to suppress terrorism but resulted in the deaths of thousands of civilians under the ruling military junta of President Jorge Videla.

Raúl Castro returned to the United States in 1980, and retired to his family home in Nogales, Santa Cruz County, Arizona.

KEY DATES	
1916	Born in Cananea, Sonora, Mexico, on June 12.
1949	Graduates with law degree.
1959	Elected judge of Pima County Superior Court.
1964	Appointed U.S. ambassador to El Salvador.
1968	Appointed U.S. ambassador to Bolivia.
1969	Returns to the United States; resumes legal practice.
1974	Elected governor of Arizona.
1977	Appointed U.S. ambassador to Argentina.
1980	Retires.

Further reading: Chanin, Abe, with Mildred Chanin. *This Land, These Voices.* Flagstaff, AZ: Northland Press, 1977.
http://jeff.scott.tripod.com/Castro.html (Hispanics in Arizona).

CAVAZOS, Bobby
Football Player, Writer

Growing up on the famed King Ranch in Texas, Bobby Cavazos rose to national prominence as an All-American running back at Texas Tech University in 1953. He later became foreman of the ranch, one of the largest in the United States. The ranch was so vast that it was made up of four divisions, and Cavazos handled the largest division, Laureles (255,000 acres/103,200ha).

Early life

Born on November 26, 1930, Cavazos was the fourth of five children of Lauro and Tomasa ("Tommie") Cavazos. Lauro, his father, was the first Mexican foreman of the King Ranch. Founded in 1853 by Richard King, the ranch is generally regarded as the birthplace of the American ranching industry; it also lies on oil-rich land. King built it up by buying the *derechos*, or land rights, from neighboring families; some had owned the land since Spanish colonial times. Among King's purchases was the San Juan de Carricitos, land given to José Narciso Cavazos by the Spanish crown in 1781.

From a young age Cavazos worked as a ranch hand, cleaning out barn stalls and helping build and mend fences. Lauro Cavazos was eager that his children have a good education; he stressed to them the importance of doing well at school. Cavazos followed his sister and two brothers to Kingsville High School in 1946. He had a passion for sports, lettering in football, basketball, and track.

All-American star

Cavazos earned a scholarship to play at Texas Tech in 1950. He majored in animal science, one of very few Hispanics on campus in Lubbock. Cavazos continued to play football, debuting in 1951 with the Red Raiders. In his three seasons as a halfback with the team, Cavazos was a three-time All-Border Conference selection and was named a third-team All-American in 1953. Cavazos rushed for 141 yards and three touchdowns in the Raiders' 35–13 win over Auburn in the Gator Bowl on January 1, 1954. He was named the game's Most Valuable Player (MVP).

Cavazos was drafted by the Chicago Cardinals (who later moved to St. Louis and then to Arizona) in the third round of the 1954 National Football League (NFL) draft. However, he suffered a shoulder injury in his rookie year and never played again in the NFL.

KEY DATES

1930	Born on the King Ranch in Texas on November 26.
1954	Named MVP of the Gator Bowl on New Year's Day.
1955	Joins the U.S. Army; spends the next two years in Korea.
1999	Publishes a memoir, *The Cowboy from the Wild Horse Desert: A Story of the King Ranch*.
2003	Is inducted into the National Hispanic Sports Hall of Fame in May.

Life after football

After his professional football career was prematurely ended, Cavazos fulfilled his Reserve Officer Training Corps (ROTC) military obligation, which had previously been deferred. He served two years in the U.S. Army's 24th Infantry on patrol in Korea's Demilitarized Zone (DMZ). He was honorably discharged as a second lieutenant. On completing his military service, Cavazos returned to his beloved King Ranch and was appointed foreman of the Laureles division, a post he held for 25 years until his retirement in the early 1980s.

Writing about his experiences

In 1991 Cavazos moved to Kerrville, Texas, northwest of San Antonio. He became a full-time author, writing three books about his experiences on the King Ranch. The most successful was *The Cowboy from the Wild Desert: A Story of the King Ranch.*

A famous family

Cavazos's older brothers also became famous. Lauro F. Cavazos was the first Latino member of a U.S. cabinet, serving as secretary of education under presidents Ronald Reagan and George H. W. Bush; Richard Cavazos retired as a four-star general in the U.S. Army.

See also: Cavazos, Lauro F.; Cavazos, Richard E.

Further reading: Cavazos, Bobby. *The Cowboy from the Wild Horse Desert: A Story of the King Ranch.* Houston, TX: Larksdale Press, 1999.
http://www.mysanantonio.com/salife/stories/1071809.html (about the King Ranch).

CAVAZOS, Lauro F.
Educator, Secretary of Education

Named by *Hispanic Business* in 1988 as one of the most influential Hispanics in the United States, Lauro F. Cavazos is a distinguished educator. When President Ronald Reagan (1981–1989) appointed Cavazos secretary of education in 1988, he became both the first Hispanic American to be appointed to that post and the first Hispanic American to serve in the cabinet. As secretary of education, Cavazos sought to address the educational needs of vulnerable groups such as ethnic minorities. He also initiated programs to fight drug and alcohol abuse and promoted parental involvement in education reform. Cavazos is the brother of Richard E. Cavazos, the first Hispanic American general in the U.S. Army.

Early life
A sixth-generation Mexican American, Lauro Fred Cavazos Jr., was born on the King Ranch near Kingsville, Texas, on January 4, 1927, where his father Lauro F. Cavazos, Sr., worked as a foreman. His mother was Tomasa Quintanilla Cavazos. Cavazos received his earliest education in the ranch's two-room school, but in the third grade Cavazos's family moved to nearby Kingsville, where he and his brothers and sisters were the first Mexican Americans to attend the town's public schools.

A career in education
After serving in the U.S. Army at the end of World War II (1939–1945), Cavazos returned to full-time education. In 1949 he gained a bachelor's degree in zoology from Texas Technology College (later Texas Tech University) in Lubbock; two years later he graduated with a master's from the university. In 1954 Cavazos was awarded a doctorate in physiology from Iowa State University. He taught at the Medical College of Virginia (1954–1964), before joining the faculty of Tufts University Medical School in Boston, where he served as professor of anatomy and departmental head until 1972. He was made dean in 1975, a position in which he remained until 1980.

In 1980 Cavazos became the first Hispanic American to be appointed president of Texas Tech University. A talented and brilliant academic, Cavazos was renowned for his work in medicine and in medical education. In 1984 he was honored with an award for Outstanding Leadership in the Field of Education by President Reagan and in the following year with a Distinguished Service Medal

from the Uniformed Services University for the Health Sciences. He was inducted into the Hispanic Hall of Fame in 1987.

Breaking boundaries
On August 9, 1988, Reagan nominated Cavazos to the cabinet position of secretary of education. Cavazos was a Democrat and was well-known for his liberal views on many educational issues. Some critics believed that his nomination was merely a Republican ploy to win Hispanic votes in the approaching presidential elections; others, however, argued that it was a long overdue recognition of the important role played by Hispanic Americans in U.S. public life. On September 11, 1988, Cavazos was unanimously confirmed in his post by the Senate.

Following the election of the Republican candidate George H. W. Bush as president in November 1988, Bush asked Cavazos to remain in the position of secretary of education. In his election campaign Bush had promised

▼ *Lauro Cavazos was the first Hispanic to hold the post of secretary of education.*

73

LEGACY

Through his academic and political career Lauro Cavazos has fought to improve education for minority groups, in particular for Hispanic Americans. He was acutely aware of the poor performance of Hispanic Americans from early childhood to postsecondary level. Low participation in preschool and college programs, effective segregation in poorly resourced schools, and high illiteracy rates were chronic symptoms of the failure of the U.S. public education system to address the needs of Hispanics. As secretary of education, Cavazo was able to highlight this crisis and to begin the monumental task of remedying the decades-long educational deficit.

During the early months of his time in office, Cavazos oversaw five regional meetings (in San Antonio, Boston, Miami, Chicago, and Los Angeles) at which students, parents, teachers, employers, and academics met with politicians to debate the causes of the crisis in Hispanic education and what could be done to rectify them. On September 24, 1990, President George H. W. Bush signed an executive order creating the President's Advisory Commission on Educational Excellence for Hispanic Americans, a body that Cavazos hoped would help the Department of Education to address the educational needs of Hispanics.

Even after Cavazos resigned as secretary of education in 1990, the commission continued to be a feature of subsequent administrations. It continues to play a vital role in enabling Hispanic students to achieve their educational potential.

that education, widely considered to be in a state of deep crisis, would be a key issue in his administration. Cavazos worked alongside Bush to produce a set of six national goals for education that would act as a blueprint for educational reform. The goals were that every child should start school ready to learn, that the high school graduation rate should increase from its 1990 level of 76 percent to 90 percent, that students should demonstrate competency at challenging subjects such as science and geography, that the United States should become world leader in math and science education, that every adult should be literate, and that the school environment should be free from drugs and violence. To these goals, Cavazos added his own, that "every child be educated to his or her fullest potential"— words he had engraved on a school bell displayed outside the Department of Education building in Washington, D.C.

Cavazos also launched special programs aimed at improving the achievements of Hispanic Americans (*see box*). He also sought to address the crisis in the federal student loan programs as well as the nationwide shortage of trained teachers. However, Cavazos's record as secretary of education was judged poor and lackluster by many media commentators. Some compared him unfavorably to his forthright predecessor William Bennett, who was seen to have taken on a complacent educational profession in his bid to make effective reforms. In December 1990 Bush asked Cavazos to tender his resignation and on March 18, 1991, he was replaced by Lamar Alexander.

Cavazos returned to the Tufts University Medical School, where he was professor and director of Graduate Programs in the Public Health Department of Family Medicine and Community Health. Cavazos has served on the boards of many international health organizations, including the World Health Organization.

KEY DATES

1927   Born on the King Ranch, near Kingsville, Texas, on January 4.

1964   Joins the faculty of Tufts University Medical School, Boston, Massachusetts.

1980   Becomes the first Hispanic American to be appointed president of Texas Tech University, Lubbock.

1988   Becomes the first Hispanic American to be appointed secretary of education and the first to be appointed to the cabinet.

1990   Under pressure from President George H.W. Bush, resigns as secretary of education; returns to academia as professor of family medicine and community health at Tufts University School of Medicine.

See also: Cavazos, Richard E.

Further reading: Ohles, Frederik, Shirley M. Ohles, and John G. Ramsay. *Biographical Dictionary of Modern American Educators.* Westport, CT: Greenwood Press, 1997.
http://www.lib.utexas.edu/taro/ttusw/00036/tsw-00036.html (Texas Archival Resources Online page on Cavazos).

CAVAZOS, Richard E.
General

R ichard E. Cavazos has had a long and distinguished career in the military. In 1982 Cavazos became the first Hispanic to be appointed a four-star (full) general in the U.S. Army. His distinguished military career has encompassed active service in both the Korean (1950–1953) and Vietnam (1964–1973) wars, as well as numerous tactical, training, and command roles. During the late 20th century Cavazos's outstanding record and high national profile provided a positive role model to the growing numbers of Hispanic men and women who were joining the United States' armed services.

Cavazos's brother is Lauro F. Cavazos, a distinguished educator and secretary of education (1988–1990) under Presidents Ronald Reagan and George H. W. Bush.

Early life
Born on the King Ranch, near Kingsville, Texas, Cavazos was the son of Tomasa Quintanilla Cavazos and ranch foreman Lauro F. Cavazos, a descendant of an old Spanish vaquero (ranching) family to whom much of the ranch had originally belonged. Although the Cavazos family lived in modest circumstances, the children were expected to excel in whatever they chose to do. After high-school graduation, Cavazos followed his brother Lauro to Texas Technology College (later Texas Tech University), Lubbock, where he studied for a bachelor's degree in geology. While a student Cavazos became a member of the Reserve Officers' Training Corps (ROTC). After graduating in 1951, he joined the U.S. Army as a second lieutenant.

A distinguished career
After initial officer training at Fort Benning, Georgia, Cavazos was appointed platoon commander with the largely Puerto Rican 65th Infantry Regiment. He was sent to Korea, where he distinguished himself for his leadership skills and his bravery. He was awarded both a Silver Star and Distinguished Service Cross, two of the highest military honors in the United States. He received the Silver Star for his conduct during an engagement near Sangdong-Ni on February 25, 1953: Under heavy arms fire he single-handedly retrieved a wounded enemy soldier.

Cavazos won a second Distinguished Service Cross during the Vietnam War for his role in the crucial Battle of Loc Ninh (October to November 1967). During the battle Cavazos, now a lieutenant colonel, commanded the

▲ *Richard E. Cavazos's military career has been full of firsts: In 1976 he became the first Hispanic to be appointed brigadier general; four years later he was the first to become a full general.*

1st Battalion 18th Infantry in assaults on enemy positions near an airstrip close to the Cambodian border. The 1st Battalion was able to inflict heavy casualties on the enemy with the loss of only five of its own personnel.

Making an impact
During the 1960s Cavazos undertook further military education, completing programs at the U.S. Army Command and General Staff College (1961), the British Army Staff College (1962), the Armed Forces Staff College

INFLUENCES AND INSPIRATION

Richard E. Cavazos has had a long and distinguished career in the military. He served as an inspiration to many Hispanic Americans wishing to pursue a career in the services, showing that it is possible for people from ethnic minorities to achieve high rank in the Army.

Throughout his military career Cavazos has stressed that the belief that a man or woman is fighting for a just cause is one of the most important weapons in modern warfare. Maintaining the moral high ground—for Cavazos the adherence to humanitarian and ethical values—is key to an effective military, at every level from the individual soldier to the government that directs military action at the global level. Cavazos believes that morality and morale are closely related.

Cavazos's beliefs were forged in the Korean War, where U.S. involvement was part of an international and UN–sanctioned response to the invasion of the Republic of Korea (South Korea) by the Democratic People's Republic of Korea (North Korea). As a platoon and later company commander, Cavazos was concerned not just with the achievement of military objectives but with the welfare of his men and also that of enemy soldiers, as seen in his actions during the Sangdong-Ni engagement, for which he won a Silver Star.

(1965), and the U.S. Army War College (1969). After his service in Vietnam Cavazos was appointed to a series of key operational posts, including chief of the Offense Section at the Army Command and General Staff College (1970–1971) and director of the Inter-American Region at the Office of the Assistant Secretary of Defense for International Security Affairs. He rose rapidly through the ranks, and in 1976 became the first Hispanic American to be appointed a brigadier general.

In 1977 Cavazos took command of the 9th Infantry Division, and from 1980 to 1982 was commander of the III Corps at Fort Hood, Texas. In 1982, the same year in which he was appointed a full general, he became commanding general of the U.S. Army Forces Command (FORSCOM), based in Fort McPherson, Georgia.

KEY DATES

1929   Born on the King Ranch, near Kingsville, Texas, on January 31.

1951   Joins the U.S. Army as second lieutenant.

1953   Awarded the Silver Star and Distinguished Service Cross in the Korean War.

1967   Awarded a second Distinguished Service Cross in the Vietnam War.

1976   Becomes the first Hispanic to attain the rank of brigadier general.

1982   Becomes the first Hispanic to become a full general; appointed commander of FORSCOM.

1984   Retires from the U.S. Army.

Making a difference

Cavazos was able to succeed in the U.S. Army despite the racism that was prevalent in the military. Although Hispanics, unlike their African American counterparts, did not serve in segregated units before the Korean War, Hispanic servicemen and women often faced prejudice in their working lives, in the duties they were assigned, in their day-to-day interaction with non-Hispanic colleagues, and in the barriers to promotion that they had to overcome. Although people like Cavazos have helped to break down many of these barriers, even in the early 21st century the proportion of Hispanics serving in the higher ranks of the military is far lower than their white peers.

After the army

In 1984 Cavazos retired from the U.S. Army, although he continued to serve in an advisory capacity in such roles as the mentoring of recently appointed generals. In 1985 he served on the government's Chemical Warfare Review Commission, and he also sat on the board of regents of the Texas Technological University. The recipient of many awards, Cavazos received the prestigious annual Doughboy Award from the National Infantry Association for a lifetime's contribution to the infantry (1999).

See also: Cavazos, Lauro F.

Further Reading: Mariscal, George (ed.). *Aztlán and Vietnam: Chicano and Chicana Experiences of the War.* Berkeley, CA: University of California Press, 1999.
www.army.mil/hispanicamericans/english/profiles/cavazos.html (biography).

CEPEDA, Orlando
Baseball Player

When Orlando Cepeda batted for the first time in his Major League career, he hit a home run. His first at-bat foreshadowed what would be a brilliant career, with nine .300 seasons, eight 25-plus home years, seven All-Star selections, and the 1967 Most Valuable Player Award.

Orlando Cepeda was born September 17, 1937, in Ponce, Puerto Rico. His father, Pedro "Perucho" (The Bull) Cepeda, was a legendary Puerto Rican hitter often called the "Babe Ruth of the Caribbean." At first the young Cepeda shied away from baseball after being told that he would never be as good as his father. By the time he was 17, however, he impressed scouts with his own abilities and the San Francisco Giants signed him for $500.

Professional career

When Cepeda arrived in the Giants' clubhouse in 1958 after rising quickly through their minor league system, manager Bill Rigney described him as "the best young righthanded power hitter" he had ever seen. Cepeda supported his manager's claim by hitting .312 with 25 home runs, and earning the 1958 Rookie of the Year Award. The next year he hit 27 home runs, with 105 runs batted in (RBIs) and a .317 average. In 1961 he moved from the outfield to first base, and his 46 homeruns and 146 RBIs led the National League. A year later he helped the Giants to their first pennant in San Francisco.

In 1963 Cepeda damaged his knee, but concealed the injury and continued to play. By 1965 he needed surgery. His recovery was slow, and in 1966 the Giants traded him to the St. Louis Cardinals. The next year Cepeda led the National League (NL) in RBIs, and guided the Cardinals to a World Series championship. He won the 1967 Most

▲ *Cepeda takes part in a preseason training session in March 1964 in Phoenix, Arizona.*

Valuable Player Award for his efforts. The 1968 season brought another pennant for the team, but Cepeda struggled at the plate, hitting .248, and was traded to Atlanta. He bounced from the Atlanta Braves to the Oakland Athletics, and in 1973 to the Boston Red Sox, where he reemerged as a designated hitter by knocking out 20 home runs. His career ended in 1974 with the Kansas City Royals.

Life after baseball

On December 12, 1975, Cepeda was arrested at Puerto Rico's San Juan Airport with nearly 200 pounds of marijuana in his trunk. He served a 10-month prison sentence for what he called "a huge mistake." After his release he said: "The best thing that happened to me was going to jail." He later developed a religious faith that helped him in his life and he rejoined the San Francisco Giants as a community liaison.

Further reading: Cepeda, Orlando. *Baby Bull: From Hardball to Hard Time and Back.* Dallas, TX: Taylor Publishing, 1998. http://www.latinosportslegends.com/cepeda.htm (biographical Web site dedicated to Latino athletes).

KEY DATES	
1937	Born in Ponce, Puerto Rico, on September 17.
1958	Homers in his debut with the Giants; wins Rookie of the Year Award.
1967	Wins a World Series championship and MVP Award with the St. Louis Cardinals.
1975	Arrested in Puerto Rico for marijuana possession with the intent to sell.
1999	Elected to the National Baseball Hall of Fame.

CERVANTES, Lorna Dee
Poet

A leading U.S. Latina poet, Lorna Dee Cervantes first came to prominence as a member of the flourishing movement of Latina writers that emerged in the late 1970s. Her lyrical yet tough-minded exploration of her complex heritage as a Latina has won her a wide, cross-cultural readership, and has played an important role in presenting Chicano and Chicana issues and identities to the American mainstream. Today Cervantes is an associate professor of English at the University of Colorado at Boulder, where she teaches creative writing, and is editor of the poetry journal *Red Dirt*.

"Orphaned from my Spanish name"

Lorna Dee Cervantes was born in 1954 in the Mission District of San Francisco, California, but was raised in San Jose. A fifth-generation Hispanic American, she has a mestizo (mixed-race) heritage combining Mexican and Chumash Native American blood. Her mother did not allow Spanish to be spoken in the family home, in an attempt to protect Cervantes and her brother from the stigma sometimes attached to speakers of that language. However, for Cervantes, her faltering Spanish caused her to become alienated both from her community and from her ancestors; she felt, as she writes in one of her poems, "orphaned from my Spanish name."

Youthful promise

Cervantes began writing at age eight, and by her early twenties her poems were being published in various magazines and journals. In 1976 she founded a poetry journal, *Mango*, to publish her own work and that of other Latinas and Latinos. In 1978 a National Endowment for the Arts grant enabled her to publish her first, much praised collection, *Emplumada* (1981), the title of which alludes to the Spanish word for a "flourish of the pen." Two further collections have followed: *From the Cables of Genocide* (1991) and *Drive: The First Quartet* (2006).

KEY DATES	
1954	Born in San Francisco, California.
1981	Publishes *Emplumada*.
2006	Publishes *Drive: The First Quartet*.

▲ *Poet Lorna Dee Cervantes uses her work to address issues such as racism in U.S. society.*

In much of her work Cervantes evokes the impoverished, embattled life she knew in the barrios (Hispanic American districts of U.S. cities), and speaks of her own need to uncover a lost sense of identity "mown under like a corpse or a loose seed." At other times she uses her poetry to address not only the racism of American society but also the sexism and machismo she sees as typical of many Latinos.

The work of Lorna Dee Cervantes has been widely honored. In 1995 she was the recipient of the Lila Wallace–*Reader's Digest* Writer's Award and two National Endowment for the Arts scholarships.

Further reading: Cervantes, Lorna D: *Emplumada*. Pittsburgh, PA: University of Pittsburgh Press, 1981. http://voices.cla.umn.edu/vg/Bios/entries/cervantes_lorna_dee. html (biography, criticism, and some sample poems).

CHACÓN, Eusebio
Lawyer, Writer

Although he spent most of his life working as a lawyer for the federal government, Eusebio Chacón is best remembered for his pioneering efforts as a writer. He was a member of a famous literary family; his father, Rafael, published an autobiography, while his cousin Felipe Maximiliano Chacón was an acclaimed poet.

A Mexican American, Chacón was born on December 16, 1869, in Peñasco, New Mexico, and was raised in southern Colorado, near the town of Trinidad. He attended the College of New Mexico and then the University of Notre Dame, where he earned a law degree in 1889. After graduation, Chacón taught English in Mexico and then returned to the United States to practice law. He became an official translator for the federal courts, and worked as a lawyer in Colorado and New Mexico until his retirement.

Writing career

Beginning in 1891, Chacón regularly contributed poems written in Spanish to local papers. In 1892 he published two short novels, *Tras la tormenta la calma* (The Calm after the Storm) and *El hijo de la tempestad* (Child of the Storm). The two novellas, printed together in one volume, are some of the very earliest examples of fiction by a Mexican American author. They were published using the printing press of a newspaper, *El boletín popular* (The Popular Bulletin), and are extremely rare today, with only a couple of copies known to exist.

In his introduction to the book, Chacón wrote that he wanted to tell uniquely New Mexican stories that did not imitate American or Spanish literature. *El hijo de la tempestad* is a supernatural story about an orphan who is raised by a gypsy and becomes a bandit under the influence of the devil. The bandit kidnaps a young maiden and is killed when a soldier comes to rescue her. Vicente

▲ *The author of two novellas and numerous poems, Eusebio Chacon is seen as an important figure in the history of Mexican American literature.*

Silva, the leader of a group of thieves who terrorized northern New Mexico at this time, probably inspired the story. *Tras la tormenta la calma* is a more straightforward love story. It is set in the Spanish communities of northern New Mexico and is the first portrayal of this distinctive culture in literature.

Chacón continued to contribute poems and essays to New Mexican newspapers into the 1930s. He died in Trinidad, Colorado, in 1948.

See also: Chacón, Felipe Maximiliano

Further reading: Meléndez, A. Gabriel. *So All Is Not Lost: The Poetics of Print in Nuevomexicano Communities, 1834–1958.* Albuquerque: University of New Mexico Press, 1997. http://www.wvu.edu/~lawfac/jelkins/lp-2001/chacon.html (brief biography).

KEY DATES	
1869	Born on December 16 in Peñasco, New Mexico.
1889	Earns law degree from the University of Notre Dame.
1892	Publishes only book, *El hijo de la tempestad y Tras la tormenta la calma* (Child of the Storm and the Calm after the Storm).
1948	Dies in Trinidad, Colorado.

CHACÓN, Felipe Maximiliano
Writer, Newspaper Editor

The late-19th century poet Felipe Maximiliano Chacón was the first Mexican American to have his verse published in book form. A member of one of New Mexico's most distinguished literary families, he was also editor of a Spanish-language newspaper.

New Mexican troubadour

Chacón was born in Santa Fe, New Mexico, on an unknown date in 1873. His father, Urbano, had founded *El Espejo* (The Mirror), a newspaper in Taos County, New Mexico, and was the superintendent of schools in Santa Fe. He died when Felipe was 13 years old, and it may have been the loss of his father that inspired the young man to start writing poetry. Just a year later, in 1887, his first poems began appearing in newspapers; like his cousin, the attorney and writer Eusebio Chacón, he also became known for his public-speaking skills. In 1911 Felipe Chacón was appointed editor of an influential newspaper, *La voz del pueblo* (The Voice of the People), which was published in Las Vegas, New Mexico. He continued his career in journalism until at least 1929, publishing many poems in newspapers.

In 1924 the printer of the *Bandera americana* (American Flag) newspaper published a collection of Chacón's works that included 56 poems and three short stories. The book, entitled *Obras de Felipe Maximiliano Chacón: "El cantor neomexicano". Poesia y prosa* (The Works of Felipe Maximiliano Chacón: The New Mexican Troubadour. Poetry and Prose), sold for $3.50 and was acclaimed by many prominent New Mexicans.

Chacón's poems expressed pride in the culture of New Mexico, lauded the sacrifices of Mexican American soldiers during World War I (1914–1918), and protested the anti-Hispanic prejudice of white New Mexicans. Of the three short stories, the most highly regarded was "Eustacio y Carlota" ("Eustacio and Carlota"). Inspired by actual events, it tells the tale of a brother and sister who are separated at birth but meet again as adults; they fall in love, and learn they are related just before they are about to marry.

During the Great Depression of the 1930s, the Spanish-language newspapers in New Mexico were severely damaged by falling circulation and loss of advertising revenue. Many of them were forced to close. Chacón's last known job as a journalist ended in 1929, and he died in El Paso, Texas, 20 years later.

Background

The region that is now the U.S. state of New Mexico became part of Mexico in 1821, when the nation declared independence from Spain. In 1848 it was ceded to the United States by the Treaty of Guadalupe Hidalgo. However, even as late as the early 20th century the dominant language in northern New Mexico was still Spanish. The region's newspapers were published in Spanish, and most government business was transacted in that language.

In these areas newspapers played a vital role in society, providing not only reports of current events, but also political commentary and literature. The papers often ran poems and short stories because there were no publishers of Spanish books in New Mexico at the time.

The work of Felipe Chacón is still widely read in Spanish, and it has influenced subsequent Mexican American writers. However, there is currently no printed translation available in English. Chacón is important historically because he straddles two eras: His early writings were published at the end of the period when newspapers were a medium for literature as well as current affairs. By the end of his productive career, newspapers carried reports and features; short stories and poetry had become the exclusive preserve of book publishers.

See also: Chacón, Eusebio

Further reading: Meléndez, A. Gabriel. *So All Is Not Lost: The Poetics of Print in Nuevomexicano Communities, 1834–1958.* Albuquerque, NM: University of New Mexico Press, 1997.
http://www.cervantesvirtual.com/FichaAutor.html?Ref=7486 (full text of Chacón's *Obras*).

KEY DATES

1873	Born in Santa Fe, New Mexico, at about this time.
1911	Becomes editor of *La voz del pueblo*, a Las Vegas, New Mexico, newspaper.
1924	Publishes *Obras de Felipe Maximiliano Chacón* (Works of Felipe Maximiliano Chacón).
1949	Dies in El Paso, Texas, on July 10.

CHACÓN, Iris
Singer, Dancer

Iris Chacón was a famous Latina dancer and singer. Known as the "Vedette of America" and "the Puerto Rican Bombshell," Chacón mesmerized TV audiences around the world in the 1970s and 1980s with her flamboyant style, miniscule costumes, and extravagant shows. Chacón also appeared in soap operas and in movies such as *Desperately Seeking Susan* with Madonna.

Early life
Born in Santurce, Puerto Rico, on March 7, 1950, Chacón and her two sisters Lourdes and Liliana showed early talent as dancers. In the 1960s Chacón began her career as a vedette, a French term for a multifaceted artist. While still a student, Chacón was hired as a dancer on the Telemundo series *Sylvia Grasse*. Chacón's sensuality and talent as a dancer made her immediately noticeable to audiences.

The "vedette"
In 1969 Chacón started working with Elín Ortiz, an actor and producer. In 1970 she moved with Ortiz to the Telecadena Pérez Perry Channel, where she hosted a daily program. In 1971 Chacón released the album *Tu No Eres Hombre* (*You Are Not a Man*), which featured her first hit "Rey de Amores." She released the album *Yo Soy Iris Chacón* a year later. Chacón had further hits with "Caramelo y Chocolate," "Mi Movimiento," "Te Vas y Qué," "Yo Te Nombro," "Libre Como Gaviota," "El Manicero," and "Tu Boquita y Me Gusta, Me Gusta."

In 1973 Chacón was given her own television show, *The Iris Chacón Show* (*El Show de Iris Chacón*), on WAPA Television. The show, which was an immediate success,

▲ **Iris Chacón performed in figure-hugging outfits, flanked by a group of exotically dressed male dancers.**

had top ratings in Puerto Rico. It aired for more than 15 years in more than 17 countries around the world and helped launch the careers of many Latin stars, including Gloria Estefan and the Miami Sound Machine.

In 1983 Chacón's appearance in a TV commercial for Amalie Coolants brought her a lot of publicity. The ad, in which she appeared in extremely skimpy clothing, became one of the most famous in Puerto Rican advertising history. It also landed her on the front page of the *Wall Street Journal*. Over the years Chacón made guest appearances in TV series such as *Tanairí* and *Escándalo*, and appeared in movies such as *Qué Bravas Son Las Mujeres*.

Chacón has received numerous awards and honors for her work, including two Gold Record Awards for her music. Chacón lives in Florida.

See also: Estefan, Gloria

Further Reading: Mendoza, Sylvia. *Book of Latina Women: 150 Vidas of Passion, Strength, and Success.* Boston, MA: Adams Media, 2000.
http://www.prpop.org/biografias/i_bios/iris_chacon.shtml (Iris Chacón's biography from Fundación Nacional Para la Cultura Popular, Puerto Rico).

KEY DATES

1950	Born in Santurce, Puerto Rico, on March 7.
1970	Begins hosting a daily program for Telecadena Pérez Perry Channel Eleven.
1971	Releases *Tu No Eres Hombre* (*You Are Not a Man*).
1973	Is given her own show on WAPA Television, *The Iris Chacón Show* (*El Show de Iris Chacón*).
1983	Sparks controversy after appears scantily clad in a TV commercial for Amalie Coolants.

CHAGOYA, Enrique
Artist

Enrique Chagoya is a leading Mexican American artist. His work invokes historical, cultural, political, and geographical references from both nations. Chagoya's art is distinctive: His art is both absurd and full of meaning, both a humorous and a serious political and social critique. His work appeals to the popular social conscience of Mexican Americans and to the sophisticated aesthetic ideals of the international art establishment.

Early life
Chagoya was born in Mexico City, Mexico, in 1953. From an early age he was interested in Mexican culture and history; he also read American comics. Chagoya's gift for drawing was encouraged by his father, a talented painter who worked in a bank to support his children.

Although obviously gifted, Chagoya did not initially envisage a career as an artist: He graduated from the Universidad Nacional Autónoma de Mexico in 1975 with a degree in political economics. After working as a rural development team leader in Veracruz, Chagoya met and married an American woman. In 1977 he moved to the United States.

Chagoya became disenchanted with political and economic theory while in the United States. He turned increasingly toward art. He studied for a bachelor's degree

in fine art, graduating from the San Francisco Art Institute in 1984, received a master's in 1986, and a master of fine art degree from the University of California at Berkeley in 1987. Chagoya went to work for the Galería de la Raza, the main establishment for Chicano art in San Francisco, where he both exhibited his work and curated exhibitions. As director, he helped establish the gallery as the city's main venue for Chicano art.

Making an impression
Chagoya's 1984 cartoon *Their Freedom of Expression ... the Recovery of Their Economy*, depicting President Ronald Reagan as Mickey Mouse for the "Artist Call against U.S. Intervention in Central America" exhibition was decisive in establishing him as a major artist and he was soon exhibiting nationally.

Chagoya's work integrates diverse elements from pre-Columbian history and mythology, Catholic iconography, and U.S. popular culture to create what he calls "reverse anthropology," as exemplified in his *Codex Books*. In works inspired by codices depicting Aztec life, he attempted to rewrite history from the Spanish Conquest onward. The 18th-century Spanish artist Francisco Goya, the early 20th-century Mexican cartoonist José Guadalupe Posada, and the Mexican muralists Diego Rivera and David Siqueiros are among his influences.

Publications and honors
Chagoya has taught at Stanford University since 1995. He has published many books, and he won the 1997 academy award from the American Academy of Arts and Letters.

▼ **The work of Mexican American artist Enrique Chagoya is influenced by Aztec codices.**

KEY DATES	
1953	Born in Mexico City, Mexico.
1977	Moves to the United States; studies for BFA (1984), MA (1986), and MFA (1987).
1995	Appointed assistant professor of art at Stanford University.
1998	Begins the *Codex Books*.

Further reading: http://www.stanford.edu/dept/news/stanfordtoday/ed/9701/9701fea501.shtml (article on Chagoya).

CHANG-DÍAZ, Franklin R.
Astronaut, Physicist

Franklin Chang-Díaz was a leading space shuttle astronaut. Born in 1950 in Costa Rica, he had a Chinese Hispanic father and a Hispanic mother. He later attended Colegio De La Salle in the capital, San Jose, then Hartford High School in Connecticut. In 1973 he received a bachelor's in mechanical engineering from the University of Connecticut. Four years later he earned a PhD in physics from the Massachusetts Institute of Technology (MIT).

While working in the physics department at the University of Connecticut, Chang-Díaz participated in the design of atomic collision experiments. His research into applied plasma physics led him to run the plasma propulsion program at the MIT Plasma Fusion Center.

Career as astronaut

Picked in 1980 for astronaut training, Chang-Díaz completed his induction course in August 1981. He participated in early space station design studies, and in 1982 he was chosen as support crew for the Spacelab mission. He has flown seven space shuttle missions, and has made three spacewalks for a total of almost 20 hours.

▼ *Astronaut Franklin Chang-Díaz prepares for a training session in February 2002.*

KEY DATES

1950 Born in San Jose, Costa Rica, on April 5.

1977 Receives PhD in applied physics from the Massachusetts Institute of Technology.

1993 Appointed director of the Advanced Space Propulsion Lab at the Johnson Space Center.

2002 Flight on board *Endeavour* on June 5 marks his seventh space shuttle flight.

Chang-Díaz's first space flight was aboard the space shuttle *Columbia*. On January 12, 1986, the crew left on a six-day flight during which he helped deploy a SATCOM satellite and conducted experiments in astrophysics. His next flight came on October 18, 1989, aboard the space shuttle *Atlantis*. One of the tasks carried out by the mission was the deployment of the Galileo spacecraft, which was set on its journey to explore the planet Jupiter. Chang-Díaz later conducted many valuable experiments and scientific observations on five more shuttle flights.

Other activities

Throughout his career Chang-Díaz has worked to forge closer links between astronauts and the wider scientific community by encouraging increased dialog and exchange of information. To that end he founded the Astronaut Science Colloquium Program in January 1987, and later helped establish the Astronaut Science Support Group, of which he was director until January 1989. He has also been actively involved in the care of psychiatric patients and Hispanic drug abusers in Massachusetts.

Franklin Chang-Díaz is currently an adjunct professor of physics at Rice University. In 1993 he was appointed Director of the Advanced Space Propulsion Laboratory at NASA's Lyndon B. Johnson Space Center in Houston, Texas, where he continued to serve into the 21st century. Chang-Díaz has received numerous awards, medals, and commendations, both from the United States and from Costa Rica.

Further reading: Cassutt, Michael. *Who's Who in Space*. New York: Macmillan, 1993.
http://www.jsc.nasa.gov/Bios/htmlbios/chang.html (official astronaut biographical Web site for NASA)

CHAPA, Francisco A.
Publisher

Francisco A. Chapa was an alderman, publisher, and journalist. A Texas-Mexican Republican, Chapa used his newspaper *El Imparcial de Texas* to further his own causes: He supported the Mexican dictator Porfirio Díaz, denouncing the Mexican Revolution. He was tried for his involvement in General Bernardo Reyes's attempt to assume power after Díaz's resignation in 1911. Chapa was instrumental in helping Gregorio Cortez obtain a pardon for murder in 1913.

Early life
Born in Matamoros, Tamaulipas, on October 4, 1870, Chapa was schooled in Mexico. In 1887 he moved to the United States, arriving in New Orleans, where he studied to become a pharmacist. After graduating from Tulane University in 1890, Chapa worked as a drugstore clerk in Matamoros and Brownsville. Later that year he relocated to San Antonio.

Entrepreneur
Chapa established his own drugstore, La Bótica del León. During the 30 years that he owned the shop it was visited by some of the most famous Mexican revolutionaries of the times, including Francisco I. Madero (1873–1913), who was later president of the republic (1911–1913). In 1888 Chapa was elected to the local board of education, on which he remained until 1906.

Influential role
Possibly Chapa's most influential role was as publisher of the conservative Republican newspaper *El Imparcial de Texas*. The *Imparcial* reflected Chapa's Texas–American Republican beliefs and called for loyalty to Mexican dictator Porfirio Díaz. The *Imparcial* also was vocal in its condemnation of the Mexican Revolution.

Conspirator
The newspaper also helped rally support for Texas candidates such as former newspaper owner Oscar B. Colquitt (1861–1940) in the 1910 Texas gubernatorial primary. Colquitt and Chapa remained lifelong friends, both men helping each other in times of crisis. When Colquitt became governor with the Texas–Mexican votes that the *Imparcial* helped deliver, he appointed Chapa a lieutenant colonel on his staff. Chapa used the post to support the efforts of General Bernardo Reyes. Following Diaz's resignation in 1911 as president of Mexico, Reyes moved to consolidate his power. Chapa set up meetings between the governor of Texas and Reyes. They hoped to prevent the Texas Rangers (the organization formed in 1823 to maintain order on the frontier) from hampering Reyes's attempts to seize political control of Mexico.

Friends in high places
When Reyes's attempt failed, more than 24 conspirators were exposed, including Chapa. Only Chapa, however, was brought to trial for violating federal neutrality laws. His case was heard in a federal court in Brownsville by Judge Walter T. Burns. Although Chapa was found guilty, his influential contacts ensured that he only paid a fine of $1,500 and that he remained on the governor's staff. Colquitt negotiated with President William Howard Taft to have Chapa pardoned of his crime. Chapa's contacts also helped him achieve a pardon in 1913 for Gregorio Cortez, who had been accused of murder.

On February 18, 1924, Chapa died. As a publisher and political campaigner Chapa was a key but largely overlooked figure in early 20th-century Mexican politics.

See also: Cortez, Gregorio

Further Reading: Paredes, Américo. *With a Pistol in His Hand: a Border Ballad and its Hero.* Austin, TX: University of Texas Press, 1958.
http://www.tsha.utexas.edu/handbook/online/articles/CC/fch50.html (biography).

KEY DATES	
1870	Born in Matamoros, Tamaulipas, on October 4.
1890	Graduates from Tulane University in New Orleans.
1911	Supports Bernardo Reyes in his attempt to assume power following Porfirio Diaz's resignation.
1913	Elected alderman of the third ward in San Antonio, Texas; joins campaign to pardon Gregorio Cortez.
1924	Dies of pneumonia in San Antonio, Texas, on February 18.

CHAVES, J. Francisco
Soldier, Politician

A dynamic statesman, J. Francisco Chaves fought Civil War battles and blazed trails through the wilderness of the American Southwest. He was a staunch Republican in both the U.S. Congress and the New Mexico legislature.

José Francisco Chaves was born into an influential Hispanic family. He attended St. Louis University, Missouri, after his father warned him that European American frontiersmen would overrun New Mexico and advised him to "learn their language and come back prepared to defend your people." Chaves then became a noted rancher. He married Mary Bowie of California in 1857.

Civil War hero

President Abraham Lincoln commissioned Chaves as a major in the Union Army during the Civil War (1861–1865). At the 1862 Battle of Valverde on the Rio Grande, Chaves led the First New Mexico Infantry. Alongside other companies, he assisted in preventing a Confederate invasion of New Mexico.

In 1863 Chaves captured Apache chief Gardo, a feat that earned him promotion to lieutenant colonel for "gallant and meritorious service." The same year, after escorting Arizona's governor to his new state capitol in Prescott, Chaves blazed a trail to Santa Fe, originating what is known today as the "Chaves Trail."

Chaves was elected in 1865 as New Mexico territorial delegate to the U.S. Congress for the 39th, 40th, and 41st Congresses, through 1871. He later studied law, and was admitted to the bar, serving from 1875 to 1877 as district attorney of New Mexico's second judicial district.

An eloquent criminal lawyer, Chaves was elected to the New Mexico territorial legislature from 1875, and

▲ *J. Francisco Chaves fought in the Civil War before becoming an influential New Mexico politician.*

remained there until his death. Contemporaries regarded him as the greatest parliamentarian of his generation. During his legislative tenure, Chaves achieved numerous outstanding successes, and helped enact 145 laws in the 28th legislative assembly alone.

Chaves opposed the notorious Santa Fe Ring, a corrupt and powerful behind-the-scenes group that controlled many officeholders in New Mexico. In 1889 he received a death threat, which he courageously ignored and carried on with his work. Finally, however, his enemies caught up with him: Chaves was shot dead on November 26, 1904. The assassin was never identified.

On June 29, 2005, the Chaves County courthouse unveiled a $41,000 sculpture commemorating the hero for whom the district had been named.

Further reading: Vigil, Maurilio E. *Los Patrones: Profiles of Hispanic Political Leaders in New Mexico History.* Washington, D.C.: University Press of America, 1980.
http://www.loc.gov/rr/hispanic/congress/chaves.html (Library of Congress page on Chaves).

KEY DATES

1833   Born in Bernalillo County, New Mexico, on June 27.

1862   Commands 1st New Mexico Infantry in Civil War Battle of Valverde.

1865   Represents New Mexico in U.S. Congress through 1871.

1875   Elected to New Mexico territorial legislature through 1904.

1904   Assassinated in Pinos Wells, New Mexico, on November 26.

CHÁVEZ, Angélico
Artist, Historian, Missionary

Fray Angélico Chávez championed Hispanic heritage in New Mexico through his art, writing, and in his acclaimed historical research. A true Renaissance man, Chávez was a writer, artist, soldier, archivist, architect, and historian. He helped translate and conserve many important historical documents. Chávez received several honors, including the medal of the order of Isabel de Católica by King Juan Carlos of Spain.

Early life

Fray Angélico was born Manuel Ezequiel Chávez in Wagon Mound, New Mexico, on April 10, 1910. He was the son of Fabián Chávez, a carpenter, and Nicolasa Roybal Chávez, a teacher, both of whom could trace their families back to Spanish colonial settlers. Chávez received his early education from the Sisters of Loretto in Mora.

As a child in a Hispanic household, Chávez grew up speaking Spanish. He soon grew to love English literature, however, and became proficient enough in the language to publish prose and poetry in English in his teens. He also began to paint during this time.

The influence of Junípero Serra

As a child Chávez visited California with his parents. They toured San Diego de Alcalá, the first mission built by the Spanish missionary Junípero Serra in 1769. Serra was a driving force in the Spanish conquest and settlement of what is today California. The story of the mission and the dedication of its founder profoundly affected the young Chávez, who vowed to follow in Junípero Serra's footsteps.

Becoming Fray Angélico

In 1929 Chávez joined the Franciscan religious order, graduating from Dun Scotus College in Detroit, Michigan, in 1933. In recognition of his artistic ability he was given the name "Fray Angélico" (Spanish for "Brother Angélico"), a reference to the distinguished Italian medieval friar and painter Fra Angelico (c. 1395–1455).
On May 6, 1937, he was ordained a Roman Catholic priest at the St. Francis Cathedral in Santa Fe; he was the first native New Mexican to be ordained by the Franciscans. Chávez retained the title "Fray" as part of his name.

Although Chávez served as a U.S. Army chaplain during World War II (1939–1945) and in the Korean War

▲ *Although Fray Angélico Chávez dedicated most of his life to missionary work, he is also known as an important historian.*

(1950–1953) and was honorably discharged with the rank of major, he dedicated most of his career—more than 30 years—to his work as a missionary. Assigned to the village of Peña Blanca, Chávez also ministered to the Pueblo reservations along the Rio Grande. He painted the walls of the church at Peña Blanca with murals and images of the Stations of the Cross. Although his work was destroyed when the church was demolished, the Museum of New Mexico managed to photograph and record the murals.

INFLUENCES AND INSPIRATION

Fray Angélico particularly inspired his young nephew Thomas E. Chávez, who grew up in awe of the renowned scholar. Chávez was so inspired by his uncle that he decided to train as an historian himself. Fray Angélico encouraged the young man in his studies.

While attending the University of New Mexico's graduate school,

Chávez studied a church that Fray Angélico had restored. Just before Fray Angélico's death, the aging priest invited Chávez to complete a manuscript he had begun. Chávez has remarked that this was one of the greatest honors of his career. The result was the book *Wake for a Fat Vicar* by Chávez and Chávez, published in 2004.

Thomas E. Chávez went on to become a respected academic. He was the director of the Palace of the Governors in Santa Fe for more than 20 years and the executive director of the National Hispanic Cultural Center of New Mexico. He has written four books, and is an acclaimed public speaker and lecturer.

A love of history

Chávez loved history and research. He was particularly interested in Spanish colonial history, and spent many hours studying the lives and families of New Mexico society and delving into the histories of local missions. He used his considerable linguistic skills—he spoke and read English, Spanish, French, German, and Italian—to translate original colonial documents, and he wrote prolifically about all of his discoveries.

Chávez's work earned him the attention and respect of two national experts on colonial history. He impressed famed historian Herbert E. Bolton, biographer of 16th-century Spanish explorer Francisco Vásquez de Coronado. Similarly, Dr. France V. Scholes, dean of the graduate school at the University of New Mexico, was so taken with Chávez's work that he mentored him in paleography—the study of ancient documents.

As part of his research, Chávez traced the movements of a famous colonial statue of the Virgin Mary titled "La Conquistadora" from the time it was brought to America in 1625 by missionary Alonso de Benavides, who mentioned it in his *Memorial* of 1630. Chávez was intrigued by the Indians' veneration of the statue, and wrote a novelized "autobiography" as "told" by the statue.

Productive retirement

Fray Angélico retired from parish work in 1972. He then devoted most of his time to research. He published more than 20 books and several hundred articles during his lifetime. His book *The Missions of New Mexico, 1776,* coauthored with Eleanor B. Adams, was featured as New Mexico's official book for the 1976 National Bicentennial of the United States. Chávez also wrote poetry and attracted such admirers as the acclaimed poet T. S. Eliot, who encouraged him to continue writing and recommended the publication of one of Chávez's poems, "The Virgin of Port Lligat."

Chávez also served as the archivist of the Santa Fe archdiocese, and lectured at the University of Albuquerque. Much of his work and his valuable archival documents are now housed in the Fray Angélico Chávez History Library at New Mexico's Palace of the Governors.

Honors

Fray Angélico Chávez received many honors during his lifetime. In 1976 he was given the Governor's Award for Achievement in the Arts. In 1987 the History Society of New Mexico presented him with a lifetime achievement award, lauding him as "the most distinguished scholar in the field of colonial New Mexico history." Chávez also received honorary degrees from the University of New Mexico, the University of Albuquerque, and the Southern University of New Mexico. He died in 1996 in Santa Fe, New Mexico, at age 85.

See also: Coronado, Francisco Vásquez de; De Benavides, Alonso; Serra, Junípero

Further reading: McCracken, Ellen (ed.). *Fray Angélico Chávez: Poet, Priest, and Artist.* Albuquerque, NM: University of New Mexico Press, 2000.

KEY DATES

1910	Born in Wagon Mound, New Mexico, on April 10.
1942	Becomes a U.S. Army chaplain and a major in the South Pacific during World War II (1939–1945).
1972	Retires from parish work in New Mexico.
1992	Receives Spanish medal of honor from King Juan Carlos of Spain.
1996	Dies in Santa Fe, New Mexico, on March 18.

CHÁVEZ, César
Labor Leader

The outstanding labor leader of the 1960s, César Chávez improved conditions for migrant farmworkers in the United States. His greatest achievement was to organize the California grape pickers into an important union. His own early experiences as a migrant farmworker, when he experienced discrimination and inequality, formed the basis of his efforts to fight for better rights for laborers. Chávez worked tirelessly on behalf of the disenfranchised and poor, adopting the personal motto "Sí se puede" ("It can be done"). He organized the first union of agricultural workers, the National Farm Workers Association, which later became the United Farm Workers (UFW). His campaigning resulted in the introduction of several laws protecting the rights of farm laborers.

Early years

Born in Yuma, Arizona, on March 31, 1927, César Estrada Chávez was one of six children born to Mexican Americans Juana and Librado Chávez. His family lost their farm during the Great Depression after Librado Chávez was unable to pay the taxes due on his land. The family was forced to move to find work, eventually settling in California. They moved from farm to farm working as migrant laborers, picking fruit and vegetables. Chávez witnessed firsthand how badly itinerant laborers were treated: Most spoke very little English, and they sometimes fell victim to unscrupulous farm owners who swindled them out of their meager earnings. Chávez himself was the victim of discrimination on the grounds of his ethnicity: At school he was often punished for speaking Spanish instead of English in the classroom.

▲ **The work of César Chávez on behalf of the poor and disenfranchised earned him many admirers: Robert F. Kennedy once called him "one of the great heroic figures of our time."**

In 1942 Chávez's father was injured in a car crash and was unable to work. Chávez quit school—by then he had attended more than 37 schools in California—but continued his education by reading widely on a variety of subjects at night. During the day he worked alongside his brothers and sisters in the fields, thinning lettuce and beets with a short-handled hoe.

Chávez became increasingly disturbed by the way in which farm laborers were treated, and by the racism and prejudice to which Mexican Americans were subjected on a day-to-day basis. In 1943 he was detained after refusing to sit in the Mexican section of a movie theater in Delano, California.

In 1944 Chávez joined the U.S. Navy, serving in World War II (1939–1945). He was distressed to find that even while serving his country he was discriminated against. After two years Chávez returned home to California to work as a migrant laborer. In 1948 he married Helen Fabela, whom he had met while working in the fields.

Becoming a labor activist

Chávez moved with his family to San Jose, California, where he worked in a lumber mill. He met Father Donald McDonnell, a Catholic priest who worked closely with the

KEY DATES

1927 Born in Yuma, Arizona, on March 31.

1962 Cofounds the National Farm Workers Association (NWFA) with Dolores Huerta.

1966 NFWA merges with part of the AFL–CIO to become the United Farm Workers Organizing Committee; six years later it became the United Farm Workers (UFW).

1970 California grape growers agree to accept a union contract for their employees and end a five-year international grape boycott led by Chávez and his union.

1993 Dies in San Luis, Arizona, on April 23.

INFLUENCES AND INSPIRATION

César Chávez was influenced by several people, including Father Donald McDonnell who gave him several books to read relating to civil and labor rights. While employed at the Community Service Organization (CSO), Chávez worked closely with Fred Ross, Sr., who was a founding member of the CSO. Ross believed that if people worked together they could bring about positive change. Ross trained many farm workers and students in the skills necessary for successful organization; he also helped Chávez set up his union.

Chávez actively promoted nonviolent protest throughout his life. He was influenced by several leading civil rights activists, including African American civil rights leader Dr. Martin Luther King, Jr., and the Indian nationalist and civil rights leader Mohandas K. Ghandi. Chávez believed that both these men best exemplified the character and strength necessary to help improve farm laborers' rights.

farm labor community. McDonnell gave Chávez various books and pamphets on labor history and civil rights leaders such as India's Mohandas K. "Mahatma" Gandhi. These works helped Chávez formulate many of his ideas about the labor movement and nonviolent protest. In 1952 Chávez met Fred Ross, who hired him to work at the Community Service Organization (CSO), a civil rights group that campaigned against discrimination and for better rights for migrant laborers. As part of his duties with the CSO, Chávez took part in a concerted drive to encourage people to register to vote. He worked hard at the CSO and in 1958 became its general director.

A union of their own

Chávez became convinced that the only way to improve the working conditions of farm laborers was to form a specialized union. In 1962 he resigned from the CSO to concentrate on doing this. Helped by Dolores Huerta, Chávez founded the National Farm Workers Association (NFWA) in Delano, California. However, efforts to organize farmworkers were initially slow: Most farmworkers were more concerned about losing their jobs or being blacklisted than improving their working conditions through unionization. In 1965, however, the NFWA was catapulted to public attention when it joined a strike with the Agricultural Workers Organizing Committee (AWOC) and the American Federation of Labor and the Congress of Industrial Organizations (AFL–CIO) against grape growers in the Delano area. The NFWA later merged with part of AFL–CIO to become the United Farm Workers Organizing Committee—after 1972 this was known more simply as the United Farm Workers (UFW).

Chávez promoted a nationwide boycott by grape pickers until working conditions for laborers improved. He advocated nonviolent protest through such means as demonstrations, sit-ins, and marches. In 1966 Chávez and other strikers took part in a 340-mile (547km) Peregrinación (Pilgrimage) from Delano to the state capitol in Sacramento. Carrying banners bearing the word "huelga" (Spanish for "strike"), the protesters aimed to put their demands in person to state officials, such as the need for higher wages. The strike, which was to last five years, drew national attention, and Chávez received support from other unions, such as the United Auto Workers, and from leading political figures such as Senator Robert F. Kennedy. The strike ended in 1970, when the grape growers agreed to accept union contracts.

Nonviolent protest

Chávez devoted the rest of his life to "La Causa," leading boycotts against grape, lettuce, and strawberry growers in order to improve labor conditions in those industries.

Like his hero Mahatma Gandhi, Chávez always used nonviolent methods of protest, often fasting to make his point. In 1968 he held a 25-day fast to reemphasize the UFW's commitment to nonviolence. He fasted again in 1972 and in 1988, when he was joined by other prominent Americans such as the Reverend Jesse Jackson and Whoopi Goldberg in a 36-day "Fast for Life," which highlighted the harmful effect of pesticides.

Chávez died in San Luis, Arizona, on April 23, 1993. More than 50,000 people attended his funeral service in Delano, California. In 1994 President Bill Clinton posthumously awarded Chávez the highest civilian honor in the United States, the Presidential Medal of Freedom.

See also: Activism; Agriculture and Migrant Labor; Civil Rights; Huerta, Dolores; National Organizations; Political Movements

Further reading: Griswold del Castillo, Richard, and Richard A. Garcia. *César Chávez: A Triumph of Spirit.* Norman, OK University of Oklahoma Press, 1995.

CHÁVEZ, Denise
Novelist, Playwright

Award-winning Mexican American writer Denise Chávez has contributed to the increased prominence of Latina letters in American literature since the 1980s. Highly acclaimed for her fiction, she is also a playwright and actress who has toured and educated Americans about the culture, people, and landscape of the Southwest.

Early life

Chávez was raised in Las Cruces, New Mexico. Her parents were both Mexican Americans—her father was a lawyer and her mother a schoolteacher. The first signs of her literary talent became evident at the age of 10, when she began to keep a diary. By the time she attended a Catholic high school she had developed a passion for the theater. She took a BA in drama at New Mexico State University, an MA in drama at Trinity University in San Antonio, Texas, and an MFA in creative writing at the University of New

▼ *Denise Chávez appears at the 2004 Hispanic Heritage Awards with TV presenter Mauricio Zeilic.*

KEY DATES	
1948	Born in Las Cruces, New Mexico, on August 15.
1985	Publishes first collection of fiction, *The Last of the Menu Girls*.
1995	Publishes first novel, *Face of an Angel*.
2001	Publishes second novel, *Loving Pedro Infante*.

Mexico. In Albuquerque she met critically acclaimed New Mexican author Rudolfo Anaya, who encouraged her to become a writer. Although Chávez is best known for her fiction, she has also written numerous plays. These performance pieces have been produced at prestigious institutes such as Joseph Papp's Festival Latino in New York, as well as at the Edinburgh Festival in Scotland and a range of small venues. She has won a National Endowment for the Arts as well as a Rockefeller Foundation award.

INFLUENCES AND INSPIRATION

Although Denise Chávez has drawn inspiration from a number of literary traditions, the author who most influenced her and encouraged her to follow her writing career is fellow award-winning New Mexican writer Rudolfo Anaya (born 1927).

Chávez is very conscious of the impact of Spanish and Latin American writers on her work. She admired Spanish poet and playwright Federico García Lorca (1898–1936) as much for his creative sensibility as for his human sympathies. She was also drawn to Mexican writer Juan Rulfo (1918–1986) by his portrayal of the people in his community, his language, and his descriptions of landscape. Throughout her education, Chávez was able to learn from drama professors from Russia and Greece as well as the United States. Her plays show great indebtedness to those of Anton Chekhov (1860–1904).

Additionally, Chávez is inspired by her Mexican heritage, as exemplified in her homage to and critique of popular culture icons such as Pedro Infante. She has also gained wisdom and strength from the women in her family, especially her grandmother and mother, and her girlfriends.

In 1985 Chávez published her first collection of short stories, *The Last of the Menu Girls*. The work addressed the trials and tribulations of growing up in a community in the Southwest as seen through the eyes of a strong Latina adolescent. As a member of a pioneer generation of Latina writers in the United States, Chávez received extensive critical recognition for this inaugural work of fiction. In 1993 she embarked on a career as a playwright and actress, performing theatrical pieces, including *Woman in the State of Grace*, which she had written in 1989, at several cultural centers and universities across the United States. In addition, Chávez has written more than 20 other works for the theater.

In her 1995 novel, *Face of an Angel*, Chávez writes about the coming-of-age experiences of a Mexican American woman who finds herself caught between an independent spirit and the traditional values of her community. Set in a small town in the Southwest, the work treats the landscape as if it were a character. As in her earlier works, Chávez is concerned above all with relationships between women, families, and friends, and draws parallels between personal interactions and the community as a whole. Furthermore, she takes into consideration the effects of gender, class, and race issues in modern American society. At the same time Chávez makes her characters come alive as if they were performers on stage because she combines much humor with drama in her fiction. *Face of an Angel* won its author a Before Columbus Award in 1995.

Mature work

Chávez's third work of prose fiction, the novel *Loving Pedro Infante* (2001), is generally regarded as her greatest accomplishment to date. The story develops as an account of a friendship between two disparate single Mexican American women who share a fascination with Pedro Infante (1917–1957), a Mexican actor and singer who became a cultural icon after his premature death. Set in a border region of the United States and Mexico, the work illustrates the complications of relationships between women, and between men and women, to draw sharp distinctions between the nature of reality and celluloid dreams in film. Even though Pedro Infante has long been dead, women and men alike continue to praise him in the United States as well as in Mexico. Using the spirit of this background, Chávez demonstrates that loyalty and sisterhood are important components of all friendships, regardless of any individual's social background and cultural heritage.

Current activities

Denise Chávez is an active member of the local community in Las Cruces, New Mexico, where she makes her home. She is married to Daniel Zolinsky. She is the director and founder of the Border Book Festival (BBF), which has been held annually since 1995 in Mesilla, New Mexico. The BBF's motto is *"Leer es vivir"* ("To read is to live"). Chávez is also a professor of creative writing in the department of English at her alma mater, New Mexico State University.

See also: Anaya, Rudolfo

Further reading: Kevane, Bridget, and Juanita Heredia (eds.). "The Spirit of Humor: Interview with Denise Chávez." In *Latina Self-Portraits: Interviews with Contemporary Women Writers.* Albuquerque, NM: University of New Mexico Press, 2000. www.ou.edu/worldlit/authors/chavez/chavez.html (Web site providing biography, bibliography, related criticism and links).

CHAVEZ, Dennis
U.S. Senator

In 1930 Dennis Chavez became only the second Hispanic American to serve in the U.S. Congress—the first was Joseph Marion Hernández of Florida in 1822.

Chavez was elected to Congress as a Democrat in 1930. He moved to the Senate in 1935, and remained there for the remaining 27 years of his life. During his long period in office he consistently backed legislation to help the poor and unemployed, and fought all forms of discrimination against women and ethnic minorities—not only the group to which he himself belonged, but also blacks and Native Americans. He helped improve economic conditions in Puerto Rico, and worked to improve relations with the countries of Latin America. He is perhaps most famous for his success in 1945 in establishing the Fair Employment Practices Commission, a body that assured minority groups of equal access to federal jobs.

Youthful adversity

Christened Dionisio but later adopting Dennis as the anglicized form of his Mexican name, Chavez struggled to better himself from an early age. He and his family moved from his native town, Los Chávez, New Mexico, to Albuquerque when he was seven. They were so poor that he had to leave school at 13 and work in a local grocery store. He remained there until age 18, when he lost his job for refusing to deliver groceries to strikebreakers. While out of work he began a course of self study at Albuquerque Public Library before starting a new job at the city's Engineering Department. There he became active in politics. A supporter of Democrat candidate Octaviano Larrazolo in his run for Congress in 1908, Chavez also served in 1911 as a Spanish interpreter for William C. McDonald, who in the following year became the first statehood governor of New Mexico.

▲ One of the first Hispanic Americans to achieve prominence in national politics, Dennis Chavez became a role model for later generations of ethnic minority citizens.

In 1916 Chavez ran for office himself. Although he failed in his bid for the county clerkship, he was not discouraged. After serving as an interpreter for Senator Andieus Jones, he was rewarded with a clerkship that gave him the opportunity to study at Georgetown University Law School in Washington, D.C. On graduating from there in 1920, Chavez practiced criminal law in Albuquerque, and in 1922 won election to the state House of Representatives. The memory of his struggles with education spurred him to sponsor a bill to make textbooks free to students in public schools. He was elected to the U.S. House of Representatives in 1930, and served two terms.

While in office Chavez worked on various committees, including the Indian Affairs Committee and the Committee

KEY DATES	
1888	Born in Los Chávez, New Mexico, on April 8.
1920	Graduates from Georgetown University Law School.
1922	Elected to the state House of Representatives.
1936	Elected to the U.S. Senate.
1962	Dies in Washington, D.C., on November 18.

INFLUENCES AND INSPIRATION

When Dennis Chavez first took his seat in the U.S Congress, the speaker of the House, Texas Democrat John N. Garner, told him: "The most successful Congressmen are errand boys for the people who elect them." The new man took the advice to heart, and never forgot that his principal duty was to the people who had elected him.

The extent to which he achieved that aim may be measured by the words of Vice President Lyndon B. Johnson (1908–1973), Senate majority leader from 1955 to 1960, who described Chavez in a funeral oration as "a man who recognized that there must be champions for the least among us." The life and work of Dennis Chavez set a standard to which subsequent Congressmen have aspired.

on Irrigation and Land Reclamation. In 1934 he ran for a vacant seat as U.S. Senator from New Mexico. Although he was defeated at the polls by Bronson Cutting, he challenged the result, charging the Republican candidate with electoral fraud. However, before the charges could be brought in Congress, Cutting was killed in an airplane crash. Chavez was appointed interim senator. In 1936 he was fully elected to the Senate, where he would spend the rest of his life.

Throughout his political career in Washington, D.C., Chavez was a staunch supporter of civil rights reform, and championed numerous legislative proposals that opposed racial discrimination in the workplace. He was an outspoken advocate of the Home Owner Loan Corporation, which paved the way for homeowners to gain access to emergency funds in order to keep their property in times of financial hardship. He was a committed supporter of the New Deal program created by President Franklin D. Roosevelt in the 1930s, and voted to enact practically every legislative program connected to it.

Postwar concerns

After World War II (1939–1945) Chavez chaired the Senate Committee on Public Works. In that role during the 1950s he helped draft the legislation that built much of the modern economic infrastructure of the United States. The committee worked on improvements to the interstate highway network and the U.S. waterways system, and oversaw the creation of post offices. He was outspoken on foreign affairs, too, supporting the active involvement of the United States in the North Atlantic Treaty Organization (NATO), which was founded in 1949. Chavez was also a consistent advocate of the concept of national education standards and the protection of Indian lands.

His strong belief in the equal treatment of all people, regardless of race, color, creed, or political affiliation, led Chavez first to challenge and later to denounce the anticommunist investigations and trials initiated in the 1950s by Senator Joseph McCarthy (1908–1957). On one memorable occasion Chavez stood on the floor of the Senate and demanded a return to the principles on which the United States was founded. His speech was a courageous and timely reminder of the tenets of Founder Thomas Jefferson: Although other Senators privately agreed with the sentiments expressed by Chavez, they were reluctant to endorse them publicly in the atmosphere of fear and suspicion created by the McCarthy witch hunts.

In the early 1960s, during the administration of President John F. Kennedy, Dennis Chavez served as chairman of the Senate Appropriations Subcommittee for Defense. In that role he secured important defense-technology contracts for New Mexico, and thereby ensured the successful economic growth of his home state for the next generation.

Death and legacy

Chavez worked almost incessantly until his sudden death in 1962 from a heart attack at the age of 74. Four years after his remains were buried in Mount Calvary Cemetery, Albuquerque, a statue dedicated to him was placed in the Statuary Hall in Washington, D.C. Hailed as "El Senador," he was further honored on April 3, 1991, with a U.S. postage stamp featuring his image.

Among other memorials to his life and work is the Dennis Chavez Foundation, which in 1991 awarded its first two scholarships to students at the University of New Mexico. The Foundation also funds a fellowship that each year enables a graduate student to complete a doctoral dissertation on a subject connected to the work of Chavez.

Further reading: Garraty, John Arthur, and Mark C. Carnes. *American National Biography.* New York, NY: Oxford University Press, 1999.
http://www.loc.gov/rr/hispanic/congress/chavez.html (Hispanic Americans in Congress, 1822–1995).

CHÁVEZ, Julz
Entrepreneur

Entrepreneur and doll designer Julz Chávez challenged the hegemony of the Anglo Saxon Barbie doll by launching a line of multiethnic dolls. Chávez, who is the second cousin of the legendary labor leader César Chávez, worked in the toy industry for more than 15 years before launching her own company, Get Real Girls. César Chávez encouraged her to challenge existing racial and gender stereotypes in the doll industry and manufacture dolls that were more ethnically diverse and true to life.

Early life
Born in Yuma, Arizona, on January 18, 1962, Julia Chávez grew up in a household of 10 children. Chávez and her siblings were raised by their father, a Mexican American farmworker. As a young girl Chávez became aware of racial inequality and prejudice. The family were often thrown out of restaurants because their father was too dark-skinned. Coming of age in Southern California, Chávez graduated from the California College of Arts and Crafts and began applying for jobs as a toy designer. Aware of a gender bias in the toy industry, Chávez shortened her name from "Julia" to the less obviously feminine "Julz." She landed her first job shortly afterward.

A career in toys
Chávez spent 16 years working for major toy companies, including Lewis Galoob Toys, Sega of America, and Mattel, the home of Barbie. As Chávez learned more about the toy world, she found herself disagreeing with what executives thought girls wanted in a doll—glamor, high heels, and white skin. At Mattel every employee was given an upscale porcelain version of Barbie but Chávez rejected hers. When asked why, she remarked that she had never owned a Barbie when she was growing up: "I made it so far without a Barbie, I'm not going to start now."

In 1999 Chávez teamed up with Michael Cookson, the former chairman of Wild Planet Toys, to found Get Real Girls. The company's first dolls were modeled on strong

▲ *Julz Chávez believes that young girls should have dolls that look and dress like them, with lifestyles to which they can aspire.*

women from different ethnic backgrounds. The range, which included six college-bound female dolls—Corey, Claire, Nakia, Gabi, Nini, and Skylar—was designed to be more sporty and fashionable than sexy: They also had more realistically proportioned figures than comparable dolls. Chávez gave each Real Girl a distinct personality and an active lifestyle. A company Web site was set up to enable children to follow and participate in the lives of their specific dolls, even down to receiving postcards when the dolls were supposed to be traveling.

Chávez believes that the toy industry has a duty to be more socially responsible. She said: "I feel that toys do have a deeper meaning for children. We need to really get girls to like who they are, and the gifts that were given to them."

See also: Chávez, César

Further reading: http://www.salon.com/mwt/feature/ 2000/10/27/real_girl (a Salon.com article that examines the Get Real Girl dolls as challengers to Barbie).

KEY DATES	
1962	Born in Yuma, Arizona, on January 18.
1984	Begins working as a toy designer.
1999	Founds Get Real Girls with Michael Cookson.

CHAVEZ, Linda
Journalist, Politician

In 1977 Linda Chavez became the first Hispanic American editor of *American Educator*, the quarterly magazine of the American Federation of Teachers. Through her controversial editorials, which dismissed affirmative action and bilingual education as detrimental to the progress of Hispanic people, she attracted the attention of conservative politicians. In 1981 she became a consultant to President Ronald Reagan. Reagan appointed Chavez to the Civil Rights Commission in 1983, and she then became director of public liaison for the White House. The Library of Congress honored her in 2000 as a "Living Legend" for her contributions to America's cultural and historical legacy. In January 2001 President George W. Bush nominated Chavez as secretary of labor, but she later withdrew from consideration after it was revealed that she had allowed an undocumented immigrant to reside in her house.

Governmental appointments

Chavez has been appointed to a number of governmental posts at the federal level. They include chair of the National Commission on Migrant Education (1988–1992), White House director of public liaison (1985), and staff director of the U.S. Commission on Civil Rights (1983–1985). She also took part in the Administrative Conference of the United States (1984–1986). In 1986 Chavez ran on the Republican ticket for the U.S. Senate from Maryland, but lost to Democrat Barbara Mikulski. In 1992 the United Nations' (UN) Human Rights Commission chose Chavez to serve a four-year term as U.S. expert with the UN Sub-Commission on the Prevention of Discrimination and Protection of Minorities.

Chavez is president of the Center for Equal Opportunity, a public policy research organization based in Sterling, Virginia. While that takes up most of her time, it is not her only activity. She also writes a weekly column, which is syndicated in newspapers across the country, hosts a daily radio show in Washington, D.C., and serves as a political analyst for the Fox News network. Television journalistic programs such as *CNN & Co.*, *The McLaughlin Group*, *Equal Time*, and *The Newshour* with Jim Lehrer have featured Chavez as a political and social analyst. Chavez's book, *Out of the Barrio: Toward a New Politics of Hispanic Assimilation*, emphasizes her perception that Hispanics can access the opportunity structure in the United States through persistence and hard work.

▲ *President Ronald Reagan accepts a placard from Linda Chavez during her 1986 Senate campaign.*

Chavez has devoted considerable energy to encouraging the education of Hispanics, but she constantly challenges the liberal perspective held by most Hispanic civil rights and political leaders. Much of her work is carried out through the Latino Alliance, which she chairs. It is a federally registered political action committee of the Republican Party. An unashamed controversialist, Chavez acknowledged that her views run against the grain of current orthodoxy in her 2002 book *An Unlikely Conservative: The Transformation of an Ex-Liberal, or, How I Became the Most Hated Hispanic in America.*

KEY DATES	
1947	Born in Albuquerque, New Mexico, on June 17.
1970	Graduates from University of Colorado.
1977	Appointed editor of *American Educator*.
1981	Becomes consultant to President Ronald Reagan.
2002	Publishes *An Unlikely Conservative*.

Further reading: Chavez, Linda. *Out of the Barrio: Toward A New Politics of Hispanic Assimilation*. New York, NY: Basic Books, 1991. http://www.stopunionpoliticalabuse.org/lindachavez/bio.htm (biographical Web site).

CHAVEZ-THOMPSON, Linda
Labor Leader

Linda Chavez-Thompson was the first Hispanic member of the board of the American Federation of Labor–Congress of Industrial Organizations (AFL–CIO). On her election in 1995, she became the highest-ranking nonwhite in U.S. labor history, and one of the most powerful, representing some 13 million workers. In her role she challenged economic, racial, and gender discrimination by championing workers' rights.

Early life

Lydia Chavez-Thompson was born in 1944 in Lubbock, Texas. Her forename, like that of many Spanish-speaking children of her generation, was soon anglicized. Her first-grade schoolteacher considered "Lydia" too difficult to pronounce, so changed it to "Linda." The name stuck. Chavez-Thompson was one of eight children, the daughter of Mexican American sharecroppers, and she herself worked in the fields from age 10. At the time child laborers were not protected by the law, and as a result Chavez-Thompson was exploited by her employers, earning no more than 30 cents an hour. While in the fields she was horrified by the ill treatment of workers, and noticed that U.S. citizens were treated as badly as migrants, whose lack of rights and subjection to abuse were even then well known. Those early experiences convinced her of the importance of organized labor.

Chavez-Thompson dropped out of high school in ninth grade to support her impoverished family. She married her first husband in 1963 and began cleaning houses for a living. In 1967 she became the local secretary of the Lubbock branch of the Laborers' International Union, where she used her language skills—she was bilingual in Spanish and English—to help Mexican American members. In 1971 she went to work for the American Federation of State, County, and Municipal Employees (AFSCME) in San Antonio, doing legislative work, educational outreach, and representation. She thought the job would give her more time with her young daughter than she had with the union in Lubbock, but again, with her talent as an organizer, she quickly became an AFSCME leader.

Union leader

Chavez-Thompson next went to work for the AFL–CIO, the largest collection of labor and trade unions in the United States. She rose as quickly through the ranks of the

▼ *Linda Chavez-Thompson (center) joins striking janitors at a picket in Boston in 2002.*

INFLUENCES AND INSPIRATION

Linda Chavez-Thompson claims that "Workers without a union are helpless people." She feels a great responsibility as the first Hispanic woman in her position, not only to represent Latinos and Latinas but also to foster fresh and diverse leadership. By the 1980s the labor movement was in decline and, in Chavez-Thompson's words, "male, pale, and stale." Her election to the board of the AFL–CIO changed that. The union began reaching out to other labor organizations and civil rights bodies, such as the League of United Latin American Citizens (LULAC), the National Association for the Advancement of Colored People (NAACP), and the National Council of La Raza (NCLR), to advocate on behalf of all workers, unionized or not. Chavez-Thompson also worked on consumer education about the importance of unions to maintaining good wages, safe working conditions, health care, and corporate responsibility for all workers. She helped the AFL–CIO form international labor alliances with the Canadian Labor Congress (CLC) and International Labor Organization (ILO). Such new alignments reflect the globalization of the workforce and the ability of companies to move and exploit workers transnationally.

organization as she had at previous unions. In 1995 she became the first woman and nonwhite to be elected executive vice president, the third-highest-ranking board member. In her new role she worked mainly on legislative and educational programs, particularly those designed to benefit fellow women and people of color. Under Chavez-Thompson's leadership the AFL–CIO grew in membership and was successful in major labor actions against United Parcel Service (UPS) and General Motors (GM). Throughout her period in office one of Chavez-Thompson's most abiding concerns was the possible erosion of members' rights. She worked on the principle that the time for discussion was past, and favored direct action by labor whenever necessary.

Progress

Chavez-Thompson fostered female and Latino and Latina leadership in the AFL–CIO, sponsoring training seminars and hiring multilingual staff to recruit and serve a workforce of rapidly increasing ethnic diversity. Her success inspired other organizations to draw on her expertise. She served on the board of governors for the United Way and as a vice chair for the Democratic National Committee, which is traditionally supported by labor. She was also a member of the executive committee of the Congressional Hispanic Caucus Institute and the Labor Heritage Foundation Board of Trustees.

Presidential recognition

Chavez-Thompson became renowned for her ability to break the glass ceiling for Latinas in labor. Her success attracted the attention of U.S. President Bill Clinton, who in 1997 invited her to join the board of his Initiative on Race, a mission designed to help the people of the United States "grow together as one." As the only Latina on the eight-member board, Chavez-Thompson's objective was to move discussions about race beyond the narrow black–white perspective that normally characterized such studies. She traveled the country listening to leaders and gathering data. The resulting report, "One America in the Twenty-First Century: Forging a New Future," recommended changes in education, civil rights law, and presidential action. In 1998 *Hispanic* magazine recognized Linda Chavez-Thompson as one of the 25 most influential Hispanics in the United States.

KEY DATES

1944 Born in Lubbock, Texas.

1967 Joins Laborers' International Union.

1971 Starts work for AFSCME.

1995 Elected executive vice president of the AFL–CIO.

1997 Invited by President Bill Clinton to join his Initiative on Race.

1998 Named one of 25 most powerful Hispanics in Washington, D.C., by *Hispanic* magazine.

Further reading: Menard, Valerie. "Lady Boss: Sharecropper's Daughter Linda Chavez-Thompson Shatters the Glass Ceiling in Organized Labor." *Hispanic* magazine, September 1998. http://www.nwhp.org/tlp/biographies/chavez-thompson/chavez-thompson-bio.html (National Women's History Project biography of Linda Chavez-Thompson).

CHRISTIAN, Linda
Actor

Despite her fame as a star of film and television, Linda Christian is best known as the wife of swashbuckling actor Tyrone Power (1914–1958).

Early life
Linda Christian was a stage name. Christian was born Blanca Rosa Welter in 1924 to a mother of Spanish descent and a Dutch petroleum engineer. Her father's job with the Shell Oil Company took the family to many places around the globe. As a consequence Christian was educated not only in her native Mexico but also in Venezuela, South Africa, and the Netherlands. On leaving school she went to work as a clerk in the office of the British government in Palestine. Later she moved to Acapulco, Mexico, where she became a fashion model and was discovered at a show by movie star Errol Flynn (1909–1959).

▼ *Linda Christian was a glamorous actor whose private life became better known than her work.*

KEY DATES

1924	Born in Tampico, Mexico, on November 13.
1947	Marries actor Tyrone Power.
1956	Divorces Tyrone Power, gets custody of both daughters.
1962	Publishes *Linda: My Own Story*.

In 1944 Linda Christian followed in the footsteps of her elder sister, Ariadna Welter, and became a movie actress. She started under contract to RKO Pictures, but when she was offered only bit parts there she became dissatisfied, and moved to MGM. Her prospects improved in 1946, when she was loaned back to RKO to appear in *Tarzan and the Mermaids* (1948), which was Johnny Weissmuller's last appearance in the main title role. The film was shot in Mexico, and after it was completed Christian returned to Acapulco, where she met actor Tyrone Power. The two became infatuated, and married in 1947 in Rome, Italy. Christian subsequently gave birth to two daughters: Romina Power (born 1951) became a singer and an actress in the 1960s; Taryn Power (born 1953) went on to become an actress in her own right.

What was billed as a fairytale marriage soon ran into trouble. Although both Power and Christian were Roman Catholics—they had gone straight from their wedding to an audience with Pope Pius XII—the couple divorced in London, England, in 1956. Christian demanded and received a settlement of one million dollars. She was also awarded custody of the children.

Linda Christian was the first Bond girl, appearing in a 1954 CBS television adaptation of Ian Fleming's *Casino Royale* alongside Barry Nelson, the original 007. Her later films included *Slaves of Babylon* (1953), *The House of the Seven Hawks* (1959), and *The V.I.P.s* (1963).

Christian was married again in 1962, to actor Edmund Purdom. The couple divorced three years later. Christian retired in Mexico.

Further reading: Christian, Linda. *Linda: My Own Story*. New York, NY: Crown Publishers, 1962.
http://www.glamourgirlsofthesilverscreen.com/show/44/Linda++Christian (biographical Web site).

CINTRÓN, Nitza Margarita
Scientist

Nitza Margarita Cintrón is a distinguished Puerto Rican American physician who has served as chief of the National Aeronautics and Space Administration (NASA) at the Lyndon B. Johnson Space Center Space Medicine and Health Care Systems Office in Houston, Texas.

During her childhood Cintrón traveled widely as she and her family accompanied her soldier father to various postings at U.S. Army bases in Europe. From an early age she was fascinated by science and mathematics, and enjoyed reading books on biology, chemistry, and outer space.

Education

Cintrón took her bachelor's degree in biology at the University of Puerto Rico in 1972, and then enrolled in a doctoral program in biochemistry and molecular biology at Johns Hopkins University in Baltimore, Maryland. After graduating she joined NASA in 1978. She wanted to be an astronaut, but her eyesight did not reach the stringent requirements for space travel. Despite that disappointment she remained with the administration while completing a medical doctor's degree at the Medical School at the University of Texas in Galveston.

▼ *Physician Nitza Margarita Cintrón has spent over 25 years working for NASA.*

Since qualifying as a doctor Cintrón has carried various responsibilities at the Johnson Space Center. In 1979 she created its biochemical laboratory and became a project scientist for the Spacelab 2 Mission of the Space Shuttle program. She was later promoted to chief of the Biomedical Operations and Research Branch in the Medical Science Division, and then served as director of the Life Sciences Research Laboratories, in which capacity she managed the operations of the International Space Station.

Recognition

After 25 years with NASA, in 2004 Cintrón was inducted into the Hispanic Engineers National Achievement Awards Conference's (HENAAC) Hall of Fame. She was also honored with the NASA Medal for Exceptional Scientific Achievement, the U.S. administration's most prestigious science credit, and the Johnson Space Center Director's Commendation and Innovation Award for outstanding achievements and contributions as a civil servant.

Nitza Cintrón has also served as co-chair of the International Space Station Multilateral Medical Operations Panel. In February 2005 she was appointed clinical associate professor of internal medicine at the University of Texas Medical Branch. Her research has involved the study of microgravity and radiation, and their physiological effects on humans in space. Her work on space medicine has greatly improved the health care of astronauts on long missions.

KEY DATES	
1950	Born in San Juan, Puerto Rico.
1978	Joins NASA.
1979	Creates Johnson Space Center Biochemical Laboratory.
2004	Inducted into HENAAC Hall of Fame.
2005	Becomes associate professor of Internal Medicine at University of Texas Medical Branch.

Further reading: http://www.henaac.org (Hispanic Engineers National Achievement Awards Conference Web site).

CISNEROS, Evelyn
Ballet Dancer

Evelyn Cisneros was the first Mexican American to be appointed a prima ballerina. Between 1976 and 1999 she enjoyed an illustrious career with the San Francisco Ballet. Since her retirement, she has worked with Latino and Hispanic communities around the San Francisco Bay area and continued to promote ballet.

Cisneros was born in 1959 in Long Beach, California, and grew up near Huntington Beach. Her grandparents were migrant workers from Mexico, and her parents raised her to understand the importance of her Chicana background. Cisneros was extremely shy as a child, and her mother enrolled her in ballet lessons to help her become more self-confident. Cisneros quickly fell in love with ballet, and her teacher, Phyllis Sear, immediately recognized her talent. By the time Cisneros entered high school, she was making a daily three-hour round trip to dance classes in Los Angeles.

San Francisco Ballet

In 1976 Cisneros graduated from high school and immediately joined the San Francisco Ballet as an apprentice. Two days after joining she made her debut when she stood in for an injured dancer, successfully learning the role in a matter of hours. The San Francisco Ballet's artistic director, Michael Smuin, quickly became Cisneros's mentor and helped develop her full potential. Before long Cisneros had become the company's most popular dancer. Her ability to dance both modern and classical roles captivated audiences.

Having established herself as the San Francisco Ballet's most famous ballerina, Cisneros used her high profile to help the local community, particularly people of Hispanic origin. In the 1980s she joined the board of Project Open Hands, a charity that worked with AIDS sufferers.

In 1985 dramatic changes at the ballet company led to the dismissal of Smuin. Cisneros remained, however, and

▲ *Cisneros performs in Caniparoli's* **Lambarena,** *a work first staged by the San Francisco Ballet.*

began working with the new director, Helgi Tomasson, who introduced more modern dance to the repertoire. Cisneros embraced the challenge, and when the company traveled to New York in 1991 she was the senior ballerina.

After nearly nine years at the pinnacle of her profession Cisneros announced her retirement, and made an emotional farewell performance in San Francisco. The decision to quit was prompted by her desire to have a child with her second husband. The couple later adopted a son, and Cisneros started to concentrate on family life. However, in the early 21st century she continued to be very active in the ballet community. From 2002 onward she was ballet education coordinator for the San Francisco Ballet, and in 2003 she co-wrote the book *Ballet for Dummies*.

Further reading: Speck, Scott, and Evelyn Cisneros. *Ballet for Dummies*. Hoboken, NJ: Wiley, 2003.
www.gale.com/warehouse.cch/bio/cisneros_e.htm (comprehensive biography of Cisneros).

KEY DATES	
1959	Born in Long Beach, California.
1976	Joins San Francisco Ballet.
1999	Retires.
2002	Takes on education role for ballet.

CISNEROS, Henry G.
Politician, Businessman

Henry G. Cisneros has achieved many firsts during his life. He was the first Mexican American mayor of a major U.S. city, and later served in President Bill Clinton's cabinet as the first Hispanic American secretary of housing and urban development.

Early life
Born in San Antonio, Texas, on June 11, 1947, Cisneros was one of the five children of George and Elvira Cisneros. He grew up in a close-knit but highly disciplined family. His parents believed in establishing rules for their children, including no television during the week, doing chores after school, and doing extracurricular reading and creative assignments. The family also visited museums and galleries and attended the opera and the symphony regularly. Cisneros initially had dreams of becoming a pilot in the Air Force, but when he graduated from high school, aged just 16, he went on to study at Texas A&M University. His interest changed to politics while he was there, and by the time he graduated in 1968 he had a new dream—to become mayor of San Antonio. He married Mary Alice Pérez in 1969 while continuing his studies. He received an MA in urban planning from Texas A&M in the following year.

The road to Washington
In 1971 Cisneros moved to Washington, D.C., becoming the youngest person to take up a White House fellowship. Cisneros gained a lot of political experience working as an assistant to Elliot Richardson, secretary of health, education, and welfare. At the end of his fellowship Cisneros decided to go back to study. He completed an

▲ *Henry Cisneros has often attributed his success to a positive attitude. Following his appointment as secretary of housing and urban development, he remarked: "We can go for years wallowing in examples of despair, but it's time to say to people: 'You can do it. We can do it. I have seen it done.'"*

MA in public administration at Harvard's John F. Kennedy School of Government, and a doctorate in the same field from George Washington University in 1975, after which he returned home to San Antonio to pursue his dream of a political career.

Career in politics
In 1975 Cisneros won a seat on the San Antonio City Council, becoming the youngest person ever to do so. He was reelected twice and served on the council for a

KEY DATES

1947   Born in San Antonio, Texas, on June 11.

1975   Awarded a doctorate in Public Administration from George Washington University, Washington, D.C.

1981   Becomes mayor of San Antonio (until 1989); he is the first Mexican American mayor of a major U.S. city.

1993   President Bill Clinton appoints him secretary of housing and urban development; forced to resign in 1997.

2000   Heads American City Vista.

CISNEROS, Henry G.

LEGACY

Despite the scandal over payments made to his former mistress, Linda Medlar, which effectively ended his career as secretary of housing and urban development, Henry G. Cisneros achieved many positive things during his stay in office. Cisneros claimed to be most proud of his achievements in reforming public housing. He changed the way in which local officials provided housing for the poor, and argued that federal laws penalized people for working by raising their rents at an unfair level as their wages rose. He supported legislation to enable local public housing authorities to have the flexibility to adjust their rents in order that more working families could stay in public housing. Housing authorities were also given the power to evict criminals and other undesirable residents from housing projects. Cisneros is credited with persuading lenders and real estate agents to help low- and moderate-income buyers become homeowners. Under Cisneros HUD also took a clear stand against home loan lenders discriminating against minority groups, making it easier for victims to file complaints, and punishing abusive lenders.

total of six years. In 1981 he decided to fulfill his dream and ran for mayor of San Antonio, the ninth-largest U.S. city. He was elected to office, becoming the first Mexican American to preside over a major U.S. city and the first to be voted mayor of San Antonio since 1842.

A dream come true

Cisneros was a popular mayor who worked hard to improve relations between the Anglo and Hispanic communities. He attracted business to San Antonio to help create more jobs in the region. He also promoted tourism to the area and campaigned to improve social services and housing. He was so successful that he was reelected to three further terms. In 1989 he decided to leave public office and concentrated instead on being chairman of the Cisneros Asset Management Company. He also sat on several boards, including that of the Rockefeller Foundation.

Return to politics

Cisneros continued to be part of the political scene, working hard on Bill Clinton's presidential campaign in 1992. When Clinton became president in 1993, he rewarded Cisneros by appointing him to the post of secretary of housing and urban development (HUD). In that role Cisneros served in the president's cabinet, a close circle of advisers who also preside over their respective federal agencies.

The new HUD secretary took charge of a department that had been mismanaged for some years, and also faced a growing number of homeless persons in the nation's cities. To meet the mounting challenges, Cisneros tore down old and often dangerous public housing projects across the nation, moving residents to better

accommodations. He also attempted to reform the HUD bureaucracy, and fought off efforts to eliminate HUD altogether. Cisneros kept in touch with the people: He walked the streets of Washington's poorest neighborhoods at night to talk with the city's homeless, and opened the HUD building on cold nights to provide shelter to homeless people. Some commentators believe that he achieved significant change during his time in office.

In the mid-1990s, however, a ghost from the past came back to haunt Cisneros. During his time as mayor of San Antonio, Cisneros had had a love affair with Linda Medlar. The relationship lasted until 1991. When it became public knowledge in 1994, during a series of background checks prior to his cabinet appointment, Attorney General Janet Reno appointed an independent counsel to investigate whether Cisneros had lied to the FBI about the amount of money he had paid to his former lover. Cisneros resigned from office in January 1997, and he was indicted in December 1997. In September 1999 Cisneros admitted to one misdemeanor count of lying to the FBI. He paid a fine of $10,000, but served no jail time or probation. Bill Clinton pardoned him in 2001.

From 1997 to 2000 Cisneros was president and CEO of Univision, a Spanish-language broadcasting network. In 2000 he became CEO of American City Vista, a venture with the KB Home company to provide competitively priced housing in central metropolitan areas for people from different backgrounds.

Further reading: Martínez, Elizabeth Coonrod. *Henry Cisneros: Mexican American Leader*. Brookfield, CT: Millbrook Press, 1993.
http://www.klru.org/texasmonthlytalks/archives/cisneros/bio.asp (features on notable Texans).

CISNEROS, Sandra
Novelist, Poet

The most critically acclaimed and commercially successful Mexican American fiction writer of the 20th century, Sandra Cisneros made a name for herself by writing about the working class and the experiences of women in Latino culture. She was one of the first Latinas in the United States to attend the University of Iowa Writers' Workshop, and the first to win a MacArthur Fellowship Award. She has also earned two National Endowment for Humanities awards.

Early life
Born on December 20, 1954, in Chicago, Illinois, Sandra Cisneros grew up on the West Side of the city in a working-class neighborhood that predominantly consisted of a Puerto Rican community. The only daughter among the seven children of a Mexican father and a Mexican American mother, Cisneros spent most of her childhood summers on family vacations in Mexico City, Mexico. She claims that her mother gave her the fierce voice to write in English, and her father the tender sweet voice of Spanish. These bilingual and bicultural experiences would later influence her fiction and poetry as she learned to mix English with Spanish words and syntax.

After completing high school Cisneros attended Roosevelt University in Chicago, where she received a BA in English. During this period she became exposed to the work of a variety of poets in the Spanish language, including the Argentine Jorge Luis Borges (1899–1986), the Spaniard Federico García Lorca (1898–1936), the Chilean Pablo Neruda (1904–1973), and the Mexican Octavio Paz (1914–1998). With encouragement from her English professors, Cisneros then enrolled on a postgraduate course at the University of Iowa Writers' Workshop, where she studied from 1976 to 1978. During those two years she wrote a thesis that would later become her first novel, *The House on Mango Street* (1984). The story concerns the urban working-class experiences of a Latina coming of age in an American city: It is partly autobiographical and partly based on the lives of the students Cisneros taught at the Latino Youth Alternative High School in Chicago. *The House on Mango Street* quickly became established as a classic of Latino literature, and won its author the Before Columbus Award in 1985. It has since sold more than two million copies in English, and has been translated into several other languages.

▲ *Writer Sandra Cisneros addresses the* **Los Angeles Times** *Festival of Books in 2004.*

The emergence of Cisneros was both a cause and an effect of a general upsurge of interest in Latina literature in the United States during the 1980s. The renaissance brought to prominence a whole new generation of writers: Among the pioneers were Cisneros herself, Gloria Anzaldúa, Cherríe Moraga, Denise Chávez, and Helena María Viramontes. Never before had Latina writers received such critical attention, and as a consequence their works proliferated. Their fiction, poetry, drama, and essays were suddenly in unprecedented demand. English-language publishers of all sizes, from the multinationals to the tiniest of small presses, saw the commercial possibilities: Many commissioned at least one writer in the genre; some even brought out Latina lists.

KEY DATES	
1954	Born in Chicago, Illinois, on December 20.
1984	Publishes first novel, *The House on Mango Street*.
1997	Becomes the first Mexican American to win a MacArthur Fellowship award.
2002	Publishes second novel, *Caramelo*.

INFLUENCES AND INSPIRATION

Sandra Cisneros revered Gwendolyn Brooks and Carl Sandburg, her fellow Chicago poets, as formative influences on her early writing. She admired above all their experimentation with colloquial forms of English. As Cisneros began *The House on Mango Street*, she was struck by the lack of literature about a Latina girl's coming of age in a major U.S. city. In response she developed a colloquial and poetic style that made her first novel accessible to audiences of all ages, from elementary school to university level and beyond.

Cisneros has also drawn inspiration from modern poets and fiction writers in Spanish, most notably Jorge Luis Borges for his concision and precision in style. She also feels indebted to women writers such as Jane Austen, Margarite Duras, Jean Rhys, and Mercé Rodoreda, solitary women writers with whom she feels a particular spiritual kinship. Although Cisneros draws from a wide range of literary sources, she is still attuned to the oral traditions of the ordinary people she meets in her daily life in Texas and during her extensive travels around the world.

Cisneros's next published work was a collection of poetry, *My Wicked, Wicked Ways*, which came out in 1987. In the volume she moved from the concerns of a Latina adolescent to those of womanhood. The themes include travels across the world, and love.

Publishing history

In the early 1990s Sandra Cisneros made a personal and historical breakthrough by becoming the first Mexican American woman writer to have her work published by a major East Coast firm. *The House on Mango Street* had been produced by the Arte Publico Press in Houston, Texas, and *My Wicked, Wicked Ways* had been brought out by the Third Woman Press in Bloomington, Indiana. Cisneros's first commission for Random House in New York was *Woman Hollering Creek and Other Short Stories* (1991). In the collection, which received national critical acclaim, Cisneros expanded her earlier portrayals of the Mexican American community by including stories of immigrants and migrants along the border region of Texas as well as in Mexico. In her 1994 collection of poems, *Loose Woman* (also Random House), Cisneros celebrated the spirit of the independent woman as she addressed the female body, sexuality, and popular culture. The work also included extensive references to various aspects of her Mexican heritage, including film and religious icons.

In 1995 Cisneros won the MacArthur Foundation Fellowship, a grant worth $225,000. Three years later she took another step toward mainstream integration when selections from her work were included for the first time in *The Norton Anthology of American Literature*. As a further reflection of the growing multiculturalism in American society, at about the same time her work started to appear on university English curriculums.

Another landmark in Cisneros's career occurred in 2002, when her second novel, *Caramelo*, was published. Her growth as an artist is shown clearly in the historical account of a Mexican and a Mexican American family's travel experiences in the 20th century. Cisneros uses the story of a young girl, Lala Reyes, coming of age in Chicago, San Antonio, Texas, and Mexico City, as a backdrop to an account of various encounters and conflicts between U.S. and Mexican cultures. *Caramelo*, winner of the 2005 Premio Napoli, was the first work of Cisneros's artistic maturity. She followed it in 2004 with *Vintage Cisneros*, a selection of her best fiction and poetry to date, through which she was able to reach an even wider audience.

The color purple

Sandra Cisneros lives in San Antonio, Texas. When she had the exterior of her house there painted purple, she antagonized some of her traditionalist neighbors, who complained that the color was "historically incorrect." With typical trenchancy, Cisneros responded that, on the contrary, purple was a pre-Columbian color that symbolized and celebrated pride in a Mexican heritage. She has been director of the Guadalupe Cultural Arts Center in the city, and is currently working on a collection of essays, tentatively entitled *From Tango to Tongolele*, in which she pays tribute to figures who have been important to her life and career.

See also: Anzaldúa, Gloria; Chávez, Denise; Moraga, Cherríe; Viramontes, Helena María.

Further reading: Cisneros, Sandra. *The House on Mango Street*. Houston, TX: Arte Publico Press, 1988.
http//: www.sandracisneros.com (biographical Web site).

CIVIL RIGHTS

The 1776 U.S. Declaration of Independence states that "all men are created equal." The Bill of Rights, the first 10 amendments to the U.S. Constitution, further protects citizens' rights, such as freedom of speech. In reality, however, minority groups, such as Hispanic Americans, black Americans, and women, have historically been treated as second-class citizens.

In the last 50 years, civil rights legislation, such as the Civil Rights Act of 1964, has offered ethnic minorities greater legal protection. In particular, people from the three main Hispanic groups, Mexican Americans, Puerto Ricans, and Cuban Americans, have achieved marked improvements in employment, education, housing, and voting. Some commentators claim that great achievements have been made and that Latinos, today the largest minority group in the United States, can achieve anything. They see evidence of this in the 2005 election of Antonio Villaraigosa as the first Mexican mayor of Los Angeles in more than 100 years, and Alberto R. Gonzales's rise to U.S. attorney general. Critics, however, argue that although Hispanic activists share certain common causes, such as bilingual education and immigration, the struggles of each group of Latinos in the United States have been unique, and their strategies for attaining equality varied. The way in which different Latino groups are perceived by mainstream white America has also differed according to their rate of assimilation and amount of politicization or protest.

Immigration

There is a long history of Latin American immigration to the United States. According to the first reliable research data, in 1820 Latinos made up 7 percent of the nation's immigrants. Although the Latin American population in the United States grew during the 19th century, the percentage of immigrants fell. By 1900, Latin American immigration stood at just 1 percent of total U.S. immigration. By contrast, in the period 1991–1996 it stood at 43.8 percent.

In 1848 the Treaty of Guadalupe Hidalgo, signed at the end of the Mexican–American War, ceded more than half of Mexico's territory to the United States. Although it theoretically gave Mexicans who became U.S. citizens the same constitutional rights as other U.S. citizens, in practice this rarely happened, and Mexican Americans were often discriminated against.

By the late 19th century, many journalists, activists, and politicians had begun to protest against the discrimination and racism experienced by minority groups in the United States. From the 1890s Nicasio Idar, for example, published articles in *La Crónica* exposing problems such as the segregation of Mexican children in Texas schools. Idar and men and women like him worked hard to

Since the 1960s, Chicana women have been heavily involved in fighting racism and discrimination.

improve the lives of Latinos. In 1911, Idar organized El Primer Congreso Mexicanista, a conference to discuss issues of racial inequality. La Liga Femenil Mexicanista, an organization that campaigned for the education and economic and cultural advancement of Tejana women, arose out of the meeting.

The late 19th and early 20th centuries also saw the development of mutualistas (mutual-aid societies) and cultural preservation societies, or honorary commissions. These organizations served to help and support the Latino population and to preserve the culture, traditions, and language of the countries from which the migrants originated.

The Orden Hijos de America (The Order of the Sons of America; OSA), founded in 1921, was the earliest effective Mexican American civil rights organization. The organization existed to promote and protect "the rights and privileges and prerogatives extended by the American Constitution." The Order achieved many things, including getting the first Mexican American onto a jury in 1927.

Some members left the OSA to form other organizations. In February 1929, the Corpus Christi chapter joined the Latin American Citizens League of the Valley to establish the League of United Latin American Citizens, better known as LULAC. With Ben F. Garza as its first president general, LULAC fought discrimination. By 1930 it had more than 2,000 members in 19 chapters across Texas.

Early in the 20th century, labor unions began to mobilize effectively to fight for Latino workers' rights. La Confederación de Uniones Obreros Mexicanos (CUOM) and the United Cannery, Agricultural, Parking and Allied Workers of America (UCAPAWA) organized agricultural workers and fought for better wages and working conditions. During the 1930s in Los Angeles, the International Ladies Garment Workers Union (ILGWU) organized Mexican and Mexican American women to combat abuses in the textile and needle trades. The National Labor Relations Act of 1935, however, excluded agricultural workers from its guarantee of the right to organize and bargain collectively.

Promoting the cause

In the 1930s Spanish-language radio emerged to discuss and promote Latino civil rights issues. Pedro J. González and his band Los Madrugadores (The Early Risers) broadcast in Spanish in Los Angeles; they reached thousands of listeners before sunrise every day.

González, who became a local star, used his program not only to promote popular Mexican music, but also to speak out against deportations in California in the 1930s, known as "repatriation." He upset many local Angelenos, particularly the district attorney. González was later accused of rape. He was tried and sentenced to 150 years, serving six years even though the alleged victim eventually admitted that she had been coerced into falsely accusing him. His supporters established the Pedro J. González Defense Committee to cover his defense costs and provide support for his family. The defense committee became a popular way to support people in the Latino community who faced miscarriages of justice. Many Latinos believed that such incidents could happen to any member of their community since the criminal justice and legal systems discriminated against ethnic minorities.

Segregation in schools

Segregation was another issue that Hispanic activists fought against. The 1954 case of *Brown v. Board of Education,* which centered on African American schoolchildren, is generally regarded as the greatest breakthrough in the struggle for desegregation. However, the U.S. Supreme Court ruling did not come out of the blue. It was the culmination of a series of smaller actions that had been brought since the 1930s in which minority groups challenged the separate education of their children.

One of the most famous incidents involving Mexican Americans occurred in California. In January 1931, Principal Jerome Green stopped 75 Mexican American students from entering

---

KEY DATES

1848	Treaty of Guadalupe Hidalgo is signed.
1929	The League of United Latin American Citizens is established.
1946	The Supreme Court rules that the segregation of Mexican children in schools is unconstitutional.
1954	*Brown v. Board of Education* ends segregation.
1964	The Civil Rights Act is passed.
1969	Él Plan Espiritual de Aztlán is formed; MEChA is established.
1970	La Raza Unida, the first Chicano political party, is formed.
1975	Congress adopts provisions in the Voting Rights Act to adopt Spanish in addition to English at elections.
1994	Proposition 187 is passed in California on November 8; it denies public benefits to illegal aliens in the United States; it is subsequently struck down as unconstitutional.

Lemon Grove Grammar School with their white classmates. Instead they were taken to a two-room barnlike building that had been constructed for their schooling. The parents refused to send their children to the new school. With the help of the Mexican consulate, they sued the school board. The board later claimed that the new building was an "Americanization" school to help children learn English and assimilate properly. San Diego Supreme Court judge Claude Chambers ruled that the school board's action was wrong.

In 1945 Gonzalo Méndez used the Lemon Grove case as a precedent to sue the Westminster School District in California. The case led to the banning of segregation in the state. In 1947 the U.S. Court of Appeals upheld the decision. The legal arguments used in the Méndez case formed the basis for *Brown v. Board of Education*.

Serving one's country?

No single event moved civil rights forward more for Mexican Americans in the early 20th century than World War II (1939–1945). While Latinos were denied vital rights at home, they were expected to defend America in times of war. Like African American soldiers, Latino veterans and their families refused to remain second-class citizens after serving their country, but many people in the United States were not of the same opinion. Veterans were routinely denied government benefits and were the victims of prejudice. For many veterans, the breaking point came when Private Felix Longoria was denied burial rights in his hometown of Three Rivers, Texas. Dr. Hector P. Garcia, head of the American G.I. Forum (AGIF), formed to defend Latino soldiers' rights, made the American public aware of the issue. Texas senator Lyndon B. Johnson intervened, and as a result Longoria was

finally buried with full military honors in Arlington National Cemetery, Virginia.

Immigration

Many activists were also concerned about the negative effects of such policies as the Bracero Program, introduced between 1942 and 1947, and again in 1951 to 1964. The program encouraged Mexicans to work on short-term contracts in U.S. industries such as transportation and agriculture, often for extremely low wages and in poor conditions. In practice the Bracero Program did not bring in enough legal labor to fill employment needs, and many undocumented workers, called "wetbacks" or "mojados" because they had crossed the Rio Grande, came to work in America.

In the 1950s immigration became a big issue. Between 1950 and 1955, the federal government deported undocumented Mexican workers in Operation Wetback. In this five-year period, almost four

THE CIVIL RIGHTS ACT OF 1964

Following John F. Kennedy's assassination, Lyndon B. Johnson became president in November 1963. Johnson announced his vision of America as a "great society," in which poverty and racism would cease to exist. In support of this dream, Johnson pushed through the civil rights legislation that Kennedy had brought before Congress in 1963, and which was still being debated when he was killed. Johnson used the American people's grief to help get the bill passed, arguing that no one

could possibly vote against an issue so close to the late president's heart.

By January 1964, more than 68 percent of the U.S. public supported a civil rights bill. Less than six months later, Johnson signed the Civil Rights Act. It gave the federal government the right to end segregation in the South; prohibited segregation in public places such as theaters, restaurants, and hotels; stated that employers had to provide equal employment

opportunities; and created an Equal Employment Commission.

The act is seen by some commentators as Johnson's greatest achievement. It paved the way for other landmark civil rights legislation, including the 1965 Voting Rights Act, which outlawed literacy tests and poll taxes as a way of assessing whether people were fit to vote. Despite this, several civil rights organizations criticized Johnson for not going far enough in protecting the rights of minority groups, particularly Latinos.

César Chávez (front right, facing camera), president of the United Farm Workers of America, fought hard to get better conditions for Latino workers.

and members of other ethnic minority groups were able to enter professions or attend colleges previously closed to them.

The Chicano movement

In the 1960s a unique Chicano national identity emerged among Mexican Americans. One of the leading activists was César Chávez, head of the United Farm Workers of America. Chávez organized grape pickers and agricultural workers in California, leading them in strikes to win better rights. Chávez's action led to similar boycotts, such as in the lettuce industry. He influenced many leading activists, particularly Chicano student protestors, who campaigned for more Latino teachers and a Chicano studies program in the late 1960s.

The evangelical minister Reies López Tijerina was another important activist. He organized the Alianza Federal de Mercedes (Federal Alliance of Land Grants). In June 1967, Tijerina and a group of New Mexicans went to Tierra Amarilla, the Rio Arriba county seat, to arrest the district attorney. They accused him of failing to enforce the 1848 Treaty of Guadalupe Hidalgo, and demanded that he restore property rights to the heirs of those people who lived on Mexican territory at the end of the Mexican–American War. Tijerina was arrested after one raid on the courthouse resulted in two people being shot.

Another key Chicano activist was Rodolfo "Corky" Gonzales, who founded the Crusade for Justice in Denver, Colorado. In March 1969 the Crusade for Justice organized the National Chicano Youth Liberation Conference in

million Mexicans were forced to return to their native country. The Asociacion Nacional Mexico-Americana, established in 1950, worked to prevent the separation of family members and the expulsion of people who had lived in the United States for several years.

Legislation

In the 1950s and 1960s, people from ethnic minorities began to mobilize. Latino activists often worked side by side with African Americans to achieve better rights. Many Latino campaigners were influenced by such black leaders as Martin Luther King, Jr.

Politicians also began to publicly support civil rights legislation. In his 1960 presidential campaign, John F. Kennedy argued for more comprehensive civil rights legislation. Kennedy presented a bill to Congress in 1963, but it was still being debated when he was assassinated in November of that year. President Lyndon B. Johnson supported the bill, which eventually passed in 1964 (*see box on page 107*). The act made racial discrimination in public places illegal; it also stated that employers had to provide equal opportunities to employees regardless of their race. More importantly, the act opened the door for further civil rights legislation to be passed, such as the 1965 Voting Rights Act. Johnson also signed Executive Order 11246 in 1965, which gave the Labor Department the power to take affirmative action to increase and improve ethnic diversity in the workplace and other sectors of society. Through positive discrimination policies, such as employment and education quotas, many Latinos

THE YOUNG LORDS

In the late 1950s, the Puerto Rican gang the Young Lords (which later became the Young Lords Organization, and the Young Lords Party in New York) emerged in Chicago. Originally formed to prevent Puerto Ricans from being forced out of Chicago's Lincoln Park by Mayor Daley's urban renewal program, by the 1960s the Young Lords had become an important political organization.

Jose "Cha Cha" Jimenez, a member of the Lords, came across the work of black civil rights activists Martin Luther King, Jr., and Malcolm X, as well as the ideas of the militant African American organization the Black Panthers, while in jail. Jimenez later met Fred Hampton, head of the Chicago chapter of the Black Panthers, and became influenced by many of his ideas. Jimenez helped transform the Young Lords into an organization committed to helping the community and liberating Puerto Ricans and Latinos in general.

In 1969 the Young Lords, the Black Panthers, and the white working-class organization the Young Patriots Organization formed the Rainbow Coalition, a nonagressive pact to stop street-fighting in Chicago. Other chapters of the Young Lords also opened that year, first in New York and later in Boston, Philadelphia, and other U.S. cities. The Young Lords set up community programs such as the provision of free breakfasts for poor children and health education and immunization programs. It also developed the 13-Point Program, which called for self-determination for Puerto Ricans and other Latinos, equality for women, and the establishment of a socialist society. The group promoted its ideas through *Palante*, its newspaper and radio program. By 1976, however, government and police repression and political infighting had led to the organization's demise.

Denver, where Él Plan Espiritual de Aztlán was drafted. Él Plan identified Aztlán, the legendary Aztec homeland believed to be located in the American Southwest, as the national homeland of the Chicano people. The conference argued that Mexican American students had been subjected to an Americanized education at the expense of their own Mexican identity. A month later, another conference was held at the University of California at Santa Barbara. El Plan de Santa Barbara set down the framework for establishing a Chicano studies program and also established Movimiento Estudiantil Chicano de Aztlán. More popularly known by its acronym MEChA, the student organization established chapters on campuses across America.

MEChA campaigns for a society free of imperialism, racism, sexism, and homophobia.

In 1970 Gonzales and other leading activists, such as José Angel Gutiérrez, president of the Mexican American Youth Organization (MAYO), established the political party La Raza Unida. In 1972 Chávez, Gonzales, Gutiérrez, and Tijerina attended the first La Raza Unida National Conference, when Gutiérrez became RUP national chairman. RUP actively supported women's rights, and more than half of the 1,500 delegates there were female. By 1981, however, the party had disintegrated.

Puerto Ricans
Puerto Ricans enjoy a unique relationship with the United States. Following the Spanish–American War and the signing of the Treaty of Paris in 1898, Puerto Rico was ceded to the United States. Since then, many Puerto Ricans have fought to be free of American control.

In 1917 President Woodrow Wilson signed the Jones Act: Puerto Rico became a U.S. territory, English became the official language of the nation, and Puerto Ricans became statutory citizens. U.S. companies actively recruited labor from the island, and by the 1930s Puerto Ricans had established communities in New York, Chicago, Boston, and Philadelphia.

In Puerto Rico, several activists, including Pedro Albizu Campos, leader of the Nationalist Party, fought to maintain the native language and culture. Numerous writers and artists, such as the novelist Enrique Laguerre, also began to celebrate Puerto Rican culture in their work.

In 1950, when Puerto Rico was granted commonwealth status, many U.S.-based Puerto Ricans were living in poverty and suffered discrimination. They were represented negatively in the press and were perceived by mainstream white Americans as troublesome. Political groups such as the Young Lords (*see box on p. 109*) arose to campaign for better treatment and equal rights for Puerto Ricans.

The plight of Puerto Ricans has also been publicized through the music and writings of Nuyorican (New York Puerto Rican) artists such as Pedro Pietri, one of the founders of

Cuban Americans protest against Fidel Castro's regime on April 10, 1980, in Washington, D.C.

the Nuyorican Cafe, and the singer La India.

Cubans

Cuba was also a possession of the United States, from 1898 to 1902. Prior to the fall of Cuban leader Fulgencio Batista in 1959, the country suffered from political corruption and U.S. interference. After Fidel Castro's coup and the adoption of a communist system in 1960, many middle- and upper-class Cubans left the island. These wealthy Cubans were largely politically conservative and were welcomed by the U.S. government. Subsequent waves of poor and dark-skinned Cubans did not enjoy the same reception, however.

Several U.S.-based Cuban organizations have supported attempts to overthrow Castro. In the 1970s, the National Liberation Movement of October

10 fostered internal dissent as a means of toppling Castro from within. The U.S. government has also sponsored cultural interference in Cuba, such as Radio and T.V. Martí, which broadcasts U.S. popular culture onto the island.

Cubans have enjoyed greater mainstream political success than the other two main Latino groups in the United States. Many Cubans are prominent politicians and judges who have been successful in gaining government support for their rights agenda, which includes immigration and bilingual teaching.

Civil rights today

Hispanics from other Latin American countries have also formed key civil rights groups, such as the Committee in Solidarity with the People of El Salvador. They have collectively helped fight for greater political representation and have successfully campaigned against such orders as Proposition 187 in California, which denied the provision of public services to undocumented people and was struck down as unconstitutional.

See also: Chávez, César; Garza, Ben J.; Gonzales, Alberto R.; Gonzales, Rodolfo "Corky"; Gonzalez, Pedro J.; Gutierrez, José Ángel; Idar, Nicasio; Laguerre, Enrique; La India; Pietri, Pedro; Tijerina, Reies López; Villaraigosa, Antonio

Further reading: Rosales, F. Arturo. *A Dictionary of Latino Civil Rights History.* New York, NY: Arte Público Press, 2006.
http://www.civilrightsproject.harvard.edu/research/latino97/latino97.php (focuses on the Latino Civil Rights Crisis).

CLARK, Ellen Riojas
Educator

A widely consulted bilingual education expert and respected sociocultural scholar, Ellen Riojas Clark is dedicated to improving education for Latino students. A professor in the division of bicultural-bilingual studies at the University of Texas at San Antonio (UTSA), Clark works to address the challenges represented in changing demographics by researching and implementing new ways of helping both students and fellow educators succeed in a culturally diverse society.

Early life
Of north Mexican descent, Ellen Riojas was born into a close-knit family in San Antonio, Texas, in 1941. Her parents were poor by U.S. federal standards, but they had solid middle-class values, an appreciation of art and culture, and believed strongly in the importance of education and community service. Instilled with an unwavering faith that they could accomplish whatever they resolved to do, Clark and her siblings were encouraged to follow their dreams, but were also reminded to stay true to themselves and close to their roots.

Always one of just a few Mexican Americans in the predominately white schools that she attended, Riojas dedicated her time to cultivating her intellect. In 1959, a few months after graduating from high school, she married a chemist by the name of Hector Clark.

A teacher
Clark completed her undergraduate studies at Trinity University in 1973, before going on to earn a master's degree in bicultural-bilingual studies from the University of Texas at San Antonio in 1974. Seven years later, she was granted a PhD from the University of Texas at Austin,

▲ *Ellen Riojas Clark has received many honors and awards for her work in education.*

where she also taught, first as a lecturer and program coordinator, and later as a professor (from 2005).

As an academic, Clark's research has focused specifically on the identification of gifted language students from minority groups, bilingual education teacher training, and cultural studies.

Clark is much more than a brilliant teacher and researcher, however. She is the recipient of several grants, a popular guest speaker and presenter, a published author, an esteemed member of many committees and advisory boards, and an outstanding community servant. Since 2004 Clark has also been the content director of Scholastic's *Maya and Miguel,* a children's program broadcast on PBS that emphasizes the importance of community and family.

Clark seeks to broaden minds. She wants to close the literacy gap between those who speak English as a first language and those who do not. Clark also believes that it is important for students to "learn to think, to question, to consistently do their best, to challenge themselves, and to gain understanding."

KEY DATES	
1941	Born in San Antonio, Texas.
1973	Graduates from Trinity University.
1981	Earns PhD from the University of Texas at Austin.
2004	Becomes content director for the children's show *Maya and Miguel.*
2005	Appointed professor in the division of bicultural-bilingual studies at UTSA.

Further reading: http://faculty.coehd.utsa.edu/EClark (Clark's home page).

CLEMENTE, Roberto
Baseball Player

Roberto Clemente stood only 5 feet 11 inches (1.8 m) tall, and weighed a mere 175 pounds (79.4 kg), but he will forever remain larger than life. He won 12 Gold Gloves, appeared in 12 All-Star Games, set a National League record for leading in outfield assists for five consecutive seasons, won four National League (NL) batting titles, and was the 1966 NL Most Valuable Player and the 1971 World Series Most Valuable Player (MVP). He is also remembered for his caring nature and humanitarian efforts.

Early life
Roberto Walker Clemente was born in Carolina, Puerto Rico on August 18, 1934, the youngest of seven children of Luisa and Melchor Walker de Clemente. His father worked as a foreman in a sugarcane mill in Puerto Rico. The Clementes lived a modest life but suffered many

▼ **Roberto Clemente spent his entire Major League career with the Pittsburgh Pirates.**

tragedies. Roberto's sister Ana Iris died at the age of five when the dress she was wearing caught fire. His oldest sister, Rosa, died in childbirth. Two brothers died at a young age of cancer. These traumatic events plainly influenced Roberto's outlook and probably inspired his subsequent philanthropy.

In his youth Clemente played several sports and threw the javelin well enough on his high school team that some observers speculated he would make the 1952 Puerto Rican Olympic squad. His true love, though, was baseball. As a child he peeked through slits in the outfield fences to catch glimpses of his favorite player, Monte Irvin. At the age of 14, Clemente was playing against Negro and Major League players visiting Puerto Rico. When Clemente was 18, the Brooklyn Dodgers invited 71 players to try out for the team. The scout conducting the trials sent 70 of the hopefuls home. Clemente alone made the grade.

Pro years
Clemente's early experience of the major leagues was quite unlike what he had expected. The Dodgers sent him to their Triple-A affiliate in Montreal. Of his time there he said: "If I struck out I stayed in the lineup. If I played well I was benched." The strange treatment baffled Clemente. What he did not realize was that the Dodgers were trying to hide his talents from other teams. Despite Brooklyn's efforts, however, the last-place Pittsburgh Pirates signed Clemente for $4,000 after the 1954 season.

Clemente returned home to Puerto Rico in the winter of 1954 to visit one of his brothers, who was dying from a brain tumor. On that visit, a drunk driver crashed into Clemente's car and damaged three spinal disks. Clemente

KEY DATES	
1934	Born in Carolina, Puerto Rico, on August 18.
1955	Appears in his first Major League game April 17 with the Pittsburgh Pirates.
1966	Wins the National League Most Valuable Player Award.
1971	Receives World Series MVP Award.
1972	Dies in a New Year's Eve plane crash en route to deliver emergency supplies to Nicaraguan earthquake victims.

suffered back pain for the rest of his career. Before he batted he always rolled his neck and stretched his back to ease the pain. These warmup exercises became signatures of his appearances on the field.

In 1955 Clemente debuted in right field with the Pirates. Although not an immediate superstar, he dazzled fans in his first season by throwing out 18 runners on the bases. The next season he displayed his arm strength again by improving the number to 20 runners. In 1958 he led the league in outfield assists, with 22. He would continue to lead the league for the next five seasons.

Hitting the heights

By 1960 Clemente was approaching his peak. The right-handed hitter finished with 16 home runs, 94 runs batted in (RBIs), and a .312 average—the lowest he would hit over the next eight seasons. He made the All-Star team for the first time (he would be picked on a further 11 occasions), and led the Pirates to the National League pennant and an upset defeat of the New York Yankees in the World Series. He hit safely in every game of the series, finishing with a .310 batting average. Clemente's hustle also marked the series when he hit a soft grounder toward the first baseman. When the first baseman moved to field the ball, the pitcher trotted to first base to cover the bag. Clemente, undaunted, sprinted to first base to beat the out. His effort allowed another run to be scored, and in the end it defeated the Yankees. After winning the World Series, while his teammates celebrated, Clemente walked the streets to thank fans for their support.

Despite his heroics, Clemente finished only eighth in the 1960 MVP voting. His pride was damaged but his resolve was strengthened. The next year he batted .351, hit 23 homers, and drove in 89 RBIs to win the first of four career batting titles.

Clemente continued to dominate the game with his usual verve. On defense he crashed into walls, bloodying his chin, to make a catch. In 1964 and 1965 he won two

more batting titles by hitting .339 and .329, respectively. Recognition finally came in 1966, when Clemente received the annual MVP award. He did not lead the league in any statistical categories that year, but hit a career-high 29 home runs and 119 RBIs. The next year he hit .357 to win his fourth and final batting title.

Nothing better exemplified Clemente's hustle than his performance in the 1971 World Series. He played what one writer described as "the kind of baseball that none of us had ever seen before—throwing and running and hitting at something close to the level of perfection." His .414 World Series average, two home runs, and spectacular catches led the Pirates to another championship and Clemente to World Series MVP.

On September 30, 1972, Clemente hit a double for his 3,000th career hit. It would be his last.

Tragedy

On December 31, 1972, Roberto Clemente boarded a DC-7 airplane weighed down with relief supplies he planned to deliver to earthquake victims in Nicaragua. Shortly after takeoff, the plane crashed into the Atlantic Ocean. His body was never found.

The Hall of Fame waived its normally mandatory five-year waiting period, and in 1973 made Roberto Clemente the first Latino to be inducted. The Pirates retired his number 21 jersey, and Major League Baseball now awards the Roberto Clemente Humanitarian Award to the player who best continues his tradition of service. As Clemente himself once said: "If you have an opportunity to make things better and you don't, then you are wasting your time on this earth."

Further reading: Walker, Paul Robert. *Pride of Puerto Rico: The Life of Roberto Clemente.* San Diego, CA: Harcourt Brace Jovanovich, 1988.

www.baseballhalloffame.org (Hall of Fame Web site with biographical information and statistics).

COCA, Imogene
Actor

Imogene Coca was a celebrated comedian, actor, and dancer most famous for her double act with Sid Caesar in the 1950s television comedy series *Your Show of Shows*. Her career spanned eight decades, encompassing vaudeville theater, American television during its "golden age," and several Hollywood movies. Coca received nominations for numerous prestigious awards, and won the Emmy for Best Actress in 1951.

Early life

Imogene Fernandez de Coca was born in 1908, the only child of José Fernandez de Coca, a Spanish violinist and orchestra conductor, and Sadie Brady Coca, an Irish magician's assistant and chorus dancer in vaudeville theater. In her formative years Coca herself became immersed in the world of vaudeville, a genre of stage variety entertainment that was popular from the 1880s to

▼ **Comedian Imogene Coca impersonates movie star Carmen Miranda in 1939.**

the 1920s. Following in her parents' footsteps, she took lessons in piano, dance, and voice. Coca's first paid dancing work came when she was 11, and by the age of 13 she had become a full-time vaudeville performer, as adept at tap dancing as she was at ballet and acrobatics.

At 15 Coca left her native Philadelphia, Pennsylvania, for New York City, where she worked as a dancer in the Silver Slipper nightclub, and in 1925 she made her debut as a chorus dancer in the Broadway musical *When You Smile*.

During the following decade Coca performed in numerous revues and musicals, meanwhile developing her own act that she perfected in nightclubs and at the summer camps of the Catskill and Pocono mountains. Although Coca had obtained some of her earliest engagements through her mother's show-business contacts, she got her big break independently and quite by chance at the age of 26 while she was appearing in the Broadway revue *New Faces of 1934*. One night the heating in the theater broke down, and director Leonard Sillman sent Coca and another up-and-coming actor, the young Henry Fonda, out front to distract the audience while the electricity was turned back on. A diminutive, wide-eyed ingenue wearing an outsized coat that looked like a prop but was in fact worn against the cold, Coca held the audience spellbound with a mime routine so brilliant that it was immediately incorporated into the show.

Part of the significance of that moment was that it taught Coca her strengths as a performer. With her aptitude for physical comedy, unconventional appearance, and remarkably flexible face, she now realized that she was most likely to achieve success in light entertainment, and it was on that area of show business that she now concentrated all her efforts. She remained busy for the rest of the decade and throughout World War II (1939–1945).

Television success

Coca made her television debut in the 1948 variety series *Buzzy Wuzzy*. Among those who saw her perform in that was producer Max Liebman, who remarked: "The great thing about Imogene is that one nostril never knows what the other is doing." In 1949 he invited her to join NBC/Dumont's Admiral Broadway Revue, in which she was first paired with comedian Sid Caesar. Liebman noted an immediate rapport between the two actors, and when the revue evolved into the weekly series, *Your Show of Shows*,

INFLUENCES AND INSPIRATION

Imogene Coca was undoubtedly influenced by a childhood spent in the theater, but it was her partnership with Sid Caesar that provided her greatest lasting inspiration. Their reciprocally rewarding professional relationship spanned six decades, and it is widely recognized that both comedians did their finest work within this double act. Although the pair rarely socialized, they held each other in high regard, Caesar affectionately recalling "a lovely little lady with big brown eyes whom I got to like immediately." They attributed their success to a shared sense of humor and an intuitive ability to anticipate each other's next move.

Your Show of Shows was immensely popular during its four-year run, causing Coca and Caesar to reprise their double act time and again. Coca has been cited as an influence by many leading contemporary comic actors including Lily Tomlin, Carol Burnett, Tracey Ullman, and Whoopi Goldberg.

he hired both Coca and Caesar in leading roles. The show satirized contemporary film and television in general, but Coca and Caesar soon proved so popular that its format was altered to spotlight their talents. Coca performed observant comic parodies of famous opera singers and prima ballerinas, and one of her most loved regular sketches with Caesar featured a battling married couple called The Hickenloopers.

Your Show of Shows was aired every Saturday night from 1950 to 1954, during the era considered by many to be the finest period of American television. Among the scriptwriters were Neil Simon, Mel Brooks, Carl Reiner, and later Larry Gelbart and Woody Allen. The series won several Emmy awards, given for excellence in the television industry, including Best Variety Show in 1951 and 1952, and the Best Actress and Actor awards for Coca and Caesar respectively in 1951.

Going it alone
When *Your Show of Shows* ended, Coca went solo with *The Imogene Coca Show*, which was less successful, running for only one season. In 1958 she again paired up with Caesar for the *Sid Caesar Invites You* show, and in the 1960s she starred in two short-lived sitcoms, NBC's *Grindl* and *It's About Time* (CBS). In 1967 the original cast

of *Your Show of Shows* reunited for *The Sid Caesar, Imogene Coca, Carl Reiner, Howard Morris Special*, which won an Emmy that year for Outstanding Variety Special.

Triumph over adversity
In 1974 Coca lost the sight in her right eye following a car accident but continued to appear on television during the 1970s and 1980s with guest appearances in *The Brady Bunch*, *Fantasy Island*, *Bewitched*, and *Moonlighting*. In 1978 she was nominated for a Best Actress Tony Award for her role as Letitia Primrose in the popular Broadway show *On the Twentieth Century*. She appeared in several movies, including *Under the Yum Yum Tree* (1963) with Jack Lemmon, *Rabbit Test* (1978), *Nothing Lasts Forever* (1984), Harry Harris's 1985 musical version of *Alice in Wonderland*, and *Buy & Cell* (1989) with Malcolm McDowell and Robert Carradine. Her best-known movie role was as Aunt Edna in *National Lampoon's Vacation* (1983). In 1991 Coca, then in her eighties, was again paired with Caesar for the *Together Again* revue, which they toured throughout the United States.

Imogene Coca was twice married. Her first husband, Robert Burton, arranged the music for many of her performances but, suffering from alcoholism, died in 1955. Coca then married actor King Donovan, with whom she performed on stage in *The Prisoner of Second Avenue* and *The Fourposter*. Donovan died in 1987. Coca lived most of her life in New York City, moving to Westport, Connecticut, in 1996 when her health began to fail. She battled with Alzheimer's disease in her final days, and died of natural causes at the age of 92.

KEY DATES

1908	Born in Philadelphia, Pennsylvania, on November 18.
1934	Appears in Broadway revue *New Faces*.
1949	Paired with Sid Caesar for the first time in the Academy Broadway Revue.
1951	Wins Emmy for Best Actress.
2001	Dies in Westport, Connecticut, on June 2.

Further reading: Smith, Ronald L. *Who's Who in Comedy*. New York, NY: Facts On File, 1992.

http://www.sidcaesar.com/imogene.html (Sid Caesar's tribute to Coca on his official Web site).

COLMENARES, Margarita
Engineer

Few women make their mark in the male-dominated world of engineering, but Margarita Colmenares is an exception. Colmenares was the first elected woman president of the Society of Hispanic Professional Engineers (SHPE) and the first Hispanic engineer to be selected for a White House fellowship.

Early life
Margarita Hortensia Colmenares was born in Sacramento, California, on July 20, 1957. Her parents immigrated to California from Oaxaca, Mexico, in their youth. Colmenares's parents impressed on their daughter the importance of education. Colmenares attended a private all-girls school and earned a place to study business at California State University. During her freshman year, however, she transferred to Sacramento City College to gain entrance qualifications for an engineering degree.

Engineering
Colmenares won five scholarships to fund her engineering degree at Stanford University. She supplemented her income by working as an undergraduate research assistant. While studying, Colmenares secured a nine-month work placement on Chevron Corporation's Cooperative Education Program. After graduating in 1981, Colmenares joined the company full time, quickly working her way up the corporate ladder. After serving as a compliance specialist in Houston, Texas, Colmenares was promoted to lead engineer of a multimillion dollar cleanup project at an oil refinery in El Segundo. In 1989 she became an air-quality specialist at the same facility.

▲ **Among her many achievements, Margarita Colmenares was named Outstanding Hispanic Woman of the Year in 1990 and 1992.**

Making a difference
During her early years at Chevron, Colmenares founded the San Francisco chapter of the SHPE. In 1989 she was elected national president of the organization, the first woman to assume the role. Colmenares took a paid leave of absence to concentrate on her presidency of the SHPE.

In 1991 Colmenares became the first Hispanic engineer to serve under the White House fellowship program. As special assistant to David T. Kearns, deputy secretary of education, she tried to reform math and science education in schools. She returned to work for Chevron on international operations in Latin America, but was rehired by the Education Department in 1999 as the director of corporate liaison. Colmenares actively campaigns to increase the numbers of Hispanics entering the sciences.

Further reading: Oleksy, Walter G. *American Profiles: Hispanic American Scientists.* New York, NY: Facts on File, Inc., 1998. www.tamu.edu/west/nwe/civil_colmenares (biography).

KEY DATES

1957 Born in Sacramento, California, on July 20.

1981 Graduates from Stanford with a BS in civil engineering; joins the Chevron Corporation.

1982 Founds the San Francisco chapter of the SHPE.

1989 Becomes the national president of the SHPE.

1991 Is selected for the White House fellowship program; serves in the Education Department.

1999 Becomes the Education Department's director of corporate liaison.

COLÓN, Jesús
Writer, Community Activist

Jesús Colón was an important figure in New York's Puerto Rican community from the 1920s until his death in 1974. A longtime member of the Socialist Party, he endeavored to improve the position of all working people, and devoted himself particularly to representing the interests of his fellow countrymen.

As a teenager Colón moved from his native Cayey to San Juan, the capital of Puerto Rico, where he attended grammar school and became editor of the school paper. He also became politically active and joined the Socialist Party. In 1917 he stowed away on a ship, the S.S. *Carolina*, thus becoming one of a growing number of Puerto Ricans who left their country in search of a better life and prospects in the United States. He settled in Brooklyn, New York, where he took a succession of menial jobs.

Once established in the United States, Colón remained committed to socialism and workers' rights. In 1918 he became a founder member of the first Puerto Rican committee of the Socialist Party in New York, and in 1930 he joined the Communist Party. A decade and a half later he was appointed as labor organizer of the Hispanic section of the International Workers' Order, a multinational fraternal cooperative. He ran—unsuccessfully—for political office on a Labor Party ticket in the 1950s, and again on a Communist Party ticket in 1969. His membership in the Communist Party, along with his support for Puerto Rican independence from the United States, led to his investigation by the House Un-American Activities Committee in 1959.

Writing career
Today Jesús Colón is best remembered for his involvement in, and writings about, Puerto Rican communities in New York. Having experienced at first hand the poverty and prejudice faced by migrants, he clearly saw the value of

▲ *Jesús Colón spent much of his life fighting to improve the lives of poor Puerto Ricans.*

community networks, and became a founding member of several such organizations, including the Alianza Obrera Puertorriqueña (founded 1922), the Ateneo Obrero Hispano (1926), and the Liga Puertorriqueña e Hispana (1928). He also used his writing to voice demands for the rights of workers and Hispanics. From the late 1920s he wrote many articles for Spanish-language newspapers published in New York, as well as the socialist newspaper *Justicia*, published in Puerto Rico. From 1955 he wrote columns in English for the *Daily Worker* and *Daily World*, Communist Party papers. His books, *A Puerto Rican in New York and Other Sketches* (1961) and the posthumous *The Way It Was and Other Writings* (1993), provide rare and valuable insights into the experiences of Puerto Rican Americans between the two world wars.

Further reading: Colón, Jesús, Edna Acosta-Belén, and Virginia Sánchez Korrol (eds). *The Way It Was, and Other Writings.* Houston, TX: Arte Publico Press, 1993.
http://www.centropr.org/lib-arc/jcolon.html (biographical information from the Center for Puerto Rican Studies at Hunter College, City University of New York, which holds a large collection of Colón's papers).

KEY DATES	
1901	Born in Cayey, Puerto Rico, on January 20.
1917	Stows away on the S.S. *Carolina* and settles in Brooklyn, New York.
1961	Publishes *A Puerto Rican in New York and Other Sketches*.
1974	Dies aged 73 in New York City.

COLÓN, Miriam
Actress, Theater Director

▲ **Puerto Rican actress Miriam Colón is here pictured attending an awards ceremony in 2001.**

A star of stage, cinema, and television, Miriam Colón has earned great esteem during her lengthy acting career. She is an inspirational and passionate advocate of the Latino arts.

Miriam Colón was born in Ponce, Puerto Rico, and grew up in San Juan. She soon displayed a prodigious acting talent, appearing at a young age in the film *Los Peloteros* (1953) and studying drama at the University of Puerto Rico. Relocating to New York, Colón cofounded a pioneering but short-lived Latino drama company, El Circulo Dramatico, in 1956. She got her first major break in the distinctive Western film *One-Eyed Jacks* (1961), the directorial debut of "method" actor Marlon Brando. Like Brando and other 1950s stars such as James Dean, Colón honed her dramatic abilities at New York's famous Actors Studio.

Colón then proceeded to alternate between minor appearances in TV series such as *Dr. Kildare*, *Gunsmoke*, *Bonanza*, and *The High Chaparral*, and acclaimed, often prominent, performances on stage. Her film credits during the 1960s include the political thriller *Thunder Island* (1963), directed by Jack Leewood and cowritten by a young Jack Nicholson, and Sydney J. Furie's horse-rustling Western *The Appaloosa* (1966), which cast her once more opposite Brando. Colón formed another dramatic organization, the Puerto Rican Traveling Theater, in 1967. With Colón as artistic director, this nonprofit touring company has enjoyed sustained success, promoting Latino talents in more than 100 productions.

Range of roles

In Brian DePalma's violent crime film *Scarface* (1983), Colón had a small but pivotal role as the disappointed yet defiant mother of a ruthless Cuban gangster played by Al Pacino. Colón gave a convincing performance despite being only a little older than Pacino (born 1940). She later shone among the sprawling cast of John Sayles's study of urban corruption, *City of Hope* (1991), and joined a talented ensemble for Sayles's murder mystery *Lone Star* (1996), playing an illegal immigrant from Mexico who has become a successful restaurateur.

Later Colón enjoyed stints on two long-running soap operas, *One Life to Live* and *Guiding Light*. In 2001 she appeared in *Almost a Woman*, a TV film adapted from the memoirs of Puerto Rican novelist Esmeralda Santiago. In the same year she also excelled in the role of a troubled mother in *The Blue Diner*: The part was created especially for her by writer-director Jan Egleson. Such powerful performances demonstrate that the indefatigable actress continues to stride from strength to strength after six decades in the often precarious world of show business.

KEY DATES	
1936	Born in Ponce, Puerto Rico, on August 20.
1967	Founds Puerto Rican Traveling Theater.
1993	Wins Obie award for Sustained Excellence of Performance.

Further reading: Fernandez, Mayra. *Miriam Colon: Actor and Theatre Founder*. Cleveland, OH: Modern Curriculum Press, 1994.
http://imdb.com/name/nm0173125/ (full TV and film credits).

COLÓN, Willie
Musician

William Colón is known as the King of Salsa. He has described salsa as "a newspaper … a chronicle of our times in a big city…. [It's] an idea, a concept, the result of a way of approaching music from the Latin American cultural perspective." Colón, who has had 15 gold and five platinum records and sold more than 30 million records worldwide, is also a leading Hispanic political and social activist.

Early life
William Anthony Colón Román was born in a Puerto Rican neighborhood in the South Bronx, New York City, on April 28, 1950. Colón grew up in an economically deprived household and was brought up by his beloved grandmother, Antonia, who greatly influenced Colón's life.

▼ **Willie Colón has received many honors, including being inducted into the Bronx Walk of Fame in New York and being featured on a postage stamp.**

Antonia first interested Colón in music; she sang him traditional songs when he was a child. She also taught Colón Spanish and made sure that he knew about his Puerto Rican heritage and culture. From a young age Colón was aware of political issues affecting the Hispanic community; he became involved in community activism as a teenager. During this time he also began to concentrate on music: His grandmother gave him a trumpet when he was a teenager, but he switched to the trombone when he was 14, inspired by the music of Mon Rivera, a trombone pioneer. In 1964 Colón formed his first band, Los Dandees.

A love of music
In 1967 Colón recorded his first album, *El Malo*, on the Futura label. He promoted himself as a "bad boy," modeling his dress, talk, and style on a gangster. The record was an immediate success, selling more than 300,000 copies, but Colón later found it difficult to shake off his "bad-boy" persona. In 1968 Colón moved to the Fania label, set up by Johnny Pacheco and Jerry Masucci in the early 1960s. Colón's second album, *The Hustler,* was released later that year to critical acclaim, and his third album, *Guisando* (Doing a Job), was released in 1969. In

---

INFLUENCES AND INSPIRATION

Among the musicians who had most influence on Willie Colón was leading Puerto Rican bandleader and trombonist Mon Rivera. Also known as "El Rey del Trabalengua" ("The Tongue-Twister King") because of his fast rhymes and alliterations, Rivera is credited by some music critics as introducing the all-trombone sound to the New York Latin scene in the 1960s; others believe that Eddie Palmieri pioneered it with his band La Perfecta.

Born Efrain Rivera Castillo in Puerto Rico in 1925, Rivera was the son of Ramón Rivera Alers, a composer of popular folk songs known as *plenas*. Although Rivera was a brilliant musician he was also a good sportsman: As a teenager he played professional baseball with Los Indios. He decided to concentrate on music, and at age 16 he began playing with William Manzano's band. Rivera quickly established a reputation and became associated particularly with salsa and plena music. He was the first bandleader to introduce a four-trombone front line. Many musicians, including Colón, were inspired by Rivera's musical style. Colón worked with Rivera in 1975, collaborating on the album *There Goes the Neighborhood.* Rivera died three years later.

---

that same year Colón first collaborated with Rubén Blades, whom he met in Panama. Blades was both a musician and a law student at the time. The two men shared an interest in politics: Colón wrote "El Cazanguero," a song based on Blades's experiences working in a prison, which the young Blades later performed. As Colón's reputation grew, he was able to work with some of the leading musicians in Latin music, including Héctor Lavoe.

A pioneer

During the 1970s Colón began to experiment musically, fusing typical rhythms from countries such as Ghana, Panama, Cuba, and Brazil with jazz elements and urban sociopolitical lyrics. During these years Colón created his own company, WAC Productions Inc., an acronym of William Anthony Colón. Not content with writing and performing his own music, he also collaborated with musicians such as his childhood hero, Mon Rivera, on *There Goes the Neighborhood.* He worked with Ernie Agosto on *La Conspiración, Ernie's Conspiracy, Cada Loco Con Sus Temas, Afecto y Cariño,* and *Ernie's Journey.* Colón also produced records in both Spanish and English: He worked on several of Celia Cruz's album's, including *Only They Have Done This, Celia and Willie,* and *The Winners.*

Colón also ventured into acting in the 1980s. He starred with Rubén Blades in *The Last Fight* (1982) and apeared in the TV drama *Demasiado Corazón,* which looked at drug cartels and government corruption. Nominated for several awards, in 1981 Colón received the Musician of the Year award. A year later he won his first Grammy for the album *Canciones del Solar de los Aburridos;* he has since been nominated for 11 Grammy awards.

Activism

As well as being a successful musician, Colón is also known both in the United States and abroad for his social and political activism, an interest he shares with his friend Rubén Blades. In 1994 Colón ran for the Democratic nomination for the U.S. Congress in New York State's 17th Congressional District primary, promoting such issues as better education for minority groups and the introduction of a higher minimum wage. He lost to incumbent Representative Eliot Engel. In 1995 Colón became the first person from a minority group to serve on the national board of the American Society of Composers, Authors and Publishers (ASCAP). A year later he made the 100 most influential Hispanic Americans' list issued by *Hispanic Business Magazine.* He ran for Bronx borough president, but withdrew from the campaign in 2001.

Colón is a member of several organizations and boards of directors, including the Latino Commission on AIDS, the United Nations Immigrant Foundation, and the Congressional Hispanic Caucus Institute. In 2005 Monroe County in New York introduced a Willie Colón Day in recognition of Colón's achievements as both a musician and community leader. In that same year Colón launched a program with the U.S. surgeon general to provide free medical insurance to children.

See also: Blades, Rubén; Cruz, Celia; Lavoe, Héctor

Further reading: Brought, Simon, and Mark Ellingham. *World Music Vol. 2. Latin and North America, Caribbean, India, Asia, and the Pacific. An A–Z of the Music, Musicians, and Discs.* New York, NY: Penguin, 2000.
http://www.williecolon.com (official site).

COMPEÁN, Mario
Political Activist

Mario Compeán was a leading member of the Chicano movement, the Mexican civil rights campaign that developed in the 1960s and 1970s. In 1967 Compeán helped found the Mexican American Youth Organization (MAYO), which became the leading Mexican American political youth organization in Texas. MAYO led to the formation of La Raza Unida Party (RUP) in 1970.

Early life

Born in San Antonio, Texas, in 1940, Compeán grew up attending public schools in the Mexican barrios of the city. He worked with his parents as a migrant agricultural laborer until 1966, when he enrolled at St. Mary's College, San Antonio. Compeán joined together with four other students—José Angel Gutiérrez, Nacho Pérez, Willie Velásquez, and Juan Patlán—to fight against the systematic repression to which Mexican Americans had been subjected for generations. They founded MAYO, a political organization devoted to getting Mexican Americans elected to public office.

Making a difference

Compeán organized pickets and demonstrations and used civil disobedience to draw attention to MAYO's aims. He used his position as a trainer for the federally funded Volunteers in Service to America (VISTA) to recruit MAYO members to work in poverty-stricken areas of Southern Texas. Early in 1968 Compeán played a leading role in the MAYO-inspired school walkouts in San Antonio's West Side by students demanding bilingual education and other reforms. After the RUP won local elections in South Texas in 1970, Compeán organized statewide campaigns. He was influential in the selection of candidates, such as Ramsey Muñiz who ran as the gubernatorial candidate. Although unsuccessful, Muñiz drew enough votes from Democrat Dolph Briscoe to almost enable a Republican to win the state house.

▲ *Mario Compeán (right) is pictured with labor leader and activist César Chávez.*

In 1973 the RUP won several local elections in South Texas. The following year Muñiz decided to again seek the state governorship. He wanted to attract the moderate vote, but Compeán insisted on a nationalistic anti-Gringo campaign. The two men disagreed bitterly and Compeán resigned at the 1974 RUP state convention in Houston. By 1978 the RUP was ailing. Compeán himself ran for governor but only received 2 percent of the vote. Subsequently he left politics to pursue his studies and to teach.

Compeán headed the Chicano studies program at the University of Wisconsin as an interim director in the 1980s, then studied for a doctorate in history at Washington State University. Later he taught at Yakima Community College in Washington State. Although his political career ended in failure, Compeán was nevertheless at the forefront of one of the most significant attempts to form a third party in the United States in the late 20th century.

See also: Gutiérrez, José Angel

Further Reading: Garciá, Ignacio M. *United We Win: The Rise and Fall of La Raza Unida Party.* Tucson, AZ: University of Arizona Mexican Studies Research Center, 1989.

KEY DATES	
1940	Born in San Antonio, Texas.
1966	Joins the Chicano movement.
1978	Runs for governor of Texas.

CORDERO, Angel, Jr.
Jockey, Trainer, Agent

Puerto Rican-born Angel Cordero, Jr., was one of the world's leading jockeys. Cordero once said, "If a horse has four legs, and I'm riding it, I think I can win." Cordero's career was cut short when he fell during a race in 1992. When he retired, Cordero had ridden 7,057 winners and ranked sixth in winnings with $164,526,217. He became a trainer and agent, influencing the careers of other jockeys such as fellow Puerto Rican John Velázquez (*see box*).

Early life
Born in Santurce, Puerto Rico, on November 8, 1942, Angel Tomás Cordero, Jr., grew up in the world of Puerto Rican racing. His father, Angel Cordero Vila, was a renowned rider and horse trainer. From a very early age the young Angel was taken to the race track, where he watched his father work. He decided to pursue a career as a jockey, working hard to achieve his aim.

At age 17, Cordero began racing in Puerto Rico, winning his first race in 1960. When he turned 20 in 1962, he traveled to New York City to become a professional jockey.

Renown
Cordero's impressive career really began in 1974, when he won the Kentucky Derby, generally held to be one of the highest achievements in horse racing. The derby is held annually on the first Saturday in May at Churchill Downs in Louisville, Kentucky. Cordero won the event on the

▼ **Angel Cordero wins the 100th Kentucky Derby in May 1974, riding Cannonade.**

mount Cannonade. In 1976 Cordero won the Derby for the second time; he also came first in New York's Belmont Stakes on Bold Forbes a few months later. Riding Spend A Buck, Cordero won the Kentucky Derby for a third time in 1985, making him only one of four jockeys to win the race three times. Among his other major achievements, Cordero took New York's Saratoga racing title 13 times, with 11 consecutive wins. He also won the Preakness Stakes twice, once in 1980 and again in 1984. He was the first Puerto Rican jockey to win the "Triple Crown"—the Kentucky Derby, the Preakness Stakes, and the Belmont Stakes— in the same season.

A fantastic career

During the 1980s it seemed that Cordero could do no wrong. In 1982 and 1983, because of his impressive record of victories and commitment to the sport, Cordero was honored with the Eclipse Award, horse racing's most prestigious accolade. In 1982 he earned more than $9 million, more than any other jockey.

Cordero was considered by some people to be one of the best riders of his generation. In 1988 he was inducted into the Thoroughbred Racing Hall of Fame.

End of career

In 1992 Cordero suffered a serious fall and was almost killed. He retired, although he still raced occasionally. Cordero's career was remarkable: From 1977 to 1990 his mounts won over $5 million each year, including three Kentucky Derbies, two Preakness Stakes, and four Breeders' Cups.

A trainer and an agent

Cordero decided to concentrate on being a trainer. In July 1994 he had his first victory when Holy Mountain won the Lexington Stakes at Belmont Park. He moved on to became a jockeys' agent, most famously nurturing the career of fellow Puerto Rican John Velázquez.

In 2001 Cordero suffered great personal tragedy when his wife, Marjorie Clayton Cordero, who had won more than 70 races herself as a jockey, was killed in a hit-and-run accident. The couple had three children, Julie, Canela, and Angel III.

Cordero, who has always supported charitable causes, raced at Philadelphia Park on October 1, 2005, to raise money for the victims of Hurricane Katrina.

KEY DATES	
1942	Born in Santurce, Puerto Rico, on November 8.
1960	Starts riding in competitions; wins his first race.
1962	Travels to New York City to become a professional jockey.
1974	Wins first Kentucky Derby on Cannonade.
1982	Sets a record with jockey earnings totaling more than $9 million.
1988	Is inducted into the Thoroughbred Racing Hall of Fame.
1992	Retires from riding after a fall at Aqueduct; becomes a trainer.
1995	Becomes a jockey agent.
2001	Wife killed in hit-and-run accident in January.

Further reading: Case, Carole. *America's Aristocrats in Thoroughbred Racing.* New Brunswick, NJ: Rutgers University Press, 2001.
http://www.racingmuseum.org/hall/jockey.asp?ID=177 (biography from National Museum of Racing and Hall of Fame).

CÓRDOVA, France Anne
Scientist, Educator

France Anne Córdova is a distinguished astrophysicist and educator. She was born in 1947 in Paris, France, where her Mexican American father was working for the Cooperative for American Remittances to Europe (now Cooperative for Assistance and Relief Everywhere; CARE), a nonprofit organization founded in 1945 to distribute food and clothing to survivors of World War II (1939–1945).

The eldest of 11 children, on the family's return to the United States Córdova quickly applied herself to study and hard work. Despite having to help care for her siblings, she earned excellent grades at high school, and in her senior year she was named one of California's "Top Ten Youths."

She then studied English at Stanford University, and during her junior year she went as an assistant on an anthropological expedition to Oaxaca, Mexico. This was a life-changing period for Córdova. On her return to the United States she wrote a short novel about her experience, *The Women of Santo Domingo*, which was one of the top-10 entries in a competition run by *Mademoiselle* magazine in New York.

New direction

On graduating with her first degree in 1969, for a while Córdova pursued two parallel careers, teaching English to high school classes by day and writing short stories for the *Los Angeles Times* at night. Before long, however, she decided to retrain as a scientist. She continued her education at the California Institute of Technology in Pasadena, and completed a PhD in physics in 1979. Her new qualification secured her a job at Los Alamos National Laboratory, New Mexico, where she became one of the first women to make a mark in the field of astrophysics, measuring the X-ray and gamma ray radiation of certain stars.

▲ *France Anne Córdova studied English as a student, but retrained to become a highly respected physicist.*

From 1989 to 1993 Córdova was deputy group leader of the Space Astronomy and Astrophysics Group. She served as chief scientist at the National Aeronautics and Space Administration (NASA) from 1993 to 1996. For 10 years she was head of the Department of Astronomy and Astrophysics at Pennsylvania State University.

In 2002 Córdova was appointed chancellor of the University of California, in which role she continues to educate others in the wonders of science and the possibilities for women and Hispanics in the fields of math and physics.

Further reading: Bailey, Martha J. *American Women in Science: 1950 to the Present: A Biographical Dictionary*. Santa Barbara, CA: ABC-CLIO,1998.
http://www.gale.com/warehouse/chh/bio/cordova_f.htm (biographical data from Notable Hispanic American Women, Gale, 1998).

KEY DATES	
1947	Born in Paris, France, on August 5.
1989	Promoted as deputy group leader of Space Astronomy and Astrophysics Group at Los Alamos National Laboratory.
1993	Appointed as chief scientist at NASA.
2002	Named chancellor of the University of California on July 1.

COREA, Chick
Musician

The American jazz pianist Chick Corea is a musician who continually reinvents his sound to create something new and fresh. In the course of a career spanning more than four decades, he has experimented with everything from jazz standards and classical composition to electric jazz fusion and Latin jazz.

Early life

Armando Anthony Corea was born in Chelsea, Massachusetts, in 1941. He was raised in a home filled with the sounds of jazz greats Charlie Parker and Dizzy Gillespie and classical composers such as Beethoven and Mozart. By the age of five he was studying piano, and as he grew he was encouraged to develop his musical talents by his father, also Armando, a jazz trumpet player who led a Dixieland band in Boston in the 1930s and 1940s.

During his high school years Chick Corea formed his own trio and began playing gigs locally. Wearing a black tuxedo given to him by his father, he covered tunes by jazz

▼ *Pianist Chick Corea rehearses with the London Philharmonic Orchestra in 1999.*

pianist Horace Silver. He soon began to work with other local musicians, including Portuguese bandleader and trumpet player Phil Barboza, and conga drummer Bill Fitch, who introduced him to Latin music. Throughout his career Corea continued to explore his Latin roots through composition and collaboration. He said: "I liked the 'extraversion' of Latin music, especially the dance and salsa-style music—bands like Tito Puente's band and Machito's band. The Cuban dance music was a great kind of antidote to some of the more serious, heady jazz that I was into."

Corea then moved to New York, where he studied music for one month at Columbia University and for six months at The Juilliard School. Having been largely a self-taught player, he found both experiences disappointing, but he remained in the city because it was at the heart of the contemporary music scene and it was there that the best prospects lay.

Turning professional

Corea began his professional career in the 1960s playing with Latin greats such as Willie Bobo and Mongo Santamaria. One of his earliest recordings was with trumpeter Blue Mitchell's quintet on *The Thing to Do*, which featured Corea's own composition, "Chick's Tune." His first album as a leader was *Tones for Joan's Bones* (1966). Two years later Corea released his legendary album, *Now He Sings, Now He Sobs*.

In September 1968 Corea joined the Miles Davis group just as Davis was beginning to experiment with electric instruments and building the fusion sound that would change the jazz world forever. Corea took up the electric piano, forming part of the rhythm section with Dave Holland, and played on important albums such as *In a Silent Way* and *Bitches Brew*. When Davis's music became more funk-based, Corea and Holland left the band to form Circle, an avant-garde jazz group, in which they continued to experiment with a free-flowing improvisational style.

In 1971 the ever-restless Corea left Circle, and formed the band Return to Forever (RTF) with Brazilian singer Flora Purim and her husband, Airto Moreira, on percussion. After two albums with that lineup, Corea began incorporating more electric instruments and took the band in the direction of rock music. RTF became the trailblazers for the mid-1970s fusion movement with innovative

---

INFLUENCES AND INSPIRATION

As an experimental jazz musician, Chick Corea's influences are diverse and wide-ranging. During his early childhood he was introduced by his father to the work of some of the jazz greats: Gillespie, Parker, and Herb Pomeroy. Another notable early influence was concert pianist Salvatore Sullo, who lectured Corea from the age of eight.

Sullo nurtured the child's interest in classical music, and encouraged him to take up composition. Later, Corea was introduced to Latin music by conga drummer Bill Fitch, and he learned a great deal during his time with Latin jazz greats Willie Bobo and Mongo Santamaria. Throughout his career Corea has been inspired by the artists with whom he has played.

Perhaps the greatest formative influence was that of Miles Davis, who encouraged him to play the electric piano, and thereby changed not only the work of Corea but also the whole direction of modern jazz. Corea's major nonmusical inspiration has been drawn from his interest in Scientology and the work of its founder, L. Ron Hubbard.

---

albums such as the Grammy-winning *No Mystery*. Corea's most famous composition, the classic "Spain," originally appeared on the 1972 RTF album *Light as a Feather*.

After nearly five years of success, RTF disbanded in 1976. Corea spent the next 10 years playing and recording with a host of different artists, including Gary Burton, Herbie Hancock, Joe Henderson, Chaka Khan, and Nancy Wilson. It was during this time that he recorded the Grammy-winning *Leprechaun* as well as *My Spanish Heart*. In the latter work Corea returned to his roots with a Latin-flavored tune dedicated to his father; another track on the album incorporates classical cellos.

The eighties and beyond

In 1985 Corea formed the Elektric Band, which has since released a series of successful albums. Its 2004 recording, *To the Stars*, is a tone poem based on L. Ron Hubbard's science fiction novel of the same name. Meanwhile, in 1989 Corea formed the Akoustic Band, in which he made a turn back toward more traditional jazz forms.

KEY DATES

1941   Born in Chelsea, Massachusetts, on June 12.

1968   Releases his second recording, the legendary *Now He Sings, Now He Sobs*. Joins Miles Davis's group to play on *In a Silent Way* and *Bitches Brew*.

1971   Forms Return to Forever (RTF), which inspires the mid-1970s electronic fusion movement.

1976   Wins first Grammy award with RTF's *No Mystery*.

1985   Forms the Elektric Band.

1999   Records his Piano Concerto No. 1 with the London Philharmonic Orchestra.

In 1992 Corea realized a life-long ambition when he founded Stretch Records, a label that, as its name implies, is committed to extending musical boundaries. After he released his final albums with GRP Records, *Music Forever and Beyond*, a five-disc boxed set of selected works from 1964 to 1996, Corea signed to his own recording company.

In the 1990s Corea enjoyed fruitful partnerships with various artists, including two recordings with Bobby McFerrin: the jazz duet *Play* and the classical *Mozart Sessions*. He also revisited his past by recording a duet album with Gary Burton and collaborating with other artists with whom he had previously worked. In 1997 Corea formed another new group, Origin, which recorded two live albums before embarking on *Change*, a collection of specially commissioned original music. The album was recorded in the Florida home that Corea shares with his wife, the singer Gayle Moran.

In 2001 the Chick Corea New Trio, with Avishai Cohen on bass and Jeff Ballard on drums, released the album *Past, Present & Futures*. All but one of its 11 tracks were written by Corea, and the work shows the composer at his most creative and energetic.

Corea's unceasing inventiveness has spawned some of the most influential recordings in the history of jazz. He has won 12 Grammy awards, including the 1999 induction into the Grammy Hall of Fame of his 1968 album *Now He Sings, Now He Sobs*.

See also: Machito; Puente, Tito

Further reading: Bogdanov, Vladimir, Chris Woodstra, and Stephen Thomas Erlewine, (eds.). *All Music Guide to Jazz. 4th Edition. San Francisco, CA*: Backbeat Books, 2002.
http://www.chickcorea.com (official Web site).

CORONA, Bert
Labor Activist

Called the father of the Chicano movement, Bert Corona established several organizations dedicated to protecting Latino rights. Corona was particularly respected for his support of undocumented workers.

Early life
Born in El Paso, Texas, on May 29, 1918, Corona grew up inspired by his father, who was assassinated because of his involvement in the Mexican Revolution. Corona was brought up partly in Mexico and partly in El Paso.

Labor organizer
In the mid-1930s Corona accepted a basketball scholarship to attend the University of Southern California, Los Angeles. He became concerned about the unfair treatment of immigrants arriving to work in the city. Corona became influenced by socialism while at college. He concluded: "Socialism could solve many of the problems created by capitalism."

He also became closely involved with some of the emerging labor unions that had been formed to fight for better wages and labor conditions. He was soon a regional president of a union for dockers and warehouse workers. After dropping out of college, Corona became the leader of an new organization called El Congreso del Pueblo de Habla Espanola. It focused on immigration policy issues and campaigned for affordable housing.

Corona served in World War II (1939–1945) as a paratrooper before leading another new organization, the Associación Nacional Mexico Americana (ANMA), which had close ties to industrial unions. In 1962 the ANMA helped bring an end to the Bracero Program, which had

▲ **Bert Corona published the memoirs of his extraordinary life in 1994.**

brought undocumented Mexicans to the United States to work on farms for very low wages; the program undermined efforts to improve worker conditions.

Unlike other leading labor organizers, Corona sought to protect undocumented workers; he attempted to unionize them through a new group named Casa. He also founded Hermandad Mexicana Nacional (HMN), the Mexican nationalist organization.

Politics
During the 1960s Corona was closely involved with the Democratic Party, serving as cochair of the California presidential campaigns of Lyndon B. Johnson and Robert F. Kennedy. In 1966, after Corona assumed leadership of the Mexican American Political Association (MAPA), President Johnson invited him to air the grievances of the Hispanic Community. This resulted in the creation of a Department of Mexican American Affairs.

A man of many talents, Corona was leader of the peace lobby SANE/FREEZE, and cochair of the National Alliance Against Racist and Political Oppression. He taught Chicano studies at several universities before his death in 2001.

See also: National Organizations

Further reading: Corona, Bert, and Mario T. Garcia. *Memories of Chicano History: The Life and Narrative of Bert Corona.* Berkeley, CA: University of California; 1994. www.laprensa-sandiego.org/archieve/january04-23/bert.htm (article about Bert Corona).

KEY DATES	
1918	Born in El Paso, Texas, on May 29.
1939	Serves in U.S. military during World War II (1939–1945).
1960	Helps found ANMA.
1962	Appointed ANMA's leader.
1965	Appointed to the California Civil Rights Commission.
2001	Dies in Los Angeles, California, on January 15.

CORONA, Juan
Murderer

In 1973 Juan Corona, a farm labor contractor, was convicted of killing 25 men, more than any mass murderer up to that time.

Juan Vallejo Corona was born in a small village near Guadalajara, Mexico. At the age of 16 he left home for California, crossing into the United States without documentation. He took odd jobs in agriculture and the construction industry for a few years before joining his older half-brother, Natividad, a labor contractor, near Sacramento. The Corona brothers helped laborers find jobs on ranches and farms, taking a percentage of their pay as compensation.

In 1956 Corona began imagining that he could see dead people. His brother had him committed to a psychiatric hospital, where he received electroshock therapy before the U.S. immigration authorities sent him back to Mexico.

Corona soon returned to California, this time with a green card that allowed him to work legitimately with his brother. In 1959 he married Gloria Moreno, a labor camp cook, and they started a family. Corona often worked two jobs to support his children. The family's standard of living improved considerably in 1966, when he became the primary labor contractor for the large Sullivan Ranch in Sutter County near Yuba City.

The crimes
One day in May 1971 a local farmer noticed on his property an oddly shaped hole that was mysteriously filled in when he came back a while later. Concerned, he called the sheriff's department. A deputy came to investigate the next day and dug up the body of a murdered vagrant. Before long a worker on the Sullivan Ranch noticed a

▲ *Juan Corona is escorted under guard from the courthouse in Fairfield, California, during his trial.*

similar hole that turned out to be another grave. An extensive search of the area turned up a total of 25 victims, almost all homeless white men. In one of the graves, detectives found a receipt on which was written the name of Juan Corona. Deputies raided his house where they found tools, knives, and clothes stained with blood. They arrested Corona and charged him with homicide.

The trial
Corona's trial drew great media attention. His flamboyant defense attorney, Richard Hawk, claimed that the case was racially motivated and tried to rally support for his client among Chicanos, but without success. In 1973 Corona was convicted on all 25 counts and sentenced to life in prison (the death penalty had been recently ruled unconstitutional). Corona appealed, and a new trial was ordered because Hawk had called no witnesses. The second trial, the most expensive ever to that point, also resulted in guilty verdicts. Corona has since been incarcerated in Corcoran State Prison near Fresno, where he has survived two serious attacks by other prisoners.

Further reading: Villaseñor, Victor. *Jury: The People vs. Juan Corona.* New York, NY: Dell Books, 1997.
http://crime.about.com/od/serial/p/corona.htm (sensationalist account of the crimes).

KEY DATES	
1934	Born in Autlán, Mexico, on February 7.
1950	Moves to the United States.
1956	Suffers from delusions; returns to Mexico.
1966	Wins contract to provide labor at the Sullivan Ranch.
1971	Arrested for killing 25 transients.
1973	Convicted of murder; sentenced to life in prison.

CORONADO, Francisco Vásquez de
Explorer

Francisco Vásquez de Coronado was a Spanish explorer and colonial administrator. His epic Royal Expedition of 1540–1542 into the American Southwest in search of the legendary Seven Cities of Cíbola resulted in the exploration of many areas previously uncharted by Europeans, including parts of Arizona, New Mexico, Texas, Oklahoma, and Kansas.

Early life
The second son of Juan Vásquez de Coronado and Isabel de Luján, Francisco Vásquez de Coronado was born in 1510 in Salamanca, Spain. Since his parents' considerable fortune was earmarked for his elder brother, he had no choice but to seek his own fortune. In 1535 he set sail for New Spain (modern Mexico) as a protégé of viceroy Antonio de Mendoza. He settled in Mexico City and married Beatriz de Estrada, daughter of Alonso de Estrada, the royal treasurer. The union enhanced Coronado's status among the governing elite. By 1538 he had assumed a prominent role with the *cabildo* (municipal council) of Mexico City. In the same year the viceroy appointed Coronado governor of Nueva Galicia. The move to the provincial capital, Guadalajara, proved a mixed blessing: Coronado had to deal with fallout from the rule of his predecessor, Nuño Beltrán de Guzmán, whose cruelty toward the indigenous peoples of western Mexico left festering resentments that

▲ **This painting depicts Francisco Coronado crossing the plains of Kansas. Coronado was attempting to find the fabled Seven Cities of Gold.**

would spark the Mixtón War in 1541. By then, however, Coronado had departed on his great adventure.

In search of Cíbola
In Nueva Galicia Coronado became intrigued by accounts of the voyages of discovery undertaken by Alvar Núñez Cabeza de Vaca in the northeast and by Fray Marcos de Niza in the north. The latter claimed that the Cíbola, or the Seven Cities of Gold, lay just north of Mexico. In April 1540 Coronado was given leave by Mendoza to lead a massive expedition into the northern frontier in search of the legendary land of riches. He assembled a team of 300 Spanish soldiers, between 800 and 1,000 native servants, three women, and 1,000 pack animals, together with Fray Marcos himself and five other Franciscan monks.

Setting out from Compostela, the expedition followed ancient native trails from the Mexican west coast through Sonora, eastern Arizona, New Mexico, and the panhandles of Texas and Oklahoma to the Great Bend of the Arkansas River in central Kansas. As the explorers advanced they

KEY DATES

1510 Born in Salamanca, Spain.

1535 Arrives in New Spain (modern Mexico) to work in the colonial administration.

1538 Appointed governor of Nueva Galicia.

1540 Viceroy Mendoza appoints Coronado captain-general of the Royal Expedition into the uncharted north (now part of the Southwest United States).

1541 Lured to Quivira under false pretences.

1542 Returns to Mexico after the Royal Expedition fails to find promised treasure.

1544 Tried on 34 charges of malfeasance and deprived of symbolic wand of office.

1554 Dies after long illness in Mexico City on September 22.

INFLUENCES AND INSPIRATION

Francisco Vásquez de Coronado was a product of the age of the conquistador. He was inspired by the exploits of such celebrated contemporaries as Hernán Cortes (1485–1547), Francisco Pizarro (about 1475–1541), Ponce de León (1460–1521), and Hernando de Soto (about 1496–1542). They were all trailblazers who set out to create an empire for Spain in the New World.

In practical terms Coronado's greatest debt was to Antonio de Mendoza, viceroy of Mexico from 1530 to 1550, who advanced his early career as a bureaucrat and later appointed him captain-general and commander of the voyage of discovery into the uncharted north. According to 20th-century historian Arthur Aiton, Mendoza's "careful preparation, instruction, and influence" were of paramount importance to Coronado. With the failure of the Royal Expedition, however, Mendoza decided that his trust had been misplaced and the two men became enemies.

split up into smaller groups, and thus managed to chart a much wider range of territory than they would have been able to reach in a single band. One of Coronado's lieutenants, Hernando Alarcón, led his men to the mouth of the Colorado River, becoming the first Europeans to set foot in what is now California. Another, García López de Cárdenas, discovered and explored the Grand Canyon. A third, Hernando de Alvarado, explored west-central New Mexico and discovered the Pueblo Indian community of Acoma, and later ventured as far as Taos.

The Royal Expedition met resistance from some of the native peoples it encountered along the way. While suppressing a rebellion in New Mexico, Coronado's men destroyed 13 Pueblo villages. In another incident, Coronado was lured to Quivira, a Wichita village, after having been assured that the settlement contained a mass of treasure. When he discovered that he had been tricked, he strangled his informant. Finally realizing that Cíbola did not exist, Coronado abandoned the mission and returned to Mexico in April 1542, despite opposition from some of his lieutenants and supporters.

Controversy and decline

On his return to Nueva Galicia, Coronado found that he was no longer a hero but an object of derision. He was held responsible not only for the costly error of the Royal Expedition, but also for the horrors of the Mixtón War that had been fought in his absence. In August 1544, Lorenzo de Tejada, the *oidor* (chief judge) of Mexico, arrived in Guadalajara to investigate, and suspended Coronado for the duration of his inquiry. He later filed 34 charges against the governor: The accusations included dicing and gambling, acceptance of bribes, and the "inhuman treatment" of native men, women, and children who labored in his mines and on his ranches without compensation, adequate food, or shelter. Although

Coronado denied most of the charges, in evidence he made many damaging admissions that led to his being placed under house arrest on allegations that he had abused natives on the Royal Expedition.

At the conclusion of the case, Coronado was fined 600 gold pesos for bureaucratic negligence. He was ruined. Although he remained a member of the Mexico City council until shortly before his death, viceroy Mendoza, originally his mentor, made sure that Coronado never again held a significant post in the government of New Spain. During the last two years of his life Francisco Coronado suffered from a debilitating illness caused in part by a head injury sustained during his great trip of discovery. He died in 1554 at age 44, and was buried in the parish cemetery of the church of Santo Domingo.

Legacy

The Royal Expedition was a folly inspired by a fanciful notion of a land of unimaginable riches. It had catastrophic consequences for the explorers themselves and many of the people they discovered. From a historical perspective, however, it is significant as the means by which Europeans first discovered California, the Grand Canyon, and the Great Plains, and charted the Colorado River and the Rio Grande. Coronado thus influenced the cartography, political and cultural geography, Hispanic colonization, and written traditions and heritage of the area that is now the Southwest United States.

See also: De Niza, Marcos; De Soto, Hernando; Núñez Cabeza de Vaca, Álvar

Further reading: Bolton, Herbert Eugene. *Coronado: Knight of Pueblos and Plains.* Albuquerque, NM: University of New Mexico Press, 1949.

CORONEL, Antonio F.
Politician, Educator

Antonio Francisco ("Franco") Coronel dedicated his life, expertise, and resources to the Los Angeles community. He was mayor, a superintendent of schools, state treasurer, and a patron of the arts. Long after his death, southern California still benefits from the legacy of Coronel's contribution to Hispanic culture.

Early life
Born in Mexico City, Mexico, in 1817, Coronel was the son of the former Mexican army officer and educator Ignacio Coronel. The Coronel family moved to Monterey, California, in 1834, at a time when Mexico still governed the region. Three years later the Coronels settled in the Los Angeles (LA) area, where Ignacio Coronel opened the first school of any consequence in the community, situated in the Coronel home. Coronel's father provided him with a good role model and taught him the importance of public service.

Public servant
Coronel thrived in Los Angeles. Initially he taught in the school, but he soon began to take on other work in the local community, taking such positions as territorial deputy, street commissioner, city assessor, justice of the peace, and superintendent of schools.

When the United States went to war with Mexico, Coronel served as a captain and sergeant-at-arms in the Mexican Artillery from 1846 to 1847. He narrowly escaped capture by the Americans. However, after the U.S. victory in 1848, Coronel redirected his efforts to serving the new American society. His mining ventures during the California gold rush netted him a modest fortune: He used his wealth generously to finance his service as a community leader and politician, while still amassing more wealth as a successful merchant and rancher.

Political and racial tensions were prevalent in Southern Californian society after the war, however. Mexican Americans proudly called themselves "Californios," while Anglo Americans used the same term derisively. Nevertheless, in 1853, Los Angeles voters elected Coronel to be the city's fourth mayor under U.S. rule, and the first Hispanic to fill the position since the U.S. victory.

Coronel established the first Department of Public Works, and as a member of the school board advocated

▲ *Antonio Coronel actively promoted Hispanic and Native American culture, staging native dances and writing books on the subject.*

bilingual education. He also served as chairman of the Los Angeles County Democratic Committee.

From 1854 to 1867, Coronel served on the city council, working actively to reduce local banditry and to promote law and order. By 1866, statewide voters elected him as California state treasurer, a position he held through 1871. He married Mariana Williamson in 1873.

Patron of Hispanic culture
Coronel's gracious nature and love of Hispanic culture led him to honor his heritage in many ways. He staged demonstrations of Mexican dance for authors and photographers. As a result, photos of Coronel and his family are included in many publications about the Hispanic frontier-era in California and Los Angeles.

INFLUENCES AND INSPIRATION

The author and civil rights activist Helen Hunt Jackson (1830–1885) visited southern California in the 1880s to look into the treatment of Native Americans, particularly the Mission Indians. During her visit she met Antonio Coronel, who was a noted authority on the area's early history and a former inspector of missions for the Mexican government.

Coronel escorted Jackson on her tour of the area. He told her about life on the ranches and the missions, and described to her the difficulties encountered by the Mission Indians after the sale of their land. On January 23, 1882, Coronel took Jackson to a picturesque ranch called "Camulos." Jackson was so taken with the place that it inspired her

to write a romantic novel set in early California.

In 1884 Jackson published the now classic novel *Ramona*, which faithfully portrays Camulos and artfully interweaves characters from local ranches and missions. The plot was inspired by Coronel's stories of California's early days. *Ramona* became a best-seller and inspired three motion pictures.

Coronel wrote *Cosas de California*, a manuscript that documents the events and customs of Mexican California in the late 1840s. Unpublished during his lifetime, in 1994 Bellerophon Books of Santa Barbara, California, released the manuscript as *Tales of Mexican California*. Noted historian Hubert Howe Bancroft also cites *Cosas* in volume two of his *History of California*, and the original manuscript of Coronel's book now resides in the Bancroft Library of the University of California, Berkeley.

In the effort to build up the area's first community library, Coronel donated many of his personal manuscripts and art works to the Los Angeles Chamber of Commerce. Many of these historical pieces, including numerous photos as well as Spanish, Indian, and Mexican artifacts, later passed to the Natural History Museum of Los Angeles County's collection. In 1873 Coronel became part owner of *La Crónica*, the leading Spanish-language newspaper in the Los Angeles area between 1872 and 1892.

Coronel was also a charter member in founding the Historical Society of Southern California (HSSC) in 1883. The HSSC is the oldest historical society in California.

Orange groves in the heart of Los Angeles

Coronel acquired a great deal of property in California. He owned land in the San Juan Capistrano area south of Los Angeles, a beautiful ranching and farming region near the Pacific Ocean, and not far from the San Juan Capistrano mission founded by Padre Junipero Serra. In addition, his friend Antonio Feliz bequeathed to Coronel the Rancho Los Feliz. This prime real estate—just north of present-day Hollywood—was later owned by Colonel G.J. Griffith and comprises what is now the more than 4,000 acre Griffith Park and Observatory, the largest city park in the country. The city limits of today's Los Angeles cover 469 square miles, an area in excess of 215,000 acres.

In Coronel's day his adobe home at 7th and Alameda Streets—including his nearby vineyards and orange groves—was very close to the city's center, called the "pueblo plaza." The novelist Helen Hunt Jackson visited Coronel and his wife Doña Mariana there in 1881. Coronel's accounts of the Hispanic and Native American culture of the region were further immortalized in Jackson's classic American novel *Ramona* (see box). Coronel gave Jackson invaluable advice, proofreading the manuscript and checking it for accuracy.

A respected politician who did much to enhance the lives of Californians, particularly Native and Mexican Americans, Coronel spent his last years on his estate.

See also: Serra, Junipero

Further reading: Griswold del Castillo, Richard. *The Los Angeles Barrio, 1850–1890: A Social History*. Berkeley, CA: University of California Press, 1979.
http://www.socalhistory.org/Biographies/coronel.htm (Historical Society of Southern California Web site).

KEY DATES

1817	Born in Mexico City, Mexico, on October 21
1853	Elected mayor of Los Angeles (until 1854).
1866	Elected California state treasurer (serves until 1871).
1872	Becomes part owner of *La Crónica*.
1882	Inspires Helen H. Jackson's novel *Ramona*.
1883	Helps found the Historical Society of Southern California.
1894	Dies in the Los Angeles area on April 17.

CORPI, Lucha
Writer

Mexican-born Lucha Corpi is a poet, novelist, and children's writer. Corpi, who writes in both Spanish and English, is also a leading mystery writer; her series of books featuring the Chicana heroine Gloria Damasco is very popular.

Early life
Lucha Corpi was born in Jáltipan, a small tropical village on the Gulf of Mexico in the state of Veracruz, Mexico, on April 13, 1945. Corpi and her two siblings grew up in an artistically rich environment; Corpi was encouraged to tell stories and to write.

When Corpi was 19, she married; giving up her own studies she moved with her new husband to Berkeley, California, where he was studying at the University of California. Corpi and her husband arrived just as the Chicano civil rights movement was taking off. Corpi found herself caught up in the struggle to attain better rights for Mexican Americans.

Becoming an activist
After a bitter divorce in 1970, Corpi brought up her son, Arthur, alone. She began writing as a means of dealing with her situation. In that same year she was awarded a National Endowment for the Arts Creative Writing Fellowship. The poems she wrote during this time later appeared in *Palabras de mediodía* (*Noon Words*).

She returned to school, graduating with a BA from the University of California at Berkeley in 1975. She received an MA in comparative literature from San Francisco State University in 1979. During the 1970s Corpi became involved in political activism: She helped found the Aztlán Cultural Service and the Comité Popular Educativo de la Raza, an organization to establish bilingual childcare centers. Since 1977 Corpi has worked as a tenured teacher in the Oakland Public Schools Neighborhood Centers program.

▲ *Lucha Corpi's books examine Chicano politics, culture, and racism.*

Establishing a career as a writer
In 1980 Corpi published *Palabras de Mediodía*, a collection of poetry, written in Spanish, that made her name as a Chicana poet. She published *Variaciones sobre una tempestad* (*Variations on a Storm*) 10 years later.

Corpi's first novel, *Delia's Song*, appeared in 1989. It followed a young Chicana's life during the civil rights movement. In 1992 Corpi published *Eulogy for a Brown Angel: A Mystery Novel*, the first in a series of detective books focusing on the feminist Chicana character Gloria Damasco. Corpi uses the Damasco books to examine such themes as race relations, myths, Chicano culture, and the nature of life on the U.S.–Mexico border for the dominant American Anglo-Saxon culture.

In 1997 Corpi published a children's book, *Where Fireflies Dance* (*Ahí, donde bailan Las Luciérnagas*), that focuses on her own upbringing in Mexico. Corpi has received several awards for her writing. She has remarked that she writes "to bring justice into the world."

KEY DATES

1945   Born in Jáltipan, Mexico, on April 13.

1976   First collection of poems appears in *Firelight: Three Latin American Poets*.

1989   Publishes first novel, *Delia's Song*.

Further reading: Corpi, Lucha. *Where Fireflies Dance.* San Francisco, CA: Children's Book Press, 1997.
http://voices.cla.umn.edu/vg/Bios/entries/corpi_lucha.html (biography of Lucha Corpi).

CORRETJER, Juan Antonio
Poet, Activist

Juan Antonio Corretjer was a leading poet who was at the forefront of Puerto Rico's movement for independence from the United States. Corretjer's writing, which included essays and protest songs, reflected his passionate political beliefs.

Early life

Corretjer was born on March 3, 1908, in Ciales, Puerto Rico, to a family dedicated to Puerto Rico's nationalist cause. Some years before his birth, Corretjer's father and uncles had taken part in an uprising. They encouraged the young Corretjer to accompany them to political rallies. In the eighth grade, Corretjer organized a student protest against U.S. control of Puerto Rico. This led to his expulsion from school: Corretjer was forced to continue his education in another town, Vega Baja.

Corretjer's literary interest was evident from an early age. In elementary school he joined a society named after the Puerto Rican poet José Gautier Benítez (1851–1880), which later renamed itself the Nationalist Youth. Aged 12, Corretjer wrote his first poem, "Canto a Ciales," ("Song to Ciales"). His first volume of poems was published four years later, in 1924.

Career and activism

By 1927 Corretjer was a journalist, working for newspapers and magazines in Puerto Rico, Cuba, and the United States. His job enabled him to travel, and he tried to gain foreign support for Puerto Rico's independence movement. In 1930 he joined the Nationalist Party. Corretjer also became interested in Cuban politics, and joined a movement in 1935 aimed at overthrowing the dictator Fulgencio Batista y Zaldívar.

Between 1932 and 1967, Corretjer published 13 collections of poetry. Some of his best poems were written in the 1930s, and were inspired by his great love of his country and by his political activism. They include: "Ageuybana," "Cantico de Guerra," and "Amora Puerto Rico."

Corretjer was jailed for his beliefs a year after his appointment as secretary general of the Puerto Rican Nationalist Party in 1936. Although he later left the organization to found the Liga Socialista Puertorriqueña (Puerto Rico Socialist League), his continuing commitment to the nationalist cause saw him jailed again in 1947 and 1950. Corretjer claimed that he was once the victim of an attempted assassination attempt as he left a Socialist League meeting. His telephone was tapped and his family placed under surveillance by the U.S. government.

Corretjer and his wife, Dona Consuelo, often struggled financially. They refused to accept welfare payments from the United States government and survived instead on Dona Consuelo's small teaching income and on the proceeds of Corretjer's writing.

Corretjer's poetry in later years reflected a new theme, the damage to Puerto Rico's countryside caused by farming and coffee production. A forest named after Corretjer has since been established near Ciales.

A nationalist hero

Corretjer's dedication to the Puerto Rican nationalist cause brought him into conflict with the U.S. administration of President Ronald Reagan (1981–1989). Juan Antonio Corretjer died in January 1985. After his death Dona Consuelo created a shrine to him as an inspiration to future generations of Puerto Rican nationalists.

KEY DATES	
1908	Born in Ciales, Puerto Rico, on March 3.
1920	Writes first poem, "Canto a Ciales."
1924	Publishes his first volume of poetry.
1927	Works as an international journalist.
1936	Becomes secretary general of the Puerto Rican Nationalist Party.
1937	Jailed for beliefs; imprisoned again in 1947 and 1950.
1944	Publishes the poem "El Lenero."
1951	Publishes the poem "Tierra Nativa."
1985	Dies in San Juan, Puerto Rico, on January 19.

Further reading: Monge, José Trias. *Puerto Rico: The Trials of the Oldest Colony in the World.* New Haven, CT: Yale University Press, 1999.
http://www.independencia.net/ingles/welcome.html (Puerto Rican Independence Party Web site).

SET INDEX

Volume numbers are in **bold** type. Page numbers in *italics* refer to captions.

Set Index

D

E

F

Set Index

Picture Credits